SKELMERSDALE

D0541389

FICTION RESERVE STOCK LL60

TITLE   Demons of Chitrakut

Lancashire County Library

30118094368150

LANCASHIRE
COUNTY LIBRARY
Bowran Street
PRESTON PR1 2UX
LL1   Recycled

By Ashok K. Banker

The Ramayana

Prince of Ayodhya
Siege of Mithila
Demons of Chitrakut

Look out for

Armies of Hanuman

Ashok K. Banker

DEMONS OF CHITRAKUT

BOOK THREE OF THE RAMAYANA

www.orbitbooks.co.uk

LANCASHIRE COUNTY LIBRARY	
09436815	
H J	10/06/2004
F	£6.99

First published in Great Britain by Orbit 2004

Copyright © 2004 by Ashok K. Banker

The moral right of the author has been asserted.

All rights reserved.
No part of this publication may be reproduced, stored in a
retrieval system, or transmitted, in any form or by any means,
without the prior permission in writing of the publisher, nor be
otherwise circulated in any form of binding or cover other than that
in which it is published and without a similar condition, including
this condition, being imposed on the subsequent purchaser.

A CIP catalogue record for this book is
available from the British Library.

ISBN 1 84149 178 0

Typeset by Palimpsest Book Production Ltd,
Polmont, Stirlingshire
Printed and bound in Great Britain by
Mackays of Chatham plc, Chatham, Kent

Orbit
An imprint of
Time Warner Book Group UK
Brettenham House
Lancaster Place
London WC2E 7EN

Ganesa, lead well this army of words.

RIP
Sheila Ray D'Souza
(1946–1990)

Outnumbered by demons,
she fought to the last
on the side of the angels.

This one's for you, maa.
Peace, for ever.

ACKNOWLEDGEMENTS

Heartfelt thanks are due to:

Tim Holman, my editor at Orbit. I doubt that either Valmiki or Kamban ever had an editor this understanding, patient, or wise. Then again, they never needed one; I did! Thanks, Tim, for always being there.

Danny Baror, the finest international rights agent in the world, who continues to build bridges across continents for Rama to cross.

The rest of the team at Orbit and Time Warner UK: desk editor Gabriella Nemeth for her Garuda-keen eyes and Jatayu-sharp red pencils. Export managers Richard Kitson and Nicola Hill, who helped take Rama and his companions across the Commonwealth. Jessica Williamson, publicity and marketing manager; Bella Pagan, editorial assistant; Ben Sharpe, website manager and all-round good bloke; Andrew Edwards, royalty manager, who treats his authors like royalty; the printing, production, distribution, sales and marketing people, for a fabulous job on every front.

Blacksheep UK, for giving the Ramayana an identity that was true to the spiritual essence of the scripture as well as one of the coolest cover designs for an epic fantasy series ever.

The book trade professionals in the UK and Commonwealth countries who don't just sell books but love them as well. May Saraswati's blessings be with you always.

In India, the folks at Penguin Books helped bring Rama home: Ravi Singh, managing editor; Hemali Sodhi, director of publicity and promotions; Sujo Jacob and Ratna Kumari.

R. Sriram, CEO of the Crossword chain of bookstores, and his wonderful team: Naresh Sharma, Jay Sharma, Gurpreet Singh, Bhaktawar, and the rest of the staff at Crossword Mahalakshmi. You make the business of being an author a pleasure.

Hemu Ramaiah, Jai, and the rest of the terrific staff at Landmark Apex Plaza, Chennai. May your sales multiply and your franchise increase!

The teen deviyan who helped bring Kausalya to life so eloquently in Chennai, Delhi and Mumbai respectively: Anuradha Anand, Lushin Dubey, and Pallavi Joshi.

Sanjeev Shankar, a brother in past lives, a friend in this one. Your chariot awaits, bhai.

My wife Bithika, my collaborator on two of the most perfect epic tales ever written: our son Ayush, and our daughter Yashka. The three of you keep me sane and happy and make life worth living. All this would mean nothing without you to share it with me.

Fellow authors Cecilia Dart-Thornton, Juliet E. McKenna, Meg Chittenden, Kate Elliott and John Marco for heartfelt encouragement generously given and gratefully received.

And last but certainly not least of all, thank you, constant reader, whomever and wherever you may be, for joining me on this long adventure from Ayodhya to Chitrakut, and beyond. For me, this journey is its own reward. I hope the same holds true for you. Stay the course. The best is yet to come.

Jai Shri Ram.

Jai Hind.

Om Bhur Bhuvah Swah:
Tat Savitur Varenyam
Bhargo Devasya Dhimahi
Dhiyo yo nah prachodayat

Maha-mantra Gayatri
(whispered into the ears of
newborn infants at their
naming ceremony)

PRARAMBH

OF MEN AND MONSTERS

I

Rama.

The word rose into the air like a cry through a mouthful of shattered bone; part lamentation, part howl. It was accompanied by a plume of smoke emerging from a crack in the blighted earth, a wispy thread of cottony white unravelled from the vast grey ash-blanket that smothered the landscape. It spiralled skywards in languorous corkscrew circles that defied the tearing wind, rising high above the ashen earth, far above the pitted boulders, the scorched trees, the stripped cliffsides; and still it rose up through the birdless and desolate sky, a white arrow against the deep crimson gash of the dawn-wounded horizon, until it reached the underside of a storm bank. It pierced the belly of the cloud, at the very last moment forking into a trishul-shaped triad of spear points, and snaked its way in, disappearing.

The wind died. The land fell deathly silent. The whip-poorwills of spiralling ash settled down.

Remotely, as if from the gargantuan belly of a beast at the bottom of some distant ocean, a deep rumbling began. It originated in the south and travelled north-wards; the direction the Asura armies had taken when swarming towards their mortal goal. It grew, building immensely until it seemed that the earth would shake itself to fragments, like an ant hill crumbling in a seismic tremor.

Rama.

With a banshee screaming, the storm cloud burst open. The hole made by the wisp of smoke in its belly spread like a spider-web of cracks. The entire cloud bank came apart at those cracks, crumbling into fragments and sods of dirty blackish grey that resembled clay rather than cumulus. The sky shattered to release an immense burden of fluid. It was no ordinary rain that fell, for this was no ordinary cloudburst. It was the work of brahman sorcery, unleashed by one of the most powerful brahmin seers that had ever lived.

A carpet of pearly-white water, drawn up by a tornado-like force in a continuous spume from the vast river that flowed only a few yojanas south of Mithila city, fell like a hail of boulders upon the blighted land. It struck the earth with the force of a thousand giants' hammers pounding, raising a sound thunderous enough to chill the blood of tigers tracking prey in the distant mangrove swamps of Banglar to the east, and startle into stillness the doughty shaggy-footed mountain ponies on the high buttes of far northern Gandahar.

The earth moaned beneath the onslaught, as every pitted boulder, twisted trunk, and jagged cliff-face was scoured clean of the scars of the Brahm-astra. The pounding went on for long moments, cleansing the land of all debris of the Asura invasion, purifying it once more. Within hours, new life would sprout from the surface of the re-sanctified soil, and in mere days, the earth would appear much as it had appeared before the Asura hordes trampled it and the Brahm-astra scoured it. Naïve travellers from foreign lands, unaware of the great Asura massacre that had occurred in this region, would marvel at the lush beauty of these climes and attribute it to the presence of the sacred Ganga. In a sense, they would not be completely incorrect: it was ganga-jal, the waters of the mother-goddess river, that was now falling like rain from the tortured skies, and would accomplish this miraculous resuscitation.

Atop the highest point in Mithila city, the tapering pillar of blue-tinted stone named the Sage's Brow, Brahmarishi Vishwamitra lowered his hands, ceasing his chanting. He stood a moment, silently examining the fruit of his efforts. Flickers of lightning from the sorcerous storm illuminated his time-weathered features. In the flashes of blazing white, his snowy beard and mane of hair glowed bluish with the light of brahman. His face, craggy and majestic as those of the ancient Arya settlers, of whom he was one, settled into a marginally softer expression as he saw the pounding waves of ganga-jal wash the land clean of the last traces of Asura residue.

For as far as his keen brahman-attenuated eyes could see, the land was carpeted by the powerful rain of sacred waters. The cleansing rain continued unabated even after the last echoes of the upanisad mantra faded from his lips. He watched and was satisfied.

As the rain slowed to a steady shower, he reached to one side and took hold of his wildwood staff, the head higher than his own and knotted with red, green and yellow thread, some threads new and brightly coloured, many more dull and frayed, evidence of ancient yagnas, long-ago balidaans. They marked the combined prayer-rituals of his five-thousand-year lifespan, with gaps marking the long centuries of penitential meditation, tapasya, that were the only hiatus in a life spent in the service of brahman. Yet, if all those threads were unravelled, it would be seen that the staff below was scarred and gouged with ancient nicks and cuts. These were the evidence of an earlier life, a lifetime spent in pursuit of kingly ambitions and avaricious gain, conquest and blood-feud, war and reaving. For this staff had once been a sword, just as the sage himself had once been a raja. And for every scar the staff bore, the man bore one as well, marked by shiny trails of scar tissue that covered his entire body.

The threads on the head of the staff were tightly wound into a thick knot. Vishwamitra gripped this knot with both his hands, reaching up to do so, and leaned his weight on the staff momentarily. It was a favourite posture, one he had grown accustomed to these past several days. There was much reason to seek respite, and little opportunity to do so. The events of these last days had been demanding, in some ways more demanding than most of his millennia-long lifespan. They had taken their toll. He looked forward now to joining the rest of his Siddh-ashramites at their summer retreat, high in the Himalayas, for a long season of rest and reparation.

For a while, he was lost in contemplation, relishing the brief pause between calamities. Time passed swiftly, for he was accustomed to measuring his life by centuries-long penances, not mere moments, hours or days.

When next he raised his head, the rain of ganga-jal had reduced to barely a drizzle. Already, shoots and tendrils of green were visible against the deep ochre of the purified, rejuvenated soil. His grey eyes watched idly as the tip of a tree-root emerged from the ground beneath a fallen boulder, then stopped, struggling against the obstruction. Vishwamitra raised a finger and gently whispered the tri-syllabic sacred Aum. A thousand or more yards away, the tree-root penetrated the boulder as easily as the trishul-shaped wisp of smoke had earlier penetrated the storm cloud. The boulder cracked and shattered into fragments, falling away to either side. The triumphant sapling grew up, up, up, rising a full yard and a half before slowing its rapid progress. Shoots of green life began to sprout on its fledgling trunk.

The seer sighed and stood, looking upon his handi-work. For miles in every direction, new growth was flour-ishing, risen up to the height of a five-year forest in the brief instant it had taken the guru to utter the sacred tri-syllables.

He stared out at the distant horizon, at the first crimson-gold flush of sunrise above the blue-ridged moun-tain ranges of north-eastern Vaideha. His eyes filled with the luminscence of first light and the wetness of the moist air. With a great sense of regret, he realised that this would be the day he would take his leave of his new protégés and resume his life of bhor tapasya. His work here was done now. It was time for him to move on.

Things had turned out well, he mused. As well as might have been expected.

And yet. And yet.

There was still so much he desired to do, so much else he would undo, if only it were possible.

But his role in this great drama must end here and now. Thus had it been ordained. To interfere beyond this point would be to court epic disaster: the kind that under-mined universes and toppled worlds. His mission had been to guide Rama thus far, and then depart. That much had been clear to him when he emerged from his 240-year-long bhor tapasya in Siddh-ashrama and began his journey to Ayodhya.

But so much more had transpired in the commission of those apparently simple tasks.

He had not only instructed Rama in the art of warring

with the Asura races, he had guided him through a dangerous rite of passage, overseeing the young boy's maturation into manhood. Thereafter, he had brought Rama to Mithila in time to face the Lankan invasion, and he had thrust upon those slender shoulders the crushing responsibility of unleashing the dreaded Brahmastra. No guru should have to hand down such a terrible burden to any shishya, however able the pupil, and yet Rama had borne the weight as if it had been his dharma to commit that most momentous of acts. As indeed, it had, for what was a kshatriya's dharma if not to ensure the protection of his people?

Yet the burden of responsibility rested on Vishwamitra's shoulders as well.

For he had not merely chosen a path to Mithila that he knew would cross the steps of Rajkumari Sita and her bodyguard, but he had also engineered events in such a manner that Rama and Sita would be thrown together for a brief but intense period, culminating in a crisis that would force them to condense what might normally have been a weeks-long or even months-long courtship into the space of a dozen-odd hours.

In short, he had changed Rama's life so dramatically in so short a period that never again could the young prince go back to being the same guileless young rajkumar he had been before Vishwamitra's coming, sitting on the banks of the Sarayu with his brothers, sucking on salted kairee and dreaming adolescent dreams.

And yet, what choice did I have? I was but a pawn in the great game of chaupat the devas play with us all. I pray you see that someday, Rama. That I too only enacted my part. Like you must. I pray that what I have taught you and given to you will be enough to see you through the dark trials ahead. Devas grant me that one wish at least: let my brief time with him be of some succour in the difficult years ahead.

False dawn turned to true. Dusk to sunrise. Full-blown day lit up the panorama beyond the seer's troubled brow and bent head until the clear light of day revealed the gangetic valley and plains to be so utterly transformed, it was impossible to tell that there had ever been anything here other than lush profuse vegetation. A million jewels of light refracted the luminscence of the risen sun. The warmth of Surya's touch crept across the stone floor of the Sage's Brow, touching the brahmarishi's feet reverentially.

He released a long-pent-up sigh. He must accept what was, and must be, and would be. No amount of thinking could change the course of the samay chakra. The wheel of time would turn. And with it, Rama's life would take its inevitable course. He had done what he could to arm the young prince and prepare him for the epic ordeals that lay ahead in his bhavishya, that immutable future that was Rama's destiny. That was his role and it was done.

His task was finished here. He must now accept it and pursue his own destiny. Rama would survive. And more important, succeed. And he would do so despite the impossible odds stacked against him.

It was best to believe that, and to move on.

Feeling every moment of his five thousand years of life on the mortal plane, Brahmarishi Vishwamitra rose with a final sloka on his lips, and began climbing down the narrow, winding stone stairs of the Sage's Brow.

2

Vibhisena manoeuvred the pushpak as low as he dared. The flying chariot responded as elegantly as it always did, hovering perfectly still, mere yards above the surface. An extraordinary aroma filled the air. A mixture of wet earth, floral scents and vegetation. He had seen the ganga-jal rain pouring down in the hours before dawn, and knew that it was brahman work perpetuated by the seer-mage Vishwamitra out of Mithila. Vibhisena had been much too far from Mithila itself at the time – almost a hundred yojanas from the Vaidehan capital – to physically see the seer-mage working his miraculous feat, but he had known it was Vishwamitra's doing all the same. No mere pundit, sadhu or rishi possessed such mastery over the force of brahman. It had drawn a murmur of admiration from Vibhisena. A rakshasa out of Lanka though he was, Vibhisena's soul belonged more to the light of brahman than the dark powers of anti-brahman. It was a guilty truth that he had attempted to conceal unsuccessfully all his life, never fooling the one person who truly mattered – his brother, Ravana.

Understanding what the brahmarishi was doing, Vibhisena had waited until the rain passed. He was uncertain whether ganga-jal, holy water from the sacred Ganges, would act upon him the way it did his fellow rakshasas. After all, he used ganga-jal daily in his morning acamana, sprinkling drops of the blessed fluid to the four points of the compass before upending the contents of his silver lota over his own long, uncut tresses. And he suffered none of the reactions that other rakshasas did. The ganga-jal didn't sear his flesh like acid, or cause his eyes to burst into flame, or his skin to peel off in layers like an overboiled potato. So had he entered the catchment of the Ganga rainstorm, it was unlikely any harm would have come to him. But he had never been showered by such a deluge of ganga-jal before; there was no telling what reaction it might have. So it had seemed wiser to wait. He had bided his time until the effect of the mantra had worn off. The rain ceased just as the first rays of the rising sun began to appear on the far horizon.

That was a while ago. Since then, he had flown the pushpak across the vast tract of land covered by the rainfall, marvelling at the sight of new growth rising up visibly before his eyes. Even the knowledge that this rain-washed region marked the remains of his brother's entire army, including several of Vibhisena's own brethren, could not assuage his sense of wonder at the sage's mastery. Nay, he reminded himself as he scoured the surface below the pushpak, moving the vehicle steadily along, it was not the sage's mastery alone that amazed him; it was the power of brahman itself. Never before had Vibhisena witnessed such an awesome display of the power of the celestial force. To have razed an area of lush countryside the size of a small nation one night, reducing an army of millions of Asuras into grey ashen dust, then washed clean that same vast region, raising new growth and life the very next day, was a feat beyond rakshasa comprehension.

Awed by the epic display of power he had just witnessed, it was very hard for Vibhisena to continue his given mission: to find the remains of his fallen brother Ravana. Even now, as his eyes scanned every yard of the ground below with painstaking care, his heart yearned to seek out those who were so in touch with this great shakti, to fall at their feet and ask for their blessings, and then to become their pupil for ever, learning first-hand the glories of brahmanism.

A thought flickered across his divided mind, as fleeting as the flash of a shadow across the ground below.

Perhaps if Ravana truly was dead . . . perhaps then he, Vibhisena, would be finally free of the service of the king of rakshasas, free to pursue his own individual life-goal . . . to dedicate himself to serving the force of brahman with the same diligence and fealty with which he now served the Asura lord, his brother.

It was too startling a possibility to contemplate.

A shadow fell over him, blotting out the slanting rays of the newly risen sun. It was an enormous birdlike shadow, quite overwhelming the shadow of the pushpak on the ground below. For a moment, the combined shadows of the chariot and the bird appeared to be a chariot with giant wings. A very apt image, except that the pushpak had no wings, nor need of them.

Vibhisena looked up, shielding his eyes against the sun to see a giant vulture-beast descending. He recognised Jatayu at once. The leader of Lanka's sky warriors was grievously injured, its proud wings in tatters, punctured in numerous places, and its powerfully muscled anthropomorphic body crusted with dried blood that masked a score of wounds. As the vulture lord descended lower, hovering parallel to the pushpak, Vibhisena saw that several of the wounds were oozing fresh blood. One injury on Jatayu's right wing-shoulder looked particularly gruesome.

'Well met, lord of the sky,' Vibhisena said formally, raising his hand.

Jatayu's almost human eyes stared back at him suspiciously from a face scarred with cuts and rents. The vulture king's voice was hoarse and ragged. 'I have seen you in Lanka. You are one of those who serve the Master.'

Vibhisena acknowledged this with a brief nod. 'A minister of his council. And his brother as well.'

Jatayu squawked. 'His brother? I did not know the Master had a brother.'

Vibhisena didn't reply. He was used to being mistaken for just another of Ravana's many minions. After all, in most ways that mattered he *was* just another of Ravana's minions. In most ways but one. 'You survived the Brahmastra then, lord of the skies? How?'

Jatayu's features were man-like, for all that its skull and the back of its head were as red and wattled as an oversized vulture's, and as the bird-beast struggled to keep aloft, Vibhisena realised that the creature's wounds were more serious than he had thought. The pain showing on Jatayu's face was more eloquent than any words. Vibhisena slowed the pushpak and gestured to Jatayu.

'You may perch on the pushpak,' he said. 'It will take your weight easily.'

Jatayu looked doubtfully at the airborne chariot even as it struggled to flap its wings to stay aloft at this low, windless height. Then, it succumbed to the invitation and leaped rather than flew to the golden railings running in parallel atop the vehicle, placing its enormous claws on the railings with an expression that revealed its doubtfulness that such a fragile, gaudily man-made creation could actually hold its considerable weight. Despite its misgivings, the pushpak didn't so much as shift a millimetre, gliding steadily along the surface at precisely the same height as before. A sparrow alighting on it would have caused as much reaction. Jatayu's eyes widened in disbelief, its beak-mouth emitting a short, high-pitched scree of surprise that made Vibhisena's ears ring, and the bird-lord gripped the golden railings harder, holding on tightly now. It released another cry, this one clearly one of relief.

'How does this gold-bird fly? Where are its wings?'

'It needs no wings, sky-lord. This is Pushpak.'

'A pushpak,' the bird-beast replied in a throaty tone. 'Yes, I recall now. A flying chariot, like the ones the devas use in Swarga-lok.'

'Indeed, and this one is not just a pushpak. It is *the* Pushpak. The first of its kind, created to carry the mighty Lord Indra himself into battle. My brother won it from him, along with many other prizes, when our armies invaded Swarga-lok and defeated the armies of the devas in the plane of heaven.' He neglected to mention that the pushpak had belonged briefly, rightfully, to his half-brother Kubera, from whom Ravana had wrested this and much else, including the island kingdom of Lanka itself, during a falling-out after the asura-deva wars. He didn't think the bird-beast was interested in a lesson in mythic history right now.

Jatayu issued further sounds of incredulity and amazement, its oozing wounds momentarily forgotten as it marvelled at the perfection and beauty of the flying vehicle.

Vibhisena gently repeated his last question. 'How did you survive, my friend? What miracle shielded you from the devastation wrought by the Brahm-astra?'

Jatayu explained how it had been flying with its warrior brethren high above the clouds on Ravana's instructions – so as not to be seen by the mortals until the very time of the attack. How it had issued the order to descend and fall upon the city of Mithila, and had seen its fellows plunge down steeply, itself staying back the better to watch the first wave of assault and judge the results. How the towering blue wave had appeared, sweeping across the assembled Asura hordes, blasting them on contact into wheeling clouds of grey ash, destroying Jatayu's winged brethren as well, and of how the bird-lord had watched, dazed and amazed, until the instant the wave had passed immediately below, striking it with a force like it had never felt before in all its centuries of existence. The next thing it knew was that it was many hours later and it was lying woefully wounded upon a rocky clearing scores of miles away, being fed upon by ravenous Asura parasites, stragglers that invariably followed in the wake of the Asura armies and fed upon the mortal and Asura dead alike after battles. If Vibhisena counted them as survivors, then those offal had survived, only because they followed so slowly and far behind that the brahman wave had not reached them.

Vibhisena nodded, sighing as the bird-lord finished hoarsely with a string of curses directed at the rodents who had assaulted his unconscious form. Jatayu was crouched over the side of the pushpak, its vulturish head craned down to Vibhisena's face level.

It asked in a cracking voice, 'And what brings you to this site of devastation, brother of the Lord of Lanka? Did you seek to count the dead? They are gone! Washed away by ganga-jal like chimney soot in a monsoon thundershower.'

Vibhisena shook his head, gesturing at the ground below. 'Nay, lord of skies. I am here on a request from my sister-in-law Mandodhari, who asked me to seek out my brother and ascertain his demise, if so.'

'Ravana is dead,' replied Jatayu sharply, his bird eyes glinting in the brightening sunlight, their wide orbs catching and throwing back the glitter of the golden flanks of the pushpak. 'He was on the ground, right in the path of the Brahm-astra's assault. No Asura could have survived.'

'And yet,' Vibhisena said softly, 'my brother is no ordinary Asura. That is why, even though a mere rakshasa, by no means the most ferocious or lethal of the Asura races, he has reigned supreme for so many millennia.'

Jatayu snorted, flecks of blood-tinged emission dripping from its nostrils. 'Supreme or no, he is gone now. I tell you, not a single one survived. Every last one of our forces was turned to ash the instant the wave touched them.'

'And you saw my brother turned to ash as well, with your own eyes?'

Jatayu paused, rubbing at an oozing wound over its right eye with the underside of one enormous wing. 'There was nothing to see. One moment there was an Asura army as had never been assembled since the beginning of time; the next instant it was a wasteland of ashes and dust.'

Vibhisena sighed, resting his hand on the railing of the pushpak. 'Even so, my friend, I must search a while longer. My good sister-in-law Mandodhari refuses to grieve until she sees her husband's corpse with her own eyes. And until she grieves, all of Lanka must wait in stasis.'

Jatayu craned its neck suddenly, its many itches and wounds forgotten again as if some new thought had occurred to it. 'You say you are Ravana's brother? Does that make you his heir as well? Is not a brother ahead of a son in line of succession?'

'It is as you say, bird-lord. If Ravana is indeed dead,

then I shall ascend to the throne of Lanka. Even after me, Ravana's sons would not yet ascend, for we have one more brother.'

'One more?'

'Yes. But he sleeps incessantly, so he would have escaped your sight on your infrequent visits to Lanka, sent forth on Ravana's orders to spy on the mortals as you often are. His name is Kumbhakarna and he is the youngest of us three, so I am ahead in line of succession.'

The expression that appeared on Jatayu's face at these words was not one that Vibhisena could have put a name to. Neither human nor birdlike, it was a strange mixture of anger and frustration, greed and hope. 'So then you will be my new master? You will raise a new army in time and lead the Asuras again against the mortals?'

Vibhisena smiled gently, his face warm in the sunshine. 'Nay, my winged one. I am no warrior. Nor do I have any enmity with mortals. I will be content to turn my people towards penitence and tapasya, in the hope that some day the devas may forgive us our many transgressions and restore us once more to the status of demi-mortals. Part of the great cycle of karma and dharma again.'

Jatayu gazed at the rakshasa for so long, Vibhisena began to fear the bird-beast had lost its damaged voice at last. Then the vulture-king said, the wonder in its tone unmasked by the harshness of its voice, 'How could a fiend like Ravana have a brother such as yourself?'

Before Vibhisena could reply, the pushpak came to a halt with a shuddering motion. At once, a terrible grinding sound began to rise from the earth below, and the sky-chariot was buffeted by winds as fierce as any ocean gale.

3

Jatayu screed and released its hold on the top railings, flapping its wings hard, adding to the force of the wind already blowing. Vibhisena clutched the railing tightly with both hands, fearing he would be blown out of the vehicle. He called out to the bird-lord, shouting above the screaming of the wind.

'Fear not, my friend. Pushpak is attuned to the heart-beat of its master. Its stopping here can only mean one thing, that it has found Ravana's remains.'

Jatayu's answering cry was louder and harsher. The bird-beast sounded enraged at Vibhisena's words. The wind of its wings battered Vibhisena hard, threatening to cast him overboard. Yet the rakshasa held on staunchly, and after a moment the wounded bird-beast regained its perch atop the flying chariot with a final scree of reluctance.

Vibhisena braced himself to look down. With an instinctive gesture of appeal to the devas he worshipped in defiance of all the laws, traditions and sentiments of his own race, the pious rakshasa gazed over the side of the pushpak at the ground below, seeking out his brother.

A wind rose from nowhere, bringing a chill that made a mockery of the bright spring sunshine. Clouds appeared in a clear sky, racing across the sun, casting giant monstrous shadows across the land. The new tendrils of growth shooting up out of the ground slowed and ceased their emergence. The stench of death, blood and iron and the pungent reek of male seed rose like a miasma from the patch of earth beneath the hovering pushpak. Vibhisena stared down, unable to believe his eyes.

'*Ra-va-na!*'

Jatayu's plaintive cry filled the air for miles around, rising to the cloud-enshrouded sky like a lament to broken gods. The cry sent a chill through Vibhisena's heart. He felt the bird-lord's frustration and rage. Only moments ago, Jatayu had been dreaming of freedom; freedom from Ravana and his Prithvi-conquering ambitions, his sadistic and humiliating leadership, his brutal ways and indomitable will. Vibhisena himself had been dreaming similar dreams; not just for himself the way Jatayu had, but for all Lanka. He had had a dream, a dream of a Lanka that lived in harmony with the rest of Prithvi-lok, that some day, through the goodness of its actions and the sincerity of its reparations, rejoined the rest of the mortal plane and abjured its demonaic history for ever.

Now he feared that he might have dreamed too much too soon.

Vibhisena continued to gaze down from the pushpak. The chariot hovered in mid-air, about five yards above the surface of the ground. The area below the vehicle was unlike the rest of the land around it. While the rest had been cleansed of its Asura ash by the purifying waters of the Ganges rain, this patch remained ash-grey, scorched and charred. The patch was no more than six yards long by three yards wide, yet it was a blot on the entire gangetic plain. The wisps of fetor that rose like steam off its scarred and ruined surface withered the stalks of new shoots nearby, wilting newborn buds before they could bloom, rotting holes in newly grown leaves. There was no question at all that whatever lay here, it was neither purified nor cleansed. If anything, it still retained the potency to corrupt the land entire, like a seed of blackness waiting to sprout and darken the earth.

Even sacred ganga-jal and brahman power could not cleanse this patch. Such is the power of Ravana, even in death. Deva save us all from his tyranny.

Vibhisena felt his voice tremble as he issued a command to the flying chariot in the secret code-tongue that Ravana had taught him. At once, the underside of the pushpak began to glow with a fierce white light, the beam directed downwards at the patch of blighted earth. The beam shone as thickly as a shaft of solid whiteness, a perfect marblesque pillar with only a shimmering at its periphery to indicate its lack of substance. The pillar of white light descended solidly to the ground, then made contact with the surface.

A deafening impact exploded into the morning sky. Suddenly, the world turned dark as twilight, the sun blotted out by a force as powerful as the brahman mantra that had brought the ganga-jal rain only hours earlier. The sky rolled and seethed with ominous colours like a vast backlit cyclorama in a Sanskrit drama: some tragic epic of warring devas and Asuras. Colours at the lower end of the spectrum – garish crimsons, purples, cerulean blues – flashed and rolled across the horizon. Explosions of blinding white light burst from the pores of the patch of blighted earth as the pillar of light bored its way relentlessly into the ground. As the pillar went down, penetrating the protesting earth, ash-grey dust billowed up, spattering Vibhisena and Jatayu, blinding their vision. The giant bird-beast screed in terror and panic and flapped its mighty wings again, churning up even more dust and ash and earth. Still the pillar of light went down,

down. Sods of blighted earth began to fly up, as if churned by an invisible plough, coating the burnished gold of the celestial chariot, besmirching Vibhisena's face and person, drawing enraged cries from the bird-lord perched above.

With a final burst of effulgence, the drama of light and noise reached a climax, and as suddenly as it had begun, the spectacle ended. The world was abruptly still. Like the stillness after the first blow of a hurricane and before the arrival of the true storm. The calm at the centre of the eye of chaos.

Vibhisena forced himself to look down again, struggling to see through the suddenly dense and polluted air. He was about to call to the pushpak to cease drilling when the chaos below resolved into a clearer insight. What he saw stilled his speech and froze his heart.

At the bottom of a deep pit scored by the pillar of white light there lay a block of what appeared to be solid red marble. Its surface was criss-crossed by a fine tracery of pink veins that glowed from within. Inside this illuminated slab lay an object, trapped like a primordial insect in crimson amber. As Vibhisena watched wordlessly, he heard a choked cry from Jatayu above him. The bird-beast had seen it too.

The beam from the pushpak grew unbearably strong, too bright to look into directly, and Vibhisena had to shield his vision and squint until his eyes were thin slits. A grinding sound rose from the pit, as if the pillar of light were grinding away the sides of the ditch, widening them to allow room for the stone block to be raised. And the earth itself seemed to resist. As Vibhisena strained to see through the flying mud and dust and searing light, he saw the earth on all four sides of the stone block falling *into* the ditch now, filling it as fast as the light pillar could excavate it. Yet the pillar continued its work relentlessly. Mud and sods flew out of the ditch in an endless upward rain as the celestial vehicle and the very earth battled. But why would the earth resist? Why would it want to keep that object within its belly?

The answer came to Vibhisena as another flash of searing light exploded from the ground below.

It's Prithvi-maa herself, the spirit of the earth. She seeks to swallow up the remains of Ravana whole, to digest them and send them deep down into the bowels of her planetary body. To bury them for ever.

And yet, even as the realisation came to him, the earth shuddered one last time with a moan of protest that was shockingly human, and the stone block came free of the soil in which it was imbedded with a sudden jerk. It rose slowly on the shaft of white light, that now acted as a passageway. As the stone slab moved steadily upward, Vibhisena saw that even now the earth still fought to retain hold of it, to bury it again. Soil rained down on it from every side with the ferocity of waterfalls tumbling from a Himalayan glacier. But the shakti of the celestial chariot was beyond resisting now, and the stone block rose inexorably.

Finally, the block emerged out of the ditch. The instant it rose above the surface, the hole it had left behind filled rapidly, growing brimful with earth. The surrounding earth seeped across the blighted patch like water spilled across a spot of wine, diluting and cleansing the darker soil. The purified earth overwhelmed the ruined soil, scouring it clean as effectively as the rain of ganga-jal had scoured the entire country earlier. With it, the very last traces of the Asura invasion passed for ever into oblivion. The earth replenished itself.

Only then did Vibhisena have a chance to look closely at the stone block. It was rising higher, even as the pushpak itself rose higher. The chariot shot upward into the sky a hundred yards, then a thousand, then two thousand, pulling the stone slab beneath it. Then the world became a blur and Vibhisena was forced to close his eyes to keep from fainting dead away. Above him, Jatayu's head was forced down over the side of the sky chariot, compelled by the pressure of their rapid ascent. For once, no sound escaped the bird-beast's beak, but its eyes met Vibhisena's and the rakshasa saw that the bird-lord was terrified witless.

He dreads what lies in that stone block more than he feared being destroyed by the Brahm-astra.

After what seemed like an interminable time, Vibhisena dared to open his eyes once more.

The pushpak had risen to a great height, far above the clouds. And now it was travelling southwards, acting of its own volition as it sometimes did. Even as he looked down in amazement, the celestial vehicle gained speed until it was shooting along with a velocity even an arrow would have been hard pressed to match. The earth blurred beneath its passing. Glancing back over his shoulder, Vibhisena saw that the gangetic plain had once more returned to its normal state, green and replete with new growth everywhere, the sky brilliantly sunlit and cloudless for as far as he could see. It fell behind with dizzying speed, and he turned to look ahead. A pale blue line blurred past below, and he knew that they had passed the Ganga and crossed over into the wild lands south of the Arya nations. A faint sensation of regret plucked at his heart. He had come so close to finding salvation . . . Now, the humps of hill ranges, the green carpet of forests, the steely-blue of lakes all shot past below at a blinding pace. Had the pushpak not been capable of protecting its passengers from the force of its passage, he would been blown off the helm of the vehicle.

He glanced up at Jatayu and saw that the bird-beast too was secure in the protective shield of the chariot, its large scarlet-and-black claws clinging fiercely to the top railings.

At this rate, Vibhisena knew, they would be in Lanka before noon, perhaps even earlier if the chariot increased its speed. It did not surprise him; the vehicle had brought him north just as rapidly earlier this morning.

At last he was able to spare a moment to look down at the burden they carried. Still fixed to its underside by the supernatural pillar of white light, the stone block rode beneath the chariot as if fixed with invisible ropes. Vibhisena leaned over the edge, unafraid of falling, knowing that the pushpak would protect him, and examined the stone block closely.

It was the size that the patch of land had been, about six yards by three. But the being trapped within it like an insect in amber was relatively smaller, perhaps three yards in length, and a yard wide. At one end, though, the creature was much wider, almost twice the width of its body. This was its head; or rather, as Vibhisena corrected himself, its heads.

The still form of Ravana, Lord of Lanka, master of the Asura races, bane of all existence, lay trapped within the block of stone. As best as Vibhisena could tell, his demon-lord brother was still and unbreathing, all his ten pairs of eyes closed in peaceful repose.

4

Rama Chandra, rajkumar of Ayodhya, prince-heir of the Kosala kingdom, and Rajkumari Sita Janaki of Mithila, princess-heir of the Videha nation, were married with great pomp and ceremony. The marriage was held on the day after what came to be known as Siege Day. Even though the princess had chosen Rama at the Swayamvara, garlanding him as her chosen betrothed, it was still customary to formally ask for the groom's hand. This request, as tradition demanded, was forwarded by Maharishi Satyananda, spiritual adviser of Maharaja Janak, to Guru Vashishta at Ayodhya. Guru Vashishta accepted the request and dispatched the messenger back to Mithila before informing Maharaja Dasaratha, still recovering from his series of calamities, and the titled queens, Rani Kausalya, Rani Kaikeyi and Rani Sumitra. Arrangements were to take a splendid groom's procession, the traditional groom's procession, from Ayodhya to Mithila.

The baaraat that arrived at Mithila had spectators gaping mutely. Never before had such a lavish procession of luxury and wealth been seen in the liberated city. If the Vaidehans were ahead in their accretion of spiritual and moral enrichment, then the Kosalans had the upper hand in material and aesthetic prowess. The five-mile-long procession took several hours to pass through the city gates. One bemused portly brahmin who watched in envious delight estimated that over fifty thousand Ayodhyan bellies would have to be fed by their Mithilan hosts that night. He promptly turned the head of his ass and joined the rear of the procession, chuckling and rubbing his enormous paunch as he contemplated the joys of feasting on the special savouries that the groom's baaraat alone was privileged to be served. He got his wish and was unable to walk for days afterward; every time he belched, he tasted the wedding feast again and blessed both groom and bride fervently. It was the best and biggest feast he had partaken of in his avaricious life.

All of Mithila feasted that night. Rivers of wine and soma flowed, thousands of heads of cattle, sheep and fowl were slaughtered and roasted, entire groves of fruit and vegetables were consumed. The milky, ghee-rich odour of mithai being prepared filled the entire district around the royal kitchens.

In the central hall of the palace, on a pandal – a platform specially erected for the occasion – Guru Vashishta, Brahmarishi Vishwamitra, Maharishi Satyananda, and a small army of purohits, pundits and other venerated brahmins conducted the elaborate rituals to propitiate the devas for the fruitful union of the princely pair. It had been decided by both families that the three brothers of Rama and Sita's sister and two cousins were to be wed as well. But it was Rama and Sita who first took the seven pheras around the sacred yagna fire, as the priests chanted the appropriate hymns.

// Iyam Sita mama suta sahadharmachari thava //
// Pratichha chainam bhadram te panim grihnishwa
panina //

//Pativrata mahabhaga chayevanugata sada//
//Ithyuktwa prakshipadraja mantraputam jalam tada.//

On completion of the ritual, Maharaja Janak, tears welling in his eyes, embraced the pink-saffa-turbaned, flower-veiled Rama and said to him, 'Ramabhadra, pray accept my daughter Sita Janaki as your saha-dharmini, your partner in dharma. May you both dwell in the shadow of the grace of the devas for ever, as closely bonded as a mortal being to its own shadow.'

With these words, Janak placed Sita's hands over Rama's and chanted suitable mantras while pouring ganga-jal over his daughter's hands. The holy water dripped through the clasped hands and into a golden bowl, formally solemnising the union. Upon this, the entire congregation chanted aloud in one enormous harmony: 'Sadhu! Sadhu!' The sound carried across the city, turning the anxiously expectant faces of the waiting Mithilans into masks of pleasure. With a sounding of conch trumpets, the celebrations began, notwithstanding the fact that only one of the four marriages was formally over. Mithilans were known for starting early and finishing late.

After the marriage of Rama and Sita was solemnised, Janak gave his daughter Urmila in marriage to Lakshman. Then, on behalf of his late brother Kushadhwaja, he gave his nieces Mandavi and Shrutakirti to Bharat and Shatrugan respectively.

The two maharajas embraced to show their joy at this joining of their dynasties; Janak expressed his pleasure at seeing Dasaratha after such a long time, and wondered if he would have to father more daughters to entice his old friend into visiting again. Dasaratha pleaded his ill health and the recent Asura threat as excuses for his not staying the customary seven days.

Maharaja Janak had much to think about in the wake of the recent crisis, so narrowly averted by the timely arrival of Rajkumar Rama and Brahmarishi Vishwamitra. It sobered him to think that had they not arrived when they had, all that he now beheld from the height of the Sage's Brow would lie in blood-spattered ruins. Still, he resisted the urging of his council of ministers and sena-patis to reform the Videhan army and build up defences. In the end, he reasoned with unshakeable logic, the city had been saved not by military might, but by spiritual shakti. That was the most powerful vindication of peace he could ask for, and so Mithila resisted all attempts to militarise and remained as spiritually pious and morally liberated as ever.

5

Dawn. The day after the wedding. They stood by the north gate, lit by the soft early light. A gentle breeze ruffled their hair and clothes. Sita's wedding bangles clinked melodiously, her silk garments shirring in musical counterpoint to the rustling of Rama's silk loincloth. Lakshman's saffron-coloured dhoti flapped lazily. Both sages were clad in saffron as well, although even now Vishwamitra was tying the mouth of a large grey shawl at the nape of his neck, sobering the effect of the saffron dhoti he had worn at the wedding. Enveloped now in grey, he stood with his cloak flapping, flowing beard and tied hair rippling in the wind.

Rama and Sita paused, exchanging an unspoken thought, then bent as one and touched the feet of Brahmarishi Vishwamitra, asking the seer-mage for the ritual blessing. 'Ashirwaad, guru dev.'

The brahmarishi spoke a Sanskrit sloka conferring long life and blessed union upon the just-wed pair.

As Rama rose, Vishwamitra reached out and caught hold of the young man's hands in his own. Rama could feel the gnarled roughness of Vishwamitra's palm, worn coarse from millennia wielding first swords and lances and now staffs and rods.

'Rama,' the sage said in a voice that for once revealed

his inner emotions. 'I have not words to tell you how deeply I desire to be at your side tomorrow. Nothing would give me greater satisfaction than to see you crowned Prince of Ayodhya. Nay, I err in saying that, for one other thing *would* give me that satisfaction – to tarry in Ayodhya even after your ceremonial ascendance, revelling in the spiritual hospitality of that great capital of the Kosala nation, until the day dawns of your ascension to the throne and coronation as Maharaja of Ayodhya, liege of the mightiest Arya nation on this mortal realm. Nothing else would give me greater pleasure than to see that glorious day dawn. Yet it is not to be. And so, my young prince, you must go on as you have up to now, and I must go my own way. Remember only this: follow your dharma. Whatever else transpires, be true unto dharma and all will be well in the end.'

Rama joined his palms together in a namaskar that attempted feebly to communicate all the gratitude, respect and love he felt for the brahmarishi. 'Pranaam, guru-dev,' he said. He would have said more but there seemed no words to express what he felt. He looked up at the brahmarishi and in those eagle-like grey eyes he saw that everything he felt and could not say was understood.

Vishwamitra's face settled into a determined aspect and he turned to face north. There was no raj-marg here; the main king's highway led out of the west gate, the main entrance of the city. This was merely a cart-track, winding up a wooded slope to the base of a hill, the first of many that grew eventually until they became the foothills of the great Himalayas. Used more by holy men than merchants or soldiers, it was little trodden, and overgrown. Even this close to the city, the woods encroached upon it from either side, elms, pines and firs leaning restrictively.

Rama couldn't help but notice that the curving line of the raj-marg resembled the letter of the Sanskrit alphabet that signified sacred Aum, the syllable of transcendence. He wondered if some Mithilan road architect, centuries earlier, had designed it thus, or if it was simply to accommodate the lie of the land. He would ask Sita about it later. The minutiae of history had always fascinated him, especially the attempts of men through the ages to shape their environs in a manner that reflected their own culture.

Brahmarishi Vishwamitra looked back one last time at the quartet gathered on the northern knoll. His eyes met Rama's gaze and for an instant Rama clearly felt the searchlight of the seer's soul pass across his mind, like the spill of a blazing mashaal in the dark of night; then, as the seer turned his penetrating grey eyes away, the sensation faded and was replaced by a new feeling, a sense of great foreboding.

The seer-mage took up his staff and strode up the winding path.

As Rama watched the tall, broad-backed form move away with powerful rapid steps, a small dust trail rising languorously in the morning air in his wake, motes of dust swirling through the beams of sunlight that fell through gaps in the woods, the sense of foreboding increased in intensity.

The feeling refused to leave him, lingering long after the sage had strode on out of sight and even the curling dust trail of his passing had faded into oblivion.

KAAND I

PEACE

I

The mountain began to move.

That was the only way that Sita could describe it to herself. The entire mass of rock, several hundred yards, shuddered briefly, held still a moment, then began to shiver like a mare in heat. A sound arose from the depths of the rocky mass, a sound like nothing else, the gnashing moan of thousands of tons of rock and earth shifting against itself, grinding and scraping right down to the bedrock. The reverberations caused the ground beneath their feet to shudder. The horses snickered nervously, tossing their heads and manes and rolling their eyes wildly. Ahead and behind, the elephants trumpeted their displeasure at this unnatural motion of the earth. And from all around, the screes and cries and screeching calls of birds and beasts filled the air.

Sita clutched hold of the nearest thing at hand; it happened to be Rama's elbow. In response, he put both his arms around her, pinning her between them as he took hold of the rail of the palanquin. The elephant they were on lurched alarmingly, then roared in dismay as pebbles, gravel and other rock debris began to slide down the sides of the ravine, spattering the royals and their protectors indiscriminately. Sita glanced back and saw Nakhudi, ensconced in the rearmost seat of their palanquin, glaring up with wide angry eyes, as if this phenomenon were somehow the fault of someone up there, and if she could just spy the one responsible, she would toss a spear through his breast and put a stop to it.

The mountain increased its shuddering. Sita looked around, seeing horses rearing up in terror, elephants lurching and striking against the sides of the pass. The orderly procession had suddenly turned into a chaotic mêlée.

'Rama,' she said, clutching his arm tighter. 'What should we do? What's happening?'

Rama shook his head. The shaking of the earth made speech difficult for him, breaking up his words into staccato phrases and fragments. 'I don't know. Best stay still. Curl up. Too dangerous to get down. Elephants. Trample us.'

The shaking and shuddering got worse, until Sita could hear her teeth chattering in her mouth. She clenched her jaws together, keeping her head down, hands above the back of her head, making herself as small a target as possible, as she had been taught to do in earthquakes. Beside her, she felt Rama do the same. His body was warm and hard against her own, and she felt the better for his presence and closeness. Beside him, Lakshman was curled up still as well. Sita tried to see the elephant ahead, to check if the maharaja and the queens were all right, but the air was filled with blinding dust from the landslides and it was impossible to see clearly.

The side of the mountain shattered beside her. Like a wall made of papier-mâché, it was ripped apart by two giant diagonal slashes. Something, *or someone*, pushed its way through the meeting point of these slashes, and burst through. Chunks of basalt rock and sheets of slate rained down the side of the ravine, striking at least one unfortunate soldier below. His cry filled the air before being cut off by the brutal sound of rock crunching human flesh and bone.

Rama stared up at the shining figure that had burst out of the mountain. It was a personage of less than average height, no more than five feet, almost a dwarf, not quite a man. Yet what he lacked in stature he made up for in width. The figure standing on the crumbled debris of the ravine wall was barrel-chested and broad enough to encompass two men if he but stretched his arms. Rama squinted up against the afternoon sun, shielding his eyes with his hands, then realised that the intense brightness was caused by the man himself, not the sun above.

He was glowing with the blue-tinged effulgence of brahman shakti. The brilliance sharpened to blinding brightness at his head, vignetting to a radiant glow around his simple but pristine white dhoti. In place of an ang-vastra, he wore only the thick black thread that marked the brahmin caste. His wide, powerfully muscled chest was matted with a profuse growth of hair, also white. His forehead was anointed with the traditional triple row of horizontal saffron smears, and a single vertical white smudge dotted with raw rice grains. This, along with his matted white hair piled atop his head, and the black chest thread, left no doubt about his status as a brahmin.

But in his right hand he held an implement that no brahmin would ever touch, let alone wield, even on pain of death.

The axe in the brahmin's right hand was nearly as tall as the man himself. Even at this distance, Rama could see with the assistance of his own awoken powers that its wooden handle was scored with countless cuts, and the Sanskrit legend carved into its heft was long since obscured by use. But the blade at the head of the axe gleamed as dangerously as the day it had been forged. an enormous curved two-edged blade, half a yard in length, almost as much in breadth, and at least two inches thick in the middle, tapering to a lethal sharpness at either end. This blade caught the light and sent back rainbow-hued explosions of blinding reflection with every movement. Rama knew from experience that an axe of that size must weigh nothing less than half a hundred kilos. Yet the squat brahmin gripped it with an easy familiarity as if the axe was a part of himself.

Lakshman exhaled beside him. 'Parsurama.'

Rama caught the cold gleam of sunlight on metal and caught Lakshman's hand, stopping him from drawing the iron-bladed arrow he was about to pull surreptitiously from his quiver. He shook his head slowly. Lakshman stayed still.

Just then the axe-wielding brahmin spoke.

'Kshatriyas!'

The voice was as deep and sonorous as an earthquake. It rolled across the ravine and down the mountainside like a small avalanche, carrying to the far ends of the Ayodhyan procession, almost a mile below in the woods at the foothill of the mountain. Rama glanced back and saw horses rearing far below, disconcerted by the power of the voice. It was a voice befitting a man who could axe his way through solid rock.

'Kshatriyas, look upon me and tremble.'

The cleaver of the mountain hefted his mighty axe, turning it this way then that to show the Ayodhyans. 'I am Parsurama of the axe.'

At the sound of his name, every last throat in the Ayodhyan procession sent up a cry of anger and dismay. The echoes clashed with the booming reverberations of the brahmin's pronouncement, bringing a fresh spattering of loose stones and earth from the mountainside. Horses reared and whinnied. Elephants lowed unhappily.

'I am he who was trained by mighty Siva Himself in the arts of warfare. This axe was forged for me by the blacksmith of the devas. And this bow' – he reached out and opened his left palm. With a flash of lightning, a huge bow appeared in his fist – 'was given unto me by the Three-Eyed One Himself. It is sister to the bow which lay in the possession of Maharaja Janak, liege of Mithila. Only yesterday did I hear the sound of that mighty bow being destroyed. That sound reached even within my retreat deep within the heart of Mount Mahendra. Siva's bow? Broken? Which mortal warrior would be foolish enough to brave such a dastardly act of destruction? It is that foul act that compels me to appear before you. In the name of Siva, who bequeathed me that mighty bow, I swear that I shall not rest until I have exacted vengeance upon the foolish kshatriya who destroyed that great weapon. I know he is amongst you. I smell the resin of the bow in the air even now. Surrender him to me and I will spare the rest of your lives. Refuse, and I shall leave no person alive. Thus speaks Parsurama of the axe.'

Rama felt Sita start and attempt to turn to look at him, while Lakshman's hand moved again towards his quiver. He admonished them both with a gesture. Behind them, Nakhudi's chainmail rattled briefly, as if the rani-rakshak had turned her bulky body to look at Rama. He sensed the minds of every Ayodhyan in the long procession turn towards him. If their eyes did not look at him at once, it was because of caution.

After a moment, in which neither bird nor beast, wind nor mortal sound was audible, the brahmin took his axe off his shoulder and swung it at the mountain, as easily as a woodsman chopping a log. A thousand shards of basalt stone exploded, showering down on the Ayodhyan lines below. Rama saw a score of raised lances bent and crushed like reed sticks beneath the falling shards. The men wielding them disappeared in a cloud of dust and debris. As the echoes of the falling rolled away, the brahmin's voice boomed out again, louder and fiercer.

'Foolish kshatriyas! You do not know whom you face. I have killed a million kshatriyas before and shall kill a million more. Seven times thrice I have cleansed the earth of all kshatriyas in retribution for a kshatriya's murder of my father. It would cause me little effort to do so yet again. For you low-caste warriors understand only the language of blood and iron, naught else. Yet still I stay my hand, for your liege is of the Suryavansha dynasty and my mother Renuka, daughter of Prasanjit, was also of the same lineage. Answer me, I say. Show me the cowardly mortal who dared to lay his filthy kshatriya hands upon the venerated bow of my Lord Siva.'

Rama stepped forward, about to speak, when the deep tones of Guru Vashishta's voice rang out with preternatural force. Heads turned to see the guru standing atop a boulder to address the brahmin on the mount. 'Parsurama of the axe,' said the sage, for that was the full meaning of the brahmin's name. 'I see you have still not satiated your thirst for kshatriya blood.'

At the sight and sound of Vashishta, the brahmin lowered his axe at once. He bowed his head and performed a namaskaram. 'Guru Vashishta! Pranaam, guru-dev! It has been a long time since we last met. Forgive me if I have offended thee with my words. They are not intended for you, nor for any brahmin in this party. My business is only with these kshatriya fools who offend me by their very presence upon this mortal realm.

I would rid the world entire of the bane of their existence yet again for the insult they have caused my Lord
Siva.'

'Nay, Parsurama,' Guru Vashishta said calmly, his
words, like those of Parsurama, carrying easily to every
Ayodhyan in the procession by the aid of brahman power.
'Do not be so quick to lay blame. Your earlier grievance
with kshatriyas was justified. I myself was present upon
this earth when Raja Kartavirya, Lord of the Haihaiyas,
abused the gracious hospitality of your father's ashram
by stealing a sacred calf, the very same calf I myself had
gifted unto Maharishi Jamadgini, for it was the offspring
of the blessed Cow-Mother Surabhi Herself. That theft
was truly ill-intentioned. Thus when you chased after the
raja, you had just cause to cross weapons with him,
cutting off his thousand arms and ending his life. You
were only redressing the wrong he had done unto you,
and reclaiming the calf that he had stolen so feloniously.
And later, when you returned from a pilgrimage and
found your father slain in his own ashram, murdered by
the sons of Raja Kartavirya, you had just cause to swear
your oath to cleanse the earth of all kshatriyas. For it
was indeed true that the warrior caste of that age had
grown unruly and arrogant in their ways and deserving
of punishment. So you took up your mighty axe and you
cleansed the earth thrice times seven of all kshatriyas.
Twenty-one times in all you massacred every last warrior
on this mortal plane. Only then did you retire to your
mountain habitat, deep within the heart of Mount
Mahendra.'

Parsurama bowed again to Vashishta. 'Great one, your
knowledge and wisdom are infinite. You alone understand my pain and motivation. Then stand by me in this
matter as well. Point out to me the kshatriya who broke

my lord's bow that I might cleave his head from his body and rid the earth of his vile presence.'

This time, Rama needed no further urging. He rose to his feet, unclasping Sita's hand from his own as he stood, and presented himself to the brahmin on the mount. He pitched his voice upwards, projecting it as far as he could, to be heard not only by the axe-wielder but also by his own countrymen.

'Brahmin Parsurama,' Rama said, his youthful voice a strange contrast to the booming baritones of the two brahmins. 'I am Dasaratha-putra Rama Chandra, Prince of Ayodhya. I am the one who strung and broke the bow of Lord Siva in Mithila. I am the one you seek.'

Parsurama's response was swift and startling. The brahmin hefted his axe on to his shoulder and leaped off the mountain. Before the astonished gaze of the watching Ayodhyans, he fell a thousand yards, landing on both feet on a large stone ledge only a little way from the ravine path. Sita shielded her eyes instinctively as the brahmin's feet struck the ledge with superhuman impact. The ledge held, barely, but an enormous rift appeared, racing across it from end to end, and the stone broke into two sections with a sound like a giant walnut cracking. A flurry of dust and small stones flew up into the air, pattering down before the Ayodhyans. The dust cloud parted to reveal the squat form of the brahmin striding forth.

Parsurama stopped with his axe raised, within striking distance of Rama.

The brahmin looked Rama up and down, scorn and disbelief mingled in his expression.

'You? A mere stripling of a boy? You could not lift an Ayodhyan longbow, let alone the celestial bow of my Lord Siva!'

Parsurama turned away from Rama, dismissing him, and faced the Ayodhyans, directing his words towards Guru Vashishta. 'Guru-dev! Tell your acolytes not to test me further. Ask them to send out the true culprit. My axe has never been so patient before. If not for your presence as mentor of this dynasty, I would have slain the lot of them already. I know you will not lie to me, Vashishta. Tell me, who is the one who broke my bow?'

Sita tried to see the guru's response, but spears bristled about her thickly, crowding her view. Before Guru Vashishta could reply, Rama's voice rang out again sharply.

'I am he you seek, axe-wielder. I alone was responsible for breaking your master's bow.'

Parsurama turned to gaze sceptically at Rama again.

'Then surely you were given the gift of brahman shakti by the great Guru Vashishta.'

'Not mere shakti, brahmin. The *maha-shakti* of Bala and Atibala. That great gift was given unto me by none other than Brahmarishi Vishwamitra himself, who was my mentor only recently.'

A change came over Parsurama's expression. 'Vishwamitra infused you with Bala and Atibala?' He measured Rama anew. 'Perhaps I misjudged your youthful appearance. But even so, I cannot believe that you could have broken my master's bow. Even if you were given possession of the maha-mantras of ultimate warrior strength, you could hardly have gained enough proficiency in their use in so short a time.' He glanced scornfully at Rama's face. 'It would take ten times your minuscule lifetime to master such maha-shakti, let alone wield it.'

Rama's reply was quiet, yet his words carried clearly down the mountainside. *Aided by Guru Vashishta's brahman power, no doubt.* Sita watched, mesmerised, unable to believe that Rama, *her* Rama, was matching wits with the legendary Parsurama himself. *As long as he's not matching blades.*

'By the grace of Guru Vishwamitra,' Rama said, 'I was

able to enter the Bhayanak-van and confront the mutant hybrid hordes of Tataka. After dispensing with her vile offspring, I challenged and downed Tataka herself. Later, on a mission from my guru, I entered the Pit of Vasuki and released the wife of Sage Gautama from her millennia-long curse. And only three days past, I confronted and bested Ravana, Lord of Lanka, in the sabha hall of Mithila, on which same occasion I strung, shot and then broke the bow of mighty Siva. Later the same evening I decimated the invading Asura hordes of Ravana by uttering the secret maha-mantra of the Creator, Brahma-dev's own weapon, the Brahm-astra.'

Parsurama started, taking a step back. 'The Brahm-astra? It cannot be! You lie! You seek to deceive me with your warrior's cunning.'

Rama shrugged. 'Do you believe that Guru Vashishta would stand by silently and permit me to utter lies of such magnitude?'

Sita saw Parsurama glance uncertaintly in the direction of Guru Vashishta. The guru's voice floated down clearly: 'Heed well the words of young Rama Chandra, axe-wielder. He speaks truth.'

Parsurama drew a deep breath and released it. Sita felt the breeze ripple around her like the edges of a gale. 'Your endorsement leaves no doubt, maha-dev. I accept the veracity of his words. Yet I can scarcely believe that a mere kshatriya could accomplish such feats.'

It was Rama who replied. 'Then test me. Give me a feat to accomplish that any mere kshatriya would find impossible. Prove to yourself that I am unworthy of such achievements – or prove yourself wrong for having under-estimated me.'

A murmer of approval swept through the Ayodhyan ranks. Sita felt a thrill course through her body. Rama, *her* Rama, challenging the legendary Parsurama himself? Her sister and cousins must surely be fainting right now!

Parsurama's face was creased in doubt and suspicion. But after a long moment he came to a decision. Reaching up, he caused the bow he had held earlier to re-materialise. With a flash of lightning, it reappeared in his left hand. Now that the brahmin was so much closer than before, Sita could see that the bow was identical in every respect to the one that had lain in her father's palace all her life. In size, appearance, design and carving, it was its exact twin.

'Two indestructible bows,' Parsurama said quietly, 'were crafted by Vishwakarma himself, forgesmith of the devas, at Brahma the Creator's command. One was given to Siva the Destroyer, the other to Vishnu the Preserver. They were used by the two great ones in single combat against each other, a tournament provoked by Brahma himself to prove once and for all who was the mightier of the two devas. Both Vishnu and Siva were determined to best each other. The combat raged for many aeons by mortal count. Finally, Vishnu unleashed his secret mantra as a war-cry, which unstrung Siva's bow, putting the Lord of Destruction at a momentary disadvantage. At that instant, seeing that Vishnu had the advantage, the watching assemblage of devas, seven brahmarishis, and others all rushed on to the combat field, separating the two devas. For had Vishnu been permitted to press home his advantage, who can say, perhaps he might have been the one to triumph, and he would then have had no choice but to destroy Siva. Vishnu was relieved at the match being ended thus. For he knew that there could be no victor in such a match. So when victory was assigned to him over Siva's protests, Vishnu refused to accept the laurel, saying that the combat had been interrupted without a satisfactory conclusion. Siva, of course, was greatly angered by the outcome, and in a fit of rage he went to Mithila City and gave away his unstrung bow to Devarata, then king of the Vaideha nation. It remained in the possession of the kings of Vaideha, passing eventually to Maharaja Janaka, the present liege.'

Parsurama paused and slipped his axe through the loop of the sling tied across his shoulder, freeing his hand to hoist the bow aloft, displaying it for all to see. It caught the light of the late afternoon sun and gleamed like burnished metal, dazzling in its finery. 'This is Vishnu's bow, the same one with which he bested Siva, albeit momentarily. Vishnu did not wish to keep it, knowing in his infinite wisdom that any astra of such potency ought not to be in the possession of one so powerful as himself. So he gave it in sacred trust to Richika of the Bhrigu clan, from whom I myself am descended. Mighty Richika handed it down to my father Jamadagni. Yet even when Kartavirya's sons came to murder him in revenge for my having killed their father, Jamadagni did not use Vishnu's bow to defend himself. For he was a man of peaceful, spiritual pursuits, a true brahmin.'

Parsurama's voice betrayed his emotion now, turning sorrowful.

'Thus he allowed himself to be killed rather than raise a hand in anger. For such is the code of the brahmins since the beginning of our proud race. Even when we found his butchered body, chopped up as cruelly and heartlessly as the carcass of any forest animal, my sister and my brothers could think only of praying for repentance on behalf of the culprits who had perpetrated that dastardly act. But I,' he paused, his fierce eyes shining with tears, 'I, Parsurama, eldest of my father's sons, could not bear to see my father's death go unavenged. For he was killed in retaliation for a deed I had committed, and I felt myself answerable to the consquences of my actions. And so I took up the axe which I used to chop wood for our cookfires, and went forth into the world with vengeance in my breast and a vow upon my lips. I vowed that I would rid the earth of every last warrior-caste that lived. And so I did, reaping a terrible harvest throughout Prithvi-lok, this mortal realm. Thrice times seven I slew the kshatriyas and their sons, sparing only those women who did not raise arms against me and who were not pregnant with male offspring. Those that bore weapons or male embryos, I destroyed as well.'

Parsurama gained hold of his emotions, lowering the bow slowly. Sita saw his hand tremble with the intensity of his passion. Parsurama held out the bow to Rama.

'If you truly are the one who broke Siva's bow, and the one who made the three worlds tremble by unleashing the mighty Brahm-astra, then I challenge you to prove it. Take this great Bow of Vishnu and use it against me if you can. Face me in single combat, I with my wood-axe, and you with Vishnu's bow, and we shall determine if you are truly deserving of your claims. To arms, kshatriya!'

And Parsurama tossed the Bow of Vishnu to Rama and raised his axe once more, as a terrible roar rose from the throats of every Ayodhyan.

Dasaratha swam up from a fog of ghoulish hallucinations to find himself confronted with yet another nightmarish scenario. He struggled to raise himself from the cushioned seat on which he lay, unable to credit the evidence of his eyes. Through the ornately carved side panel of the palanquin, he could see the amassed PFs veterans of the last asura wars, and soldiers of the First Akshohini ranged in a defensive phalanx. The familiar wrestler's physique of their commander left no doubt that it was Senapati Dheeraj Kumar, which gave some idea of the serious nature of the crisis. The general stood off to one side, sword drawn but lowered. Despite having only just regained consciousness and having his field of vision restricted to this sideways view through the gaps in the carved side panel of an elephant-top palanquin, Dasaratha's military mind grasped at once that their procession had been attacked.

But by whom?

Slowly, painfully, he forced his eyes open once more. The nausea seemed to have passed momentarily. But all he saw was the same puzzling tableau. The only added detail he was able to glean was the red-hooded figure of Rajkumari Sita, his new daughter-in-law, standing in the front line of the phalanx, close behind the senapati, who seemed to be barring her way deliberately. Dasaratha tried to turn his head, risking another attack of nausea, but the ornate pattern of the sandalwood panel carving hid anything further from his view. He would have to raise himself to see above the side of the palanquin.

His elbow groaned in protest, and with a disproportionate sense of achievement he managed to raise his head a few inches higher. At once he heard a gasp from behind, and the tinkling bangled arms of Kausalya caught hold of him, bearing him up. To his left, acting just as quickly, Sumitra's delicate hands also added their own strength, and with the help of his two queens, he was able to sit up against the side of the palanquin. One of the maharanis placed a bolster behind his head, so he could rest it and yet look around. He started to ask a question, then found himself able to see over the side panel at last, and all questions became redundant.

Rama stood on a ledge beside the rock-strewn mountain

path, holding a great longbow, the likes of which Dasaratha had not seen except in paintings of legends and myths. The bow was a magnificent creation, its enormous span seemingly constructed for three men rather than one. From the unnaturally gaudy way in which it reflected the afternoon sunlight – sending shooting arrows of pain into Dasaratha's eyes, forcing him to raise his trembling hand to shield himself – its celestial origins were unmistakable. Dasaratha had seen only two such bows in his life before, both depicted in the great fresco of the Battle of Siva and Vishnu portrayed on the northside ceiling of the vast dome of Suryavansha Hall, back in the Palace of Ayodhya, painted a hundred years earlier during the reign of his grandfather Raghu. A veteran of the arts of war, Dasaratha had looked up at that magnificent portrayal too many times not to recognise such a weapon when he saw it in reality.

But he did not have time to admire the bow, or the ease with which Rama hoisted it high, as if he was accustomed to using such celestial astras daily. It was the figure standing directly opposite his son that now caught Dasaratha's attention and held him enraptured in breathless awe. A figure out of yet another painting in Suryavansha Hall.

Dasaratha knew at once that the white-haired brahmin, with his distinctive pug features and stocky appearance, could be none other than legendary Parsurama himself. The axe on the shoulder of the dhoti-clad brahmin left no further doubt as to his identity. And in that same instant, Dasaratha recalled where they were: halfway up the side of Mount Mahendra, where legend had it the axe-wielder had retired after his last cleansing of the earth. With that, the final piece of the puzzle clicked into place and Dasaratha recalled the explosion that had shocked his ailing brain into unconsciousness. The brahmin had burst out of the mountain itself – and there, high above, was the splintered maw marking the place he'd emerged.

Without needing to speak a single word to the two maharanis standing beside him in the palanquin, watching his son as anxiously as he was now, Dasaratha grasped the significance of the entire scene at once.

Rama was facing Parsurama in single combat.

Suddenly the tableau on the rocky ledge exploded into action, and Kausalya realised with new horror that Dasaratha was not saying a word to stop it – or perhaps he could not. She began to rise again, to cry out, but controlled herself. It would not do to intervene now. She might distract Rama by calling out. And there was the matter of honour to be considered: after all, the brahmin had challenged Rama fairly and openly, in front of fifty thousand witnesses. For her to intercede now on his behalf would be dishonourable, humiliating. She had no choice but to brace herself and watch . . . but there was one thing she could do honourably.

Kausalya prayed to her patron deity, the mother-goddess Sri in her supreme incarnation, the original creator of all, the One True God to whom even mighty Brahma bowed and paid homage. *Let this end now. Let it end without anyone else coming to harm. But most of all, let Rama be safe and well.*

Then she watched as the brahmin hefted his axe and charged at Rama.

Rama was prepared for the assault.

Ever since the brahmin's first appearance, he had missed the power of the maha-mantras Bala and Atibala, that fiery shakti that had flowed through his body and brain, igniting every cell, firing it up to that hot-as-ice, cold-as-flame preternatural state that had so quickly become as familiar to him as the tensing of his own muscles, the feel of his own skin.

But the shakti of brahman had been stripped from him. Taken away as the price for wielding the Brahm-astra. He had known the consequence of unleashing that great celestial weapon. Yet he had accepted the responsibility and fulfilled his dharma, saving the lives not only of those who resided in Mithila City, in the direct path of the Asura invasion, but of all mortals who would eventually, inevitably, have faced the death-wrath of Ravana.

And now he stood before Parsurama without any force other than his own mortal strength.

And what good was mortal strength before the legendary power of the axe-wielder? He who had cleansed the earth of kshatriyas so many times before?

How could one solitary warrior stand before such a legendary challenger?

All these thoughts flashed through Rama's mind in the fraction of an instant.

And then the time for thinking was past.

The brahmin attacked.

Parsurama charged at him, his axe swinging at Rama's neck with enough force to carve another passageway through the mountain. The brahmin moved with preternatural speed, belying his white-haired ancientness, the stockiness of his physique and the heavy mass of his upper body. There was no time at all for the young rajkumar to dodge the blow, nor did Rama have any weapon with which to deflect the swinging axe. The Bow of Vishnu, however potent its celestial origin, was but a bow after all, not a shield or sword. So fifty thousand breaths caught in as many throats as the watching Ayodhyans saw their prince face the rushing gleam of that legendary blade without moving an inch.

Rama simply stood his ground.

He let the axe come flying at him with all the force of Parsurama's headlong-rushing swing. He let the blade of the axe strike his exposed neck, catching it on the right side of that narrow stem, midway between his delicate collarbone and strong jawline. An artery pulsed once in the instant before the blade struck the dark, almost bluish skin. Sita's eyes were among those that saw the throb of Rama's lifeblood in his bared neck, as distinct as the flutter of a bird's heart in its exposed breast. A single pulse, like the beat of an unheard dhol-drum at some distant funeral procession. And then the blade struck home with enough impact and shakti to shatter a mountainside of basalt rock into smithereens.

3

The axe struck Rama's neck with a sound like nothing human ears had ever heard before. It was less a sound than an absence of sound. An utter blankness, as if the axe had struck the trunk of a tree so thick and soft that it had penetrated right up to the haft. But even the softest treetrunk would have issued *some* sound, the faintest of pulpy thumps perhaps, or the tiniest thwack as the enormous axe-blade imbedded itself in its bed of living cellulose. Whereas when the edge of that legendary blade hit Rama's neck, it gave off no sound at all. Or rather, no audible sound.

What ensued instead was a vibration that began at the exact point where blade met skin, and spread outwards in ever-widening concentric circles, like a boulder flung into the midst of a placid pool. The edge of the blade hit the dark skin of Rama's neck and shivered visibly. Sita could see the blade blur with the force of the vibration, like the wings of a hummingbird. She saw the vibration travel back up the haft of the blade all the way to the hilt, into Parsurama's fingers, his hirsute forearms, his muscle-knotted arms, all the way up his thigh-thick shoulders, up his own bullish neck, to his teeth, which were set to keening, and his face, which twisted into a paroxysm of agony and disbelief as the vibration shuddered through his entire being, his eyes widening not with anger now but with shock. At the same time, she saw also the air itself, the very air around both combatants, filled with motes of dust from the rockfalls in the slanting afternoon sunlight, tremble as the wave of vibration passed through it. She saw the concentric circles of unheard sound spread outwards from Rama until they encompassed the entire ledge on which both men stood, outwards to the tips of the lowered lances of the front-liners – these shivered briefly, startling the men who held them – and then, with the sudden impact of a whiplash, the wave struck the Ayodhyans themselves, herself as well, rippling back behind them, passing through them like some invisible force. And she felt the keening in her teeth, a screaming absence of sound that filled her brain with agony, and her heart clenched tighter than a smith's bellows for one frozen instant, before the vibration moved through her and past her and behind her, spreading throughout the silently watching lines of Ayodhyan soldiers and their beasts of burden.

At that same instant, Parsurama was flung back across the length of the ledge, a distance of some twenty yards, his body bending over as it travelled, until his back struck the side of the mountain with a shuddering impact. A crack appeared in the mountainside, causing entire plates of stone to shiver and crackle all around, and the white-clad brahmin fell to the ground, landing, appropriately enough, upon his knees. A cloud of dust from his impact with the mountainside drifted down like powdery snow, coating his bare sweat-glistening shoulders and hirsute body.

He remained there in that behumbled posture for a long moment, his face still twisted in the expression of agony with which he had reacted to the keening vibration of the axe striking Rama's neck. Then his face cleared, and realisation came to him slowly, in stages. First, the disbelief. Then the shock. Then the anger, sudden and white-hot, flaring in his eyes and nostrils. Then the fear, unfamiliar and long forgotten, a stranger to his indestructible heart. Then, finally, like a shedding of scales, the understanding, clear as water, upon his face.

Parsurama rose slowly to his feet, setting first one heavy foot upon the surface of the ledge, then the other, pushing himself upward as if the very effort of fighting gravity was too much all of a sudden. He stared across the sun-drenched ledge at Rama, standing exactly as he had stood all this while, slender, a mere boy, clutching the Bow of Vishnu in his right hand.

Parsurama said softly, yet loudly enough to be heard by every set of ears throughout the ravine, 'Who art thou?'

There was no reply. Rama remained standing as he was, staring at Parsurama with that expression of calm serenity that Sita had already begun to recognise as his *look*.

Parsurama asked again, louder: 'Who art thou? Tell me truly.'

Still Rama stood motionless, serenely silent.

'Who *art* thou? I beg you, answer me.'

The entire ravine was silent now, listening. For the urgency in the brahmin's voice, the tone of panic, was alarming. They were watching a demi-god brought down to his knees.

Finally, when nobody expected a response any longer, Rama replied. His voice was as soft as a gentle breeze, carrying the lilt of distant birdsong, so soft one barely knew if one heard it or imagined it, like the imagined sound of the ocean echoing deep within a large seashell.

'I am Rama,' he said simply.

Parsurama stared at him. The brahmin's eyes were as stunned as those of a lion bested by a gazelle. The axe in his hand still trembled faintly with the aftermath of the supernatural vibrations.

Rama fitted an arrow to the Bow of Vishnu. Sita started as she realised that the arrow had appeared out of nowhere. She knew quite well that there had been no arrow or quiver when Parsurama had tossed the bow to Rama earlier. Then again, there had been no bow either a moment before that. If the bow itself could materialise out of thin air, why not an arrow?

Rama pulled the cord of the bow back with the familiar leathery sound of hide being stretched to its limits. Sita could almost smell the resin, feel the coarse grip of the curved wood, hear the minute sounds the wind made as it thrummed on the taut bowstring. And she could feel, as if she was within Rama's mind for that fraction of a second, the utter raptness with which the archer set his eye on the target, a drawing of all focus on that one arrowtip-point to which the missile must travel, the fading away of all other sights and sounds, all other sensations, leaving one in a capsule outside human time and space, outside one's own self almost. It was a sensation that Sita had adored since the first time she had experienced it, standing with a tiny child's bow to her small shoulder at the tender age of three, Nakhudi and the bowmaster of Mithila Palace standing to either side, whispering instructions in her infant ears.

Rama spoke again, quietly. 'You know this arrow.'

Parsurama was still standing as before, his axe clutched in his right hand, slightly trembling, his face and stance that of a man who had suffered a mortal blow to the nether regions yet would not look down at the damage.

'It is the arrow with which my Lord Siva razed Tripura to the ground. That single arrow was sufficient to bring the city crashing down to dust and cinders.'

After a pause, Rama said, 'Then you know what will happen if I loose it at you.'

'One of two things,' Parsurama replied. 'Since I am given the gift of invulnerability, it may not destroy my being. Yet it may take away all the accumulated penance I have acquired over millennia of bhor tapasya. Or it may destroy my ability to move through worlds as I do now, simply by cleaving through barriers with my axe.'

After a moment, the brahmin added slowly, 'The choice is up to the one who looses it.'

The silence on the mountainside was palpable. If this were a katha told by a daiimaa at bedtime, Sita thought, no child would have believed that fifty thousand watching people could make so little sound.

Rama said, 'You are a brahmin, and I have been raised to honour and respect all brahmins. For kshatriyas have changed much since last you set foot upon this mortal realm, axe-wielder. It is true that once our caste was arrogant and thoughtless, that we were raised as brute hunters and warriors, slaves to our baser instincts and incapable of understanding the Vedas, let alone reading them. But that has all changed in the millennia since you last cleansed the earth. Now kshatriyas have come to accept their secondary status to brahmins. Some, like my father-in-law Janaka, whom you know well, are as learned in the Vedas as any maharishi and as pious in their lifestyles as any tapasvi sadhu. The code of Manu Lawmaker, founder of my dynasty and builder of mighty Ayodhya, is followed religiously by all kshatriyas. Thus have countless kshatriyas offered their swords, their wealth, their kingdoms, their daughters, and even their lives to brahmins on demand. My ancestor Raja Harishchandra did so, and was ever exalted in the annals of Suryavansha history. So did my grandfather Raghu fulfil a brahmin's demand for guru-dakshina even though it bankrupted him. Only a fort-night past, my father surrendered my brother's life and my own unto Brahmarishi Vishwamitra, sending us untested into the Bhayanak-van to battle Tataka and her hybrid hordes. I could relate countless instances, yet let one last one suffice.'

Rama had not relaxed his hold upon the arrow as he had spoken this long speech. But he had let the arrow point upwards, towards the sky, the better to enable himself to address the brahmin. Now he lowered the bow and aimed it once more at the axe-wielder before he continued speaking.

'I could wreak a terrible fate upon you if I so choose, with the use of this astra. Yet I shall honour your caste and knowledge by giving you the choice. What would you have me do, brahmin? Destroy your ability to move through the seven worlds, rendering you as immobile and hapless as a broken-winged bird fallen to gritty earth? Or shall I decimate the accumulations of all your millennia of hard penitential meditation? Answer me quickly, for this weapon, once armed, must be used.'

The slanting sun had descended and now shone directly at the western face of Mount Mahendra. Its rays found the white-clad brahmin, turning his beard and hair into wreaths of flame, and his eyes into glittering hot diamonds. For a moment it seemed that the legendary one, pinned down by the searchlight beam of the sungod, was about to burst into flame himself.

Parsurama raised his axe, his eyes glinting with moist-ness in the hard sunlight. 'I pray to you, do not deny me my ability to move through worlds. For then I shall die slowly but surely, just like that broken-winged bird you spoke of. But since you must unleash the weapon of Lord

Vishnu, then use it to destroy my penance and all the boons I received as benediction for that penance.'

'So be it,' Rama said, and without another word he loosed the bow-cord. The arrow left the Bow of Vishnu with a sound like a comet streaking over the earth's surface, close enough to be heard yet not close enough to touch. The sound was a boom that filled the entire sound spectrum. The arrow ignited in mid-air at the instant it left the crescent of the bow, and Sita found herself, as if in a dream, able to see every yard of its progress, as if time itself had been stopped still by the arrow's loosing. It blazed fiercely as it travelled, with a fiery white-hot light, and the air warped around it, turning rainbow-hued and rippling angrily like the corona of distortion around an intense flame. It seemed to take aeons to reach its destination, and when it did, she saw the result with dreadful clarity.

The arrow encountered something *around* Parsurama, some invisible force sheathing the brahmin. It paused briefly, and a screaming, banshee-like sound rose from its point of contact, as if this unseen barrier was unimaginably hard to penetrate. Then, with a noise like the tip of a blade piercing a wine-bladder filled to bursting point, the arrow penetrated the invisible bubble and entered the person of Parsurama himself. But even as it entered, the arrow passed through his being, leaving no puncture wound nor releasing any blood or causing physical damage. Whether thereafter it entered the face of the mountain or simply evaporated, she did not know. That was all she was given sight of.

The return to normal time and awareness was as wrenching as a collision with a stone floor after a long fall. Sita put a hand up to her head to steady herself,

disoriented and shaken. Every soldier around was similarly disoriented. *Mortals are not meant to witness such
sights. Yet we were given sight of this in order that we
might provide witness.*

Parsurama staggered forward, head lowered. Liquid
dripped steadily from his forehead, and at first Sita
thought it must be blood, that the arrow had caused some
bodily harm after all. It seemed as though his very face
was melting. Then, as the brahmin used his axe to stop
his forward fall and rested his weight upon the weapon,
raising his head fractionally with the force of the effort,
she saw that the wetness was caused by his caste-marks
melting and sloughing off his face. The shame and humiliation he felt were clearly visible in that moment of utter
defeat, and despite his earlier arrogance and avowed
intention to kill her companions and destroy her blame-
less husband's life, Sita could not help but feel a softening of her resolve. A great urge overcame her fear and
caution.

The soldiers around her were still reeling from the
disorientation caused by the loosing of the arrow, and
she took advantage of their lapsed attention to dart
forward, passing between a momentary gap in the closely
packed ranks to break through the front line, beyond the
ranks of lowered lances, to where Rama stood with the
bow in his right hand. He turned his head at her approach,
sensing rather than hearing her, and she was relieved to
see that his eyes did not shine any longer with that peculiar inhuman blue glow. She gestured towards the
brahmin, hoping Rama would comprehend her intention,
and he understood at once, nodding his approval.

She ran past Rama, to where Parsurama bent over
almost double, his arm holding the axe trembling with
the effort of keeping himself upright. She took hold of a

corner of her sari and, pulling hard, tore it off raggedly. Parsurama stirred at the sound of cloth ripping. Sita bunched the soft fabric in her hand and leaned over, showing it to the brahmin. He glanced up at her, and she was shocked to see his grey eyes filled with tears. She daubed gently at the melted caste-marks on his forehead, wiping away the stains from his cheeks and beard. Cleansed of the marks of his brahmin stature, his face seemed old and weary, long past its point of endurance. He could have been any elderly brahmin in some neglected temple of a forgotten deity, eking out his days on charity and forage. He could have been her father. In that moment, she knew that for all their bluster and arrogance, all men were but motherless boys in their moment of defeat. Perhaps that was the reason for their arrogance and bluster in the first place. She wiped a last stain from his shoulder and then backed away, joining her hands in respect of his status. A brahmin was more than his caste-marks.

He bent his head once, thanking her, then tried to straighten. She knew better than to offer to help him in that action. He managed to stand upright with a great effort, looking now like the old brahmin he truly was rather than the legendary avenger and slaughterer of countless warriors. Sita backed away, then turned and went to stand beside Rama.

Rama's face remained the same, yet she felt that he acknowledged her gesture towards Parsurama and approved of it. She stood close to him, feeling the warmth of his body and the warmth of the sunlight, both intermingled inextricably.

Parsurama inverted his axe with visible difficulty. He held it now with the blade down and the handle aloft, the traditional gesture of surrender.

'Rama Chandra of Ayodhya, aeons ago, after I had cleansed this earth the last time of kshatriyas, mighty Kasyapa requested me to cease my slaughter. He asked me to give this Prithvi-lok, Mother Earth, a season of rest, to give mortalkind a chance to prove their worthiness once more by giving birth to a new generation of honourable, respectful kshatriyas. I see now that this has come to pass. I had promised Kasyapa then that I would not spend a single night here on earth again. I returned on this day because I heard the sound of Siva's bow breaking and mistakenly believed that my axe was needed again to teach kshatriyas a lesson. Instead, it is I who have learned a lesson. Young master, had you even a shred of impurity in your thoughts or feelings, any lapse in your fulfilment of your dharma, you could not have escaped the bite of my axe. Even now, your severed head would lie in the dirt and dust at my feet. Your very survival proves your purity of thought and intention, your perfection of your duties, your adherence to your dharma. Never before have I encountered a kshatriya as dedicated and selfless as yourself, one who is so true to his vows and to the code of the kshatriya. Truly, I say upon this very axe with which I have dispatched so many of your caste-comrades to the netherworlds of Yamaraj, Lord of Death, you are worthy of all honour and admiration. You have redeemed my trust in the warrior race, and in mortalkind as a whole. I bow before you and acknowledge that my vengeance is finally done. No more shall I return to Prithvi-lok and lay waste to kshatriyas. By your leave now, wielder of Vishnu's bow, I shall return to the heart of Mount Mahendra whence I came, there to dwell eternally, for I am still blessed with immortality, and there will I stay in perpetual meditation, offering penance for all the blood-letting I have committed, until the end of time, or until such time as my lord and master Siva Himself sees fit to send Yamaraj to escort me on that final journey to the afterworld. I pray, my honourable victor, give me leave now to depart from your presence.'

Parsurama turned to face the mountain once more, lifting his axe only when his back was to Rama, and placing it upon his shoulder.

'Maha-dev,' Rama said, striding forward. Sita remained where she was, watching him walk over to the mountain face before which the brahmin stood. Rama held the bow out to Parsurama.

'You have forgotten to take Vishnu's bow,' Rama said.

'Nay,' Parsurama replied, without turning around. 'I have no further need of it. It belongs to you, Rama Chandra. It has always belonged to you. Do with it as you see fit.'

The brahmin stepped directly into the mountain, passing through the solid rock like water absorbing into cotton, and vanished completely from sight.

4

Lakshman's horse crested the rise and he sat speechless for a moment, enraptured by the vision of the Sarayu Valley spread before him for as far as the eye could see. *Home at last*, he thought. Despite the delay caused by the encounter in the ravine, Guru Vashishta had worked his magic. Their passage over the back of Mount Mahendra and through the ravine had brought them out not on the far side of the same range, but a good fifty yojanas further north and west, into the heart of the Kosala nation. Lakshman's heart leaped with sudden joy as he recognised familiar landmarks and realised that they were almost within sight of Ayodhya.

With an involuntary whoop of joy, he spurred Marut forward and downward, negotiating the winding path that would connect up soon with the raj-marg, the king's highway that led straight to Ayodhya. Now, as the procession descended the far side of the mountain range, he found himself longing with all his heart to see the familiar spires and marbled domes of Ayodhya once more. Could Rama and he have been away only a mere fortnight? Surely it was longer than that! It felt like an eternity now.

Behind him came the chanting legions of the First Akshohini, raising a new round of jubilation as they spied the familiar vista too. For hours now the Ayodhyans had shouted themselves hoarse, cheering and chanting praises to their prince and saviour. If any of them had felt some disappointment at not staying in Mithila for the full duration of the wedding feast days, it was more than made up for by the extraordinary encounter on the mountain. Already riders were splitting away from the main company, setting off towards Ayodhya at double speed, dispatched by the captains to carry the news of Rama's historic duel with Parsurama to the capital city before their arrival. One more legend to add to Rama's growing list of achievements.

Lakshman rode towards the head of the long procession, to join his family and share with them the glorious thrill of returning home to Ayodhya once more.

As they came on to the last straight stretch of the king's highway, Sita braced herself, her mind swirling with long-remembered images of towering spires, vaulting arches, looming domes, and, most of all, the lights, the fabled jewelled lights of Ayodhya. That was what she remembered best from her childhood visits to Mithila's sister city: that breathtaking panorama of lights glittering like a regal crown astride the roaring Sarayu.

If anything, she expected to be regaled by an even more fabulous view than the one from her childhood memories. Coming here after eight long years, she expected to find the Kosalan capital even more resplendent and regal. The years of peace had been good to all the Arya nations, and most of all to Ayodhya. She had heard so much about the richness of Ayodhyan fashion, jewellery, lifestyle, architecture, culture and goods. She had grown up hearing the glowing accolades paid to the growing prosperity of the Kosalan nation by the many diplomats and delegates who returned to her father's court with chests overflowing

with gifts and samples; had read about it in the trave-
logues of scholars and sadhus who made the long trek to
study the wisdom of Ayodhyan seers; had been discreetly
shown the advances in military technology and technique
by the weapons masters and few veterans who still clung
to the old ways even in peaceful Mithila. Except for spiritual and philosophical learning, the capital of the Kosalan
nation had clearly outstripped even its neighbouring
Vaidehan sister in its accumulation of wealth and magnif-
icence. As Mithila had progressed spiritually and cultur-
ally, Ayodhya had enriched itself literally. And while she
had been her father's good daughter, taught to respect
Vedic learning as being more important than the garnering
of wealth and fine things, she had been made naturally
curious by those tales of Ayodhyan luxury. And of course,
there had always been her sister and cousins, ever eagerly
gossiping about wildly exagerated tales of the decadent
Ayodhyan lifestyle.

But in her heart, it was still that first clear sight of the
lights that she sought. To measure the now against the
then, complete the long circle of time, pin past with the
present, and see with her newly matured eyes if the fabled
city could truly measure up to the one of her childhood
memories.

All that cumulative expectation came to a head as she
brought her horse in line with Rama's as they took that
last turn together and came into the straight.

From the elephant palanquin she heard Rajkumar
Bharat shout proudly: 'Princesses of Mithila, behold the
jewel in the Arya crown . . . Ayodhya!'

'Ayodhya!' echoed Shatrugan.

A chorus of excited squeals rose from Sita's sister and
cousins and their maids. Normally Sita would have felt
irritation at such a show of girlish giddiness, but now,

after all that had transpired, she couldn't help but feel a certain surge of excitement too. The air was thick with anticipation; the soldiers had stopped their singing a moment ago, growing silent all of a sudden as they came around that last bend. Now she could feel the hastening rhythm of fifty thousand hearts beating faster as they came within sight of their beloved capital. She found her own breath caught in her throat and reached out without realising she was doing so, catching hold of Rama's sleeve.

He glanced at her, allowing himself a small smile, brought her hand up to his lips and kissed it gently.

'Su-swagatam,' she heard him say. *Welcome.* 'Welcome to your new home.'

Airavata, the lead elephant, raised his trunk and bellowed a loud tribute of his own, answered down the mile-long procession by his close to two hundred fellow elephants. After travelling tens of yojanas to Mithila and back these past two days, and losing a dozen-odd fellows in the avalanches and earthquake on Mount Mahendra during the skirmish with Parsurama, even the bigfoot were pleased to be coming home. As the last elephant bellows faded away, echoing off the high rises of the dense woods that flanked the Sarayu Valley, the entire procession fell silent, marching in perfect step along the last stretch of the raj-marg.

The front line came into the straight, and were immediately buffeted by a cool wind blowing down the length of the Sarayu. The voice of the river, ever present since Mithila Bridge, now became a resounding roar, dimmed only by the height of the king's highway above the bed of the river. To her right, Sita saw the road fall away sharply to the river twenty yards below. The far bank was a good thirty yards or more distant, heavily wooded with a profusion of trees. The glacial tang of the river filled her nostrils, assailing her senses with its powerful perfume redolent of Himalayan ice-glaciers and a mineral content so rich that the royal vaids in Mithila claimed that simply drinking Sarayu water would cure all minor ailments. Unlike the gentle oceanic swelling and ebbing of the Ganga in her own kingdom, the Sarayu was a potent force of nature, wild and robust, crashing and shattering its white glacial waters upon the splintered dark rocks that lined its lower banks. Far ahead, she could hear angry rapids and cascading waterfalls. The very air blowing off the river was so sharp and sudden that she knew her delicate sister must be shivering at the abrupt drop in temperature.

But while her ears and other senses absorbed all these thrilling observations about the river, it was her sense of sight that was commanding her attention.

She peered ahead, at the glittering light-bejewelled city of her childhood memories.

And was shocked to see . . .

Nothing.

Nothing more than the dim dominating silhouette of the Seer's Tower, twin to the Sage's Brow in her own home city, limned by the soft red glow of the just-set sun. The sky above was a painter's mad flourish of colour: bright robin's-egg blue shot through with startling streaks of scarlet and crimson and fiery orange. In the far northern distance loomed the foothills of the north-western Himalayas. The thin, tapering, swordlike tip of the Seer's Tower interesected these three vistas, the distant mountain ranges, the sky and the lush growth of the Sarayu Valley itself. Below that, where there should have been lakhs of blazing fireflies, hundreds of thousands of city-illuminating lights clustered in a river-striding span, there were only the dim crouching shadows of darkened structures.

Ayodhya lay in darkness. Not a single wall-light, not one mashaal, not even a tiny diya – the clay lamps used as traditional lights of greeting – shone out from the city. Like an Arya widow veiled by a white shroud of mourning, Ayodhya lay still and dark upon the banks of the Sarayu, its lofty ivory towers and gleaming white structures devoid of any illumination.

The ensuing silence in the ranks of the procession was deafening. The roar of the Sarayu, the cries of the large flocks of wheeling birds in the darkening sky, the cricking of a particularly persistent cricket: these sounds filled the silence, accentuating the shock and disbelief.

Pradhan-mantri Sumantra broke the spell. The prime minister spurred into movement, riding a few yards ahead, then turning the head of his horse around to enable himself to look up at the palanquin of Maharaja Dasaratha.

'Maha-dev,' he said anxiously, 'perhaps I should send ahead to see what the matter is. We have had no word from Ayodhya since yesterday after all.' He gestured at the darkened city, lying gloomily beneath the pallor of dusk. 'This does not bode well.'

Sita glanced up at the ponderous form of her father-in-law, peering down at his prime minister. Even in this dim light she could read his anxiety in the slowness of his response and the doubtfulness of his tone.

'Guru-dev,' Dasaratha said hoarsely. 'What do you advise?'

Guru Vashishta's voice sounded unconcerned. 'Ride on regardless, raje. All is well at Ayodhya. You need fear nothing.'

There was a brief moment of silence, then Pradhan-mantri Sumantra said hesitantly, 'Parantu, maha-dev, there must be a reason for this unusual phenomenon. Word must surely have reached of our homecoming. It's inconceivable that the city lights should be so extinguished. Why, let alone the homecoming effulgence, even the routine wall-lights are not lit. Surely something is amiss. Not even during the Last Asura War—'

'Shantam,' the guru broke in. *Peace.* 'Be not alarmed, good Sumantra. Take my word for it. Ayodhya is safe and well. We shall all be welcomed home with due pomp and ceremony as merits our maharaja's return, and as befits the triumphant homecoming of our two brave young champions. Mark my words, this homecoming shall be recorded in the annals of Suryavansha history for millennia to come.'

'Guru-dev?' Even Sita could tell that Dasaratha's voice sounded more suspicious than anxious now, as if the maharaja, like herself, had heard the unmistakably playful undertone in the great seer's voice. 'Do you have anything to do with this . . . unusual welcome?'

Even in the dimness of the dusky evening, the smile on the guru's white-bearded face was unmissable. 'Pride is not considered a virtue amongst us seers, raje. Yet it would be immodest of me to deny my part in this. Yes, indeed it was I who asked that the lights of Ayodhya not be lit at sunfall this evening, for I knew that our return would be at this exact moment.' The guru gestured toward Sumantra. 'I chose not to tell you either, good Sumantra, as I wished it to be a surprise.'

Sumantra was still riding at the same awkward angle, trying to keep his face to his king and the royal seer. His horse whinnied as he forced her to ride virtually sideways and backwards. Sita resisted the urge to giggle at the ludicrous sight. Even the pradhan-mantri's perplexity was amusing to behold. 'But, great one, what possible reason could you have to issue such a command? What kind of greeting would it be for the king and the princes and their new brides to come home to a city shrouded in such inauspicious darkness?'

Guru Vashishta raised his hand. 'Not darkness, Sumantra. A show of light, the likes of which you have never witnessed before. And most blessedly auspicious. It shall be our tribute to the Lord of Light himself, our great god Vishnu the Preserver. For as one entrusted with the sustenance and continuance of all life upon this mortal realm, it is He who ensures that life-giving light bathes us constantly. And so, it is to His great grace that I dedicate the spectacle you are about to witness.'

The guru then raised his hand, indicating a halt to the entourage. Word was passed on swiftly down the ranks, elephants, chariots, cavalry, foot-soldiers, bullock-carts all coming to an orderly halt within moments. It was not difficult: since the sighting of Ayodhya, shrouded in shocking dullness, progress had slowed to a virtual crawl anyway.

When the procession had halted successfully, Guru Vashishta uttered a mantra to enhance his voice. Sita recognised it as the same mantra used by her father when declaiming his daily pravachans to the populace, those religious sermons that were so renowned throughout the Vaideha kingdom. By the time the two-line mantra was ended, the guru's voice could be heard clearly by even the nethermost riders in the Ayodhyan procession.

'Ayodhyans, listen well, and hear the music of Rama's achievements, chanted aloud by the citizens of our proud city. The gayakas of our great capital, pride of the Kosala nation, have assembled today on the first wall to regale us with the richness of their talent, as well as to demonstrate the shakti of a people united in their common love for a liege who loves them just as much in return. In honour of our princes' homecoming, I present the music of Ayodhya.'

As if on cue – and, Sita reflected astutely, that *was* probably the precise cue decided upon by prior arrangement – the sound of sonorous chanting rose from the first wall of defence of moated Ayodhya. Through the dim gloamy light of darkening dusk, she could just make out the tiny silhouettes of figures on the high first wall, holding what seemed to be musical instruments in their hands. It was an unusual sight. She had expected to see lances and longbows on the walls of Ayodhya, not tanpuras and sitars. As the opening chant of the sacred syllables of Aum rose in harmony, even the procession behind her joined their voices to the utterance. She heard Rama add his own voice to hers, intoning the trisyllabic word that was the essence and core of all Arya worship.

'Aum.'

The melodious trisyllable rose to the darkening sky. The vivid colours of sunset were fading fast, giving way to the dull grey tones of nightfall. Even the birds wheeling across the sky and calling from the thickets on either bank seemed to grow quiet, as if in awareness of what was to come. The roar of the river itself seemed to die down. The insect sounds and twilight noises faded away. The persistent cricket made one final stubborn call, then fell silent.

The muscians of Ayodhya began to sing.

At first Sita heard only the musical alphabet in which the music was being intoned, the sweet-sad, heart-tugging harmonies of the evening raag. The voices from the first wall rose in perfect harmony, carrying across the magically hushed Sarayu Valley like a kusalavya bard's ballad in a respectfully quiet crowded tavern hall on a winter's night. The voices rose and fell in cadence, the beautiful notes blending one into the other in a wave of harmony that flowed like a constant-running river rather than separate waves. It became impossible to tell one voice apart from the others, male from female, sweet from sad, bass from tenor, high-pitched from low. They all fused into one enormous orchestra of rhythm and melody, a Sarayu of music that washed through the valley, filling every living heart with the blessed grace of human art.

And then, as the voices rose to a peak, climbing the high intertwining notes of the raag's mid-point, Guru Vashishta spoke softly, his voice somehow audible, despite the music, to every last person in the long procession.

'In honour of Prince Rama's return after his victorious mission, on behalf of the citizens of Ayodhya I present this new pinnacle of Arya talent and artistic achievement: Raag Deepak.

'Behold,' the guru went on, his voice harmonising and blending with the voices of the distant singers. 'Our brilliant tribute to the Lord of Light.'

And Vashishta joined his own voice to the others, raising the entire performance to a new level, a pinnacle – to use his own word – of musical epiphany, the effect profoundly moving, like the sound of a million human souls reaching for something long denied, a touch of the bleeding, thorn-encrusted foot of a martyred saint, a brush of the lips of a devi whose trishul delivered life and death together in the same paroxysm of ecstasy, a quest for a boon from a dark three-eyed deva who sat on a stone ledge high atop Mount Kailasa and from whose brow the mighty Ganga eternally flowed. The voices rose until it seemed they must surely touch the belly of the sky, bring down a shower of fragrant blossoms, or a terribly beautiful blizzard of blood-ice, or at the very least prise open the long-locked doors of Swarga-lok, that realm of the gods long denied to mortals.

With a sensation akin to stepping under a waterfall of near-freezing white water, Sita realised that the lyric of the song was but a single word repeated over and over, stretched in the Arya musical fashion into a thousand and eight syllables and more, intoned in more different ways than one could imagine possible. The word was *Rama*. And the raag, as the guru had stressed so significantly, was no ordinary evening raag. Deepak. Literally, *Light*.

And in the instant that she realised these two things, all across Ayodhya the lights began to come on.

It began with a single clay lamp – diya – atop the first wall, held upon the outstretched palm of a little girl. The flame came into being at the tip of the wick of the tapered clay lamp, and even at this distance it was evident that no hand had lit that flame. A fraction of a moment after, a row of diyas lit up, perched atop the palms of a hundred little girls, standing upon the first wall. Then a row of mashaals ignited at the first gate, blazing up as fiercely as if struck by a bolt from the bow of Indra, lord of thunder and lightning. Two large fires, placed at either side of the first gate, roared into life, illuminating row upon row of young men and women lined up, awaiting the return of their victorious princes and their companions, gleaming steel thalis piled high with pooja articles, diyas – which also lit up – and sacred prasadam, sacramental foods consecrated by priests at poojas conducted earlier. Now the entire first wall, stretching to either side as far as Sita's eye could see, was illuminated with light, and she could see and admire the intimidating fortifications of the most militarised nation in the Arya world.

Lights began flaring into life across the city. Atop buildings, on the six inner walls of the city, set in concentric circles, and set off by three enormous moats filled with Sarayu water and teeming wild carnivores (or so Sita had heard and read so often before). Mashaals blazed into brilliance, storm lanterns clutched in the hands of tens of thousands of waiting citizens, enormous lamps specially mounted for the occasion atop towers and spires, streetlights raised high on poles, even the bonfires of rakshaks on the hills and rises around the city; and towering above all these countless fires, at the very peak of the spire of the Seer's Eye, a great blueish-orange ball of flame sprang into being with a sound like a thunderbolt cracking, coinciding with the final syllable of the Raag Deepak, sung by the assembled gayakas of Ayodhya with passionate fervour. For this was not brahman magic at work: this was the result of pure musical prowess. The lights of Ayodhya had been brought to life by the succession of notes in a certain order, performed with enough sincerity and devotion to please Agni himself, god of fire. In other words, these lights were living proof of Ayodhya's intense love for its prince-heir. *Rama*. The final syllables faded into a blessed awe-struck silence.

As a rising murmur from the Ayodhyan procession turned into a roar of exultation, Ayodhya lay clothed in a garment of benign flame, blazing brightly enough to turn the night just fallen into gaudy day once more. A day created by the power of human song.

Guru Vashishta, his voice fallen silent along with those of the other singers, turned to face the procession. His eyes sought out and found Sita in the forelines.

'I welcome all of you, Mithilans and Ayodhyans alike, to Ayodhya the beautiful, the unconquerable, the effulgent. Let this display of our passion and art be proof positive of this fact: that as long as we continue to light up this proud city's name through adherence to karma and dharma, so shall mighty Ayodhya shine on eternally.'

5

When the sound of distant shouts and cheers woke Manthara, her first thought was that Ravana had arrived at last. Her lord and master had finally triumphed and taken Ayodhya. She was filled with vindictive triumph: now these stupid mortals would learn what it meant to challenge the Lord of Lanka!

The next instant she was filled with bone-numbing, heart-chilling terror. Fear at the realisation that she had not completed the task Ravana had entrusted to her. And when it came to fools and failures, as Ravana had often remarked to her, he suffered neither gladly.

She groaned and sat up slowly, cursing her throbbing head. The first thing her eyes came to rest on, swimming into focus, was the guard by the door of her sleeping chamber. He stood with his left shoulder to her, sword held loosely in his right hand, pretending to be looking at nothing in particular.

She cursed him and his sisters, then his mother as well for good measure.

He ignored her. Like all the other guards assigned to guard her in her own chambers, he was used to her foul tongue.

The sound of dhol-drums erupted from outside – they seemed to be coming from the palace courtyard itself.

The dhol-drums were soon accompanied by the almost cheerful lowing of conch trumpets. Far in the distance, the sound of singing could be heard. She realised with a sinking heart that an Asura invasion would hardly be greeted with celebratory music.

'So what is it this time?' she snapped at the guard. 'Did some Arya raja father his five thousandth illegitimate child?'

The guard glanced at her sharply, and made as if to answer her. Then he seemed to think better of it and turned his back deliberately on her, facing the outer chamber.

She spat at him, the spittle landing far short.

She lay like that sullenly, licking at her mental wounds and thinking of all the ways she could torture the man – and everyone else who had ever said or done anything to offend her in her lifetime. It was a long list and would have occupied her the rest of the day at the very least, but at some point something clicked into place in her mind. What better time to attempt an escape than during a celebration? She had already figured out that the jublilation outside was occasioned by the return of Rama and the rest of the royal family. It hardly took a genius to realise that.

But it did take a genius to figure out what she had just come up with. A plan so simple yet devious that it might just work. There might yet be a way for her to fulfil her mission and propitiate the Lord of Lanka. Even if his invasion had not succeeded, he would certainly appreciate her loyalty. And who knew, perhaps her little scheme might even open a new door of possibility for the Lord of Asuras himself.

Rising with difficulty, she shuffled with exaggerated effort towards the door, clearing her throat noisily to alert the guard. He turned at once, sword barring her way, eyes narrowed with suspicion darting to each of her hands in turn as if seeking out the weapon he half expected her to be holding. She kept her wrists bent, the bare hands twisted arthritically.

Aloud she said, 'I must needs partake of some nourishment. Pray, ask a serving girl to fetch me something from the bhojanshalya.'

He looked at her warily. He wasn't suspicious of the request – she hadn't eaten since being confined and it was only natural that she should be feeling some hunger – but it was her unexpected politeness that was making him stare so. That was easily corrected.

'Get a move on then, dolt. I'd like to have it for supper and not breakfast!'

He grimaced and nodded curtly. Then he struck his sword hilt against his helmet twice, alerting his fellows throughout the chamber. Manthara rolled her eyes in exasperation. These kshatriyas and their idiotic military rituals. She wished there was a spell she could use to simply vanish them all out of existence.

The guard's fellow from the outer chamber came in and both men spoke briefly, keeping their voices low – as if they were trading national secrets! – then the guard from the outer chamber returned to his post while the guard from her sleeping chamber left the apartments. She slouched her way to the door of the room, peering out. The guard at the outer door was standing with his back to her, facing outwards as he usually did. The bhojanshalya was a fair distance away, which meant it would take the other guard several minutes to return. She had that much time at least to attempt her escape.

Now kill the remaining guard.

For an instant, she almost turned her head to look

around. The voice had risen so easily within her mind, it was almost like hearing Ravana speak again. The way he had spoken to her at her secret rites, cursing and torturing her, yet commanding and cajoling her as well. She shuddered, holding on to the memory of those encounters, and gathering her strength together for what she was about to do. *This is for you, master. That you may see how I serve you yet.*

She licked her parched lips nervously. The guard still had his back to her. He was a large man, broad through the shoulders, and armed with the shortsword that the palace guards favoured. After all, as guardians of the royal family and attachés, any fighting they were likely to engage in would be at close quarters. Like this very situation. She took another step closer, unable to keep her mind from visualising how easily that gleaming half-yard of Kosala steel would slice through her reedy tendons and emaciated flesh, hewing through the thin bone beneath without much effort. Then, with a prayer to one of her nameless gods, she raised her forefinger and aimed it at the guard.

A green flame shot out from the tip of her finger, streaking like a blowdart to the back of the guard's neck. It entered the base of his skull, making a slight sizzling crackle. A faint, indistinguishable rotten odour filled the air briefly, and the guard clutched the back of his neck with his free hand, gasping once. He swung around, his sword still clutched in his right hand, and his eyes, very wide and afraid in his helmeted face, found Manthara. He staggered forward, stumbling as the spell rotted his brain. Already, greenish mucus was dribbling from his nostrils, mouth and ears, and as he took yet another step, Manthara saw greenish goo seep from the corners of his eyes.

She backed away until her shoulderblades struck a

wall, shuddering briefly in terror. The dying guard's mouth opened and closed as he fought to release a cry to warn his colleagues outside the apartment. Only choked gasping sounds emerged from his dribbling lips, too faint to be heard over the raucous cheers that had broken out throughout the palace complex. He tried to raise his sword hand, to strike it against his helmet, but his arm seemed to be caught in a rictus, spasming with a life of its own. He stumbled forward again, closer to Manthara, now barely three yards away, then two yards, then . . . She raised her hands, biting back the urge to scream aloud. Just as it seemed he was certain to run her through, all awareness vanished from his face, his eyes rolled back in his head lifelessly, and he collapsed on the thick pile rug. The rug absorbed any sound his half-armour or weapons might have made striking the ground. The guard lay still, a puddle of greenish fluid seeping around his head.

Manthara released a tightly held breath, lowering her shaking hands. She was shivering all over, like a leaf in a monsoon gale. Her brain felt wrung out, like a towel squeezed dry of all moisture. It was hard to use sorcery again, after the tremendous amount of energy she had expended to work that last illusion, changing the very architecture of this section of the palace to put a lie to Rani Sumitra's words. The effort hadn't succeeded entirely – Rani Kausalya had still had her placed under house arrest – but it had saved her from being proven outright guilty and executed on the spot. Now, even this minor death-spell had sucked her dry. She needed to hide, to recover her energies. And to work her magic from some hidden place away from prying eyes.

She was shuffling towards the doorway when the guard jerked upright, rising from the waist, suspended impossibly without the support of either hands or feet, raised his sword-hand, and plunged the blade into the emaciated flesh of her thigh.

It was all she could manage not to scream out with agony.

The sword point entered her inner thigh, penetrating through the thin layer of flesh, passing right through her leg, emerging out the other side, and striking the wall behind her. It made a dull wet sound as it went through her flesh, ending in a metallic thump as it emerged from her thigh and struck the wooden wall.

The dead guard bent his neck impossibly, raising his head to stare up at her. His face, oozing fluid and blood from every orifice, was a gruesome mask at some carnival nautanki side-show. His eyes remained rolled up, the whites showing, his open mouth gaped, greenish-black tongue lolling to one side, and when he spoke, the words came directly from somewhere deep within his innards. 'Jai Shree Ram.'

Then he collapsed again, falling on to her right instep, the rim of his helmet cutting her foot as sharply as any kitchen blade slicing a mutton joint. The sword remained embedded in her thigh, pinning her to the wall.

'My lord,' she sobbed, barely aware she was speaking the words aloud. And lost consciousness for a moment.

When she came to her senses again, she was looking down at the hilt of the shortsword sticking out of her thigh.

Pull it out. Quickly. The other guard is already at the bhojanshalya, giving instructions for your supper.

Manthara stuffed one hand into her mouth, biting down hard enough to draw blood. With the other, she reached down and took hold of the hilt of the sword. It still retained warmth from the grip of the dead guard.

She clutched it as tightly as she was able, then pulled. It came out of the wall with a jerk. The pain in her thigh was excruciating; it felt as if an iron pike had been driven through her heart. She tugged again, and for an instant the sword would not budge. Then, with a liquid sound, the blade passed back the way it had entered, and popped out of her body. Because of the angle at which she was gripping it, the edge of the blade sliced upwards as it emerged, enlarging the wound further. The cut travelled all the way up to her hip, grating against the bone, causing another explosion of pain. She stared at the sword, its blade smeared with dark-maroonish blood. Her blood. With a grimace, she dropped it on the rug. It fell with a muffled thump, lost in the jubilation ringing out from all sides.

Then she bent down, face contorting as the thigh wound screamed pain, and tugged at the dead guard's helmet. Pulling it off her foot, she shuffled to one side. Finally, she was free.

Now go. Get out of here quickly before the other guard returns and it's too late.

For an instant, in her pain and delirium, she forgot that it was only her own voice speaking within her head, not Ravana. She sobbed through clenched teeth, straining to keep herself from screaming out with pain. 'But where shall I go? The guards at the entrance to my apartment—'

And almost as if it was he replying, the answer came back at once.

You won't get out that way, old crone. Go to the south corner of the apartment. To the window.

She limped and shuffled to the far corner of the chamber. Manoeuvring around each item of furniture was a chore in itself, even though her chamber was barely furnished. She reached the southern wall. An open window was set in the wall, looking out on to the inner court-yard. Through it she could see large numbers of serving girls, maids and untitled queens mingling together, expres-sions of great joy on their faces. Several women were preparing pooja thalis to anoint soldiers returning home. She didn't have to be told what the scene meant: Maharaja Dasaratha and the rest of the wedding party were returning home from Mithila with the four princes and their new brides. She fought back the urge to put her head out the window and spew vomit over the jubila-tion, leaning against the wall instead, struggling to stay conscious through the pain of her wounds. Blood seeped steadily down her thigh, drenching her sari.

Now go through the window.

She raised her head and stared up. Only the ceiling met her dazed eyes. Go where?

The window, hag. Climb through it.

She stared out of the window again. It was a fall of perhaps fifteen yards to the courtyard below. That didn't concern her in itself. With her shakti restored, she could cushion her own fall magically. What was puzzling her was why Ravana would wish her to leap down into the midst of that mêlée. How could it possibly help to jump into a courtyard full of witnesses? Then she remembered feverishly that it wasn't Ravana, it was her own voice telling her to do this insane thing. Or was it?

Jump now.

Manthara swallowed. Tears poured down her wizened face, almost as profuse as the blood dripping from her wound. She went to the window, holding on to the jamb as she tried to figure out whether it was best to go through head or feet first.

Quickly, witch. The guard is returning from the bhojanshalya now. You must be gone before he arrives.

She decided it didn't matter either way. The fall would smash her withered bones no matter which way she went. And if this was the punishment Ravana had in mind for her, then perhaps it was best she go quickly and as decisively as possible. She stuck her head through the window, pushing herself through with an effort. Her hunch stuck for a moment, and she saw a young serving maid glance up. Their eyes met for an instant, and recognition spread across the pretty young woman's face. Her mouth opened to say something to her companions. Just then Manthara applied one final burst of willpower and squeezed herself through the narrow window, striking her injured thigh on the upper jamb and crying out involuntarily with pain. As she fell, she saw the stone ground of the aangan below rush up to meet her head.

'Oh master,' she whispered. 'Save me.'

6

Manthara.

This time, she could not tell if the voice came from within her own fevered, tortured brain, or from some other source.

She opened her eyes to find herself enveloped by pitch darkness. The absence of light was so complete, she could not see even her hands in front of her face. Her first instinct was relief: she had learned to love the dark ever since, as a child, she had begun to see through the eyes of others around her the hideous ugliness of her hunchbacked deformity. Darkness was her friend, her ally. It was the light that she feared.

She clawed at the ground with her sticky, bloodsmeared hands. Even without light to see, she could tell at once that it was tiled with the same immaculately smooth hand-polished redstone that adorned the floors of every chamber in Suryavansha Palace, not the coarser grey flagstones that were used in the courtyards and outer areas. This meant that she hadn't fallen into the chaukat after all. She was still within the palace somewhere. *But where?*

Then her fingers found the place on her thigh where she had sustained the sword wound, and she gasped with disbelief. The gaping wound was closed, the skin uncut and unblemished except by the normal parchment-like coarseness of age. Her hand flew to her face next; she touched her eye accidentally in the darkness and it began to water as she blinked rapidly. It was true. She was healed again. She could feel the strength returned to her limbs, the crushing void gone from her mind, life filling her veins and senses once more. She thanked him silently for the miracle: no matter how many times they repeated this cycle of torture and restoration, it never ceased to evoke her deepest awe.

'Master! It is you, then! You have healed me. Thank you, swami. You are truly magnificent.'

The room flared to life around her. Manthara blinked, dazzled. She forced her eyes to open, squinting against the brightness. A figure stood before her, familiar in silhouette yet too brightly backlit for her to be able to focus her vision upon it.

'Manthara,' said a voice she knew almost as well as her own. 'It's me.'

And the sari-clad figure of Maharani Kaikeyi strode toward her, heavy gold jewellery clinking noisily.

'My lord?' Manthara said shakily, almost doubting her own mental equilibrium for once. 'Is it thou?'

Kaikeyi paused, threw her head back and emitted a low throaty laugh, her mouth reddened with paan-chewing. 'Very good, Manthara. You see through this guise then. But will anyone else?'

Manthara raised and lowered her eyes, turning her head this way then that as she examined the Second Queen as closely as she could manage. 'My lord, your art is beyond compare. The perfection of the illusion—'

'Spare the superlatives, hag,' Kaikeyi said with a startling red-toothed smile. 'There's work to be done. And since you've foolishly exposed your role in our great campaign, it's up to me to finish the task we began.'

The Second Queen paused to adjust her sari, drawing the pallo up to her head, covering her gleaming burnished dark hair with the end of the silk. 'And now,' Kaikeyi said, 'I will show the young prince that one battle alone does not win the war. He will pay for the decimation of my forces on the fields of Mithila. He will pay by losing everything he holds dear.' She added with a chilling grin, her eyes reflecting the dancing fire-light, 'And every*one*!'

And then she turned and walked away, vanishing instantly. Manthara was left in darkness once more, alone.

Kaikeyi was awakened by the sound of dhol-drums pounding a martial rhythm. They were all around her, beside her bed, upon the sweat-drenched mattress, filling the darkened boudoir in which she lay, their heavy thunder reverberating in her chest, making her collar-bones and breastplate ache, hammering at her temples, filling her skull with their remorseless monotony.

She rose slowly to her feet, prepared to feel the rest of the familiar morning-after symptoms of her nightly excesses, even to empty the contents of her bilious belly and void her bowels before starting to feel something akin to human.

Several moments passed, and to her surprise, nothing of the sort occurred. Neither nausea nor rising bile. No knifing pain in the bowels nor the old swimming blurri-ness before her eyes. Instead, she found herself steady on her feet, able to see the room well enough, and her head clearer than it had been for days . . . or years even.

Then she remembered: she hadn't been out carousing the night before, or the night before that. She had been here these past two nights – or was it longer? She couldn't recall exactly. But she was certain of one thing. She had been nowhere but here. In her own bedchamber, lying on this very bed, brain feeling as if it was being pressed down by a hundred-kilo weight. She glanced around the boudoir. As if in confirmation of her recollection, there were no telltale depleted jugs of wine, no half-quaffed goblets cast aside, dribbling soma on to the richly brocaded rugs.

She sniffed, and smelled only the fragrance of orchids and incense which was usual to her chambers, and below that, the faint odours of her own exudation, understandable after a long sleep. She certainly needed to bathe herself, but nothing worse than that.

So it was true. She had slept sober and woken clean. If so, it was a first for her in a long time. Years certainly.

What day was it anyway? She recalled it being Holi feast day only two days earlier . . . three days at best. So much had happened that day, her mind was still filled with little flickering fragments of images. The last of which was the sight of Rama and Lakshman departing with the seer Vishwamitra while she watched them from a window, Manthara beside her, saying something nasty as usual. After that, everything was a blur. She strained and struggled, but nothing else came to her mind. How long could she have been asleep to not remember anything at all? Not more than two days surely, or simple hunger and thirst would have woken her earlier, wouldn't they?

As if hearing his name being called, Annapurna, deity of food and drink, began working upon her appetite. Her stomach churned suddenly, reminding her that it hadn't been fed for a while, and her throat was parched with a thirst so great, it felt as if she must have water at once or die for want of it.

She started to call for a serving maid, then thought better of it. There was a jal-bartan right there by the bed. She drank deeply of the cool rose-scented water, relishing every gulp more than she would have relished the finest Gandahari red right now. When she set the copper-bottomed silver jal-bartan back on its bedside stand, it rang hollowly, empty.

The dhol-drums had continued unabated all this time. Now, their steady marching rhythm sounded less hostile and menacing, more festive. She caught the sound of conches blowing, and the shirring ocean-like roar that could only be the sound of large numbers of people cheering. Somewhere in the city, a celebration was in full spate. A celebration of what? There was only one way to find out. She called for a serving girl and waited, patiently for perhaps the first time ever. When nobody responded to her calls the third time, she began to feel uneasy. This was strange; surely someone ought to have heard her and responded by now.

Her feet felt as if they had been freed of lead fetters. After a few steps, a light sweat broke out on her face and upper body, and once she had traversed several rounds of her boudoir, she felt she had regained enough confidence in her ability to navigate the outer world once more. She went to the door of her bedchamber and pushed it open, expecting serving maids to come rushing at the sight of her. Instead, an explosion of light assailed her. She blinked, her eyes adjusting to the gaudy brilliance after the unilluminated dimness of her bedchamber.

The outer chamber was arrayed with a profusion of diyas, each painted a different colour and lined up in neat rows along the walls. The effect was dazzling, like Deepavali, the festival of lights. But that was ridiculous. Deepavali was celebrated on the last moonless night before winter, not in early spring! There must be some other reason for this light show. Obviously it was related to the commotion going on in the city outside. She couldn't think what it might be, but there must be *something*. Some formal occasion she had forgotten probably. Manthara would know. Manthara always knew. Speaking of which, where *was* Manthara? For that matter, where was everybody? She had only just realised how deserted her chambers were. At first she'd assumed that everyone was in the outer chambers, but there was not a soul in sight here either.

It took her a full circuit of most of the main level of her palace, some two dozen large rooms with antechambers, offshoots, and intersecting corridors, before she would admit to herself that there was nobody around. Her chambers were deserted.

This was unusual in itself. With a personal retinue of fifty-odd serving girls, and as many guards, all hand-picked from her own clans, kith and kin from her native Kaikeya, there ought to have been at least a dozen around to cater to their mistress's needs at any given time. But all she found were more diyas blazing away brightly in every corner and cranny. She even stopped at the pundit's desk to consult a panchang, the religious almanac of moon phases by which all Arya festivals were assigned. No, there was no special occasion listed for several days after Holi. What was going on?

When she found that even the guards at the outermost door to the apartment were missing, a cold prickle of fear ran down her spine. She sat down on a diwan in some antechamber and tried to think, to remember. What had happened before she lost consciousness? What had she done? She knew that she had done something wrong, something bad. But what?

Her hand struck something metallic, causing it to echo hollowly. She glanced down reflexively, and recognised the beaten-gold-plated breastplate that she always wore to feast-day mêlées. The rest of her armour was here as well, beside some soiled rags and a mud jar filled with vile-smelling metal-polishing fluid. Some maid had been shining her armour before putting it back into storage until the next occasion.

She held the breastplate in her hands, turning it over. Unexpectedly, the corner of the lower end scraped her forearm, drawing blood. She peered at the metal, seeing that the latch that locked the two halves together had been twisted out of shape, as if the person who had last worn it had taken it off carelessly, undoing the latch with more force than was necessary. She put the armour plate down on the diwan, examining the cut. It was barely a scratch, only a thin, faint line of blood visible below the first layer of skin. Not worth washing even. She raised the hand to her lips and instinctively licked the scratch. The salty taste of her own blood filled her palate, startling in the strength of its flavour. Her senses were attenuated by her long sleep-fast.

The taste of blood stirred something deep within, awakening some hidden memory. Something that had happened recently. At the mêlée? She vaguely recalled taking part in the event, riding hotly down the track, lashing this way and that with her cat-o'-nine-tails, downing opponents one after another, wounding some severely – she remembered liking that, laughing at their screams of agony. Then a memory of herself riding and flinging a spear at the stuffed-dummy target, an effigy of a rakshasa – again that old nemesis – before being distracted by the glint of fading sunlight off a chariot too richly gold-plated to be any other but royalty. Dasaratha, riding off the field in the direction of the palace, and following close on his heels, Kausalya. And like a tidal wave rising out of the heart of the ocean, it all returned with shocking intensity.

She remembered feeling a sudden red-hot rage. So Dasaratha and Kausalya were leaving the Holi festivities early, no doubt to sit together in some cosy nook and resume their dalliance of the morning, leaving right in the middle of Kaikeyi's own event, as if she were nothing but one of the many hundreds of kshatriya contenders seeking a purse of gold and a little name-glory, not the Second Queen of Ayodhya, and by rights the *First* Queen.

As she sat there, holding the armour in her hands, pressing it tightly enough that the jagged corner of the clasp dug into the flesh of her forearm, drawing blood, it all burst into her brain like a wave in a monsoon-maddened ocean battering a rocky cliff. The clasp dug deeper, gouging through flesh, but she was barely aware of the pain and the blood, the shakti of her mind's eye more powerful than the two feeble organs of contemporary vision. She saw herself, like a player in someone else's dream, face puffed and swollen with excess, red-cheeked with fury, striking aside a companion in the mêlée, breaking left into the stands, leaping over the audience with no heed for the safety of the watchers, numbering children among them, then riding off the field in the wake of Dasaratha and Kausalya. She saw the scene in the Seer's Tower several minutes later, herself flinging abuse and accusations at both her husband and his First Queen. Remembered with terrible clarity the wretched things she had mouthed, those foul words and fouler insinuations. Ending with her about to cast the spear at her real-life nemesis, stopped in the nick of time by her son Bharat.

Kaikeyi came to her feet. She dropped the armour plate and backed away sightlessly. Blood dripped in a steady stream from the gouge in her forearm. She put a hand before her face, gesturing, as if trying to dismiss the tumult of images that rolled through her fevered brain now, begging for mercy, mercy.

The images rolled on. The memories seared her with their sharpness and unbearable clarity. It had been years since she had seen so clearly. Not since she'd been a child, a girl in her father's court. Had she been blind all these many years? Surely she must have been, to have done so many terrible things, felt such nameless, meaningless rage. A demon had possessed her then, a rakshas born of some nether realm, captaining her body and mind like a mahout on an elephant's head, guiding its every move. Why else would she have indulged in so many petty deceptions, committed such venal sins, manipulated and connived? That could not be her doing. She was not a bad woman, she was just a . . . needy woman. A woman who wanted what was hers.

Yes, a rakshas must have taken over her body and soul. Nothing else could explain all those years of excess and self-indulgence and . . .

The images cascaded before her mind's eye like a waterfall at Gangotri, mystical, mythical source of the sacred Ganga. She bathed in its wash, the memories fermenting and foaming thickly around her, purging her of every last crime of omission and commission. She laughed hysterically, then wept profusely, then shook her head like a madwoman, then ranted and raved and foamed at the mouth like a tantrik in a trance, wandering through her desolate palace, striking a vase here, shattering a mirror there – who was that wild-eyed witch anyway? – breaking her glass bangles, symbols of her status as a married woman, then walking upon the shards of glass until her bare feet bled all over the marbled floors. She left a smear-trail behind her everywhere she left, like the track of some gargantuan dying snail.

Somehow in her delirious rage of recollection, she wandered out into the chaukat of her palace, the square courtyard in the centre of the royal residence. She stumbled and fell against the fountain, striking her forehead on the foot of the statue, then broke yet again into uncontrollable sobs. The blood from the forehead cut trickled into the fountain and swirled in the eddy. Outside the palace walls, the roars of happy citizens, the festive pounding of dhol-drums, the palpable thrill of some momentous event continued unabated, an unfeeling backdrop to her solitary pain.

At one point, she thought she heard her name being called out. She raised her head and looked up – directly into the eyes of Lord Shiva, standing in his one-footed posture atop Mount Kailasa, the serpeant Takshak wound tightly around his blue throat, his trishul in his right hand, the other hand held palm outward as if offering a benediction and blessing. It was only the fountain statue, of course. The Ganga flowed out of his coiled locks into the fountain where she lay bleeding.

She thought she saw him smile down at her in sympathy, then say, 'Awaken, Kaikeyi. Awaken with grace.' But when she listened closely, she heard only the ragged rhythm of her own tortured heart. Slowly, as if she was an actor in a nightmare dreamed by someone else, she stumbled out of the chaukat, towards the gate of the palace, towards the sounds of celebration outside.

7

Sumitra was the first to see her. Kausalya felt the Third Queen's arm on her shoulder, tugging urgently. She turned, expecting Sumitra to be pointing to some new show of adulation by the assembled citizenry of Ayodhya, a group of children chanting the praises of Rama and Lakshman perhaps.

The city seemed to have turned into one giant mad festival of lights, the people thronging the thoroughfares and margs by the tens of thousands at every turn, slowing the progress of the procession to a crawl. A distance that ought to have taken minutes to traverse had already taken up the better half of an hour since sunset.

Yet Kausalya would not have hastened their progress for anything in the world. It was thrilling to witness this show of joy and celebration, the sheer delight the people took in their prince's victory, *her son's* victory, the open-hearted love they displayed.

Effusive as ever, the city's outpouring of love and admiration was flagrant in the extreme. The royal elephants were already festooned with gaily coloured streamers made from strips of tie-dyed cloth, the air glimmered with descending chamkee, tiny pieces of glittering tinsel fluttering everywhere, conch shells sounded constantly from the highpoints, kusalavya bards sang loudly new ballads

lauding the achievements of the rajkumars Rama and
Lakshman in the Bhayanak-van, on the road to Mithila,
at Mithila, on the slopes of Mount Mahendra. At every
crossroad, scores of red-faced children yelled their throats
out endearingly. There were groups from every caste and
guild. Kausalya even spotted a black crowd of tantriks
raising a ganja-fuelled chant, swaying like rubbernecked
dolls, slashing themselves with razor-edged whips to prove
their devotion, whirling in a paroxysm of ecstasy.

And then there were the young women, or even older
women for that matter, trying desperately to catch the
eye or ear of the two princes. These were by far the most
vigorous of all. She watched the antics of this particular
type at various points on the march, marvelling at the
brazenness of some of the bolder women. Didn't they
know that Rama was married now? Certainly they did.
Didn't that dissuade them from seeking his affections?
Not a whit. After all, she mused, if their beloved maharaja
could have three titled queens and three hundred and fifty
untitled concubines, why, then by that measure of reckoning, Rama was practically a virgin!

Kausalya saw that while Rama waved cheerfully to all
his admirers, he didn't have the lingering gaze and raised
eyebrows of his brothers Bharat and Shatrugan, or even
the occasional wide-eyed glance of Lakshman. Yet she
knew that it was Rama who was unusual in this respect
rather than his brothers: it was no shame for an Arya
prince in the first flush of youth to dally with any number
of women he pleased, even to seed them with his children. It was considered natural to do so. Even the three
giggling princesses of Mithila, Urmila, Mandavi and Kirti,
seemed unabashed by the eager female attention showered on their new husbands; if anything, they actually
seemed delighted that they had husbands who were so

hotly desired. But they weren't fooling Kausalya at all; she knew from long and bitter personal experience how that initial pride would fade and turn to self-doubt and then apathy after a hundred or so nights spent in their lonely boudoirs knowing that their husbands were in the arms of some other woman that night, and most other nights.

Rama, though, sat with his wife Sita, both waving and issuing namaskars of acknowledgement in perfect unison, as if they were one person, wedded not just in sacred matrimony but also in heart-lock. Lakshman still retained his seat by Rama's side – or rather, by Sita's side now – rather than on the other elephant palanquin with his brothers and his own wife, not seeming to mind that Rama's attention was clearly focused on Sita. Even at the height of the frenzy, when they passed a crowd numbering easily a lakh or more at the concourse of Raghuvamsha Marg and Harischandra Avenue, Kausalya saw the little exchanges of words and touches that continued unabated between her son and his new bride. Yes, there was love there already. More than that, there was a bond.

She sent up a silent prayer to Sri the mother goddess for having brought home a bride who was not only well born and gifted with many physical and mental talents, but whom Rama had fallen so much in love with so soon. She had noticed the little intimate huddles and affections they had shown each other as children before Rama's gurukul years, but after all, children who loved one another could as easily grow up to become indifferent strangers in adulthood. It was not so with Rama and Sita. Clearly, whatever bond of personality and soul they had shared in those tender years still remained, rendering them dear friends already. She had heard about their travels and adventures together, and wondered if those days and experiences had hastened this union of hearts and minds. Probably it had played its part; she knew how common battlefield romances could be, especially between kshatriya men and women who fought side by side. But surely it couldn't be the whole of the matter – that would be too simple an explanation. No, she decided firmly, there was clearly some deeper-rooted force at work here. She saw the way Rama pointed excitedly to the palace complex, looming now ahead of them as the elephants turned ponderously on to Raghuvamsha Avenue, pointing out to Sita the various palaces and other structures. She saw also the way Sita looked up adoringly at Rama as he spoke. That was no simple road-romance; that river ran deep.

A pair of young dev-daasis broke through the PF cordon to run after Rama's elephant, and when one of the young girls threw up a bunch of flowers, it was Sita who bent low enough to catch it in time, before passing it on to Rama. She laughed and waved back at the girl, who was shouting up incoherent endearments to Rama. Sita turned and said something to Rama, who laughed in return and, tossed the flowers back into the crowd on the other side of the marg. The whole exchange took place so smoothly that Kausalya couldn't help but feel the faintest twinge of admiration. Look at how perfectly attuned to one another they were already: she and Dasaratha had never been like that, had they? Not that she could recall. Not even in their young, wanton days.

She put a hand to her sari-clad breast in dismay as she realised that she was actually feeling envy of sorts at their happiness. She resolved at once that she would perform a special haven rite to ward off any ill-luck occasioned by any hostile observers. If she, Rama's foremost well-wisher, could feel even the faintest touch of envy for him, then imagine the host of uncharitable thoughts that must be winging their way from other, less well-disposed minds.

Such a perfect mating would certainly bring its share of envious onlookers, starting with the many royal and noble houses that had hoped ever since his birth to make Rama their son-in-law. They would still hope, she knew, and would not expect that Rama might refuse to entertain any other matches. Yet, knowing her son and seeing how content he was, she felt instinctively that he would be unlikely to take another wife any time soon, if ever. That would bring a small avalanche of envy and resentment, and the warding ritual would be worth undertaking in advance. She must do all she could to preserve and sustain this nascent love. She knew how precious and fleeting it could be. Hai, Devi, bless us and preserve us in your grace.

She sat contented and occupied with these thoughts in her own palanquin, keeping one watchful eye on Dasaratha beside her while basking in the glory of her son's newfound popularity and adulation. The procession was approaching the main palace now, the gates already wide open to receive them. A fresh burst of noise, colour and revelry rang out in the square as the citizens and military declared their love for their champions one final time.

In moments they would be home, and she would welcome her daughter-in-law into her house for life. To think that she, Kausalya, had gone from being the neglected wife and anxious mother of two weeks ago to the ceremonially reinstated First Queen and proud mother of this great night. How strange were the ways of the devas. Who could have foreseen such a dramatic chain of events only half a moon ago? And yet she tried not to gloat at her newfound success too much. One never knew what new changes the samay chakra could bring with the next turning of that great wheel of time.

She was still basking in the roars and cheers when Sumitra caught her arm. 'Kausalya. Look!'

She turned, expecting anything but what Sumitra was pointing to.

Rani Kaikeyi was running after their elephant. At first Kausalya actually mistook the Second Queen for some penitent driven mad by religious ecstasy. Kaikeyi's appearance was shockingly dishevelled, her waist-length hair flying like a dark cloak behind her, her sari unravelling unheeded, her breast half bared . . . and was that blood on her forehead? What had she been up to? She was barefoot, and apparently her feet were wounded too, for Kausalya could see splotches of drying blood on them. If Kaikeyi had been carrying a weapon of some sort – a dagger, or perhaps even a lance, she wouldn't have put that past the woman – then Kausalya would have assumed that this was a continuation of the hostile rage displayed on the eve of Rama's departure to the Bhayanak-van.

But the Second Queen was empty-handed and clearly in great distress. Now, as she came up alongside their elephant, Kausalya could see the smears of tear-tracks down the woman's face, the smudged kohl around her eyes, and the dripping wet sari hanging soggily from her buxom body. Something had happened to Kaikeyi.

She was shouting now as she ran, yelling hoarsely. Kausalya could just make out the sounds and catch an occasional word, but it was impossible to understand what she was saying. Kaikeyi stumbled over her own feet and for a moment Kausalya's heart was in her mouth as it seemed that the Second Queen would surely roll under the elephant and be crushed to death. But ever-vigilant Airavata rolled his lumbering bulk and stepped over the

fallen rani, the rear edge of his enormous foot landing
on the corner of Kaikeyi's unravelled sari pallo. Beside
Kausalya, Dasaratha groaned at the sudden sideways roll
of the palanquin and grumbled aloud about bigfoot and
their insufferable ways. He hadn't noticed Kaikeyi yet,
his attention being occupied by a bravely saluting row of
disabled PF veterans lined up on the left side of the procession. Kausalya glanced at him but didn't draw his attention to the little drama unfolding on this side. She was
still trying to understand what Kaikeyi was up to, and
why.

The royal procession had reached the palace gates –
out of which Kaikeyi herself had emerged – and a fresh
wave of conches were being sounded triumphantly and
deafeningly by a row of purple-and-black-uniformed PFs,
bringing the long welcome to a culmination. Just as this
new assault of sound exploded, filling the air for miles
around with the sheer bullhorn fullness of its volume,
Kausalya saw Kaikeyi rise to her feet, her sodden sari
now caked with the dust and dung of the avenue, and
reach out to the elephant ahead. She said a single word
that Kausalya could make out, 'Rama!', and then the rest
was lost in the bone-vibrating contralto of the conches.

As the maharaja's elephant trundled through the gates,
Kausalya saw Senapati Dheeraj Kumar ride up alongside
Second Queen Kaikeyi, dismount, and begin speaking
gently to the distraught rani. She looked around wildly,
as if only just growing aware of her surroundings, and
stared dumbly at the general. The senapati directed
Kaikeyi's attention back towards the marg on some
pretext, preventing her from following the procession into
the palace gates, and held her attention for another
moment. The last Kausalya saw was a trio of agitated
daiimaas rushing out through the gates, dodging the

oncoming elephants, and going to Kaikeyi's side, taking hold of her arms. None of them was Manthara, but then Kausalya had never seen Manthara-daiimaa rushing to intervene in one of Kaikeyi's 'scenes'.

Kausalya turned back and saw Sumitra looking at her. Sumitra's delicate face, as light-boned and fragile as a bird's, was pinched with concern. Her eyebrows rose, asking the same question that Kausalya was asking herself: what is Kaikeyi up to this time?

Kausalya had no answer, but the question worried her a great deal.

On the elephant ahead, Rama touched Sita's hand gently. She looked up at him, smiling. The smile faded slowly as she saw the expression on his face. A moment ago, his dark-complexioned features had been lit up by that luminous blueish glow that she was already coming to love. Now, he looked suddenly grim.

She followed the direction of his gaze. He seemed to be looking at a tiny knot of women beside the palace gates through which they had just entered. It appeared to be three elderly matrons – daiimaas, she thought instantly – herding a strikingly beautiful if somewhat overweight woman away from the royal procession. The woman was in quite a state, her sari dripping wet and filthy, as if she'd been rolling in a ditch somewhere, her long lustrous hair knotted and billowing wildly, the front ends of her blouse unknotted and open to reveal her ample bosom. Sita took her to be some madwoman, one of the many driven to ludicrous ecstasy by the sight of Rama or one of the other princes. Rama, probably, for even now the woman's eyes were focused clearly on the foremost elephant, looking directly at them. The daiimaas attempted to lead her away, in the direction of the palace no less, but she twisted and turned, her eyes riveted to Sita's husband.

Just then, their elephant lurched to a halt, and began performing a peculiar sideways shuffling movement, turning to bring itself in line with the palace steps, where its occupants would dismount. Sita lost sight of the madwoman for a moment. Then, as the elephant finished its half-turn, she was given a last glimpse of the lady – for she was clearly of noble lineage, judging from the cautious manner in which the daiimaas were handling her – and a tiny dagger of ice entered Sita's breast, piercing through to her heart, the same sharp pinprick of coldness that she had felt as a girl when she had learned that she had no mother.

The woman was shouting a single word over and over again, her head lolling madly like a jogini in the grip of an ecstatic trance. Even without being able to hear her voice above the deafening sounds of the conches, Sita was certain that the word was 'Rama'.

8

From the edge of his aerie atop Lanka, the king of vultures brooded angrily.

The aerie of the bird Asuras was set upon the highest tower of the black fortress, a thousand feet above the ocean battering the rocky shores of the island. On the north side it overlooked one of the many volcanoes on the island-kingdom of Lanka. One of the more active ones, constantly spewing forth great geysers of blazing lava. The heat reached all the way to the aerie, warming the very stone of the tower. It kept the younglings warm and the other ground-bound Asuras at bay, and these were good enough reasons to suffer the stench of sulphur and gouts of black smoke that drifted up night and day, obscuring the rest of the island of Lanka.

On the south side, the aerie overlooked the ocean itself, brackish and perpetually angry, like the Asura king who made his home upon its waters. Turned blood-red by the angry light of sunset, the ocean stretched to infinity in every direction. Running parallel to the shore, spanning the length of the curved sticklike shape of the island, the black fortress rose like a living thing, a dark grimy pile of greatstone, like the carapaced shell of some titanic ocean creature.

Nestled upon the open ramparts, the aerie was laden

with enormous stacks of hay, saplings and bushels of leaves, hauled up by the bird-beasts and tamped down with their beaks and talons until the tower top resembled some lofty Himalayan nest rather than the roof of a fortress.

At present the aerie was occupied by only a few dozen younglings and a half-dozen decrepit and crippled old bird-beasts, the pathetic remnants of what had once been the greatest flying warrior host on earth. The air was filled with the cranky calls of the younglings as they fought and scrabbled around for scraps. A pair of slightly more mature vulture-gryphons were daring one another to take the first leap off the rampart wall, egged on by the rest of their younger cousins. The resulting cacophony was almost loud enough to drown out the gnashing and booming of the primordial juggernaut below Jatayu's talons.

Almost, but not quite. From time to time, Jatayu could feel the solid rock beneath its claws tremble with the vibrations from the volcano below, and the tips of its wings, hanging a good thirty feet down, shivered with the searing heat. A fresh geyser erupted, throwing up great gouts of red molten magma shot through with black slag, and the fledglings squawked nervously and leaped back into the aerie. They cackled to each other about Jatayu's fearlessness in staying poised there despite the ferocity of the eruptions.

Jatayu barely heard their awed squawking and cackling. The bird-beast was angry, and it had been angry for the whole of the day. On its arrival at the island-kingdom three days earlier, it had found only the old ones of its flock in the aerie, those pathetic youngling-minders that had been too badly crippled, old or feeble-minded to undertake the long flight north for the Lord of Lanka's invasion.

The olduns had nevertheless received their vulture-king

with a mixture of superstitious awe and fear. Once they were reassured that it was indeed Jatayu itself and not their lord's aatma returning to haunt its last roost, they had welcomed it back as best as they were able. Jatayu had been consoled and fed and had its wounds tended to, and even rested these past two nights and days. It had stayed in the large tower-roost long enough to grow weary of the fledglings' constant squawking and squabbling. When it slept, the little ones crawled and flapped and leaped over its large body with an utter disregard for Jatayu's lordly stature or its currently injured condition. Normally, Jatayu would have occupied the far side of the aerie, surrounded by the pick of the plumpest females of its flock, all its needs tended to with lavish care. But there were no females now, nor any males, and the younglings had the run of the entire aerie.

Physically, Jatayu felt almost normal, and it was certain that a few moon-spans of rest and feeding would restore its robust health in full. What it was unable to accept was the loss of its entire flock. It had been bitterly disappointed to find that not a single one of the winged warriors that had set out with it on the flight to Mithila had returned. Every last one had been wiped out by the Brahm-astra. Even though it had witnessed the awesome ferocity of the celestial weapon, it had still harboured a faint trace of hope that somehow, somewhere, a survivor had managed to escape the dragon breath of the mantra and would find its way home.

But three entire days had passed, and just today, Jatayu had made a few brief flights to chase down and interrogate many of the southward-flying birds who had fled the environs of Mithila in sheer terror. All those it questioned roughly were unanimous on one count: there had been no survivors. When Jatayu had told one of the birds, a particularly pompous white swan leading its harem, that it, Jatayu, had managed to survive the Brahm-astra, the puffed-up fool had cocked its head in mock dismay and issued a cackling call that was echoed all down the curving line of its harem flock. Jatayu had wanted to tear off the stupid bird's head with one snap of its mighty beak, but its strength was still depleted and it had already flown far from the island in its chase after the swan flock. It chose instead to turn back, its heart leaden enough to weigh it down until its wings brushed the tips of the foam-flecked waves all the way back to the black fortress.

Clearly, the swan-king had been wrong in its assumption: after all, Jatayu itself had survived, but as its interrogations continued and the same message was repeated by a variety of other south-flying species, Jatayu was forced to admit that it was probably the only survivor of the devastation wrought by the Brahm-astra.

Apart from one other.

Jatayu's mannish features darkened to an ugly grimace as it recalled the block of glassy red stone that had accompanied it on the return voyage home to Lanka. The block had been suspended beneath the pushpak, and from its perch atop the celestial vehicle Jatayu had been able to look down directly at the form murkily embedded in the heart of the veined stone. It had taken every ounce of its willpower to retain its grip on the pushpak instead of letting go as it dearly longed to do. Had it possessed the strength to fly on its own to some other safe clime where it would be rid for ever of the king of rakshasas, it would have done so. But its oozing wounds and loss of feathers and wing muscle had compelled it to cling on to the speeding air-chariot and endure the ten faces of Ravana staring up at it all the way to Lanka. At least the Asura lord's eyes had been closed, all twenty of them.

Besides, it had had no other place to go, Jatayu mused now as it raised its bald head to peer around the dark roost filled with squabbling, crying younguns. The last of its breed were all here in Lanka. Apart from this pathetic clutch, there were no more of the giant bird-beasts that had once dominated the skies. This was all that remained of a proud ruling clan, a few tottering old fogies that could barely spread a wing, and a score and ten younguns too small to know a jatayu from a garuda if they ever saw one.

The thought of Garuda brought to mind the recollection that the lord of winged beings still lived, and ruled over a flourishing and prosperous clan, or even a number of clans by now, up in Swarga-lok, the heavenly realm. But that celestial plane was long since barred to Jatayu. No, here on Prithvi-lok, this was all the family it had left. And the only hope it now clung to was that some of these spitting, quarrelling young brats would grow up to breed a new dynasty of bird-beasts as magnificent as the ones Jatayu had grown with.

The image of its youth brought back a flood of memories of times when Jatayu had basked in an eminence second only to Garuda itself, father of all birdkind. Ah, those had been the days. Before these wretched warmongering Asuras had appeared on the scene, when the name Ravana hadn't been in the vocabulary of any language yet known.

Jatayu was torn out of its memories by a blood-chilling sound. At first it assumed that one of the younglings fooling about on the rampart had fallen over and its wings were too badly frozen with fear for it to lift itself in time to avoid the leaping geysers of lava below. It turned and scanned the aerie. No, the younguns were still safely in the nest, all looking as startled as Jatayu itself, peering around to identify the source of the scream. The olduns shuffled and hopped around agitatedly, calling out to each other and to Jatayu. The bird-king felt sick of their constant mewling and complaints. Was this its future? To live amongst feebles and younguns too nervous to take their first leap? Bah. It should never have flown towards the pushpak in the first place. It would have been better off battling the crab-rats, or even rksas if it came to it. Anything would have been better than this wretched existence.

Then it raised its head to peer in the direction of the setting sun and saw something that made it change its mind all at once. A pair of kumbha-rakshasas had emerged on to the ramparts a few hundred metres west of the aerie. Had they been closer, Jatayu might have suspected them of coming up here in search of younguns – rakshasas would eat anything if they were hungry enough. And those damn nagas and uragas salivated – if snake-Asuras could be said to salivate – at the very scent of young jatayus.

Jatayu scraped its talons along the rim of the rampart, issuing a screeing cry that lacked much of its former vigour but was nonetheless piercing enough to make the younguns cower nervously and a distant flock of swallows, some two yojanas out to sea, veer away and take a major detour from their flight path. For good measure, it raked its claws along the edge of the rampart at an angle designed to cause the most nerve-grating sound. It scored deep long scars in the ancient volcanic rock, cracking one corner and sending it hurtling into the red-orange maw of the belching monster below.

The kumbha-rakshasas glanced up, peering in Jatayu's direction, then turned back and resumed whatever it was they were doing. Satisfied that this wasn't another snack-quest, Jatayu flapped its enormous wings and rose several yards into the air to gain a better angle to see what they were up to. Asuras never came up here if they could help it. The only thing the demon races loathed more than fresh running water was sunlight. For the kumbhas to brave even the dim glow of the waning sun meant that their chore was urgent.

Silhouetted against the fading orb, the pair hunched over something, vigorously working their disproportionately long ape-like arms. Jatayu flapped its way a little closer, its curiousity aroused now. What were they doing?

After a moment, the kumbhas stood upright again, raising up what seemed to be a very tall and thick pole with some kind of banner at its top. It was the banner that they had been struggling to fix upon the top of the pole. They embedded the pole into a depression in the rampart specially provided, and then checked to make sure it was firmly fixed.

That task accomplished, the two rakshasa-sergeants stepped back, lumbering in the leering, simian manner of their sub-species, and peered up at the banner atop the pole. It rippled desultorily in the slow wind for a moment, then a stronger gust caught it and snapped it fully open. It caught the gust and flapped noisily, surprisingly large once unfurled. Jatayu estimated that it was easily ten yards long and half as many in breadth. It had never seen a banner of this type before.

It flew closer, swooping directly over the heads of the kumbhas and giving them a very satisfactory alarm, sending them scurrying back to their trapdoor, hands flapping furiously over their misshapen heads. They popped into the trapwell like rats into a snake-hole, cursed loudly in their grunting-roaring tongue, and slammed the door shut with a resounding bang. Back in the aerie, the younguns and old feebles cackled merrily, applauding their lord.

Jatayu turned back in a wide sweep, craning its wattled neck to see the sigil on the banner. It was black as pitch with red markings. The markings were meant to represent bones and a skull. Jatayu called out in shock as it recognised them. That was no ordinary war banner. It was a death-flag, hoisted to mark the passing of a great lord or king.

This particular death-flag belonged to the lord of Asura races, king of rakshasas, master of the black fortress, ruler of Lanka. If it was flying now, it could only mean one thing.

Ravana was dead.

9

Sita knocked over the golden kalash with her bare foot, spilling raw rice and wheatgrains across the threshold of Suryavansha Palace and into the house. She stepped into a thali filled with water mixed with sindhoor, taking care to let as much sindhoor powder as possible stick to the soles of her feet, then walked across the marble foyer, leaving a trail of wet red footprints across the white stone floor. A roar of cheers erupted from the watching throng of untitled queens, palace staff and even the guards, echoing off the high vaulting dome and travelling through the vast halls of the royal complex. The celebration was echoed by the crowd outside, as the word was passed on that the goddess of wealth and prosperity had entered the royal house in her current form as Sita Janaki, wife of Rama Chandra.

Sita's sister and cousins followed suit, each repeating the rite, and cheers sounded for them as well. Then the four princes of Ayodhya entered the palace formally and took their places beside their respective wives, and each couple in turn paid their respects to the queen-mothers who had preceded them into the palace for this reason.

By rights, Bharat and Mandavi ought to have been received by Rani Kaikeyi, but after seeing Kaikeyi's distraught state, Guru Vashishta had suggested that they continue with the ritual without delay, and Rani Kausalya and Rani Sumitra had stood in for their sister-in-queenhood. So it was Kausalya's feet that Bharat and his bride first touched.

Bharat rose with his head bowed and hands joined. Kausalya felt a lump in her throat as she saw the pain in his eyes. *Oh, Kaikeyi, what use are all our vanities and ambitions if we cannot be there for those who love us truly? These are the moments that we live for as mothers.* Her rivalry with the Second Queen seemed so paltry and insignificant just then; her heart went out to the handsome young man before her, a man so desperately in need of a mother to touch his head and wish him the blessings that only a mother could confer. *Never mind,* she thought, *I'll be a mother to him as well.* She reached out her hand, about to complete the formality, when a voice rang out across the large foyer.

'If you please, Kausalya, I prefer to bless my own son and daughter-in-law.'

Heads turned all across the chamber. Captain Drishti Kumar took two quick steps forward, arm raised in the stand-by gesture that would pit a dozen quads of palace guards against any potential threat. Kausalya saw an expression of extreme puzzlement appear on the captain's stern face. Drishti Kumar blinked rapidly, then his eyes narrowed in suspicion. Bharat and his wife were the only other ones in her line of sight, and the expressions on their faces were those of surprise as well.

Kausalya turned her head to see Rani Kaikeyi coming down one of the two semicircular stairways that joined at the top and bottom to form the periphery of the Suryavansha sun sigil. She blinked, unable to believe her eyes. Kaikeyi was clad in the finest of silk saris, adorned with gold ornaments fit for a bride. With every step, jewellery jangled, bangles clinked, payals tinkled. Her long hair had been freshly oiled, the lustrous tresses glowing with vitality. Her eyes were kohl-rimmed, her lips painted, red sindhoor applied dutifully to her forehead . . . Kaikeyi looked like the epitome of Arya queenhood, resplendent as any of the Suryavansha queens depicted in the frescoes on the ceiling of the domed roof of the palace foyer.

But she was a muddy mess only moments ago. How could she have bathed and remade herself this quickly? It's impossible!

Out of the corner of her eye, Kausalya could sense the excited flurry the rani's unorthodox entrance was causing. It was hardly customary for a queen-mother to arrive at this late juncture, interrupting the threshold-crossing ritual of her own daughter-in-law. Yet, she realised as she scanned the half-envious, half-admiring reactions of the aristocratic families of Ayodhya, the very unorthodox boldness of the action matched Kaikeyi's character perfectly.

Everyone thinks she's making a dramatic late entrance on purpose.

And who could blame them for thinking that way: every pair of eyes was riveted on the Second Queen, magnificent in her bejewelled finery as she descended to the bottom of the stairway, hips swaying in that cocky, swaggering sashay that only Kaikeyi could do so well.

But it couldn't be her. No human being could have achieved such a transformation that quickly.

As the Second Queen began walking towards her, Kausalya's eyes met Kaikeyi's for an instant. She clearly read the arrogant challenge in the woman's eyes. It was as if Kaikeyi were telling her directly, *Go ahead then, say what's on your mind. See where it gets you.*

'I told you, she's bewitched. How else could she have changed herself this quickly? This woman isn't Kaikeyi, it's an Asura posing as her!'

Every pair of eyes in the crowded foyer turned to the speaker. Kausalya turned as well, looking at the woman who had spoken the words that had been on the tip of her own tongue. Third Queen Sumitra stepped forward, eyes flashing angrily, and pointed an accusing finger at Kaikeyi.

'This time she can't deceive us. We're all witnesses. How could she have washed off the mud and dung, changed her sari, painted her face so painstakingly, and adorned herself with all those ornaments in the few minutes since she was taken away ranting and raving?'

A new flurry of reactions broke out, racing through the crowd of court nobles and aristocrats gathered to receive the princes and their new wives home. But it was Dasaratha himself who spoke first. The maharaja, seated on his travelling chair, half rose to his feet, face contorted with incomprehension.

'What are you talking about, Sumitra? What deception are you referring to?'

Sumitra pointed again at Kaikeyi. 'Dasa, Guru Vashishta and Kausalya know what I am referring to. When your condition, instead of improving, grew worse and you fell into a coma, it was not your illness that was the cause. It was poison administered by this shrew in human form.'

Shocked gasps rose from the ladies of the assembly. Dasaratha frowned and looked at Kaikeyi. The Second Queen was standing calmly, eyebrows raised in an expression of mock-surprise.

'You are surely mistaken, Sumitra. How could you possibly believe that Kaikeyi would ever do such a thing?

The setback to my health came as a result of my being attacked by a twice-lifer sent by the Asuras. Guru Vashishta himself freed me of the wretched thing's hold and saved my life. Kaikeyi had nothing whatsoever to do with it.'

Sumitra shook her head. 'Not that, my lord. I speak of another, earlier incident, before the twice-lifer's attack. Kausalya knows of that, but we were loath to tell you about it earlier because, because . . .'

Because the evidence we found pointed to you, Sumitra, being the one who administered the poison, not Kaikeyi. But of course Sumitra could hardly say that now.

The maharaja frowned. He had resumed his seat but still leaned heavily to one side, as if favouring his right arm. 'I still don't follow. What does this incident have to do with the accusation you are levelling at her now?'

'It's no accusation, Dasa,' Sumitra said earnestly, her high-pitched voice cracking as she grew more agitated. 'It's a fact! We all saw her as the procession entered the palace gates. She was running by the side of Rama's elephant like a madwoman, her breast bared, hair untied, sari drenched and filthy with the dirt of the marg. Why, she was led away by the daiimaas only a few minutes ago, just before we performed the griha pravesh ceremony and entered the palace proper. It's physically impossible for any person to have changed her appearance from that state to *this* in so short a while.'

Sumitra emphasised her point by indicating the calmly watching Kaikeyi again. 'I tell you, this woman standing before us is not Kaikeyi. It is an Asura in disguise, another imposter seeking to get close to the royal family and do us all bodily harm.'

At the mention of the word 'Asura', Drishti Kumar's entire contingent drew their swords, and by the time

Sumitra ended, the captain and two quads had taken two steps forward in Kaikeyi's direction, ready to strike.

Dasaratha pounded his fist on the armrest of his chair. 'Enough! Sheathe your swords!' When the guards looked uncertainly at their maharaja, then at their captain, Dasaratha shouted agan, spittle flying from his mouth, 'Sheathe your swords!'

As one man, they obeyed the order, but the captain remained standing where he was, his eyes on Kaikeyi with the canny alertness of a mongoose crouched before a snake-hole.

Dasaratha looked at Sumitra. 'What madness is this, Sumitra? Do you realise what you are saying? You are accusing Kaikeyi, mother of Bharat, of being an Asura in mortal disguise. Do you think I would not know if she were such a being? Or Guru Vashishta?'

Sumitra joined her hands in supplication. 'I beg you, Dasa, believe me. I have seen her with my own eyes, transforming into a nagin and attacking you upon your sickbed. I have seen the hidden chamber where she offers vile sacrifices to her secret deity, the dark Lord of Lanka himself, Ravana!'

At the mention of the rakshasa king's name, the entire congregation exploded in a shockwave of horror and disbelief. People turned to stare at the Second Queen and Third Queen both, backing away in repulsion as if fearing that either might be an Asura in mortal disguise. The memory of Kala-Nemi's wily intrusion was still fresh in their minds.

Dasaratha looked at Sumitra in exasperated bewilderment. 'Is this true? You have seen these things with your own eyes?' He searched around for support or denial. 'Guru-dev? Royal Preceptor? You confirm this too?'

Guru Vashishta, standing at the head of the brahmin

panel that was reciting the sanctifying mantras of the griha pravesh at the north-east wall of the foyer, replied quietly, his voice carrying easily to every ear in the palace conclave. 'I have not had time to verify these things myself, Ayodhya-naresh. Perhaps they may be true, perhaps not. What is true, though, is that there are great forces at work here in this palace, and they are not all directed at the betterment of this family, nor even this kingdom.'

A fresh wave of anxiety swept the congregation. What exactly did the guru mean? Was he confirming Sumitra's accusations, or was he offering a counter-accusation? Several seemed to think aloud that the guru was accusing Sumitra herself of treachery!

Kausalya came to Sumitra's aid, knowing that if she didn't intervene now, the tide would turn any which way. 'My lord,' she said firmly, walking forward to stand beside Sumitra. 'I have seen some small evidence of these matters. Yet as the guru says, the truth was so shrewdly concealed that it was impossible to verify it either way.'

Dasaratha's thick brows beetled. He shook his head in exasperation. Sweat trickled down his face.

Kausalya went on. 'Be that as it may, one thing about which I am fully in agreement with Sumitra is the current deception. Only moments earlier, when our procession was arriving at the palace gates, both of us saw Kaikeyi-rani run out of the palace compound and attempt to come close to the elephant carrying Rama and Sita. She was in a distraught state and excessively dishevelled. Senapati Dheeraj Kumar himself prevented her from coming to certain injury beneath the pads of the bigfoot. She was led away by a trio of daiimaas. Moments later, we entered the palace to perform this griha pravesh, and lo and behold, Kaikeyi appears before us, bathed and bedecked as she is now. Decide for yourself then, Ayodhya-naresh. Is such a thing possible? Surely there is reason to doubt whether this is the real Kaikeyi or not. I suggest that without further ado we request Guru Vashishta to confirm for us whether she is truly what she appears to be, or some other personage. I await the wisdom of your judgement.'

The silence that followed this small speech was as heavy as a stone wall. While Third Queen Sumitra was well respected and loved, there was no question that it was First Queen Kausalya who was the mother-figure of the Kosala state. Women across the kingdom kept her clay image or painted portrait in the north-east corners of their houses, beside those of their own mother-goddess deities. If anything, Kaikeyi's years of cavorting publicly beside the maharaja had only drawn greater loyalty and support for Kausalya. And today, of course, with Rama's glowing accomplishments, it was Kausalya who held the floor.

Even Kaikeyi's face acknowledged the turning of the tide by a faint twitching downturn of her mouth. The Second Queen's eyes flashed briefly, smouldering in their sockets.

The entire assembly looked to Maharaja Dasaratha for his response.

10

Jatayu descended cautiously through the labyrinth of inner towers and fortifications that crisscrossed the heart of the black fortress, following the kumbhas in its quest for an answer to the riddle that now dominated the course of its future history.

The bird-beast had folded its wings firmly upon its back, and appeared strikingly human at first glance. Except for its bald misshapen head and oversize wattled neck, the vulture-king could have passed for an oddly configured mortal. Its anthropomorphic appearance was enhanced when it passed through the long stretches of shadowy dimness that dominated the Asura stronghold.

Only when it chanced upon an occasional – and rare – demonlight casting its garish fluorescent green light from a high crevice did the illusion vanish, to reveal nothing more than a giant creature with the body of a bear-like animal and the head and wings of a giant vulture. But it pleased the bird-king to maintain the illusion when it could; it enjoyed the look of blank incomprehension upon the face of the rakshasas it passed when they came upon Jatayu. It took them several moments to understand what it was, and that it was not what it seemed at first to be – a human wandering casually through the lair of Ravana. Then they gnashed their curved fangs, slammed their hooved fists together and went on their way, cursing Jatayu in their harsh rakshasa tongue.

Jatayu was descending a flight of stone stairs that seemed to go down endlessly. It had lost track of time, and even though it knew only a little while had passed since sundown, it seemed as if it might wander these dark passageways eternally.

It shivered at the thought and hastened its pace. Its talon-tips clacked and clattered noisily on the dark lohit stone, the sounds rising behind and above it to the distant rooftop trapdoor it had used to enter the fortress. Here and there, slashes and streaks of rusty red scored the dark walls. Lohit stone was literally ironstone, rich with the raw element, and it tended to rust when exposed to the air, or to salt water. Fresh air was not much to be found in the depths of the black fortress, but salt water there was plenty of, and these patches on the walls marked the places where countless Asuras of every species had scratched or scraped on their way up or down these stairs, exposing the stones to the corroding salt air.

Jatayu heard something and paused.

Strange echoes and distant reverberations sounded from deep within the bowels of the fortress. Most of these Jatayu took to be simply the sounds resulting from the endless war preparations of the demon races, their giant smiths working to produce armour and weaponry for those Asuras who needed to enhance their natural killing endowments. But some of these noises were mystifying to the bird-beast. Like the deep rhythmic groaning it heard now, rising steadily until it seemed to fill the entire stair-well with its sonorousness, then fading away into the distance. What could *that* possibly be? Jatayu wasn't sure if it even wanted to know.

It shivered and continued its downward descent. After what seemed like another thousand yards, the stairwell finally let out upon a horizontal level. Jatayu heaved a sigh of relief as it stepped on to flat ground again. It resisted the urge to unfurl its wings and peered down a dark corridor. This seemed like the way to the Hall. It recalled a level much like this one following a similarly harrowing descent. It pattered cautiously down the gloomy passageway. The sickly glow of the demonlights illuminated only a featureless antechamber like a thousand thousand others in this vast fortification. It was said there were a million million Asuras in Lanka, and there was a chamber to house each one of them in the black fortress.

Now, of course, the first figure would have to be severely amended – very severely – but the fortress itself remained, vast and impenetrable, so labyrinthine that to be lost within its endless passages and halls was not just likely but inevitable, which was why Jatayu never ventured down here except when following those given the way by the demonlord himself. And Ravana, for reasons best known to him, had long ago chosen only to let the kumbha-rakshasas know the way through the fortress. It was rumoured that even the brutal overseers often lost their way in these countless mazes, usually those ones who had fallen out of favour with their master. It was said that there were thousands of wretched outcasts and hapless ones wandering these corridors endlessly in search of the way out. For when it pleased its master, the black fortress was given to altering its own architecture and interiors.

Jatayu went to the end of the antechamber and peered through the archway to the next chamber. It looked exactly like the first. It hesitated a moment then decided to continue. Something smelled familiar about this place, and it was quite certain the kumbha-rakshasas it had followed down from the rampart rooftop had come this way. It could still smell traces of their distinctive odours, especially the older one, whose scent clearly indicated a vile case of uraga-bite which had begun to fester.

The antechambers flowed for several hundred yards further, ending abruptly. The demonlights also ceased, and Jatayu suddenly found itself plunged into total darkness. It skittered nervously to a halt, its talons seeking purchase on the slimy floor. It paused, craning its neck this way, then that. The only thing it could make out at first was that the chamber was vast even by the standards of the black fortress, enormous beyond all measure. It could feel currents and eddies of wind sweeping from different directions, travelling in a complex interweaving.

The vulture-lord's leathery wings shuddered, eager to unfold, to take it high up to the rafters and explore this vast open space, but it forced them to remain closed. It shut its eyes, making the darkness redundant, and used its bird senses to explore the room. By studying the wind currents flowing across its bald head and fine, profuse antennae-like hairs, it could form a virtual mental image of the chamber's dimensions and broad measures. After a moment, it opened its beaked mouth and issued a sharp piercing screech. The sound raced away into the darkness, seeming to lose itself in the vast empty spaces. But to Jatayu's finely attuned avian senses, the sub-sonic echoes of the call reverberated for several moments afterwards, adding depth, dimension and even texture to the sketch formed by the wind-current image. It opened its eyes, blinking its heavy lids in amazement. If its senses were right, and there was no reason to doubt them, this space was two whole yojanas in length and a full yojana in width!

Jatayu squawked again, expressing its sheer amazement at the discovery. A chamber eighteen miles long and nine miles wide? Impossible! It had flown over entire island-chains in the Lakshadweep archipelago that were not this large. But once the first flush of surprise passed, it realised that anything was possible in Lanka. If the portals of hell themselves could be kept open in a place in the mortal realm, allowing the free passage of dead Asuras from the nethermost levels of Patal and Narak, then what was a minor architectural miracle or two? Besides, it was well known that the black fortress had been built by yaksas for Kubera, Ravana's half-brother, from whom he had wrested the island-kingdom. And yaksas had built cities such as Amravarti, Alkapura and Indraloka, the celestial cities of the devas themselves. Surely a room a few hundred square miles large would pose no obstacle to those gifted builders.

After a moment of indecision, Jatayu began walking through the chamber. The scent of the kumbha-rakshasas led through here, unmistakably, and it still needed to verify the news heralded by the raising of the flag. If Ravana truly was dead, Jatayu wanted to see his corpse with its own two eyes. Spitting was optional.

It walked for another thousand yards or so without meeting anything or anyone. That was not surprising in itself: it hadn't expected to find *furniture* in this place! This was probably some holding area where Asuras retrieved from the hell worlds were brought and kept awhile until their obedience and loyalty to the Lord of Lanka was established beyond doubt. Hence the overpowering stench of kumbha-rakshasas in the place: the overseers and their vicious knife-tipped lashes were most needed here. But what Jatayu didn't understand was why there was no corresponding stench of other Asura species.

After all, if a million or two demons had been assembled here, still writhing and smouldering from their time spent in the hell worlds, surely the resulting smell should be overpowering? Yet Jatayu could detect no trace of anything but kumbha-rakshasa. It didn't give the matter much thought: intellectual analysis had never been the vulture-king's strong point. What mattered was that the kumbha it was seeking had clearly passed this way, so this was the way Jatayu would go.

It passed a row of enormous round objects, each looming up to rise high out of sight. They gleamed with a metallic dullness in the faint illumination that crept in from cracks and crevices in the vaulting rock walls of the chamber. Jatayu paused to peck at one with its beak; it resounded with a startling sound that made it back away hurriedly. The sound was curiously like striking a metal vessel filled with water, but on an immensely larger scale. Jatayu debated a moment, torn between curiosity and caution, and finally decided that flying was the only way it would get where it was going within a reasonable time.

It spread its wings with a sensation akin to sexual relief. It felt so good to be able to fly again, even if only for short intervals. The wounds on its body still hurt horribly, but they were healing fast. And while some damage was permanent, leaving Jatayu a pale shadow of its former self, at least flight was still possible. Among its kind they had a saying: *If it can fly, it's still alive.* A flightless jatayu or garuda was better off dead, which was why its fellows pecked and clawed it to death, mercifully saving it from years of landlocked misery.

Jatayu found the currents surprisingly powerful and rose quickly. By its earlier estimate, the roof of the chamber was as high as its width, namely a full yojana. With that much space, a whole flock of jatayus could live down here. Not that any bird-beast would want to live out of reach of the blessed life-giving rays of Surya-deva, the sun god. But it was a sobering thought. Once this vast place had probably contained lakhs, or even crores of Asura species. Now, it was deserted. That was how dramatically Lanka's fortunes had changed.

It turned in a wide arc as it reached the top of the curved metal object it had pecked at earlier. It took it a fraction of an instant to recognise the object, and several stunned moments to let its mind accept the reality.

It was a jal-bartan.

An enormous drinking-water receptacle.

Jatayu screed with surprise as it rose higher and saw, stretching out for miles and miles, an endless row of identical jal-bartans, all as impossibly huge as the first.

It veered left, flying to the far side of the chamber's width. As it came within sight of that side of the enormous hall, it saw what it had expected to find: a row of small hill-sided heaps of oddly familiar stick-like objects. It took only a sniff to confirm with its keen sense of smell that the mountains were in fact mounds of discarded bones. The gnaw marks on their centres and edges were clearly visible as Jatayu flew closer then swooped overhead.

Suddenly, it realised with a shuddering shock that it was dangerously mistaken. This was no ordinary chamber at all. Nor was it a holding pen for retrieved Asuras.

As if in confirmation, the groaning sound it had heard earlier on the stairwell began again. Except that this time it was sounding from *this* level of the black fortress, from this very chamber. With the evidence Jatayu now had, there was no disputing the nature of the sound. It was the sound of something snoring. Something so huge that it took a bedchamber eighteen miles long and nine miles wide to accommodate it comfortably.

The snoring grew louder as Jatayu flew further. The bird-beast knew that it was committing perhaps the most foolish act of its long life, yet it felt compelled to go on. Now that it knew where it was, in the forbidden chamber, it couldn't resist the fascination of exploring further. It executed another turn, finding a wind current that was as warm and sultry as a South Seas breeze. But unlike those balmy wind waves, this one had the foulest stench imaginable. More peculiar, it seemed not to bear any relation to the other currents and eddies in the chamber. If anything, this malodorous wave seemed to originate from a point within the room itself, about a mile off the floor.

Jatayu peered down through the slatted dimness. Slits of light from other torchlit chambers filtered through into this vast space, illuminating long, slender bars of the room. There was something there, Jatayu could see now, something rising from the floor to about a mile's height. Could it be a volcano? It was certainly large enough to be one! But a volcano would emit light as well as heat, and the stench was nothing like any other volcano on Lanka.

Suddenly a mashaal flared somewhere down below, off to one side, about two miles or so from the western wall of the forbidden chamber. It sent flickering fingers of yellow light racing across the breadth of the vast space, illuminating the enormous humped object that lay on the floor of the room. A moment later, it was joined by another mashaal, then yet another.

Jatayu flew higher on the warm, smelly draught, craning its neck to gain a better perspective by which to make sense of what it was seeing. It almost cried out in terror as its mind finally assimilated and accepted what its eyes were perceiving.

Illuminated by the light of the mashaals, the largest

rakshasa Jatayu had ever seen – or imagined in its wildest nightmares – lay sleeping on the floor of the chamber. The warm, malodorous eddy on which Jatayu was riding was the exhalations of the rakshasa's breath as it snored raggedly.

Jatayu squawked like a pigeon in a cat's lair and changed direction quickly, seeking a way out. Suddenly it knew why the forbidden chamber was forbidden. It was the private chamber of Kumbhakarna, brother of Ravana.

Dasaratha sighed. The weariness of the maharaja was visible to all as they awaited his decision on the conundrum. Sita's heart went out to him. She knew what he had been through these past few days and could see that the canker ravaging his body had only gained a greater hold. This was not the Dasaratha she remembered from her girlhood visits. The illness had reduced him to a pale shadow of his former self, turning the lion-strong warrior-king into a wounded old cat.

As she watched her father-in-law struggle to pronounce judgement on the matter at hand, she was reminded powerfully of her own father. She had watched him age and change as well. But there was a difference. While Maharaja Janak had grown leaner, more austere and more calm with the passing of time, Dasaratha seemed to have grown wearier and more burdened. The sunwood crown was a heavy weight to bear on that ageing brow.

It vindicated her father's lifelong belief that the body was indeed a temple, and ought to be treated as such. Her father had been stout and mild-mannered in his youth, or at least that part of his younger life that she had witnessed, but unlike many of his contemporaries, Janak had grown leaner and stronger both physically and spiritually with the passing of time. She had often admired his self-discipline and ability to adhere to his rigorous routine

Dasaratha, though, had clearly suffered adversely from the excesses of living, and had allowed his virile manliness to waste away into decrepit palsy.

She wondered briefly – just a fraction of a lightning-second – if Rama would become like this some day in the distant future. An ageing, weary king, too ravaged even to rise to his own feet, crushed beneath the burden of kingship.

For some reason, she didn't think so. Rama was Dasaratha's son, true, but he was also Kausalya's son. And looking at the three of them now, Sita saw at once that it was Kausalya's steel-strong fortitude that Rama had inherited, rather than Dasaratha's leonine forcefulness. And as for the other fleshly indulgences, well, in that respect Rama compared favourably with Sita's father rather than his own. Looking at Dasaratha in this moment of weakness, it seemed that he had treated his body more like an ale-house than a temple over time.

Enough, she told herself sternly. *You're being too harsh*. All right, so Dasaratha had been careless about his health, and perhaps he should have paid more attention to spiritual contemplation than fleshly indulgence, but who was she to judge him? He was once the greatest warrior-king in the seven nations. Her father had only one victory to his credit, that a disputed battle against a petty despot. And that paltry lack of battlefield prowess didn't trouble Janaka in the least; he had always been a pursuer of spiritual gains rather than military ones.

On the other hand, Dasaratha, this weary, ageing king seated before her, had kept the Asura hordes from the borders of the Arya world and raised the Kosala nation into the greatest power on earth today. Whereas when death came stalking up to Mithila's door, her father could barely summon up enough military resources to man the gates of his home city. It had taken a prince from another kingdom, this same Dasaratha's son, to save the King of Vaideha's kingdom and people.

As for past errors of youth and indulgence . . . which man did not have his weaknesses? For that matter, which deva? Arya scripture was rife with the many instances of devas and devis faltering, succumbing to vices and temptations, committing grave errors and mortal sins. This man, why, he was just a man. A king. A great king and a great provider and protector. What more could one ask for? Perfection? Sainthood? *In that case, go create your own dream-world, Sita Janaki; this one belongs to those whose feet still gather dust and mud when they walk the marg, no matter how lofty their thoughts and ideals.*

Even her father was wise enough to know and accept that, through all his spiritual austerity and religious dedication. He had said as much to Brahmarishi Vishwamitra, and to Rama, her Rama, when giving his daughter away in the kanyadaan, the gift-of-the-daughter ceremony at their wedding. 'Today I do not give away a daughter, I gain a son, a son I could not be more proud of had the devas themselves given him over as a dakshina for my long piety.'

It had been a shining moment in her life, that realisation that her father, despite all his peaceful spiritualism, still accepted the need for warriors and heroes in this troubled mortal realm.

She watched Dasaratha now in this new perspective, his bowed head weighted down by the burden of his difficult decision, and saw the man within the king, the soul beneath the crown. It was a heroic soul, battling manfully with larger-than-life challenges, and bravely triumphing.

No wonder that he had produced such a son. For Rama was his son too, just as much as he was Kausalya's.

Pradhan-mantri Sumantra was at his maharaja's side, looking anxious. Unlike his counterparts in other Arya states, politically ambitious players that they all were, Sumantra seemed content to focus his energies on administration and organisation, working discreetly by Dasaratha's side like a charioteer by his lord, steering the rath adeptly through treacherous ways and leaving his master free to concentrate on more important intellectual decisions. Sita guessed they must have been very effective partners in the governance of the Kosala nation, judging from the city she had just passed through.

She was still recovering from her passage through mighty Ayodhya, the sheer spectacle of colour and noise that had assailed them. Such a display would have been considered wastefully extravagant, even decadent, back home in spiritually enlightened Mithila, but she understood and appreciated the need for the Ayodhyans to express their gratitude and admiration for their liege-heir. And Mithilan though she might be, she was not too enlightened to recognise that Rama's victories had been no ordinary trophies won at a feast-day mêlée. This was history in the making. Ayodhya was everything the legends claimed, a lion among Arya nations.

And yet, here was the dark blight on Ayodhya's sun-bright face. Sita already knew about the history of Dasaratha and his three wives, his succumbing to Kaikeyi's amorous charms to the woeful neglect of his lawful first wife Kausalya, and even the delicately girlish Sumitra. Rama had been reticent about the actual day-to-day relationship between the queens, but Sita was woman enough to understand that however polite and well-mannered things might be on the surface, the three ranis, and the first two in particular, could hardly be gaily contented in one another's company.

Dasaratha coughed feebly. Sumantra bent forward quickly, and the maharaja took the napkin the pradhan-mantri handed him, using it to wipe his mouth. Sita was startled to see a distinct tinge of red on the cream-coloured cloth. Dasaratha moved his hand in a gesture of thanks to Sumantra, who offered him a goblet filled with what Sita hoped was water. Dasaratha sipped gingerly, with the painful slowness of someone whose every physical action has become a living torture, and then seemed ready to speak.

'This dilemma is beyond the powers of any ordinary mortal to solve,' he said hoarsely. 'And it is hardly meet for me to make such choices amongst my own queens. I urge you all to contain yourselves and wait until we have completed the ritual welcoming of our daughters-in-law into their new house. Thereafter we shall . . .' interrupting himself to release another volley of heart-rending coughs, '. . . we shall retire to the sabha hall and debate the matter in private session.'

Sita resisted the urge to frown. She sensed from the turning of heads and sharing of glances that everyone else in attendance was as puzzled by the maharaja's response as she was. Dasaratha's words were extraordinarily obtuse and vague in the circumstances. Rani Sumitra's accusation had been blatantly unambiguous: she had accused Rani Kaikeyi of being an Asura in disguise! Few allegations could have been more urgent. Rani Kausalya had seconded Sumitra's accusation, adding to its gravity. Yet here was the king asking them all to wait and talk about this later.

Then Dasaratha punctuated his words with a look at Kausalya. The expression in the maharaja's shining, beady eyes, the ghastly pallor on his sweat-washed face, the involuntary rhythmic shaking of his jowls, these told Sita what the maharaja's words could not express.

She saw the truth beneath his diplomatic words. Dasaratha was even sicker than he looked. The maharaja was at the end of his resources, and was asking Kausalya, as the senior queen, to give him a little respite, buy him a little time. An outright call of help could hardly have made his condition plainer. The look in the king's eyes was as close to a plea as one could expect to see. Sita felt ashamed at all the criticisms of Dasaratha that had passed through her mind only moments ago. In the end, he was just an ailing man on the verge of his end.

Kausalya's face softened immediately. The First Queen's quick eyes caught the plea in her husband's response and look, and she responded at once. 'Of course, my lord. If that is your will, we shall discuss it later.' She looked around, aware of the several hundred pairs of eyes upon them both, analysing and judging shrewdly. A nation was watching its king in his last days, measuring how these words and decisions might affect them individually and universally. Kausalya raised her voice. 'Truly, you speak wisely, Ayodhya-naresh. As ever your adherence to dharma is beyond reproach. Verily do you insist that tradition and ritual must come before all personal considerations. Our private family matter would best be discussed behind closed doors later tonight.'

Sita distinctly heard a sigh of frustration rise from the aristocratic ranks. A private sabha would mean that none of them would be able to see how the drama unfolded.

Kausalya touched Sumitra's arm gently. 'My sister-queen, I urge you to withdraw your accusation for the nonce. We shall debate this issue within the chambers of the sabha hall after the completion of this rite.'

Another look passed between the two queens, this one of empathy and understanding. Sumitra glanced at Dasaratha, her own face reflecting her concern for her husband's well-being, and she nodded. 'Of course, my sister. A few more moments will hardly matter.' She hesitated, then glanced over Kausalya's shoulder at the other queen. Her expression hardened again. 'I ask only that Rani Kaikeyi be placed under . . .' she seemed to weigh her words cautiously, 'under close watch until such time as this matter is resolved. If it pleases you and our lord?'

Kausalya hesitated a moment, as if debating how to agree to Sumitra's request without launching them all upon yet another stage of accusations and counter-accusations. Then, before the First Queen could say another word, Kaikeyi herself spoke. Silent this past spell of time as her identity was being questioned and then disputed, the Second Queen now leaped back in the saddle. She took a step forward, raising an arm heavy with glittering gold.

'Justice.'

Heads turned to look at Kaikeyi.

The Second Queen's voice was fraught with a haughty air of righteousness that even Sita, who did not know Kaikeyi well, thought was obnoxious.

'My honour has been sullied in public. I protest against this barbaric offence and demand redress at once. Clear my name before we proceed further.'

Kaikeyi looked at the four princes with their new brides, all watching anxiously as the drama unfolded. 'I apologise for first interrupting and now delaying your rite of welcoming, my sons, my new daughters. But I was not the aggressor here. I have been wrongfully accused in a shocking and reprehensible manner.'

She gestured at the watching aristocrats, nobles, ministers

of the court and other onlookers. Sita sensed their glee at the continuance of the drama, an interest that Kaikeyi was milking for all it was worth. 'The accusation was made publicly. To take the matter under private advisement would be to deny me my opportunity for vindication. I demand therefore that the matter be settled here and now, this very minute. An injustice was done unto me and it must be undone before we can proceed.'

Sumitra's delicate features sharpened into a birdlike ferocity. 'You see? She does not even have a heart in that breast, or she would understand why it is we are willing to postpone the matter. I tell you, Kausalya, this witch—'

Kausalya pressed down on the younger queen's shoulder, cutting off Sumitra's outburst. The senior queen spoke with a tight-lipped formality that sharply rebutted Kaikeyi's overblown tone of self-righteousness. 'Rani Kaikeyi, you heard the maharaja's decision. Once spoken, his word is law. Is it now your desire to invoke the charge of treasonous disobedience by ignoring his judgement? For that is what you appear to be doing by refusing to accept his decision.'

Bravo. Sita wished she could applaud. Kausalya's response was as masterful as anything she could have wanted. *That'll put the shrew in her place.*

Kaikeyi's smile showed that she was undaunted. 'Come, come, Kausalya. How could I possibly deny the authority of our lord? Of course I abide by his decision in every respect. What I am saying now is no contradiction to Dasaratha's pronouncement, it is simply an expansion. The maharaja himself said that we should finish the rites first before continuing this discussion in private. And part of these rites includes my welcoming my own son and his new bride into our household. A right that you seek to deny me.'

Kaikeyi pointed at Bharat and Mandavi, who were standing even now before Kausalya. 'I should be the one receiving Bharat and his beautiful wife. By standing in my stead, you dishonour me and sully my untarnished name. I demand that you apologise and step away at once, and then repeat the rite once more with me present.'

People gasped openly. Sita heard her sister and cousins turning their heads with alarm, peering out through the flower-veils that hung from their foreheads. For a new bride to repeat her griha pravesh was considered very bad luck. *But so is being interrupted in the midst of the rite, which is what's already happened here.*

A commotion broke out, this time among the brahmins clustered to one side, still dutifully reciting the mantras of welcoming. Kausalya had fallen silent and Sita could understand why. The senior queen was in a fix now. If she denied Kaikeyi her right as mother and mother-in-law, it could be seen as a violation of Arya tradition, and a personal insult against Kaikeyi. But if she repeated the ritual, it would only delay the whole process further, restore the face Kaikeyi had just lost, and fatally undermine Sumitra's allegations. She could hardly claim the Second Queen was an Asura in disguise if she permitted her to go through the rite now!

And she can't arrest her either, Sita thought, *because that would also be a violation of the maharaja's decision.* What would Kausalya do? Sita glanced discreetly at Dasaratha, and saw that the maharaja's head was bowed painfully low as he coughed again into Pradhan-mantri Sumantra's napkin. This time, the splotches of blood on the cloth were unmistakable. Sita saw Sumantra take the cloth from Dasaratha and replace it with another. Dasaratha remained hunched over, like a man on whose shoulders a great new burden had just been placed.

Beside her, Rama moved briefly. Sita sensed he wanted desperately to go to his father's side and support him. Escort him out of this debate and to his sickroom, where he could rest and be tended to in comfort. Even Sumantra seemed to be debating whether or not to put his arms around his king to hold him upright, for it seemed sure that Dasaratha would keel over at any moment.

Into this miasma of tension, Rani Kausalya's voice spoke quietly.

'Very well, Kaikeyi. As queen of this kingdom, it is your royal right to participate in the ritual. And you are Rani Kaikeyi after all, are you not? So why should you not exercise your right? Go ahead then, rani. Offer your pranaam first to Guru Vashishta as is customary, and then you may take my place here and welcome your son and your bahu home.'

And Kausalya indicated with her hand the place where the great preceptor stood before the brahmins of the palace, inviting Kaikeyi to come forward.

Except that it wasn't an invitation. It was a challenge. Sita rejoiced inwardly again at her mother-in-law's ingenuity. Pressed to the wall, Kausalya had found a way to expose Kaikeyi as well as end this debate swiftly. By reminding Kaikeyi to offer pranaam to the senior brahmin present, she was challenging her to touch the guru's feet. At that point, if she was indeed an Asura in human guise as Rani Sumitra claimed, she would be exposed beyond doubt. There would be no concealing her true identity from Guru Vashishta.

To Sita's surprise, Rani Kaikeyi only smiled, bowed her head gracefully, then walked across the marbled foyer, watched closely by everyone present. The Second Queen of Ayodhya went to the preceptor of the kingdom, bowed deeply, and touched his feet. The guru in turn touched her head and gave her the ritual ashirwaad. Then Kaikeyi straightened, turned around, and walked towards Kausalya and Sumitra, her eyes glittering with triumph as she approached.

'Ranis,' she said in a dangerously soft voice. 'Make way for your sister.'

And to Sita's chargin, Kausalya moved aside, her arm compelling Sumitra to move with her, and made way for Kaikeyi to stand on the high step to take her place in the rite of welcoming.

12

Jatayu almost flew into the sleeping rakshasa's face. The creature was lying prone on its back, occupying most of the enormous chamber, its prodigious snores filling the air with the warm stinky gusts that Jatayu had foolishly mistaken for a wind current. Further down to the south, its belly rose impressively, curving roofwards like the rise of a ridge of mountains. Beyond that, the far reaches of the chamber were too dark to make out how long it stretched.

By the vulture-king's estimate, the beast's nose alone was at least half a mile off the floor. And its belly at its peak must rise to two or three miles. Jatayu shuddered to imagine how high the creature might be when it stood up. Something close to nine miles, or why else would the chamber be built a yojana high? Now it understood why this room had such fantastical dimensions and why it stank only of kumbha-rakshasa and nothing more. This sleeping giant could be none other than the legendary Kumbhakarna, brother of Ravana. And Kumbhakarna, as legend had it, slept for three score years, then rose and feasted for as many years, before going back to sleep.

This cycle had continued for some millennia, to the best of Jatayu's knowledge. But in the relatively brief time it had served the demonlord of Lanka, a mere four hundred years or so, it had not yet had the experience of setting eyes on the legendary giant himself. Because Kumbhakarna had not left his chamber deep within the black fortress for almost a thousand years! Or so it was believed.

Jatayu saw the lights of the two mashaals flickering still by the western wall of the chamber. That was where it was headed now. It had a sense that the torches were held by the same two kumbha-rakshasas it had followed down here. In moments, as its flight carried it swiftly across the murky expanse of the chamber – and high above what it now saw was Kumbhakarna's rising and falling chest – it came within sight of a pushpak flying towards it.

The air-chariot was nothing like the pushpak that Jatayu had hitched a ride on three days earlier. That one, the first of its name, Ravana's personal vehicle, driven by his other brother, the more normal-sized Vibhisena, was glorious in its beauty; after all, it was the personal vehicle of Lord Indra-deva Himself. This rath, in stark contrast, was dark, ugly and menacing in appearance. It befitted the two foul-looking and even fouler-smelling kumbhas that rode in its cradle, peering and waving angrily at Jatayu as they approached. The bird-beast sniffed disapprovingly. The kumbha whose stench it had tracked was one of those in the approaching pushpak – there was no mistaking that festering uraga-bite stench.

The pushpak slowed as it approached the vulture-king, then started to execute a turn that was apparently meant to intercept Jatayu. Abruptly it lurched and dropped several dozen yards, before stopping its fall. The two black-hide kumbhas manning its controls seemed to be having some difficulty manoeuvring the air-chariot. No doubt because they were more intent on cutting off Jatayu's flight path.

Foolish wretches. Did they think that any vehicle could

ever match the flying ability of the lord of birdkind? Even depleted and damaged as it was, Jatayu could still have danced rings around the pushpak. Even Ravana's pushpak, if it came to that. For all the celestial vehicle's pyrotechnics, it was ultimately just a device. And as for being divinely created, well, what was Jatayu then? Puffed rice?

The pushpak lurched violently, then flew forward and back in fits and starts. The two kumbhas were desperately attracting Jatayu's attention. One of them seemed to be trying to do something to the controls. It lost its temper and kicked hard, and with a whoosh the pushpak rose and shot upwards like a flung spear. Jatayu flapped its left wing hurriedly as the air-chariot shot past it, its rusting iron frame brushing the vulture-king's wingtips. It screed in indignation, forgetting where it was and what lay below, and turned to follow the kumbhas, folding its wings and shooting after the pushpak like a bat out of hell, quite literally, considering that it had in fact been released from Narak, the first level of hell, by the Lord of Lanka. In the thrill of the chase, its healing wounds and painful scars were forgotten, and there was only the wonderful waft of the wind upon its face and body, and the sense of power in being able to change direction or speed simply by elevating or declivating certain wingtip feathers.

It caught up with them a mile higher, still shooting madly towards the ceiling. As Jatayu raced closer, it could hear their gruff voices yelling furiously. Closer still, it could see them fighting each other as well as the pushpak, mashaals flaring and flickering as they battled in the brainless way of all rakshasas. Cruds! Dolts! Imbeciles. At the rate they were accelerating they would reach the roof in moments. High as the chamber might be, it was not infinite, no matter how great the illusion of infinity might be. If they struck the roof at this velocity, they would be smashed beyond all recognition, the pushpak itself crumpled into a twisted mass of rusted metal that would fall and probably be lost within the valley of Kumbhakarna's navel miles below.

Jatayu came up from below them and caught hold of the pushpak's sides. At the same instant, the bird-beast opened its wings and used all its strength to slow both itself and the shooting vehicle.

The air-chariot resisted its efforts fiercely for a moment. Then, with surprising meekness, it relented and lay limp in Jatayu's grip. The vulture-king screed triumphantly and flew towards the far end of the chamber, carrying the chariot.

A while later, it descended to a spot on the floor close by the northern wall of the enormous chamber. It had passed Kumbhakarna's feet a couple of miles back, large and hairy and thirteen-toed, like all rakshasas. It had glanced down briefly and by the light of the flickering mashaals in the pushpak had seen what looked like lice scrambling over the giant Asura's hirsute feet. That was the last it had seen of the mountainous brother of Ravana. It realised now that those could not have been lice: the creatures it had seen had been huge, larger than most Asuras. It shuddered in distaste and put the memory out of its mind. It had other matters to deal with now.

It set the pushpak down on the floor with a softly ringing clanging and let go of it. Its feet were glad to be free of that filthy iron monstrosity. The pushpak was all but falling apart from rust and neglect. The two kumbha-rakshasas tumbled out of the air-chariot, falling over each other in their haste to look up and face the vulture-king properly.

'You!' the larger, uglier one rasped. 'You in trouble! Master teach! Master punish! Dare enter forbidden chamber! Dare defy kumbhas!'

Jatayu raised one of its feet menacingly. The bird-beast was no Kumbhakarna, but the kumbha-rakshasas were barely five yards tall apiece, while Jatayu itself was twice as high at the head. Each of the bird-king's talons was a yard and a half long, enough to cut one of the blustering buffoons in half if it wished; all it would take was a single flick of its talons.

At the sight of the raised foot, the kumbhas sputtered and protested again, but they quietened down. These were the languages they understood: threats and intimidation.

Jatayu crooked its head. 'What master? No master have you no more, kumbhas! This Jatayu saw the flag you raised atop the ramparts. And saw as well Ravana dug bodily out from ground by Vibhisena. Dead as good was he. Frozen bug in amber like.'

The kumbhas stared up at Jatayu. Slowly, smiles of wicked delight spread across both their faces. Their outer mouths opened to reveal second and third mouths within, all three opening and closing, emitting choking, gasping sounds. It took Jatayu a moment to understand that this was the sound of rakshasa laughter.

'What laugh at, you two?' Jatayu asked angrily. 'Drop you like rats to smash your brains out Jatayu could have, up there. Answer! Command you!'

One of the two rakshasas, the one without the sickening uraga-bite stench, paused in its merriment long enough to waggle a horny arm and six-fingered hand at Jatayu.

'Master drop *you*! Smash *you*! Say master is dead, do you? Fool! Flying fool! Flag we put on the roof was to show mourning for comrades killed by vile mortal treachery at Mithila battle. You thought it was for master? Master alive and well, preparing new plans, new war campaign already. Wait till we tell him what you said about him being dead as bug. You birdbrained fool! *You* dead then!'

And that set them off on a fresh wave of laughter. But Jatayu didn't care any more. It was too stunned by their words. *Master alive and well.*

Ravana was alive!

13

Bharat's maternal uncle Yudhajit, Kaikeyi's older brother, was waiting to speak with them when the welcome rituals were over. A handsome, big-built man, Yudhajit had a striking similarity to his sister. They shared the same arrogantly handsome features, a small forehead with wiry brows, and intense eyes set wide apart, set off by prominent cheekbones. They were quintessential north-western faces, eye-catching in their forceful lines, yet hinting at brutal wills and violent histories.

'My father and brothers could not come for the wedding in Mithila,' he explained to Sumantra in lieu of Dasaratha, who had retired to his sickroom so that his vaids could adminster yet another dose of ayurvedic herbal potions. 'The seers may have cleansed Mithila and the Ganga valleys of the main Asura force, but up northwest there are still sizeable numbers. They lurk in the wadis and by the riverbanks, preying on smaller groups of travellers. It is important that we flush them all out before they grow into a permanent menace.'

Yudhajit paused to wait for an attendant to hold up a spittoon for him to dispense a mouthful of blood-red tobacco juice. 'My father and brothers are about that work even as we speak.' He indicated his own metal-reinforced leather apparel. 'I came directly when I got the news.'

He paused to spit again, glancing briefly into the spittoon to see the result of his emission. Turning back to Sumantra, he put his arm over the prime minister's shoulder. 'My father wishes that Bharat and his bride join us at Kaikeya, that the family may meet her too and see the bearer of our future heirs with our own eyes.' He added, 'With Aja-putra's leave, of course.'

The Kaikeyans referred to Dasaratha as Aja-putra, literally 'Aja's son', because it was at the then Maharaja Aja's insistence that the match with Kaikeyi had been made. In fact, the Kaikeyans always maintained that their daughter was by rights the first wife of Dasaratha. It was only Kaikeya's remote geographical location, and the continued skirmishes with stray Asura gangs, that kept them from coming east to complete the formalities. It was in those years that Dasaratha had taken Kausalya for his first wife, and only later, when the Kaikeyans had pressed his father's assigned match upon him, had he conceded and taken Kaikeyi for his bride as well, allotting her the second title, a fact that had always rankled with the proud Kaikeyans.

Now, Sita detected the underlying rancour in Yudhajit's tone as he pretended coarse familiarity with Pradhan-mantri Sumantra. A tactic which clearly wasn't working, judging from Sumantra's clear discomfort. The prime minister moved away to speak to one of the vaids exiting the maharaja's chambers, making it necessary for Yudhajit to release his hold on him.

When Sumantra returned his attention to Yudhajit, the prime minister had a studied absence of expression on his lined features. 'It is quite unorthodox to take the boy on his wedding night, Lord Yudhajit,' he said. 'The Ayodhyan tradition places great emphasis on the first nine nights after the wedding vows.' He smiled. 'But you know this already.'

Yudhajit paused to empty his mouth for the umpteenth time since stuffing his cheek with the paan. His first word was lost in the action of spitting. '—the Ayodhyan way. We have our own traditions in Kaikeya. It's considered inauspicious for a son of Kaikeya to bed his new bride before the elders of the family and the royal preceptor have examined her first.'

'Examined her?'

Yudhajit's face darkened, mottling with spots of colour that spoke eloquently of a temper thinly checked. 'Met her. You know what I speak of, Sumantra. Besides, why are we bickering like merchants at a village bazaar, haggling over the price of gobi or bhindi? Bharat has already expressed his keenness to ride home tonight. We could be there in a few hours, time enough to complete the formality of showing her to the elders and then consummating the wedding before sunrise. He will still be under his own roof, in a manner of speaking, and your Ayodhyan tradition will not be too badly botched. All I need is the maharaja's formal consent. If you are unable to help me—'

'Calm down, my lord,' Sumantra said quietly. 'There is no need to raise your voice here. Nobody is trying to stop you from taking Bharat home. He is as much your son as ours. If he has already agreed, then there is nothing further to be debated. As you yourself said, there is only the formal question of getting the maharaja's consent. Unfortunately, the vaids have just told me that he is napping after taking his medicine and should not be disturbed for another few hours.'

Yudhajit slapped his thigh with the shortwhip he carried everywhere, another arrogant affection that the Kaikeyans favoured, showing off their pride in their nomadic roots, 'a country on horseback' as they liked to call their equestrian nation. 'Another few hours? By then it will be too late for either Ayodhyan traditions or Kaikeyan! You might as well just say nay, and deny me the right to take my own sister's son home to meet his grandparents!'

'I say no such thing,' Sumantra replied calmly. 'But there is one thing I can do. In the absence of his majesty, I can take the leave of Rani Kausalya. If she will allow it, you and Bharat may saddle and ride for Kaikeya at once without further ado.'

At the mention of Kausalya's name, Yudhajit's face darkened again. Two brights spots of colour danced high on his protruding cheekbones. Yudhajit had been present in the palace foyer when the scene between the queens had unfolded.

With an obvious effort, he said in a choked voice, 'If we need to ask Rani Kausalya—'

'You do not need to ask me anything,' Kausalya said from behind Yudhajit. Sita had seen the rani emerging from the maharaja's chamber and was hoping beyond hope that the Kaikeyan would say something stupid before she spoke up and was noticed. But Kausalya was not the kind of woman who stood even a moment eaves-dropping. 'I could not but help hearing Sumantra's last words as I approached,' she said, gazing steadily at her husband's brother-in-law. 'If it is permission you seek, you have it. Bharat has already spoken to me of your desire to have him spend the nights of fertility under your roof. So be it. The maharaja has no objection.'

Yudhajit seemed vaguely suspicious. He looked at Kausalya closely. 'I thought the maharaja was uncon-scious yet?'

'He is. As First Queen, I speak on his behalf. I think you should be aware of that by now, Yudhajit. I've been First Queen for sixteen years, if you'll recall. Do you object to that?'

'Object?' Yudhajit was staring blankly, taken aback by Kausalya's directness and her icy formality.

'To my speaking for the maharaja,' Kausalya said, watching as Yudhajit's mind caught up finally with his ears. 'No? In that case, you may do as Sumantra said. Saddle up and ride. It's a difficult ride through the pass at night. Go safely and with the blessings of the Devi our Mother Sri.'

At the mention of the Devi, Yudhajit looked flustered again. The Kaikeyans favoured the theory that the original creator was a male entity, and to enforce their belief they conferred the title Sri upon all males, instead of using it as the name of the Mother-Goddess Creator which it originally represented.

He retorted gruffly, under his breath, 'And may the devas protect you as well.'

Bharat came forward with Mandavi, Shatrugan and Shrutakirti close behind. Bharat bent to touch Kausalya's feet.

'Maa,' he said.

Kausalya caught his shoulders and raised him up. A lock of his hair fell forward on to his forehead and she pushed it back. There was more motherly caring in that small, seemingly insignificant action than in all of Kaikeyi's blustering arrogance at the welcome ceremony. And yet Kausalya was but a clan-mother to Bharat, while Kaikeyi was his birth-mother.

'My son,' she responded. 'Go with the Devi's grace. Care for your wife. Remember that you are no longer a youthful brahmacharya! Act and speak accordingly.'

Bharat's hands remained folded in a namaskar still. 'Maa,' he said softly, 'is it all right, my leaving Father at such a time?'

Kausalya glanced back over her shoulder instinctively.

The vaids had all departed the maharaja's chambers a few moments ago while the First Queen and Yudhajit had been speaking. She took a moment to respond, her eloquent deep brown eyes – exactly Rama's eyes, Sita noted – softening visibly.

'Life must go on, son,' she said. 'That is the way of the world. Your father would want you to go as well, since that is your desire. These past few days have been taxing in the extreme, but now the stormclouds have passed, he will rest and recover his strength. He will be here when you return.'

Bharat nodded uncertainly. 'I am yet in two minds, Maa. On one hand, I want Grandfather and Grandmother to meet Mandavi, and yet . . .' He gestured generally.

'I understand, son, but such is always the way. Life pulling us five different ways at once. There are always choices, sometimes impossible ones. That is why we have been given the laws of dharma, to help us choose.'

'Then tell me, Mother, what would dharma prescribe in this situation?'

She paused, as if that was the last question she had expected him to ask. 'You have changed much, Bharat. That is a very good question. But we have already answered that. You must do what you feel is right. Follow your own heart.'

Bharat looked back, at his impatiently waiting uncle, his brothers clustered around expectantly, then returned his gaze to Kausalya. 'My heart tells me different things. I cannot decide which is the right course to follow.'

Kausalya turned her gaze upon Bharat's bride. 'Then ask your wife to help you. She is now your partner in dharma. For both your destinies are joined hereafter.'

Mandavi seemed taken aback at the suggestion. She blushed immediately, lowering her plump face. 'Great mother,' she said through her flower-veil, 'what can I say? It is not my place to speak before my husband and his clan-mother.'

'Nonsense.' Kausalya placed her hands on Mandavi's rounded shoulders, straightening them. 'Let no one tell you so. You are a daughter of Vaideha and a bride of Kosala. Bahu of the Suryavansha line, and wife of Kaikeyi-putra Bharat. You have the right to speak your mind freely and act just as independently as Bharat himself! We of Ayodhya do not brook this modern notion of women tiptoeing and sitting silently around their menfolk. Do you follow me?'

Mandavi's eyes were large and wide in her round face. Sita almost felt sorry for her sister, but at the same time her heart surged with gladness: she hoped her cousins were taking notice too. If they didn't heed Father's sermons on the same topic, perhaps they would pay attention to Rani Kausalya at least.

Behind the group of princes and brides, Yudhajit spat angrily and messily into the spittoon. Kausalya went on, ignoring the Kaikeyan.

'Let all of you pay heed to that. Woman or man, you are Arya. Our forebears fought and died and paid a price of blood and pain to wrest us this patch of middle-world on which we dwell. The Great Mother Sri did not differentiate between males and females when she created the world, so why must we? Stand by your husbands as equals, partners in dharma and karma. I bless you all with long life and happiness. Ayushmaanbhav.'

They all paid her respect with namaskars once more, thanking her for her words of advice. Yudhajit, looking like he needed to spit out more than any ten spittoons could contain, called out harshly to Bharat.

'Putra, are you coming, or should I ride back home

alone? It is a moonless night as it is and Ravana's stragglers will be looking for easy pickings on the passes.'

'Just a moment, mama-shri,' Bharat said politely,
pointedly addressing Yudhajit by the formal title of
'revered uncle'. He gestured to Shatrugan, who came
forward with Shrutakirti. 'Mother, Shatrugan wishes to
accompany us. With his wife, of course. Will you give
him your permission as well?'

'Please, Maa,' Shatrugan asked earnestly, his biceps
flexing as he raised his hands in a pleading gesture. 'I
would ask my mother but she has locked herself into her
chamber and left word not to be disturbed for the next
hour. If I wait, it will be too late to travel.'

Kausalya sighed softly. 'Your mother has had a difficult week, young Shatrugan. I sympathise with her need
for a little time to herself. Of course, I am sure her doors
are never barred to you. Or to your wife, Kirti.'

'Even so, Kausalya-maa, I do not wish to disturb her.
She is already upset enough tonight, as you yourself
admit. If you can give me your blessings to leave, it would
be most gracious . . .'

Kausalya lowered her head, thinking. 'I cannot imagine
that she will find any objection. After all, ever since you
were able to stand and hold a finger, it was Bharat's finger
you held on to, even if he dragged you all over the play-
ground!'

Smiles erupted at the comment. Sita couldn't imagine
Bharat dragging equally well-muscled Shatrugan by the
finger even a yard, but she had already noticed how
closely the two stuck together, almost in parallel to Rama
and Lakshman's own brotherly bond.

'Go with grace, both of you,' Kausalya said. 'And do
not tarry so long that you return as fathers rather than
sons!'

A round of laughter met that comment. Except from Yudhajit, who grimaced instinctively and spat yet again – *why doesn't he simply hang a spittoon from a chain round his neck?* – before frowning and slowly, almost reluctantly, breaking into a smirking smile. Sita guessed that the Kaikeyan had belatedly realised that Kausalya had actually paid tribute to his nephews' virility. One last round of tearful yet smiling goodbyes between the sisters and cousins, and then the two brothers and their brides were swept away excitedly by their uncle, all disappearing down the corridor in a wave of rustling silks and swishing saris. Finally, only Rama and Lakshman and their wives were left with Rani Kausalya.

'And as for you lot,' she said, addressing the rajku-mars but including Sita and Urmila in her look as well, 'don't you have better things to do than stand around here all night chattering with your old mother? In case you've forgotten, it is your suhaag raat! Go on, get to your apartments and spend some time pampering your-selves and your new brides. Go on now.'

She added softly, 'You've more than earned the right.'

14

Dasaratha was sitting up in bed talking to Sumantra when Kausalya returned. They stopped the minute she entered. She smiled as she took her seat beside the bed.

'Was it that enjoyable?'

The maharaja managed to sketch a mock-frown through his weariness. 'Was what?'

'Eavesdropping on my talk with your sons.' She gestured at Sumantra, who was sitting on the far side of the maharaja's bed. The pradhan-mantri smiled gently, unoffended by her implication.

'Oh, that,' Dasaratha said dismissively, trying to wave his hand but managing only to wiggle a finger or two. 'What good would a king be if he didn't use his spasas to keep an eye on his kingdom?'

'Spasas?' Kausalya raised her eyebrows at Sumantra. 'You hear that, Sumantra. Now you're a spasa. A common spy!'

The prime minister shrugged good-naturedly. 'If the sandal fits, I'll wear it . . . I do confess, though, rani-maa, I was quite impressed by the way you handled that arrogant ass.' He coughed quickly. 'Pardon my commonspeak.'

'No apology necessary,' Dasaratha said hoarsely. 'He *is* an ass. The backside kind more than the four-legged kind.'

'Dasa!' Kausalya's eyes twin
better if you're able to make n

The maharaja raised a hand
fingers nonchalantly through his
was anything ever wrong with me
gesture didn't quite come off, his
to reach its destination. He settled
into a shrug, but the shocking trer   side
undercut the attempt at humour. H glanced down irri-
tably at the shaking hand and tried to still it without
success.

Kausalya sat on the bed beside him, clasping the
offending limb tightly between her own hands, massaging
it gently. 'Dasa, your sons did you proud today. You
should have seen them, so handsome and strong, and
their wives so beautiful and proud beside them. It made
my heart burst with pride and joy.'

He coughed once, violently. She put a napkin to his
mouth, bringing it away bloody. A glance passed between
her and Sumantra. The lines on the prime minister's face
deepened.

Dasaratha said hoarsely, 'I did see them. I was there,
remember? Or did you think I was an Asura in disguise
as well?'

Kausalya sighed. 'Are you still angry about that? It
was an honest mistake. Even I saw Kaikeyi running beside
the procession and thought—' She shrugged. 'In any case,
it's no use belabouring it now. I just don't want you to
be angry any more. It's not good for you.'

'You think I enjoy being angry?' Dasaratha shook his
head, or it shook involuntarily – it was getting hard to
tell now, as the maharaja's condition deteriorated further.
'Well I don't. No more than I enjoy being humiliated
before the entire aristocracy of Ayodhya. What were you

Kausalya? And what got into Sumitra ...ought she was too meek and mild to boo a

...hat tells you how provoked she must have been, to ...urst out in public that way. But it wasn't her intention, nor mine, to humiliate you or cause you any discomfort. We were only trying to—'

'What? What were you trying to do?' Another succession of coughs, another napkin stained with bright red lung blood. 'All because I was too weak to protest loudly enough and put an end to the farce? I expected better of you, Kausalya.'

Kausalya took a deep breath. She really didn't want to have this argument at all. Best to end it quickly. She used her most contrite and conciliatory tone. 'I'm genuinely sorry about it, Dasa. It was not meant to happen. Can we please put it behind us now? I don't know how—'

'I know how,' he said sharply. 'Sumitra and you have been harbouring far too much hatred against Kaikeyi. It had to come out sooner or later.'

Kausalya sat back, releasing her hold on Dasaratha's arm. 'Dasa, my king, how can you say that? You know—'

He rode over her words. 'I know that I spent far too many valuable years with Kaikeyi when I should have been sharing my attention equally between the three of you, and if I could but turn back the samay chakra I would do it in an instant, trembling palsy or no. But I cannot change what happened. And neither can you. So let it go now, Kausalya. Let bygones be bygones, or this poison will seep into all our lives and taint them for ever.'

She placed her hands firmly in her lap, resisting the urge to knot them into fists. 'This poison, as you call it, has already tainted all our lives for ever. I wanted to forget as much as you do. Otherwise I would not have taken you back when you came to me on Holi feast day.' She glanced up at him sharply. 'You do recall that you came to me, do you not?'

'Yes,' he said shortly, then rasped in a long, harsh breath. 'I hope I do not have cause to regret it now.'

She stared at him, filled with an urge to shake him. Across the bed, Sumantra rose nervously.

'I should go now,' the prime minister began.

'Sit down,' Dasaratha said harshly, coughing once.

Sumantra looked at Kausalya uncertainly, then resumed his seat.

'Dasa,' she said softly, picking her words very carefully. 'I have forgiven you a long time ago. I didn't do it for you. I did it for Rama. For if I had retained the hatred and the bile all these years, it would indeed have poisoned me, tainted my very soul. Hate and love are good house-keepers; once let in the door, they tend to become masters of the house. I did not want my son to grow up under the blight of his mother's hatred for his father's other wife. I have seen sons like that. They do not grow into good men, let alone good kings. So I let the anger go. I turned hatred out of my doors. And I locked my heart away, never believing that it would ever be called into use again by you. Yet you were the one who came calling one day without warning or preamble. You knocked upon my heart's door, and when I opened, you asked me for shelter. For forgiveness.' She reached out and touched his hand lightly. 'For love even.'

Dasaratha turned his face away, his expression inscrutable, his eyes shiny with some undefinable emotion. His jowls shook with the continuing tremors of his condition. Kausalya went on.

'And I gave you what you asked from me, as best as

I was able.' Her voice sharpened despite her effort to control it. The steel crept back into it, hardening her tone. 'But that does not mean I gave you an empty scroll upon which you could scribe anything you pleased. Our reconciliation does not give you the right to assume that you know me so well as yet. You can never know the Kausalya of all those lost years. That Kausalya is forever barred from you, locked in an abandoned prison of your own design. But this Kausalya,' she looked down at her own hands now, seeking to control the emotions warring within her, 'this Kausalya is yours. She belongs to you entirely. She lives only to serve you and to see her son rise above the downturns of her own past misfortunes. I think, if nothing else, I have proved that much to you at least. Do not question my loyalty ever again. Not even by mistake. For that is a mistake I cannot forgive.'

There was a long, heavy moment of silence after she had ended. The prime minister had taken to staring at the floor mutely, trying desperately to make himself invisible. But after Kausalya finished speaking, his eyes flickered to her face, then to Dasaratha's sweating pale features. He seemed to want to say something, then thought better of it. He sighed a long, deep, unhappy sigh and clasped his hands together, staring down once more. A serving maid, no doubt waiting for a pause in the conversation, crept in quickly, picked up a pile of bowls that had been used to towel-wash the maharaja before he changed and took to his bed, and scurried out quickly as a mouse, never once raising her head to look at any of the three.

After the maid had come and gone, Dasaratha spoke quietly into the ensuing silence. He kept his face turned towards the far wall, his chin trembling as he attempted to form words and phrases without slurring them.

'I did not question your loyalty. That has never been an issue between us. I only questioned the propriety of your adding your own voice and weight to Sumitra when she had that hysterical outburst. Bad enough that she should succumb to whatever nervous imaginings that have been plaguing her of late. But I was shocked that you should give credence to them as well.' He added more tenderly, 'That was all I meant to say. I intended no insult or injury to you, dear one. If I sounded like I did, then forgive me that trespass as well.'

He leaned back against his bolsters. Kausalya looked up and saw that his face was all but dripping sweat. She took up a fresh napkin to wipe him clean, then offered him a jal-bartan of cool water. He bent forward to sip it desultorily, then lay back again.

'When does the fighting stop, Kausalya? When do these endless conflicts end and peace truly begin? Not just for our nation, or even for our family. I mean for our hearts. When will these wretched organs ever find lasting peace?'

Only in the grave. For that is the only time we finally travel beyond reach of mortal errors, beyond regret and reproach, sins of commission and of omission, free, if only briefly, between our countless physical lives and their inevitable conflicts of karma and dharma.

But of course she couldn't say that aloud. Instead she said, 'You should be at peace. You have earned the right.'

He looked at her, his chest rising and falling irregularly, breath wheezing raggedly from his partly open mouth. 'You think so? I have earned the right to a little space to rest? A small season of peace and recovery?'

'Indeed,' she said, stroking his brow gently upwards, pressing back his sweat-oiled hair. 'As much rest as you need. I did not understand it earlier when you told me.

But now I do. You were right in your decision to announce Rama's succession. He will lift the burden of kingship from your shoulders. That much at least he can do.'

But not the burden of husbandhood or fatherhood.
Those will weigh you down until your very last breath,
and nobody can help that, my love.

'Yes,' he sighed. 'You are right. It is time. I have already spoken with Sumantra. All the arrangements are ready. The council has already passed a formal motion accepting Rama as my heir-successor. Tomorrow I will pass on my crown to him at the sabha and step down from the sunwood throne.'

He paused, reaching up to grasp her hand. She could feel the shaking in his fingers. It took all her strength to keep her own steady as well as his.

'Kausalya, I don't understand all that has happened these past days. I have no conception of sorcery and the evil it can wreak. It has always been beyond my comprehension. I am a man of the flesh, of the earth, of the elements. But this much I know: you have raised a great man. You have moulded him into a person like few others that have ever walked this earth. That credit is all yours.'

She thought for a moment he was speaking of himself; then, with a warm flood of pleasure, she realised he was talking of Rama. She bowed her head, kissing his hand. 'He is your son as well, my lord. He carries your blood, and your great heritage. It takes a lion to father a lion cub.'

'Perhaps,' Dasaratha rasped, his lungs clouding over again audibly. 'But it takes a lioness to raise him like a lion.'

She accepted that gracefully. Across the bed, Sumantra released yet another long sigh. This one sounded less unhappy, more relieved. Kausalya looked up to see the lines on the prime minister's face a little lighter. 'If you will permit me, then, my liege and my lady, we have a few minor matters of formality to discuss concerning tomorrow's coronation.'

Dasaratha rolled his eyes in mock exasperation. 'Trust you to bring everything crashing back down to Prithvi-lok again, Sumantra! Don't you enjoy visiting Swarga-lok when you get the chance? These moments of reconciliation are rare enough as it is without cutting them even shorter!' He glanced at Kausalya with the faintest trace of mischief in his eyes. 'If you were not here in the room, perhaps I might even learn just how fully recovered I am!'

Kausalya slapped her husband's arm lightly. 'Dasa! If the royal vaids hear you, they'll have you chained to your bed for the rest of your life!'

'Just as long as they chain you with me,' he said, half seriously. 'Close to me.'

Sumantra emitted a disbelieving laugh that turned immediately into an embarrassed cough of apology.

Dasaratha looked into Kausalya's eyes with that intense, searching look, part forgive-me and part love-me-for-ever, that she knew so well. She shook her head, wagging her finger in warning, and was about to make some throwaway comment about how invalid kings ought not to attempt amorous forays into hostile territory when she saw Sumantra react to something behind her. The prime minister's expression changed suddenly as a strange twisted shadow fell upon the bed, backlit by the mashaals in the outer room.

Dasaratha looked up too, and Kausalya, who had her back to the doorway, saw his face lose its playful, smiling mischievousness at once, so abruptly that it seemed a mask had been pulled from his face. Or perhaps a mask had been put upon his face. The shadow of the person who had entered behind Kausalya fell partway across Dasaratha, dissecting him in half.

'My lords, my lady, pardon my interrupting,' said a voice that was oddly familiar yet not instantly recognisable. 'But I must needs have a word with the maharaja at once.'

It was the way the intruder said the word 'maharaja' that made Kausalya identify her. Kausalya did not wish to turn around, did not want to confirm what her ears were telling her. It couldn't possibly be who she thought it was. And yet, now that she had heard that peculiarity of speech, she could not doubt it. An instant later, Sumantra confirmed it when he rose to his feet and spoke stiffly, almost harshly, quite unlike his usual impeccably polite official manner.

'What could be so urgent that you need disturb the king in his sickroom at this hour of night? You could have discussed it with the preceptor, or if Guru Vashishta were not available, then you could have asked for me, surely?'

Now Kausalya did turn her head, if only to see how the visitor reacted. She saw the haggard pale face of the hunchback Manthara curl in a sly smile that barely concealed her snide disagreement with the prime minister's words.

'That would be impossible, Pradhan-mantriji. For this matter concerns the maharaja alone. You see, my lord,' she went on, addressing Dasaratha directly without further preamble, 'my lady Kaikeyi wishes you to come see her at once.'

Kausalya noticed the darkness spread across Dasaratha's face, creeping to cover both sides now, leaving only part of one eye and a bit of his forehead illuminated.

Manthara had taken another step into the room as she spoke, elongating her shadow.

Dasaratha raised himself to his elbow with an effort. 'As you can see, daiimaa,' the maharaja replied harshly, 'I am not at my best for paying late-night visits at present. If the matter is urgent, Rani Kaikeyi will have to take it up with the preceptor or prime minister.' He added, after a pause, 'Or, if it is of a personal nature, it might be best if she addresses herself to Rani Kausalya directly. The First Queen has charge of all palace affairs while I am indisposed.'

Kausalya saw the gleam in the old woman's eyes. For a second she almost thought the daiimaa's eyes were green. But that couldn't be. Manthara had plain black eyes, didn't she? She put it down to a trick of the light and the angle.

'That would be quite impossible, my liege.'

'I see,' Dasaratha said with a weary but unmistakable trace of anger in his tone now. The maharaja had never brooked subordinates who spoke back after being told what to do. Kausalya prepared to place a hand on his arm to coax him to calm down. It would not do for him to lose his temper at some tottering old wet-nurse and worsen his already deteriorated condition. 'And why is that?'

'Because,' Manthara said with a sound somewhere between a sigh and a sly chuckle, 'my lady has taken the vrath vows and retired to the kosaghar. She intends to remain there until she is parted from her mortal form. In short, she will starve herself to death unless your majesty goes at once and stops her.'

15

The moment Vibhisena entered the Hall, all conversation ceased. Actually, you could hardly call it conversation; cacophony was a more apt term. When you had a hundred different Asuras from a dozen different species gathered together in one place, talking nineteen to the dozen all at once, that was what it sounded like.

Vibhisena walked toward the dais at the far end, taking care to avoid stepping on the long central carpet that traversed the length of the Hall. It was difficult to tell from its present soiled and scuffed condition, but the carpet was made from human skin. It gave Vibhisena the willy-nillies to imagine how many unfortunate mortals had died to make the six-inch-thick hundred-yard-long carpet. He felt worse when he recalled that the skin used was all taken from human infants while still alive.

Vibhisena kept his eyes raised to avoid having to look at the carpet. The seats of the great Hall were filled, every chair occupied by an Asura chief. Unlike previous sessions, he failed to recognise any of those gathered here today. That was probably because most of the Asura lords he knew had perished in the battle of Mithila, as it was now being called. These Asuras gathered here today were the lowest-rung specimens of their species, catapulted overnight to chieftain status because of the sudden void in their leadership. Even so, Vibhisena was surprised to see any Asuras here at all. The massacre of Mithila – as he preferred to call it – had been brutally efficient in its decimation. He presumed that these survivors must be from the few groups that had been sent north-west to Kaikeya and Gandahar, or perhaps even part of the contingent that had remained to guard Lanka itself. If so, they should count themselves doubly lucky, once for having escaped the fate of their fellows at Mithila, and once more for being rewarded with these promotions.

They watched him with hostile curiosity as he passed by. Vibhisena was a curious object in Lanka even to those who knew him well, and to these Asuras he must seem like a most exotic specimen. He was certainly not what any of them might have expected. This was not the image that came to mind when one said the words 'Ravana's brother'.

He could imagine what they saw with complete clarity. A stick-thin albino-skinned rakshasa clad in brahmin-white dhoti and kurta and toe-grip wooden slippers, choosing to walk the length of the Hall rather than be borne aloft by the servants at his disposal. It was an image they would be having a hard time reconciling with their expectations.

But the physical imperfections apart, what would baffle most of them was his outward appearance. How could Ravana's brother, a rakshasa, be dressed like a mortal, a brahmin no less? Why, he even had the caste marks of a real brahmin, and the rudraksh maala around his neck, and to those who were sharp-eyed enough to note, the black janayu thread around his torso, wound diagonally over one shoulder and tied at the waist. From the clicking and hissing and gruff mumbles all around, he could tell what they must be speculating.

There must be some subterfuge here, they were thinking, a part of some devilish new ploy of the demonlord to trick the mortals of Prithvi-lok. This brahmin bhes-bhav was no doubt intended to be a disguise that Vibhisena would use to infiltrate some mortal city, most likely Ayodhya, in order to eliminate some mortal enemy. They were even speculating as to the identity of the target: Rama Chandra was by far the favourite choice.

He felt the hooded beady eyes of the nagas and uragas watching him suspiciously, their forked tongues flickering in and out of their slitted maws, hissing sibilantly. The danvas, pisacas, ditis, daityas, vetaals and other related sub-human species all stared with glittering red-veined eyes as he passed them by. The yaksa chiefs were morphing through various forms as they pleased, depending on their moods and whims, one in the process of turning from a tiger into a rhinocerous, another seemingly content to stay half gharial and half albatross, with the wings of a garuda. The rakshasa chieftains were as surly and bloodthirsty-looking as ever, licking their fangs and tusks in restless anticipation. A trio of them, two females and a male, were engaged in fervent copulation as he passed, or perhaps they were resolving some dispute the rakshasa way.

Vibhisena's wooden slippers clattered on the stone floor as he approached the dais. The Black Throne of Lanka sat empty as it had these past three days. He climbed the stairs to the top of the dais slowly and cautiously. This entire area was always slippery with blood and various internal fluids from the unfortunate Asura chiefs that Ravana routinely slaughtered for their various lapses and inefficiencies. The stench was incredible and the floor squirmed and writhed with a profusion of maggots, death beetles and other offal-feeders. Perhaps he ought to have the place washed down? He wondered how that would abide with the Asura chiefs. It would be a stark contrast with Ravana's methods.

He turned and faced the Hall, which had suddenly fallen still and silent once more. Every pair of eyes – and various other kinds of vision organs – was focused on him. He raised his voice to be heard, grateful for the sorcerous spell that made the speaker's voice audible to everyone across the large Hall.

'Friends,' he said, 'I am Vibhisena, brother to Ravana, Lord of Lanka. It was I who brought back my brother's body from the place at Mithila where he fell.'

He paused to let them react. Not a single one gave him the satisfaction. He mused that they must already be aware of these basic facts at least. They would be wanting to know something more, something they did not already know. He obliged them.

'My brother is not dead. Whatever you may have heard and believed, hear this first: Ravana is alive and well.'

That got a reaction. A burst of exclamatory sounds and noises erupted around the Hall. The trio of copulating rakshasas ceased their sexual activity. At least, two of them did; when the third, a female who didn't want the male to stop his action, growled and bit him impatiently, the male rakshasa used his talons to slash her throat and let her body roll down the steps from his seat to the floor below; it writhed and shook in its death spasms, shaking exactly as if it was experiencing some macabre orgasm. Perhaps it was; with rakshasas, eroto-necrophilia was a finely developed art. Some orgasms were considered worth dying for.

Vibhisena averted his eyes from the thrashing naked female form before the dais and continued his speech. 'He has asked me to speak to you on his behalf and let you know that Lanka remains in his command. Let none of you think otherwise. He retains his position as lord of the Asura races and master of the island-kingdom.'

A pisaca chieftain, its ghostly white eyes glowing in a

rotting face, called out seductively, 'If this is true, why does not the demonlord appear to us in person? Why does he send you poor fool to speak on his behalf?'

A danav further down the line made a tearing, ripping sound with its tooth-rimmed maw. 'Perhaps Ravana has lost his voice!'

That drew honks and roars of laughter all around. An uraga turned abruptly and lunged at its companion, a diti, swallowing the angelic horse-Asura up in two quick gobbles. Vibhisena didn't dare ask what the diti had done to aggravate the uraga. The giant serpent uncoiled to allow for the animal it had just ingested, which slid down the python-like body with lurching progress as the diti suffocated to death within the uraga's gullet. The uraga's little-girl face beamed beatifically, in start contrast to its horrific body.

Vibhisena raised his hand, asking for silence. It was slow in coming. He could see that the chiefs were not impressed or intimidated by his appearance or manner. That was to be expected: they had been accustomed to millennia under the yoke of the cruellest Asura ruler that had ever existed. A rake-thin albino rakshasa dressed and marked like a mortal brahmin would hardly cause them any consternation. For all his religious piety, Vibhisena was still a rakshasa. He could smell from the mélange of odours in the Hall that the chiefs were bordering on open mutiny. He must bring the sabha under control and quickly, or his very life would be forfeit.

He went on, trying for a sterner, more commanding tone this time. 'My brother is still indisposed, that is why I speak for him. But none of his power is diminished in the slightest, so, friends, let me warn you—'

'What do you mean, indisposed? Does he just have a cold and a fever, or did he grow wings and fly away?'

Vibhisena wasn't sure where that question came from, but it seemed to have originated from the rakshasa section. That was a very bad sign. If the rakshasa chiefs were losing respect for Ravana, then the other Asuras would pounce on the lohit-stone throne in a trice. The fact that the rakshasas had outnumbered the other Asura species by a factor of ten was one of the things that had kept the rest of them in check; after the massacre at Mithila, that safeguard had been lost. As the vanguard of the attack, the rakshasa clans had been the most badly hit. The rakshasa races, so long the masters of their Asura associates, were no more superior in numbers. And with Ravana's powerful sorcery and brutal leadership absent, it left no check on any kingly ambitions the other chiefs might have.

The lurid remark drew another mangled burst of Asura laughter. On the floor below, the female rakshasi had finally stopped writhing and lay spreadeagled in a grotesquely inviting sexual posture. If she wasn't moved soon, he wouldn't put it past some lusty Asura chief to cover her and use her for his necrophilic satisfaction.

Vibhisena looked around for the kumbha-rakshasas that customarily stood by when Ravana held his sessions. Not a single one was in sight, yet another telling sign of the rapid deterioration in morale and discipline. If he didn't act quickly and decisively, the Asura races would soon break out into open mutiny. From there to outright inter-species war would be a short step. And much as Vibhisena deplored his brother's excesses and brutalities, he had never doubted that without Ravana the Asuras would all go their separate ways. There was good reason why no one master had been able to command all the species until Ravana came along and dared to attempt the feat. To rule over a million million demons, you had to show that you were more demonaic than them all.

Vibhisena raised his arms, holding them out before him, palms facing upward.

Someone saw him and commented boldly, 'Now the brother is praying for rain. Quit it, white-face! All the waters of the world won't revive your brother now!'

Something exploded like a blast of thunder from the heart of a barkha cloud. A lightning bolt, jagged black edged with crimson, shot out from the roof of the Hall and struck the vetaal who had spoken the last comment. It was indeed the last comment that wretch would ever speak. The bolt of black lightning entered his mouth and impaled him on the point of its jagged tip. The vetaal's skinless body crumpled in a single burst of flame, then dissipated into a hundred thousand flakes of ash. The flakes flew apart and were lost in the murky light of the mashaals that lit up the Hall.

The voice that spoke into the ensuing silence was as deep and sonorous as the distant rolls of thunder fading away.

'I am Ravana, Lord of Lanka. Who dares show me disrespect in my own house?'

This time, Vibhisena noted with relief, there were no vulgar retorts or comments. Every Asura chief in the sabha stared transfixed at the object that had appeared in the centre of the Hall.

Ravana, still embedded within his block of transparent red stone, floated in mid-air, several yards above the ground. The enormous block rotated rapidly, turning on a diagonal axis to allow a view to every chief in the assembly. Frozen within the heart of the redstone, the demonlord's body was still suspended like a beetle in glass, but his eyes, all twenty of them, were open and glaring.

16

'Dasa, don't go,' she said, catching his arm as he rose wearily from the bed. The attendants had brought the travelling chair into the sickroom and had set it down beside the bed. Dasaratha, a shawl wrapped around his chest, was preparing to move his ailing self from the bed to the chair when Kausalya stopped him.

He looked up at her with woeful large eyes, rimmed red and shot through with a fine tracery of veins. The irises seemed as if ringed by filmy white orbs, like cataract-ridden pupils, even though Dasaratha had not complained or displayed any loss of vision. 'Kausalya,' he said softly. Sumantra had left the chamber, escorting Manthara out, and Kausalya could hear his voice berating the daiimaa in the antechamber for the way she had barged into the maharaja's private chambers unannounced. But the attendants who would carry the chair were yet here, and it was to avoid them overhearing that the maharaja kept his voice low.

'You heard the daiimaa,' he said now, his eyes pleading. 'She has taken a vrath vow and locked herself into the kosaghar. You know what that means. If I don't go to her, then she will allow herself to die of starvation and thirst.'

'Even if she does, which I doubt,' Kausalya said softly

but urgently, 'she's hardly likely to die this very night. Why not go see her on the morrow, after a night's rest?'

Dasaratha shrugged, although it came off as the merest twitch of his shoulderblades. The powerful arm, shoulder and upper back muscles that she had once stroked with such pride and pleasure were dissipated and sagging with disuse. It was all he could do to continue speaking hoarsely. 'Why put off what must be done anyway?'

'Because I don't trust her,' Kausalya said. 'Because her timing is so bad. You saw her this evening, strutting about at the griha pravesh welcoming rite. Did that seem like a woman about to take a fast-vow unto death? On her son's wedding night?'

Dasaratha sighed, his eyes flickering weakly. 'That is what I must go to find out, Kausalya. Sitting here, how can these questions be answered?'

'But why would she do this if not to rouse you from your sickbed?'

His mouth twitched. 'Sumitra and you did give her cause for upset.'

'Cause enough to take her own life? Come on, Dasa. Even for Kaikeyi that's making a Himalaya out of an antheap. Besides, it still doesn't make sense for her to do it at such a time, when she knows that you are so ill and in need of rest. Why tonight? Why now? Why not wait until you are stronger to take up the matter formally? After all, she won her vindication before everyone present. She proved her identity beyond doubt when Guru Vashishta recognised her and blessed her. She has already won that little battle. Why drag you out of your bed?'

'As I said already, Kausalya, we'll never know if I don't go.'

She clutched his arm, gripping his flabby flesh through the sleeve of his ang-vastra. 'Then do it for my sake.

Don't go tonight. Send back word that you are too unwell to move about. Let the daiimaa take the message back to her that you will see her on the morrow. Then, after the coronation, you will be up and about anyway, and you can go meet with her then.'

He shook his head doubtfully. 'I don't know, Kausalya. I have already said I will go, I told Manthara.'

'Forget Manthara!' Kausalya glanced around, aware of the attendants standing with eyes averted, waiting. 'I told you about Sumitra and her experience with that old hag. Surely you believe that there was something wrong, even if we could not track down any hard evidence of actual wrongdoing. Where there is smoke, there must be fire.'

'But there was no smoke,' he said wearily. 'Not even a wisp to be seen, from what I gathered. And she has been under close guard ever since. It was the guards who escorted her here to my chambers. Besides, she has nothing to do with this. This is between Kaikeyi and me.'

Kausalya was about to speak again, marshal a new line of argument, when he raised his eyes sternly, silencing her.

'Kausalya, listen to me. I spent fifteen years with Kaikeyi. She gave me a son, as you did. I shared my life, my kingdom and my bed with that woman every night for those many hundreds of moons. I cannot simply detach the rope and set myself adrift without so much as a backward glance. If this were simply some tantrum, I might have protested. But a vrath-vow is a serious act, to be taken seriously. I must go to see her in the kosaghar. The moment I am done, I will return here to you. It will be you I share this bed with tonight, and every night here-after. But first I must perform this one last duty as a husband to his lawful wife. I must go minister to Kaikeyi and see what ails her.'

I know what ails her, Kausalya wanted to scream. *She cannot accept the loss of you to me. And she will not accept it, no matter what you do or say to placate her. She is a warrior-queen, the daughter of a long line of raj-kshatriyas. Defeat is not in her vocabulary. This is the only reason she has staged this new drama tonight. Stay here with me. Let this night pass.*

Dasaratha was shuffling toward the chair. It broke Kausalya's heart to see him hunched like a vanar. The attendants stepped forward but Dasaratha gestured them away as fiercely as ever – *he has more pride than strength left now* – and made it to the seat on his own. He sat down with a great sigh, face flushed and dripping sweat. He accepted the napkin given by one of the attendants and nodded.

'Kosaghar le chalo.' *Take me to the anger room.*

The attendants bent as one and raised the poles on which the chair was hung. Moving in perfect tandem, they strode swiftly out of the chamber. Sumantra's voice broke off in the antechamber and he said something to which Dasaratha replied.

Kausalya didn't hear their words. She was absorbed by a fresh thought that had struck her. She would tell Dasaratha to ask Guru Vashishta to go to Kaikeyi in the kosaghar. It was an old and accepted practice for the preceptor to intervene in such matters. Kaikeyi could not refuse the guru's requests; in fact, with Vashishta she would not have the emotional hold she had over Dasaratha. Then, after the guru had ascertained what exactly the Second Queen was demanding this time, Dasaratha could decide whether or not to see her on the morrow.

Kausalya raced out of the chamber to stop Dasaratha and tell him of this strategy. But the chair was already far down the long corridor, and as she watched, it turned the corner and disappeared from sight.

It was too late to stop him now without causing a hullabaloo that would awaken the entire palace. She could hardly go running after the chair through the heart of the palace, yelling out suggestions to thwart Kaikeyi.

She stood at the aangan and twisted the edge of her sari pallo into a knot, struggling to control the wave of anguish that threatened to drown her.

She was not given to over-emotionality. But this once, she could not stop the small inner voice that kept repeating over and over again that she had lost some crucial battle she had not even known she was fighting.

And that this lost battle would cost her the war entire.

17

The sabha had ended. The Hall of Lanka was empty once more. Even the naked dead rakshasi had been dragged out by the kumbha-rakshasas who had appeared magically the minute they were given evidence of Ravana's continued existence.

Now Vibhisena was alone in the vast echoing expanse of the great Hall. He felt ashamed of himself. Ashamed and unclean. He took two steps back, unable to believe that he had just done what he had done. Forgetting where he was, he continued stepping backwards, as if trying to physically retreat from his own actions and words. The back of his knees struck the edge of the lohit-stone throne and he sat down heavily, gasping with surprise. The iron throne was cold as ice, and he sprang back to his feet at once. But somehow the frozen consciousness that was all that remained of his brother spoke once more into his mind.

Brother, you play the part of a tyrant well. Perhaps you should have your own throne.

Vibhisena looked up at the block of redstone, still rotating slowly in mid-air. Ravana's splayed arms and feet were motionless, but in those terrible commanding eyes he thought he saw a flash of life.

'Brother,' he said softly. 'You know I will never sit a throne or command others. It goes against my principles.'

*Ah. Of course. You are that rarest of rare creatures,
a rakshasa with scruples. A brahmin, no less. How did
I ever grow a brahmin rakshasa under my own roof, I
wonder?*

'You had nothing to do with it. If anything, you were
even more pious and devout in your worship than I
was when we were children. It was only later in puberty
that you began to change. But you and I are still grandchildren of Pulastya, don't forget that, brother.'

*How can I, when you never let me forget! You and
my wife Mandodhari. Sometimes I think that you should
have been the brother she married, not me! The two of
you would have gone through life happily together,
chanting the praises of the devas.*

Vibhisena clicked his tongue disapprovingly. 'Ashubh,
ashubh!' *Inauspicious, unsuitable.* 'Do not speak of my
sister-in-law in that manner. She is a paragon of moral
virtue, as you well know.'

*Oh, I do know. Which is why, when I desire true
womanly passion, I have to seek it in the arms of one or
other of my sweet rakshasi mistresses. Which isn't always
easy, there being so many to choose from! And any of
them are far more enjoyable to mate with rather than
your too-sweet sister-in-law.*

Vibhisena pinched his earlobes, then turned and made
a throwing gesture in the general direction of Varanasi,
seeking to cleanse himself thus of Ravana's vulgarity.

*Did I cause some offence? Excuse me if I don't apol-
ogise. As you can see, my resources are limited and I
must make the most pertinent use of the only shakti I
seem to have access to – communication. To the point
then, brother. You did well today with the Asura council.
Those bottom-feeders would have eaten you alive if you
had shown the slightest bit of weakness. By putting them*

*in their place so effectively, you held my kingdom together
for a while longer. I have to admit, I would never have
thought that you would be the one to help me thus. Tell
me, what made you rise to the occasion so admirably?
If anything, you've always sought to thwart my desire to
destroy the mortals. Why do you help me now?*

'I help you because nobody else can, brother,'
Vibhisena said. 'Because you are my brother after all. It
becomes my dharma to do whatever I can to save you.'
He gestured at the empty Hall. 'As for the kingdom, it
was a matter of survival. Had I not held the Asura races
together, civil war would have broken out. And in that
infighting, even the devout brahmin rakshasas of my order
would have been destroyed.'

*Most certainly. They'd be the first to be butchered.
Their very presence is an affront to any self-disrespecting
Asura. Why, there are times when I feel like taking a
mile-long rod, skewering them all through their bellies,
and roasting the whole clutch over a spit. Kumbhakarna
would feast well on them! You know how he relishes
roasted brahmins!*

'Brother,' Vibhisena said grimly, 'if you persist in
making such talk, perhaps you should turn to
Kumbhakarna for assistance. Whatever evils you may have
done before, you know I cannot even brook talk of them,
let alone stand by and watch the act itself committed.'

Vibhisena began walking down the dais steps. 'I will
order your kumbhas to go awaken our eldest brother.
You and he can savour such vulgar talk to your heart's
content. I have not the stomach for such discussions.'

Stop, Vibhisena!

Vibhisena paused on the third step.

*It would take months, even years, to rouse Kumbha-
karna. You know that. I must be freed of this cage of*

stone much sooner. I have unfinished work to see to. You may have held the hounds and bitches of our allies at bay for now, but very soon they will understand that I am trapped physically within this block of brahman-created redstone, unable to do more than cast a few feeble spells like the one I sent through your hands to kill that snivelling vetaal. By the way, thank you for allowing me a channel to rid myself of that blood-sucking scum. I hate vetaals! So, as I was saying, if I am not freed from this cage before the chiefs realise my limitations, they will revolt in force. And then there really will be brahmins roasting on spits in Lanka, Vibhisena.

'Your sons are great warriors, Jay,' Vibhisena said, looking unmoved. 'Meghnath isn't called Indrajit for nothing. It was his victory over Indra, Lord of Devas, in your great campaign against Swarga-lok that earned him that title. And your younger son Akshay Kumar's prowess on the field has never been matched by any warrior, Asura or mortal, till now. They have both been most anxious about your condition and have repeatedly offered to help. I will send them to speak with you here.'

Vibhisena. Great warriors do not always make great leaders. My sons are brilliant in the field, but duffers at court. That is why they're not permitted to set foot in this Hall, by my own order. Were they handling today's council session, they would have created more chaos in the Asura ranks, and worse, they would end up fighting each other, just to answer the old question of which of them is the better warrior. No, my sons cannot help me now. Only you can. You know this as well as I do, so why do you try my patience, brother?

Vibhisena smiled, shaking his head. 'It's you who is trying my patience, Jay. You know I will not stand by and hear vulgarity and abuse, especially directed at brahmins.

Either you control your tongue – or your mental voice, as the case may be – or I will walk away at the next insult and leave you to fend for yourself, whatever the consequences.'

There was a long moment of sullen silence during which time the Lord of Lanka spun slowly in his bed of redstone, his eyes glaring with equal ferocity and barely suppressed anger. Finally, the response came, reluctant and recalcitrant but unmistakably clear.

Very well. No more brahmin jokes. Now can we get on with it?

Vibhisena thought for a moment, one foot still on the lower step. Was he being a fool? Surely it was asking too much to expect Ravana to change in the least degree. And yet this was such a deva-gifted opportunity to try to mellow the demonlord's rapacious ways and bring some small measure of morality into Lanka's evil excesses. Perhaps he couldn't change his brother substantially, but even if he could play a small part in reducing the blood-shed and horrors in some way, it would be worth it. He had no doubt that once restored to his full strength Ravana would return at once to his brutal, murderous ways. Which was why it was essential to press home his advantage here and now, while the demonlord was still relatively helpless.

What's going through your mind, brother? What's taking you so long? Do you have another appointment you've suddenly recalled? A brahmin priestess you promised to bed before daybreak, perhaps?

'Brother,' Vibhisena said admonishingly.

Scratch out that last carving. I forgot, no more brahmin—

'I have a condition.'

So. Spit it out.

'No more invasions of Prithvi-lok. Ever.'

Another moment of silence. The block spun slowly, casting a long shadow that twisted and changed shape ominously.

Now you're the one making vulgar jokes, brother. You're asking an elephant not to breathe through his trunk, an ant not to seek out honey, a gandharva not to play music.

'That's my condition. No invasions of the mortal realm. Ever again.'

The reply came back sullenly, if a mental voice could be said to express itself sullenly.

You might as well ask me to slice off my manhood and eat it with butter and salt. Once made, the arrow must fly, the sword cleave, the typhoon rage. I exist to destroy and strike terror. It has been this way ever and shall continue ever more. You know this, as well as you know the history and cause of my quest for vengeance.

'Even so, this is my condition. If you will not concede, then I leave you to work your own way out. I shall send for our brother, and for your sons.'

Ravana spoke again before Vibhisena could move another step.

Very well! No more invasions. What about forays? Skirmishes? Minor campaigns of conquest and subjugation? You would not deprive a boy of all his toys, would you?

'No unprovoked acts of violence against mortalkind. You will under no circumstances attack humans singly, in groups or in larger numbers. I do not wish to play with semantics, brother. I mean that you and your Asura followers should not in any way assault or attack any human in any manner henceforth.'

What about provoked attacks then? If the humans

*attack me or invade my kingdom, how can I not be
expected to defend myself? As you well know, I lost
almost all of my army strength to the Brahm-astra. What
if the mortals decide that now is the best time to invade
and cleanse the world once and for all of all Asuras?
Even your holy Vedas do not prescribe that a person
under attack should quietly offer his other side to be
stabbed and slashed!*

Vibhisena smiled. 'In that highly unlikely event, if the
mortals themselves inflict bodily harm upon you or your
followers anywhere, then yes, you may defend yourselves.
But you and I both know that the mortals will not invade
Lanka. You may have lost your army, but once released
from this brahman cage, you will begin at once to
replenish your numbers. In a decade at best, you'll have
enough to begin thinking of invasion once more.'

*In a decade I'll barely have a few million Asuras. At
best a crore. You overestimate my abilities, brother. Even
the hell worlds grow empty of new reinforcements, Lord
Yamraj grows more difficult to bargain with each passing
century. This is no longer the prime of our glory, which
is all the more reason why we must go on fighting the
mortals. Otherwise they will overrun this whole plane
and we will all be forgotten. Even you wouldn't want
your own race extinguished, would you, Vibhisena?*

Vibhisena shrugged. 'We are all one in the flow of
brahman. Merely occupying different forms.'

*I doubt you'd be as equanimous if you were occupying
the form of a naga or a vetaal. But nevertheless, I won't
waste further energy arguing. It's blasted hard enough
communicating through this damn stone. I'm asking you
again, please, set me free and I will agree to whatever
contract you draw up.*

'First tell, do you agree to this bargain? No more

attacks on humans? No more invasions, intrusions, assaults, or—'

Yes, I follow. I won't even scratch their backs unless they scratch mine first. Get on with it. I feel my strength fading. It's happening again like it did this morning, I'm finding it more and more difficult to reach you with every passing minute.

'It's the moontides,' Vibhisena said. 'The flow of brahman has ever been linked to the flow of energy from the sun and the moon. This is why the Suryavansha line and the Chandravansha line on earth have always produced the most powerful champions, for their blood-lines are most directly linked with the solar and lunar energies of—'

Vibhisena . . . enough talk. Free me . . . fading fast . . . quickly! Act . . . brother!

Vibhisena nodded, even though Ravana's back was to him at the time. The redstone block was pulsing with a blueish-tinted glow that cast a strange mixed-colour palette of rays across the Hall. This had happened twice each day since he had brought his brother home. It meant that the time was ripe for him to perform the rite he had planned. If he let this window of opportunity pass, he would have to wait till the next moontide, twelve hours hence, to act. If it had to be done, then this thing was best done sooner rather than later.

He summoned the pushpak from its perch by the northern end of the black fortress. It arrived in moments, entering the chamber through one of the enormous open spaces that had been especially created to allow its passage. The golden air-chariot glimmered dazzlingly in the light show cast off by the rotating slab. The slab had begun to turn faster now, its progress hastened by the rising of the tide. Vibhisena had studied its movements closely. It would turn faster and faster, reaching its peak at the height of the moontide, spinning so rapidly as to be only a red blur.

He boarded the pushpak and commanded it to take hold of the redstone slab. The slab continued to spin even after the chariot gripped it with its invisible shakti. Then Vibhisena instructed the celestial vehicle of his desired destination. The vehicle took flight without hesitation. If he had asked it, it would have taken him to Swarga-lok itself, realm of the devas, or conversely, to Patal-lok, the lowest netherworld of all. But his destination was nowhere near that ambitious; it was on the island of Lanka itself. He arrived within moments.

Vibhisena peered down from the height of a thousand yards, looking down into the maw of the largest, most violent volcano on Lanka. This was no ordinary volcano. This was the portal to Narak itself, the entrance to the hell worlds.

It was into this dread place that Vibhisena would have to take his frozen brother in order to free him of his stone cage. For only here could he summon up the heat and pressure that were required to release Ravana from the brahman cage. And even so, it would take all his vidya and shakti to accomplish the feat.

The brahmin rakshasa sent up a fervent prayer to the devas that he might succeed in his mission. Not for himself: the pushpak would ensure that its occupant was protected from the toxic dangers and heat of the volcano's heart. It was for Ravana that he offered his prayers. He was keenly aware of the irony involved in his asking the devas' grace to help the most terrible demon that had ever walked the earth. But Vibhisena's faith was absolute. Moreover, he believed sincerely that if he succeeded in this task, he would achieve his larger goal: to recast

Ravana in a more mellow form, leash his brother's savagery and rein in the brutal destruction that he had wrought for millennia. Vibhisena was one of those who still remembered Ravana's great austerities and penances of aeons past; those memories still inspired hope that he could make Ravana walk the path of brahman once more. He took the Lord of Lanka's present predicament, and his ironic reliance on Vibhisena and his brahman-shakti, as a significant omen. The samay chakra had turned, bringing yet another change in the affairs of mortals and demonkind. It could, he believed, mean only one thing: that the end was near. The end of war and violence, and the birth of a new age.

Chanting a potent mantra from the sacred secret work known as the Smriti-Upanisads, he commanded the pushpak to descend into the volcano. The golden air-chariot descended swiftly into the heart of the simmering open-mouthed mountain, the redstone block spinning at breathtaking speed.

As if in response, the volcano belched a gigantic gout of molten magma, emitting a roar like a sea-beast awakened.

Lanka shuddered.

18

The night was cool and dark when they rose from their flower-bedecked bed and stood on the veranda.

The city still echoed faintly to sounds of revelry. The grooms' wedding procession might have been deprived of a full seven-day feast in Mithila, but they were more than making up for it back home in Ayodhya. And with the coronation tomorrow, it seemed as if two weeks of festivity that had begun at Holi were finally coming to a climax. But the eyes of both young lovers were drawn upwards. The sky was rich with stars, and their thoughts and emotions were high above the everyday affairs of the mortal world in which they dwelt by day. The distant sounds of merriment only enhanced the cocoon of privacy in which they stood, nestled in each other's arms on the quiet veranda. Somewhere to the northern side of the palace, unseen except for the occasional flash of white foam breaking the blackness, the Sarayu sang her eternal song.

Sita broke the silence first, her voice soft and melodious on the still night air. '"Forget the singer but not the song. The lute but not the wood. The forest but not the tree. There was the place I gave you my heart, and you gave me yours in return. Then was the time, and that was the night."'

Rama said, '"Will you not deny this sun that shines above, this canopy of cloud, this panoply of gold and bronze? Or are these more deserving of your witness than that one sweet night of wedlock?"'

'"For even though the eyes grow dim, the mind falter, the head dizzy from the elixir of wealth and power, yet does the heart remember truly, and your lips, and your tongue, and every flame-singed hair on your skin recall. So ask your body, what the body remembers, what the soul holds tight in its fist, and come back, come back to me again."' Sita finished with a long sigh. Resting her head on Rama's chest, she said, 'Why are all the most beautiful love poems so melancholy?'

'I don't know. Remind me to ask the poet.'

'Ask your guru.'

'Guru Vashishta?'

She pinched his arm, laughing. 'Brahmarishi Vishwamitra. You know that! It's his daughter's tale, isn't it? Considerably embellished and dressed up suitably for presentation before patrons and kings by the poet laureate, no doubt, but still the tale of Sakuntala, and her tragic love for Dushyanta. Their son was Bharata, the father of the Arya nations.'

'Really?' Rama said, feigning innocence. 'How remarkable is that! Tell me more, maiden from Mithila.'

She smiled, untroubled by his teasing. She loved the story enough to tell it a hundred times – or hear it being told. 'Sakuntala lived and served her widowed father Vishwamitra in his forest hermitage in remote Kanwavan. One day she went down to the stream to fetch water as usual and found a handsome man lying unconscious. He was Dushyanta, a raja wounded during a hunting accident. The sage's daughter tended to him until his wounds healed. Now do you remember the story?'

Rama frowned, tapping his cheek with an expression of mock-concentration. 'Not really. It sounds vaguely familiar, but . . .' He shook his head. 'Not a thing. Must be that blow on the head I took when my horse rode under a low-hanging bough the other day, hunting wild stag in the woods.'

She tousled his hair affectionately. 'I'll give you such a blow—'

'Okay! Okay!' he said, laughing as she resorted to tickling next. 'I remember now! How could I forget? It's taught at every gurukul in the seven nations. It is the story of our founding father's birth after all!'

He leaned closer to her. 'The truth is, I like hearing you tell it. The sound of your voice . . .'

'Yes?'

He gestured to the north-west, towards the unmistakable sound of the river. 'It harmonises with the song of Sarayu. As if you were speaking with the voice of the river herself.'

Sita was silent for a moment. Rama turned his head to examine her profile in the dim light of the city. She looked more alluring to him than any portrait of apsaras or gandharvas, those celestial temptresses that adorned the palace of the Indra-dev. Yet there was something in that profile that also reminded him of the likeness of the devi his mother worshipped. Goddess and celestial beauty: surely it was conceivable that both qualities could be contained in one womanly form? The proof stood beside him, made flesh.

'That is the first lover's compliment you've paid me since we met.' Her voice was soft, an undertone to the murmuring song of the Sarayu.

He leaned low, breathing warm against her cheek. 'But not the last.' He nuzzled her cheek. 'Our marriage may have taken place expediently, but our courtship shall last a lifetime.'

She laughed softly. 'Now you're getting carried away, my lord. You don't need to be that lavish with your compliments to get me to recite the tale of Sakuntala!' She added softly, 'Although the compliments are welcome.'

He smiled at her in the darkness, white teeth flashing in his dark face. 'And well deserved. I meant what I said about your voice and the river. You two might well be sister-bards. Were you ever a river in your past life? Or a waterfall?'

She rolled her eyes in mock exasperation, then realised he probably couldn't see the expression. 'Back to the story, my lord. As I was saying, Sakuntala tended to the wounded king until he effected a complete recovery. In the process, he grew enchanted by her lustrous beauty.'

'Lustrous beauty,' Rama repeated softly, lifting her hair off her shoulder. 'That describes you well.'

She brushed his hand away gently but firmly. 'Dushyanta induced Sakuntala to enter into a gandharva vivah with him.'

Rama touched the nape of her neck. 'Gandharva vivah? A fancy euphemism that simply means they exchanged vows without witnesses or pundits present, probably before a stone lingam in the forest.'

She continued smoothly. 'Intoxicated by their mutual passion, Dushyanta and Sakuntala dallied together, desiring only to stay thus for ever, content with the simple forest life and each other's love. But of course, he was a king. And for a king, dharma came before self. Finally the day arrived when his mantris and senapatis, after a long, exhaustive search, sought him out in that deep forest.'

'If I was he,' Rama commented, 'I would have taken her and gone someplace where they could never be found.'

'But then what of your dharma?' she asked, only half teasing.

He sighed, nodding to her to go on.

'Raja Dushyanta gave Sakuntala his ring and vowed to her that he would return very soon and take her home as a queen-bride to his palace, there to reign beside him to the end of their days. Then he rode away.'

'Ah,' Rama said. 'And then it all turns sad. Like all Sanskrit dramas, and . . .'

And life? Is that what you meant to say, my love? But he didn't complete the sentence, and she went on.

'Weeks passed. And then months. And then years went by. And still Sakuntala waited patiently, secure in her love. But still Dushyanta didn't return. Finally, she decided she must go to him. And after a long and arduous journey—'

'Why do the protagonists always have to suffer at this point in the story? Is there some kind of formula that all playwrights employ, or—'

'After much hardship, Sakuntala reached the court of Raja Dushyanta and presented herself before him. But because of a curse cast upon her by an irate sage—'

'Another staple of Sanskrit drama! The shraap by the offended sage!'

'Because of Sage Durvasa's curse, the raja failed to recognise her and flatly denied their relationship as well as their child, Bharata. Then, in that speech we mauled a little while earlier, she lamented his loss of memory and their forgotten love.'

Rama feigned a melodramatic sigh, holding a limp wrist to his forehead. 'I'm lamenting, lamenting.'

'But her love was too great to deny, and the devas saw fit to reunite them against all odds. Sakuntala's ring, lost by her in a river crossing en route to see the raja, was swallowed by a fish. The fish itself was fortuitously caught by a fisherman, who brought it to the same court on the same day, as a humble gift to the raja.'

'How convenient,' he murmured. 'But how poetic as well. Go on, my love, finish the fish-tale.'

'When the fish was cut open, the ring was found within its belly, with the raja's seal upon it. The instant the raja laid eyes on the ring, the curse was circumvented, and his memory returned at once. He realised how terribly he had acted by spurning Sakuntala. He rode into the forest after her with an army and full entourage, and came upon her in the Kanwa-van, raising the product of their love, little Bharata.'

'Father of our nation, if he only knew it.'

'Dushyanta fell to his knees before Sakuntala, begged her forgiveness and entreated her to return to Ayodhya with him. She relented, and they rode back together as king and queen, exactly as she had once dreamed, at the head of a great procession. And Sakuntala got everything she had ever desired, but most of all she had the love of Dushyanta.'

Into the silence that followed, a nightbird called mournfully, as if asking for something it knew it could never have.

Rama said, 'And did they live happily ever after?'

'What do you mean?' she asked. 'You know the story as well as I do.'

He was silent for a moment, then turned and faced her. 'Of course they did. Otherwise the poet who composed that drama wouldn't have got paid a single coin for his work!'

Sita laughed. 'Maybe so. But maybe it was also because it's true. They did live happily ever after.'

'A tragedy with a happy ending.'

'A what?'

'That's what Guru Vashishta once said to us, when explaining prosody and the art of composition. He said that to be truly memorable, a story must be in essence a very sad tale, a great tragedy, but with a happy ending.'

'Why?'

He shrugged. 'Because that is the kind of story that pleases the human heart the most to hear. Great sadness, great suffering, great odds, but in the end, jaya.'

'Triumph.'

'Yes.'

Rama sniffed the air, suddenly distracted. A raat ki rani had just blossomed somewhere, its eloquent fragrance whispering softly on the night wind. He looked at Sita to see if she smelled it. She nodded, inhaling too. They stood, enveloped in the perfume of the night.

The river sang to them.

19

Dasaratha woke to find himself lying on a bed of dried rustling leaves with the taste of blood and iron in his mouth. He groaned and tried to raise himself. He was disoriented and confused, unable to remember anything at first. All he knew was that he must get up at once, *move*, get away from this place, *get to safety*. There were Asuras here, he was surrounded and in great danger. *Move! Flee!*

As he put weight upon his feet, a searing pain in his right leg pierced through the fog that filled his brain. Suddenly he remembered everything with crystal clarity. The flurry of arrows, the sharp agony in his right shoulder as an arrow struck deep enough to hit bone, the bristling staffs of half a dozen arrows embedded in his charioteer's face, neck and chest – poor devil – and the screams from all around as his rally was broken by the unexpected fury of the Asura rebuttal. *Yaksas*, he remembered himself thinking as he clenched a fist, *the pisacas have been reinforced by yaksa longbows*. The yaksas were deadly with their enormous curved bonewood bows, deadlier even than Mithilan bowmasters.

He heard the ghoulish cries of the pisaca and yaksa forces as they came thundering down the gorge, and heard his own voice calling out to *hold fast, hold fast*, even as his lead horse whinnied and succumbed to its own arrow-wounds. The other horses lost their rhythm and stumbled chaotically, tumbling pell-mell on the steep crumbling way. Dasaratha saw that there was no help for it, the chariot would go over regardless of what he did, and leaped just in time. As he flew, the corner of the foot-board of the chariot slashed his leg, gouging flesh from his calf, and threw him over on to his head.

He fell badly, partly upon his wounded shoulder and head, cracking or breaking his collarbone as well. The arrow snapped off, the point digging deeper, probing bone. The voice of Sumantra called out from somewhere close behind, shouting his name, calling out that the maharaja had fallen, rally to the maharaja. A great cloud of dust swirled up the gorge like a dervish out of hell, and through the seething, boiling cloud, Dasaratha saw the Asura forces emerge, roaring and gnashing their teeth. He groaned, not for his own wounds and pain, which he hardly felt at all in the heat of his battle-fury, but for his exhausted forces. The reinforced Asura numbers would surely break the back of this rally as well now. Would this battle never end? How much more must Dasaratha pound these wretched beasts, pound them with all the might of his army, the dwindling forces of Kaikeya and Kosala, the beleaguered and all-but-besieged men and women exhausted and depleted after three days and nights of sleepless, endless battle.

He started to rise, to reach for his sword, his lance, anything. But his foot would not take his weight, his shoulder refusing to respond, the arrowhead driven into some vital muscle juncture that left his arm dangling uselessly. And in that moment, the worst of all such moments he had faced in his time, Dasaratha knew that he would die here in this dust-riddled gully close to a strategic plateau. He knew yet again, a thing so easily known and even more easily forgotten, that the only true rewards of war were ash and dust, nothing more. Not gold, not glory, not peace – that most foolishly sought prize of all, as if wholesale butchery and hatred could ever engender a thing as bloodless and innocent as peace – only blood, and dust and ash. The Asura forces had engaged with the front line of his host, Sumantra bravely and desperately struggling to hold a brutally battered line against the juggernaut. Dasaratha had found and gripped a throwing spear and now he clutched it in his left hand, ready to go down, taking as many as he could with him. The roar of battle filled his ears, the dust and stench of death his nostrils.

Then he heard a thundering of hoofs and wheels as a chariot rode up alongside him, enshrouded in its own cloud of dust, but before he could turn and see who it was, the first of the enemy was upon him, and he was battling for his life. He saw one pisaca go down in a screaming, writhing bundle, then another's throat slashed to bloody ruin by the spear he was swinging like a sword, then he glimpsed one clever bastard leap down from the ridge, upon him.

A blow struck him full in the mouth, the lunging pisaca's hammerhead shattering two teeth and filling his mouth with the rusty, oceanic flavour of Asura ironrock, the dread lohit stone, and he lost all awareness.

He breathed heavily now, half kneeling, half crouched, trying to overcome the swimming of his senses, the flaring behind his eyes. His mouth still dripped blood, his lips swollen fat and feeling like wine bladders filled to bursting. He wiped the blood and spittle and dust from his eyes with the back of his cuff, careful to avoid the swollen mess around his mouth. Then he looked around.

What place was this? How had he got here? It seemed to be a tiny clearing, thickly shrouded by bushes and the thin, sturdy soldier pines that were such an integral part of the Kaikeya landscape. The ground around him was bare except for pine cones, and the pile of leaves on which he had lain.

He remembered nothing of this place, nor of how he had got here. Yet from the stillness of the forest around him, and the faint mewling cry of a khushibird somewhere not far away, it was easy to deduce that it was safely distant from the battle. He tried to stare up at the sky, barely visible through the close-growing trees, new agony shooting through his shoulder and leg, his vision blurring and swimming, and all he could tell was that it was either very early morning or close to end of day.

Then he heard the unmistakable sound of someone coming, the familiar jangling, slapping sound of chain-mail striking leather. The swishing of a blade as it cut through undergrowth. He hopped back, resting his back against a pine for support, seeking a place to hide, a weapon, something to defend himself with, even as the khushibird grew silent, and the visitor appeared, cutting a swathe through the dense bush beside which he had just awoken. Dasaratha exclaimed.

'Rajkumari?' He dropped the dried branch he'd picked up in sheer desperation. 'What are you doing here?'

Kaikeyi strode towards him, her handsome face wreathed in that sly smile that was so talked about amongst the kings of the seven kingdoms. Any of those young kings with whom he sat on the war councils would give an arm and a leg for the hand of Kaikeya's princess. But one rumour had it that she had sworn never to wed, while another, more malicious, suggested that perhaps she preferred to be wedded to a sword than a man. She smiled that smile at him now, resting a hand on her hip. Even through the armour and battle leathers, her buxom rounded body was unmistakably feminine. She swung the sword in the other hand with practised ease, reminding him that he was looking at the most accomplished woman swordmaster in the seven kingdoms, winner of every mêlée worth entering.

'Who do you think it was that carried you from the gorge and brought you here, Dasa?'

He stared at her, uncomprehending. 'You? But you were only to lead the rearguard. The last I saw of you, you were far behind. On the plains.'

She shrugged, the gesture a curious mixture of feminine delicacy and kshatriya strength, the quintessential mix that marked the best and bravest warrior-queens of Arya. In that moment, Dasaratha saw the queen she would become. A legend among legends. He saw the vision even before she spoke the next words.

'Rearguard, vanguard, what's the difference?' she said. 'Fighting's fighting.' She flicked her sword past his right ear, so close he could feel the wind of its passing, then wiped the blade clean on the tree trunk behind him. He glimpsed blood and smelled Asura innards on it, then she withdrew it as smoothly as she had drawn it, and sheathed it in a single action without even glancing down at her scabbard. 'You'll be pleased to know we cast them off the canyon and the plateau. Our flag flies from the high ground now.'

She came closer. Dasaratha could smell the sweaty, womanly odour of her now. It was powerfully exciting. He had fought alongside women before, but never had he been rescued by one. Let alone one who then went on to win the battle that he himself had struggled at for three long days.

'But it was you that broke the back of their host,' she said softly. 'All I did was push the blade in one final time, and twist hard.'

She used her hand to demonstrate, making a jabbing and twisting gesture at his midriff. Her other hand touched his bare chest and remained there. Her palm felt cool and hard on his fever-hot skin. She leaned closer, her palm sliding up to grip his shoulder.

'You did your father and your kingdom proud,' he said. 'And I owe you my life.'

She leaned closer, her palm sliding to encircle his waist. Her armour jangled. 'Not a whole life. But perhaps a part of it, yes.'

'How will I repay you, rajkumari?' He wondered if his breath was as harsh as it sounded, his heartbeat as loud. His head had stopped swimming, but now it was fogging over in a completely different way, not the mist of disorientation but the miasma of arousal.

'By making me a queen,' she said, and pressed her lips against his. The pain in his mashed mouth was tremendous. Blood seeped out of his split lips and into her mouth. Her body drove him back against the tree, hard. The angles of her armour dug and poked his limbs, pinning him immovably. He placed a hand upon her and she gasped.

After that, everything was a blur. Just like after he was struck by the pisaca's hammer in the gorge. Except that this time he knew he would remember every single thing that followed.

Dasaratha came awake with a start and reared up.

'Deva,' he said, gasping for breath.

The chamber was dark and still around him. The only illumination came from diyas strategically placed at intervals behind pillars, so that their soft, flickering glow backlit everything but fell directly on nothing. It made for an unsettling, gloomy obscurity in which one could see people and things but not their finer details. After all, this was a place one came to when one wished to retire from the world, when one had a grievance with things or people; a place where one didn't want to see anyone clearly.

He was in the royal Anger chamber, or kosaghar as it was called in Sanskrit, a remote section of the royal annexe where members of the royal family came when seriously aggrieved about something. Except that he couldn't recall anyone using the chamber for years.

He sat up, trying to make sense of his condition. He appeared to be lying on the floor. His ang-vastra was half draped carelessly around his waist, his dhoti lay flung to one side. His shawl appeared to have fallen several yards away. His travelling chair was set by the doorway of the chamber. Even from this distance, in this gloom, he could tell at once that the doorway was barred shut. There was no way to tell time in here, but he had the impression that several hours had passed. Nothing made sense.

He tried to recall what had happened and found his mind a blank.

'Deva!' he exclaimed again in frustration.

The sound of payals approached, tinkling softly. The sound was hypnotic. Dasaratha sat entranced, his eyes lowered. For some reason, vision was clearer there. As if in a dream, he saw a pair of shapely feminine feet come into view, saw the gleam of the gold anklets with their tiny bells encircling two exquisitely curved calves. They approached him, stopping a yard away. Then the woman knelt before him in a supplicating gesture, offering him something in her outstretched palms, a jal-bartan of some sort. Her jewellery resounded musically in the echoing emptiness.

'Kausalya,' he said with great relief. 'I must have fallen asleep. I had the strangest dream.'

The woman leaned forward slightly. Her face came into the flickering light cast by one of the hidden diyas, limned in the grainy half-glow like a figure in a painting blurred by water.

'A good one, I trust, my lord,' she said.

Dasaratha rubbed his face, wishing he could remember something, anything. 'I don't know if you could call it good. Intense, surely. So real. So immediate. I could even taste the blood on my— Kausalya?' He reached out, a sudden doubt assailing him. His heart clenched in the vice of an invisible fist. 'It is you, isn't it, my love?'

'Your love, yes. Your only true love. Then, now, and always.' She raised the jal-bartan again. 'Take some more tonic, my lord. It has done you a world of good already. I cannot last recall when you were so amorous.'

He frowned. 'Amorous? But—'

'Drink.'

He was thirsty, no doubt. He took the jal-bartan from her palm, raised it to his mouth and took a sip.

His gorge rose in his throat. He turned and spat out the mouthful, spilling the container on the floor in the same motion. 'The devil take me! What is that foul thing?' Even in the dimness, he could see the strange viscous way the fluid puddled and scattered, its dark maroon shade lending it a macabre texture. For a second it almost seemed to move of its own volition, like a living thing in fluid form. He swore and snatched up the ang-vastra, and wiped his mouth, rubbing hard. 'Are you trying to poison me?'

'The precise opposite, my lord. It is an elixir. An elixir

that restores life and energy, giving you the strength and potency of a man ten years younger. Prepared from an old and timeless recipe. Of course, I cannot vouch for the taste being as palatable as one might wish. After all, it is a medication of sorts.'

He stared at her. That voice. It couldn't be – wasn't – and yet—

He lurched to his feet, the ang-vastra slipping to the floor, leaving him completely exposed. But his nakedness was the least of his concerns. He stumbled around a pillar, found a diya and picked it up carelessly, spilling its oil on his hands as he turned back. Ignoring the scalding oil dripping from his fist, he held the little clay lamp up, casting a clear pool of light upon the woman who still knelt, smiling up calmly. How could he ever have thought she was Kausalya? This was—

'Kaikeyi? But how?'

She stood, raising her eyebrows. 'How, my lord? You came to me here, in the kosaghar. Do you not recall?'

He looked around, still feeling as if his dream had been the real experience and this was in fact the dream. But then it came to him: Manthara's unannounced entry into his sickroom, Sumantra's ire at her disturbing Dasaratha at that late hour in his ailing condition, Manthara's insistence that he come to see Kaikeyi at once in the kosaghar, his deciding to go against Kausalya's strenuous objections . . .

Of course he was in the kosaghar. Where else would he have been? In a forest clearing near the border of the Kaikeya kingdom? That was years ago, another place and time. Just an old memory of a younger man.

He looked down at his nakedness, suddenly more aware of it than of the hot mustard oil scalding his hand and wrist. 'How did I fall asleep? My garments?'

She picked up his ang-vastra and dhoti and stood, stepping towards him, the payals tinkling. 'You were tired, exhausted really. I gave you a goblet of my tonic to drink. It soothed you. Soon enough you fell asleep.' She held out the clothes. 'Shall I garb you, my lord? Give me the lamp. It must be very hot.'

He handed her the lamp without protest, still unable to shake the sensation that the dream was still continuing. She even looked slimmer, younger, her face smoother and unwrinkled, her limbs more slender and shapely, much as she had looked that day in the Kaikeya woods years ago. *It's the light in here*, he told himself. *And your illness. That's all it is.*

She took the lamp from him and set it gently on the ground. As she bent over, the pallo of her sari came undone, the top turns of the upper part of the garment falling loose, baring her ample breasts. His breath caught in his chest. He stopped, his dhoti only half wound around his waist, and was shocked to feel his manhood respond with an immediacy that he would not have believed possible any more.

She stood, not yet adjusting her sari. He covered himself with a flick of the dhoti, but he could tell from the way her eyes widened that she had seen the evidence of his sudden arousal.

He covered his embarrassment with a question, brusquely asked. 'How long have I been here?'

She replied sweetly. 'But a few hours. In another hour or two it will be dawn.'

'Dawn?' He was shocked. 'But that's impossible. It was early yet when I came to the kosaghar. How could so much time have passed?' *And why is it that I don't recall a single detail of what transpired here?* The last, unspoken question was the one that troubled him the most.

She unravelled her sari further, preparatory to winding it properly again. She took her time about it, unashamed of her nakedness before her husband. He tried to ignore the dryness in his mouth as he watched her adjusting her garment leisurely. She talked as she redraped herself. 'We talked a great deal when you came. And then, afterwards, we—'

She glanced up at him, one breast still uncovered, the end of the sari in her hand. 'Surely you recall the rest, my lord?'

He tugged the end of the dhoti, tightening it harder than usual against his taut abdomen, answering her with frosty silence.

With a sly smile, she went on. 'After that, you did what any husband does to his wife.'

He froze in the act of draping his ang-vastra, the dressing forgotten, everything else forgotten. Suddenly it all made sense, the strange, pleasurable ache in his groin when he had awoken, the absence of clothing, even the dream . . . But how could it be? He remembered his decrepit state when he had been carried into the kosaghar. He was on the verge of total collapse. No, this couldn't be possible. This was some deception of her devising.

'You're wrong,' he said harshly. 'I was in no condition to lie with you when I came in here. I could barely stand on my own feet.'

She continued smiling with the supreme composure of one who knows she is beyond all reproach. 'When you came in here, you were ill disposed, it's true. But after the elixir, once the tonic took effect, you were as amorous as Indra-deva himself, my lord. And as priapic as well!' She indicated his midriff with a coy gesture, her armlets sounding. 'As you still are.'

He ignored the stubborn hardness in his groin. 'What

madness or magic is this? How could I have recovered simply after having your vile tonic? I know you well, Kaikeyi. What are you not telling me? What are you trying to conceal?'

'Conceal?' She spread her arms, allowing the top of the sari to fall once more, exposing her nakedness to the waist. 'I have nothing to conceal, my lord.'

He slammed a fist against the nearest pillar. 'Impossible! If what you say is true, then why can I not recall any detail of these events you speak of? Why is my mind a complete blank since the time of my entering the kosaghar?'

She shrugged. 'Perhaps your hunger is clouding your mind, my liege?'

'Hunger?' He started to roar at her, then stopped. Now that she mentioned it, he did feel a keen appetite. It had been months since he had felt so great a need for victual nourishment. An overpowering hunger throbbed in his belly.

She smiled as if understanding exactly what he was experiencing. 'The tonic leaves one feeling inordinately hungry and thirsty. If you will sit calmly and partake of some nourishment, it will do you good. After all, now that you have regained your strength, your appetite will have returned with it as well.'

He flung the end of the ang-vastra over one shoulder, angrily. 'Stop speaking of food, woman. I wish to know why it is that I cannot recall any of our dicussion. Did we really speak of anything, or did I just fall asleep after entering this chamber? Answer me truly, Kaikeyi. I am in no mood for games. Tell me, why did you summon me here? Why did Manthara say you had taken your vrath-vows and were fasting unto death? Nobody who takes their vrath-vows partakes of health tonics and cavorts with their husband amorously!'

She turned, looking over her shoulder as she adjusted the final fold of her sari, tucking the end into her waistband. Her hair falling across her face, caught in the dusky light of the concealed diyas, added to an effect that he found powerfully arousing, despite his anger and confusion. *Why are all my lusts and needs so powerfully aroused? Could her stupid tonic truly have revived me this much?*

'I did indeed undertake a vrath-vow, my lord,' she replied. 'A vow to fast unto death if my wish was not granted. And once that wish was granted, quite naturally I ended the vow. You and I partook of the elixir together. And after that we cavorted amorously, as you so mischievously put it, my lord.'

He shook his head, trying to clear it of its foggy obscurity. 'I don't understand yet. What was this wish you had that was worth dying for? Which deva was it addressed to?'

'To the only mortal deva I worship,' she said, coming forward and unexpectedly prostrating herself before him, touching his feet. 'You, my beloved husband.'

He stepped back hurriedly. 'What tomfoolery is this, Kaikeyi? I am asking a serious question. What is this talk you keep referring to? What wish? What did we discuss here tonight?'

She looked up at him from her supplicant position. 'You still do not recall, my lord?'

He all but snarled at her. 'If I did, why would I ask, foolish woman!'

She rose to her feet elegantly. *She has regained her former slimness and grace. How is this possible? What sorcery is at work here? No elixir can accomplish such wondrous results!*

'I am certain it will all come back to you.' She gestured

oddly, fingers performing some arcane action not unlike the mudras of a classical temple dancer performing a dance of divine adoration. 'In fact, I would not be surprised to know that you are starting to remember everything even as we speak now.'

He staggered back, raising a hand to his head. The hand stank of mustard oil; it was the same one with which he had carelessly picked up the burning diya. He felt as if he had received a blow to the head – but on the inside! His shoulder struck a pillar and he leaned against it, bending over. 'Deva!'

'My lord?' Her voice sounded anxious, concerned now. 'Are you well?'

He straightened up with an effort, staring at her. As suddenly as it had struck, the pressure was gone, leaving only a sense of great foreboding and regret. 'What sorcery is this? What have you done to me, Kaikeyi?' He looked down at himself. Suddenly, he realised fully what he had only been dimly aware of since awakening. 'My body? My strength?'

'Is returned to you. Yes, my lord. This, you see, is the magic of the elixir. Wonderful, is it not? To have the health and virility of a man ten years younger once more?' She feigned a coy blush. 'Perhaps even fifteen years younger, to judge by the way you covered me so vigorously.'

'Enough!' He pounded the pillar with his fist. 'This is impossible! My vaids and even Guru Vashishta have tried for years to reverse or slow my canker. No elixir can achieve what they could not achieve, in just a few hours!'

She shrugged. 'If you will take another draught, you might find that much more can be accomplished. I for one certainly intend to partake of another serving. Shall I fetch you goblet as well?'

'Silence,' he said. 'I am—' He was remembering it all now. Not just the drinking of the elixir, in the belief that it was truly some herbal concoction, but also the sudden surge of power and virility that had swept him like a torrent. And the rest as well: his savage lust for Kaikeyi, the way he had taken her in his arms and ravished her—

And then it came to him, with the striking immediacy of a vajra bolt flung by Indra himself, lord of thunder and storm. The talk they had had before the drinking of the elixir, before the lovemaking. The way Kaikeyi had lain on the floor of the kosaghar when he had entered, distraught and dishevelled, face puffed with tears. His bending to console her, ask her what ailed her mind. The long, tortuous talk that followed, at the time seeming so like a nightmare that he had wanted only to forget it for ever. It was to drive the memory of that talk from his consciousness that he had consented to drink the elixir, had in fact quaffed it like water without so much as tasting it. And it was that same talk that flooded his consciousness now, roaring through his mind like the Sarayu in spate during spring thaw, great chunks of glacial ice crashing and shattering down its turbulent course.

'Kaikeyi,' he said, dropping to his knees in disbelief and shock. 'Kaikeyi, I beg you, tell me it is not true. I did not promise you . . . It was but a dream, was it not? We did not have any such discussion. You did not press me to – to—' He sobbed, unable to say it. 'Tell me it isn't true!'

'What isn't true, my lord?' She had draped the sari around herself, covering her nakedness. Now she looked at him as calmly as if he had just made a comment upon the coolness of the night air, or some such irrelevance. 'What are you trying to deny?'

'What we talked of, before I drank the elixir,' he cried.

'The boons you reminded me of. The promises I made to you years ago, the vows I swore to you in exchange for saving my life on those two occasions. You asked me to recollect those vows. When I did so, you told me you wished to collect the boons I had promised to give you unconditionally. You demanded your right to claim anything you pleased, upon my honour. I could not refuse you. I said yes, of course, I made you those vows and you may collect upon them if you please. Whatever you wished, I would grant to you unconditionally. And then you said—' He lowered his head, unable to stop the tears, the tearing anguish that threatened to rip out his heart and slash it to shreds. 'You said—'

She looked at him with an expression of utter serenity, like a palace cat that had partaken its fill of milk and cream and fish. 'I said that I wished for Rama to go into exile for twice times seven years. And for my second boon, I wished to have my son Bharat crowned prince-heir on the morrow.' She whispered the next words, though they seemed to echo resoundingly in the vast, empty pillared chamber. 'And you said you could not refuse me anything I desired. And so the pact was struck.'

20

'Rani? Pardon my disturbing your rest.'

Kausalya came awake with the swiftness of one accustomed to caring for the sick and ailing, used to waking at all hours to tend to her husband's medical needs these past several nights. The lamps in the chamber had burned down. The serving girls had probably neglected to refill them, believing that she was asleep for the night. But she had only been dozing here upon this diwan, unable to sleep properly, restless in the knowledge that Dasaratha was taking an inordinately long time in the kosaghar.

She sat up and looked around. The old daiimaa who had woken her had a kindly face. She was one of several who had cared lovingly for Rama and his brothers during their tender formative years. Kausalya nodded in acknowledgement. 'Susama-daiimaa. What is it? Has the maharaja sent for me?'

'No, my lady. Forgive me for interrupting your nidra. But the matter seemed to warrant some attention. I would have come earlier, but you were engaged in conversation with the maharaja, and then, after he left, you and the pradhan-mantri were in discussion until very late. So I thought it best to return in the morning. Only,' she paused, her voice trembling to match the shiver in her wrinkled arm, 'it would not wait. So we decided to send for you at once.'

'We?' Kausalya sat up and looked around. There was nobody else in the chamber.

'Vandana-daiimaa and Karuna-daiimaa are in the outer chamber, with her. If you will but accompany me, I will take you to them. We have a strange thing to show you, my rani. I trust it will not disturb your dreams tonight, for it will surely trouble us for many nights to come.'

Kausalya frowned. 'What are you talking about, Susama? What thing?'

The daiimaa looked at her strangely. 'It is best if I show you. Please, if you will come this way . . .'

Kausalya rose and followed her. She paused as she left the chamber, shocked to see the time in the large water-clock in the anteroom. Whatever was keeping Dasaratha so long? Had he fallen asleep in the kosaghar? Yes, perhaps he had. She felt a touch of unease, like the tip of a cold blade pricking the back of her neck. Then she dismissed it as idle anxiety. He must have grown weary after cajoling and coaxing Kaikeyi out of her latest tantrum, and then had no energy to make the long journey through the palace complex back to his chambers, so he had fallen asleep right there in the kosaghar, stretched out upon a mat on the floor, for the kosaghar had no furnishings. She hoped Kaikeyi had kept him warm.

The palace corridor was empty and still, in eerie contrast to the hustle and bustle of just a few hours past. Only the ever-vigilant palace guards stood at three-yard intervals, alert and silent as ever. The serving maids were all asleep, but several had remained within calling reach, in case she or the maharaja required anything during the night. She let them sleep. They would need to be rested. Tomorrow would be a long, busy day, with the coronation, and the rest of the traditional post-consummation marriage rituals. She glanced out at the dark starlit sky and wondered if Rama and Sita were still awake, looking out at that same sky, or blissfully asleep. She hoped it was the latter; they would need their rest too. Thinking of them gave her a warm, comfortable feeling, like sinking into a rock-heated bed on a snow-bound winter's night, with a blizzard raging outside. She vowed to make some time to spend alone with Sita. She had so much she wished to share with her new bahu. So much to say, and so much to know. The culmination of generations of female wisdom to be handed over to the woman who would some day bear Kausalya's grandchildren. She smiled at the thought, at the thought of herself as a grandmother. Yes. It would be nice. To have little Ramas and Sitas running around this palace, filling the air with their milky cries and little pattering footfalls.

The daiimaa led her into a receiving chamber, one of several that were intended for visitors to wait in until the maharaja was ready to see them. At one time there had been visitors sitting here all night, and Dasaratha would even receive some of them at ridiculous hours and spend his rest-time hearing matters of state or regional interest. But that was a different Dasaratha, at a very different time. A younger, more idealistic Dasaratha, with enough energy to put into running the kingdom the way he believed it must be run: not as a fiefdom inherited from his illustrious forebears, but as a great tradition entrusted to him for safekeeping and continuance.

Two other daiimaas stood by a diwan, below a life-size portrait of Aja, father of Dasaratha, and Kausalya's own father-in-law, although she had never known him too well. Aja had decided to take vanaprasthashrama, forest retirement, and had unexpectedly handed over the

reins of kingship to a very young Dasaratha almost immediately after his marriage to Kausalya. All she recalled of
her father- and mother-in-law was that last glimpse of
them, clad in spiritual white symbolising their departure
from worldly affairs, as they were carried by the chariot
out of the city. They had passed away peacefully in the
forest a short while later, not even living long enough to
see their grandsons. Whenever Kausalya saw his portrait,
it always evoked a silent prayer from her that she at least
would be here to see and hold *her* grandchildren in her
arms. She took it as a propitious sign.

There was a woman seated beneath the portrait.
Kausalya blinked in surprise as she took in the woman's
dishevelled state, her torn and muddy sari, the bruises on
her arms, a recently bandaged cut on her forehead. She
was leaning back against a stack of bolsters the daiimaas
had propped up to support her. She seemed to be unconscious. Kausalya could smell dung on her, stale, dried and
encrusted elephant dung. The woman's mouth lay partly
open, and she snored lightly, like a person who had
consumed far too much soma.

'This woman,' Kausalya said. 'I know her. Who is she?'

The three daiimaas exchanged a look. Kausalya caught
the tenseness in their manner and the fearfulness in their
eyes. *They're scared witless.* Susama-daiimaa spoke for
them.

'She is a serving girl, my rani. She works in the Second
Queen's palace. But mostly she serves . . .' The daiimaa
looked around at her companions for support.

'Whom does she serve, Susama? Speak freely, you need
not have any anxiety when addressing me.'

The old woman nodded gratefully. 'She serves
Manthara-daiimaa.'

Kausalya frowned. 'Manthara. Then . . .' She stopped,

unable to complete the thought aloud. *Then she might be the one Sumitra spoke of, the serving girl she saw in the hidden chamber where Sumitra too was kept prisoner that day. Then again,* she thought, *Manthara might have a dozen serving girls running errands. I must learn more before I say something that I cannot withdraw from gracefully.* The memory of the humiliating scene at the welcoming ceremony was still fresh in her mind. Poor Sumitra had retired to her chambers and hadn't been seen since. *Should I have Sumitra roused? No, not just yet. Let me find out a few more things first.*

Aloud she said, 'Why is she in this state?'

Susama replied haltingly, 'Rani, we were watching the royal procession approach the palace when we happened to see her, running out of the palace gates like a madwoman.'

One of the other daiimaas piped up in a thick southern accent. 'She all but came beneath the bigfoot, she did. Running wild.'

Susama went on, 'She fell in the mud and must have got the cut on her forehead when she fell. We were called by the palace guards to go fetch her and take her into the palace. So we did, all three of us, and it was all we could manage to drag her away from the maharaja's elephant.'

'No,' said the third daiimaa, silent until now. 'It was Prince Rama's elephant she was after, I tell you again. Prince Rama.'

Susama nodded. 'Or perhaps it was the rajkumars', I don't know for sure. I was too shocked at the time. You see, milady, at the time we went out into the avenue to fetch her, we all three of us,' indicating her companions, 'never thought she was a serving girl at all. We thought for certain she was—'

'Rani Kaikeyi, Second Queen of Ayodhya,' Kausalya said quietly.

The southern-accented daiimaa reared back in surprise. All three of them stared up at the First Queen with identical expressions of shock. Susama-daiimaa touched her hand at once to the amulet hanging around the withered folds of her neck.

'Isn't that who you thought she was at first?' Kausalya asked gently. 'Rani Kaikeyi running wild in the streets, probably distraught over some perceived slight, or simply drunk and out of her senses? It wouldn't be the first time, after all, would it?'

'Indeed, no, my queen,' replied Susama, her breath coming faster and heavier now. The daiimaa still had her hand on the amulet, clutching it tightly. 'We have often tended to her at such times. Rani Kaikeyi is . . . how shall we say it . . .'

'High-strung,' said one of the others.

'Aye,' Susama agreed. 'And the way she was calling out, the things she was saying, her very voice too . . . it was all exactly Rani Kaikeyi to the core. So we naturally took her to her own palace, calling to her serving girls, all of whom had abandoned their posts to see the parade.'

'They will do that at such historic times,' the south-accented one said apologetically. 'It's not to be condoned, of course, but it's not worth punishing harshly either, my rani.'

Susama continued. 'But after we brought her into the palace and sat her down on a diwan, only then did we see her . . .' glancing at the others with that same fearful look, 'change somehow. As if some invisible hand were re-drawing her features to make them less like Kaikeyi and more like . . .' gesturing at the woman asleep on the diwan, 'like the serving maid she truly is. It happened very quickly, in a trice, but we all saw it, and we all knew that something sorcerous had occurred. The only thing was, we didn't know what exactly had happened.'

'Aye,' said one of the others, muttering a two-line sloka from the Devi's Kavach, a common prayer of protection recited daily by women, literally 'Goddess's Shield'. 'Devil's work it was, though,' she added.

'What did you do next?' Kausalya asked. She motioned to the daiimaas to take a seat, taking one herself as she did so. They elected to squat on the floor on their haunches, as daiimaas were wont to do. 'After you saw Rani Kaikeyi change into this . . . serving maid? You couldn't have left her in the Second Queen's palace then, could you?'

'No, we couldn't, my lady,' Susama said, giving Kausalya a grateful look for being so understanding. 'For she clearly was not the Second Queen, not any more at least. So we took her to the witch's chambers—' She stopped, a hand covering her mouth reflexively. 'I mean, Manthara-daiimaa's chambers.'

'That's all right,' Kausalya said, gesturing to the woman to go on. *I think she's a witch as well.*

'But there we had another setback.' The old woman's eyes flashed with something akin to anger. After all, she might be a daiimaa by profession, but by birth she was still a kshatriya, even if only a kshatriya serving other kshatriyas. A trace of her birth-pride still burned in her. 'The hunchbacked daiimaa refused to recognise this woman as her maid; she said that she had never seen her before in her life, and that we were feeble-minded to think that she was her servant.' She shook her head, remembering. 'She said many other words besides.'

'Foul words all, for no songbirds sing in a dragon's cave,' said one of the others.

'So we took the poor wretch to our own chambers, and tried to put her to bed. But about an hour or two ago she woke with a scream that near killed us with fright, and when we fetched a lamp to her bedside, she began shuddering and shaking like a thing possessed.'

Susama paused, glancing fearfully at the woman lying unconscious on the diwan. 'After we calmed her down, she began speaking. And once started, she could not seem to stop. Like a waterfall, she gushed words. She was not speaking to us so much as speaking things that weighed heavily upon her young heart, poor soul. She spoke of terrible things, my rani.' The daiimaa looked up hesitantly at Kausalya. 'Horrible things that make us ashamed even to repeat them.'

'Tell me,' Kausalya said reassuringly. 'Tell me everything. I must know.'

Susama nodded and glanced at the other daiimaas as if to say, *See? I told you she would listen.* After a moment to clear her throat, she went on. 'From the torrent that came out of her mouth, we understood some but not all she said. One thing that recurred several times was how she served Manthara, Manthara, Manthara.'

'Every third word she said was the witch's name,' said the southern daiimaa, looking as if she would rather spit than speak the hunchback's name herself.

'She spoke of foul things done in the dark of night. Of visits to tantriks. Of deals struck over silver coin. Of brahmin orphans stolen from ashrams. Of rites performed in praise of the Dark Lord.' She looked up hesitantly at the First Queen again. 'Balidaans!'

Sacrificial offerings. Kausalya's blood ran cold. So, the things Sumitra had claimed to have seen, the secret pooja room with the yagna chaukat still filled with ash and half-burned human bones, that was all true. The old crone was offering human child sacrifices to the Lord of Lanka right here under this very roof! *Sri have mercy on our souls.*

'And at the very end, when she was winding down, like a child at the end of a long night of fevers and chills, she spoke of the evening of the procession, this past evening itself. Of how she had been trapped still in the hidden chamber, half starved and out of her mind with delirium and sickness for the past several days – she had lost count how many days – when suddenly she found herself free and at large. Only this time she was upon the street, in our clutches, being dragged towards the palace. And then she understood what had happened, for she knew enough of the witch's workings to follow her evil schemes.'

Susama paused to cough twice, hoarsely, clearing her throat. One of the other daiimaas offered her a bud of clove, pointing to her throat, but Susama shook her head in refusal. She went on after clearing her throat once more.

'She believed that Manthara had somehow projected the Second Queen's soul into this body,' pointing at the serving girl asleep on the diwan, 'and had taken Rani Kaikeyi's own body and used it for some nefarious deed. She didn't know what that might be, but she did know that during the time she was running about the street shouting madly, she *was* Rani Kaikeyi. Even below the consciousness of the rani's aatma she was still herself, present in that body. The rani's presence in her physical form caused her to look almost like Kaikeyi-maa, transforming her very flesh and features, but after a while she could not sustain that bhes-bhav and so she reverted to her natural form . . . *this* form.'

Kausalya nodded to show she understood. 'During that

time, when Rani Kaikeyi's soul inhabited her body, where was Rani Kaikeyi's own body? Did she know that?'

The daiimaa shook her head. She glanced at the other old wet nurses. Both of them looked blank as well. 'No, my rani. She did not say.'

'And this nefarious deed for which Manthara needed Kaikeyi's body, did she give any hint what it might have been? After all, when Kaikeyi's aatma was transplanted into her body, she might have been able to learn that from Rani Kaikeyi perhaps?'

'All she said, my queen, and I quote her as well as I can recall, is this: "Kaikeyi goes to do the Dark Lord's work now."'

Kausalya stared at the daiimaa.

21

Dasaratha took a step towards Kaikeyi. His hands were shaking with rage. His entire body felt as if it had been set on fire, and the fire threatened to engulf and consume him completely.

'You witch!' he roared. 'You drugged and duped me somehow, using what vile sorcery I know not. That is why I was not aware of anything we said or did. You tricked me like an Asura in human guise. Sumitra and Kausalya were right. I should have cast you into the royal dungeons rather than hear a word you spoke!'

She stood her ground calmly. Her expression hadn't changed a whit. When she spoke, her voice was just as composed as before. 'Is that how you will honour your vows, raje? Is this how you fulfil your promises to one who saved your life not once but twice, and risked her own life both times?'

He faltered. 'What promises, what vows? I made no vows to you, you Asura in mortal guise! I made those oaths to a mortal woman. You are no more mortal than the King of Lanka himself!'

Her eyes gleamed darkly. 'Did you not see me touch the guru's feet earlier tonight? Did he cast me off with a brahman mantra and declare me anything but that which

I am? Do you doubt the evidence of your preceptor's divine intuition and vidya, raje?'

He crushed his own hand into a fist. The bones of his knuckles crackled. 'How do I know that the woman I saw is the same one that stands before me? I have seen much sorcery at work these past few weeks. I trust no one and nothing any more.'

She was silent for a long moment. Finally, she seemed to arrive at some inner conclusion. Her silence and calm unsettled him more than any amount of shouting or hysterics would have. A seed of doubt planted within his heart began to grow steadily, sprouting roots. *What if she is Kaikeyi? I did promise her two boons once. What if she is telling the truth?*

'Very well,' she said at last. 'I respect your anxiety. These are warlike times again, and I understand the pressures and strains of kingship during a time of war better than any other woman. Did I not witness the manner in which the Last Asura War crushed my own father's spirit and resolve? And when the other Arya nations threw up their hands in despair and pleaded their inability to send their forces to our aid, did I not see with what terrible self-affliction my father fought tooth and nail to keep the Asura wolves from our door? Yes, I understand warlike times. Your anxiety is justified, Ayodhya-naresh. Go on, then, set your mind at rest. Call Guru Vashishta this very instant and prove to yourself for the second time tonight that I am indeed Kaikeyi, your queen, wife and long-time lover. Go on then, for our business here is by no means done, and already the moonless night creeps steadily towards the new dawn.'

Dasaratha stared at her, his anger fading in sharp, hot pulses. Would an Asura speak thus? He recalled the twice-lifer that had attacked him in his own sabha hall. Ravana,

come in the garb of Vajra lieutenant Bheriya. That one
had been quick to take advantage of his isolation and
weakness, wasting no time on mere talk and rhetoric.
Again the doubt assailed him. What if this really *was*
Kaikeyi?

She read his indecision upon his face. 'What stays your
hand, raje? Why do you not unbar the door and call for
your attendants and guards? Why do you not send for
the guru at once?'

She took a step towards him, her payals tinkling melodiously, incongruously. 'Could it be that you harbour a
doubt yet? A suspicion that I might actually be who I
appear to be in truth?'

By way of answer, he looked down at his clenched
fists, cursing the star beneath which he had been born.

She laughed. An unaffected, open-mouthed, heedless
laugh. Not unlike the Kaikeyi he had met and loved once.
In another time, another place. 'What a fine dilemma we
are faced with then! And how is it to be solved, pray
tell?'

'The boons,' he said too loudly, then lowered his voice
before going on, forcing a rein upon his emotions. 'The
boons I granted you. When and how did the event occur?
What was the day, where was the place? What were the
circumstances?'

She stopped laughing, but a trace of a smile lingered
still. She was not afraid, he saw. An Asura would surely
be afraid if it was in danger of being exposed. Even
Ravana himself, were the dark lord returned yet again in
human garb, would not waste time laughing and talking
when he could eliminate his greatest foe in a few quick
moments. For that matter, Ravana would have killed him
as he slept, naked and defenceless. The doubt grew as
she replied confidently and easily.

'It was at the same shrine of Vishnu, deep in the Kaikeya-van woods where I had sheltered and nursed you back to health the first time you were struck down in battle. We had fought back the Asura forces and retaken the plateau of Kanwa after days of bitter fighting. Your first wounds had somewhat healed but you were too quick to return to battle. And then, on the sixth day, when we began to believe that the tide had turned at last, the Lord of Lanka himself appeared at the head of a great host. And the battle began anew. This time, to the death. For we knew that either we must break their resolve or we ourselves would break upon that resolve.'

And a terrible battle it had been, Dasaratha remembered. Filled with more bloodshed and brutality than any he had ever fought before. He remembered himself doing things he would never have dreamed of doing, violating every rule of war in the Arya code. He had set aside his great ancestor Manu Lawmaker's own rules of morality during warfare, had thrown away all considerations except the burning need for victory. And he had set about orchestrating a massacre like nothing else witnessed before. At the end, he had seen the tide truly turn, a victory within his grasp, and despite the awful price he had paid – by violating his own moral principles as well as by sacrificing so many brave kshatriya men and women – at that crucial point where every commander sees a battle turn decisively, Ravana had launched a personal attack.

Dasaratha, he who had been named by his parents for his future prowess in warfare, literally 'he who rides ten chariots at once', had been caught in a pincer movement by the demonlord and his two sons, Meghnath and Akshay Kumar, and cut off from the rest of his army by a force of Asuras that had crept up from behind specially for this mission. Within moments, their purpose had been crystal clear. Eliminate the leader of the mortals and the mortal armies would lose heart and falter. And their plan had been faultless. That day, for the second time in the same battle and perhaps only the third or fourth time in his entire military career, Dasaratha knew he faced certain death. But he fought on relentlessly, a force of nature as unconquerable as the sun whose effulgent disc he bore upon the armour of his House Suryavansha shield.

But Ravana had been smarter and more vicious than anyone could have expected. The demonlord violated a basic rule of combat when he cut down Dasaratha's horses beneath him, then smashed the King of Ayodhya's chariot to smithereens with mighty blows from the maces and clubs in his twenty arms. Dasaratha still recalled the screams of agony of his magnificent Kambhoja stallions as they were butchered before his startled eyes. He had leaped from his shattered chariot to engage in hand-to-hand combat with the lord of demons then, challenging him as one commander to another. And that was when the rakshasa king had committed yet another violation of the rules of conduct: he had refused Dasaratha's challenge and ordered his Asura forces to converge en masse on the mortal.

Dasaratha might still have fought his way out of that impossible situation. The devas knew he had done so before, partly by sheer bravado, partly by his prodigious skill at facing large numbers single-handed. But Ravana's ingenuity still had more arrows of brilliance in its quiver. The Lord of Lanka also joined the fray, attacking Dasaratha from one side while his forces covered the other three sides. Using a constant series of plunging and withdrawing attacks, in the manner of hyenas or wild dogs attacking a mighty lion by nipping it constantly in the nether parts, the Asuras and their commander had inflicted many wounds upon Dasaratha, until he knew that soon he would fall from sheer blood loss if not from a fatal blow. Once he fell, his armies would withdraw, shaken by the loss of the leader whose sheer courage and iron control had held them together thus long. And Kaikeya would fall as well, lost for ever.

And at that crucial moment, again she had appeared, like an apsara out of Indra's court, bent on being his salvation and his avenging angel both at once. He saw a flurry in the Asura ranks, and then the creatures began flying left and right, cut to bits by a chariot that rolled over them like the celestial juggernaut, Jagganath himself, riding out of Swarga-lok to avenge the destruction of that heavenly realm by the Lord of Lanka. And then Sumantra had appeared in his chariot as well, leading the maharaja's first Vajra, commanded by Captain Bejoo, attacking in their devastating four-way action, using a combination of elephant brute strength, chariot speed and power, lethally accurate shortbow archers, and armoured cavalry. They had cut a trail wide enough to extract Dasaratha. But it was Kaikeyi herself who reached him first and pulled him aboard her chariot. And it was Kaikeyi who faced the brunt of the Lord of Lanka's wrath when he saw his prize wrested from under his very nose – or noses. Dasaratha recalled standing shoulder-to-shoulder alongside Kaikeyi as they fought back the demonlord's crushing blows from the helm of her chariot, Kaikeyi driving her horses forward at the same time. And somehow, miraculously, with the aid of Sumantra's death-defying loyalty, and Captain Bejoo's ferociously disciplined Vajra, Dasaratha had left the field for the second time in that conflict.

And once again he had been unconscious when he was driven away, succumbing to his multitude of wounds.

This time when he had awoken, in the same serene

spot in the Kaikeya-van, the battle as well as the campaign was over. Reinforcements had arrived from Gandahar and Banglar in the nick of time. Ravana's forces had pulled back, unable to face such large numbers of fresh kshatriyas. The battle was credited solely to Dasaratha, for Kaikeyi had downplayed her role – with Sumantra and Bejoo's willing support. And so it was that, having won the last battle of the Last Asura War, he had lost his heart to the princess of Kaikeya. And there, in a shrine to Lord Vishnu and Devi Lakshmi in those very woods where she had taken him to safety the first time, Kaikeyi and he had sworn their vows of marriage alone together. And he had sworn two further vows: two boons that he would grant her in exchange for saving his life. No matter what they might be, or what their price.

'And I said I did not wish anything from you then apart from my desire to become your queen,' she said now, watching him with much the same expression that had been on her face that memorable day in the forest. 'But you insisted that some day, whenever I pleased, I could ask you to honour your vows, and you would grant me those two boons without question or debate.'

He looked at her, weighing her words, his life, the years between then and now, the things he had done and said and the things he had meant to do and had never done; the many, many things he had left undone.

'Did you not mean those vows then?' she asked.

And what could he say? He brushed away the tears rolling down his face, hot salt tracks searing his cheeks. 'You know I did, Kaikeyi! And honour them I must, as the devas are my witness. But these things you have asked of me, tell me, what good are they to you? How will it serve you to send my Rama into the forest for fourteen years of exile?'

She shook her head. 'Do you think I wish that? Do you think I would ask these things if there were some other way to accomplish this? All I wished was to be a queen, raje. Not the first, second or any other number. Just a queen. Your queen. You did not grant me that wish, because you did not admit to me then that you were already betrothed to another, to Kausalya of Banglar. Had I known that, I might not have given you my heart so readily. Nor bared my body to your needs.'

She looked away, her eyes brimming with tears now. And he wondered, *Can Asuras cry?* 'But I bore that lash all these many years. In the certain knowledge that when the time came, you would make my son king.'

'But Rama was born first,' he cried. 'He is the eldest. He must be the one to succeed me!'

'Have younger sons not ascended the throne of Ayodhya before?' she demanded fiercely. 'Have they not done so in other kingdoms where the oldest were either too feeble or too weak in the arts of war, or simply uninclined to kingship? There are many precedents for it; even the Lawbook of great Manu allows for exceptions. And my Bharat is only younger than Rama by a few days. But above all, heed this, Dasaratha: *There would have been no Rama had I demanded my first boon then and asked that you set aside Kausalya for ever and share only my bed.*'

'Would that you had done so,' he said, burying his face in his hands. 'Would that you had done so. Then at least I would not have lived to see this day.'

She was silent then, waiting for him to go on. When he did not speak again, she said softly, 'Whether you remember or not, you agreed tonight to grant me these boons. And if you intend to honour them, I demand that you now do so at once.' She raised a hand and pointed at the door. 'Summon Rama and tell him that he is exiled. And on the morrow, tell the council of ministers and the preceptor that my son Bharat is to be crowned liege-heir, to rule in your stead when you are gone.'

'What? Now, at this hour?'

She smiled sadly. 'Do you think the burden will grow easier if you wait a day? Or a month? It is decided, these things have been said, now they must be done.'

He joined his hands then, pleading beyond all hope. 'But he has only been wed a day. At least give him time to savour his matrimony. Do not be so cruel, Kaikeyi. Have some care for a boy who was once like your own son.'

She said sadly, 'He is still and ever will be my son. It was you who has cast him out of his marriage bed, his inheritance and his kingdom. You should have accepted a long time ago that what Manu said was always true: a man cannot serve two mistresses, nor two queens wear the same crown. You brought this upon yourself, Dasaratha. You were named for your ability to fight in ten directions at once, yet it was in ten women's beds that you lost your name and honour. This is all your doing, the day you set Kausalya above me and failed your vows to me in that forest shrine. Did you think none saw us or bore witness? The devas saw. Devi herself was my witness. And today they have asked you for their dakshina. One last time, Dasaratha, will you honour your vows or will you dishonour your race for ever?'

He fell to his knees, broken then, and cried out in a lost, desolate voice, 'I cannot say it. You tell him then. Tell him what has been decided and do what you must do. But do not ask me to say the words. That is beyond me.'

She looked at him for a moment, her eyes dark and

merciless. 'Have no fear, husband. It has long been the lot of women to do what their husbands fear to do. This is the true reason why men delude themselves that they are braver than women, because the truth would crush their fragile egos. Fear not. I will tell Rama and the council and the guru as well, to remove any last doubts you may have about my identity or my resolve. I will do all that must be done this dark night.'

And she strode to the doors and unbarred them.

22

'Hurry, maha-dev,' Kausalya gasped as she strode quickly through the corridors. Alert guards, surprised at seeing such activity at this late hour – or early hour, for it was close to dawn – glanced sharply in their direction as they approached, then snapped their eyes back to the fore as they went past. The serving girls had already begun rousing, their work begun well before the royal family even woke, and several curious heads gaped astonished as they saw the First Queen rushing past, followed by the guru.

'This is a most serious claim, rani,' Vashishta said as they strode along. 'You are certain that it is not some misconception on the part of these old women?'

'I told you, maha-dev, I saw Kaikeyi with my own eyes, running alongside our elephant. You were already dismounted and in the palace, overseeing the preparations for the welcome ceremony, otherwise you would have seen her yourself.'

'Would that I had,' he said gruffly. 'It would have settled much. For when Rani Kaikeyi stepped forward to take my blessing at the rite, I all but wished that she was indeed an Asura in disguise.'

Kausalya glanced hopefully at the guru's flowing mane of white hair and beard. 'But she was not?'

'Entirely mortal, I assure you, good Kausalya. The day an Asura is able to approach and touch me without my knowing it is the day I will fling my staff upon a funeral pyre and myself after it.'

She didn't know how to respond to that. As they rounded the corner, approaching a junction between two wings, the delicate small form of Rani Sumitra raced out to join them.

'Kausalya,' Sumitra said breathlessly. 'Is it true? You have caught the real Kaikeyi, disguised as a serving girl?'

'Not exactly,' Kausalya said, clasping Sumitra's hand to help the smaller woman keep pace. 'It's complicated. But I think I have got hold of the same serving girl you spoke of. If you recognise her as the one you saw in the secret chamber, then we have a direct link to Manthara's witchery. And a witness to all those unholy doings.'

'But no direct connection with the Second Queen,' Guru Vashishta said admonishingly. 'Despite the hunchback being Rani Kaikeyi's personal attendant, we have no proof that they were in connivance on this dark plot. If anything, I severely doubt that Rani Kaikeyi herself played any active part in the worship of the Dark Lord, human sacrifices, and all such doings. I believe we will find only that Manthara was up to this dire mischief to serve her own ends. And if so, then it is something I have suspected for a long time, for I have sensed the presence of evil forces close to the royal family long before these recent events. Only I did not know the identity of the person or persons involved.'

'Now you have her,' Kausalya said, 'caught red-handed.'

The guru grunted in response. Kausalya and Sumitra exchanged a worried glance. Surely this would be all the evidence they needed to point the finger at Manthara? Surely this time too the daiimaa could not go scot-free of her crimes? But even if Manthara was found to be guilty of her evil-doing, what good was it if Kaikeyi were not convicted as well? Too much was happening too soon. Kausalya felt as if events were hurtling, just as they themselves were rushing, at breakneck speed towards some unforeseen conclusion that none of them could have imagined or dreamed. What that would be was anybody's guess. She thanked the Devi that at least Rama was safe in bed and far removed from this new turn of events. Little harm could come to him in the arms of his lovely bride at least. She glanced at Sumitra and sensed that much the same thought was crossing the Third Queen's mind just then. She squeezed Sumitra's hand again, glad for her presence, and together they turned the last corner towards the wing where she had left the daiimaas and the serving girl.

The daiimaas were sitting on the ground, looking as anxious as before. They rose hurriedly to their feet when they saw the two queens and the guru approaching. They bowed at once, prostrating themselves before the preceptor, who briefly acknowledged them, then turned toward the object of their gathering.

Without preamble, Guru Vashishta went to the diwan where the serving girl still lay unconscious. He sat beside the woman and leaned forward. To Kausalya's surprise, instead of speaking to her or attempting to rouse her, the guru simply sniffed, around her face, then her nostrils, then her ears. Kausalya was struck by the notion that the girl was so redolent of the stench of dung – the odour was palpable even from here, two whole yards away – that it was unlikely the guru could smell anything besides that pungent reek. But after a moment of close sniffing, the guru turned his head and beckoned to Kausalya. She went to him, her heart pounding.

'This woman has been possessed by a spirit,' he said quietly. 'This much at least is true. The stench of occupation is unmistakable.'

'So then it's true what the daiimaas said,' Kausalya said excitedly, glancing back at Sumitra, who stood right beside her. 'Kaikeyi's spirit was transferred into this body while another Asura spirit took over Kaikeyi's own body.'

The guru raised an eyebrow. 'And yet the woman who paid her respects to me at the griha pravesh welcoming ceremony was none other than Rani Kaikeyi herself. Which is why I now deduce that Rani Kaikeyi was indeed in her own body, but was under great duress on some account. And so, for a brief period, Rani Kaikeyi's soul fled her physical form, and took up occupation of this form, using it to try to warn those who were to be harmed by the other force.'

Kausalya stared at the guru. This was not the answer she had expected to hear. 'You mean that their souls exchanged bodies, don't you, maha-dev?'

The guru shook his head, replying patiently, 'Nay, Rani-maa Kausalya. As I said, Kaikeyi was indeed Kaikeyi. But she was operating under the influence of some other entity, whether mortal or Asura I am not certain yet. That intense pressure of outside control drove Kaikeyi's aatma out of her body for a brief while, during which time she came upon this woman's body and occupied it, hoping that in this way she would be able to undo the goal that the outside influence was working to achieve.'

Kausalya pondered this for a moment then replied slowly, 'So if we assume the outside influence was Manthara . . .'

'Very good, rani. That is what I am favouring as well at present. Go on.'

'Then Kaikeyi was herself but under mental pressure from Manthara. And that severe pressure—' Suddenly it all made sense to Kausalya in a weird, twisted way. 'Do you see it, Sumitra?'

'Not really,' the Third Queen replied timidly. 'But am I understanding you correctly when you say that this woman was Kaikeyi for a while, but the real Kaikeyi was also herself?'

'That's it exactly!' Kausalya said.

'Under duress,' the guru added quietly, 'a mortal mind is unable to retain its hold upon the physical form. It must have taken a great pressure indeed to drive Kaikeyi's aatma from her body, even if for a short spell of time. During that period the real Kaikeyi's body would certainly have lain asleep, for no outside force can operate even an occupied body without its own aatma present.'

Kausalya felt a tug on her sari. She turned to see Susama-daiimaa staring wide-eyed at her.

'Rani,' the old woman said. 'She's awake now.'

Kausalya frowned. 'Rani Kaikeyi?'

The daiimaa pointed over Kausalya's shoulder. 'This one. Whoever she may be. My lady.'

Kausalya turned and saw what the daiimaa had been pointing to. The serving girl, lying with her head back on the bolsters, was staring at them with wide-open eyes.

They were both roused by the knocking on the door. Sita sat up first, looking around. She was briefly disoriented by the strange surroundings. Then she remembered everything at once: the wedding, Ayodhya, Rama. He sat up beside her, then stepped out of bed in a swift, smooth motion that she had to see to believe possible. Before she had rubbed the sleep from her eyes, a sword was in his hands.

She raised a hand. 'It must be Nakhudi. A security sweep. Or something.'

His face was dark in the blackness of the chamber. The lamps had sputtered out hours ago, before they had fallen asleep in each other's arms, exhausted and sweaty from passion play. 'I doubt even your bodyguard would interrupt our suhaag raat to check on our well-being.'

He moved towards the door. She had a sudden vision of him and Nakhudi facing off with one another on her balcony back at Mithila. She got out of bed quickly, joining him at the door just as he was about to pull back the bolt. He glanced at her briefly, then opened the door.

She saw Nakhudi's face looking down at her anxiously. 'My prince, my queen,' the Jat bodyguard said in an uncharacteristically worried tone. 'Rajkumar Rama has been summoned to the kosaghar on urgent business. He must come at once.'

The kosaghar? Did they still have that here in Ayodhya? Sita had thought that archaic custom had been discontinued in all civilised cities. But then again, not all cities were as civilised as Mithila. 'Now?' she said. 'Can't it wait till morning, Nakhudi?'

The rani-rakshak shook her head. 'Apparently not. The queen's words were quite clear to the two guards who brought the order.' She gestured over her shoulder. 'It took much persuading to get me to wake you.' She touched the hilt of one of her curved swords. 'I almost had to tell them to get lost.'

Rama and Sita exchanged a glance. 'It must be to do with Father,' he said quietly. 'I must go at once.'

'I will go with you.'

Nakhudi cleared her throat. 'Forgive me, my queen. But Rani Kaikeyi's order was quite explicit. Prince Rama, and Prince Rama only, will accompany the guards back to the kosaghar.'

'Rani Kaikeyi?' Sita watched, puzzled, as Rama went back into the room to lay down his sword and re-tie his langot in two quick, efficient tugs. He was back at her side before she had finished speaking. 'Not Rani Kausalya? Are you sure?'

'Certain, my lady,' Nakhudi said, standing aside to give Rama room to pass, but possessively crowding the doorway so that the guards could not get past her. 'You must stay in your chambers. I will wait inside with you. I do not like after-midnight calls. Especially on wedding nights. It is most inauspicious.'

Rama turned to glance at Sita. He gave her a brief reassuring smile, conveying more than any words could have done, and left, pulling the door to behind himself. Nakhudi came into the room, conspicuously avoiding looking at the tousled and rumpled bed. 'While we wait, my lady, it might not be inappropriate if you elect to garb yourself. Just in case.'

The woman on the diwan issued a long hissing sigh. Then she lunged forward, grabbing hold of Kausalya's arm and neck in a fierce grip. At once Kausalya was assailed by the stench of dung and damp and vomit and something else, something she had never smelled before on human breath. It smelled like . . . brimstone?

'Kausalya,' said a voice that sounded exactly like Kaikeyi's, except that each word was elongated, as if the person were struggling to put out one syllable at a time. 'Paaaaaay heeeeeed . . . nooooot muuuuch tiiiiime noooooow . . . Saaaaaave . . . Raaaaaama.'

'Guru-dev,' Sumitra shouted behind her. 'The witch will kill her! Please, save her!' Behind her the daiimaas erupted in a chorus of alarmed exclamations and muttered mantras.

But Guru Vashishta only stood immobile beside Kausalya, watching and listening intently, his whole attention focused on the serving woman.

'It . . . waaaaaaas . . . nooooooot . . . my . . . dooooing,' said the tormented Kaikeyi-like voice. The woman's eyes were bulging now, the red veins sharply defined. And Kausalya could see a trickle of blood seeping slowly out of one flared nostril. 'I . . . truuuuusted . . . the . . . witch . . . Manthara . . . buuuuuuttt . . . sheeeeee . . . serves . . . anooootheer . . . maaaaaster . . .'

Kausalya could feel the grip on her arm growing stronger, crushing her flesh and bone. She resisted the urge to cry out for help, knowing that if she was in any real danger the guru would not simply stand and watch as he was doing now. For some reason he wished to let the woman speak her piece. And, Kausalya sensed, that piece was almost said.

'Fooooooorgggiiiive meeee . . .' the woman moaned.

And then, with a torrent of life-blood pouring out from her nostrils, her ears, her eyes, and her open mouth, the woman released her hold on Kausalya and slumped forward, falling face down on the ground. She lay there still and unmoving, a pool of blood forming quickly around her flared tresses.

The guru knelt down and touched the woman's neck. 'She is dead,' he said quietly. Only then did he stand up and look directly at Kausalya. 'Are you well, my rani?'

She nodded, unable to speak at once.

Sumitra hugged her tightly, weeping copiously. 'Oh Devi, Kausalya! I thought she was going to kill you just now!'

'No,' the guru said. 'Poor soul. She was already as

good as dead. She stayed alive only that she might convey that one last message to you. A message that achieved two goals at once. One, it put the finger of blame squarely upon the hunchbacked daiimaa. And two, it told you something you would not otherwise have believed, that the real Kaikeyi, trapped within her own body and mind under the crushing influence of the daiimaa's evil shakti, does not endorse or desire what her physical form has been given to accomplish.'

And what is that? Kausalya asked herself silently, still recovering from the shock of the assault. *That is the real question. What is Manthara using Kaikeyi to accomplish?*

She searched for an answer in the words emitted from the dying woman's throat. Cleansed of its sibilant syllables, the message was simple enough: *Kausalya. Pay heed. Not much time now. Save Rama. It was not my doing. I trusted the witch Manthara but she serves another master. Forgive me.*

Save Rama.

The door of the kosaghar was open when Rama arrived, flanked by the two palace guards. They had walked in silence all the way. Rama knew better than to ask questions of them; they were simply following orders. But he sensed a tenseness about them even as they walked the long corridors to the kosaghar. An air of great unease, quite unlike their usual smooth efficiency. He had lived among armed kshatriyas all his life, and he could read their outlook simply from the way they moved and spoke – or did not move and speak. These two men were exceedingly unhappy about something. But they could not say what it was, and he did not wish to waste time by asking.

They stopped at the door of the kosaghar, and one of

them rapped quietly on the outside. Then they stepped
back to allow him passage.

Rama took a quick deep breath as he went inside. In
another moment or two he would know why he had been
summoned here at this odd hour. And why the two guards
had been so unhappy performing a simple duty.

'Shut the door behind you,' said a female voice.

He did as he was told, then turned and saw Rani
Kaikeyi standing with her arms folded across her chest.
Further along the chamber he saw his father, seated on
the ground like a child with his legs sprawled wide, his
head in his hands. Was he weeping? Surely not. Oddly
enough, the maharaja seemed otherwise quite all right.
Rama could clearly see his chest rise and fall with the
lurching motion of someone who is trying hard to still
his own crying.

'Kaikeyi-maa,' Rama said, performing a namaskar out
of respect for his clan-mother. 'You sent for me?'

'I did,' she said softly, walking closer. 'I have a message
from your father for you.'

Rama blinked. His father? But his father was right
here in the same room. Why would Dasaratha ask Kaikeyi
to speak for him when he could address Rama himself?
'Is my father indisposed? I am concerned for his health.
If he has lost his voice again, as he did on Holi day, I
can fetch him some herbs that will soothe his throat.'

She smiled oddly. 'Your concern is well intended, but
misplaced. Your father is well, better than he has been
in years. His health need not concern you now, only his
words. For these express his desires. Now heed me well.
For he has asked me to speak on his behalf, and I do not
wish to have to repeat these words. Are you listening
closely?'

What was this? Some kind of test? Rama glanced at his

father. Dasaratha remained as he was, but he seemed to have stopped crying. Instead, he was sitting very still, as if listening to every word they were saying. It was very strange indeed, but if Dasaratha was not objecting by word or gesture, then clearly Kaikeyi was speaking the truth. Rama followed Kaikeyi's example by using Sanskrit highspeech, taking care to employ all the formal terms and phrases.

'Speak, Rani-maa. I am listening intently to your every word. Say it but once and it will be done as you wish. Speak my father's wishes to me.'

Kaikeyi said in a clear and ringing voice, audible throughout the chamber even though Rama was only standing a yard or two distant, 'You are to go into exile at once. Do not stop to take any clothes or belongings. Say no farewells to anyone, but leave this very minute with the clothes upon your back, no weapons or tools or possessions except what you now carry. Go to the heart of the Dandaka-van and reside there off the fruit of the land for twice times seven years, and by doing so cast off all claims to your inheritance and the throne of Ayodhya for ever. Do you understand what you have just been told, Rama?'

He stared at her silently for a moment, not daring to move, or even breathe. 'Yes, I do.'

'Then go now,' she said flatly, without trace of either cruelty or regret. 'And do not return until fourteen years have elapsed.'

He kept his eyes on her, riveted, unable to move or even blink. 'These are my father's wishes?'

'They are,' she replied as flatly as before. 'Do you debate them?'

He looked at his father, sitting like a child on the floor, head in his hands. Dasaratha made no word of denial or protest. 'I do not.'

'Then obey your father's wishes. Go into exile now. And remember well the terms I spoke of.'

And with those words she turned on her heel and walked back across the chamber to the spot where Dasaratha sat.

Rama stood for one endless moment, his entire world set ablaze, his mind and heart and very soul on fire, and then, with one lurching step, he started towards his father, his knee already bending in anticipation. Then her words came back to him, ringing in his ears like temple bells. *Say no farewells to anyone.*

After another moment, seeming aeons but only a fraction of a second, for Rani Kaikeyi had not yet covered the few dozen strides to the maharaja, Rama turned and walked towards the door of the kosaghar. He opened the door and went out, neither looking behind him nor stopping.

KAAND 2

THE DISPOSSESSED

I

Sita was dressed and pacing the chamber. She turned and ran to him as he entered, barely waiting for him to shut the doors, throwing her arms around his neck and lavishing kisses as if he had been gone for a month rather than a mere half-hour.

Then she saw his face and stopped. 'What is it?' Then, when he didn't respond, more urgently, 'Rama, what is it? Tell me, my love!'

He still didn't answer.

He had held himself together all the way back through the long winding corridors of Suryavansha Palace, grateful for the early hour and the relative absence of palace staff. But now that he was here, alone in his chambers, in these familiar rooms where he had spent so many sheltered years of his life up to now, and in the circle of these arms where he felt he had spent all his previous lives up to this one, in these twin overlapping circles of warm familiarity the strength ebbed from his limbs at once. He felt barely able to stand. Fighting Tataka had not been this hard; releasing the Brahm-astra was surely easier; facing Parsurama was child's play in comparison.

He unwound Sita's arms from round his neck, as gently as he could manage, and went to the bed. He turned and sat on its edge, almost slipping down to the floor but catching himself in time. He rested his elbows on his knees, leaning forward, striving to focus on the simple impossibility of the art of breathing. Only breathing, breathing as if his life depended on it. And it did. His life did depend on this simple act of taking in air and exhaling it, an act so simple he had repeated it millions of times since emerging from the womb. Then why did it seem so difficult now? Why was it suddenly like trying to breathe through crushed glass? Every breath an agony, every exhalation requiring a lifetime's energy to expend, every pause between breaths an eternity. What had happened to all those years of pranayam training? Of yogic mastery? Why had all his skills and learning fled him now?

'Rama,' she said, slipping to the floor, clutching his feet. 'Please, tell me. What did your father say?'

He shook his head. His eyes felt cold and dry, as they should feel if he had been walking on the high slopes of Gandahar in the deep winter. That was odd. He had expected tears by now. Indeed, they felt ready to come. But none did. He seemed to have forgotten how to initiate the act of crying, just as he had misplaced the art of breathing. Perhaps he had only strength to manage one at a time. Perhaps if he stopped breathing, then the tears would come. And with them, blessed oblivion, an end to all questions and feelings.

'Rama!' She tugged at his arm. 'Speak to me!'

He shook his head again, trying to make her understand how impossible speech was at such a time. How futile. What could he possibly say? How could he explain that all his dreams, his aspirations, his hopes had been savagely ripped out from his heart like an uprooted tree in a monsoon storm? How could he make her understand that nothing he said would make any difference at all?

To his surprise someone spoke in a voice exactly like his own, speaking on his behalf.

'I have to go,' this voice said aloud. It sounded detached, remote, almost beyond caring. 'I must leave you and go.'

Sita reared back, her eyes wide with fright. 'What do you mean? Go where? Why? For what? Is there a new wave? Did someone bring news of it just now? Where are they attacking?'

It took him a moment to understand that she was referring to the Asura invasion.

He shook his head yet again. It was becoming quite a habit. Again the voice spoke, and this time he recognised the familiar vibration of cords in his throat, felt the reverberation of sounds in his chest cavity. It was he speaking, yet he still felt as if it was another he, a physical he that he was detached from and could float loose of the real Rama at any moment. 'I am to go into exile. Into the Dandaka woods. At once. Now, this very minute. I am to say no farewells, take nothing except whatever clothes I am wearing now. No jewels or ornaments, weapons or things. I am to stay there in exile for twice seven years. Fourteen years in all. In exile.'

He had repeated 'in exile' several times. He felt like saying it over and over again, like a mantra that could ward off some evil spell. Or perhaps by saying it enough times he could break the spell he seemed to be under. This state of being without feeling, speaking without being conscious of the act, seeing without being able to make sense of what he was seeing: what else was it if not a spell? A spell cast by life itself, by the turning of the great wheel of time.

She stared up at him for one long, breathless moment. Then she rose and stood before him, looking down at him. He had to lift his head to look at her now. He did so with the same remote detachment, as if he were moving someone else's head.

She slapped him.

She put all her strength behind the blow. His face was flung sharply to the right, his vision blurring out of focus before the world swam back into view, accompanied by several motes of swirling light, and he found himself facing the wall. He turned back to look at her. Something told him that he should raise his hand and touch his cheek, to feel where she had slapped him. But his hand felt as if a mace and lead-weight ball had been chained to it, and his face, which should have burned agonisingly from the blow, only felt numb. As if he had fallen asleep in a cavern of grey ice and had just awoken. That would explain the frozen feeling in his entire body.

'Stop it,' she said. 'Stop teasing me like this. I've heard about the games some clans play. I thought the Suryavansha Ikshwakus were above such petty chicanery. Don't insult my intelligence with such a feeble trick.'

He hesitated. He wasn't afraid of another blow. He was afraid of how she would respond when he didn't burst into embarrassed laughter and admit sheepishly that it had been just a post-marital game – he had heard of such games too; they were immensely popular in Kaikeya, played with great enthusiasm, bordering on cruelty – as she expected him to do now. Finally, he spoke, because there was nothing else to be done, bracing himself for another slap, keeping his voice surprisingly quiet and calm. It felt as if he was speaking through an ice-numbed mouth.

'Kaikeya-maa, my stepmother, once saved my father's life. Actually, she saved his life twice. In exchange, he granted her two boons. She could ask anything of him her heart desired, at any time. She chose to withhold her privilege until today. Today she asked him to honour his promise and grant those boons. The first boon she desired was that Bharat, her son, should be crowned prince-heir. The second boon was that I, Rama, should go into exile in the Dandaka woods for fourteen years.'

She slapped him again. Harder this time, although he wouldn't have thought that possible a moment ago. He still didn't raise his hand to his cheek, but this time he did feel some sensation. Like ants crawling over the skin, or under the skin.

'I told you, no games.' Her voice was deathly quiet.

'It's no game, Janaki. This is exactly what I was told when I went to the kosaghar just now.'

'Your father told you this?'

'No. But he was there. He heard every word. He did not deny it or stop her. Kaikeya-maa told me this, and then dismissed me.'

'It isn't true,' she said. Her voice faltered slightly for the first time. Ever so slightly, but he caught it. Already he was attuned to the nuances of her emotions, as if the intensity of the events of the past few days had bonded them in some way that was more powerful than a lifetime of normal marriage. 'It can't be true. Dasaratha-chacha would not do such a thing to his first-born.'

'He didn't do it, you're right about that much. Rani Kaikeyi did it.'

'He wouldn't let her! He would have stopped her!' Her voice rose sharply.

Rama shrugged. 'He was bound by an oath.'

'Even for an oath, he would not turn his own son out of doors.'

'He had no choice in the matter. Kaikeyi had every right to demand the boons he had promised her. It was a blood-oath, given in exchange for the saving of a life. Not once, but twice.'

'Even so . . .' Sita turned around where she stood, like a dancer performing a step, banging her foot down hard. Her payals shuddered discordantly. 'He was under pressure of a blood-oath. You are not. You have no obligation to respect his promise. You need not go at all! There!' She flung out her arms triumphantly, as if by coming to this rational conclusion the matter was settled there and then, just like that. 'You need not do what she bade you. She is only your stepmother. Your father did not tell you these things himself.'

'I am my father's son. I must respect his wishes, no matter if they are conveyed by some other medium.'

'They're not his wishes! You said so yourself. They're her wishes! Hers!'

'But the right to ask them was granted to her by my father. He was present in the kosaghar when she addressed me. He heard and was aware of the whole transaction.' He rose to his feet slowly, reaching out to take her into his arms. 'Sita, listen to me. There is no way around it. I must respect my father's wishes. I must go into the Dandaka—'

'No!' She backed away, pushing his hands away roughly. 'I will not let you! I will not allow you to go! I will fetch Kausalya-maa. Guru Vashishta. I will tell your brothers. I will go to the king himself if I must. To Rani Kaikeyi! I will prostrate myself and beg for her mercy. If she wishes her son to be king in your stead, so be it! She can have him crowned king and reign as queen-mother! Everyone knows that's what she's always wanted. But she doesn't need to send you into exile to achieve that!'

He let his arms fall limply. 'It doesn't matter what she needs or doesn't need. This is her wish, she has spoken it. It is my dharma to follow it through now. You may call upon whomever you please; nothing they say either will sway me. If anything, Guru Vashishta himself will agree that I must obey my father's command.'

He looked around the chamber. He was shocked to see gloamy light seeping in from the veranda. Dawn had crept up on him unawares. 'I should not have come here. I was specifically forbidden to say any goodbyes. I will honour that, by saying no farewell to you. Only this will I say: you will be well cared for here until I return.'

'I won't hear this!' She put her hands over her ears, like a child shutting out a parent's voice.

'You will live like a princess, no matter whether Bharat reigns or I. My brothers are great and honourable men, each one of them. They will ensure that your every need is met, your every desire fulfilled. The entire kingdom and wealth of the Suryavanshas will be at your disposal from—'

'I don't want any of it,' she yelled, tears streaming down her face now. 'None of it! Do you understand? Are you listening to me? Or are you just going to drone on without hearing a single word *I'm* saying?'

'I'm listening,' he said quietly. 'And I understand your pain and anguish. But there is no way to undo this. Understand that first and foremost. I must fulfil my dharma, I must obey my father's wishes, and honour the vow he once made. In fourteen years, when I return, I will try and make reparations for your long—'

'I won't be here,' she cried, shaking her head from side to side over and over again. 'In fourteen years or fourteen days, I will not be here. Do you understand? I'm not going to sit in this palace and wait for you.'

He was silent. Shocked. He had thought he had been shocked sufficiently for one lifetime – or at least for one night. But apparently the human heart had a greater capacity for hurt than he had believed possible. Still, with the shock and pain came relief as well. For her answer assuaged his guilt, the guilt that had been the reason he had come back here to his chambers rather than proceeding straight to the gates and out of the city as he should have done in the first place. If she would not stay, then she would not suffer, and he would feel a little less horrible.

'That is understandable,' he said. 'You have every right. No Arya wife in her youthful prime could be expected to stay fourteen years without her husband. Under Manu's Law, a wife whose husband takes sanyas from the world can seek to marry again if she pleases. An exile is akin to a sanyas, for what is exile if not a total renunciation of all one's worldly possessions, habits and desires? I will free you from our marital vows before I go. In fact, I will do so this very minute, by reciting the slokas of disavowal. After I have spoken them aloud, you shall be free to remarry and seek your own happiness.'

She flew at him then. He thought surely this time she meant to kill him, or wound him deeply at least. The rage in her beautiful face, the heat in her eyes, the hand raised in a clawing gesture . . . Instead, all she did was clap her hand upon his mouth and shove him back upon the bed, straddling him, her tears dripping as hot and thick as spilled diya oil upon his forehead.

'If you utter that sloka,' she said hoarsely, her throat constricted by her emotions and tears, 'I will kill myself. I swear it. Don't you dare utter a single syllable of disavowal! I'll die before I marry another man!'

'I was only suggesting it for your own good,' he said. 'It would be better if you try to put me behind you and live your life afresh.'

'Haven't you felt anything at all? Don't you see what we share together? Is it only my body and my youth that you see before you? Do you not see the heart that beats within this breast, the mind that ticks behind this face, the soul that floats within this cage of flesh? Don't you feel what I feel for you?'

'Of course I do,' he said softly. 'That's the reason why I don't want you to suffer alone.'

She slapped him, harder than the first two times. This time the slap stung. He felt its impact sear into the pores of his skin, like liquid metal seeping in. It freed him of the spell of numbness and detachment, breaking through to the core of his own anguish and anger. The dam burst, and his emotions flooded his mind in a white-hot wave.

He gripped her tightly in his arms and swung her to the side. She gasped as he pressed her down on the bed, kneeling beside her, feeling the heat in his own eyes now, the constriction in his own throat.

'Then what do you want of me?' he said. 'Why don't you understand? I have to do this! Accept it and get on with your life, Sita Janaki! There's nothing more I can say or do for you. Do you understand? I must go into exile! This is my fate. It cannot be undone no matter what you say or do,' his voice broke, 'or what we feel and share with each other, no matter how extraordinary that feeling happens to be.'

They stared at each other, breathing harshly. After an instant, he realised that the rhythm of their breath was perfectly matched. He clambered down from the bed and regained his feet, careful to keep his back to her. He feared that if he looked at her face, he would not be able to do what he now must do. It was time.

'Rama,' she said. There was no pleading or cry in her voice. She only said it with love, more tenderly than he had ever heard his name said before, except by his mother.

Don't turn. Just walk to the door, open it, and keep walking. Don't look back. If you look back, you will be lost for ever.

But she didn't repeat his name. Only said it that once, and then fell silent. He heard the sound of her payals and jewellery clinking and tinkling as she rose from the bed and stood behind him, but she didn't speak his name again. As if she knew that no amount of crying and wailing could persuade him to turn now that his mind was made up, now that his foot was set upon the path of dharma. She said his name that one time, and waited. And in the end, it was that perfect faith, that blind belief, that made him turn. For how could he ignore she who loved him dearly enough to respect his wishes and let him go, even though it meant the certain destruction of everything she had hoped for and aspired to? How could he just walk away from a soul-mate so perfect that her very sorrow harmonised with the pain he himself carried in his own breast like a dying broken-winged sparrow?

He turned. And found her tearless and calm once more. She raised her arms to him, asking, not pleading.

'Then let me go with you,' she said.

2

The kosaghar doors stood open by the time Kausalya and the rest of the party arrived. The two guards on duty saluted Pradhan-mantri Sumantra, Guru Vashishta and the two queens but barred their way. Sumantra was rapidly approaching his endurance limit.

'We have urgent business with the Second Queen, soldiers. Move aside and let us pass.'

The two Kaikeyans, part of the Second Queen's personal rani-rakshak regiment, looked at each other nervously. They both had the trademark curling moustaches of the western kingdom, shined to perfection by the daily application of clarified butter. 'Rani Kaikeyi has left the kosaghar,' one of them said. 'She has gone to the sabha hall, we believe. Before she left she sent couriers to the houses of the ministers, calling for a special plenary session of the council.'

Sumantra stared at them, flabbergasted. '*She* has called a session? Have you two been sipping soma on duty?'

They looked at each other again, unhappily, as if coming to a harsh decision. Then, with one movement, both men prostrated themselves before the prime minister. 'Great one, we beg to be relieved of our duties as Rani Kaikeyi's bodyguards. Pray, grant us sanctuary in the ranks of Kosala's army.'

Sumantra looked even more bewildered. 'You no longer wish to serve your clan-queen? Do you know what this means?' He added impatiently, 'Rise to your feet, men!'

They stood up, putting their lances aside. The way to the kosaghar was unbarred now. Seeing her opportunity, Kausalya moved past them and entered the chamber of complaints, followed by Rani Sumitra. The guru and Pradhan-mantri Sumantra remained with the guards. Sumantra was very curious to know their story. Kaikeyans were famous for their national fealty. Why, even the Second Queen's personal bodyguard consisted solely of men, in keeping with the Kaikeya nation's chauvinistic conviction that the only true kshatriyas were men. For these two to have cast aside their clan-oaths and sought refuge in Kosala's army indicated some great crisis.

'What occasions this behaviour?' he asked them sternly. 'Why do two Kaikeyans sworn to protect their queen wish to leave her service thus? You know that as a consequence of this desertion your names will be forever cast out of the annals of Kaikeyan kshatriya clans and seven generations of your descendants will be forbidden water, food, or shelter beneath any Kaikeyan kshatriya roof? In effect, you will be as if in exile the rest of your natural lives.'

'We know this, my lord,' said the first guard. 'But we cannot serve our duty any longer. There are some things that are beyond a clan-oath and fealty.'

'Such as?' Sumantra's heart was pounding now. He thought he glimpsed what might have upset these men so deeply, but he wished to hear them say so in as many words. There were only two acts which could cause a Kaikeyan to break his clan-oath and forswear fealty to his queen. Two acts which no Kaikeyan could condone, whatever the circumstances, and which absolved even the extreme betrayal of desertion.

'Denial of a mother's duties,' they said with one voice, naming the first, most heinous of crimes that could possibly be committed by a Kaikeyan woman. And as he had feared, they went on, naming the second of those unforgivable acts, 'And king-slaying, my lord.'

Kausalya entered the kosaghar first. The pungent reek of some foreign agent assailed her nostrils, and the miasma of misty vapour that filled the air irritated her eyes, causing them to sting and water at once. Her entire being cringed and crawled with an unpleasant sensation, as if she had passed through a thicket of poisonous bramble-flowers and her skin had been afflicted by their noxious pollen. The kosaghar was gloomy and silent as ever; this was not a happy place at the best of times. But there was something more than the usual oppressive atmosphere that hung over a chamber reserved for mourning, grieving, or wretched retreat from the world at large.

She stepped into a viscous patch of something wet and unpleasant and recoiled. At first, in the gloomy murk of the sputtering diyas – almost all of them had burned down to the wick – she was certain the stain on the carpeted floor was blood. A terrible vision filled her mind's eye, of Kaikeya dressed in her tight-fitting armour suit, flinging the gleaming spear she had carried back from the Holi mêlée. Only this time the spear was directed not at Kausalya, as it had been that day in the Seer's Tower, but at Dasaratha himself. She pictured the spear striking Dasaratha and driving him back, to fall to his knees, spilling his life-blood.

She bent and felt the patch with great reluctance. She had to know. The relief that she felt as she recognised the familiar greasy feel and smelled the unmistakable odour of mustard oil was out of all proportion to the simple act.

But the sense of dread she felt remained. Like the tip of a thorn broken off deep inside an impaled thumb. She rose to her feet and resumed her course down the long pillars of the kosaghar. Behind her, footfalls sounded lightly.

'Kausalya?' Sumitra's voice betrayed her fear.

Kausalya gestured at the Third Queen to wait there by the door. She could hear Sumantra's voice speaking to the guards outside, then Guru Vashishta intoning in his quiet, calming way. Then she took another few steps further into the chamber and the voices faded to a distant murmur. This section of the kosaghar was duskier than the area by the doorway. Here, the diyas had almost all been extinguished, and the only light came from a single lamp flickering in the wind brought in by the open doors. As Kausalya approached this solitary flame, hidden yet behind a row of pillars, she saw a distorted shadow cast upon the floor and left-hand wall, as if a person were bending over with the diya in hand. She felt a flush of relief, her footsteps hastening to cover the last few pillars to the flickering source of light.

'Dasa,' she said. 'Are you well? We were so worried. What happened—'

She came around the last pillar and stopped dead in her tracks.

The hunchbacked form of Manthara-daiimaa reared up before her. The daiimaa was holding a diya in her hand, and the light cast upwards by the little clay lamp threw her wizened features into garish relief. Normally, Kausalya was not offended by the sight of an ageing face – if anything, she loved the careworn lines of an ancient visage just as much as the wrinkled pinkness of a newborn babe – but there was something in Manthara's sneering features that put her in instant remembrance of those childhood tales of chudails and vetaals. An expression of utter disgust for everyone and everything that could not be considered lovable by even the most trusting person on earth.

The daiimaa straightened as best as she was able, given her deformity. 'Rani Kausalya. You have come at last. And about time too. The maharaja was just asking for you by name.'

Kausalya saw the huddled form leaning against the pillar behind Manthara. The daiimaa's lower body concealed most of it from her view, but she saw enough to know it was Dasaratha. Why was he just lying there? Was he unconscious? But Manthara had just said that he was asking for her, Kausalya.

Caution bade her keep her distance until she learned more about what was really going on here. The guru and Sumantra would be with her in moments. She bit back the accusations that were boiling up in her throat and spoke to the daiimaa as levelly as she could manage under the circumstances.

'What are you doing here, Manthara?'

The words came out harsher than Kausalya had intended, she realised. But it was too late to take them back. She let them hang in the air, like a challenge. *Let her make something of it if she wants to. Maybe she'll show her hand at last, reveal her true self and condemn herself once and for all.*

Manthara sighed with the utter weariness of one who has suffered long and hard under the yoke of royal servitude. 'Tending to the maharaja, of course. Rani Kaikeyi asked me to stay and adminster to his needs as long as he chose to remain in the kosaghar.'

'Chose to remain?' This time the sharpness in Kausalya's voice went up a notch. She took a step closer to the daiimaa as she spoke. 'He was not the one who came voluntarily here. You said so yourself earlier. It was Kaikeyi who shut herself up here, after taking her vraths. It was at your behest that he came here at all.'

'Surely.' Manthara tilted her head, reminding Kausalya of a carrion bird she had seen once as a child, gazing greedily across a battlefield strewn with grisly dead, as if deciding with which poor fellow's innards to start the feast. 'But his majesty's health seemed to take a turn for the worse after his arrival here. I was only adminstering this herbal tonic to revive him somewhat.'

The daiimaa held out a glass jal-bartan with her left hand, showing Kausalya the dregs of some dark fluid within.

A cold fist grasped Kausalya's heart, squeezing until she could barely breathe. Suddenly she understood the reason for the sense of dread she had felt upon entering. It was more than just the serving girl's dying words, or Kaikeyi's words as spoken through the medium of the dying serving girl, whichever one believed. 'Where is your mistress?' she asked harshly, not caring about her tone any longer. 'Where is the Second Queen? Why did she send for my husband and then leave him here alone with you? What have you two wrought this dark night in this cursed chamber of pain and sorrow? Answer me!'

The daiimaa sketched a brief bow. It came off as a grotesque mockery due to her dwarf-like stature and protruding hump. 'My mistress is in the sabha hall, as the guards outside, treacherous oafs that they are, have already informed you. *First* Queen Kaikeyi is overseeing an emergency samiti of the council of ministers even as we speak. As for why she sent for Maharaja Dasaratha, *her* husband, why, that is a matter you must discuss with her directly. Or with him, if you can rouse him now. And to answer your final question, well, she and I have been doing exactly what you and your son Rama Chandra have been doing these past weeks, securing our rightful place in the kingdom after his majesty's passing.'

The daiimaa paused, a scornful smile flickering across her distorted face. 'And now that I have answered your queries, *Second* Queen Kausalya, let me add this one further statement. You have enjoyed the luxury of reigning supreme for these past years despite the maharaja favouring my mistress in the boudoir. But now, with the balance of power suitably redressed, I urge you not to address me as offensively as you have done till now. Before, I may have been a humble daiimaa. Now, I am the governess-regent of a king of Ayodhya. It gives me great pleasure to inform you that you are now addressing *Lady* Manthara!'

There were bounds even to Kausalya's legendary limitless patience, and she might have flown at the woman had a voice not spoken from behind just then. Guru Vashishta's booming baritone carried the length of the kosaghar, preceding the sage as he approached.

'Enough! You have spoken too much already, old crone. I command you to silence, in the name of the founder of this great dynasty, might Surya-deva himself! Shantam!'

Before Kausalya's startled gaze, Manthara's eyes flashed green. If she hadn't seen it herself, she wouldn't have believed it. But there was no mistaking that emerald gleam that lit up the daiimaa's normally black pupils when the sage called out his command. They positively blazed with green fire. Kausalya took a step back, and was caught by Sumitra's feverish-hot hands.

Manthara had finally decided to show her true colours.

3

The daiimaa's voice was as soft as the hiss of a serpent, yet no less deadly in its challenge. 'You dare to command me to silence, sage? I advise you to stay silent yourself!'

Kausalya heard Sumitra emit a startled gasp at the daiimaa's effrontery. Neither of them had ever heard anyone, leave alone an ageing wet-nurse, speak with such rude arrogance to the seer-mage Vashishta. But that was only the first salvo in the old hunchback's arsenal. She went on, her voice rising with unleashed fury, her eyes blazing sorcerous green, the green of Asura shakti, as Kausalya knew from a thousand childhood tales. A corrosive, searing green flame that seemed to issue from as well as consume the daiimaa's eyes like a pair of oil-dipped cotton wicks.

Manthara raised a clawlike finger, pointing it at Guru Vashishta. 'Be warned, whitebeard! Your powers will not serve you in this matter! Too late you see fit to intervene. Too late you arrive like an unwelcome guest at a wedding feast after the last course has been served and eaten. Too late to save your precious Ikshwaku clan, your exalted Suryavansha dynasty, your feeble, fickle, faithless friends. With one masterstroke, your great child-champion has been disinherited from his throne and kingdom, cast out into exile, condemned to fourteen years in a place no less perilous than the nethermost region of hell. What use your great brahman shakti now? Your yogic mastery? Your millennia of maha-vidya and wisdom? Dust and ashes, offal and filth! That will be your lot henceforth!'

As she spoke, the green blaze in Manthara's eyes grew brighter, filling the entire orbs, until their garish light fell upon the daiimaa's face and upper body, overwhelming even the pure yellow glow of the diya.

Kausalya glimpsed Guru Vashishta's white-clad form sweeping past her. The guru seemed taller than usual, looming above them all, but especially above the daiimaa, who seemed further dwarfed in comparison with the tall sage.

'You have done enough damage already,' the guru said, his gravelly voice a sombre and dignified contrast with the daiimaa's hissing, spitting tones. 'I should have suspected your evil ways earlier and acted sooner. But you were cloaked by the presence and protection of your mistress. Fool that I was, I neglected to look past the brightness of Kaikeyi's obfuscating aura, or I would surely have glimpsed how deeply your black heart and sin-soaked aatma were steeped in the dark arts. Instead, I misread the signs and omens and failed to perceive your role in this villainish conspiracy. For that failing I must pay penance.'

'Yes!' the old hunchback screeched. 'Penance you will pay! While I rule the roost like a queen in all but name. Do not delude yourself. You could no more have seen through my outer guise than a greybeard goat can see through its mountain! My master's shakti is supreme in all the worlds. His time is come. While you and the rest of your clutch of seven, your time is nigh past. Go on then, whitebeard. Cast off your glowing robes and put on a hair-coat. Go out into the wilderness and seek the repentance you deserve. Suffer another millennia or two in silence while my master and I build a new world order, a world where your pathetic devas and devis will be forgotten, their idols smashed down and trampled into the dirt beneath the passage of our triumphant armies!'

Guru Vashishta advanced a step further upon the woman holding the diya. Manthara's face was all alight with the green glow from her eyes now, Kausalya saw. It was as if the daiimaa had been set ablaze by some sorcerous flame and was literally burning in its rapture. Inside the cocoon of green flame, the old hunchback's face and body were limned in black, like an outline sketched with a charcoal grease-stick.

'I will brook no further blasphemy from your withered lips, old hag,' the guru said. 'Until now, you have worked your evildoing in darkness and in secret. But you stand exposed now, and you will not escape justice. I command you, yield this instant or face the shakti of brahman.'

Standing behind the guru, with Sumitra in turn behind her, clinging to her arm, Kausalya saw the look of rage that passed across Manthara's wizened features. The old daiimaa glared at Vashishta with an expression of such intense hatred that even Kausalya had to force herself not to turn her face away. The very fact that the old woman had stood up and confronted the legendary seer-mage so boldly thus far was itself shocking. Their worst fears had finally been proved beyond doubt. Manthara was in the thrall of the demon-lord of Lanka, that much was clearly evident now. No other force in the three worlds would defy Guru Vashishta face to face, nor be able to accomplish so many dastardly deeds so near to the great seer's presence. It was shocking to see that the daiimaa was so foolish, or so powerful, that she would dare to stand up to the guru himself. It made Kausalya cry out in the fastness of her own besieged mind:

How could we have raised this serpent under our own roof and not seen her for what she truly was all these years? Yet the answer was as simple as faith itself: *Because we trust our own. We trust them unto death.*

For several moments the confrontation teetered on a knife-edge. The witch, for that was how Kausalya knew she would think of her henceforth, stayed deathly still in her sorcerous cocoon of green Asura fire, glaring at the sage as if she would do battle with him to the very end before yielding so much as an inch. Nor did the guru himself yield an inch, his eyes flashing blue with the cold fire of brahman, his white beard and flowing mane of hair lending him a terrible grimness.

Then, before Kausalya's astonished eyes, Manthara turned around, putting her back to the guru and the two queens, and bent down. The daiimaa shattered the glass jal-bartan she was holding on the floor of the kosaghar, splitting it into jagged halves. She took one wickedly curved half and put it to the throat of the unconscious maharaja. The hand she used was encased in a mashaal-like blaze of green flame, casting a horrible deathlike pallor upon Dasaratha's face.

'Come then,' she hissed at the sage. 'Let us see how powerful your brahman shakti truly is when matched against my master's powers. Let us see if you can save the life of your precious Aja-putra before I turn him into yet another blood-sacrifice to my master, Ravana!'

'Release him at once,' the sage thundered, his voice echoing and reverberating off the walls of the narrow confined chamber, ringing up and down the corridor-like length of the kosaghar. 'In the name of almighty Brahma, I command you on pain of death!'

Manthara sneered, lifting part of her upper lip to reveal a mouthful of ugly yellow-black teeth. 'Brahma will soon be a forgotten god, seer. By the time the kalyug comes, even his most ardent devotee will have to search the land to find a single shrine. Name some more powerful deva if you will. Or better still, admit defeat and back away.' She turned her hand then, showing them a glimpse of the maharaja's neck. A small drop of blood emerged from the spot where the tip of the jagged glass was held to his throat.

'NO!' Kausalya screamed. Sumitra's voice clashed with hers as the other queen added her own plea. 'Don't hurt him!'

Manthara leered up at them. 'You see, sage? How something as worthless as a single mortal life can undo all the efforts of mighty Brahma? That is why your deva will be forgotten in time, while my lord will be worshipped well into the last yuga of the world, until the final turn of the samay chakra itself. As long as the wheel of time turns, Ravana's name shall be set above all.'

The guru's voice was quiet and calm. 'You delude yourself, witch. Or your master deludes you. What has he promised you in exchange for all this evildoing? A beautiful form, unmarred by your childhood deformities and misshaping? Power and wealth? Adulation and glory?'

Manthara cackled. 'More than you will ever have, whitebeard. My master is generous in his gifts, just as he is cruel in his punishments. He is not one of your devas, who demand eternal service and suffering without ever rewarding you for your servitude.'

'That is because we know, as does every good soul that has ever existed, that serving the force of brahman is reward enough,' replied the sage calmly. 'But your master deceives you. Did he ever tell you that it was he who gave you those deformities and inflicted upon you such hideous misshaping? Did he reveal to you that he picks upon mortal souls at random, inflicting such adversities upon them in order to twist and warp their minds and hearts, making them all the more pliable to his vile purpose? Did he reveal this to you as well?'

For the first time since entering the kosaghar, Kausalya saw the daiimaa's face lose its snarling expression. The look of shock that replaced the snarl was heart-rending to behold. The daiimaa's hand, pressing the jagged glass-edge to the maharaja's bleeding neck, faltered and moved away, shaking in a spasm as if it would drop the makeshift dagger. But almost immediately the woman caught herself, and a wry grin replaced the look of abject shock that had been upon it a moment earlier.

Then a subtle shift took place in the balance of shakti between the two opposing forces. Something flickered in the daiimaa's eyes, a blurring, as if she were distracted by some inner thought. As if she heard a voice speaking inside her mind, Kausalya thought. And slowly, like an oil fire that had been starved of fuel, the daiimaa's green aura receded. In a moment, Kausalya could see Manthara's face and body again. The last vestiges of the sorcerous light flickered at the periphery of the daiimaa's head, then faded away, leaving a few straggling motes of emerald light that swirled and were lost in the long shadows of the kosaghar.

'Well tried, whitebeard,' she hissed softly. 'You almost had me with that lie.'

'It is no lie, Manthara,' Vashishta said with new gentleness. 'You know it as well as I do. Use your newfound powers to examine the veracity of my words. Look back upon your own past. See the exact moment when Ravana reached out with his vile sorcery and twisted you within your mother's very womb. Witness each new blow and misery he inflicted upon you during your tender years, corrupting you further, alienating your from your fellow mortals. Trace the whole history of his workings upon you, as he has worked upon countless other weak souls before you. See it all for yourself and judge whether I speak truly or no. And then decide whether you are truly going to be gifted with all the foolish baubles he dangled before your mesmerised eyes, or cast aside like any of his other minions after they had completed his work. For make no mistake of it, he will cast you down as he would cast a gnat or an ant, not even looking to see if you remain alive or broken. For once you finish his work, you are finished in his eyes. He has no more use of you.'

Now it was Manthara's turn to scream, 'NO!' The cry was magnified by her sorcery, filling the kosaghar with an ear-splitting echo that seemed to go on for ever. When it ended, the daiimaa was on her feet again, the glass shard tossed aside with a clatter. 'I will not stay and be duped by your brahman sorcery, whitebeard. I don't know how you began to weave this spell, or by what mantra you caused it to enter my mind, but I will not stay to be further deluded by its influence. But mark my words, we shall meet again. And the next time, I shall finish with you. Then we shall see whose shakti is greater!'

With those final words, the daiimaa turned and shuffled towards the wall of the kosaghar, heading directly for it without stopping. Just when it seemed she would strike the wall and be thrown back, a blinding flash of green flight seared Kausalya's vision, causing her to fling her arm up to shield her dazed eyes. When she could see again, her eyes adjusting once more to the dim gloom of the chamber, only a few motes of green light swirled at the far corner. Manthara was gone.

'Her power is great,' the guru said. Kausalya was shocked at the weariness in his tone. 'Truly, I was deceived by some great master of Asura sorcery all this time. How could I have allowed her to grow into such a sorceress under my very nose?' He sighed deeply. 'And yet, this too is part of mighty Brahma-dev's great plan. In his infinite wisdom he has found a place for her too, as much a pawn in the great game as I myself.'

Before Kausalya could speak in response to these strange comments, her eyes adjusted sufficiently to the gloom to see the figure that lay beyond the guru. All this while he had been concealed by Manthara, but now Kausalya could see him clearly. Dasaratha lay with his back to a pillar, feet sprawled out before him, head bowed on his chest.

She flew to him, crouching down beside her husband, feeling his cheek, his face, trying to see his eyes in the dimness. 'Dasa? Oh, Dasa, say something. Speak, Dasa!' Sumitra was with her too, saying much the same words, touching Dasa with anxious hands, trying to evoke a response from the maharaja. But Dasaratha only lay there with half-open eyes, barely breathing, his skin as cold and clammy to the touch as a fish freshly drawn from the Sarayu in the last chill of springmelt.

'Guru-dev,' Kausalya said, turning her face up to the guru now standing beside her. 'Your ability to see transcends our weak mortal vision. Tell me truly, what ails my beloved husband? Why does he not respond?'

From behind her, the guru said softly, 'Good Kausalya, gentle Sumitra, brace yourselves. I fear our beloved Dasaratha has run his course. He is alive yet, but his time with us has been reduced considerably by the trauma of this night's events. Even our great Aja-putra's mighty heart will not recover from this final betrayal. I am sorry to say that Maharaja Dasaratha will leave us before the sun sets tonight.'

4

Rama and Sita were almost at the rear gate when the shouting broke out. In her anguished state of mind, it took Sita a moment to connect the outbreak with herself. It was taking all her energy simply to keep placing one foot before the other.

But when Rama paused and glanced around, keeping his head low and covered by the cowl of his shawl, she realised that something was happening in the city. Something that must be connected to their plight, for surely there were no coincidences today.

She glanced back at the rear wall of the palace complex, where they had just exited a servants' entrance. There was nothing amiss here. The shouting was on the far side, at the front entrance of Suryavansha Mahal. It seemed hard to believe that only hours earlier she had entered through that grand portal as an honoured new bride and future queen of the dynasty. And barely before the night was fully ended and dawn's first flush on the horizon, here she was skulking out the rear way like a common thief. Her tightly fitting garments chafed at her skin as she turned, though she hardly noticed.

At Rama's urging, both had exchanged their rich royal silks for simple roughcloth garments, secured for them by a visibly suspicious Nakhudi. The rani-rakshak had looked even more suspicious when Sita had invented a story about their having to travel incognito to avoid being recognised. When the bodyguard pressed her mistress for details of their destination, Sita had spun an impromptu yarn about Rama and she wishing to visit the shrine of Vishnu-Lakshmi, the Divine Preserver and his consort, without the whole palace and the city entire getting wind of it.

At that, Nakhudi had nodded and relaxed visibly. It was considered highly auspicious for a newly married couple to visit that particular shrine the morning after first consummating their new union. And as a hard-bitten northern tribeswoman, Nakhudi didn't truly approve of the brouhaha these Ayodhyans made over their liege. Among her folk, a king was merely a clan-chief, to be treated like any other kshatriya, no better, no less. The display of luxury and sheer glamour the night before had far surpassed the surly Jat's sense of what constituted decent behaviour.

She approved of their quiet assignation and fetched the garments from her own quarters in a trice. Back in Mithila, Sita and she had often moved about the common-folk incognito, and these garments were intended for Sita. Fortunately, Rama's waist was scarcely wider than Sita's slender dimensions, and the dhotis fitted both of them equally well. To disguise their faces, Nakhudi had fetched them shawls, a mite unseasonal since the weather had begun turning warm early this spring, but not unusual. So here they were now, sneaking out the rear entrance with their faces and heads covered by the thick woollen shawls.

Rama took a moment to assess the situation before turning to speak quietly to Sita. 'The palace guards are quarrelling amongst themselves for some reason. We should move quickly before Drishti Kumar gives the order to shut the gates.'

Sita nodded, and they moved across the enormous concourse, heading for the rear gates, which were still a good three or four hundred yards away. They had to pass the royal stables to get there, and the overwhelming odour of horse, elephant and donkey assailed them as they walked briskly. They were passing a horse stall when the beast within, a beautiful white battlehorse with a deep scar across his forehead, raised his head and whinnied loud and long. Several other horses responded in like voice, and even the elephants joined the fray.

Beside her, she heard Rama catch his breath. 'They recognise me. Keep walking.'

She did, thinking as she went of her own favourite horses and elephants back in Mithila. They were to be brought here in a few days, following the usual three-day route rather than the magical half-day journey that Guru Vashishta's brahman shakti had made possible. She wondered what would become of them now that she would no longer be here to receive them. Who would ride them? Or would anyone ride them at all? Would they spend the rest of their lives in stables, emerging only to be exercised occasionally by some ostler? When she returned, how many would still be alive? How many would die of old age before that? And even when she did return, would they still recognise her scent, as these animals did Rama's, and neigh and stamp their feet and trumpet loudly to show their recognition? Or would she be a stranger to them after such a long absence?

She stumbled and fell against Rama. He caught her arm. 'Are you all right?'

She nodded, not trusting herself to speak.

He looked at her closely, trying to see beneath the

shawl's cowl. After a moment he turned and they resumed walking. An ostler emerged from a barn-like structure up ahead, a pitchfork bristling with hay held over his shoulder. He peered down the length of the stalls, then at Rama and Sita with obvious hostility.

'How many times have I told you low-castes not to throw stones at the horses? They may look like dumb animals to you, but they have feelings too, you know. How would you like it if someone came to your window and threw stones inside at you and your family, hey?'

They reached him and continued walking past. He blinked, offended, and came after them. Beneath his breath, Rama said to Sita, 'Keep walking.' She did.

The ostler caught up with them and took hold of Sita's shoulder. She guessed that beneath the shawls it was impossible for the man to tell which of them was male and which female. She shrugged off his grip. He swore and caught her shoulder again, this time too hard for her to wrench free. She tried, but nearly wrenched her shoulder socket out of joint. The ostler pulled hard with the brute strength of a man whose livelihood depended on handling strong animals every day of his life. Sita swung around, the shawl falling from her face.

The ostler stared at her in amazement. 'What is this? Some kind of joke? Who are you, and what's your business going through here, dressed like chamars? You're no chamar, lady. I know you. You're . . .'

He squinted, trying to place Sita's face.

Rama pushed his shawl back on his head, just enough to show his face to the man. 'This is Rajkumari Sita Janaki, Sameer. My new bride. We threw no pebbles at your horses. They smelled me and recognised me. Sadly, I have no time to stop and return their greetings.'

The ostler dropped his pitchfork and fell to his knees,

prostrating himself before Rama. 'My prince! I had no idea! If I had known—'

Rama caught him by the shoulders before he could kiss his feet, and helped him up. 'No apologies required, Sameer. It was an honest mistake. You're right about the janitors throwing pebbles at the horses. I've seen them do it. At the elephants too.'

Sameer wiped tears from his eyes at the thought of having insulted his prince and princess. He bowed before Sita. 'My princess, forgive me.'

'It is nothing,' she said, although her shoulder felt as if it had been wrenched by a rope tied to a logging elephant.

The ostler accepted her reply with an expression of undying gratitude. Sita understood the poor fellow's plight: in less tolerant kingdoms, he would have been flayed alive or quartered by elephants for speaking thus to his prince and for laying hands on her.

'My prince, why are you dressed like this?' the ostler asked, taking in their garments. 'And where do you go at this hour on foot? Would you not like to take a chariot? Or at least two horses? I have a fine mare for Rajkumari Sita. And for you, Rajkumar—'

The shouting from the far side of the palace had grown louder all this while. Now it was joined by the unmistakable sound of weapons clashing. Sita flinched at the sound of steel striking steel, so cruel and remorseless even at this distance. Rama spoke quickly and urgently to the ostler.

'We have no need of mounts or chariot, thank you for asking. The rajkumari and I must leave the rear gates at once on a most urgent matter. One more thing. It would be best if you do not tell anyone of our passing at least for some hours.'

'Not even me?'

They all turned in surprise at the voice. Lakshman was approaching from the other side of the palace complex, which explained why they hadn't seen him. He was bare-chested, clad only in a gold-embroidered silk dhoti. His rig was slung on his back, and in one hand he had his bow and in the other two swords.

Lakshman's face was dark with an emotion Sita couldn't identify. There was anger there. But there was disbelief as well. And pain, a great deal of it. It was all directed at Rama.

Lakshman moved one sword to the hand holding the bow and held the other out to Rama as he came abreast of them. 'You forgot your sword, bhai. I found it in your chambers.'

Rama made no move to take the weapon. 'I am not permitted to take it with me, brother.'

'And what about me? Were you not permitted to tell me as well before you left? You were going to leave without even a word?'

Rama sighed. 'Luck, I was ordered not to say any farewells. To leave without speaking to a single person.'

Lakshman glanced at Sita. 'Even my bhabhi?' He used the colloquial word for sister-in-law.

Rama nodded. 'I had to go back to change my garb, for those were my given orders. So I had to tell her. She insisted on coming with me. But to come to your chambers and speak with you would have amounted to disobedience of my orders.'

Lakshman was silent as if weighing this in his mind.

Rama gestured in the direction from which the sounds of fighting still sounded. It had now progressed to men crying with agony and horses screaming. 'What's happening?'

Lakshman pursed his lips as if reluctant to answer. 'The Kaikeya guard has been given command of the palace complex. The new First Queen has demanded a complete reshuffling of the command chain. The old guard aren't taking it very well. Some disagreements broke out. There's no doubt about who's going to come out on top. The Kaikeya guard are barely a few thousand strong.'

The sound of a conch shell sounding rose on the still early-morning air, wafting across the city. It issued a brief burst, followed by two long blows. It was answered by conches farther away, in like style, a succession that receded into the distance. Rama and Lakshman exchanged a worried glance.

'The army is being called out,' Rama said shortly. 'That's the signal for a palace riot.'

A palace riot? In Ayodhya? Sita glanced at the face of the ostler, who was still standing with them. The man looked flummoxed. 'Rajkumars, what is happening? Why—'

Before he could finish the sentence, the sound of pounding hoofs came from the far side of the palace, the direction that Lakshman had come from. A moment later, four quads of armed men clad in the traditional uniform of the palace guard, sixteen in all, rode into sight, heading directly for them.

Lakshman glanced back at them. 'I told them to follow me as soon as possible. And to get word to Pradhan-mantri Sumantra and Senapati Dheeraj Kumar.'

Rama frowned. 'Luck, what are you up to?'

Instead of answering, Lakshman looked at Sita. 'Janaki. My sister. Would you have my brother abdicate his throne and his birthright at the merest command of a woman—'

Rama broke in mid-way, speaking over Lakshman's

words. 'Lakshman, this matter is not open for discussion.'

Lakshman continued as if Rama hadn't even spoken. 'A woman acting under the influence of our greatest enemy himself?'

Sita stared at him. 'What?'

'Yes. Did you know that, sister? The green witch Manthara has been found out! She admits freely to her connivance with the Lord of Lanka in this plot to destroy our people. What Ravana could not accomplish by direct warfare, he tries now to do by stealth and deception.' Lakshman gestured at Rama as the horsemen rode up and reined in their mounts. One of them dismounted and came up to take Lakshman's weapons from his hand at his gesture. Sita saw with no surprise that the man was none other than Senapati Dheeraj Kumar himself. 'My brother is a paragon of dharma,' Lakshman continued. 'He wishes to carry out our father's wishes. If that were all he were doing, I would gladly let him go. But there is more to this whole plot than meets the eye. Manthara was using her dark shakti, Asura-shakti, to control Rani Kaikeyi. Even Guru Vashishta says so himself. I have just come from speaking with them after they left the kosaghar, where they found our father in a near-death state. And they say—'

Rama's face flinched at the mention of his father. Lakshman paused briefly, then went on, 'And even as we speak here, Kausalya-maa and my mother have gone to the sabha hall, where Kaikeyi is trying to push through the council's formal approval of Bharat's ascension.'

'Lakshman,' Rama said sternly.

Lakshman raised his voice. 'Rama has but to stand up and claim his right, and I swear, every Ayodhyan, nay, every Kosalan will support him to the bitter end. Our father wished for Rama to be prince-heir, and to be king after him. Rama, not Bharat!'

'Lakshman!' Rama put a hand on Lakshman's arm.

Lakshman shook off the touch. He had tears rolling down his face now, Sita saw. Tears of rage and pain. 'Our father did not wish for this to happen. Whatever vows he may have made to Kaikeyi, she has had a lifetime to claim them. Why now? Why these demands? Isn't it obvious? It's only because it serves the Lord of Lanka's purpose!'

Lakshman turned to Rama, addressing his brother heatedly. Tears spilled hot and fast from his angry eyes. 'Don't you see this, brother? Whatever her faults, Kaikeyi-maa loves you like her own son! She may not be a perfect mother, but she *is* a clan-mother to you as well as me! Yes, she has wanted to be first-titled queen for as long as we can remember. Yes, she resents your mother's power and popularity. Yes, she would want nothing more than to see her own son Bharat crowned heir today. But not like this! Not by sending you into exile. *And surely not at the cost of breaking our father's heart and killing him.* Because that's what this has done to him, Rama. Our father isn't dying now of any canker or ailment. He's dying of a broken heart. Aja-putra Dasaratha has a great heart and it is breaking now because he has been tricked into sending his own son into exile, punishing your great achievements with this brutal reward, tearing a family to pieces, a kingdom to shreds, and doing exactly what the king of rakshasas wishes him to do. Is this what you want, Rama? For Ravana to win and us to lose?'

'No,' Rama said very quietly. Everyone present heard him. The ostler standing by, watching with gaping mouth and wide round eyes, the growing crowd of palace guards and soldiers – more had come whilst Lakshman was speaking – all watching the scene with eyes and demeanours as fierce as Lakshman's. 'No, my brother, I want none of this.'

Lakshman fell to his knees, clutching Rama's thighs. 'Then come back with me. We will have Kaikeyi and Manthara arrested. You will be crowned heir. Bharat will never object. He will support us all the way, you know that! He knows you have the rightful claim, and once he hears the circumstances of these events, he will—'

'I can't do that,' Rama said, just as quietly.

Lakshman stared up at him. Rama bent and raised his brother up. 'I cannot come back, brother. I have given my word. I must obey my father's wishes. To refuse now would dishonour him.'

Lakshman looked as if he would hit Rama. Sita stepped forward. 'Bhaiya,' she said, using the colloquial word that could mean brother as well as brother-in-law. 'Rama is right. I argued with him as well, and cried and fought, but in the end I accept his decision.' She felt tears start from her eyes. 'His father was present when Kaikeyi gave Rama the order to go into exile. Maharaja Dasaratha did not object or rescind the order, as he could well have done. Whatever the influences on Kaikeyi, whatever Manthara's witchery, whatever the plot behind these doings, the fact is that your father agreed to Kaikeyi's demands and gave her those two boons that she rightfully demanded he fulfil. He stood by and let her send Rama into exile without saying a word of objection. She spoke in his name, and once issued in his name, that command cannot be disputed. It would be against dharma to do so. Rama is right. Now that he has been ordered into exile, he must go. And as his wife, I go with him as well.'

Lakshman stared at her for a long moment, then turned

back to Rama, his eyes brimming over with fresh tears. 'Bhai,' he said. 'You cannot go. I won't let you go! I will kill Manthara! The witch will not go unpunished.'

Rama placed a hand on Lakshman's mouth, silencing him. There were tears in Rama's eyes too, Sita saw. But he was holding them back somehow, using what strength of will she did not know.

'She will not go unpunished,' Rama said. 'You may be certain of that. For karma and dharma govern us all, my brother. But those are matters beyond our control. For your own part, you will do nothing to dispute our father's wishes. If what you say is true, and I do not doubt it, then these may well be his very last wishes. Honour him then, honour Aja-putra Dasaratha. He once granted two boons to a woman who saved his life. Today he repaid those two boons by sending his own eldest son into exile. So be it. Let the name of Dasaratha be praised and remembered always, for he was an honourable man who kept his vows and fulfilled his promises, even at this terrible cost.'

'But Rama,' Lakshman said, weeping against his brother's hand, clinging to it like the last reed in a sinking swamp, 'it's an evil conspiracy. A plan engineered by Ravana through his witch Manthara. Don't you see?'

Rama nodded slowly. 'I see it all. But it doesn't change the fact that our father was honour-bound to fulfil those vows, and he did so. *Whatever the consequences, we must honour our father!*'

Lakshman shook his head, unable to accept it still.

'Rajkumar.'

Rama looked over his shoulder at the man who had spoken, at the ageing general standing behind Lakshman. Senapati Dheeraj Kumar had handed over Lakshman's arms to another man. His age-lined face was creased with unhappiness and anger. Sita could scarcely imagine what the man must feel at this moment, what every Ayodhyan would feel when the news spread.

'Senapati?'

'I understand that you are fulfilling your father's wishes. Upholding his honour. But bear with me a moment. Already the Kaikeyan guards have tried to take over the command chain and been thrown down. They are under arrest, and their colleagues across the city are being dug out and put under arrest as well. Just before I rode out here at Rajkumar Lakshman's request, I received news that Rani Kaikeyi herself has just secured the required mandate from the council for her son Bharat's ascension. It is official now. I do not blame the council. They could not but vote otherwise, since the maharaja himself willed it so. Even Pradhan-mantri Sumantra and Guru Vashishta have agreed that despite the sorcery used and the undue influence applied, Maharaja Dasaratha did indeed grant Rani Kaikeyi her two rightful boons. And in accordance with his wishes, those boons must be honoured.'

The general paused as a fresh flurry of activity broke out from the direction of the palace. It was Pradhan-mantri Sumantra, Sita saw, riding towards them at a breakneck gallop, followed by a throng of PFs.

The senapati went on in his measured military way. 'But as a Suryavansha prince, you are also obligated to the people of this great kingdom. Not just the army, but the citizenry as well. To every man, woman and child of this great nation. I do not doubt that a sizeable section of the army as well as the general populace will dispute the council's decision. They will not accept the argument of vows being fulfilled and dharma being followed. Many may interpret this very act as being against dharma, for dharma demands that a king's first duty is to his kingdom, not himself. Even as we stand here debating these issues, the news is spreading like wildfire through the cities. People who had expected to wake to the brightest dawn in Kosala's history are being rudely accosted by this harsh, terrible sandesh. *Rama is exiled! Bharat is to be king!* The people will not accept these things as easily as you did, my prince. They will insist on seeing you personally and knowing that you are well and unharmed, that you choose to go into exile willingly, and are not being coerced at sword's point as some will suspect. that you—'

'Then tell them,' Rama said as Sumantra reined in his horse and dismounted, breathless. 'Tell everyone that I do this of my own free will. That I myself choose to go into exile to honour my father's wishes. Tell them that Bharat, my brother, is a capable and honourable heir and he will make a great king. I take pride and pleasure in his ascension and will not return to contest it. And even at my exile's end, after fourteen years, I will not contest it. Bharat will rule until the end of his days or as long as he wishes. Tell the army, tell the people, tell one and all that Rama Chandra says this. Tell them that there are to be no riots, no disputes, no more fighting amongst ourselves. Only yesterday we had an enemy at our gates; this is no time to be fighting one another.'

Rama stopped and looked over the faces of the size-able crowd now assembled before him, soldiers and ostlers, palace guards and PFs, all watching Rama as if they were seeing their own hopes die with his departure. They had come up in ones and twos and groups, and had stood silently and listened raptly to the last wishes of a prince they might never see again. Several of them, soldiers as well, were weeping openly, tears glittering like steel as they fell on burnished armour.

'Spoken like a king,' Senapati Dheeraj Kumar said into the silence that followed Rama's speech.

Rama acknowledged the praise with a bow of his head. 'Then carry out these last orders,' he said to the senapati, and to the pradhan-mantri standing beside him. 'Do so in the interests of my people and my kingdom. Let no drop of blood be shed in my name.'

He looked again at the crowd that now faced him, and nodded briefly at them. *You shall say no farewells.*

'Come, Janaki,' he said to Sita. And began walking towards the rear gate.

Sita walked with him.

After a moment, the sound of bare feet pattering on the hardened mud-road grew, and Lakshman appeared alongside them, walking on the far side of Rama. Rama and he exchanged a glance, and Sita saw that something passed between them that words could never express. Rama put his hand out and squeezed his brother's shoulder. Behind them, the crowd was murmuring and talking discontentedly. Someone began to wail, as in a funeral procession.

Sita and her husband and brother-in-law walked until they reached the rear gate. The guards posted on duty saluted them. She saw that they had shock and disbelief written across their faces, and tears glistening in their eyes, reflecting brightly in the daylight that had crept stealthily across the land. The three of them passed through the gates of Suryavansha Palace and walked on without looking back.

5

The doors to the sabha hall were open when Kausalya entered. She had already met the agitated council ministers outside, and Sumantra, who was leaving at a frantic run to catch up with Rama and Sita. Guru Vashishta had gone to speak to the shocked crowd assembling outside the city gates, to help prevent the riots that seemed certain to break out across the city. Sumitra was with Lakshman's bride, Urmila, comforting her, for it was a foregone conclusion that if Lakshman could not persuade Rama to return, then he would follow him into exile. *Or unto death*, Kausalya thought grimly. *That is true fealty. A brother and a wife who will leave everything at a moment's notice and go with Rama into fourteen years of exile as if it were but a visit to—*

'A flower-vale,' she said, realising that she was speaking her mind's innermost thoughts aloud as she walked up the long red carpetway to the royal dais at the far end of the vast hall. The sabha hall was deserted despite the enormity of the crisis going on. This was by order of the new First Queen herself. Kaikeyi had seen fit to suspend the council of ministers and disband the sabha samiti until after Bharat's ascension. Of course, she had done this only after the said council had formally approved the maharaja's decision to crown Bharat, not

Rama, as heir. Mantri Jabali, usually the most conservative, surly and reticent minister on the council, had flared up at Kaikeyi's high-handed pronouncement. *Suspend, disband and command all you like now*, he had said to Kaikeyi in the foyer outside, in full view of the watching palace guard, the rest of the council, and several sabha samiti representatives from across the kingdom. *Those who raise the sword of law to suit their own needs end up on the receiving end of the same sword before long.*

Virtually every last one of those present had applauded and cheered his words. Furious at this public rebuke, Kaikeyi had ordered the watching palace guards to arrest the mantri at once and throw him in the dungeons. When Captain Drishti Kumar had cleared his throat and informed the First Queen that this would violate law, since a minister of the council could only be arrested on certain grave charges, insulting a royal personage not being included in said list, Kaikeyi had ordered *him* arrested. Not surprisingly, this had evoked no response either.

And that was when Kaikeyi had ordered that the guard be changed at once; ordering her own Kaikeya personal guard to replace the Ayodhyan palace guard. That move had since backfired, and after a brief but not entirely bloodless clash, the security of the palace and the royal family was once more in Captain Drishti Kumar's able hands. But everyone knew that Kaikeyi was smarting from the series of rebukes and her first failure at power-play. Which was why the sabha hall was empty. Half the people who had business here now disdained to enter it, for fear of coming on the receiving end of Kaikeyi's ill-placed wrath, and the other half were not permitted to enter, by the maharani's own command. As Mantri Ashok had commented caustically, it was a fine way to run a kingdom.

But Kausalya was determined to do what she felt she had to do. She might have been divested of her title, reduced to Second Queen in one flash of an instant, her husband in a comatose state, her son thrown into exile, her world upturned and shaken out with brutal injustice, but she still had her strength, her will and her tongue. And she would not rest until she had shown Kaikeyi what it meant to play this game of thrones.

'Ah, the wronged mother comes to plead on her son's behalf.'

The voice dripped with all the sarcasm Kaikeyi could infuse into the words. The new First Queen looked shockingly out of place seated on the sunwood throne. Not only because the throne, an ancient and massive artefact carved from a single trunk of the rarest of rare trees and as much a part of Suryavansha history as the Seer's Tower, was reserved solely for the liege of the time, which in this case was still Dasaratha. Once Bharat was crowned liege-heir and formally sworn in as maharaja, he would earn the right to take his place up there on the great throne, but that had not happened yet. And no matter who the liege that sat upon it, the sunwood throne deserved more respect and dignity than Kaikeyi was conferring upon it. The new maharani of Kosala was sitting in a grossly disrespectful posture on the seat of power, one leg curled upon the throne, the other carelessly flung out at a rakish angle. Her blouse was askew, as if she had been recently engaged in some particularly passionate bout of love-making, revealing part of one breast and almost all of the other; her limbs were so weighted down with heavy jewels that were she to be put on a scale right now and her jewels on the other side of the same scale, the ornaments would easily outweigh her.

As she approached the dais, Kausalya didn't notice all

these finer points so much as take in the overall picture. The import of it was clear: Kaikeyi didn't care a fig for the seat she sat on, nor for the great tradition she had succeeded to today.

She was chewing paan, and after she spoke those galling words, she spat into a spittoon set by the left hand of the throne, the tobacco juice splashing partly on the rim of the brass container, mostly down its side, to drip disgustingly on to the tiger-skin pelts that carpeted the royal dais. A hundred of Bengal's finest striped beasts had died to make that pelt-pile, but to Kaikeyi it was no more than a rug.

'Come, come,' she said, making a slurping sound as she relished her betelnut and tobacco savoury. 'Bow, beg, prostrate, crawl, whatever you like. It won't make any difference. Your son is lost to you for ever.'

Kausalya reached the end of the dais and continued up the steps. She took them easily, despite their majestic height. Kaikeyi looked up at the last moment, saw her adversary climbing the dais rather than stopping before it as she had expected, and sat upright. Her blouse flaps fell open, revealing her breasts. 'How dare you?' she screeched, her voice rising two whole octaves with surprise. 'You can't come up here! Get away! Get away!'

Kausalya reached the throne and stopped. She had no desire to get any closer than this. For one, she had no wish to be spattered by the paan flecks that were flying from Kaikeyi's mouth as she yelled shrilly.

'You think this is a game,' Kausalya said, fighting to keep her voice level. 'A game of thrones. But it isn't. It's a game of souls, Kaikeyi. Souls.'

Kaikeyi had drawn both legs up on the throne, rearing back until her head touched the hard carved wood of the backrest. She was dwarfed by the seat despite her ample bulk. The sunwood throne had a way of making those who were small at heart seem small in stature as well. She saw that Kausalya wasn't attacking her physically as she'd expected, and relaxed slightly, resuming her chewing.

'Souls?' she said, then giggled hysterically. Betelnut juice oozed from the corner of her mouth. 'What's that supposed to mean? A game of souls?'

'It's the game you chose to play when you danced with the lord of demons, Kaikeyi,' Kausalya said. 'The game that brought you from lying drunken and naked on your back in my husband's bed to this great seat of power. Do you follow what I'm speaking of now, *First* Queen?'

Kaikeyi's eyes narrowed at Kausalya's words. 'Still jealous over that, *sister*-queen? Get over it. I was Dasaratha's first lust, and his last. His last, Kausalya. Do you follow what I'm speaking of?'

The revelation hit Kausalya like a slap. She had noticed Dasaratha's dishevelled clothes and untied langot when she had had him removed from the kosaghar back to his chambers, but the maharaja's very condition had made it impossible for her to think of such a thing. Now she knew. So the second queen and the daiimaa had somehow bewitched Dasaratha into performing the conjugal dance one final time with Kaikeyi. Devi alone knew what vile sorcery they had employed to achieve such an end.

Kausalya had also noticed the strange phenomenon of Dasaratha's appearance in the kosaghar. Despite his collapsed condition, the maharaja nevertheless seemed to look younger than he had done only hours earlier. She had put that down to her own stressed state at the time, but now it all made sense. The jal-bartan with the last dregs of some potion that Manthara had been clutching when they entered. The daiimaa had been pouring the last of it into Dasaratha's mouth when they had come into the kosaghar. And who knew how much more of the vile stuff Kaikeyi herself had made Dasa drink earlier? What the potion was, it was impossible to tell, after Manthara had shattered the vessel to shards, spilling the last of the concoction. What was certain was that it was no herbal mixture. Kausalya's memory still held fresh, vivid images of the day she had found Dasaratha lying in his bed, lips blue allegedly from the poison in the fruit punch Sumitra had mixed for him. A whole lot of things had become clear since the serving girl's appearance and demise, and any last vestiges of doubt were decisively swept away by Manthara's 'coming-out' in the kosaghar. The shrew and the witch, that was the enemy within that they were faced with, had been faced with for devi knew how long without their knowledge; they were the ones within the royal family that Guru Vashishta had sensed and spoken of at the secret meeting he had called in the seal room the night of Rama and Lakshman's departure to the Bhayanak-van. But even the great seer's powers had been obfuscated by the potent shakti of the Lord of Lanka. Ravana's armies might have been decimated by the release of the Brahm-astra at Mithila. But his spasas were still active and alive, here in the very heart of Ayodhya.

Not for long, Kausalya vowed. Not for long. If I have to fight them with my last breath, so be it. Whatever else happens, I will see to it that they do not prevail in the end. As the gods are my witness, I will rid Ayodhya of this unholy duo or die fighting them.

'You may have sapped him of his seed,' she said aloud now, giving Kaikeyi no opportunity to take pleasure in her vulgar revelation. 'But in doing so, you have also sapped him of his life. Do you know that your own country-men now speak of you with shifty eyes and low voices as a result of your doings in the kosaghar? They call you "king-slayer". Are you pleased?'

'Who says that?' Kaikeyi rose to her feet, stumbling over her own sari's hem. 'Which son of a whore dares to speak of me that way? Show him to me! I will have him torn apart by stallions and feed the remnants to the city dogs!'

Kausalya took care to stay out of range of the betelnut spittle issuing from Kaikeyi's mouth. The new First Queen's breath, even from a distance of almost two yards, stank vilely of alcohol and some rancid thing she couldn't identify. What was in that paan anyway? The stuff dripping down the sides of the spittoon didn't look like normal betelnut and tobacco juice.

'How many will you torture and execute, Kaikeyi?' she asked. 'All of them? And once you're done dispensing this brutal brand of injustice, what then? Who will stand by you and help you rule this vast kingdom? Sitting the sunwood throne is no mean task. Women have sat it before, and ruled as wisely as men. For the kshatriya code does not distinguish between sexes. But man or woman, it takes a person of rare strength of character to wear that heavy crown and wield the sword of justice. Are you capable of taking on that task, and ruling under the shadow of accusations of murdering your own husband—'

'I didn't mean to kill him,' Kaikeyi screamed, her mouth an open red-black hole in her face. 'I told him to have the tonic. The tonic made him younger and healthier! He was so virile, so strong again . . . it was like the years, the illness, everything had fallen away. But he vomited it out. He put his fingers down his throat and induced himself to bring it all up! And he would not take any more, even when I begged and pleaded. Manthara said—'

She stopped abruptly. Looked around and seemed to

grow aware of her surroundings, her situation. She looked down at the gold thali lying on the armrest of the throne. It was half filled with paans. They all seemed to contain the same purplish-red stuffing that produced the peculiar juice Kaikeyi had been spitting out. A look of horror came over Kaikeyi's face. She raised a hand and slapped the edge of the thali. It flew up into the air, cartwheeling front over back, spilling paans everywhere – Kausalya stepped back hurriedly to avoid a few – and flew to the left-hand side of the dais, there to crash and crash again until it came to a rolling halt and fell, ringing out one final time. Kaikeyi turned, and before Kausalya knew what she was doing, she was before her, clutching her hand tight enough to hurt, her eyes brimming with fat tears.

'You don't understand,' Kaikeyi said in a voice wholly unlike the arrogant loftiness with which she'd greeted Kausalya only moments earlier. 'She drugs me somehow. And controls me. Her voice is inside my head all the time now. Telling me what to do. And if I try to resist or fight her . . . she . . . she . . .'

Kaikeyi screamed. It was the banshee wail of a lost soul. Heart-rending and horrible, it raised the hackles on Kausalya's arms and the back of her neck. It was the kind of sound you might expect to hear from a mother whose only child had just died, not a queen-mother on the day of her son's coronation.

'Help me,' she sobbed, falling at Kausalya's feet, clinging to her hopelessly, helplessly. 'Help me, please. She makes me do these things. She made me do it all. I tried to reach out to you, to warn you, to warn Rama . . . in the street last night . . . the procession . . . you saw me . . . And later, before the wretched servant girl died . . . But it was too late already. She had a hold of me.' Kaikeyi shuddered. 'She was inside me, Kausalya! I can't describe how it feels. It's horrible! She's completely mad now, I think. Driven crazy by . . . She kept talking to me as if I was her master, master this and master that . . . but it was only her, speaking through me, answering herself . . . and all the while, I could only watch and hear and feel my body being used, but I had no control . . . except for moments like this, when she's distracted by something, or really communicating with her master.'

Kaikeyi clutched Kausalya's feet, striking them with her forehead repeatedly. 'I can't fight her any more, Kausalya. Help me. Save me. I'll die before I go on like this another moment. Please!'

Kausalya bent down, putting her arms around the shuddering, shaking woman. Her own mouth was dry, her heart thudding. Kaikeyi's scream had chilled her to the core; her confession had set her ablaze. She didn't know how much of this to believe and how much might be part of some new sinister scheme the duo had cooked up. But despite her better sense, she believed Kaikeyi. Most of all, she believed that this woman, the woman lying at her feet and sobbing her guts out, was the real Kaikeyi, pleasure-seeking, self-centred – even now Kaikeyi only thought of herself, not what she had done to Rama or Dasaratha under Manthara's evil influence – but not the arrogant, supremely in-control bitch who had greeted Kausalya when she had entered the sabha hall. *Yes*, she thought, *this is the woman who spoke to me through the mouth of the dying serving girl. This is our Kaikeyi, not Manthara's and Ravana's Kaikeyi.*

She was about to speak, to comfort and reassure the sobbing queen, when a brilliant flash of green light exploded, blinding her momentarily. She gasped, taken by surprise, and peered through the darkness that had suddenly descended.

Manthara stood on the royal dais. A corona of green flame flickered at the periphery of her contours, then faded away.

6

'Stand up,' the daiimaa said to Kaikeyi. 'Stand up and step away from that woman. She cannot help you now. Nobody can. Only I have the power to save you, Kaikeyi. Only I.'

Kaikeyi remained prone on the dais at Kausalya's feet. She looked up at Kausalya, her face streaked with smudged collyrium and ornamental colours, the sindhoor in her parting oozing like blood down her forehead. 'No! I won't do it any more. I won't let you use me! Leave me alone, Manthara!'

Manthara chuckled softly, the sound echoing in the vastness of the great hall. 'Come now, my queen. There is much to be done yet. Your son will arrive soon, to be crowned liege-heir. And before the ending of this very day, he shall inherit the throne and become king as well.' Her eyes looked slyly at Kausalya. 'For we all know that his highness will not last this day. It is your good fortune to see your son rise to the stature of prince-heir and then king within the space of a single day. Rise and embrace your fortune.'

'Bharat's gone to his grandfather's house,' Kaikeyi said, her voice turning falsetto with stress. 'He knows nothing of what happened here. He will not return in time for any coronation.'

The daiimaa clucked her tongue disapprovingly. 'Don't you remember anything, my rani? You had riders sent to Kaikeya the instant Dasaratha caved in and granted you the two boons. Bharat would have received the news and left Kaikeya hours ago. He will be here at any moment. Would you have him see you in this sorry state? You are a queen-mother now. If you cannot act like one, for his sake at least look the part!'

Kaikeyi stared up at Kausalya, pleading with her eyes. She shook her head from side to side, repeating over and over again, 'Save me save me save me.'

Kausalya swallowed and looked up at the daiimaa. Manthara was standing beside the sunwood throne, dwarfed by its stature. Her bent grey-haired head came barely to the pedestal of the throne. She had her hand on the pedestal, carved to resemble a lion's foot, and was stroking and caressing it slowly, like one might pet a favourite dog or parrot.

'You have what you want already,' Kausalya said. 'Leave Kaikeyi out of the rest. Set her free from your power. Let her be herself again.'

Manthara smiled and frowned at the same time. 'Herself? And who might that be? What woman is it you speak of, Rani Kausalya? A snivelling, self-centred, self-indulgent, hedonistic woman whose only goal is to pleasure herself into oblivion from dawn to dusk? A spoilt overgrown brat of a girl who has never truly matured over the mental age of fifteen? A selfish bitch of a she-whelp who cares about nothing and nobody but herself? Is that the woman you want her to become again?'

'If that is all she was, then yes, let her be just that,' Kausalya said. 'But a lot of those faults were encouraged by you. That's very clear now. From the outset you were manipulating and shaping her to suit your own dark purposes, just as you yourself have been manipulated by your evil master.'

A dark cloud passed across Manthara's sneering features. 'I've had enough of your rubbish talk about manipulations and misshapings. First old whitebeard, now you. I'll advise you to watch your tongue when speaking of my master, Rani Kausalya. Even being Rama's mother won't help you much if he takes offence at your blasphemous accusations.' Her lips curled in a snarling smile. 'After all, he can hardly come running all the way from Dandaka-van every time you are in trouble, now can he?'

Kausalya bit her cheek to hold back the retort that was on the tip of her tongue. No, she admonished herself. It would not do to cross words with this vile creature. Manthara was only a tool in the hand of a greater power. If she was to win this war, if not this battle, then it was against that greater power that she must pit her strength.

'I have a message to give you, Manthara,' Kausalya said quietly. 'A message you must pass on to your master, wherever he might be at this time. Can you do that?'

Manthara peered at her suspiciously. Her eyes were filmed over with some condition of her age, Kausalya saw. By rights she should have been partly or wholly blind, yet she was able to see. Then Kausalya realised that the occlusions had not been there before. As recently as Holi feast day, she recalled seeing the daiimaa's eyes quite clear and grey as ever. The explanation for this unnatural phenomenon came to her in a flash of insight. *He has blinded her, that she might see only that which he wishes her to see. So he has given her cataracts in both eyes and made her blind to human reality. Everything she sees is distorted by the Asura shakti she uses in place of natural eyesight. And the more she uses that unholy shakti, the more he corrupts and controls her.*

'What message might that be?' Manthara asked suspiciously. 'You'll be sorry if you try to pull some sorcerous trick on me, rani. Don't go underestimating my powers. I may have laid low all these years, but every moment, every season, I was gaining great vidya and shakti from my master. Now I am able to take on any seer you pit against me, no matter how much brahman shakti he may wield.'

Kausalya held out her hands, palms facing up. 'Do I look like I mean to attack you?' She indicated the empty, cavernous sabha hall. 'Do you see anyone else here besides me? Or perhaps you think I might speak a simple mantra and call upon the devi to grant me her strength.' Kausalya paused, indicating a portrait of the devi that hung on the wall behind the dais. 'And her trishul as well.'

Manthara started. For a second, her eyes flashed to the portrait, reacted, then blinked rapidly. The daiimaa visibly fought to regain control of her emotions before she glowered again at Kausalya, her eyes flashing green this time. 'Don't patronise me, rani. You had your say, now speak your message and get lost from here. I have better things to do than to stand around and banter with you all day. Speak!'

Kausalya took a deep breath and released it slowly, using the pranayam method to calm her senses and slow her metabolism. If her judgement was correct, she ought to have bought enough time by now for the others assembled outside to play their part. Yes, it was time to act now, before the old witch grew more suspicious and simply blew her away with a blast of her Asura sorcery. She wasn't afraid of personal harm coming to her as much as she was anxious not to lose this precious opportunity to disarm and disable this cursed thorn in the side of her family and future. Manthara must go, and she must go now, before she turned Ayodhya itself into a seething swamp of Asura evil.

And the burden of ridding the land of the witch fell to Kausalya. Now. Here. At this very place and time.

'Listen well then, old woman. This message is for your master, he who calls himself Lord of Lanka. Ravana! Hear these words now! And feel the power and might of brahman towering before you!'

She stepped forward and bent down to pick up the still weeping Kaikeyi lying on the floor. 'Rise, sister,' she said gently. 'The time has come for you to think and act for yourself, not as a pawn in this game of thrones and souls.'

And before Manthara could grasp what she was doing, Kausalya placed her hands tightly around Kaikeyi's head and began to chant the Sanskrit slokas Guru Vashishta had infused into her mind before she had entered the sabha hall.

// Asuryah namah tey loka aandhyen tamasavratya //
// Tan asthey preytyabhigshanthi yet keych atma-
*   hanah janah. //*

Manthara screamed. The foulest curse Kausalya had ever heard was spat from the green witch's lips, aimed at Kausalya's heart. It was less an abuse than a spell. Something struck Kausalya directly in the chest with the impact and unbelievable painfulness of a dagger flung at her breast. She staggered back, teetering on the brink of the dais. Manthara screeched again, furious at being outwitted, and threw her hand out, palm facing Kausalya, making a shoving gesture. Kausalya felt as if the hand were at her breast, pushing with savage force, rather than ten yards away. She lost her balance and fell violently off the dais, arms cartwheeling instinctively.

Devi protect me! she cried silently, then she hit the ground with a bone-crushing crunch and lost consciousness.

She came round a few seconds later to see Manthara dragging Kaikeyi by the hair towards the throne. She blinked, and stars flashed before her eyes, blazing white and then black and then red. She tried to feel if she had broken anything. She couldn't tell for certain, but she didn't think so, although the back of her head ached terribly, and her elbow was sore too. Luckily for her, the sabha hall was carpeted from wall to wall to accommodate all the samiti representatives who sat cross-legged on the floor.

She struggled to her feet and called out, 'Kaikeyi, listen to me. The spell was broken the instant I uttered that mantra. You have been freed of the witch's curse. Resist her, fight her if you must. She has no more power over you.'

'SILENCE!' Manthara screamed, turning to point one gnarled finger at Kausalya. A spear of light as thin as a longbow arrow shot from the tip of her finger straight to Kausalya. It even felt like an arrow when it struck her in her right shoulder, the impact powerful enough to lift her off her feet and fling her further across the sabha hall. She landed several yards away, but regained her feet almost immediately. Agony exploded at the juncture of her right shoulder and collarbone.

'Kaikeyi,' she shouted. 'Fight her!'

This time Manthara could take it no longer. She let go of Kaikeyi and turned fully towards Kausalya.

'Enough!' she cawed. That was what it sounded like to Kausalya, like a crow cawing in indignation. 'This time you transgress too far! For twenty years I've watched you prosper and grow from strength to strength, prancing around like the gods' own gift to the world. Acting as if you're better than all of us lesser mortals. Who do you think you are anyway? Just because you bend your head in prayer, that doesn't make you pious and free of sin!'

'No,' Kausalya replied, standing as straight as she could without revealing any of the pain she felt from the sorcerous blows. 'That comes only from really being pious and free of sin. Are you free of sin, Manthara? When the devas weigh your sins against the rest of your karma, do you think they'll be pleased with all you've done? Do you think you'll be rewarded or punished?'

'The devas have no hold over me,' the green witch said scornfully. 'I am in the employ of the Dark Lord now. His power is greater than any other. He protects and rewards me. You dare to doubt his shakti? You dare to defy him? Then it's time that you learned just what he is capable of.'

And Manthara raised both her hands and began chanting a mantra aloud. The language she spoke was alien and terrible to human ears. Beside her, Kaikeyi cried out and clapped her hands over her ears, her face twisting with pain. Even at this distance, Kausalya's ears were assailed by the sound. It was the most awful, bestial tongue she had ever heard spoken. *Rakshasa, she's speaking rakshasa.*

A ball of fire the size of a wine-bladder coalesced between Manthara's parted hands. It blazed green and black and tiny lightning bolts flashed within its core. The sabha hall was filled with a roaring wind, as every atom and molecule in the air was dragged inexorably towards the unnatural phenomenon called up by the Asura mantra. Manthara turned the burning ball of sorcerous fire around, not actually touching it with her hands but able to manipulate it somehow. It grew stormier, like a thundercloud building up an electrical charge before unleashing its fury. Kausalya raised her hands instinctively before her breast, then lowered them slowly. *I can't fend off that thing like a pillow thrown at me.* She saw the difference in scale between the two earlier blows Manthara had flung at her, and estimated that if they were respectively a dagger-throw and then an arrow-shot, by that reckoning this weapon would be akin to a lead weight flung at her by a siege machine. *It will shatter my bones like glass.*

Manthara reached a climax in her chanting, concordant with the ball spinning faster, like a dervish out of control. The lightning in its core flashed brighter and louder, filling the entire sabha hall with its blinding green blaze and billowing like a gale through the chamber.

Kausalya braced herself for death. *If this is how you wish me to go, then so be it, maa.*

At the very last moment, just as Manthara raised her hands to unleash the ball of Asura witchfire, a figure staggered across the dais and fell on the daiimaa. Manthara was too absorbed in her chanting to see Kaikeyi come at her, and the rani shoved Manthara hard enough to throw her off balance. The witchfire ball spun out of control momentarily, shooting up to strike the ceiling above. The plaster and stone of the sabha hall ceiling shattered at the impact, showering down chips and shards and debris over both women. Manthara howled in frustration and rage and lashed out at Kaikeyi. Her hand struck the queen across her exposed midriff, leaving four sharply defined slashes, like those made by an animal's talons. *Or an Asura's.* Kaikeyi gasped and fell to her knees, clutching her belly. Blood welled up in the cuts. She looked up and her eyes met Kausalya's. *She's herself now, the spell is broken.* Then Kaikeyi keeled over and fell on to her face on the dais floor.

'No!' Kausalya shouted, running towards the dais. 'You've killed her! You'll pay for this, you witch!'

The ball of witchfire had bounced off the ceiling and fallen down again – straight into Manthara's hands once more. The witch shuffled forward, snarling in rage at Kausalya. 'She'll live,' the hunchback screamed. 'But you won't!'

And with all her strength she flung the witchfire ball at Kausalya.

Kausalya stopped dead in her tracks. *Devi help me*, she cried silently. But the words came out aloud. 'Devi help me!' she heard herself say above the roaring of the wind and the green fire. And then the witchfire ball came at her like a thundercloud sent down to wreak death and destruction.

7

A sound like a thunderclap exploded in Kausalya's ears. Her vision was seared by a light so dazzling she could see only whiteness for several moments, whiteness tinged by a corona of flickering green. She thought she had lost consciousness, had lost life itself, but when one moment passed, then another, and she realised she still stood on both feet, still felt her heart thumping like a dhol-drum in her chest, and smelled the same acrid odour that had pervaded the kosaghar after Manthara had used her Asura sorcery to vanish, only then did she accept that she was still very much alive.

She opened her eyes and saw a chiaroscuro of flashing, flickering lights, winking in and out of existence. She waited, praying for it to pass, and in another moment or two she began to discern faintly, as through a thick fog, the outlines of the pillars of the sabha hall, the royal dais with the great silhouette of the sunwood throne, and two figures, one standing, one lying prone on the dais. She blinked and squinted, straining to see, and like a miasma out of swamp-mist, her vision swam back into focus.

Manthara stood over the prone, still form of Kaikeyi, her hands clawed into a bestial rictus. The green witch-flame that had blazed in her eyes and fingertips and at her contours had vanished. She stood in her usual hunched posture, grimacing in Kausalya's direction. It took Kausalya a moment to understand that what she had taken for a grimace was actually intended to be a smile. Who was she smiling at? Kausalya? No, her gaze was directed slightly to Kausalya's right.

Kausalya turned her face.

And only then did she become aware of the figure standing beside her, a figure that had at least a head of height on her, and was powerfully muscled and well built, wielding a mace in one hand and a shield in the other. A shield that was now cracked and splintered, its shattered front smouldering with the last vestiges of the witchfire. Then the whole situation became crystal clear. While Manthara and she had waged their ill-balanced battle of wits and words, someone had entered the sabha hall, unseen by both women in their emotional distress. This person had seen Manthara wield the witchfire, and had covered the distance just in time to put his shield between Kausalya and the flying ball of destruction. As Kausalya tried to make out the features of the face of her protector, standing with only part of his left profile visible, the man let the broken shield's leather grips slip loose of his forearm and the shield dropped to the floor, breaking into three separate pieces on impact, each one smoking like lightning-scorched wood. Then the man raised his mace and stepped forward, towards the dais.

'Bharat, my ward,' Manthara called plaintively, raising her hands in feigned supplication. 'You return not a moment too soon. There is much need of you here, my boy. So much has happened this past night.'

'So it would seem,' Bharat said in his rough baritone, so much like his father's voice, so unlike Rama's ear-pleasing tenor. 'And all wrought by your Asura sorcery, I warrant.'

Manthara's face twisted in a parody of dismay. 'My Asura sorcery? No, my lad. You have been deceived. Did the old preceptor tell you that lie? Do not believe it. It is she who wields the sorcery. She is the Dark Lord's spasa! *She!*'

Her finger pointed, not surprisingly, at Kausalya.

Bharat turned to look at his stepmother. His face and voice were gentle as he addressed her with genuine concern and affection. 'Maa, are you all right? Did she hurt you with her witchblast?'

Kausalya reached out and touched him on the forehead with her fingertips. 'I am well, now that you are here.'

'I would have entered sooner, but there was a commotion outside. Thank the devas I arrived when I did. She meant to kill you with that last blow.'

'No matter,' she said. 'It served its purpose. Now, do you believe what I tried to tell you when you arrived?' She had tried to explain the complexities of the situation on his return from Kaikeya – without much success.

'I did not doubt it then, but now I am armed with the undeniable evidence of my own eyes.' He gestured towards Manthara. 'How could we have allowed this evil to flourish within our midst?'

'We did not, son. Evil insinuated itself into the cracks of our home's foundation. Even Guru Vashishta's visionary powers could not identify it before now. But now that it is exposed, it must be destroyed. You know what to do. Go with Devi's grace and my blessings.'

'Mother.' He straightened and turned back to face the dais.

'What are you two whispering over there in the shadows?' Manthara cried out. 'Bharat, my boy, do not listen to her lies and half-truths. She seeks only to deceive you and regain the kingdom for Rama!'

Bharat's voice resounded through the hall. 'The kingdom *is* Rama's. As the eldest, he is the only one entitled to sit the sunwood throne. Dharma demands it.'

She cackled. 'Not any more. Dharma has seen fit to send him to the Dandaka woods, into exile. You are now the prince-heir, to be sworn in today. And if your father's sad decline continues, then you may well find yourself sitting on this very throne today as well!'

Bharat took two steps forward, hefting his mace. 'Do not speak of my father thus! May he live a thousand years more than you. You cannot deceive me any more. Everyone knows what you really are now, *green witch*!'

At the use of that name, Manthara's face hardened into a mask of fury again. For an instant, Kausalya was certain the woman was going to unleash another blast of witchfire, this time directed at Bharat. But with visible effort the daiimaa regained control of herself and smoothed her face as best as she could into an approximation of hurt. 'You would call your old daiimaa a witch? Mantharadaiimaa? I who bathed and fed and clothed and cleansed you through your childhood? Sang you lullabies and played with you in the gardens of Suryavansha Palace? Bounced you on my knee until you grew too big for me to carry?'

Bharat took another step toward the dais, gradually closing the distance between himself and the daiimaa – and his unconscious mother – without making it too apparent. 'You played the part well, old crone. But I'm no longer fooled. An old daiimaa doesn't cavort upon the sunwood throne, and use Asura sorcery to strike down her own mistresses!'

Manthara glanced down at the prone form of Kaikeyi lying at her feet. 'What? No, my son. You have it all wrong. Kausalya-rani and Kaikeyi-maa were having a squabble here. Kausalya was loath to let Kaikeyi become queen-mother and wrest her power away, so she approached your mother and attacked her on false pretexts. I was only using the limited brahman powers I have acquired over the years to fend her off before she finished the job and did your mother further harm!'

'Enough, hag!' Bharat moved closer yet, now only a few yards from the stairwell of the dais. 'Unbeknownst to you, while you were wielding your sorcerous blasphemy, Shatrugan and I were watching from without the hall, aided by the true brahman shakti of Guru Vashishta. Give up your feeble excuses and tales, I have already heard you incriminate yourself with your own vile tongue.'

Manthara stood silent. Bharat took her silence to mean surrender of a sort and moved openly now towards the stairs leading up to the dais. When Manthara spoke again, it was without the affected whingeing tone she had assumed earlier, but in a level voice that crackled with menace.

'So what of it?' Manthara said. 'What if I am the green witch? Is not your guru a sorcerer too? Is not your beloved brahman shakti a form of magic as well? Why should it be that when an ordained brahmin sage, a *man*, mind you, wields the power, it is a thing to be lauded and admired. But when a mere kshatriya, a *woman*, does so, I am a witch?'

Bharat shook his head, holding his mace in both hands as he placed his foot on the first step. 'This has nothing to do with being a man or a woman, as you well know. It has everything to do with fealty and treachery. Instead of obeying the tenets of dharma and being loyal to my mother and our family, you chose to go over to the side of our greatest enemy. Not just the enemy of this house, but the enemy of all mankind. It is that which condemns you, Manthara!'

'Who are you to judge me, whelp?' she said, and a cold chill seized Kausalya at the changed tone of voice. Until now Manthara had shown Bharat a certain grudging respect, but with these words the bile and venom in the daiimaa's heart finally rose to the surface. 'You, who have everything to gain from my work. See what I have done for you. I ousted Rama and put you in his stead. I have made you crown-prince of Ayodhya, heir to the greatest Arya kingdom!'

'Hear me well, green witch,' Bharat said, matching Manthara's bilious outburst with an iron grimness. 'I will not wear a crown wrested from my brother's brow. I love Rama more than you can ever know, or understand. By unseating him from his legacy, you have roused my wrath. I will never sit that throne as long as Rama lives.'

Manthara stared at him, her eyes goggling with disbelief. 'You would deny all this?' She flung her hands out, encompassing the hall and the palace around them. 'All the wealth and power and honour in the world? For what? What will you get by defending your brother's birthright? He is gone into exile, without even a word of farewell to his own mother! He is a slave to dharma! Do you think he will return to accept the throne and the crown now? Never! If you believe this, then you understand Rama even less than I do! Rama is gone, you fool. But Ayodhya remains. Take it. Grasp the goddess of opportunity with both hands and put her on your lap. She is yours now! Yours!'

Bharat stepped up on the dais proper, looming over Manthara even from yards away. 'The goddess belongs to no one, witch. She comes in one door and goes out the other. But fealty, brotherhood, filial love, kinship, these last for ever. These are the true rewards of dharma, not gilded thrones and elephant-loads of gold.'

'What would you have then?' Manthara demanded, her voice rising in accompaniment with her temper. 'Brahmins chanting your praises in the temples? Bards singing odes to your great deeds and victories in the taverns? Phaw! A thousand years from now, your deeds and your victories will be forgotten, boy! Your filial love and devotion to your brothers will be a mere footnote in the annals of history.'

'At least it will be a footnote. You will not even merit that much, traitoress.'

Manthara screamed then, screamed at the top of her lungs, as loudly as she could manage without the use of actual sorcery, '*I am doing all this for you! Only for you, you ingrate of a whelp!*'

Bharat's answer was deathly quiet. 'No. You are doing it all for your master, the lord of Asuras.'

He had reached within striking distance of her. He stood only a yard away from Manthara, less than that much from his unconscious mother. He hefted the mace, raising it in his right hand. He towered above the hunchbacked old daimaa like a giant before a misshapen dwarf. The contrast was so stark that if Kausalya had not known what treacherous evil that deceptively feeble-seeming old woman was capable of doing, she would herself have cried out to Bharat, begging him to stop. As it was, her heart was in her mouth when Bharat raised the heavy mace, its plating of beaten gold gleaming in the torchlight. It was one thing to defend oneself against Asura sorcery, wholly another matter to strike down a defenceless woman.

But she's not defenceless, she told herself severely. *She could strike him down in a trice if she chose. The power she wields is no less destructive than that great mace he holds.*

As if sensing this, Manthara made no move to defend herself. No green flame flickered in her eyes, no witch-fire blazed between her palms. Her hands lay by her sides, twisted into fists but doing nothing except kneading themselves.

Bharat hesitated. Kausalya could almost feel the doubt prickle in his mind at that instant. *He feels the shame of it too, the shame of striking down an unarmed, deformed old woman in cold blood.*

Manthara sneered up at him. 'Go on then. Smash me down. Lift your mace and destroy me with a blow. Let us see how dharma justifies the murder of an unarmed woman, that too one who cared for you as her own child through your growing years. Go on, Dasaratha-putra! Kill me now and earn your place in history for ever!'

Bharat glanced down at his unconscious mother, his eyes lingering on the welts that criss-crossed her belly, the blood pooled beneath her body on the tiger-skin rug. *He's trying to find a valid justification for what he's about to do,* Kausalya thought. Then, as if coming to a decision, he raised the mace again, his handsome face set in a grim mask of determination. He lifted the great metal weight high above his head, his back and chest and shoulder muscles standing out in clear relief, bunching powerfully. For one endless moment he stood poised that way. Despite her bravado and venomous diatribes, Manthara cringed at the sight, at the certain death that hung above her head, preparing to come crashing down like the hammer of Indra, meting out bloody justice. A sickly look came over the old crone's face, and in that instant Kausalya saw what might have been genuine fear and remorse in the daiimaa's expression.

Then, with a great sigh, like an elephant setting down the heaviest load, Bharat lowered the mace and stood aside, hanging his head with regret. Manthara, staring blankly up at the spot where the mace had been a moment ago, lowered her eyes. Understanding flooded her face, filling it with colour and life once more. 'Bharat, my son, you see the light at last. I did it all for you, my boy. Only for you. If you will but accept these gifts I have wrested for you—'

Bharat raised an arm, warding off her words, blocking his view of her, as if he could not bear to look at Manthara's face. 'I do not hear you any more. I do not see you any more. You are no longer human. No more one of us than a mist-wraith or a graveyard ghoul. I banish you from this house for ever. If you ever cross the threshold of Suryavansha Palace again, may Devi herself strike you down in her fury, for I will not spare you again as I do now. I bid you go from this place at once. Take nothing, for you have taken enough from us already. Go from here and never return.'

Silence hung from the eaves of the cavernous hall when his words had faded. Manthara stood gaping at him with her mouth open and her hands hanging limply by her sides, stunned.

'Go before I kill you,' Bharat said, not shouting, but speaking in a voice so potent with threat that even Kausalya's hackles rose. Manthara staggered back, falling over her own feet in terror. She stumbled and struck her head against the pedestal of the sunwood throne. Recovering, she stared one last time at Bharat's face, as if convincing herself of what she was seeing and hearing.

A look of pure hatred came over her face, a look so evil that Kausalya almost cried out to Bharat, *Strike her down, strike her down now, or have her shadow hanging over us for ever; kill her and be done with it.*

But she could not bring herself to say the words aloud. Because she knew that what Bharat had done was right. Whatever the hag had done to them, whatever evil she had wrought, it would be ten times worse for them to stain their own hands with her blood. Bharat had done the just thing in sparing her. A painful and immeasurably difficult thing, but the right thing. Even Rama would have done no differently. *He will make a good king*, she thought, even in that moment of desolation and loss. As good a king as Rama would have been. The realisation pierced her heart, causing a moment of pure agony. In that instant, Kausalya truly accepted her loss, and the kingdom's loss as well. Rama was gone. And yet Bharat had done right in sparing the life of the witch who was responsible for Rama's absence.

Upon the dais, Bharat, finished with Manthara, set his mace down and knelt before his mother, checking her pulse and breath in anxious concern.

That was when Manthara struck back.

The green witch raised her clawed hands and screamed again, as she had done before raising the witchfire ball to strike at Kausalya. Then she began to chant some arcane Asura mantra, perhaps the same one she had uttered earlier, it was impossible to say. She chanted and raved, spittle flew from her lips, and her hands rose and fell in a rictus of rage and frustration.

But nothing happened.

No green fire flashed.

No witchfire ball appeared.

No invisible darts or daggers struck at either Bharat or Kausalya.

After a long moment of shocked silence, Manthara lowered her hands, staring at them in disbelief. 'My lord?' Her voice cracked in dismay. 'My lord, why have you deserted me now of all times? Now when I need your shakti most? Give me power, my lord. Let me complete the task you have entrusted unto me. Let me destroy this family and wipe their last traces from the face of the earth!'

She fell to her knees, sobbing and raising her arms to the ceiling as she screeched her banshee screech again. '*Give me shakti, my lord!*'

But nothing happened. Nothing extraordinary took place. The green witch was gone. In her place there was only an old hunchbacked, wizened daiimaa, kneeling at the threshold of her own ruin, weeping tears of angry frustration.

8

They were outside the city and on the raj-marg when Sumantra caught up with them. The pradhan-mantri rode up alongside, reining in the six-horse team pulling his personal chariot. He stepped down on to the king's road, paying no heed to the dust of his own passage swirling around him, and strode to where they had stopped at the sound of the chariot's approach. The prime minister prostrated himself on the road, touching Rama's feet.

'Rama!' he cried. 'Rama!' When he looked up, his age-lined face was wreathed in tears. 'Grave injustice has been done today. A grave injustice.'

Lakshman fought back his own emotions as he watched Rama raise the broken-hearted man to his feet. Blinking away more than mere dust from his eyes, he saw that several pedestrians and mounted travellers had stopped to stare at the odd sight of the country's foremost statesman prostrating himself before what appeared to be a lowly janitor, for Rama and Sita were still cloaked in the garb of chamars.

Lakshman glanced around, keeping a wary eye on the crowd that began to gather quickly. The raj-marg was unusually busy for this hour. After the curfews and omnipresent threat of Asura invasion that had darkened the Arya nations these past weeks, the clouds had parted to allow the sun of peace to shine through. Today's coronation had put the silverfoil on the mithai, officially lifting all curfews and travel restrictions. These people gathering around curiously were from all over the kingdom, come to Ayodhya for trade, exchange, as well as to see the future king being crowned. He wondered how they would react if they knew that their future king was right here amongst them, clad in a cleaner's grimy clothes and the dust of the road, making his way into exile?

'Sumantra,' Rama said, embracing the weeping prime minister. 'Good Sumantra. Whatever is done is done. It is not meet that you follow us like this. You must return to the palace at once. My brother Bharat will have need of your decades of experience and your sage counsel. Ayodhya and Kosala have need of you. The sunwood throne and Suryavansha Palace need you.'

'I do not serve brick and stone, gold and dust,' the prime minister said, uncaring of the tears flowing freely down his face. 'I serve the Ikshwaku Suryavanshas, the noblest Aryas since the beginning of time. And you, my lord, are the descendant of Surya-deva and Manu, the great progenitors of that great dynasty. You are the true heir to the Suryavansha throne. Therefore, dharma dictates that I serve you, my lord Rama.'

Rama reached out, gently wiping the tears from Sumantra's lined cheeks with his bare hands. 'Weep no more, chacha. For you are as a brother to my father, and so have my brothers and I called you chacha since we were able to speak. Listen well to my words now. You will still serve me by serving my last wishes. Go now, return to Ayodhya and await my brother's return. Help Bharat rule wisely and well, long may he prevail.'

Sumantra seemed to regain a measure of control at Rama's strong, calming words. *When Rama speaks, even wild beasts cease to roar and snarl*, Lakshman thought.

It was an old saying in Ayodhya, one that had some measure of truth, for when they were boys in Guru Vashishta's ashram, Rama had displayed an extraordinary affinity with animals and a remarkable talent for soothing even the wild beasts of the forest by the hermitage. But grief was a more difficult animal to soothe.

'Will you not reconsider?' Sumantra asked, looking up at the face of his prince with heart-rending pathos. 'Will you not return and save us all from the darkness that looms endlessly ahead?'

Rama lowered his hands, still damp with Sumantra's tears. 'What looms ahead is merely destiny, chacha. As long as my brother rules, the sun will continue to shine brightly on the sunwood throne and those who seek out its justice. If there are shadows, they are only those cast by the sun itself, for wherever there is sunlight, there must be shadow as well, its twin in nature. As for my path, it is set upon this road that leads eventually to the edge of the Northwoods, thence to proceed to the remote jungle of Dandaka-van, according to the terms of my exile decided by my father and my mother Kaikeyi.'

He raised his chin, indicating the marg ahead. 'And now we must resume our journey, good Sumantra. For we have a long way to go yet, and I wish to cross the Kosala kingdom's border before nightfall.'

'Hold but a moment, Rama,' Sumantra said, putting his hand out. 'If you must go, if you will brook no other alternative, if this is the karma that you have chosen to accept for yourself,' he dipped his head respectfully to Sita and Lakshman, 'and for your new bride and your good brother, if this is what you must do, then at least let me carry you in my chariot as far as the road allows.'

Rama hesitated, glancing at the chariot. Lakshman used the brief pause to look around once more. The crowd had swelled surprisingly fast. Or not surprisingly, when you considered the exceptionally busy traffic on the raj-marg today, and the fact that it wasn't every day people saw their prime minister weeping at the feet of their prince-heir on the public highway. From the whispers and looks being exchanged by people in the crowd, he could see that their identity was no longer a secret. Had Sumantra not appeared, they could have continued to walk unrecognised down the road. But now, after hearing the words spoken by the pradhan-mantri and Rama, nobody remained in any doubt as to who they were. In another few moments this crowd would begin to clamour and demand to know what was going on. Why was their prince travelling in this lowly garb? Where was he heading with his wife and brother on his own coronation day? What was going on in Ayodhya?

So it was with great relief that Lakshman heard Rama say at last, 'I see no violation of my orders in doing so, chacha. On behalf of all three of us, I shall be glad to accept your offer.'

As Sumantra ran to unlatch and lower the foot-steps that made boarding the chariot easier, Lakshman sidled closer to Rama.

'Bhai,' he said softly, 'it would be best if we depart as quickly as possible. There is no telling how these people may take the news of your exile once their hearts accept the evidence of their ears.'

'Fret not, Lakshman,' Rama replied just as quietly. 'They are all good Kosalans. Whatever their reaction, it will be motivated by love and concern, nothing more. We have nothing to fear from our own people.'

Lakshman wasn't very sure of that. Even as Sita climbed aboard the chariot, followed by Rama, he glanced nervously around at the considerable crowd that now filled the highway. They were all murmuring and muttering unhappily, bending mouths to ears and debating the extraordinary scene that had unfolded before them, and what it might mean. A portly trader with a wagonload of grain called out anxiously as Lakshman climbed up on the chariot. He spoke in one of the regional dialects, obscured by a thick western accent. Lakshman didn't understand anything he said except the one word, 'Rama'. The man was answered by a group of carpet-makers with the tools of their trade slung around their waists. Instantly, pandemonium broke out. The crowd surged forward, reaching out for the chariot, calling out plaintively.

Rama looked as if he would speak to them, but Lakshman gestured quickly to Sumantra. The pradhan-mantri caught his meaning and nodded. With a deft flick of his wrist, the prime minister drove the horse-team forward, setting the chariot rolling down the raj-marg. The crowd fell back, but some ran after their dust-wake as if meaning to follow them. Soon the chariot caught speed and outpaced them easily. Lakshman breathed more easily as he turned to look forward. It felt good to be mobile again. *For probably the last time in fourteen years*, he thought bitterly. *There will be no chariots, wheelhouses or horses in the Dandaka-van. Your weary feet will be your only transport hereafter, Shanks's mare will be your only mount hereafter, so enjoy this ride while it lasts.*

All four of them were silent as the chariot rolled on down the king's road. They passed many people on the way, most on foot, the traders riding heavily burdened carts of goods and produce for selling at handsome Ayodhyan profits, and even a caravanserai or two, long lines of camel-borne tribes and enormous extended families numbering a hundred or more, all winding towards Ayodhya on this momentous day.

After a while, they passed the point at which their procession from Mithila had stopped on the way back home to Ayodhya, when Guru Vashishta had initiated the lighting up of the city before their astonished eyes. Glancing back, Lakshman could still picture the glorious effulgence of that magnificent display. Now the city lay shrouded by an early-morning mist wafting off the river, like a widow veiled in mourning. The brilliant lights, the cheers, the fluttering banners, the showers of rose petals, the shouts and chants of the crowd, the cries of the children, the yells of the maidens, all that seemed a memory of something that had happened several lifetimes ago rather than just yesterday. So much had changed in a single night. And, Lakshman thought grimly as he stood astride the rumbling chariot, gripping the hilt of his sword in an anger-tightened fist, much more would change yet. This was only the beginning. Fourteen long years stretched before them, like a desolate highway leading into a barren wilderness.

So this is the wages of heroism, he thought, and almost laughed aloud at the ludicrousness of their lot. *This is how we are repaid for risking our lives to serve our people? Your justice is great indeed, devas.*

Beside him, Rama stood in a silence matching his own, staring out at the road ahead, his profile carved in granite, smooth and unyielding. Not once during that long ride did Rama ever turn his face back to gaze upon the city. But Lakshman looked back several times, as if drawn by some powerful urge that would not release its hold on his heart.

Kaikeyi regained consciousness with a great inhalation of breath, as if she had been trapped in a windless tomb and was only now able to breathe freely once more. She gasped and coughed, choking in her eagerness to gulp in air. 'Jal,' she said as soon as she could manage speech again, 'jal.' *Water*.

Bharat offered a jal-bartan of water to her and she tried to take it, but her hands shook and the water spilt on the front of her sari. Bharat held the jal-bartan to her lips and she drank gratefully, emptying the vessel and then most of a second one. The simple act of slaking her thirst calmed her and she shut her eyes, leaning back against the cushioned head of the bed. She sat still a few moments, breathing.

When she opened her eyes again, there were tears in them. 'Dasa,' she said with more pain and regret than Bharat had heard her express before. 'Dasa!'

Her eyes turned to Bharat's face, searching, questioning. Her hand gripped his arm, fingernails digging into his flesh. 'It was a nightmare, only a nightmare. None of it was true, was it?'

Bharat couldn't bear to look at her face any more. At the anguish and regret of a woman who had been in the taloned grasp of a nightmare in which she committed unforgivable deeds; and now, awake again, could not live with the memories of those deeds. He glanced up at Shatrugran, standing on the other side of the bed. Shatrugan's eyes were still red from comforting his own mother. Kaikeyi followed Bharat's gaze, saw Shatrugan and turned on him, desperately pleading, 'Shatrugan, my son. Tell me. It was not true. I did not do such a thing, did I? I could *not* have!'

Shatrugan looked away as well. Kaikeyi gazed around, but there was nobody else in the room, only a palace guard at the door – not one of her own clansmen. He stood indifferently, uncaring of the rani's emotions, staring straight ahead as his duty warranted. Yet even in that unknown guard's face and demeanour, Kaikeyi seemed to see something. A cold aloofness, a remoteness that went beyond discipline. An air of uncaring that verged on outright loathing.

She struggled with the bedcovers, almost falling over herself. The dressings on her abdomen wounds began to unravel.

'What are you doing?' Bharat asked, catching her before she could tumble headlong out of bed.

'I must go to him,' she said, her voice rising in hysteria. 'I must go to him and apologise at once.'

He restrained her firmly. 'Father is very ill. In a coma. He cannot see anyone. Only Guruji and Maa are with him, trying to do what they can to ease his passage to the afterlife. He has only a little while longer.' Bharat's voice was polite and well modulated, but there was no attempt to soften the blow, to break the news gently. *After all*, the implication lay in his words, *you are more than partly responsible for his condition.*

Kaikeyi stared up at him. 'Maa?'

He frowned. 'What?'

'You called Kausalya maa and addressed me directly, without once calling *me* mother.'

Bharat looked away, his face showing no regret. 'She is as much my mother as you are.' He added slowly, 'Perhaps more so, these past weeks.'

Kaikeyi stared up at him, seeing that he meant the words, that they were not spoken merely to hurt her – Bharat actually felt more like Kausalya's son than her own. If anything, that honesty hurt her even more than any display of pique would have. She reached out, taking his face in her hands. He had so much of her in his features, his craggy jawline, those high, wide cheekbones, the ever-so-slightly slanting eyes set together predatorially close, the narrow, low forehead with its bushy brows.

'Putra,' she said, her voice trembling. *Son.* 'Putra, look at me.'

He looked at her reluctantly.

'Do you . . . hate me very much?' she asked.

He reached up and took her hands away from his face, returning them to her lap. 'This is no time to sit around talking,' he said gruffly. 'I have much to do. There is trouble in the city. Riots threaten. The council have offered their resignations. The mountain clans are calling for a referendum to—' He shook his head. 'This is the worst day of my life.'

'Just answer me that one question,' she cried as he started to rise. 'Do you hate me for what I did?'

He looked down at her hand, grasping his ang-vastra. 'How can a son hate his own birth-mother?'

She shook her head. 'That is no answer. I want to know, Bharat. I want to know if you can live with the knowledge of what I did.' When he didn't answer immediately, she went on, 'It's true I was under the influence of that witch, that Manthara was drugging me and controlling me through her Asura sorcery. But even before that,' she released his vastra and covered her face, 'even before that, I was filled with so much anger and hatred. I wanted more, more, more. Whatever I got, it was never enough, only a stepping stone to the next object of desire. And so it went, endlessly. Yes, Manthara controlled me and manipulated me, I realise that now that I'm free of her spell. She used me to her own ends. But she could only push me further towards a direction I wished to go anyway. She wielded me like a sword to penetrate to the heart of this great family, just as her dark master used her as the hilt of that same sword. But a sword is made for killing, or she would not have been able to use me. Her influence would have been useless on Kausalya . . . or Sumitra. That would have been like trying to use a flower to do a sword's work.'

Shatrugan shifted uncomfortably. Both princes were loath to hear this outburst, yet were too well mannered to walk out on her. Kaikeyi saw this and went on quickly, as if afraid that at any moment their deep-rooted conditioning would snap and they would stalk out without further regard for social mores.

'But the worst thing of all, my son, is that I wanted this to come to pass.' Kaikeyi's voice was one notch short of an outright cry. 'In my heart of hearts, I wanted it all. I wanted you to be prince-heir, and maharaja some day. I wanted to be First Queen, and to hold the keys to Ayodhya in my fist. I wanted to see my grandchildren inherit the sunwood crown and become the forebears of the future Suryavansha dynasty. I wanted it all, and Manthara only manipulated me into using wrongful means to get what I wanted. But,' her voice broke, 'and you have to believe me, putra, when I say this, I did not want it *at this price*! I did not want Rama . . . or your father . . . I did not want any of these things to happen. This was not my ambition, to cause all this pain and damage. I only wanted the good things, not the bad. Try to see that. I need you to see that, as my son.'

Bharat stood silently throughout this long speech, listening with his eyes averted. At the end, when his mother began to regret aloud the things she hadn't wanted, he turned his gaze back on her. His eyes were hard and remorseless.

'And in the end,' he asked quietly, 'did you get what you wanted? Are you pleased with what you accomplished? Are you content?'

She shook her head, crying freely. 'No,' she said over and over again, 'no, no, no. How can I be?'

'Then what is it you wish from me?' he asked. 'Forgiveness?'

She raised her eyes to his, hope sparking in her orbs.

He shook his head. 'I cannot give it.'

She stared at him wordlessly.

'I cannot forgive you. The things you did to my father and my brother, these are beyond my ability to forgive. Perhaps they are beyond forgiveness itself! But that is not my place to judge. The devas will consider your actions and weigh your karma in due course, be certain of that. Be certain also of this now: I will fulfil all my duties to you as befits an Arya son. But do not expect anything beyond duty. Do not expect understanding, or compassion, or trust. Above all, do not expect love. That I will not hate you, nor act out of hatred, is all that I can promise. But beyond that, you will have nothing from me. I will serve you as any other servant in your retinue.' He pointed at the guard by the door. 'I will serve you as efficiently as that guard at your threshold. But expect no more.'

'I expect only a son's love and forgiveness!' she wailed, beating her breasts.

'Then you expect more than you deserve.'

He bowed his head curtly, performing a dutiful namaskar that would have suited his greeting of a strange courtier in a sabha session, turned smartly on his booted heel, and left the chamber, Shatrugan in his wake.

9

They left the raj-marg and turned west at the northern crossroad. Going straight would have led them eventually to Kaikeya Pass. The by-road was bumpier, being less travelled, and then rarely by royals. The traffic dwindled to a few bullock carts driven by farmers carrying their produce to Ayodhya market. Several were piled enormously high with sugarcane stalks, seemingly too great a load for two oxen or bullocks to carry. Yet the beasts trundled along, their horned heads lowered, pulling with untiring energy. The farmers must have distinguished the royal chariot from its rapid dust-churning progress up the road, for all of them were standing up on their carts by the time it reached them. They performed namaskars and called out the traditional four-word greeting, 'Dasa naam satya hai!' *Dasaratha's name is truth*.

Fields of freshly cut sugarcane rolled by, the late-morning air thick with the scent of the syrupy sap. Scorpion birds hovered, sipping from cut stalks, snakes slithered in the bushes alongside the marg, and across the marg at times. They were quick enough to get out of the chariot's way in time, warned by the vibrations in the ground well in advance. At a small pond, children and oxen milled together in the muddy water, splashing about happily. They saw the chariot and waved excitedly, shouting simply, 'Ram-rajya!' *The reign of Rama*. Clearly, news of the dramatic events in Ayodhya had not reached these backwaters yet.

After another yojana, they began to pass villages. Some were barely a dozen thatched mud huts built on either side of the marg itself, their occupants busy binding together sugarcane stalks and loading them on to carts. Women and men, old and young, all worked together, unmindful of the sun. It had been a harsh winter, well below freezing until little more than a fortnight before Holi feast day, and people were happy to be out baking carelessly in the affectionate warmth of Surya-deva once more. An occasional dharamshala passed by, its mud roof bearing the saffron pennant that announced to passers-by that they could find free food and shelter here. Brahmins came out at the sound of the approaching chariot and made genuflections, conferring long life and honour on the maharaja and his lineage.

As they climbed higher into the western hills, the road grew less populous. For a full yojana or more they saw neither a cart nor a house. Then, as they descended the far side, the vista spread open before them, and they began to glimpse distant smoke-puffs rising into the ice-blue sky. These were villages and hamlets, some sprawling across entire valleys or over clusters of hills, thousands-strong clans living together harmoniously, linked by their varna or occupational caste, each self-contained tribal township or village engaged in its own hereditary line of work, be it tanning, harvesting, threshing, or sword-making. Hills rose and fell as the chariot trundled on; the road grew rough and stony, then turned smoother and less gravelly, then wound up and down over ghats and hillocks. Once, they passed a grove filled with musicians playing happy, carefree songs, presumably stopping to rest while en route to Ayodhya. From the snatches that could be heard over the thundering of the chariot, it appeared they were singing the praises of the new crown prince Rama Chandra. They all waved happily at the chariot passing by, dipping their heads in allegiance.

Shortly after midday Sumantra suggested that they stop briefly for a rest, more for the sake of the horses than for themselves. None of them felt much like partaking of any nourishment. Rama would not even take a sip of water. Sita and Lakshman ate some fruit, at Sumantra's insistence, but left most of what the pradhan-mantri offered them. The land here was abundant with fruit and fowl and game, and in younger days, the prime minister informed Sita as they sat beneath the shade of a banyan tree and tried to eat their noon repast, Rama and his brothers would often ride out here and hunt for days.

They would set themselves a target, he told her, smiling wistfully at the memory of those bygone days, always picking species that had overbred lately and needed culling – or, quite frequently, assorted predators that had turned man-eaters and were preying on the nearby villagers, and so needed to be exterminated. The four brothers would split up into two pairs – he hardly needed to tell her which two went together in each pairing – and would enter the dense hilly woods on foot. They would hunt over the next several days, surviving on the land itself, and occasionally on some of their own game. All the while, Sumantra had to send out men to follow on their heels, collecting the animals they had killed, carrying the carcasses back to the city. The princes would continue to stalk and kill and even be stalked at times – he narrated a chilling yet ludicrously funny anecdote of a panther that had kept on their trails for three whole days one time – and at the end of the tour, Rama and Lakshman and Bharat and Shatrugan would all return to an appointed spot on an agreed-upon day to compare their kill-tallies.

'Who mostly won?' Sita asked Sumantra, not because she had a burning curiosity but because the pradhan-mantri seemed to expect some query or response at this point. Rama and Lakshman sat with heads bowed, presenting a polite listening stance yet clearly not engaged by the telling.

Ah, winning was rarely easy to judge, Sumantra recalled, chuckling and shaking his head. For it wasn't a question of mere numbers but size and age and species as well. 'For instance,' he pointed out, after all three had declined the fruit he was offering for the third or fourth time, 'Rama and Lakshman might have ten fully grown adult boars, three pantheresses, two male leopards, a lioness, and a few dozen stag and deer. Bharat and Shatrugan, on the other hand, might have seven female leopards but only three adult boars, a panther or two, a young lion, a hundred fowl, duck, geese, peahens.' He laughed. 'Either one a cache deserving of a whole royal hunting party, not just two young boys armed with nothing but simple steel knives.'

Sita frowned. 'They killed all that game with just knives?'

Sumantra chuckled. 'I wouldn't put even that past them. But no, I meant that they went into the woods armed only with knives. They then used the knives to carve bows and cut and shape arrows. It was with the bows and arrows that they carried out the actual hunting. That was always the way they liked to stage their contests, pitting not only their hunting abilities but their survival skills against one another.'

After waiting a moment for someone to comment or question him, the pradhan-mantri went on with exaggerated enthusiasm, 'So it was almost impossible to measure and compare their tallies exactly, some kills clearly being more difficult to attain than others. And naturally enough, that led to arguments, growing more and more heated until it seemed inevitable that both pairs of brothers would come to blows.' He shook his head, smiling wistfully. 'But it never came to such a pass. Because, in the end, they would always turn to their father and ask him to decide. And Dasaratha, when he had a few minutes free from matters of state, would look over the two caches carefully, and pronounce his judgement. And once he had spoken, no matter which pair he had judged the winner, his verdict was accepted without objection or debate. And all four were friends once more. That night they would all feast and carouse over the roasting joints of their own catch, along with most of the city!'

There was a long silence after the prime minister had finished the story. All four of them sat silently, looking at the ground, at the squirrels dancing up and down the massive gnarled banyan trunk, listening to the calls of the monkeys rampaging through the treetops, the distant roars, grunts of boars and other assorted sounds from the wooded hills. Their horses snorted and neighed, having finished the oats that Sumantra had obtained from a nearby farmer while they had waited here beneath the tree at Rama's request. Sumantra unpeeled a banana and raised it to his mouth, then paused and looked around. Except for a bite or two, none of their fruit had been touched. He put aside the banana uneaten.

'I suggest we rest awhile now, rajkumars, rajkumari. The day grows exceedingly hot, even for early spring. Had I time, I would have fetched a covered chariot, or even a wheelhouse, but even now it would pose no difficulty to find a suitable lodge where you may lay yourselves down for a few hours. After the sun has grown less stringent, we may resume our journey once more.'

'Sumantra,' Rama said quietly, 'we cannot wait. We must continue on our way within the hour.'

Sumantra nodded, as if he had expected this response. 'You wish to reach the Tamasa by tomorrow then?'

'I wish to cross the Tamasa before sundown, and leave the borders before sunrise.'

Sumantra's brow creased. 'That would mean travelling without another halt. And . . .' He shook his head, disapproving. 'You would travel all night? But what purpose would that serve, my lord? Why not stay and camp by the Tamasa tonight? It is most pleasant there. I am sure Rajkumari Sita Janaki would enjoy—'

Rama placed his hand on Sumantra's shoulder. 'Good Sumantra, my mother Kaikeyi's orders were crystal clear. I am to leave the borders of Kosala this very day. And I am to enter the Dandaka-van as fast as humanly possible. If it is not possible to do so tonight itself, then with the help of your speedy rath, we can certainly do so before sundown tomorrow. That will fulfil my mother's wishes.'

Sumantra shrugged in acceptance. His face clouded briefly. 'I do not know, though, how you can continue to call her mother. Even a clan-mother, which is all that Kaikeyi ever was to you, and even that in name alone. When a clan-mother acts as she has acted, she deserves no respect. By sending you into exile in Dandaka-van, Kaikeyi-rani—'

'Enough.' Rama rose to his feet. 'I will hear no word against her. She only fulfilled the boons my father owed her. You will not sully her name by speaking ill of her to me or to anyone else.'

Sita and Lakshman had stood with Rama. Sumantra came to his feet too, wearily. He dusted crumbs of soil from his garments. 'If that is your wish, then it will be as you say, my prince,' he said.

'That is my wish,' Rama said. He turned to go.

Sumantra caught his arm, stopping him. 'Rajkumar, hear me out. The Dandaka-van is no place to take a newly wed wife, a princess of Mithila no less. What life would you have there? Fending off wild beasts and Asuras every hour? The demons of that dark forest are almost as legendary as Tataka's brood in the Bhayanak-van.'

Rama did not speak, he only looked at Sumantra without any expression. It was Lakshman who asked curiously, 'What would you have us do then, chacha?'

Sumantra gestured at their surroundings. 'Why not stay somewhere in these very hills? They are remote enough for you to stay incognito. I can have a small lodge built in a few days in a location that does not come easily to human eyes. There is a clan of sutaars nearby, they are among the best house-builders in the kingdom. You can reside in that lodge and live out your exile. That way, you shall be close enough to Ayodhya to have all your needs supplied by me. Rani Kaikeyi need never come to know of it as long as she lives. Only say the word, and I will have it done.'

Rama looked at the pradhan-mantri a long moment, saying nothing. Finally, the minister released the prince's arm and looked away, lowering his eyes. Rama turned and walked back to the horses, putting the yoke on them himself without waiting for Sumantra. Lakshman glanced back at Sumantra, as if wanting to say something, then went to help Rama. Sita hung back a moment, long enough to give Sumantra a squeeze on his shoulder, affectionate and compassionate. *As if I am the one who needs compassion rather than they.*

Sumantra fought back the tears that had started to brim in his eyes, and went to help the brothers horse the chariot.

10

It was early evening by the time they came to the Tamasa.
They heard its roar and smelled its flower-strewn banks
almost a mile before they reached it. Lakshman had taken
the reins of the rath since midday and he brought the
team to a gentle halt, turning the vehicle around in the
clearing used by those who waited to take the ferry across.
There were no people here at present: almost all travellers preferred to use the newer, manned ferry boats
plying across the wider strait a mile or two downriver.
This was precisely why Lakshman had suggested they
cross at this relatively abandoned old crossing, to avoid
meeting any more citizenry.

A thick jute rope was tied to trees on both riverbanks,
and passed through poles at either end of a large ancient
balsawood raft. One had to pull oneself across the river
by hand. Normally, Tamasa was a gentle, quiet river, but
this was spring, and melting ice had given her more force
than usual. There was also some danger from debris from
the logging mills upriver, where the woods clans toiled
to supply Ayodhya's unceasing construction needs with
timber.

They de-yoked the horses, and tied them to a tree to
give them a few moments to adjust to the river. It was
decided to take the rath across first, with Sita and

Sumantra holding it firm and Rama and Lakshman pulling the rope. The trip went without too much trouble, although the river's force was hard to fight and both princes were hard pressed to pull the loaded raft the last few yards. Sita and Sumantra trundled the chariot off the raft, inadvertently bogging one side down in a wet muddy patch, and both Rama and Lakshman had to disembark as well to lend a hand. They got in the mud pit and pushed while Sita and the pradhan-mantri pulled the yokes. By the time they got the stubbornly stuck chariot wheel out of the mud patch, the two brothers were spattered from head to foot. Sita turned around and took one look at them and burst out laughing. Both grinned sheepishly, and washed themselves off in the river, each holding the other's hand to keep from getting swept away.

Sita stayed on the west bank, while the three men went back for the horses. From the outset there was trouble. The lead horse, a beautiful black stallion named Kamabha, was skittish around white water, and neighed and stamped his feet stubbornly when he was taken down to the river's edge. Sumantra tried to coax him down, to no avail. It was Lakshman who was able to talk the horse into going down the bank, holding his head firmly when he flared his nostrils and tried to wheel around, and managed to get him on board the raft. The others followed Kamabha nervously but obediently. Rama poled them away from the bank, then pulled on the rope. Sumantra pulled as well, but Lakshman stayed with Kamabha, who was still exceedingly skittish and snorted every time the raft jiggled or shook.

They were halfway across when the logs came downriver. From the looks of it, a rope must have snapped, or more likely an elephant had dropped its load at the sight of a water-snake or river-rat. The elephant seemed the more likely explanation: there were about a dozen roughly cut logs, just about what an elephant would be expected to carry at a time. They came sweeping around the bend, rubbing noisily against one another, striking the bank and pinwheeling around, climbing over each other with harsh rapping sounds.

Sita saw them first, the three men being wholly occupied with the twinfold task of pulling the raft across as well as keeping the horses in control. She yelled a warning to them. Rama looked up and saw the oncoming logs and assessed the situation instantly. They were a little more than halfway across, too far to go back, not far enough across to be out of harm's way. He shouted to Sumantra to pull harder, harder! Sumantra did so, his muscles standing out in corded relief as he strained with all his energy. Rama pulled too with all his might. But Lakshman's hands were full with the skittish stallion, who had sensed danger in the air and chose that moment to start kicking out in panic.

Sita sent a prayer to her devi as Rama dodged the stallion's powerful back-kicks, while struggling simultaneously with the rope. If one of those kicks landed anywhere on Rama, they would smash bone certainly, likely do worse damage. But Rama had nowhere else to go to avoid the flailing hoofs. All he could do was hang out over the edge of the raft, pulling away on the rope without a pause. Worse, the other horses picked up on Kamabha's panic and began turning their heads, tossing their manes and threatening to kick out at any moment. If they joined in the fray, there would be no way for Rama to avoid them.

The logs chose that precise moment to strike.

The bulk of the load had managed to get snarled up in a nasty tangle at the bend, rolling over each other noisily, scraping and groaning as they struggled to resume their downward course. They were all on the east bank, and with every muscle-wrenching yank, the raft pulled farther away from them and closer to safety. But when they were two-thirds of the way across, almost close enough for Sita to run and jump on to the raft, a solitary log freed itself from the tangle and swung round in elliptical circles, gaining momentum as it whirled around in the roaring torrent. Sita saw it and held her breath rather than yell another warning: the three men were struggling to cope with their existing problems, there wasn't anything further they could do. She thought at first the log would turn around a few more times, then make its way downriver, bypassing the raft. And that was what seemed likely to happen. But then a fresh wave of melt water joined the flow, creating an eddy. And at the last possible moment the log came around with greater force, and struck Rama's side of the raft a hard glancing blow.

The entire raft shuddered at the impact, starting to swing around at once. Sumantra lost one hand-grip on the rope, and the raft was twisted right out from beneath Rama's feet. The horses went berserk, flailing like wild things rather than thoroughbred Kambhojas. Sita watched, horrified, as Rama clung to the rope for one agonising moment. She was at the water's edge already, calling out to Sumantra, who was poling the raft the last few yards. The pradhan-mantri's face was bathed in sweat, his cheeks red from the effort. Lakshman had grabbed the rope and pulled it as hard as he could, keeping out of the way of the snapping jaws of the horses. He was facing the wrong way to have seen what had happened to Rama.

Rama swung out over the river, the raft already too far for him to reach with his feet. He managed to put one hand over the other on the rope, and Sita's heart leaped with relief as she saw that he was going to pull himself to shore. The rope was strong enough to carry his weight easily – it had to be, to be able to pull a raft-load across the river. Rama put another hand over, then yet another . . . he would have made it in another two or three hand-lengths. But that was when the rest of the logjam chose to free itself from the tangled snarl, and resumed its downriver journey. The rolling logs swung out into the river's flow, stretching out across the Tamasa's width, and their far edges passed directly beneath Rama. Even though he had raised his feet to keep them well out of the water, two logs were still tumbling over each other as they turned, and the higher one struck the back of his ankle a slight blow. At that force and speed it was enough to dislodge him. Rama lost one hand-hold, then the other immediately after, and the next instant he was in the river, washed downstream along with the pile of logs.

Sita screamed.

Lakshman turned and saw Rama gone. He stopped pulling and would have raced to the far side of the raft, but by then the horses were completely out of control. Sumantra called to him to finish pulling and get them to the bank. Lakshman froze for a moment, then he saw Rama's arm break the surface, flailing above the white rush. Sumantra shouted to him again to bring the raft to shore first, or they would all go into the river.

Working with demonic strength, Lakshman pulled on the rope, bringing the raft the last yard or so to the west bank. The minute it struck shore, Sumantra ran the lead stallion on to solid ground. Kamabha's fellows followed him in quick succession, leaping on to the bank. But the last horse's rear hoofs slipped on the wet edge of the raft, knocking the vessel away from the bank, and as Sita watched, the beast slipped into the gap and fell into the river. It screamed in terror as the powerful current caught hold of it and yanked it away, kicking out madly, striking the muddy bank underfoot. But the current drove it away from the bank, and in another moment it was lost, floating downriver after Rama and the pile of logs. Barely a second or two had passed since Rama had fallen in.

Lakshman shouted Rama's name and let go the rope. He would have leapt into the river after Rama, but Sita shouted to him to stop.

'The horses!' she yelled above the roar of the river. 'Faster by land!'

Lakshman caught her meaning and instead leapt to the bank. Both of them caught hold of two of the unsaddled horses and, gripping their manes, vaulted on to their backs. The horses whinnied, startled, but they were on dry land again, and knew better than to throw off human riders.

Sita turned the head of her horse and pressed him to a gallop, racing around the horseless chariot and the lead stallion, still fretting and giving Sumantra a hard time. The pradhan-mantri turned as they rode past. He shouted something incoherent to Lakshman that Sita didn't catch, then she was well away and riding like the wind.

Except for the low, muddy site of the raft crossing, the riverbank was a good yard higher than the water. Trees grew along the west bank but not very closely. Sita forced her horse to ride along the narrow patch of crumbly bank directly beside the water, bending to avoid the low-hanging boughs that stretched out over the river. Leaves caught in her hair, and branches raked her back, but her eyes were fixed on the roiling white water, searching for sign of Rama. She saw the horse first, snorting desperately as it struggled to keep its head above water. She scanned the river ahead anxiously, kicking her heels to keep her horse from slowing.

Then she saw him, a dozen yards ahead. He had caught hold of a loose log and was clinging to it. She shouted excitedly to Lakshman, who was close on her heels, and pointed. He shouted back in acknowledgement. Rama was using his strength to swing the log around, trying to turn it just enough for the current to catch it and do the rest. It was a battle he was losing. Sita reined in her horse – despite the river's force, it was slowing at this point, its banks growing wider apart. If only she had a rope she could toss to Rama to pull him ashore. Before she could even glance around for a tree with vines that could be used, she heard a loud splash just behind her and turned to see Lakshman in the river. He had leapt off his galloping horse!

Sita raised her head to watch, and almost got it knocked off by a low-hanging bough. She ducked just in time to avoid it, feeling a strand of her hair yanked out by the roots by the greedy branch. When she was able to look up at the river again, Lakshman had reached the far end of the log and, as she watched, put his weight against it. It swung all the way around, as Rama had desired, and Lakshman let go at once, striking out for the bank but looking back over his shoulder. Rama was carried around by the river's force, and at the appropriate point he struck out for shore as well. Lakshman reached out and grasped his hand. Rama took it with a teeth-flashing grin, and both brothers hauled each other ashore.

Sita jumped from her horse and half tumbled, half bounded down the crumbling wall of the east bank. She landed in the water beside her husband and brother-in-law, and all but leapt on to Rama, embracing him, kissing him, rubbing her hands across his face and head. Her tears fell on his wet cheeks.

'You fool,' she said. 'You fool, you fool, you fool.'

He kissed her back, gently first, then with a passion that matched the river's rage. 'No more than you.'

They stayed that way for several minutes, clinging to the roots of a tree that had broken through the underside of the bank in their effort to reach the river, the water tugging furiously at their legs as if wishing it could have them again. A loud snorting came to them from upriver and they glanced that way wearily to see the horse that had fallen in clambering on to the bank again. Its fellows, the horses ridden by Sita and Lakshman, came to its aid, tugging with their teeth and pushing at its flanks. The three horses nuzzled each other affectionately, glad to be reunited.

Sita looked at Lakshman and touched his cheek, thanking him wordlessly for going to Rama's rescue. No words were needed. She knew he had done it for himself, not for her, but wanted him to know that by doing so he had saved her life as well. He nodded, wiping a tear from his own eye; or perhaps it was only river water.

After a while, Lakshman said to Rama: 'If we still had the shakti of the maha-mantras, this would never have happened. Even a hundred logs wouldn't have been able to dislodge you from the raft.'

Rama didn't speak, only kept looking out at the river surging past them.

Sita glanced at one brother, then the other.

It took her a moment to understand what Lakshman was saying. Rama and Lakshman had been stripped not only of their kingdom, inheritance and family, but also of their acquired gift of brahman strength.

She recalled Guru Vashishta's words on the last leg of their journey from Mithila to Ayodhya: '*Rama lost all access to brahman shakti the instant he unleashed the*

*Brahm-astra. As did you, Lakshman, for you also shared
in that unleashing. That was the price you both paid for
uttering the celestial maha-mantra of destruction. The
moment the two of you used the Brahm-astra to destroy
Ravana's invading armies, you lost forever the chance to
tap into and channel the shakti of the force that binds
the universe. You were returned to your former state of
normal mortality. Never again will you be able to achieve
superhuman feats of strength, skill or speed.'*

At the time, she had not realised the full import and
implications of the seer-mage's words. But now, with their
mortality brought home so brutally by the encounter with
the raft, it seemed almost like another level of punishment. As if losing everything else hadn't been enough.
After another moment, the full implications hit her with
a force equal to the log ramming the raft.

They were entering fourteen years of exile in a jungle
almost as notorious for its perils as the dreaded
Southwoods. A place known to be rife with berserker
rakshasas. And probably more infested now than ever,
with the straggling survivors of the eastern forces of the
Asura army left here and there, as Yudhajit of Kaikeya
had explained just last night. To the Rama and Lakshman
who had been infused with the maha-mantras Bala and
Atibala, even an army of rakshasas would have posed no
mortal danger. But they were no more that Rama and
Lakshman. The shakti of the maha-mantras no longer
flowed through their veins.

*They're only human now. And what chance do mere
mortals have in a place like Dandaka-van?*

No chance at all, whispered a little voice inside her
head. *Not a chance in hell.*

II

Kausalya turned and saw Bharat standing inside the threshold of her antechamber. She hadn't heard him enter, which meant he must have done so very quietly indeed. That itself was such a change to the Bharat of just a few weeks ago: it seemed inconceivable that the old boisterous, loud Bharat could have been replaced by this silent, gentle young man with an air of almost regal dignity and quietude about him. The thought wasn't very comforting. He's holding himself too tightly, she thought as she looked up at his sweat-wreathed face. *Let some of your pain go, Bharat, release it before it cuts you up inside.*

Seeing that he had her attention, he came forward at once and bent to touch her feet in genuflection. She laid her hand on his head in the customary gesture, and as he rose she was disturbed to see his handsome young face carrying lines of weariness that had been absent only the night before. *He has aged an era in just one day,* she thought sadly. It reminded her painfully of two occasions on which she had seen Rama after a long absence: the first was when her son had returned home after his seven years at Guru Vashishta's gurukul. The second was after a mere two weeks' separation – this past week when she had arrived at Mithila for Rama's marriage – yet it was after this second time that the change was the most strikingly evident. The first time, she had seen that her little child had become a full-grown boy. The second time, she had seen the boy grown to manhood, matured and wisened by his experiences in the Bhayanak-van and in the battle against the Asura invasion.

She saw the same look on Bharat's face now. *He has become a man today.* He had been forced to become one. In his own way, Bharat had endured a lot: seeing his mother exposed as the pivot of a devilish plot to unsettle the sunwood throne, bring his father to the brink of early death and send his brothers and sister-in-law into long exile, these were no less a challenge than battling Asuras. In a way, this battle was a much harder one to fight. At least in a physical challenge you could use a sword and dhanush-baan to bring down your enemies, all of whom were horned or physically distinctive enough to set them apart from human allies. Here, your enemies were your own people, those you loved and trusted most, and your weapons were only endurance, fortitude and spiritual resilience. It was a war Kausalya had been fighting all her life, and she felt and empathised with Bharat's burden.

'Maa,' he said in a voice so weary it tugged painfully at her heart. 'I have dealt with the situation as best as I was able. But there are still pockets of trouble throughout the city. Senapati Dheeraj Kumar has made sure that there will be patrols constantly monitoring every trouble-prone locality, but—' He sighed, rubbing his eyes. 'It is difficult even for our good soldiers to fight their fellow citizens. They have no stomach for this kind of fight. Besides, there is unrest in the ranks of our own army. Many feel that grievous wrong has been done here and that the Suryavansha line cannot brook such injustice.'

'Even so,' she said gently, trying to reassure rather than

disagree, 'as long as the Suryavansha line prevails, they must serve it without question or doubt.'

He inclined his head. 'That they do, Maa. That they do. It is what makes the whole situation so painful.'

He looked at a diya burning nearby, in the pooja thali she had set down only a moment ago. She waited for him to continue. When he did so, his voice was steadier. 'Our spasas have just brought us word that the news has spread to other parts of the kingdom, and there is unrest in the north of Kosala.'

Kausalya noddd. The foothills of the Himalayas, marking Kosala's northern border, had always been a contentious region. The mountain clans, or pahadis as they were commonly known, tended not to accept any kind of leadership easily, even of their own tribe or clan, let alone that of a king in distant Ayodhya.

'They say that the pahadis may press home their advantage by attacking the plainsfolk over the river waters dispute. You already know the trouble we've had there in the past year. Anticipating trouble, I have ordered the senapati to send a full akshohini there to pre-empt and prevent any outbreak of violence. But we cannot patrol the entire kingdom as we do Ayodhya. Before the night is over, it seems inevitable that we shall see Kosalans shed Kosalan blood on our own lands.'

His voice cracked slightly at the end, betraying the emotional toll this admission cost him.

Kausalya spoke gently. 'Son, you have done your best. Whatever happens, I know you shall deal with it honourably and justly.'

'Yes, Mother. But there is so much resentment. So much doubt. And anger. And suspicion everywhere. Even my own companions look at me strangely and ask me how I could not have known that my governess was a witch and my mother a pawn in the control of the Lord of Lanka.' He looked at her, his face twisted with pain and confusion. 'How do I even begin to tell them anything? As it is, nobody seems truly to want to hear my side of the story. It's as if they have already judged me and deemed me guilty! And the citizenry . . . they are so pitifully confused and angry.' He indicated a purpling bruise on his shoulder. 'Someone in a crowd threw a stone at me. The lieutenant of the PFs riding with me wanted to charge them with lances drawn, to teach a lesson. I stopped them by putting my own horse and person in their way. It was a lesson I would not see taught, not today, not ever. But when I dismounted and tried to explain myself to the people huddled on that street corner, they began dispersing without listening to me.'

She put a hand on his shoulder, not knowing what to say. There was nothing to be said.

He shook his head as if trying to clear it and not quite succeeding. 'But I did not come here to burden you with all these matters. I came here to see my father. How is he now?'

She couldn't have hidden the truth even if she had wanted to do so. Her face would have revealed what her words tried to soften or deny. 'Not good. Still unconscious. Our best hope now is that he passes away peacefully in his sleep. He has suffered much.'

Bharat nodded, his face impassive now. *This pain is greater than all the others combined, and so he has no face to put upon it.* She was struck by how much he was like Dasaratha in such moments of crisis. Dasa too had reacted strongly, emotionally, to the smaller, more niggling problems of statecraft, but when confronted with the truly large issues, or a great crisis, he had always grown quiet, almost withdrawn and detached. *The heart can only bear*

*so much and no more, so at this point it resigns itself to
destiny.* Now that the thought had occurred to her, she
could see that young Dasa in his son standing before her.

At that instant, the thought came to her, clear as the
sound of a temple bell in a silent forest glen.

*He will make a good king. A better king than his
father. A wise and just king who feels passionately for
the plight of his subjects and yet has enough iron in his
blood to mete out justice when it needs must be done.*

Bharat said, 'May I see him now, briefly?'

She nodded. 'Do not try to wake him or provoke him
to speech. Those were Guru Vashishta's orders.'

He passed into the innermost chamber, where the
maharaja lay attended by vaids and Kausalya's most
trusted servants. Guards stood obtrusively at every turn,
but they were only for protocol; nobody had any real
fear that an attack would be mounted here and now. *Why
kill a dying king when Yamaraj himself is already on his
way here, riding his black buffalo, carrying the bag that
will bear Dasa's aatma?*

Kausalya sat immersed in her thoughts in the
antechamber. She was not aware of Shatrugan's entry into
the room until he bowed before her and touched her feet.
He too had grown more silent and withdrawn, mirroring
his brother. 'Maa,' he said softly.

She blessed him and told him that Bharat was within,
with his father. He was about to go inside when Bharat
emerged, wiping his cheeks with the end of his sweat-
stained ang-vastra.

'Bhai,' Shatrugan said, 'there is news of Rama.'

At once Bharat's face lit up. He caught hold of
Shatrugan's shoulders. 'Where is he? Take me to him at
once!'

Shatrugan nodded vigorously. 'First at least listen.' He

included both Kausalya and Bharat as he went on, explaining about the spasas who had reported in only moments ago, speaking of a great crowd amassing on the banks of the Tamasa river. Apparently, Rama had broken his journey there to camp for the night, and word had spread like wildfire. That was perhaps an hour or two earlier, said the last spasa, who had nearly killed a horse getting to Ayodhya with the news, and it was nearing sunset now. Pradhan-mantri Sumantra, Sita and Lakshman had been with Rama.

When Shatrugan was finished, Bharat turned to Kausalya. 'Maa,' he said, 'give me your ashirwaad once more. For I am about to do that which my dharma demands I must do.'

'You have my ashirwaad in everything you do, as always. But what is that you wish to do, my son?'

Bharat looked at her with an inscrutable expression. 'Depart the city with as large an entourage as I can collect within the hour. If I can take the whole population of Ayodhya with me, I will.'

Kausalya's heart clenched in shock. 'Where will you take all these people?'

'To Tamasa's banks. To Rama.'

When she did not answer immediately, he went on, his words almost stumbling over each other in their eagerness to convey his intentions. 'I have not had time to speak with you further of the evil that was wrought here by Manthara and . . . and her accomplice. But I must say to you what is in my heart now.'

'Speak your heart freely then,' she said quietly.

'Then this is what my heart says, and what dharma demands. If there is to be a prince crowned heir in Ayodhya, it will be Rama alone. I will not wear the Suryavansha crown and sit the sunwood throne as long as my brother Rama still draws breath. This I swear by the ashes of all my Suryavansha and Ikshwaku ancestors back to the beginning of time. Rama is the only true king who will succeed our father.'

Kausalya fought to control her own emotions. 'What can I say to such a pronouncement, Bharat? What would you have me say?'

He knelt before her then, with Shatrugan kneeling at the exact same time, as if sharing his every thought and emotion. 'Say only that you bless me in this undertaking. Give me your ashirwaad to go and bring my brother back home. I intend to undo the evil that Manthara wrought. I will bring Rama home and see him crowned king-heir. If you abjure me from doing this, then I must obey you. But I plead with you to bless me and permit me to do this for the sake of my own honour and for the sake of every Ayodhyan and every Kosalan.'

She stared down at his bowed head, then at that of his brother beside him. Tears welled in her eyes yet again – *will this river never cease to flow?* – and she saw herself reach out and touch first Bharat then Shatrugan on the head as custom demanded.

'If this is what you wish, my son,' she said, 'then go with Devi's grace and my heartfelt blessings.'

As Bharat rose, she stopped him and embraced him. Suddenly, she was no longer a queen, but simply a mother. Just a mother crying out to him, 'Go, Bharat, and fetch your brother home. Heal the wounds of this terrible night. Make this family whole again. Bring Rama home!'

12

They were still recovering from the mishap in the river when Sumantra appeared, using the remaining horses to pull the chariot. He cried out when he saw them, heaved to, and rushed to embrace Rama with fresh tears spilling from his eyes. After thanking the devas profusely for sparing Rama's life, he renewed his pleas for them to return to Ayodhya. The journey was ill begun, he insisted, the omens were very bad. He carried on about birds flying in the wrong direction, and predators heard roaring in daylight, and all the other augurs, until Rama put his hand gently but firmly on his shoulder and said that they would go on by foot if they must, but go they would.

At that, Sumantra's face fell and he broke off his litany. With a resigned air, the pradhan-mantri nodded and said he would go as far as Rama took him. They started to yoke the horses to the chariot with every intention of resuming their journey right then, but just as they were harnessing the last horse, Lakshman noticed something odd about the way the animal moved and bent to check its hoofs.

The horse's left rear shoe was missing.

'It must have come off when they were kicking up a storm on the raft,' he said in disgust.

Sumantra looked abjectly downcast again. Rama

expected him to renew his talk of ill omens and bad augurs, but the prime minister simply looked to Rama for his decision. Rama looked at Lakshman, soaked from his dip in the river. He looked at the horses, still skittish and nervous from the unfortunate crossing. He looked at Sita, at Sumantra, then at the surrounding grove, and up at the fading sunlight.

'It is almost sundown,' he said, weighing their options. 'We are across the Tamasa at least. Perhaps we had best rest awhile. We have a long way to go yet, and a little refreshment and a short rest might do us all good before continuing our journey. In the meanwhile, perhaps you can find a new shoe for the horse, good Sumantra.'

Sumantra stared at Rama in dismay. 'The shoe will not be difficult to replace, my prince. But would you truly wish to travel these backroads under darkness?' He gestured at the sky. 'It will be an awamas night. Not even a sliver of moon to light our way. And the way to Dandaka-van is a difficult one, fraught with many perils.'

Rama nodded. 'I am aware of that. But what must be done must be done.' He hesitated, then added with a wry smile, 'That which is least palatable is best done quickly, lest by putting it off we lose our drive to do it at all. Was it not you who taught us that procrastination is a vice, old friend, and that for warriors and kings it is a fatal vice?'

Sumantra sighed and nodded. 'That I did, rajkumar.' He looked around briefly, scanning their surroundings, then indicated the way ahead. 'There is a grove a little way from here with a dharamshala. Travellers often stop there before crossing the Tamasa to go to Ayodhya. With luck we may find an ironsmith with a horseshoe or two in his bag. You could rest and partake of some refreshment at the dharamshala. It is run by your mother's order. Every Arya kingdom builds dharamshalas to cater to the needs of travellers, but Rani Kausalya makes it a point to see that each and every one of Kosala's free-houses are always equipped and manned.'

Rama smiled at his wife and his brother. 'So we shall have the pleasure of partaking of my mother's hospitality then. Let us proceed there at once.'

Neither Sita nor Lakshman offered any comment. They were still shaken from the incident in the river. Rama knew that for them to come so close to losing him on this ill-fated day, in such a meaningless, unexpected fashion, was a greater shock than if he had been cut down in battle against Asuras. Both Lakshman and Sita were trying to deal with the implications of that mishap. Was Sumantra right after all? Were the omens and augurs really that ominous?

It was a sober and silent foursome that walked the half-mile to the dharamshala. They led the horses on foot, to avoid harming the shoeless one's hoof. It was still an hour or so before sunset, and the sun slanted gently through the trees, casting long shadows. Butterflies and insects whirred and chirred around the path. Birdsong filled the forest to their right. The path twisted through a dense grove of eucalyptus trees interspersed with a few coconut trees and date-palms by the water's edge, then came out into a large man-made clearing. To the left was the other, larger ferry crossing, its ground tramped by the feet and wheels and hoofs of a steady daily stream of traffic to and from the capital city.

They had expected a few travellers, perhaps even a few dozen, but the sight that met their eyes stopped them all short.

The clearing was filled with people of all castes, creeds, ages and occupations. They stood by the water's edge, helping ashore the new arrivals who were disembarking from the fully loaded ferry boat; sat around the thatched hut, which was a dharamshala providing free food and shelter to travellers; and milled about the clearing. All of them wore the faces of people who had just been ousted from their homes, or suffered a tragedy of like proportions. Rama had seen people like this uprooted by clan-wars, migrants with no definite destination or future, their faces reflecting the bleak despair of their situation. They sat cross-legged, their heads bowed towards the ground, as if mourning some lost cause. Even at a glance, he estimated several hundred people, perhaps even more than a thousand.

At the sight of Rama and his companions, heads turned at once. A hush fell across the clearing. An awareness spread wordlessly through the groups and pairs and clusters of folk, rippling across them all the way to the ferry and beyond, to the far side of the river. As he brought the horses to a halt, Rama glanced that way, and saw that there were even greater numbers of people on the east side of the river, waiting their turn to cross. If there were hundreds here, there were certainly thousands there. And from the spirals of dust rising from the road on that side, more were arriving.

The people in the clearing rose to their feet and began surging forward. They did so slowly, blankly, like mourners at a funeral, not quite sure how to show their grief, how to begin to express their pent-up emotions.

As they crowded closer, Lakshman stepped in front of Rama protectively. He had his hand on the horn of his bow, the other hand darting toward his quiver in readiness.

Rama laid a hand on his shoulder. Lakshman glanced at him questioningly. Rama shook his head. Lakshman nodded and dropped his hands, but remained standing between Rama and the approaching commonfolk. Sumantra did likewise, with Sita staying by Rama's side. He felt her warm breath on his bare shoulder and put his arm around her, squeezing her reassuringly. She glanced up at him with a nervous smile.

Rama saw that the people were Kosalans all, but not all were Ayodhyans. These were inhabitants of the villages and hamlets they had passed en route to the Tamasa. People who had heard somehow of the events in Ayodhya this morning, and had come here, probably in expectation that Rama would pass this way. There were elders, their wizened heads shaking with disappointment. Little ones, their wide eyes staring up in perplexity. Mothers with infants on their hips, tears rolling down their cheeks – the mothers' cheeks as well as their babies', in maternal empathy. Young women and men, singly or in couples, holding hands and looking lost and forlorn. Carpenters, smiths, washerfolk, woodworkers, tanners, hunters, and a wide assortment of castes and varnas, all carrying some evidence of their trade or occupation stuck in their waistbands or hanging from their shoulders, as if they had left their work and rushed here without a second's hesitation. All had the same desolate look on their faces. The same air of mourning and grieving.

Rama held up his hands in greeting, joined together in a namaskar.

'Good Kosalans,' he said quietly, yet loud enough to be heard above the birdsong and rush of the Tamasa fifty yards away. 'Well met.'

They all greeted him with namaskars. But instead of the usual spoken response, they got down on their knees as one person, amid a great rustling of clothes and clanking of tools. 'Rajkumar Rama Chandra ki jai ho. Siyavar Rama Chandra ki jai.'

Praised be Prince Rama Chandra. Praised be Rama Chandra, husband of Sita.

Then, instead of rising to their feet again, they remained on their knees, looking up at Rama and his companions with a look of abject misery. Lakshman glanced around nervously, not sure what to make of this odd scene. From the riverbank, more people kept arriving, offloaded by the constantly moving ferry boats, which were working overtime to keep up with the demand for their services. The new arrivals dropped to their knees as well, faces gazing reverentially towards Rama.

Sumantra had gone to a group of white-haired brahmins standing by the dharamshala whence they'd emerged. He spoke to them quietly for a moment, then listened carefully to their words before returning to Rama's side.

'They do not believe the news, my prince. They are unable to accept that such a thing could have come to pass.'

Rama looked at Sumantra. 'I understand their feelings, Sumantra. But how will collecting here help anything? What is it they mean to do?'

Sumantra glanced back at the growing crowd. A band of sudra hunters had emerged from the forest to join the throng, their sickle-spears still held by their sides. One of them had a deer carcass thrown over his shoulder, while two others carried a live leopard between them on a pole. They were looking at Rama with a fierce light in their eyes.

'I do not think even they know why they are here,' Sumantra said sadly. 'Most of them have left their work undone and simply come here when they heard the news. The brahmins say that if you are to go into exile, they will go with you.'

Lakshman looked around uneasily. 'There is an air of impending violence here as well. If their mood turns, this crowd will as easily follow you back into Ayodhya to lead a revolt.' He glanced meaningfully at Rama. 'And I warrant that half the kingdom would follow as well.'

Rama shot Lakshman an admonishing look. 'There will be no talk of revolts. These people must be dispersed quickly and peacefully. They cannot follow us into the forest, into exile. The order was for me to go on my own. It is bad enough that I am taking Sita and you with me. I cannot have all these people's lives on my conscience.' He passed a hand across his face, as if trying to wipe away unseen grime. 'Would that this day would end and be done with.'

Sita said gently, 'Perhaps if you will speak to them, a few words to comfort them . . .'

Rama looked at Sumantra, then at the large crowd of anxiously waiting people, then at Sita standing beside him. What was he expected to say to all these people that would make them go home and resume their normal lives? What if he said the wrong thing and they misinterpreted his intent or implication? Lakshman had spoken honestly, if roughly: these people could as easily be incited to riot as into exile. He remembered the riot of the tantriks on Jagannath Marg on Holi feast day. How had he dared to step into the midst of that mêlée, between the angry PFs and the bhaang-enraged tantriks? How had he dispelled that crisis by singing a song? He didn't know. That Rama seemed like another person now, that time another time. Right now, here in this clearing by the Tamasa, he felt no more a prince than that hunter there with his black panther-pelt coat and the gutted deer over his shoulder, dripping a few last drops of blood on to the ground.

He looked again at Sita. She nodded her head very slightly, as if encouraging him to go ahead and speak. He had to say something. It seemed to be expected. But what? He cleared his throat, searching for inspiration. For great thoughts and noble sentiments, the kind that the history scrolls were always filled with, the deathless rhetoric of his Suryavansha ancestors that he had pored over in the palace archives as a boy, dreaming of standing some day on a marble pedestal and speaking such lofty words himself to a crowd that covered the earth for miles, his voice enhanced by Guru Vashishta to carry to the farthest listener.

Now, here, his pedestal was a grassy knoll that rose a yard higher than the surrounding ground. No legendary seer-mage stood by his side, enhancing his voice. No deathless rhetoric came to mind. But still, he had to speak. He would not have a riot on his conscience, much less a revolt.

'Desh-vasiyon,' he began. *Countrymen.*

A gentle wind sighed around him. It took him a moment to realise that it was the collective exhalations of the people themselves, not a river-gust. They had been waiting anxiously for him to speak.

He looked down at Sita on his right. She smiled up at him reassuringly, giving him love and encouragement. Lakshman on his left nodded brusquely, reminding him of the need for strength.

He went on with greater confidence.

'Countrymen. The king has chosen to make my brother Kaikeya-putra Bharat his successor. Bharat is an honourable and generous man, and he will make a good king. Though he is young in age, he is old in wisdom. He is strong of hand, yet gentle of touch. He is quick to root out injustice and evil, yet careful to nurture knowledge and art. In every way possible he is the ideal king. I believe with all my heart that he will make a great ruler, and do his lineage proud. Now that he has been chosen as the crown prince, we must all respect the king's decision. My father was wise to choose Bharat over me, and I am happy with his choice. If you love me, if you wish to see me happy, if you wish to see Ayodhya and every other city, town, hamlet, village and home in this great kingdom rise to even greater heights of peace and prosperity, then do this much and no less. Take all the love you feel for me. All the joy, the affection, the admiration, the pride, the respect, the honour, and the willingness to obey, and give it to my brother Bharat. He is your crown prince now. He is *my* crown prince as well. Honour and love him, for in doing so, you honour and love me as well. When I return, let me hear that you behaved as good Kosalans, that you worked with Yuvraj Bharat to keep this nation as great as it is today. Do this for me, and fourteen years in the forest will pass as if they are fourteen months, nay, fourteen days, and I shall be proud to return to this land I call my home.'

In the utter silence that met the end of his speech, Rama bent down and grasped a handful of dry earth. Tendrils of grass were uprooted, snapping off in his hand. Mud trickled from his clenched fist as he raised it high above his head for all to see.

'Bharat-rajya satya-rajya hai, Kosala ke vasiyon, sada sukh raho!'

Bharat's rule is the just rule. People of Kosala, stay content for ever!

With a roar that filled the clearing and the forest for miles around, sending flocks of settling birds fleeing into the sunset sky, the crowd of commonfolk surged forward, touching, holding, embracing, kissing Rama. Before he could shout a word of protest, they had caught him up in their arms and raised him aloft. With one voice they shouted a variation of the chant he had heard ever since he was a child. The original chant had always been 'Dasaratha-naam satya hai', literally 'Dasa's name is truth.'

What they shouted now was: 'Ram-naam satya hai! Ram-naam satya hai!' over and over and over again, until the rhythm reached a frenzied pitch, rising to a deafening climax.

Rama's name is truth.

13

'Rani, make haste. He calls for you now.'

Kausalya started, almost spilling the thali with which she had been performing the aarti pooja. There were aartis being conducted throughout Suryavansha Palace this evening; the sound of pooja bells and chanting voices filled the entire palace complex. Every one of Dasaratha's three hundred and fifty untitled wives was assembled in the large aarti hall of the neighbouring concubines' palace, performing a rigorous ritual, chanting in a final appeal to the devas to spare their husband-liege. The melodious music of their voices raised in ecstatic harmony filtered all the way up here; it almost drowned out the sounds of restless angry crowds on the avenue outside, the shouts of enraged citizens, and the all-too-frequent clash of steel upon steel. Almost, but not quite. As Mantris Jabali and Ashok had said, speaking on behalf of the rest of the council when they came earlier to visit the maharaja and pay their respects, 'Half of Ayodhya is shrouded in grief today, and the other half is clouded by anger.'

She turned, expecting to see the guru at the threshold of the pooja room. But only the palace guards that Drishti Kumar had insisted stay close by her side stood there, their hardened faces intently watchful. The pooja room itself was filled with the women of her staff, their soft

Banglar voices kept low to avoid disturbing the maharaja. There was no sign of the guru or of anyone else who might have spoken her name. But Kausalya knew better than to question her instincts. She was knowledgeable enough to know that a blind insistence on rationality could cloud one's mind as easily as superstition. She handed her thali to an associate, indicating to her and the other women to continue with the aarti. It was important to complete the cycle of repetitive chanting without any interruptions.

As she left the pooja room, making her way quickly down the corridor towards her private chambers, she was glad of that: at least the aartis kept occupied the incessant flow of visitors and well-wishers whom she had to receive all day long. With everyone inside the aarti halls, the corridors and hallways were virtually deserted. She did not have to offend anyone by rushing past without accepting tearful regrets at the events of this morning. If she heard one more such regret voiced, she believed she would scream loud enough to shatter crystal.

The guru was indeed waiting for her at the door to the innermost chamber. 'Rani,' he said, speaking normally now. 'It is good you came at once. He is conscious, but he will not be for long.' He paused briefly to make sure she understood his meaning. 'He has returned to us only to speak his last words. Heed them well and say your farewells. He will come no more to you henceforth.'

She was silent a moment. Then she nodded briefly, silently: there were no words to express what she felt at this moment. She touched the guru's feet, taking his ashirwaad, and then passed into the chamber. Her own bedchamber, the very same one where Dasaratha had come to her only a fortnight ago, like a whirlwind. Tonight, that whirlwind was dying down at long last, preparing to leave these shores.

She adjusted the pallo of her sari, as befitted an Arya wife in her husband's presence, and made her way to the man lying on the bed. He was breathing raggedly, in slow, hitching gasps, like a pair of smith-bellows unable to fill themselves with sufficient air to keep the fire alive.

'Kausalya,' he said, staring up at the ceiling yet somehow aware of her presence. 'Forgive me, forgive me, forgive me, my love, I beg of you, forgive me . . .'

She fell to her knees beside the bed, grasping the hands he held out to her, joined in supplication. 'There is nothing to forgive, Dasa. You did what dharma demanded.'

He turned his head from side to side, still staring up wild-eyed at the ceiling. His face was wreathed in sweat, his mouth open in a grin of agony. 'I owed her two boons . . .'

'Yes, yes,' she said, fighting back the tears that threatened to wash her away like the Sarayu in spate. 'You had no choice.'

He gripped her hand in an iron fist, crushing it. He turned his face to her, snarling like a wild beast. *'We always have a choice. Always!'*

She was chilled by the fury in his face and voice. Yet she knew that his anger was directed not at her but at himself. His grief and guilt and rage had awoken this savage beast within the failing body, a ghoulish echo of the young virile Dasaratha she had first met and loved.

'I should have denied her the boons. Should have struck her across the face and thrown her aside like the whore she is and always will be!'

She cried out, as much on account of the pain of seeing his state, as at the agony in her crushed fist. 'Dasa!' she sobbed.

Almost at once he fell back, releasing her hand, lapsing back into delirious, maudlin self-pity. 'But I was bound by dharma. And I could not deny its call. I could not . . . could not . . . And so I destroyed it all, by the granting of two simple wishes. Denied my true heir, destroyed my legacy, and played into the hands of our enemies, all with two simple boons.' He laughed the laughter of a maniac who has forgotten everything except pain. 'The ancient Asura gods must be laughing today, high upon their craggy perches, laughing at Dasaratha for doing what no Asura army could ever accomplish . . . laying waste to Ayodhya the Unconquerable!'

'Dasa,' she said desperately, trying to break through his self-obsession. 'Don't torture yourself thus. You did nothing wrong. It was all Manthara's doing. She was manipulated by Ravana, and with the use of Asura sorcery she manipulated Kaikeyi, who in turn manipulated you . . .'

'YES!' he shouted, almost gleefully. 'But in the end it was not any of them who banished Rama into exile. It was me! Dasaratha! Your Dasaratha!' He turned his head to look at her with the pitiful gaze of a loyal dying beast. 'This man you once loved. This king you once married.'

'And still love. And am still married to.' She caught his hand, ignoring the pain in her own fist. 'Listen to me, Dasaratha. Bharat is an honourable man. He has gone to the forest to bring Rama back. To reinstate him as prince-heir.'

A light of hope flashed in the maharaja's eyes. 'Bring him back then. Place me under arrest. Put me in the dungeon on charge of treason!'

She stared at him, wondering if he had gone completely insane. 'Treason?'

'Yes,' he said eagerly. 'That will negate my promises to Kaikeyi! Better still, have him declare me insane. That way nobody can fault me for breaking a boon I made when not in my right mind.' He cackled like a crone suddenly, sending a chill through her chest. 'And was I not then in my right mind? Am I not now? Do this, Kausalya. Throw me in the deepest dungeon and place Rama on the throne.'

'But . . .' She did not know how to respond to this, so unexpected was it. Yet a part of her also acknowledged the fiendish brilliance of its simplicity. Declaring either a charge of treason or one of royal insanity would decisively negate any rule of Manu that Kaikeyi might invoke to enforce her boons. Then she remembered. 'But it won't be necessary. Kaikeyi has relented. She is out of the witch's spell now, Dasa. Perhaps . . . perhaps she was always under her spell to some extent. Now she is free of it, she regrets it all. She herself wants Rama to be crowned heir.'

'Not heir,' he rasped feverishly. *'King!'*

'There is no need to take such drastic measures as imprisoning you,' she said. 'Not that any of us would ever do such a thing, whatever the cause or provocation. Kaikeyi has repeatedly expressed her wish to take back her demands, freeing you of the boons you promised her, and reinstating Rama to his rightful place.'

Dasaratha chuckled. It was a low, throaty chuckle, like a man who has been taken by surprise, having been told a rich joke by the one person he least expected to tell such an anecdote. 'You should know better, Kausalya. It does not matter what Kaikeyi says now. The deed is done! In the foul darkness it was committed, and the pact sealed with an act of passion and an exchange of bodily emissions. It was no less than any blood pact! My promise was made to Kaikeyi, but Kaikeyi was under the thrall of Manthara, and Manthara was in the thrall of whom? Tell me?'

'Ra-va-na,' she whispered, the word sticking in her throat like a handful of thorns.

'Exactly,' he said. 'The Kaikeyi who wrested the boons from me last night in the kosaghar, that was not the Kaikeyi I once loved and married, nor the daughter of noble Bharadwaj of Kaikeya, nor even the sister-queen who lived beneath the same roof as you all these years. That was the lord of Asuras himself, merely acting through a mortal agent. Last night it was Kaikeyi, tomorrow night it will be someone else.'

'What are you saying? That Ravana was the one to whom you made your promise?'

'As good as,' he said, sombrely now. 'He was the engineer who built the siege machine that stormed the impregnable walls of Ayodhya last night, and he will not let his work go unfulfilled. That is why I say to you, arrest me, fling me into prison, declare me a traitor to the kingdom, insane, incompetent, anything! But act!'

'I cannot do such a thing,' she cried out. 'You know I cannot! Nor will anyone else in this house!'

He slumped back lifelessly. 'Then we are doomed.'

He repeated the word over and over again, like a child's litany at a forest gurukul. 'Doomed. Doomed. Doomed.'

She almost didn't hear the voice at the door, so shaken was she by his brutally honest and incisive perspective on the whole situation.

'Dasa,' said the voice again, for the third or fourth time. 'Please . . . may I . . .'

Kausalya turned to see Kaikeyi standing at the door, begging for permission to enter like any common serving maid.

'Vishnu's blessings be upon you,' Rama said, pleasing the farmer who had brought a stack of half-inch-thick maize rotis with a handful of parrot-green chillies. Sumantra took the rotis and mirchis from the farmer and set them on the large cloth spread out upon the knoll, along with the several dozen other items of food given by the other commonfolk. They were all homely preparations, evidence of the rustic simplicity of their givers. There were no elaborate dishes or princely preparations here; it was a far cry from the sumptuous table-crushing spreads that were laid out in the royal bhojanshalya at every meal, a veritable banquet of culinary delights. Yet in Rama's eyes, these simple items of food were no less sumptuous in their generosity and richness of soul. Already there was enough food here to feed a hundred. And the line of people waiting with offerings in hand stretched to the clump of coconut palms at the far end of the clearing.

Rama looked at Sita, seated cross-legged beside him. 'These people are giving me their evening meals,' he said. 'The food they would normally eat at the end of a hard day's work. On what will they and their children sup tonight?'

'I don't think any one of them will sup tonight, Rama,' she said. 'Look at their faces. They look like pilgrims on their way to a shrine to ask the Devi's forgiveness for past misdeeds.'

Rama looked. Despite the rousing reception his speech had elicited, the people were still dejected and forlorn. He had succeeded in calming their anger and clearing their confusion; nobody doubted now that he would go into exile and that he was doing so of his own free will, uncoerced. But that still did not mean they were ready to accept the facts of the matter. The crowd, swelled now to well over five thousand, filled the entire clearing and the surrounding palm groves, seated cross-legged in the manner of devotees awaiting a darshan of a beloved deva, their faces still turned hopefully towards Rama, as if praying that somehow, by some miracle, he would relent and change his mind. A dhobi, his wife and their large clutch of children of various ages sat with their knees up, gazing desolately at Rama. They were among those who had given him their meal and now sat fasting like the others. Several yards to the right, a young pubescent girl sat by her father, their rigs and bows indications of their occupation: Mithilan archers, two of several hundred who had joined Ayodhya's armies after Mithila began laying off its armed forces years ago. The girl stared at him with complete concentration, her heart-shaped face streaked with the tracks of dried tears, as if willing him mentally to take back his words, turn back to Ayodhya and kingship.

He looked away, unable to see any more. To his left, Lakshman stood on the eastern side of the knoll, staring out at the river. The crowds kept coming, thousands upon thousands seeking their banished prince, seeking answers, hope, salvation, and devas knew what else. They were giving him their day's food; they would give him their lives if he but asked. What did he have to give them? Nothing but words and promises, ideals and inspiration. A poor substitute for wheat and rice and a king's grace.

He rose to his feet abruptly, walking to where Lakshman stood. To the right, downriver, where the Tamasa veered sharply westwards, the saffron rays of the setting sun slipped through gaps in the trees of the palm groves, igniting the contours of Lakshman's body and face. They had performed their eveing sandhyavandana a few minutes ago, accompanied by the whole gathering of Kosalans, all squatting by the edge of the riverbank and following Rama's every action and gesture to perfection. Droplets of water still lay beaded on Lakshman's arms and back. His fists and jaw were clenched. He flinched when Rama laid his hand on his shoulder gently. His eyes when he turned were filled with shadows cast by the sun at his back.

'Bhai?' he asked.

Rama glanced around. Sita had risen to join him and Lakshman. Sumantra was continuing to accept offerings of food from the endless line of commonfolk, trying to find room on the already over-full shawl.

'These people will not let me go alone into exile,' he said.

'Nor will we,' Lakshman said.

Rama smiled. Lakshman smiled back, a dark smile that told Rama of the darker shadows lurking in his brother's heart.

'There is no way to make them return to their homes and leave us to journey onward to Dandaka-van,' Rama said.

'If you ask me, I think they would rather die than let you go on alone.'

Rama looked at him closely.

Lakshman indicated the crowded clearing. 'I mean these people, of course.'

'Of course,' Rama said quietly. 'Their mission is to try to make me change my mind and turn back to Ayodhya, to restore myself to my former place and inherit the kingdom.'

Lakshman shrugged. 'I couldn't have said it better.'

Rama nodded. 'And I will not do that.'

Lakshman looked at him intently for a long moment, then looked away. 'You will not.'

'That is why,' Rama said, turning to look at Sita and include her in the discussion, 'it would be best if we wait until they are asleep, then slip away quietly in Sumantra's chariot. If we ride all night, by morning we will be too far ahead for them to catch up with us.'

Lakshman and Sita were silent.

Rama went on after a pause, 'The Dandaka-van is a big place. Once we enter the forest, they will hardly be able to find us. Although I hope that they will not try to follow us at all.'

He glanced back at Sumantra. 'To be sure that they do not follow us into the jungle, we will send Sumantra back to dissuade them and tell them which way we went.'

'Tell them which way . . .' Lakshman began, then stopped. 'While we actually take another route into the jungle?'

Rama nodded. 'That is all we can do. The rest we must leave to the devas and the common sense of these simple folk. I trust they will not do anything foolish after we are gone.'

Sita said softly, 'Whatever they do, it is not your fault. You cannot protect them any more. After all . . .' She hesitated before adding, 'They are no longer your people to protect.'

He looked at her sadly, the dusky light of twilight casting her lovely features into shadow as well. 'You're right. They are not my people any more.'

14

They made their move late into the night. It had taken several hours for the gathering to subside into something resembling sleep. A large throng of new arrivals had broken down, distraught, at the sight of Rama, and their weeping had set off a chain of wails and chest-beating and hair-pulling throughout the clearing. By then, the crowd on the west bank was easily ten thousand strong. The ferries had stopped plying because the river's spate had made it dangerous to do so in the dark of night. But from the thickening masses of shadows and the sounds from the far bank, Rama estimated that another ten thousand or more would accumulate by morning. At one point, he thought he caught the distant rumbling of wheels and hoofs, as if a large, heavy contingent was on the move. It carried in the stillness of night even above the ceaseless roaring of the river. He turned uneasily in the dark, reminded for some inexplicable reason of his distant memories of childhood, when his father used to ride out to quell regional disturbances and enforce the peace among the quarrelsome pahadi clans. A part of him longed for the simplicity of that childhood, when the days seemed to last for ever, the nights passed in a wink, and the sky appeared to him to be the blue-tinted palm of a benevolent deva who would protect the world from all threats.

Where was that deva now? The sky had turned dark and pressed close upon his face, threatening to suffocate him.

He sat up slowly. Sita was instantly alert and whispered, asking for the third time that night if he would eat something before they left. He had already told her twice earlier that he would take only water until they were in Dandaka-van and he had fulfilled Kaikeyi's orders to the letter. He made no answer this time, and crept quietly to the tree trunk against which Lakshman sat, watching. Lakshman turned his head before Rama could touch his shoulder and rose to his feet.

They went down the far side of the knoll, walking through the grove until they found the open spot where Sumantra waited with the chariot and a lantern set to the smallest wick to prevent the light from being seen by any of the commonfolk. He raised the lantern, twisting the knob that widened the wick slightly, producing a brighter spill. Rama saw that the pradhan-mantri had already harnessed the horses in preparation. His lined face gazed at Rama silently, with the faintest trace of hope.

'We must leave now, Sumantra,' Rama said very softly, putting to rest any further arguments. 'We will lead the horses as far as we can, then ride. If it is all the same to you, I will take the reins.'

Sumantra offered no argument. Since sunset, the prime minister had settled into a kind of resigned acceptance that was in some ways worse than his earlier resistance. They walked for about a mile, far enough to be out of easy hearing of the crowd by the river. When they were all mounted and ready to ride, Rama looked at Sumantra by the light of the lantern.

'Old friend, perhaps you should stay here and reassure the people when they awaken. Your place is with them, not in the jungle where we go now.'

Sumantra looked ahead at the dark, narrow mud-path winding between closely pressing rows of dense forest.

'I don't know where my place is any more,' he said in a broken voice. 'Or even if I still have a place in this world. If I do, then that place is with you, Rama. I will ride with you as far as you will let me.'

He turned to look at Rama, his eyes rheumy and jaundiced in the yellow glow of the lantern. 'If you command me, I will dismount at once.'

'No,' Rama said. 'It is our privilege that you ride with us tonight on this last journey out of Ayodhya.'

He raised the reins, making sure that the team understood his intent and were ready to obey. They had settled well since the brush with death and the river. They raised their heads, snorting softly, awaiting his command. He tugged the reins, then flicked them forward, giving the animals their head.

'To Dandaka-van,' Rama said, to nobody in particular. The lead horse, Kamabha, whinnied softly, as if acknowledging their destination. *This time*, he seemed to say, *I will not let you down, my lord*. Rama flicked the reins again, setting the chariot into motion. *Ride then, my beauty, ride with all your strength and speed*.

The chariot moved forward, rolling quietly into the dark night.

The very humility in the queen's face, the abject self-effacement of her deglamorised appearance and apparel, all brought home the change in her with painful impact. Could this truly be Kaikeyi? Proud, beautiful, arrogant Kaikeyi? She of a thousand charms and a million desires? *No. This is Bharat's mother Kaikeyi, Dasaratha's wife, my sister-queen*, Kausalya thought.

'Please,' Kaikeyi repeated. 'I only wish to say—'

Dasa sat up in his bed, sweat flying off his face. 'Get this woman out of my sight at once. Guards!' he roared. 'Take her away.'

Kaikeyi ran to the bed, breaking away from the guards before they could take proper hold of her. 'Please! I beg you. All I ask is your forgiveness. I knew not what I was doing.'

'You did it,' he said savagely. 'That was enough.'

She stared up at him as the guards descended on her, grabbing her by either arm, remorselessly. Every soul in the palace knew the details of what had transpired in the kosaghar last night and early this morning; Kaikeyi's own guards had made certain of that, turning coat upon their own sigil in sheer disgust at the monstrous injustice wrought by their clan-queen. Kausalya would have stopped them, or at least ordered them to handle her less roughly, but Kaikeyi worsened her own lot by straining at their muscled arms, crying out to the bed-ridden maharaja with all the manic hysteria of a crazed woman.

'I RELEASE YOU,' she cried. 'I RELEASE YOU OF YOUR BOONS!'

'Ah,' he said, as if a dart had found its way to his heart. 'But that release is no longer yours to give, my beautiful one.'

'I love you, Dasa,' she sobbed then, as the guards began to drag her away by the arms, pulling her across the floor to the entrance. 'I love you, my prince!'

For a moment his face crumpled, and Kausalya bent forward, thinking to catch him before he fell. But he only swayed from side to side momentarily, like a drunken man staggering at the threshold of his home, and grinned a lopsided maniacal grin. 'If only that was all it took to make the world turn,' he said. Then, to the guards, 'Hold her a moment. I wish to speak words.'

They stopped at once, but retained their iron grip on Kaikeyi's arms. She flopped miserably like a rag doll in their grasp. 'Scribe,' Kaikeyi heard one of the guards say, turning his head to address one of his fellows outside the door. Almost at once, a court scribe appeared, his pigtail bobbing upon his shaven pate, the wooden scribe-board, scroll and other instruments clutched eagerly. He sat down on the floor at the foot of the bed, virtually out of sight of the king and Kausalya, and was ready to take dictation in a moment. Scribes were ever present to transcribe the maharaja's words, but tonight, Kausalya guessed, they were that much more alert. Tonight they would transcribe a maharaja's last words.

Dasaratha bent his head for a moment, as if in some deep contemplation. When he raised his brow again, Kausalya saw, he almost appeared normal. Her Dasaratha. The maharaja who looked exactly this way when he pronounced judgement in his court on any one of the innumerable cases brought before him in his decades of service as a king of the realm.

'Rani Kaikeyi, I divorce myself of our nuptial bond. From this moment on, you are no longer my lawfully wedded wife, nor I your lawfully wedded husband. You are free to return to your father's roof, or to any other place you desire. You have no place here henceforth. In my reckoning, you have broken the vrath you made at our nuptials, so many years ago. You have brought great pain and humiliation and shame to me and to my family, as well as to my people. I do not wish to see you ever again, whether I live a thousand years more, or merely another instant. Go from my sight, and do not return. This is my aadesh, my royal decree, both as your husband and as your king. For a king is always king first, husband second.'

And he turned his face away from her, towards Kausalya.

Kaikeyi screamed. Her long wail of grief rang through the corridors of Suryavansha Palace and passed out into the late-evening air. The scream lingered in Kausalya's memory a long time after the Second Queen was dragged away by the guards, long after the scribe had picked up his implements and returned to the antechamber, long after Dasaratha reached out to her and gripped her arm with shaking hands. Dragging himself across the bed, he laid his head upon her lap. A sigh rose from him, as a traveller might make when laying down his head at the end of a long, arduous journey.

'How could I grant her forgiveness?' he said in a voice that shook as much as his hands. 'I who am so urgently in need of being forgiven myself.'

She laid a hand upon his brow, feeling the intense heat of his fever, her heart aching to imagine the blazing agony of his condition. From time to time he writhed and twisted, racked by pains within his vitals. 'You have no need of forgiveness,' she said, breathing warm and soft upon his unshaven cheek. 'You have redeemed yourself already a thousandfold.'

She felt him struggle to turn, even this simple action suddenly become too great an effort. *His heart broke at last just now*, she thought. *It broke when he sent Kaikeyi away and accepted his own responsibility for all that has happened.*

'Redeemed myself?' he stuttered. 'H-h-how?'

She wiped the sweat from his brow, pushing his straggly grey hair back off his face. 'The day you fathered Rama.'

He grew suddenly still, and remained that way for a long time. When he spoke again, it was in the whispering tone of a much older man. 'He will return, will he not? To succeed me? To accept his place as king of Ayodhya?'

'I vow to you that he will,' she said. She, who never made a vow idly. 'Rama will return and be crowned king of Ayodhya.'

His breathing seemed to grow easier then, less ragged. His shaking gradually ceased. His writhing stopped. He lay peacefully with his head upon her lap a long time, perhaps hours or minutes, she could not tell. Outside, the sky grew dark and night fell upon Ayodhya, upon them all.

Sometime towards morning, he took one final gasping breath, said a single word, and died. The last word he spoke was the name of his eldest son.

It came first to Rama as a sense of breathlessness, a choking sensation that threatened to drop him there and then, at the helm of the chariot. His hand shook, and he almost jerked it to the right, almost twisted the tightly held reins the wrong way. Had he done so, he would have turned the heads of the team, driving them off the edge of the ghat they were travelling over now. Chariot and all, they would have plunged into the valley below. *And would that be so bad? Better a sudden quick death than fourteen years of slow dying.*

Then a wave of black despair passed over him like a monsoon cloud over a mountain, engulfing him, smothering him with darkness. He cried out despite himself, and the reins jerked again. This time, the horses did turn, and the chariot veered towards the edge, closer to the crumbling rim of the dirt-path cut into the side of the ghat, shifting towards the yawning gulf. Lakshman came to his rescue. He snatched the reins from Rama's hands, shouting to Sumantra and Sita to grab hold of Rama. It was well they did so, for the next moment Rama all but collapsed in the well of the chariot. His legs lost all strength and he slumped down. Sita gripped his arms with fierce strength, squatting down to put herself between him and the open rear of the swaying, bumping chariot. Looking at the road fleeing behind them, Rama saw the course of the chariot change slowly, steadily, as Lakshman drove the team with the practised expertise of one who had loved and communicated well with animals all his life. The chariot regained its position in the centre of the mountainous path, out of harm's way.

Sita peered into Rama's eyes as if she would see right through into his mind. 'What is it?' she asked urgently. 'What's happening, my love?'

He shook his head, opening his mouth, but found himself unable to speak. He tried to gesture with his hands, but it came out only as a fish-like flopping. She frowned, struggling to understand him.

'What is it? Say something, Rama.'

He tried to open his mouth again, but no words emerged. It was as if the cloud had enfolded him in its cold wet embrace, and darkness filled his brain and vision, a roaring emptiness that threatened to wash him away, dash him on the rocks of oblivion and shatter him to fragments. He moaned, clutching his head with both hands, and Sita cried out with alarm. She shouted something to Lakshman that Rama did not catch above the noise of the chariot and the roaring in his own head. But several moments later the chariot began to slow, until finally it rolled to a gentle halt.

Rama tried to stand. Sita and Sumantra helped him, clutching his arms. His vision swam as he rose to his feet, his knees buckling. He managed to get to the edge of the chariot with their aid, then off it and on to the ground.

They had stopped almost at the top of the ghat, near the peak of the dusty mountain marg. Looking back, he could see the dust-cloud of their trail still hanging in the air. Far beyond and below was the vast undulating northern forest they had ridden through the night before. Somewhere beyond that were the rivulets Vedasruti, Gomatic and Syandika which they had crossed without any difficulty in the early hours. They were well beyond the borders of Kosala now. They had mounted these ghats an hour ago. Beyond them lay the Ganga valley, and the glade of Sringaverapura, also known as Hunter's Glade. In less than an hour, at the rigorous pace they had maintained all night, they would breast that peak and ride down the far side, into the sacred arms of the Ganga.

He realised that it was almost daybreak; that was how he was able to see so far.

He also realised that his limbs had stopped trembling and had lost their gelid weakness. The cloud still loomed over his mind and soul, but the physical debilitation was gone. He could stand and speak again.

They were all staring at him, concerned, frightened. Sumantra had his hands clasped, like a man standing before a deity with only one desperate prayer.

Rama braced himself, taking a deep, long breath before saying what he knew to be truth with every fibre of his being. Only Lakshman's face suggested that he had some inkling of what his brother would say next, as if he too had been brushed by the belly of the same cloud.

'Our father is dead,' Rama said. 'Maharaja Suryavansha Manu Ikshwaku Raghuvamsha Aja-putra Dasaratha is no more. I felt his aatma pass me only moments ago, on its way to Swarga-lok.'

15

It began to rain as they entered the Ganga valley. A rain-cloud appeared out of the clear dawn sky, showering them with a gentle drizzle. Lakshman was driving the chariot still, to give Rama a respite. Sumantra, standing beside Rama and Sita, raised his arms to the sky, sending up a prayer, and voiced his thanks to the gods, his tears mingling freely with the first droplets. It was considered very auspicious for rain to fall on a death day; the brahmins took it as an omen that the person's aatma would certainly ascend to the heavenly realms for the duration of its stay between worlds, until the time of its next rebirth. The devas crying, it was called in Mithila. Sita licked a droplet that fell on her upper lip and felt that no water ever drunk had tasted so pure and sweet.

The devas cried all the way to the Ganga. When they came within sight of that great concourse of water, even Rama's heart seemed to lift. Sita sensed it immediately, as if he felt not happier but less burdened. Another auspicious omen, for to visit the Ganga after a loved one's death was to wash oneself clean of the detritus of past lives and gain forgiveness for any wrongs or hurts one might have committed against the departed one.

The lush green valley glowed with fertility in the dawn light. Everything was wet and fragrant with the natural aromas of earth and fresh rain, flowers and growth. The air above the river was filled with life: swans, cranes, cakravaka birds and a wide assortment of songbirds flew in great wheeling circles, celebrating the new day's dawning. As they rode the path alongside the river itself, Sita saw the shapes and colours of a multitude of life forms in the waters: porpoises performed their sinuous gleaming dance, crocodiles crawled lazily on their long bellies on the mudbanks, kachuas floated upstream sleepily. And fish of course, a teeming myriad of species and sizes, turning the river into a glittering silver necklace.

They halted the chariot at a small Gangetic settlement that was more resting area than village. It was an outpost of the Nisada clans, Sumantra informed Sita, who hadn't visited these parts before. There were rishis and sadhus and brahmins of all orders sitting and walking about the few timber-plank structures beside a wide, slow section of the holy river. Most of them were engaged in their morning acamana, either about to enter the water or emerging dripping from it. A stone stairway, ten yards wide, descended gradually into a small pool that drained off the main river, lagooned by a border of time-eroded stone blocks. Even so, the fauna of the river could easily have slipped over the stone border, like the water that constantly slopped over its top, to find easy pickings in this pool. But it was a well-known fact that even predators did not prey on those who came to the Ganga with genuinely repentant hearts. Gazing across the river at the line of crocodiles lying on its banks, Sita wondered at the truth of that belief. In any case, she would have a chance to verify it herself in a few moments.

They took their acamana together, the brahmins around them unperturbed by the presence of a woman in their midst: all were as one here in the arms of the blessed Ganga. Brother and sister suckled together at the breasts of the divine mother. Sita was astonished at the purity and clarity of the water. How could there be no mud or silt? And with so many bodies wading in and out at all times, what kept the water so clean? She had a feeling that if she were to ask those questions, she would not receive a satisfactory rational answer from even the wisest brahmin present.

As she immersed herself in the waters, a great calm came over her. Beneath the surface of the river, sitting cross-legged on the stone steps, Rama to her left, Lakshman beyond him, she felt a sense of elevation that transcended the mere physical sensation of the water pushing her upwards. Speaking the sacred Gayatri maha-mantra in her mind, she felt tranquillity pervade her pores, releasing the unbearable stresses that had ravaged her mind this past night and day. At the very end of the last recitation, when her held breath ought to have been exhausted, she felt as though she could go on thus indefinitely, breathing the very molecules of the river to gain the nourishment she needed. It was only when both Rama and Lakshman got to their feet, breaking the surface, that she thought she ought to rise as well. But just before she did so, something caught her eye, at the extreme periphery of her vision. She turned, seeking out the distraction, but saw nothing. She continued turning, executing a full circle. All she saw was the rough-cut stone of the steps, worn smooth in the centre by the treading of countless feet over the centuries. She saw the dhoti-clad legs of Rama, standing on an upper step, saying the end of his prayer as he offered water to Surya-deva. She completed the turn and finished the circle. That was when she saw it, or thought she did, just for a flash of a second.

A woman, walking towards her, at the very bottom of

the steps, five yards below the surface. She was dressed in a red sari, so vividly coloured that it actually made Sita squint. On her feet were silver anklets, not payals but bracelet-like ornaments. She walked with easy grace beneath the water, coming towards Sita. She had something to give her, Sita knew. Something to hand over for safe keeping. Sita raised her eyes to the woman's face, to see who this exotic creature might be who walked the floor of the mighty river as if strolling through a princess garden.

Abruptly, she found herself above the surface, gasping in air, choking on swallowed water, the crisp early-morning air blessedly warm after the chill of the river. She smelt lotus and other assorted flowers, from the garlands the brahmins floated upon the water. Rama was holding her tightly, in both arms. She wiped her face, clearing her eyes. 'What . . . what happened?' she asked, sputtering water.

'You were drowning,' he said, sounding puzzled.

She looked around. Nobody was paying attention to them; all were busy with their own ablutions. Only Lakshman was watching from a few steps up, concerned but not overly anxious. 'That's impossible,' she said. 'I was holding my breath.'

'It was too long to hold your breath, Sitey,' he said, using the affectionate 'ey' suffix for the first time since she had known him.

She looked at him, then glanced around again. A line of cranes left the surface of the river, rising slowly into the sky, their white spans catching the first rays of the rising sun. They glowed golden for a moment, then moved out of her line of vision. 'But . . .' she said. 'But I saw . . .'

He waited patiently.

How could she describe the woman she had seen? She

hadn't even seen her face. Only her bright red sari and her anklets, like thick bracelets a man might wear rather than the delicate payals Arya women favoured.

She shook her head, saying nothing. He didn't press her further. They went up the steps, treading carefully, and made their way back to the place where Sumantra had left their chariot. A pair of strangers were with the pradhan-mantri, listening as he talked softly. From the manner in which the prime minister spoke, Sita could tell he was discussing Rama and the events in Ayodhya. But then, what else would he speak about? Every Kosalan in the kingdom, nay, every Arya in the seven kingdoms, would be talking about nothing else.

The two strangers were clad in the garb of sudra hunters. Animal pelts were their only clothing, worn diagonally over their shoulders and around their waists. Necklaces of animal teeth – at least Sita hoped they were animal teeth – and assorted small bones hung in layers around their necks. One of them had small, straight bones piercing his nose laterally, and both had several other metal and bone piercings on their ears, brows, arms, navels, and everywhere else visible. Among hunters, the body piercings indicated status. These two were no ordinary men; they were village panchs at the very least, part of the five-person village committee that constituted the basis of Arya rural self-governance. They were strong and well built in appearance, not in the oiled and muscled manner of rakshaks or the austere leanness of trained military men, but rather in the vigorous manner of naturally robust men who worked hard, lived well, and enjoyed their meat and drink as well. They were short by Arya standards, both no more than Sita's height and perhaps half a foot shorter than Rama and Lakshman.

They turned as Rama approached, and Sumantra

introduced them at once. 'These are Neelkant and Ninaad, tribe-chiefs of the Vegrath-Nisadas.'

The hunters came forward to greet Rama, bowing their heads but not their knees in respect. As freemen, they were not strictly bound by Arya law, and so did not consider Rama or any other Arya royalty as above them. They gripped Rama's hand first in a double-handed clasp, then embraced him warmly before repeating the welcome with Lakshman.

'On behalf of the Nisada free peoples, we welcome you to Sringaverapura,' said the one named Ninaad. 'There is no doubt that Chief Guha will be most pleased to offer you the hospitality of his clan-house.'

They said nothing about the banishment or Ayodhya, which, Sita thought, was a welcome thing.

They crossed the river with the Nisadas on fishing boats that smelled richly of fresh and stale catches alike. Halfway across, Sita realised that the 'stool' she had been sitting on was a turtle shell, and that the turtle in question was very much alive. Her squawk of alarm when the amphibian moved elicited smiles from the Nisadas. Only Rama and Lakshman remained expressionless, their lack of visible emotion barely concealing the pain she knew they must feel at their father's passing.

The Nisadas brought their chariot and horse-team across on pull-rope rafts but without the kind of mishaps Rama and his companions had suffered crossing the Tamasa. Sita was charmed by the way the men and women accompanying the horses seemed to speak gently to the beasts, soothing them expertly. It was only when one of the women made a comment about how just one of the horses would make a grand feast that she remembered that the Nisadas only bred animals for their meat, never as beasts of burden. She wondered if strong-headed

Kamabha, set to browsing on the rich green grassy bank, knew that he was being eyed as a possible main course for tonight's evening meal. She thought not, or the horse would not be munching so calmly.

It was a long walk through the woods, since Nisada law did not permit wheeled or mounted travellers in their heartland. Along the way, Sita saw several of the forest folk going about their daily work.

Chief Guha was a large man, not only in girth but in voice and manner as well. He roared with pleasure at the sight of Sumantra, greeting him like a long-lost friend, embracing the poor distraught pradhan-mantri in a bone-crushing grasp. He was disproportionately taller than the rest of his people, towering at least three heads higher than the other Nisada men around him, and a head higher than Sumantra as well. Bearlike in appearance, his chest and limbs matted with a dense profusion of black hair tinged only slightly with strands of white, he resembled the predators his people hunted and for which they were renowned. His jaw was wolf-like, his mane of hair leonine, his eyes glittering like the beady orbs of a cobra, his arms simian like a gorilla's, and his overall look that of wildness. Sita half expected to find roots sprouting from his feet, snaking into the earth.

Heads poked out of the huts sprawled about the clearing and nestled among the trees, stretching as far in every direction as Sita could see. There were even dwellings in the trees, round platforms made of wood and bamboo and hemp rope, and people seemed to live or work on these as well. She was taken aback by the sheer profusity of the population; she had always assumed that the Nisadas were little more than a hamlet of a few hundred folk. As Chief Guha performed the arghya ritual for Rama and Lakshman, he himself volunteered the information, proudly, that the Nisadas now numbered over five hundred thousand.

'And growing by the hour,' he said, winking boldly at Rama before breaking out into yet another forest-shaking burst of throaty laughter.

A great feast was prepared in their honour within the hour, with every conceivable kind of flesh served up on huge wooden platters, steaming and sizzling in fragrant juices. After looking at the long table piled high with the flesh of assorted species, Sita felt she would rather continue to fast than eat any of it. In the end, she followed Rama's example and took a little of this and that, pretending to eat out of sheer politeness while actually breaking her hunger-fast with simple fruits. Moving the food around on her plate with the cores and remnants of the eaten fruits, she thanked their host for the sumptuous meal.

After the meal, Guha and the rest of his highest-ranked men and women listened with rapt attention as Sumantra told them of the events preceding their exodus from Ayodhya. When he came to the part where Rama stopped their chariot on the ghats and said that he had sensed Dasaratha's passing, Guha's face darkened and he slammed his fist on the rickety wooden table, knocking food and plates off.

'Who will light the maharaja's byre now?' he said, shaking his wild mane. 'His eldest son sits here in Sringaverapura, a long way from Ayodhya. What will happen to the funeral rites of Dasaratha when Rama is no longer there to even put flame to his bier?'

Nobody answered him. The Nisada chief raised his hands to the skies. 'Everyone calls us savages, because we make our living hunting and killing the beasts of the land. Indeed, we are savages, for you cannot catch wild predators by acting in a civilised fashion! But then what does that make the Arya nations? What has our world come to when a father banishes his son to exile at the behest of a jealous wife?'

Guha gestured with one large hairy hand, indicating the women and children sitting to one side of the table. 'I have a hundred wives, or perhaps two hundred, I lose count. Thrice as many children. If I were to listen to every one of my wives who wishes her first-born declared clan chieftain after my passing, I would be banishing one or two sons into exile every day!'

He laughed at that, and was echoed by the other Nisadas. He pointed to Rama.

'Here is what I have to say on your banishment by Dasaratha, my young prince of Ayodhya. I say that when Kaikeyi told Dasaratha to send you into exile, your father should have slapped her hard and sent both her and her milk-fed son away instead!'

This also elicited much laughter, especially from the smaller children, who were gnawing toothlessly on joints that were almost as large as themselves.

Sita glanced at Rama and saw him sitting rigidly upright, in that expressionless way that made it clear he disapproved of Guha's words and manner of speech.

Rama spoke stiffly after the laughter died down. 'My father is an honourable man. He owed his second wife two boons for having saved his life. When she demanded that he honour his word, he had no choice but to comply.'

Guha laughed scornfully. 'A man always has a choice!' He winked at Sita openly. 'Perhaps a woman sometimes does not, but a man, he can always choose. Am I right or am I right, my pretty princess?'

There were sniggers and smirks from the men and giggles from the women. Sumantra looked unhappy at the comment, while Lakshman actually started to rise to respond to the innuendo that would be considered offensive in civilised Arya society. *But we're not in civilised Arya society any more*, Sita reminded herself. *We're amongst the jungle clans now. They are rough people, with rough talk and rougher ways. Chief Guha does not mean to offend, only to provoke an honest response.*

Sita stopped Lakshman with a hand placed on his arm, and responded undaunted. 'Perhaps among the forest clans, Chief Guha. But in Ayodhya or Mithila, a woman has every right to say no. Men and women, young and old, all have equal rights under Manu's Law.'

Guha gazed at her keenly, his beady eyes glinting in the firelight. It had grown dark as they feasted, and night had fallen while they talked. 'All except prince-heirs? Is that what Manu's Law says? That the eldest son can be deprived of his birthright, or his . . . what is that word you civilised Aryas use? His dharma! Is that acceptable under Arya law then?'

Rama replied quietly. People leaned forward, straining to hear his words, the gathering quietening the instant he spoke. Sita glimpsed mothers hushing their children as they listened intently to Rama. There was more than idle interest in the eyes and body language of the younger, unmarried tribal women, she noted. One particularly attractive specimen, her bare torso bedecked strikingly with bronze and copper body-pierce jewellery, was clearly trying to catch Rama's eye with her sinuous movements and adoring sighs. But Rama's eyes were fixed on his host as he spoke.

'My father was oathbound to my clan-mother Kaikeyi. She had saved his life on the battlefield a long time ago. He had promised her two boons for her acts, one for each time she had saved his life. When Kaikeyi demanded that he fulfil his oath and grant her those two boons, he was honour-bound to do so. Any honourable man would do the same.'

Rama emphasised the word *honourable* in a manner that could only be termed provocative.

Guha frowned slowly, reading the unmistakable challenge in the words. He glared at Rama from across the table. 'Are you saying I am not honourable?'

'I do not comment on you or your ways, Chief Guha,' Rama said quietly. 'I would be most grateful if you do not comment on mine.'

There was silence in the clearing for a moment. Sita could hear the distant chittering of bats high above the trees, and the chirring and clicking of insects around them.

Guha sat absolutely still. His entire clan seemed to hold their breath as they waited for his response to this acrid comment, easily possible to interpret as an insult, or at the very least a challenge to the chief's own honour.

In the deathly silence Sita heard the angry cry of a peacock deep in the forest. It was followed almost immediately by another answering cry, as angry as the first. A mating fight.

The Nisada chief rose to his feet. His enormous belly struck the edge of the table, setting it to a shudder that almost knocked it over. He stood, towering over his guests, glaring down at Rama. Then, just as Sita was certain that he was about to give the order for them to be trussed and executed summarily, he threw his arms out.

Rama stared at the chief's outstretched arms for a moment, incomprehendingly. Then he rose and came forward in response. Guha embraced Rama in the bear-like manner with which he had greeted Sumantra earlier, clapping him hard on the back. Rama's slender form seemed to vanish into the hirsute folds of the tribal chieftain's enormous body.

After what seemed like an eternity, Guha released Rama. Flashing a wide, toothy grin, he called out to the expectant spectators, still waiting uneasily for some verbal confirmation of the chief's response. 'Look well at him, my people. Look long and hard. For here is a son who honours his father even after being cast out of his house. Who among the forest clans . . .' He stopped and shook his mane. 'Nay, who among all mankind would turn his back on his inheritance, his regal right, his entire kingdom, just to uphold his father's honour and his own dharma? No man I know of. Can you name any such man . . . or woman, for that matter? Even one living soul who would sacrifice so much only for the honour of his parent?'

He looked around, waiting for a response. There was none. He nodded, indicating Rama again.

'Hence I say, feast your eyes upon a true prince, not only of Ayodhya, but of all mankind. A prince of dharma! And repeat after me, Siyavar Rama Chandra ki jai!'

Praised be Rama Chandra, husband of Sita.

With one gruff, booming voice, the entire clan leapt to their feet, repeating lustily after their chief, 'Siyavar Rama Chandra ki jai!'

They repeated it thrice, each time louder than before, until Sita's ears rang with the resounding echoes. Birds, disturbed from their night roosts, flew up in alarm everywhere, roused by the stentorian cries of fifty thousand voices.

Guha embraced Rama yet again, then he all but shouted above the echoes and cries of complaining birds, 'Son of my friend, now my friend as well, I am humbled by your loyalty to your father. Accept my apologies if my words have caused any offence. I am a rough-spoken man.'

'No apology is needed, good Guha,' Rama said, as the

echoes died away. 'Your heart is true. And as soft and tender as your words are rough and coarse.'

Guha laughed with delight, clapping Rama hard on the back. 'My friend. Now I know truly that Dashrath was a wise and great king. I know this because he has fathered a great and wise son!'

Rama bowed his head silently, smiling even though Sita knew how painful it must be for him to endure all this needless talk. She wished she could tell Guha to shut up and leave them be. She wanted to be alone with Rama. She needed to lay her hot cheek on his cool shoulder and take comfort in his strength. It was all she could do to keep her senses about her.

Guha clapped his hands loudly, then emitted a shrill, ululating bird-cry. It was answered from all points, then passed on deep into the forest.

'Tonight,' Guha boomed out loudly, as if addressing the forest entire, 'we shall honour our great guests by keeping a night-long vigil. Rama Chandra ki jai!'

The answering cry was deafening.

Above the sounds of the crying and complaining birds, Sita heard another sound, growing steadily louder.

Guha raised his head, hearing it too. Lakshman stirred uneasily, his hand moving to his bow and rig. One of Guha's lieutenants said something in their tribal dialect that didn't need translation. Everyone present had heard that distinctive ominous rumbling often enough to know it for what it was.

Guha frowned and looked at Rama.

'That is the sound of an army approaching,' he said. 'I do not think this is good news, my friend.'

16

Bharat gazed out at the Ganga valley spread before him like a promised land. The very sight of it made him ill to the core. The last time he had come here, it had been with his brothers and his father, on a hunting expedition. They had stayed with Guha of the Nisadas and enjoyed a holiday filled with wonderful, unforgettable memories. To be here again now, under these circumstances, was unsettling enough to make him want to turn his horse around and ride home.

But he had a mission to complete. *Bring Rama home*, Kausalya-maa had said, sealing his intent with her words. *Make this family whole again*. Bharat didn't know if he could accomplish such a task, in the wake of all that had transpired. His heart still ached for his departed father. The news had reached them when they had stopped by the Tamasa and found Rama departed from there. He had heard also of his father's dying disenfranchisement of Kaikeyi. How could Bharat possibly make this shattered family whole again now?

But one thing he could and would do: convince his elder brother to return to Ayodhya and reclaim his rightful place. That was why he had travelled this long way with a full akshohini of Ayodhya's finest. The long lines of cavalry and bigfoot rumbled down into the valley before him, raising a dustcloud and thundering reverberation that could be seen, heard and felt for miles. Nothing and nobody would prevent him from fulfilling this mission. *Bring Rama home.* Yes, Mother, he said silently, touching his forehead where she had blessed him. I will not return home except with Rama.

He turned the head of his horse, nodding to Shatrugan, who was waiting nearby. Together they rode down past the long winding lines of mounted and armoured Ayodhyan soldiers, a host large enough to start a war. He prayed it would be large enough to bring one exiled prince home.

They emerged from the trees and came upon the Ganga again. Sita caught her breath at the sight before them. Guha was right. An army had come to Sringaverapura. It was assembled on the far bank of the Ganga, rows upon rows of cavalry, chariot, elephant, and infantry, their burnished armour gleaming in the noonday sun, sending dazzling reflections and refractions through the misty vapours rising from the river. The sigils of Kosala, Ayodhya, the Suryavansha dynasty, and the Ikshwaku clan were clearly visible even at this distance, the banners flapping proudly in the steady breeze that blew downriver. Sita's heart thudded in her chest. Why was this army here?

Guha answered the question aloud, speaking for them all in a sober tone wholly unlike his earlier boisterous belligerence. 'It appears your brother Bharat is not content with having the throne to himself, Rama Chandra. See. He comes after you with the might and steel of Kosala. He seeks to remove any potential threat to his ascension, now or in the future.'

'I would not have believed it if someone had merely

told me so, Rama,' Lakshman said in a choked voice. 'But I think Chief Guha speaks the truth. Why else would Bharat come here with such an army if not to wage war upon us and wipe us out?'

'Heed your brother, if not me,' Guha said. 'He sees the threat and recognises it for what it is. Your brother knows that some day your exile will end, and you will return to claim the throne you were born to inherit. By stamping you out today, he stamps out all future risk to his kingship.' The Nisada chief sighed, massaging his belly. 'I cannot blame him. Even after fourteen years, your people will welcome you home as if you had been gone only fourteen days. Even we Nisadas know how much Ayodhya loves its prodigal son.'

Across the river, Bharat and Shatrugan had dismounted and were striding forward, approaching the line of boats pulled up along the bank. They were accompanied by quads of soldiers on either side. A captain of PFs shouted some order to the fisherfolk squatting by the boats, and soldiers showed their lances, ready to prod the boatmen into action if needed. It was impossible to hear any words across the two-hundred-yard breadth of the river, or even to see individual features of faces clearly, but Sita sensed that Bharat was staring across at them directly, looking straight at Rama. She glanced at Rama and saw that he too was gazing directly at Bharat.

Lakshman unslung his bow and put an arrow to the cord. The muscles of his jaw were clenching with anger.

'He means to launch an assault now, Rama,' Lakshman said. 'Let us prepare to fight back. We can pick them off more easily while they are in mid-crossing. That way, we negate their superiority in numbers.'

'Good thinking, rajkumar,' Guha said. 'Your best chance would be to kill as many as you can before they cross. Once that great host is on this bank, you stand no chance in hell.'

Rama said quietly, 'They have bowmen too. Long Mithilan bows. If they wished, they could have done the same to us, firing across the river and picking us off where we stand. As you can see, they are not doing so. Only Bharat and Shatrugan intend to cross, with maybe just a quad or two.'

'Even better,' the chief said. 'Kill Bharat and you eliminate the whole threat. I warrant that every soldier on that bank of the Ganga would fall at your feet and accept your right to the throne once Bharat is gone. Aim your arrows well, princes of Ayodhya. Win back the kingdom you have lost!'

Rama turned to look at the Nisada chief. Guha stood on Rama's far side, so Sita could not see Rama's face when he turned to him. But she could see Guha's face clearly, and from the way the hunter-lord flinched, she could imagine the grim look he had just confronted.

'Hear me well, Chief Guha. I would rather remain in exile until my dying day than wrest back the throne by shedding a single drop of my brother's blood.'

Guha looked nonplussed, then an expression of sudden exasperation passed across his fleshy face. 'I do not understand you, Rama Chandra. You are too great a man of dharma to survive this world! It is one thing to have such lofty ideals when you are a brahmin, freed of all wordly responsibilities. But you are a kshatriya. A warrior-prince who was raised to be a king. It is your destiny to be king! Even your father willed it so.'

'If it is destined, it will be so,' Rama said. 'All things will come to pass in their own time and way.'

Guha gestured at Sita. 'And what of your wife? And your brother? Will you make them suffer these long years in exile as well? And what of your future offspring as and when they come? Will you condemn them to grow up in that wretched haunt of rakshasas and predators? Do you understand what it means to spend even one night and survive the perils of Dandaka-van, let alone *fourteen years*? If one of our young boys ventures mistakenly into that place and comes out alive a day later, we offer bull-sacrifices to Agni-deva to thank him for the boy's safe return. Our greatest warriors dare not venture in there for more than two nights at a stretch. It is a well-known fact that by the third night, every savage creature, animal or Asura, in that dread place comes to know of a new arrival, and descends upon it with no pity or mercy. The only people who have ventured in there voluntarily are outcasts and condemned outlaws who are doomed anyway – and even they are never seen or heard of again. Would you raise your children in such a place?'

'If it is their karma to be raised there, so will it be,' Rama said, his eyes on the river again.

Guha made a sound of disgust. The Nisada chief hawked and spat on the ground at his own feet, then stamped the place where he had spat. 'I do not understand such stubbornness,' he said loudly, his face and neck flushed with frustration. 'What good is your karma and dharma and artha if they do not serve you and your loved ones?'

When Rama gave no answer to his question, he threw up his hands in despair and turned abruptly on his heel, stalking back towards the forest. His men, confused and alarmed by the escalating events, ran after him. Sita turned to watch. The Nisada chief strode a dozen or two yards towards the forest, then turned as abruptly as before, and walked back to the river's edge. His men overshot him and then scuttled back after him.

'I do not know why I even make this offer,' he said tightly, addressing Rama's granite profile. 'But if you have need of it, my clans are yours in this battle. For the sake of your father, who upheld our right to live as free people and never once tried to force us into subjugation as so many other Arya kings would have done. For Dasaratha's sake, I will give my warriors to fight for his son's right to the throne.' He gestured at the army arrayed across the river. 'We may not win the day. Indeed, I do not know if we will even survive a clash with such a host. But Nisadas are men of honour too and we do not think twice of our own welfare when our friends are in need. If you have need of our swords and our lives, they are yours.'

Rama turned to look at Guha. From the softness of his voice, Sita could guess his expression. 'I have need of your friendship, good Guha,' Rama said, clearly enough to be heard by all. 'Your friendship and the friendship of the Nisada clans. That is all I desire.'

Guha stared at him. 'Then you will not fight? You will not defend yourself against your brother's aggression?'

Lakshman spoke heatedly, the muscles of arms, shoulders and back tense with the effort of holding the bow stretched to firing readiness, his eyes fixed on the boat crossing the river. 'Bhai, his boat approaches. He will be with us in moments if we do not act quickly. Give the word now, and I will put an arrow through his traitorous heart. And then I will put another arrow through his accomplice's heart as well.'

Rama turned to Lakshman. 'You would kill our brother Bharat? And your own twin Shatrugan?'

Lakshman replied tightly, 'If they attack us, we must fight back. It is only natural.'

Rama shook his head. 'What is natural and what is

not depends on one's own nature. Put back your dhanush-baan, Lakshman. Let us go down to the water and greet our brothers.'

And Rama walked down to the bank, waving to the boat that was now only yards from the shore. As he walked, he cut across Lakshman's line of fire without once glancing back. With a great sigh of frustration, Lakshman released the tension in the cord carefully, stared at Rama's back for a moment, then swiftly replaced the arrow and the bow on his rig, leapt down from the mound and went to join Rama. As Sita debated whether to follow them, she felt Guha come up to stand beside her. She smelled the ripe, acrid odour of the forest chieftain's unwashed furs and the powerful reek of his breath.

Guha spoke from beside her, his voice as gruff and gravelly as a rksa-maa guarding her cubs against human aggressors. 'It is a strange man you have chosen to spend your life with, Rajkumari Sita. I have lived many years by my own reckoning, and seen many strange sights and met many extraordinary personages, friends as well as foes. Yet I have not met such a man as your Rama Chandra in my whole life.'

'Yes,' she said gently and sadly. 'And I do not think you will meet such a man again.'

She went down to the bank to join Rama and his brothers.

Bharat leapt from the boat, not waiting for it to be pulled ashore. He waded through the shallow muddy shoals, spoiling his silk attire, and as soon as he was on dry land he fell at Rama's feet.

'Bhai,' he said. 'Forgive me. Forgive us all. Forgive my mother and the witch that corrupted her mind. Forgive my father for acceding to my mother's ill-thought demands. Return home to Ayodhya with me at once. Regain your place on the sunwood throne. I ask this on behalf of not just our family, the council of ministers, the noble houses of Kosala, the army and the Purana Wafadars of Ayodhya, but also the people, every last one of whom clamours for your return and weeps without ceasing.'

Shatrugan came up beside Bharat, prostrated himself before Rama, and then held out an object covered in a satin cloth banner on which the sigil of House Suryavansha had been embroidered with gold thread. Bharat unwrapped the cloth carefully, then held up the object. It caught the afternoon light and glittered like fire. Sita gasped as she recognised the yard-long jewel-studded wooden staff capped with gold at either end. It was the legendary raj-taru. The royal sceptre of Ayodhya, believed to have been cut by the hands of great Manu Ikshwaku himself, later embellished by his descendants. It was the mark of the true king, handed over to a new maharaja upon his crowning. The Sanskrit word, raj-taru, literally meant 'king's rod'.

Bharat held out the raj-taru to Rama.

'Behold,' he said, making his gestures large and simple so that the army on the far bank could see what he did even if they could not hear his words. 'I give the sceptre of our ancestors to my brother, the true king of Ayodhya, Rama Chandra.'

A loud cheer rose from the far bank as the assembled forces applauded Bharat's gesture.

Bharat waited for Rama to take the sceptre, keeping his head bowed and his knee bent. After a long pause, he grew aware that the raj-taru was still in his hands. The cheering from the far bank died out slowly as the watching host saw that Rama had not taken it.

Bharat looked up at Rama, his eyes brimming with tears. 'Bhai?' he said.

Rama gazed down at his brother with an expression of infinite sadness.

'I cannot take it, Bharat. You know that. I must do as my father said. I must honour his last command. I thank you from the bottom of my heart for this grand gesture. You have proved beyond doubt that you are indeed fit to rule Ayodhya. For only a king who does not seek power for his own selfish ends can be a good king. I can say now with full conviction that you will be a wise and just king, a great king. Make our ancestors proud, Bharat. Rule wisely and well. I wish you long life and happiness. Even when I return, fourteen years hence, I will be happy to live as your dependant, safe in the comfort of your just kingship. I ask only that you care well for my mother, for all our mothers, and treat our people with grace and justice. I beg of you now, do not follow me further than this point. If you love me, honour these last words of mine. Let me go into exile as our father promised your mother. Honour him just as I honour him with my implicit unquestioning obedience. To honour our elders and ancestors and live our life in accordance with the precepts of dharma, karma and artha – these are the only things that lie within our power. The rest we must leave to the devas. Go in peace, my brother and my king. Go back to Ayodhya and fulfil your destiny, as I go now to fulfil my own.'

And with those terrible, uncompromising, final words, Rama turned, took his wife's hand and his brother's hand, and walked into the forest.

It was night when Kausalya heard Bharat return. The rumbling of chariots and thumping of elephants was a familiar sound, one she had grown used to hearing in Ayodhya, but never before had those sounds awakened such hope in her breast. She was waiting at the threshold of the palace, unable to eat or sleep or rest since two nights ago. No heralds had returned to bring word of Bharat or Rama, but she knew that Bharat himself would be riding as fast as any herald could hope to travel, and the lack of news had not worried her. What had worried her was the knowledge she had of her own son. Of his uncompromising adherence to dharma. Yet still she had hoped, prayed, wished. These hopes and prayers and wishes had been her only sustenance since the night of Dasaratha's passing, the night her entire world had tilted from its axis and spun out of control.

When she saw the gleaming armour-clad lines rolling up Suryavansha Avenue, she caught her breath, her eyes searching keenly for Rama's familiar crow-black hair, his straight aquiline features, his strong jaw. But she found only Shatrugan's stricken face riding at the head of the column. He dismounted without any appearance of pride or triumph and came walking to her with rounded shoulders.

'Maa,' he cried, falling at her feet in a boneless heap. 'Maa, I am sorry. We could not do it. We could not bring Rama back.'

Kausalya felt as if the ground had melted beneath her feet and she would fall through into the bowels of the earth itself. Into the arms of Prithvi-maa.

But she had to be strong yet. For so many others, if not herself. For Rama's sake, and Kosala's future.

'Do not fret, my son,' she said, raising him up gently. 'You did the best you could.'

He looked up at her with anguish. 'But I failed, Mother!'

She shook her head gently, fighting back the tears that threatened to rush to her eyes. 'Nay. It was not you that failed. It was Rama's dharma that won.'

He was silent, his head lowered. But he seemed to take strength from her acceptance.

She scanned the avenue. The rows of mounted cavalry, elephant and chariot stood silently, their very silence revealing their bitter disappointment. There was not a single raised helmet in those endless rows. Even the elephants kept their trunks straight and low, sensing the mood of their mahouts.

'Where is your brother Bharat?' she asked.

Shatrugan looked up, raising his hands to show her. In his arms, she saw, he was clutching two bundles. One was the silk banner in which the royal sceptre was kept. She could not tell what the other bundle was.

'He has gone to Nandigram,' Shatrugan said.

'Nandigram?' Kausalya knew only that the town was a small, unexceptional place, squalid and rustic to the point of backwardness, totally unlike the rest of prosperous, advanced Kosala. It was notable only for its extremely northern position, on the very tip of the border between Kosala and the northern kingdoms, a rugged and harsh climate adding to the town's long-time poverty and abjectness. 'What business did he have in that wretched place?'

'He has gone there to live,' Shatrugan said slowly, as if each word was a weight he could no longer carry. 'He asked me to tell you that this is his decision. If Rama will not rule in Ayodhya, neither will Bharat. He will live at the border and await Rama's return from exile. Only when his brother returns home will Bharat re-enter Ayodhya. He has sworn this vow before the rock of Shanideva at Sringaverapura, in the presence of Guha, lord of Nisadas, Pradhan-mantri Sumantra, and myself.'

Kausalya's head reeled. Bharat, self-exiled to Nandigram? Was there to be no end to the misfortunes that would befall this house?

'But my son,' she said, fighting to keep her voice from turning into a wail of protest. 'Who will rule Ayodhya now? Who will man the sunwood throne for the fourteen years until Rama's return? The kingdom must have a king, the people a ruler!'

Shatrugan unwrapped the two parcels he was holding. From one he took the raj-taru, gleaming in the light of the mashaals. From the other he took a pair of wooden slippers, cracked and stained with dried mud and grass. 'These are Rama's slippers, left behind at Sringaverapura when he departed for Dandaka-van with Sita and Lakshman. Bharat has asked that you place them upon the seat of the sunwood throne. Let them symbolise Rama's true claim to the throne.'

Kausalya took the slippers, her head reeling. They were rough to the touch, yet the first thought that struck her when she felt them was: *Rama walks barefoot over the thorns and sharp stones of the forest paths. My Rama, exiled into Dandaka-van.* The touch of those rough, mudcaked wooden slippers almost undid her resolve. It took a new surge of determination to keep her from crumpling right there and then.

Shatrugan handed her the gleaming king's rod. 'And here is the raj-taru, which Bharat has asked you to hold for Rama.'

'Me?'

'Yes, Maa. For as Rama's birth-mother, you alone must carry the burden of his absence. You must rule as regent in his stead, until his return. There is no other way to prove Bharat's honesty to the world and keep peace in the kingdom. With Rama's slippers upon the seat of the throne, and the raj-taru in your hand, nobody will dare revolt or attack Ayodhya. The army also will obey your every command, for you shall rule in Rama's own name. Bharat will be in Nandigram to support your governance and will add his seal to anything you present. But this heavy burden you must bear on your own shoulders. Bharat and I have debated much on the way back from Sringaverapura. It is the only way to maintain peace and keep Kosala united until Rama returns to claim his throne.'

Kausalya took the raj-taru as well, feeling the odd inequity of the cold gold-capped weight of the sceptre in one hand, and the grimy roughness of the wooden slippers in the other. And yet both were evenly balanced. She even found space in her mind to admire Bharat's wisdom and foresight. Yes, he might be right. This might yet be the way to keep the kingdom peaceful and united. But *fourteen years*? She could hardly conceive of continuing thus for fourteen days! Merciful Devi give her shakti.

Shatrugan touched her feet reverentially. 'Now give me leave, Mother. For I go to Nandigram as well, to join Bharat. We shall live as ascetics there until Rama's return. On the day he comes out of exile, we shall return to honour and celebrate his crowning. Until then, I beg you, give me leave.'

As distantly as an actor in a Sanskrit drama, she gave Shatrugan the ritual blessings and watched him walk down the steps. He mounted his horse, turned its head, and rode away. Only a handful of his closest men followed him. The seemingly endless rows of armoured soldiers stood silently beneath the flickering lights of the mashaals of Raghuvamsha Marg, waiting for her command. She grew gradually aware of the weight of the raj-taru in her right hand. Now she was the closest thing to a ruler the land had left. She must do what must be done. *So this is to be my dharma then. So be it.*

She gripped the sceptre tightly. It was cold and hard to her touch. Silently she renewed the vow she had made to Dasaratha on his deathbed, Dasaratha who now lay embalmed in oil until his eldest son returned home to perform his funeral rites. Dasaratha who would lie thus until Deva knew when, for none of his four sons remained here to perform his rites any more. She missed him so much at this moment, as if a part of her own heart had been torn from her breast and embalmed with him. She would have to appeal to Bharat to return home to complete his father's last rites at least. If he still remained steadfast, well, then . . . then under certain alleviating circumstances the scriptures did allow for a wife to perform the rites. *My beloved Dasaratha, whatever happens, you will be given due honour, I promise you that.*

And when all the rituals were done, and the official mourning period was over . . . what then? How would she go about the business of governing a kingdom without a king? Without even a prince-heir, or a prince? Bereft and begrieved as she was, could she bear this heavy burden? The raj-taru seemed to grow heavier by the second, bearing the weight of all of Kosala, in addition to her intimate grief. Yet she refused to yield to its pressing pull, steeling her arm to hold it firmly, strong and steady as her kshatriya calling demanded.

The army waited for her next command. For she was all the authority that remained in Ayodhya now.

Steady, my queen.

The words were so gentle, so close, she did not have to turn her head to know it was Guru Vashishta who had spoken.

You hold not just the fate of a kingdom in your hands but also your legacy. Gather your strength and do what must be done. Fulfil your dharma.

She did not turn her head, for she was afraid that she would find that he stood not beside her, that the voice in her head was just that, a voice in her head. But how could the guru speak directly into her mind space? Then she remembered the shakti that Vashishta commanded. The shakti of brahman; the power of belief manifested. And with that came flooding back the shakti of her own beliefs, her own bedrock of faith. Her arm gripped the raj-taru tighter, higher. Her chin rose, firm and without a quiver.

She remembered the words she had spoken. *Rama will return and be crowned king of Ayodhya.*

Even if she had to wait fourteen years to see that happen.

Rama will *be king.*

Slowly she raised the heavy sceptre as high as her hand would go. A sense of anticipation grew in the watching, waiting ranks. An elephant stamped its foot and raised its trunk, trumpeting once, commandingly.

She raised her voice to be heard all down the silent avenue, infusing her words with every ounce of strength and confidence she now felt. She spoke now not as a mother, or a queen, but as regent, wielder of the sceptre of power and heritage, upholder of dharma. She spoke now on behalf of Rama himself, the rightful ruler of Kosala.

'Yuvraj Rama Chandra ki jai!'

Praised be the new king Rama Chandra.

The forces of Ayodhya echoed her words with all the energy and strength born of their grief and disappointment. The words were taken up by the citizenry next, echoing from the rooftops, the towers, the mansions, the hovels, the smallest hut and the largest palace. The echoes rang through the avenue, beyond its walls, rippling from marg to marg, house to house, neighbourhood to neighbourhood, across the seven walls and beyond them, to the farthest borders of the kingdom. And the words she did not speak aloud nevertheless rang out as clearly as the words of the guru spoken silently in her mind's ear, filling every citizen with a sense of unwavering certainty.

Rama will return.

17

Manthara stood in the Seer's Tower, her arms held out to the wind and rain and elements. Her hair flew behind her, billowed by the powerful gusts of the stormy rain. It had been difficult getting up here. She had managed to stow away these past weeks somehow, hiding from the enraged citizens who sought to kill her for her role in Rama's exile and Ayodhya's misery.

Unexpectedly, the tantriks had come to her aid. Not all of them, just the few fringe ones who worshipped the older pagan gods, like the man who had helped her procure the brahmin boys for her sacrifices – and whom she had killed for his part in her forbidden practices. The tantriks didn't know that she was the murderer, of course; she had fooled everyone into believing that his death was the result of his attempt to blackmail one of the king's concubines. To the tantriks, she was a celebrity. Just being thrown out of the palace had won her their eternal support: or so she'd thought. They had kept her hidden until now. But today, they had told her she had to leave. The captain of the palace guard, Drishti Kumar, had come by some information through the city spasas. A raid was expected at any time. That was how far their devotion to the old gods extended – only so far as it didn't endanger their own precious hides. So they had turned her out as well, and with them she had lost her last allies. Where could she have gone next? Out of Ayodhya? To wander the countryside for ever, living in rags and picking at berries? She might have done that if she could. But with her distinctive appearance, even that option was denied her. A white-haired hunchback with a limp could hardly be missed. She would be stoned at the first village she passed, or speared by the first sudra hunter who laid eyes on her. To the tantriks Manthara was a celebrity; to the rest of the world she was a witch and a traitoress.

So she had come here. To play one final hand. Here, in this place of power, she would offer one last sacrificial rite, a final balidaan to the Dark Lord of Lanka. If Ravana yet lived, as she still fervently believed he did, then he must hear her plea. The Seer's Tower was known for its ability to amplify prayers, shakti and supernatural force of any kind. Why not Asura sorcery? So what if she no longer seemed to have the ability to cast even the simplest cloaking spell. She would do what she had done a hundred times before: cause herself untold pain as a means of showing Ravana how dearly she was devoted to his cause. And by doing it here, in this powerful place of magic, he would not be able to ignore her demonstration. He would come to her again, as he had before. And all would be well again. After all, she mused as she readied herself for the final sacrifice, she had carried out his plan with brilliant effectiveness. Rama was exiled, doomed to battle the rakshasas of Dandaka-van. He would barely survive the month, let alone fourteen long years. The Suryavansha family was broken, shattered to shards like a crystal goblet. So what if Rani Kausalya ruled as regent in Rama's name? If Ravana granted her shakti once more, Manthara would undo that as well. The fate of mortalkind hung by a thread. What Ravana

himself could not accomplish with the largest Asura invasion ever mounted, she had achieved with simple harem
politics and shrewd deceptions. And now, with her
master's aid, she could finish the job she had so well
begun.

'Hear me,' she said aloud, removing a dagger from her
waistband as she moved to the edge of the rampart, to
the place where the stone floor ended and nothingness
began. Far below her the lights of Ayodhya gleamed,
subdued but still brighter than the lights of any other
mortal city. 'Hear me, my lord, hear the plea of one who
has served you loyally and truly. Give me your shakti
once more. Infuse me with your strength and let me serve
you once again.'

And she slashed herself with the dagger. The blade bit
deep and hard, drawing a gush of blood. *Ah, lord, that
hurts.*

There was no answer. Only the wind, howling like a
pack of wolves about her ears.

'See my devotion, master,' she called out, her words
whipped away by the wind. 'See how I suffer to serve
you. Answer my plea. Give me your shakti again.'

Still no answer.

She cut herself again, a mortal wound this time. She
staggered, barely able to remain upright. Somehow she
managed to stay on her feet, her vitals a nest of fire-
serpents gnawing and writhing. She put the last of her
failing strength into one resounding wail of utter desolation.

'HEAR ME, MASTER! SAVE ME! I GIVE MYSELF
INTO YOUR HANDS.'

And then she jumped.

The night air was cool and pleasant on her face as she
went down. Her blood gushed around her, flying up into

the air, catching the bright lights of the city below, like a shower of rubies raining upwards to heaven. She fell towards the city.

Ravana! she cried out. *My Lord, catch me!*

There was still no reply.

The night receded into silent darkness around her, a black shroud falling over the universe entire. Her bowels gave way, her bladder lost control, her life-blood poured out of her gruesome wounds and was whipped away by the tearing wind, and then she was screaming wildly, knowing at last what she had not known all these years, seeing the truth beneath the pathetic ritualistic barbarism of her dark devotion, the skull beneath the skin of her foolish faith. She screamed, and for an instant, a sliver of a fraction of a second, she glimpsed the larger purpose behind it all, the great hand that moved the forces that moved those who thought they controlled all others. She glimpsed the face of brahman itself, manifest and terribly physical. And for that brief flash of an instant, she knew all. And the knowing was more terrible than the ignorance that had shrouded her mercifully all her life. For complete knowledge cannot be contained within the constraints of a mortal mind, just as divine love will not be confined within the tiny sphere of a mortal heart. And in that penultimate moment, Manthara was given possession of both, complete knowledge and complete love. Love and knowledge, the most terrible of all burdens.

Then she struck the pavement three hundred yards below, and all knowledge, love, and life ended.

KAAND 3

A PLAGUE OF DEMONS

I

Ravana.

The cries resounded through the ash-filled skies of Lanka. As the pushpak moved smoothly above the ramparts and abutments of the fortress city, a million Asura eyes turned skywards, gazing with fearful awe at the returning sky-chariot. Spirals of smoke rose desultorily from parts of the city where violence had erupted. The inter-species skirmishes and mini-battles that had begun breaking out even before Vibhisena had entered the volcano were still raging unchecked. They fell momentarily still as the shadow of the gliding pushpak passed across them. To those below, the celestial vehicle must have made a compelling spectacle, its intricately designed structure gleaming burnished gold, silhouetted magnificently against the angry orange-red sky.

The volcano had ceased its eruption but the lava spewed out by its explosive spurts still flowed red-hot, winding its slow, sluggish way to the ocean. At the edge of the turbulent coast, flowing lava and raging sea met in a sizzling clash, exuding boiling gouts of ash-filled smoke that rose in thick, ominous coils. At the contact line of lava and brine, massive hundred-foot-high spouts of spray flew into the air like eruptions from a geyser. Steam roiled off this line of contact. The ocean was strewn with corpses of various species of Asura killed by their rival species in the ongoing battle for control of Lanka. These corpses, as well as the carrion birds and sharks that fed greedily on them, floated on the incoming tide, igniting on contact with the lava. Many burst into flames. As Vibhisena glanced back, several carrion birds and a herd of shark writhed furiously in their death throes, burning black; their fellows feasted on their charring remains even before the flames could die out.

The odour that rose from this combination of toxic slag, volcanic smoke and Asura offal would surely be life-threatening. Vibhisena turned his face away from the dark cloud through which they now flew, compelled by an instinctive urge to hold his breath, even though he knew full well that the pushpak kept clean fresh air circulating for its passengers through its inscrutable mechanisms. As the cloud obscured the external view, he turned his head to glance at the figure seated within the central palanquin-like deck of the chariot.

The king of rakshasas sat exactly as he had been placed when extricated by Vibhisena's brahman shakti from the stone cage in which he had been imprisoned like a primordial insect in amber. He had not stirred or spoken a word since being freed. Vibhisena had thought it simple exhaustion at first. After all, it had taken an epic effort on Vibhisena's part, and the application of all his knowledge, skill and physical strength, as well as the evocation of the natural forces of the volcano and the fumes and vapours exuded from the supernatural opening to the hell worlds. Vibhisena himself was exhausted by the time the deed was finally accomplished.

He took a moment to savour his accomplishment, even as a shadow of a doubt clouded his joy. Yes, Ravana was alive and whole, flesh and bone once more. He looked much the same as before, exactly as he had looked the day he left to invade the world of mortals. Vibhisena's mind probed and swiftly returned the conclusion that, physically, the Ravana seated in the pushpak before him was as healthy and robust as ever.

But other than that, he might as well be dead.

There was no similarity to the Ravana whom Vibhisena, and so many countless others, knew so well. This being that sat on the golden bench of the pushpak a few yards from him, while outwardly identical in every way, was no more than a pale effigy of the Ravana that had been left to conquer Prithvi and subjugate all mortalkind. Strictly speaking, he was alive, if the action of a chest moving with the intake and output of breath alone could be taken as proof of life.

But simply living and breathing alone did not make Ravana Ravana.

The demonlord had not spoken a word since being freed from the brahman cage. Not so much as one curse had left his leathery lips. His heads drooped inwards like wilting lilies, their faces blank and expressionless. All of the ten pairs of eyes were closed, even the central face slack-jawed and lifeless.

As he continued to observe his brother, Vibhisena felt a twinge of concern. Had he truly succeeded in resuscitating Ravana? Or had he only freed a wisp of shadow, fleshbound and alive only in its vital signs, a soulless walking corpse?

A piercing scree penetrated the dense smoky air, coming from somewhere high above. At the same time, the pushpak was engulfed by a thick cloud of smoke and ash, partly the product of the volcano, partly the offal of some Asura clash below. Vibhisena glanced skywards but saw only the blurry haze of the morning sky full of smoke and steam and ash. The sun was a miserable gold disc skulking in the east, obscured by the malicious fog that cloaked Lanka. The penetrating cry was repeated, and this time Vibhisena recognised the familiar pitch and tone of Jatayu. Like its earthbound Asura colleagues below, the vulture king was expressing its agitation at the unexpected return of Ravana. There was more than a trace of acrimony in the cry. Ravana dead was better loved than Ravana alive, it seemed.

The pushpak cleared the cloudbank, allowing a relatively more lucid view of the ground below, obscured only by twisting ribbons of smoke. Something had changed in the few moments that it had been hidden by the cloud. The sound of violence, suspended until now, seemed to have resumed with even greater ferocity than before. The naga and uraga quarters of the city were ablaze. Through the shifting curtain of smoke, Vibhisena glimpsed flashes of combat: metal weaponry glinting in the cold inhuman light, the glistening scales of striking serpent-demons, the ichor-splashed hoods of the enormous uragas battling their serpentine naga cousins.

Vibhisena shuddered as the sound of exultant roars and the terrible screams of victors and victims wafted upwards. The absence of any action or command from the pushpak had been taken as a message of sorts by the feuding species below. Ravana would not have simply flown overhead and allowed such unbridled mutiny to go unchecked. The Asuras of Lanka had tacitly decided that Vibhisena had failed in his task: from below they could not see the ten-headed figure seated silently in the pushpak. They assumed their master was dead. Finally. And so the killing went on unabated.

But it will stop. I will find a way to make it stop, he

promised himself. *Perhaps in a way it is better that Ravana is so changed by the imprisonment; perhaps now I can bring peace to this tortured land at last.*

He admonished himself guiltily for seeking gratification in his brother's deathlike condition, but the thought persisted. *Finally, the era of violence approaches an end.* The bulk of Ravana's blood-thirsty hordes had perished at Mithila, wiped out by the Brahm-astra. If these last few hundred thousand survivors decimated one another, so much the better. It would make his task that much easier for him. Now there would be a chance, however slight, to bring peace back to Lanka. And from the ashes and ruins of this new inter-species civil war, he would build a new Lanka. A Lanka pointed firmly towards peace and prosperity, and the pursuit of brahman.

His eyes watering from the smoke, he peered out across the city. The dark mossy structures of the island-kingdom extended like a living carpet, roiling and undulating over seventeen volcanoes, most dead or sleeping. Every square inch seemed to be covered with the grotesque architecture of Asura habitats, misshapen and deformed in design to the normal eye, a nightmare necropolis of strange slithering creatures, writhing monstrosities, and bestial species. Ringing the whole netherworldly map was the black fortress, a gigantic stone serpent coiled roughly around its possessions. The fortress's size was deceptive: it was far larger within than its outside extremities suggested. Even Vibhisena, brother of its lord and master, did not have full knowledge of its countless labyrinthine chambers and dark monstrous secrets. Over time, the Asura sorcery that had raised the fortress had spread like a virus to infect its neighbouring inhabitations, those residential quarters nearest to its forbidding walls, turning even thatched shanties and tiled roofs to the same blackish-greyish-red stone-like substance of which the fortress was made. Now, the entire island-kingdom seemed to be made of the same wretched material, one giant nest in which the offal of demonkind bred and brawled, fornicated and reproduced, and otherwise maintained the ceaseless engine of war that was Lanka under the iron rule of Ravana.

But the engine will stop now. It must, with its main force gone and its lord disabled. Vibhisena glanced at Ravana again: there was no change in his brother's condition. The same deathlike pallor. The same palsied lifelessness. This Ravana did not look as if he could quell this rebellion among his own forces, let alone launch an invasion of the realm of the devas, as he once had. Vibhisena attempted for the third time since emerging from the volcano to communicate mentally with his brother, with the same negative result. Since his release, even Ravana's mental sandeshes to his brother had ceased abruptly. Again the same twinge of unease passed through Vibhisena's mind. Would it have been better to have left Ravana suspended eternally in that brahman stone cage? But then it had been Ravana himself who had compelled Vibhisena to release him, whatever the cost.

They were approaching the southern ramparts of the black fortress now. The promontory normally used for landing the pushpak swarmed with kumbha-rakshasas and their smaller rakshasa brethren. At first Vibhisena mistook their agitation for enthusiasm. Then, as the pushpak brought him closer, his eyes widened as the horrible truth struck home.

The kumbhas were slaughtering the rakshasas. Even at this distance, almost half a mile away, he could see the unmistakable frenzy of conflict. Red splatters stained the dark crenellations of the city-fortress, victims fell from the ramparts screaming, disappearing into the foggy confusion of the riots below.

If even the loyalist Asuras of the black fortress were rioting, it could mean only one thing. One of the other Asura leaders had gained the upper hand for the moment. Vibhisena scanned his limited – by choice – knowledge of Lankan politics to think who it could be. Surely not Kumbhakarna. Ravana's brother, while ostensibly the leader of the kumbha-rakshasas, was still asleep in his subterranean chamber; were he awake, he would be visible for yojanas around. Kumbhakarna was a giant among giants. Nor would any of Ravana's sons take any part in this foul treachery. In any case, they were all in distant realms at this time, sent there by Ravana himself for different missions, the main purpose being the development of their education as warriors. Only Mandodhari and Ravana's enormous harem of concubines remained, and they were not players in the morass of Lankan politics. So it was certainly one of the other Asura chiefs.

They were close to the southern ramparts now, and a shower of spears, some ablaze, began arcing towards the pushpak. They clattered harmlessly off the invisible field of protection that the chariot maintained, but the sight of javelins and barbed steel weapons flying directly at him still gave Vibhisena a queasy feeling.

Suddenly he realised that it was no longer feasible for him to land on the fortress and simply take Ravana to his chambers as he had planned. These rebels, which seemed to include all the Asuras in Lanka, would probably cheer and applaud at the sight of Ravana thus incapacitated. Vibhisena shuddered at the thought of what they might do to the former tyrant in his present hapless state.

Only a few dozen yards from the ramparts now, he

could see the kumbhas turning to roar their bestial challenges, their quadruple-hinged jaws snapping forward as if they would grasp the pushpak and tear it to bits in mid-air. Not that such a thing could be achieved, but once Vibhisena and Ravana left the celestial vehicle they would be on their own again, and there was no longer any doubt as to what their fate would then be.

He willed the pushpak to change direction at the last minute, causing the sky-chariot to bank and turn sharply away from the black fortress. A roar of dismay and protest rose from the ramparts, and a fresh volley of missiles came speeding at them. All were deflected easily by the sky-chariot's invulnerable defences.

Vibhisena willed the pushpak to fly in the opposite direction: northwards. As they turned away from the fortress and traversed the city once more, awful cries of violence and torture rose from the yaksa quadrant below. The pisaca-rakshasas were settling some old score with the yaksas, judging from the numbers of shape-shifters spreadeagled on torture racks in the yaksa quarters, their writhing bodies worked over by the enthusiastic carapaced pisacas. At the sight of the pushpak passing overhead, the pisacas clicked and chirred in their insectile dialects. They began to spit up at the passing vehicle, royal carriage of their lord and master: blood, body parts and bodily fluids were spewed up into the air, spattering disgustingly against the undercarriage and sides of the pushpak, only to slide greasily off the invisible protective shell of the celestial machine. As they passed over hordes of warring vetaals and gandharvas in the twisting, sloping streets below, both groups paused in their mutual decimation to send up a chorus of curses and abuses. Spears and discs sliced the air beneath the vehicle, accompanied by derisive roars and mocking jeers. Vibhisena willed the

pushpak to fly even faster and higher, speeding them out
of reach of the immense volley of hate and rage directed
at the lord of the land, Ravana. The sky-chariot sped
across the two-hundred-and-fifty-mile length of Lanka in
mere moments, and only then did Vibhisena permit it to
slow down. He was still shaking from the outrage and
shock of the experience.

Barely had they begun to leave the city limits behind,
the terrible sounds of violence dimming to a dull blur,
than a new series of sounds caused him to turn sharply
and look back in surprise.

He was shocked to see bright red gouts of fire and
dense black smoke clouds erupting like boils across the
island-kingdom. The sound of powerful explosions ripped
through the air, producing shockwaves that he could sense
if not actually feel, thanks to the pushpak's protective
field. He stared horrified as the explosions went on relentlessly, raging from one end to the other of the island-
kingdom, filling the sky and ocean for yojanas around
with enormous reverberations and dense, evil-looking
clouds of smoke.

An aerial bombardment could not have produced a
more effective carpeting, he thought, clutching his chest
and settling himself on the pushpak's luxuriously padded
seat. His hands shook and his legs trembled. Vibhisena
was unused to war. And this . . . this was beyond war.

Riots were one thing. Internecine blood-feuds were
another. Even civil war was understandable. But this was
self-genocide, if such a term existed. The Asuras seemed
hellbent on wiping themselves out. This was not the work
of any one species or political faction: the whole of Lanka
would have to be involved in staging such a massive series
of explosions, ripping the very fabric of life itself. As he
watched, the explosions continued, tearing apart entire

neighbourhoods, demolishing whole kasbahs with each gut-wrenching outburst.

He looked again at Ravana and saw that his brother sat as slack-jawed and glassy-eyed as before. Even the sight of his entire nation being demolished evoked no response from Ravana. Whatever the damage to his mind and vital functions, it was indeed great, or surely the demonlord would have shown some flicker of response, some reaction to this holocaust.

And what of your plans now, Vibhisena? Your own dreams? What of the new Lanka you intended to build?

He sat, sobered, and saw his grand plan shattered by each successive explosion.

Few Asuras would survive such mass-scale destruction. The few who did would be broken beings, devoid of all else but the simple instinct to stay alive. Survival itself would be a challenge. In the charred and ghastly ruins, the remnants of Ravana's once-great force would eke out their last days like rats and roaches after a holocaust.

Well, now at least the mortal realm need fear Lanka no more. The terrible might and awesome fury of this once-powerful Asura stronghold was gone at last. There would be no further threat from Lanka.

Vibhisena glanced at his brother again.

Nor from Ravana.

They flew northwards, away from the burning, seething blister that was once Lanka.

2

Around late afternoon, Guha gruffly requested Rama to halt. The chief gestured at an ancient tree that dominated the clearing into which they had just emerged.

'This marks the southernmost border of my dominion. I cannot go any further, or I would violate my own sanction. It is forbidden to my people to hunt or fish beyond this point.'

He went to the skirt of creepers and touched one affectionately, as a man might touch the flank of an old and faithful cow. The creeper was as thick as the trunks of most younger trees, easily a man's width across. 'This is Nyagrodha, a great totem of power in these parts. He marks and guards our southern border. It will be auspicious to spend the night in his shadow.'

They looked at the tree. It was a magnificent being, towering higher than the tops of all its brethren. Like all others of its kind, it was as squat and broad as it was tall, seeming to crouch and touch the land with its root-tips. These root-tips, appearing more like creepers or vines, hung thickly from the edges of its looming branches, forming an almost impenetrable fencing. Guha went easily to a place where the hanging roots had not yet reached the ground, and parted the curtain-like downgrowth to reveal a shadowy bower within, into which strands of sunlight fluted in obliquely.

'My Ayodhyan friends, you may sleep here tonight as you would in your own akasa-chamber, unafraid of the forest elements. Nyagrodha is a great deity and protects all who offer him suitable obeisances. We will sacrifice to him before nightfall.'

He let the natural curtain fall again, glancing up fondly at the ancient banyan tree. 'His roots extend for five dozen yards on every side. He moves himself some fifteen yards every year, sometimes twice as far. It is believed among my people that he was originally from a land far south, and walked his way up here because he sought the sacred Ganga. It has taken him nine hundred years to come this far.'

He patted the tree affectionately. 'You do not have far to go to reach your goal, old one. Only a few yojanas more now.' He continued speaking softly to the tree, lapsing into his forest dialect, falling into a hypnotic devotional rhythm. After a little while, he sank to his knees and clasped the roots of the tree, touching them to his forehead and chest. His bear-like voice assumed a piquantly melodious tone of reverence.

Rama, Sita and Lakshman stood uncertainly for a moment, waiting for Guha to finish. Lakshman used the time to string his bow and rehitch his rig properly.

When the chieftain had finished his little ritual and rose to his feet, Lakshman said, 'I will go hunt for our meal now. There should be ample game in these woods.'

Guha frowned at him. 'Do you seek to insult me now? Have I not been hospitable enough to you, my prince?'

He laughed at the nonplussed expression on Lakshman's face. 'There will be no need to hunt so long as you are still on Guha's lands. If it is nourishment you seek, it is provided for already. Pray, settle yourselves down, my Ayodhyan friends, take some rest after your day-long trek.'

Lakshman exchanged a glance with Rama, who nodded. Lakshman shrugged and began unstringing his bow. Sita went to the gap in the hanging roots that the tribal chieftain had indicated and passed through into the shelter of the tree. Rama thought about whether to follow her. He decided to allow her some moments of solitude. He knew he could use some time alone too. *And I will have it soon,* he mused. *Fourteen years of solitude.*

Lakshman finished unstringing his bow and turned to Rama to speak. He had barely said, 'Bhai—' when Guha put his fingers to his mouth and emitted the most piercing junglecat-call either of them had ever heard before: it carried far through the woods, and was distantly echoed by other identical calls.

Satisfied, Guha crossed his oaky arms across his burly chest and grinned. 'My people are as the birds in the branches. Always near, yet never easily glimpsed.'

Sita's head emerged from between the hanging roots, eyes wide with curiosity, seeking out Rama. He shook his head, giving her what he hoped was a reassuring smile. She affected a pale, tired ghost of a smile and retreated into the bower once more. He thought of telling her to rest now. Sleep if she could. Sleep was the best immediate treatment for their present state of apathetic listlesness. But again he restrained himself. Leave her to find her own method of dealing with her condition. She was as strong in her own way as he was; she needed no manful over-protectiveness.

A moment later, a trio of Guha's clansmen appeared. Two of them carried a heavy basket slung on a rod borne on their shoulders. The third carried a bag hitched on his back. The basket was opened to reveal a fresh catch of river fish, the bag a large jar of honey. They laid the food before Rama and Lakshman, bowed until their heads touched the dust of the forest floor, then backed away. In moments they had vanished, melding seamlessly into the undergrowth. A moment later, a bird call so natural that even Rama doubted whether it was man-made issued, was answered by others, and faded away. They were alone once more, yet not alone, as Guha had said. Rama had no doubt that were they to encounter any kind of peril here, a hundred, or perhaps ten times as many, armed tribesmen would burst out of the forest and ensure their rescue.

Guha unfolded a stack of banana leaves wrapped in a wet cloth. He looked up at the princes. 'We will eat now.' His voice was authoritative. 'You have not taken anything since I do not know how long. Even last night at my feast, you did not partake sufficiently of my hospitality.' The words were meant for all three of them, but the chief's eyes met Rama's briefly, communicating his knowledge that Rama had not eaten a morsel since the previous day. Rama did not argue the point; it was true. He had eaten only some fruit, and that out of sheer politeness.

He carried a banana leaf laden with fish covered with dollops of honey to Sita, using his shoulders and head to part the curtain of hanging roots. It was shockingly cool and pleasing in the shade of the ancient one, sufficient sunlight filtering in to suffuse the bower with soft, diffused light. The heavy overhanging acted as a buffering against the sounds of the forest as well, providing a sense of deep calm restfulness. The trunk of the tree was as massive as its exterior promised. Enormous, gnarled like the intertwined feet of a hundred elephants, it straddled the forest floor authoritatively, claiming its territory. And yet there was a sense of readiness in its curved and upward-springing lines, as if it could uproot itself and step away this very instant, moving northwards toward its destination, the sacred Ganga. Rama paused and admired it for what it was, an epic self-made sculpture wrought over nine hundred years. He bowed his head reverentially, sending a silent prayer to Nyagrodha. The Aryas did not worship trees or the deities of natural objects any more, had not done so for millennia. But they paid homage to the great force that was responsible for the creation of such objects, of nature herself. After all, one of the many names of the One God was Prakriti. Creation, or Nature. A gentle wind soughed softly through the unseen upper branches of the forest giant, as if acknowledging his show of respect.

He found Sita standing on the bent foot of a gnarled root, reaching up to the trunk. She was tying a thread unravelled from her own garment to a part of the trunk. She finished knotting it tightly as he watched, then touched her forehead to the tree and uttered a soft prayer.

She showed no surprise when she turned to find him standing there. He watched her leap down lithely, the muscles of her thighs and haunches tensing as she landed. She glanced at the contents of his outstretched palm.

'Fish and honey?'

She started to take the laden leaf from his hand, then hesitated. 'And you?'

He looked pointedly at the food.

She nodded and dropped cross-legged to the ground.

He assumed a similar position, close enough to eat from the same leaf.

They ate silently. The fish, surprisingly fresh, was lightly grilled. It fell apart in their fingers and melted in their mouths. The honey added a sense of balance to the crumbling white flesh, adding not just sweetness but satisfaction in the absence of wheat or rice. The whole tasted heavenly. Rama found a choice morsel, smeared it lightly with honey and offered it to Sita. She opened her mouth and ate it. He fed her another mouthful. She nibbled affectionately at his fingers, then fed him a morsel too.

A twig cracked nearby with curious deliberateness, as if it had been snapped by hand rather than underfoot.

Lakshman's voice was hesitant, awkward. 'Bhai, I would go with Guha and hunt some game for tonight. We require a sacrifice to offer to Nyagrodha. We have a long journey tomorrow, we must eat to keep up our strength.'

Rama started to rise. 'I will go with you.' He looked at Sita. 'We could all go.'

Lakshman cleared his throat. 'There is no need. Guha and I are sufficient. He says the game is so plentiful in these parts we will be back well before sundown.' He paused, then added, as if by afterthought, 'We shall return and build a fire in the clearing nearby, and begin the sacrificial ritual. There is no need for you to make any effort. Bhabhi and you can rest as long as you please.'

Rama glanced back to see Lakshman disappearing through the root curtain. He looked at Sita. She caught the expression on his face and nodded. 'He wants something to do,' she said. 'It is better to let him go with the chief and hunt. It will do him good.'

Rama nodded and sighed as he wrapped the remains of their repast, bunching the banana leaf filled with the fishbones into a bundle. He dug a small hole with his hands and buried the leaf and bones in it, to return it to the earth. 'What were you doing when I came?'

She frowned. 'Doing? Oh. I was . . .' She pointed up

at the thread she had tied to the tree trunk. 'Tying a knot.'

He smiled. 'To hold Nyagrodha together? Was he broken?'

She smiled back, responding to the jest. 'It's an old Mithilan tradition. Or superstition. Call it what you will. Tie a thread from your garment to a banyan tree and make a wish.'

He took her hand. 'Doesn't that normally apply to lovers seeking to wed? Or married couples who are facing some threat to their unity?'

She clasped his hand tightly. 'And to newly-weds praying for a long and harmonious union.'

'Then shouldn't the couple walk around the tree, as a parikrama? To strengthen the bond symbolised by the tying of the knot?'

She looked up at him with a doe-eyed softness that he had seen only once before: their wedding night. In that all-too-brief idyllic time between their arrival home and his fateful call to the kosaghar. She put her other hand on his, pulling him towards her.

'The walking must be accomplished by mutual desire,' she said. 'That is when it becomes a true parikrama.'

He clasped her hands with his other hand as well, bringing himself close enough to feel the warmth of her breath. 'Then we shall walk together.'

The sun was low in the sky when they finished. He did not feel tired. If anything, he felt refreshed and more vigorous than before. The meal they had taken together, the parikrama performed, their hands clasped as they walked around the massive trunk of the ancient banyan, the knowledge that they were two beings united in spirit, all added to strengthen their already growing bond. When he had walked away from the banks of the Ganga last evening, turning his back on Bharat and his princely heritage for ever, he had felt as if that was the last meaningful thing he would ever do, as if from that moment onwards everything else would be without significance or sense, merely existence.

Even Lakshman's presence by his side had weighed heavily on his conscience: why had he allowed his brother to accompany him into exile? Why had he not been stronger, firmer, even crueller if that was what it took? All day today he had thought of a suitable argument he could pose to his brother to persuade him to turn back even now. But he had not felt the same way about Sita. He was glad of her presence. Where with Lakshman he felt guilty and irresponsible for letting his brother come, in Sita's case he felt relieved and blessed. It was a strange thing. Not two weeks earlier he would not have felt this way; would have turned his back on his wife as Lakshman had turned his back on Urmila, and gone to the forest to pay his dharmic debt. But so much had changed so swiftly; in a way, he was no longer the Rama who had left Ayodhya with Brahmarishi Vishwamitra less than two weeks ago. And neither was Lakshman the same. They had both changed in some deep, immeasurable way that could not be explained, nor discussed openly. It was not that their relationship was any less strong; it was that their brotherly bond no longer occupied the same central position in their mutually shared universe. Rama already cherished his bond with Sita just as much.

He looked at his wife's face, flushed and glowing from their long parikrama – each circuit of the banyan trunk was a hundred yards at least, and they had completed a hundred and eight such circuits, as was expected. What was this invisible force that had bonded her to him so swiftly and strongly? Mere days earlier she had been only a name from his childhood, a fond memory. Now, she was already as close to him as his brother. He would not have believed that to be possible days ago; now he accepted it was inevitable. *It is in the nature of the relationship itself*, he told himself. This is what it means to be wedded to someone. It is not beyond brotherhood, it is simply something else.

He reached out and gently brushed a wisp of sweat-dampened hair from her forehead, tucking it behind her ear as he had seen her do. She nodded absently, lost in some deep thought.

'I am glad you came,' he said softly. 'I did not wish it, for your sake, but I am glad you did, for mine.'

She looked up at him. 'I too am glad I came. But for my sake, not yours.'

He smiled. 'So we both had our own reasons. So be it.'

She did not say anything to that. There was no need to. He clasped her to his chest and embraced her, embraced the wonder that was his first love, his wife, in the gentle shade of Nyagrodha, who watched impassively and silently, as it had watched lovers like them for close to a thousand years.

3

Guha emerged from the darkness of the woods into the circle of light cast by the fire, his dark skin rendering him almost invisible except for the glowing whites of his eyes and his flashing teeth. The chief bore more firewood. He dropped the bundle, chose a sizeable log and placed it into the heart of the flames. Then he sat back, stirring the fire with a long stick, until he was satisfied by its colour and warmth. The aroma of roasted meat still hung sweetly in the air, along with a sense of contentment that Sita would not have believed possible at the end of such a day, or in such surroundings.

Partly it was the good meal and the fire. The night was cold here, colder than it had been back in Mithila – or in Ayodhya for that matter. She did not know why that should be, unless there had been an unexpected spring fall up in the Himalayas. She supposed it was always possible. If so, it was a bad omen and would be taken as such by the farmers of Vaideha, who would otherwise have been preparing to sow their monsoon crops.

As if reading her thoughts, Guha spoke. 'Unnaturally cold this night,' he said. 'A bad omen, my prince.'

Rama leaned forward to place a hand on the chief's shoulder. 'Just Rama, old friend. You can drop the "prince" now. I left all titles back in Ayodhya.'

Guha guffawed. The chief's laughter was gloriously unaffected and ribald, as shocking as a profane word on account of its sheer vigour and bawdy boldness. 'Such titles cannot be shed like silk garments and gold ornaments, my Ayodhyan friend! You are crown prince of Ayodhya and will remain so for ever. You may have wished you had left the title behind, yet it follows you as loyally as a milk-fed puppy into these Nisada lands.' He gestured with the stick, sending sparks scattering within an inch of Sita's feet. She drew her feet up hurriedly. 'And it will be with you when you go into the Dandaka-van, or wherever else you may journey in your long exile.' The tribal chieftain shook his head, baring his teeth like a cougar shaking a dead rabbit by the throat. 'The burdens of kingship do not come off when a king is exiled. They only grow weightier on his shoulders.'

There was only the sound of the fire crackling softly for a long moment, then Rama replied, 'You seem to have spent some time contemplating such matters, my friend. I cannot disagree with your reasoning. What you say is true: I am yet and will always be a prince of Ayodhya. Yet I only meant that it would please me more if you called me by my birth-name. For right now I am a prince without a kingdom, or a throne. And as such, I am Rama, your good friend, as Dasaratha my father was once before me. I ask only that you treat me with the same rough warmth you gave him, as a man rather than a king.'

Guha turned to stare at Rama. The chief's broad bulging features hid no emotion. Sita could read his surprise as clearly as if he had spoken his state of mind aloud. 'Wherefrom does such nobility arise, tell me then. What meat or milk were you fed by your mother's hand that you turned out to be thus?'

He dropped the stick with which he had been prodding the fire and turned to face Rama fully.

'You said that I should not speak of it again and I agree that I should not. You have made your decision plain on the matter. Yet I still cannot accept your acceptance of this banishment. I do not believe that if Dasaratha were here with us tonight he would permit you to continue on this journey into darkness and anonymity. You, prince of Ayodhya, heir to the Suryavansha throne! Your place is there in the capital of the Kosala nation, ruling justly and wisely as your father always wished. I swear, Rama, if Dasa was here he would rescind every oath he has sworn to your stepmother and command you even now to return home and take your rightful place at the reins of power. Do you doubt it?'

Rama sighed, leaning forward. The shawl he held loosely around his shoulders fell open. 'I do not doubt it, my friend. But Dasaratha is not here. My father died after pronouncing this exile upon me, and it is all I can do to fulfil it.'

He raised his hand before Guha could answer. 'Yet stay your arguments, Guha. You are a great man and a wise king. But once my feet are set on a path, I will not be turned back. End this debate now, as it should have ended when I left the gates of my city. Accept me as what I am now, a prince in exile.'

Guha exploded. Rising to his feet, the chief turned to face Rama. Yet despite his imposing size, the Nisada king's attitude was imploring rather than intimidating. Sita could clearly read the chief's frustration and anger on his fleshy features.

'So be it!' he said, his barrel-chested growl counterpointing the crackle and snap of the fire. 'Rama, I do not claim to understand your godlike adherence to dharma.

Nay, even the gods, your sacred devas, would be shamed by your dharmic diligence, for did not they stray from their own dharmic paths from time to time? A mistake or three is permissible to us mortals, let alone our devas. But I do not question that stubborn adherence which you displayed so astonishingly on the banks of the Ganga. I stood by silently as you sent Bharat back with the raj-taru, denying your own brother's wishes that you rule Ayodhya. You did not see what transpired after that, and you did not wish to know it, but I will tell you nevertheless.'

He squatted before Rama, peering into his face. 'Do you know what Bharat did after you, Lakshman and Sita went into the woods? He wept inconsolably. Then, when Shatrugan asked him what he desired to do next, he looked at me and asked if there was any object belonging to Rama that remained in my possession. I went and looked, and lo, I found your slippers, Rama. For you had shed them before seating yourself at my table for the repast, and had not had an opportunity to wear them again. They remained there exactly as you had left them, mud-crusted and worn at the heels. I showed them to Bharat, and do you know what he did then?'

Again Rama did not respond, and the impassive expression on his face was one that even Sita could not read. She wanted to put her hand in his, to feel his touch, but she did not want to interrupt the debate. Guha's words were heartfelt and passionate, and she was moved by the emotion the chieftain exuded.

'He kissed them, Rama,' Guha went on. 'He kissed those mud-spattered slippers and clutched them to his chest as lovingly as any religious icon. And then he said to Shatrugan – and I will never forget the look on his face or the determination in his voice when he spoke – "Shatrugan, my brother, take these slippers belonging to our brother Rama, the true prince and king-in-waiting of our nation, take them to Rama's mother Kausalya. Tell her that they are to be placed upon the sunwood throne as symbols of Rama's continued sovereignty. There they must stay until Rama returns from exile and replaces them with his own person." While he himself intends to reside in common style at Nandigram, the remotest border town, sworn never to enter Ayodhya until Rama's return to claim his rightful place on the throne.'

Guha shook his head, wiping the spontaneous tears that had sprung to his eyes. 'Such fraternal devotion and love never have I seen before. And do you know what thought passed through my mind at that moment? *Greatness inspires greatness!* If Rama sets so noble and self-sacrificing an example, can his brother do any less? Why, at that moment I wished I could be one-tenth as great a king as you are. To take such a harsh decision and embrace it to my breast as if it were a rose-petal garland, not the briar necklace you have worn. For then truly should the Nisadas be a great people, and this land as great as any Arya nation.'

'You *are* a great king, Guha,' Rama said. 'And the Nisadas are a great people. How can you even doubt that? Why else do you think my father always took such pleasure in coming here, in consorting with you, hunting and feasting with you? Do you know, my friend, he always thought of you as dearly as his own blood. He told us once that he had five sons, not four. For Guha was no less dear to him than we, the sons of his own body.'

Guha stared at Rama. 'He said such a thing? In his own words?'

Lakshman spoke from across the fire. 'Indeed, chief. He said it more than once.' Lakshman exchanged a glance with Rama, grinning wryly. 'He even used to joke that if Guha ever left his forest kingdom by the Ganga and chose to come to Ayodhya, we brothers would lose a great part of our legacy. For he would grant you any wish you desired, even if it were part of the kingdom itself.'

Guha had turned to stare at Lakshman. The fire underlit his features, burning them into a mask of incredulity and sorrow. He turned back to face Rama. 'I knew he loved me, as I loved him too. But that he felt this way . . .' He shook his wild locks. 'He never said such things, not even when drunk like a coon, which he was much of the time in my company.' He emitted a short choked laugh at the last memory.

Rama sighed. 'For him to say it here would have been inappropriate, Guha. But he meant it, of that much you can be certain. He made me promise once, for he knew that I would be king after him, that if you were ever in need, whether in time of war, pestilence or famine and drought, I must give you whatever aid you desired. Not that I should give you what I could, but whatever you desired.'

'Whatever I desired . . .' Guha repeated the words like a sacred litany. His eyes, large and moist in his dark face, glowed like fireflies in a dark bush. He gripped Rama's arm, his large hairy fist encircling Rama's slender wrist easily. 'And what did you reply then, my friend?'

'I said that I would give you not only whatever you desired, I would personally care for the Nisadas as if they were my own family.' Rama paused, looking directly into Guha's eyes. 'For if my father regarded you as his son, then that made you my brother as well. And brothers must share the responsibility of caring for their families, must they not?'

Into the crackling silence that followed, Lakshman said softly: 'Rama was only ten at the time. I remember it.'

Guha leapt up and embraced Rama. It was like watching

a bear leap upon an antelope, so different were their physical structures. Yet Rama was as quick to respond, and he rose to meet Guha's bearlike embrace with swift felicity. The two men, so unlike in appearance and upbringing, embraced chest to chest with all the passion and enthusiasm of blood brothers. Lakshman rose to his feet in accord with Rama, but stood where he had sat, watching. Sita couldn't help but notice the quick, impatient gesture Lakshman made as he swiped at his face, as one might if wiping away an inadvertently shed tear.

Guha roared his pleasure to the night. The forest shuddered in response, sleeping birds and skulking creatures raising a brief, irritable response before returning to their nocturnal occupations. 'This is a great night, my friends . . .' He roared again. 'My *brothers*! It calls for a celebration!'

In his own tongue, he called out several quick, sharp words. Lakshman raised his eyebrows, glancing around. Not long after, Guha's men appeared – another set of men, different from the ones who had brought the fish earlier and those who had helped skin and clean the meat that Guha and Lakshman had hunted – bearing several earthen flasks. They set them down carefully, and retreated into the darkness of the benighted forest as swiftly as they had appeared.

Guha uncapped and poured the wine from the flasks into goblets, handing them round to each of them. Sita took hers without protest, knowing that to refuse it would offend the Nisada chief mightily. When each had a goblet in hand, Guha raised his high above his head, roaring a tribute: 'To my brothers Rama and Lakshman, and my sister Sita, fellow warriors of the Nisada clan!'

Quaffing his drink in one enormous swallow, the chief beamed his pleasure at Rama. 'I have the answer to your problem, Rama. A beautiful and simple answer that will fulfil your father's vow as well as retain your dignity and honour.'

Rama asked with genuine curiosity, 'What have you thought of, my brother?'

'Stay here.' The chief expanded his arms, encompassing the forest around them. 'Stay and rule the Nisadas with me. Both of you. Your wife will live like a queen of our tribe, you will enrich our lives with your great Vedic knowledge and guru-taught wisdom, and we will treat you like the kings you rightfully are. Stay here for fourteen years and rule beside me.' The chief took up a flask and poured fresh drinks into their goblets. Rama had room only for a few drops, Sita noted: he had barely sipped the first drink. Lakshman, though, seemed more than willing to refill his. The chief raised his own goblet, eyes shining with pride at his ingenious solution. 'What say you?'

Rama handed his goblet to Sita – she took it and set it beside her own untouched drink on a flat patch of ground. He went to Guha and embraced the burly man passionately. 'Brother, my brother . . . I love you dearly. Even had my father not proclaimed you akin to a son, still would I have thought you my brother. The Nisadas are fortunate beyond words to have as fine a man as you for their chief.'

Guha broke the embrace, holding Rama at arm's length. 'But?' He added impatiently, 'There is a "parantu" in your tone, Rama. I can hear it even though you leave it unsaid. Finish your thought. I am a great chief . . . a brother to you . . . *but*?'

Rama shook his head sadly. 'But it cannot be as you wish. I must rise tomorrow at daybreak and go into the Dandaka-van. It has been decreed, and it shall be done.' His face brightened momentarily as a new thought struck him. 'Yet listen, Guha. When I return fourteen years later . . .'

Guha released Rama, turning away roughly. 'When . . . and *if* . . . you return, I do not know if I will be here. We ordinary mortals cannot predict our lives as clearly as you can, Rama. We live from day to day. Our bellies must be fed each day or we pine and waste. Do not speak of what will be or might be fourteen years hence. I speak only of tonight, of the *here and now*.'

He turned suddenly to face Rama once more. 'Yet reconsider but once. Is it so wrong? You will be in exile from Ayodhya. You need never set foot within the seven-walled city until the end of your time. Stay here with me, with the Nisadas; we will eat fish and honey and meat every day, and at night by the fire we shall partake of this wonderful mead and laugh and speak of happy things. You will bring great prosperity and enlightenment to our people, Rama. I know this as surely as I know that going into the Dandaka-van will sour you and turn you into a pale shadow of the man you are now. Stay! For the sake of your brother, stay with me here! I do not ask for whatever I desire. Just this one thing. By your father's oath, grant me this one wish, my brother Rama.'

Rama was silent too long. Guha's stance changed from imploring to dejected as he waited for the answer that never came. The next person who spoke was neither Rama nor Guha, but Lakshman.

'Bhai,' he said uncertainly. His eyes glistened in the light of the fire. Not with tears, Sita thought, but from the mead which he had drunk two goblets of in quick succession. He had needed it in order to work up the courage to say these words to Rama. 'It is not my wish to attempt to change your mind from its fixed path . . .'

Rama turned his eyes to Lakshman. 'Then what is it

you wish, Lakshman?' His voice was soft and calm, yet Sita saw Lakshman wince.

'Only that . . .' Lakshman seemed to search for the right thing to say, revealing in that brief pause how desperately he wanted to persuade Rama. 'That you give due consideration to our brother Guha's words. You need not reply at once. Tomorrow morning . . .'

Rama sighed. The log Guha had put on the fire not much earlier shifted and settled as it burned, issuing a flurry of sparks that rose in a spiral, swirling around the three men. None of them blinked or moved to avoid the sparks, even though Sita clearly saw some settle lightly on their bare shoulders and torsos.

'Tomorrow morning,' Rama replied, 'we have a long way to go. We must retire early to keep our strength. I will take your leave now, my brothers Guha and Lakshman. Come, Sita, if you will, let us take our rest. Tomorrow we go into the forest of exile.'

Sita rose from her place, carrying the shawl that Rama had left behind when he stood to embrace Guha. He took it from her and both of them walked to the spot they had prepared earlier by laying down grass pallets.

Rama began spreading his shawl over his pallet. Sita followed his example with her own. In moments they were done. Rama lay down upon his pallet and she did the same. She glanced briefly back at Guha and Lakshman. They were not far away, but they might as well have been a hundred yojanas distant. The look of abject sorrow on both their faces, in their very stance, was heartbreaking. She had guessed that Lakshman and Guha had had a great deal of discussion while on their hunting trip earlier that afternoon. She had seen it on their faces when they returned, bright-eyed and red-cheeked, bearing proudly their spoils from the hunt.

She turned her face to Rama. He was still awake, she knew. She could sense it from the way he lay, stiff and ill at ease. He was profoundly disturbed by the passion of Guha's argument and the desperation of Lakshman's last, half-coherent plea. 'Rama,' she said softly, too softly to be heard by Guha and Lakshman.

He did not reply but she knew he was listening.

'Don't worry,' she said. 'I'm not going to add my voice to the argument. I know your mind is made up about going into the Dandaka-van, and I agree with you on that count. It is the only honourable thing to do. What I wished to say to you is that I fear for Lakshman. Perhaps you should speak to him. Perhaps he might be better off staying with Guha during the time of exile. After all, he finds solace in the idea, clearly. And he is not taking this with the same equanimity as yourself. See the way he is quaffing mead even now. And weeping openly while Guha puts his arm around his shoulder and comforts him. He is very troubled, Rama. It may not be the best thing for him to go into exile with us.'

Rama was silent for so long, she thought he would not answer her. She had given up all hope of a response when he said, 'I will talk to him in the morning.'

That was all he said. It was enough. She nodded silently, then realised he could not see her in the near-darkness. Over by the fire, Guha said something in a bitter tone and Lakshman issued a laugh that was more a cry.

Both men echoed each other hollowly, and Sita heard the sound of another flask being uncorked and more mead being poured. She lay a long time, listening to the sounds of their voices, unaware of when she finally drifted off into sleep.

4

The hill Nikumbhila rose like a lush green miracle, a stark contrast to its surroundings. The ground around it was the same reddish-black as the rest of the island, a crustacean amalgam of rock and earth fused together by the unholy forces wielded by the kingdom's lord and master. The cliffs of Lanka rose sheer and jagged on the northern coast, half a yojana beyond the sacred hill, barring the way to any who sailed from the sub-continental mainland that lay but thirteen yojanas distant in that direction. Any such unfortunate sailors approaching Lanka would see only the dark hellish face of those forbidding cliffs, winding their jagged way around the coast on both eastern and western sides of the island until they reached the black fortress and melded into its sorcerous stone. Even the sparse patches of rocky beach at the foot of those towering cliffs were lined with black sand that shifted and bubbled like an unnatural quamire. To the seaborne observer, all was the same unrelenting black, craggy volcanic hell that Lanka was famed to be.

But nestled within the hammer-shaped northern head of the island-kingdom was the hill of Nikumbhila. Seen from the vantage of the pushpak's aerial approach, it shone like a jade stone set in black opal. The hill was lushly carpeted with dewy green grass, a startlingly normal contradiction to the unnatural menace of its surroundings. Vibhisena made a gesture of genuflection as the pushpak sped him close enough to glimpse the small stone structure on the very top of the gently sloping hill. That was the shrine of Shiva, the patron deity of all rakshasas, as of their lord Ravana. For Shiva was the Destroyer, and were not rakshasas dedicated to destruction?

As the pushpak slowed and began to descend gradually, Vibhisena mused on the irony of the present circumstances that brought him and his catatonic brother Ravana back to Nikumbhila. It was on this sacred hill that Ravana himself, long millennia past, had performed his fabled tapasya. Those terrible penitential meditations, some lasting several thousands of years, had resulted in Ravana being offered fabulous boons by Brahma and Shiva. From those great boons had come the power and invulnerability that enabled him to embark on his unprecedented spree of conquest, invading the kingdom of the very devas who had granted his powers, wresting the island-kingdom of Lanka from Kubera, his yaksa half-brother, who dwelled in the foothills of the Himalayas. Since Kubera was also the treasurer of the devas, invading his northern retreat and defeating him had secured for Ravana fully half the immense celestial treasury and many other rich prizes, including this very pushpak itself. After which Ravana had returned here, to remake Lanka in the image of his dreams . . . or more accurately, his nightmares.

Yet it was the tears and sweat and spilled blood of those long penances that had preserved the sanctity of the Nikumbhila hill long after Ravana had recast Lanka into the effigy of hellishness that he desired, transforming the beautiful island paradise of Kubera into an unspeakable volcanic nightmare and a gateway to the netherworlds. Even now, after all this time, the sentient stone of the black fortress, forged from Ravana's own living flesh, had been unable to corrupt the natural grassy lushness of Nikumbhila. This supreme irony brought a small spot of hope to Vibhisena in this moment of abject depression. It proved that brahman did and would triumph in the end, despite all odds. If these tender blades of grass could still grow and flourish mere yards from the corrupt sorcery that pervaded Lanka's soil, then what might not a living, sentient, mobile being like himself be able to achieve?

As the pushpak descended to a relatively flat spot on the top of the hill, the downwind generated by the celestial vehicle rippled across the grassy slopes, like waves rolling across an emerald ocean. In those waves, Vibhisena spied the flash of a tawny hare's long ears, twitching, then swinging as the little creature leapt nimbly downhill. A cluster of butterflies, succouring themselves in a patch of sunflowers, rose in confusion, dispersed by the force of the pushpak's displacement.

The sky chariot came to a halt so gentle Vibhisena had to look down to be sure he was indeed on solid ground once more. He descended the extruded ramp alone. He would return in a while for Ravana. His brother remained as mindlessly spastic as when he had first emerged from the stone cage, with not a flicker of change in his slack visage. He would be safe here alone in the protection of the pushpak. There was something Vibhisena wished to do before disembarking him.

Vibhisena stepped on to the springy surface of Nikumbhila with a sigh of relief. He was still shaken from the sight of Lanka's destruction. It was hard to accept the fact that the only land he knew as home was destroyed. His thoughts flashed again to his sister-in-law Mandodhari and the rest of Ravana's family. They would be safe, he knew, nestled deep in the protective heart of the black fortress, guarded by rakshasas whose loyalty was guaranteed by sorcery: those poor fools could no more turn against their master and mistress than plunge a heated blade into their own vitals. Ravana's near and dear would survive the holocaust of Lanka without question, sequestered by the sorcerous protection of the fortress. Later, when the fires had died out and nervous peace had returned, Vibhisena would return in the pushpak and seek them out. Then would begin the painful task of restabilisation and, eventually, reconstruction.

But that was later. Now, he had only one purpose.

To find a way to heal his brother.

He strode across the whispering grass-covered ground, approaching the monolithic structure that rose from the centre of the hilltop. It was not particularly large or imposing. In times past, one did not build ostentatious structures for public worship, nor did one gild idols with gold and precious stones or clothe them with gold-embroidered finery as many did now, for such things were considered vulgar and contrary to the spirit of simple devotional prayer that was the heartstone of brahmanism. One simply provided a stone shelter from the elements, a little corner of quietude where the true believer could immerse the self in the vast contemplation of brahman. The specific deity housed in that shrine was also not significant, for all deities were merely perceptual forms of the same One God. But over time, it had become accepted that the presiding deity here at Nikumbhila was Shiva, if only because it was Shiva who had become manifest in answer to Ravana's epic penance, granting him the great boons that spelled the salvation and eventual rise of the rakshasa race.

He touched the exterior wall of the shrine. The stone was cool and granular, only slightly weathered by the

elements over the millennia. Ravana himself had carved
this shrine from a single great granite boulder. Even the
boulder had not been in this place: he had rolled it all
the way from its original home, several miles away.
Merely bringing the stone here and carving it out
painstakingly had taken one hundred and five years, more
than an entire mortal lifetime. And even back then,
Ravana was not without power; he had only to command
it, and his followers would have toiled night and day to
roll the boulder up the slope. But he had accomplished
that arduous task himself; then, once the boulder was on
the highest point on Lanka, he had proceeded to carve
the shrine with his own hands, working with such reverence and application that the finished structure vied with
any monolithic mandir in the world. The fact that it stood
here, solid and majestic despite the passage of time, was
testament to the demonlord's dedication. That was one
thing Vibhisena had always admired about his rakshasa
brother: whatever Ravana did, he did with such utter
devotion, even the devas watched and wondered.

Vibhisena removed his sandals and climbed five steps
up to the threshold of the temple. Five steps led down
again, into a rectangular pool placed precisely beneath
an identically sized gap in the roof of the temple. Rain
water collected here and remained a long while in Lanka's
humid climate. Vibhisena waded through the ankle-deep
water, his feet washed without any effort on his part,
then stepped up on to the temple floor, cleansed and purified by this simple yet ingenious architectural design. The
granite floor was surprisingly warm underfoot, perhaps
because of the coldness of the water. The approach to
the deity was purposely oblique, encouraging the
worshipper to walk around the little palanquin-shaped
carving that housed the statue. He performed a full circuit

– a parikrama of sorts – and found himself facing towards the north-eastern end of the shrine, the most propitious place for the deity to be housed. Rows of slender pillars, their heads carved to resemble the heads of various beasts, for Shiva was also Pashupati, Lord of Beasts, marked his progress down the last stretch. The palanquin, exquisitely carved from the floor of the rock, blossomed before him like a creation of nature herself. His eyes filled with spontaneous tears. *What art, what devotion, what love you poured into the making of this temple, my brother. Where did all that love, that devotion go? What happened to that Ravana?*

He approached the central pandal, lowering himself to his knees, and prostrated himself full-length, touching his forehead to the floor. Then he rose and went forward, close enough for the sacred act of gazing reverentially upon the face of the deity himself: darshan. The stone idol was as simple and basic as could be. Another significant difference between the ancient ways of worship and the more modern, emerging trends. In those days it was not considered seemly to carve a humanlike effigy, as some cults now preferred. To cast the devas in the image of their worshippers was not only foolish and needless, it bordered on sacrilege. Vibhisena himself abjured the methods of some believers, who even went to the extent of clothing their deities in little doll-like garments, adding jewellery and accessories. That was against the spirit of darshan itself, he felt. To have a rough image carved of stone, suitably placed and ritually propitiated, that was what the Vedic rites prescribed. Perhaps some day, when the rites and prayers were all collected and bound together in one comprehensive manuscript, it would be possible for all followers of brahman to stick to the letter of the laws of dharma, neither exceeding the prescribed methodology of rituals nor avoiding the more arduous parts. But who would undertake such a great and difficult task? It would take a great seer to collate the scriptures of Vedic learning and write them down in one complete book. Or two books, or even four . . .

Until then, true believers like himself would hold those rituals in their heads and follow them to the letter, knowing that in the perfect practice of ritual the soul found the freedom to soar free of the cage of flesh and bone, to explore the mighty infinity of brahman.

He would have lost himself in prayer and contemplation for hours then, completely detached from his physical self, feeling neither hunger nor thirst, not any other bodily need. Achieving a oneness with brahman that only the most pious achieved, and that too rarely. A rakshasa he might be by birth, but by vocation he was no less than a brahmin. After all, he was of the line of Pulastya, one of the first brahmins, they who first spread the knowledge and practice of brahmanical worship.

But a voice cut into his worship at the very outset, before he could immerse himself so completely in the ocean of brahmanic contemplation that to emerge would itself take a long while and considerable effort. The voice spoke with just the right intonation and inflection required to hold him back, like a hand placed gently but urgently on his shoulder.

'Vibhisena.'

5

Vibhisena opened his eyes, seeing only the effulgent vision of Shiva atop Mount Kailasa with which his darshans always began. Lord Shiva, with his matted locks piled high on his head, the king of serpents Takshak wound round his neck like a living garland, tiger furs wrapped around his waist, seated cross-legged in yoganidra, the sacred transcendental contemplation of brahman, upon only a thin worn fur-mat on the ice-encrusted peak. Distant snowy peaks were visible in the backdrop, and somewhere, not far from here, Vibhisena could even sense the Lord's wife Parvati and their sons Ganesha and Kartikeya, as well as Shiva's vehicle of choice, the black bull Nandi, borrowed from its original master Yamaraj. So intense and vivid was the darshan he was blessed with.

Then his vision cleared and he saw again the simple black-stone Shiva-lingam carving, its sloped head anointed with red-ochre stripes like the forehead of any brahmin would be, nestled in a pestle-shaped open-ended circle. He smelled the unmistakable fragrance of devil's orchid blossoms, the trademark of only one woman he knew . . . his sister-in-law, Ravana's wife.

'Mandodhari?'

He turned and saw her standing by the pillar that had concealed her from his view when he had approached the deity. So great had been his desire for darshan that he had failed to allow the meaning of that fragrant odour to penetrate, but now that he was aware of it, it pervaded his senses, filling his olfactory channels with the same pervasive authority with which Mandodhari filled any chamber she entered.

She took a step forward, then another, stepping into the light, the silver payals on her feet tinkling melodiously. She was clad in the same manner as always, except for one notable difference: her sari was white with a simple blue border. Had that touch of blue been absent, her garb would have been indicative of the status of widowhood. He did not think that her choice of sari was accidental. Few things were not carefully thought out by Ravana's wife.

The almost-white sari was tied at the bottom rather than left loose, its top draped tightly around her womanly form. Her beautiful long, lustrous hair was wound tightly into a braid that dangled by her knees. The devil's orchid flowers whose scent pervaded the temple were imbedded in her hair, at the top and by the ears.

She came forward like an apsara entering Indra's court, filled with the beauty of night and darkness and all that was most alluring about the rakshasa race. Mandodhari was considered the most beautiful rakshasi ever to have lived; how else would she have caught the ever-roving eye of Ravana? Yet she possessed that certain quality of beauty that was attractive not only in a sexual way but in a complete, holistic sense. She was a perfect mother; a wonderful daughter; a fine sister; a great queen. Her sense of dharma showed in the way she instantly bent to touch her brother-in-law's feet, as tradition demanded when approaching an elder in sanctified surroundings.

He bent and caught her arms, raising her up before she could prostrate herself.

'Brother . . .' she began, her voice filled with sorrow and fear. The emotion revealed by that single word shook him. It was not often one saw Mandodhari brought to the point of either emotion.

'Nay, wife of my brother. Do not let yourself be overwhelmed. I know it seems like the end of the world, but it is only a beginning, a new beginning.'

She looked up at him, her beautiful dark eyes large and searching in her ebony face. 'But Lanka is burning.'

'It will be rebuilt.'

'But the Asuras, our people, are at war with one another. They seek to wipe each other out.'

'Even war must have an end. The greater the violence, the greater the calm that follows.'

She shook her head, unable to find consolation in his wisdom. 'My husband . . . I saw him when you landed. Saw how he sat in the flying vehicle. I came here when you took him away to the volcano, to pray for his full recovery. But when I saw how he sat, lifeless and mindless, I could not even go to him. Instead, I waited here, like a coward, unable to face the corpse of my own beloved.'

'He is not dead, Mandodhari. Only drained by the effort of escaping the brahman stone cage. Together, you and I, we can revive him, help him recover to his former strength and vigour.' He gestured at the stone temple. 'Here, where he first gained his powers, we will help him regain them. His patron deity will preside and guide us. We will revive Ravana.'

She looked up at him, wiping the tears from her eyes. He saw a spark of hope light in her face. 'You believe this is possible?'

'I believe it is inevitable. It is our dharma, yours to save your husband, mine to save Lanka.'

She nodded, her face regaining its strength and

determination. He saw Mandodhari, the terrified wife and hapless mother, transforming back into the woman he had come to know and love and respect, Mandodhari the wife of the greatest Asura lord, wife of Ravana, mother of champions.

'Then it shall be done,' she said. 'Come, lead me to my husband. Let us bring him within these sacred walls. Let us begin by asking He Who Wields The Dumroo to play his drum for my lord and master, to bring back the strength to his limbs.'

Vibhisena nodded, pleased at her quick recovery. Mandodhari had always seemed so strong and immutable, he had felt a twinge of terror at the thought of her breaking down before his eyes. 'And the rest of the family? Your father, my nephews, our loyal retainers?'

She gestured downwards. 'They are safe and well. There is a secret passageway that leads from the black fortress directly into the heart of Nikumbhila. There are caves there. We have moved into that habitation until such time as the civil violence ends.'

He nodded, recalling the ancient passageway. It had been designed for precisely such a time, in the highly unlikely event that Lanka was overrun by war or disaster, that the royal family might be able to make their way safely to their patron shrine. This was the first time it had ever been used in all these millennia. That itself bespoke the rarity and magnitude of the current crisis.

As they walked back to the temple entrance, he wondered aloud: 'I don't understand though . . . those explosions? Why would the Asura races try to destroy the whole city? Rioting and fighting I can understand . . . they have a great many old scores to settle. But to undermine the kingdom itself? Which faction would take such an extreme step?'

She replied easily, almost nonchalantly, as they exited the dim, gloamy light of the temple and emerged into the gaudy daylight outside. The enormous cloud far south marked the aftermath of the very explosions he had just spoken of, vying with the effusion of the volcano's eruption in density and toxicity.

'The explosions were done at my bidding.'

He stopped short, staring at her. She paused, turning. 'You, Mandodhari?'

Her profile was a classical portrait against the backdrop of grey sky. The billowing cloud visible in the far background only added to the allure and mystique of her exotic features. Her slanted pupils, not wholly like an animal's yet quite unlike any human's eyes, nictitated sideways as she gazed into the distance, replying,

'Yes, brother-of-my-husband. I ordered them set off.'

He felt his knees buckle beneath his weight. A temple pillar provided support for his arm. 'But why? Why would you devastate our own kingdom, decimate our own people?'

She replied calmly with the same demureness with which she had bowed to touch his feet. 'The riots were uncontrollable. Despite my best efforts, the warring factions would not cease and desist. They thought that with Ravana gone, the strongest force would rule Lanka . . . and share my bed. I thought of all the options, waking Kumbhakarna, sending my sons forth to quell the rebellion, calling up more Asuras from the netherworlds . . . but in the end, this was the only viable option.'

He gestured at the distant cloud. 'This? Total annihilation? How could this be an option?'

She shrugged. 'Desperate times call for desperate measures. I did what had to be done.'

He was at a loss for words. Not only because it shocked

him to know that it was she who had ordered the destruction of Lanka, but because of the calm, steadfast way she admitted to having done so. He began to look at her in a new light. Perhaps he had not understood Mandodhari after all. Perhaps the quiet, docile façade he always saw was nothing more than a mask for the blood-thirsty rakshasi that lay beneath. He shook his head. He could not believe it. After all, was she not the island's next most diligent adherent of dharma? Next only to himself? No, there had to be some more rational explanation for her act.

'You feared for the welfare of your family,' he said, seeking some glimmer of insight, of empathy. 'You feared that the rebels would seek revenge on yourself and your family for Ravana's excesses. That is why you took this extreme step. Fear always breeds destruction, my sister. Your actions, though contrary to your dharma, are understandable in that light. You must atone for your acts, of course. I will aid you in that atonement. But . . .'

She turned her face fully to him. With the sky behind her and the darkness of the temple at his own back, her features were shadow-smeared, obscure. Only her eyes glinted in that shadowed visage.

'I did not do it out of fear, Vibhisena. I had my family removed at the very outset of the riots. Otherwise my sons would never have stood by quietly and let a chance at armed combat pass by. No, my brother-in-marriage. I did what I did because it had to be done. When I saw the lust and rapaciousness in the eyes of the rebels, in those who were formerly most loyal to my husband, those who had sat by his feet and fed on his scraps like hounds, fawning on his slightest favours, it filled me with loathing and disgust. I decided then and there that if those wretches could not be loyal to Ravana, if all they sought was to usurp his authority shamelessly and repay his governance with open treachery, then they might as well all die. It was a difficult thing to order, but order it I did. So hear me well now. I ordered the destruction of Lanka for one reason and one reason only. *If Ravana cannot rule Lanka, then nobody will.*'

And then she turned on her heel and walked on towards the pushpak, leaving Vibhisena standing in the dim half-light of the temple threshold, stunned and dismayed beyond belief.

6

Lakshman stood on a boulder upon a ridge, silhouetted against the faintly reddening sky. A soft breeze rustled the grassy meadow around him. His rig was on his back, his bow in hand and tightly strung, an arrow notched at the ready but held loosely; only the cord remained to be drawn. As Rama approached, Lakshman raised the bow, forming a perfect silhouette against the lightening pre-dawn sky, and drew the cord taut to its limit. If it had been a statue, Rama would have named it *Ayodhyan Bowman*. There were moments, not as rare as one might expect, when he caught himself wishing he had been born into the house of some artisan in the guilds of Ayodhya. A sculptor's would have done. He had always had a good hand for carving and sculpting, clay-modelling even. In these day-dream moments outside the normal span of consciousness, he imagined what it might be like to be *that* Rama, a shilpi by birth, a professional sculptor for hire. He would have carved flattering busts and repre-sentations of rich noblemen and vaisyas who commis-sioned them, and in his spare time he would have wrought pieces such as this one. *Ayodhyan Bowman*. An attempt to capture the grace and agile beauty of an anonymous young hunter. Yes. Sometimes the day-dream seemed almost desirable. What did paupers dream of? Becoming princes. What did princes dream of? Becoming kings, of course. But what did kings dream of? Becoming . . . someone else. Anything but kings. Even commoners would do.

He paused below the boulder and waited.

Lakshman loosed his arrow, the sound of the cord echoing like a whip-crack in the placid morning. High above, a flock of birds cried and altered course. A moment later, a heavy object fell fluttering to land with a muffled thud in the thick overgrowth across the clearing.

'Yes, bhai.'

Lakshman's voice was as taut as the cord had been, held by an invisible hand.

Rama looked up.

Lakshman remained standing, still staring upwards at a diagonal, scanning the dark skies intently. 'Speak if you wish.' He added after a moment, 'It will not disturb my shooting.'

'Why do you hunt?' Rama said. 'We already have food to break our sleep-fast. Guha provides generously.'

'And should we not repay his generosity?' The question contained the faintest trace of a challenge. 'These fowl are to replace the fish and meat he gave us. Were we not taught by our guru to repay every debt, be it ever so small, at the earliest possible time? For debt unpaid becomes debt unbearable over time. That is all I am doing. Repaying Guha for his hospitality.'

Rama chose his words carefully, knowing that the wrong choice of phrase could turn his brother's barely contained sullenness into belligerence. He had no stomach for an argument with Lakshman, not at this early hour, not at any time. 'That is good,' he said, using honest praise. 'I should fetch my rig and do the same. Or . . .' He allowed himself a brief pause, hoping that Lakshman would catch his meaning. When that did not happen, he continued, 'Or perhaps you will allow me to use your bow to down a bird or two.'

Lakshman found a new target, sighted intently, pulling the cord taut once more, then released. 'I can down enough for all three of us.'

Rama nodded, then leapt on to the boulder. 'I have no doubt you can.' He stood beside Lakshman, compelling his brother to pay attention to him by entering his private space. There was very little room on the boulder for one bowman, let alone two. Lakshman was forced to lower the bow and stare at Rama. Rama deliberately did not meet his gaze but looked towards the east, where a crack had opened in the deep blue sky and strange hues were leaking out, heralding the new day.

'Lakshman, my brother,' he said.

'Yes, Rama?'

'I wish to ask you a question.'

Lakshman kept his eyes on the sky. 'Yes, brother, speak. I am listening.'

'What Guha said last night . . . It was a generous invitation, and a wise one too.'

'I thought so. But I did not think you felt the same.'

'It was not an invitation I could accept. Not for myself at least, for the terms of my banishment are crystal clear. I must go to the Dandaka-van. But Lakshman, you are not bound by those same terms. You may stay here freely of your own choice. Why, if some calamity were to befall Ayodhya, or, the devas forbid, our family, you would be free to ride back to the capital and deal with it as you will. Guha's ties to our nation are strong, and communication between Ayodhya and his lands is easy and frequent. You would be in a position to travel to Ayodhya whenever you wished. If Bharat spoke truly in Guha's presence, and I have no doubt that he did, then our brother intends to take up residence at Nandigram. Which means that he will not set foot in Ayodhya again until I return from exile. You know our brother well, Lakshman. He will do as he has vowed, no matter what it costs. Even open civil riot would not draw him back against his word. Given these circumstances, it would be a blessing to our mothers if you were to remain here, accessible to Ayodhya and our family.'

Lakshman looked down. When he spoke, his voice was almost a whisper. 'You wish me to remain here in the land of the Nisadas while Sita and you travel to Dandaka-van to live out your exile?'

'I wish it, yes, for then I could rest easy knowing that at least you, my brother, are at hand to raise your sword in Ayodhya's and our family's protection should such a need arise.'

Lakshman turned to look at him. Even without seeing his face, Rama could feel the accusation in Lakshman's eyes, burning into him. 'Do you not wish me to go with you? To travel by your side? To sit by your cookfire at nights? To hunt shoulder to shoulder? To face whatever dangers – and surely the Dandaka-van is far more dangerous than civilised Ayodhya – in that forest of banishment alongside you? As we have faced so many dangers and shared so many days together? Are you so weary of my companionship and brotherhood that you wish to have done with me now?'

Rama sighed. 'How can you even think such things, Lakshman? You know I love you as much as my life itself. I would spend every living moment with you if I could.'

'Then why do you wish to separate us?' Lakshman hesitated, then asked, 'Is it because you are married now?'

Rama frowned, turning to look at him. 'What does my

being married have to do with this, or with anything else? Am I not still your brother now that I am married? Do I not love you as much?'

'Yet you will take Sita with you into Dandaka-van today but you ask me to stay behind.'

'You cannot compare the two things, Lakshman. She is my wife. You are my brother. One is neither more nor less than the other.'

'Yet you are treating us differently. By asking me to stay and allowing her to accompany you.'

'Lakshman, her dharma is different from yours. Her dharma demands that she follow her husband wherever he may go, in sorrow or joy, sickness or health, wealth or poverty . . . these are part of our wedding vows. But your dharma commands you to protect your family and your kingdom, to serve our people.'

'And your dharma does not?'

Rama sighed. 'I am already following my dharma.'

'And so am I.'

Rama shook his head vehemently. 'No, Lakshman. You are thinking now like a brother, not a raj-kshatriya. Not like a prince of Ayodhya. You forget: you have not been exiled. I have. I must go. And for the same reason, you ought to stay.' Rama glanced at the eastern sky. 'Already it's nearing daybreak. In a little while we must start out, before the sun rises too high. Give me your answer swiftly, my brother. What will you do?'

Lakshman stared at the horizon for many moments. Rama let him think his way through the decision. The sky grew steadily lighter, the crack opening to fill the whole world with new light. Even so, it was still not fully daybreak yet. Mere moments had passed, though it felt like a lifetime. Rama's heart ached with too many unspoken words and feelings. *My brother. I wish I did not have to burden*

*you with such decisions. But such is the burden of princes
and some-day kings.*

Finally Lakshman asked simply, 'Rama, can I ask a
question?'

'Of course.'

'If I were the one banished into exile, and you were
my brother, our positions reversed, and I said the same
things to you that you have just said to me, then would
you have agreed to stay, and let me go into Dandaka-
van without you?'

Rama nearly smiled, but caught himself in time. *Clever
Luck. A mind as quick as your bow.* 'What I might or
might not have done is not relevant. You have to decide
for yourself.'

'I have already decided. But I still want to know what
you would have done.'

Rama looked at him. He could just make out
Lakshman's features now. Staying awake all night and
drinking with Guha seemed not to have marked
Lakshman's face too much. His eyes still seemed clear,
though filled with that heartbreaking sorrowful look that
seemed to have become part of his appearance since
leaving Ayodhya. 'If I answer that question, it will influence you.'

'It won't. I will not change my decision either way.
You have my word on that.'

Rama hesitated, then nodded. He trusted Lakshman.
'If our places were reversed, then I would have stayed
and let you go into the Dandaka-van without me.'

Lakshman nodded, smiling in triumph. 'I knew you
would say that. It is exactly your way. You would have
stayed because you believe in the truth of your words:
that my dharma would be better served by staying here
with Guha, within reach of Ayodhya. And you, Rama,

would always follow your dharma, even if it meant letting me go into exile alone. That is always your way.'

Rama didn't say anything. There was no need to.

After another thoughtful pause, Lakshman went on, 'But I will not do as you would have. Rama, I will not stay here with Guha. I will come with you into Dandaka-van, if you will have me. If you still want me to, my brother.'

Rama looked at him, his eyes softer now. 'When did I say I did not want you? That was never the issue.'

'Then I can come with you?'

Rama sighed. He was caught now, between brotherly love and dharmic duty. 'You do not intend to follow your dharma then?'

'Of course I do.'

Rama blinked. 'But then . . .'

'My dharma is to stay beside you, Rama. Always. No matter what happens, this one thing will always be true. Lakshman will stay beside Rama for ever.'

'But what about our mothers? Ayodhya? Your respon-sibility to the people?'

Lakshman spread his palms. 'I serve them all by serving you.'

Rama stared at him.

Lakshman put a hand on his brother's shoulder. 'To you, Rama, the people will always come first. Even before our mothers, even before me, or Sita . . . That is why you are Rama.' He shrugged. 'And to me, *you* always come first. Do you see now? You serve dharma, and in doing so you serve the people of Ayodhya. I serve you, and in doing so I serve my dharma, which is *you*. Rama is Lakshman's dharma.'

Rama stared at him. Then, overcome by emotion, he embraced Lakshman tightly, fiercely. Lakshman embraced him back, just as fiercely. Behind them, the dawn broke quietly.

Rama finally ended the embrace. He gestured towards the shrubbery into which he had seen the bird fall. 'Now, my brother, I think we should go fetch the gifts you captured for Guha before some other predator takes them and has them for breakfast!'

Neither of them noticed the pair of eyes watching them intently from the shadows of the nearby thicket as they walked back to their camp, carrying four fat geese slung over their shoulders, talking and chatting amicably. That was not surprising in itself; even the most cautious of hunters would hardly bother with a mere doe skulking shyly. But when the doe transformed a moment later, changing in the same muscle-wrenching, bone-reshaping manner as the famed shapeshifters of her mother's race, the yaksas, were wont to do, it was well that neither brother was within sight. For they would have certainly been on their guard against the formidable creature that now stood in the thicket, her half-rakshasi, half-yaksi form terrifying enough to send the squirrels scurrying up the branches of the highest trees to be well away from her.

Supanakha sighed, stretching her limbs, cracking her joints with relief. It was convenient to take the form of a doe for the ease with which it allowed her to follow Rama and observe him from the closest quarters. Even at the moments when she had been seen by him, or merely sensed, she could be bold in her proximity, safe in the knowledge that he would take no offence at her presence or her watchfulness. But it was hell on her body when sustained over long periods of time. This was the longest she had stayed without changing: all the way from

Ayodhya, where she had caught Rama's scent within moments of him leaving the city, up to here. Usually she tried to change back into her natural rakshasi form – or yaksi-rakshasi form, if you preferred – with each phase of the sun. It gave her some respite.

Still, she mused as she teased out the more painful cramps in her powerful muscles and tendons, it had been worth it. She had learned so much just by being close and listening carefully. So cousin Ravana's plan had been successful, in part at least. Though he had not succeeded in the invasion, his little scheme within Ayodhya had borne poisonous fruit. Rama was exiled. Ravana would have been in a paroxysm of joy had he but known. But alas, Ravana was no longer in a position to feel anything any longer, neither joy nor sorrow. If her understanding of the situation was correct, Vibhisena's attempt to free his brother, and her cousin, from the brahman stone cage had not been entirely successful. Which suited her just fine. She had begun stalking Rama on Ravana's orders. But her pursuit of the mortal had continued purely because of her own growing affection for him. And now fate had turned things to her advantage, with Ravana no longer in a position to order her around, or penalise her for deviating from his elaborate plan. And with Rama exiled and en route to Dandaka-van. Supanakha had wanted to cry out with sheer joy when she had understood that much. Conversely, she had pouted when she realised that Rama's new wife – *wife!* – would indeed stay the course with her husband, as would his brother. She could have done without their tagging along, frankly. It was only Rama she had eyes for. *Her* Rama. Not that mortal hussy's!

But that little inconvenience could easily be removed. Once within the Dandaka-van proper, so much could happen. Rama and Lakshman had no notion what they were about to face in a short while. Or how easy it would be to dispense with that meddlesome brother and that worthless wife once within the environs of the forest of exile.

She licked her lips, imagining how she would relish the moment when Lakshman and Sita were killed and removed from her path, and Rama was alone, completely alone. Hers for the taking. How she would finally bare her heart to him, and win his heart in return. Theirs would be a match made by the devas themselves! And what a wedding dowry she had to gift unto Rama. He had no conception of what was in store for him. Soon . . . very soon.

She finished licking herself, in the manner of the jungle felines with whom she shared more than a few affinities, and debated whether to continue following her beloved for just a little while longer. No, she shook her large head regretfully, slobber dripping from her open jaws. She had to make sure she reached Dandaka-van before they did, and they did not seem inclined to tarry much longer now. She would have to cut across the woods, and even then she still had to ferret out her brothers Khara and Dushana. They might be anywhere within Dandaka-van. Their division, and the rakshasas that had followed them, had been delayed in Lanka itself when their ship had been forced to turn back because of a run on an undersea reef; which had resulted in their leaving just after the Brahm-astra had struck and decimated the rest of the invading Asura forces. Upon landing on the south-eastern shores of the sub-continent, they had taken refuge in the Dandaka-van, an old bolthole of rakshasas, and waited there even now, leaderless and missionless.

Except that now she had a mission for them. One so

simple to fulfil that it was almost laughable. She had no doubt that Khara would laugh when she told him what she wanted him and his rakshasas to do. Dushana might listen more sympathetically; he had always been her favourite brother out of the litter of twenty-four in which she had been born. But she would convince them using whatever argument was needed. And with their help she would gain Rama for herself. And once Rama understood the magnificent genius of her plan . . . !

She roared her joy and anticipation aloud, forgetting for a moment that she was in enemy territory.

The sound echoed for miles around, making every Nisada within earshot cringe. Then, with a great leap, she bounded away through the thicket, heading southwards, towards Dandaka-van. Each lunging step carried her closer to her ultimate goal. *Rama!*

7

They reached the hermitage of the sage Agastya around noon.

The chief had wept when he took his leave of them, at the banks of the Jamuna. He had rowed them across in one of his own boats, eschewing the help of his many aides to perform this last service with his own hands. The crossing was conducted in utter silence, the rising sun only just over the horizon warming their backs. Arriving on the far side, he had grounded the boat then fallen at their feet, weeping. Rama had raised him up and embraced him. There were few words spoken. Everything of consequence had already been discussed before they had broken camp by the Nyagrodha tree. Lakshman had cut a vein in the Nyagrodha's trunk and collected the sap. As they used the sticky sap to mat their hair into the coiled fashion of forest hermits, Guha had made one last attempt to sway Rama's mind.

The chief had again extended his invitation to the princes and Sita to stay with him and rule alongside him, and had been rejected, gently but firmly, yet again. This time, Lakshman had not supported him. Then Guha had offered to send a considerable number of his best and bravest warriors, both men and women, into the Dandaka-van with them, for their protection, and that had been refused as well, just as firmly and gently. Finally, when all overtures were rebuffed and nothing else remained but to take their leave, Guha had shaken his head and taken a feather from his chief's turban. The feather Rama had accepted, as a token of his brother-hood and as a sign of the alliance between their nations. Then they had left on foot, arriving at the Jamuna very shortly after, for the place where they had camped was almost at the verge of the river. On the far side, they had entered the valley of the Jamuna and proceeded at a brisk pace, following the directions Guha had given them towards the sage Agastya's hermitage.

The journey was not unpleasant. The countryside was beautiful, the new spring growth decorating everything in sight with colours as bright as the plumage of a peacock. They passed ponds overgrown with lotus creepers, went by groves with swans preening, walked through thickets filled with newly flowering trees, brooks bubbling quietly in their shade.

Their route took them almost parallel to the Jamuna itself, and at one point they heard the lowing of buffaloes and saw a large herd bathing in the rushing waters. One enormous bull stood half immersed in the river, facing upstream. The water struck him and fanned out like glittering plumage in the morning sun. Lakshman pointed the sight out to Rama and Sita, and Sita laughed in amazement. They passed a thickly shaded grove filled with a deafening buzzing. Looking up, they saw at least a dozen visible beehives, each as large as one of the buffaloes they had just passed, suspended from the thick branches of vanash trees. The full cluster of pendulous hives must have housed crores of bees, all told. The air swarmed with their busy activity. Rama shushed his companions to silence, leading them quietly through the grove. Bees buzzed curiously around their faces, some settling on Rama's bare neck and back, one daring to explore Lakshman's face. When two settled on Sita's cheek, she held her breath inadvertently, afraid that they might enter her mouth. She could smell the faint aroma of lotus on the bees – they did love to feed on lotus nectar. When they had passed through the grove and the bees flew away, no longer interested, she gasped in relief, pausing to refill her depleted lungs. She continued rubbing her face where the bees had settled for several minutes afterwards, eliciting amused laughter from both boys.

As the morning wore on, they laughed a little less and talked almost not at all. It was difficult to forget that they were not embarked on a pleasure trip. At the end of their road lay a place that no sane Arya would want to visit, by choice or compulsion. After a while, the path through the woods grew more placid and devoid of natural distractions, and their journey more mechanical and duty-bound.

The sun was directly overhead when the path widened. They could hear the sounds of human habitation from up ahead; more specifically, the typical sounds of a gurukul. The unmistakable rote-chanting of brahmacharya acolytes reciting the day's slokas over and over dominated all other sounds. A drum was being beaten monotonously, as if by an acolyte who was being trained to master the four-by-four beat to which all Arya rituals were performed – except that the drummer seemed to resent his task, or perhaps it was a punishment, for the count tended to slow down gradually, then suddenly pick up again, as if the acolyte had been corrected sharply, then gradually dwindle to a slower count again . . . It made Rama smile, remembering similar punishments meted out to fellow pupils in his time.

They reached a fork in the path. One well-trodden

way led down to the river, the mud of the path as well as the bushes on either side dampened by water spilled while being carried back to the camp; the other way led right, growing wider as they went. Rama expected the path to widen into the usual large clearing with a cluster of thatched huts, the template for any number of similar gurukuls across the Arya nations.

Instead, the path widened but led to a pair of high bamboo gates, barred shut.

They stopped, Lakshman and Rama exchanging glances. It was hardly customary for forest hermitages to build gated settlements. They examined the shrubbery on either side of the gates – a bamboo wall, each pole sharpened to a point at the top, wound its way in a roughly circular shape. The wall and the gates were noticeably high, at least fifteen feet. The brothers exchanged another knowing glance. The height of the walls told them two things. One, these walls were intended to keep more than human predators out. Two, the brahmacharyas of this kul had gone to great trouble to fortify their habitat. Rama touched the bamboo wall, made up of poles as wide as his fist, tightly lashed together with strong vines. Yes, a great deal of trouble.

Sita voiced what they were both thinking.

'Why would a sage fortify his ashram?'

It was a good question. One that demanded a satisfactory answer. And there was only one way to learn that answer. Rama nodded once to Lakshman.

Lakshman called out, loud enough for his voice to carry over the bamboo gates – and over the rote-chanting of the acolytes within the compound.

'Namaskar to you within the ashram Chitrakut! We come in peace to take the blessings of the great sage Agastya. Pray, permit us entry within your ashram!'

The first thing to stop was the drumming. The drummer struck one much louder stroke, then went silent. Rama could almost picture the boy standing there wide-eyed in his dhoti, the weighted stick in his fist, staring. The rote-chanting continued for a half-sloka, then tapered off, one of the reciters stubbornly persisting to the end of the sloka before stopping. Now there was a true rishi in the making.

After a pause, in which Rama could discern much hushed whispering, a voice called back, 'All who seek the sage's blessings are twice blessed. We shall open our gates to you in just a moment. Before we do so, strangers, in the name of Brahma the Almighty Creator, we humbly request you to identify yourselves.'

Lakshman replied, 'We are three travellers from distant Ayodhya. Our names are Rama, Lakshman, and Sita.'

There was a great flurry of consternation within the settlement. Then the sound of distant cries and shouts of excitement, these last issued by very young throats, and the gates flew open, followed by a belated warning: 'Take care. The gates . . .'

'. . . open outwards!' Lakshman finished, leaping back nimbly. Rama and Sita were standing far enough back to avoid the swinging gates.

A horde of excited, wide-eyed young brahmacharyas were clustered at the entrance to the settlement, staring out. They looked much the same as young acolytes anywhere else: pates shaven clean except for a single lock of hair which was allowed to grow into a low chotti that was oiled and braided; upper bodies bare on most, except for a few older boys, who wore woven-hemp ang-vastras, lower bodies clothed in either bare functional langots or rough cloth. They were of all ages, from seven upwards to Rama's and Lakshman's own age. One older brahmacharya, his chotti almost entirely white with age, stood with a large staff, trying to quieten them down. Rama guessed that he was the person who had spoken to them before ordering the gates opened.

As Lakshman stepped forward, issuing introductions, several of the young brahmacharyas gasped and pointed. Clearly their reputations had preceded them, even in this remote corner.

'Greetings, namaskar, well met in the light of brahman,' Lakshman said with a flourish. 'I am Sumitra-putra Lakshman. This is my brother Kausalya-putra Rama Chandra. And his wife Sita Janaki, formerly of Mithila.'

'Rajkumars!' The word was shouted from somewhere in the back of the cluster of younger brahmacharyas, causing the others to blush and giggle in embarrassment. 'You are princes of Ayodhya!'

Lakshman cocked his head, playfully pretending to contemplate the statement. 'Well, yes. My brother and I are princes of Ayodhya. You are well informed in that respect, young sir. However, my sister-in-law would be more accurately referred to as a princess, if you please.'

That brought a great burst of laughter.

The elder brahmacharya stepped forward, shushing the crowd sternly. 'Shantam! Shantam! Is this how you treat royal visitors? Standing here and giggling like a gaggle of geese? Go and fetch the arghya implements! Quickly! And move aside. Make way for our honoured guests to enter the ashram!'

He greeted Rama and his companions with a namaskar and a deep bow. 'Su-swagatam, my lords, my lady. I apologise for the frivolous words. Our young acolytes are unaccustomed to such princely visits. We are a humble kul, isolated and detached from the glamour of city living.'

'No apologies are needed, rishi-dev,' Rama said. 'We

are grateful to you for permitting us entry. It is our honour
to be able to visit the famous hermitage of Maharishi
Agastya.'

Another commotion ensued from within the compound.
A larger group of brahmacharyas were approaching the
gate. These sadhus were much older than the ones around
the gate, several with grey hair matted in the style of ascetics – the same style in which Rama and Lakshman and
Sita now wore their own hair, piled in coils atop their
heads. Leading them was a gaunt, large-framed man with
a complexion almost as dark as Rama's, striking features,
and an aura of great spiritual power. Undoubtedly Sage
Agastya. Like all sages, he had shed his true name and
family links the day he entered a life of spiritual penance.
His name, the title by which he was thenceforth to be
known, had been chosen by his gurus, based on his own
intrinsic qualities. The name Agastya literally meant an
august personage, one who commanded respect and admiration. In keeping with his given Sanskrit name, Agastya
was truly august in every sense of the word; he approached
with a dignity that transformed his simple walk across the
ashram compound into a royal reception.

'Sadhu, sadhu,' he said, greeting the visitors with a
smile. 'This is a great honour. Today a great follower of
dharma graces Chitrakut ashram with his presence. Join
me in greeting the legend-in-his-time Rama Chandra, heir
to the throne of Ayodhya. Jai Shri Ram.'

Every single brahmacharya, all twenty score of them,
said in perfect unison, 'Jai Shri Ram!'

'Om Shanti Shanti Shanti!' chanted the senior rishis,
sprinkling Rama, Lakshman and Sita with sacred Ganga
water, as Sage Agastya himself bent to wash their feet in
the arghya ritual. More ritual words were said, slokas
recited, and the various spiritual obligations fulfilled.

The ritual finished, Rama prostrated himself before the maharishi, taking his blessings. Lakshman and Sita followed his example.

'Sadhu,' said the maharishi, touching their heads and uttering the appropriate benedictions.

He then led the way to his own hut, at the rear of the ashram. Not surprisingly, it was neither the largest nor the most striking; in fact, it was no different from any of the twenty-odd other huts aligned in neat rows across the compound. Behind the huts was a small thicket that had been included in the fencing-in, and Rama was pleased to see tame deer roaming freely. One doe nibbled tentatively at what looked like a lettuce patch. An elderly rishi waved a stick unaggressively at the nibbling doe, and she skittered away a step or two before turning her large round eyes back on the enticing green leaves peeking out of the ground. The elder rishi shook his head despairingly; clearly, this was a fight he was accustomed to losing, and the doe, emboldened by his gentleness, snatched a quick mouthful of crisp green lettuce, munching contentedly. Rama and Sita both noticed the little theft and smiled. The elder rishi saw them and smiled back, sighing as if to say, *What to do?*

At the north-eastern wall of the compound was a row of immaculately maintained shrines dedicated to various deities. Rama glimpsed shrines honouring Brahma, Vishnu, Indra, Surya the sun god, Chandra the moon god, Bhaga, Kubera, Dhatr, Vidhatr and Vayu. He noticed Sita genuflecting as she saw the shrines. He made a note to make time to pray before they continued their journey to the Dandaka-van.

'My roof is yours,' the sage said, gesturing them within the open uncurtained doorway of his hut.

They entered, bowing their heads to duck below the

low lintel. The interior was as Rama had expected: bare
and devoid of all but the most essential requirements.
Pallets of darbha grass for sleeping, a mud pot filled with
water for drinking, and naught else. The unmistakable
pungency of cow urine hung in the air. No doubt the
floor had recently been sanitised by a good washing-down
using the usual antiseptic mixture of cow urine and water.
Rama glanced at his brother. If Lakshman had any
response to the odour, he didn't show it on his face.

The sage indicated the floor, upon which had been
placed straw mats. 'Please. Sit.'

They made themselves as comfortable as was possible
and were served water in clay cups by three visibly
nervous young brahmacharyas. One of them was shaking
so much with excitement, he spilled most of the contents
of one cup on the floor before handing it to Rama.

Barely had the brahmacharyas been dismissed when
the maharishi spoke softly but with unmistakable urgency.
'Words cannot express my great joy at your arrival, my
lords. Since the day I heard the news of your journeying
in this direction, I have said to my acolytes, indeed, mighty
Brahma is magnificent in his vision. See how he turns
two great princes out of their homes so harshly, and yet
in doing so he provides us, the beleaguered ascetics of
this region, with two great champions. Truly, rajkumars,
we are greatly blessed that you have arrived here in time
to save us from the evil menace that plagues Chitrakut
vale.'

8

Sage Agastya was about to continue when more acolytes entered the hut, bearing bowls of fruit, puffed rice, and similar simple fare. The maharishi commended the food to his guests, and they ate some gladly, for they had begun their journey at dawn on empty stomachs, taking only a little water from the Jamuna en route, and had traversed over three yojanas that morning alone.

Rama sensed Lakshman's curiosity to his left, and Sita's concern to his right, and at the first available opportunity he asked politely, 'Maha-dev, I do not follow your meaning. What evil menace plagues this place?'

An acolyte, no doubt the same one who had spilled the water earlier, almost dropped the bowl of puffed rice he was carrying. Lakshman's hand shot out and caught it in the nick of time. The brahmacharya smiled nervously at Lakshman, who nodded and took the bowl from the boy's nervous hands, setting it down on the mat. As the brahmacharya scurried out of the hut, Rama heard him saying, 'Guru-dev is asking the rajku-mars for help! Now we will be free of the menace at last!'

Agastya gestured at the food. 'Pray, supply yourselves first. I know you have come a long way and must be sorely in need of rest and nourishment. We can speak of these matters later this evening, after you have rested. Or even on the morrow if you prefer.'

Rama glanced briefly at Lakshman, who was clearly bursting with curiosity. 'Maha-dev, we thank you earnestly for your hospitality. The terms of our exile require us to live deep within Dandaka-van. If I am correctly informed, Chitrakut vale is on the outskirts of the forest proper. We still have further distance to travel before we reach the heart of the forest, and it is only our great desire to pay our respects to your holiness that caused us to divert our path briefly.'

The faintest trace of surprise touched the sage's face. He blinked once, then recovered his equanimity. His gaunt cheekbones moved slowly above his white beard as he spoke. 'I see. Then clearly I was mistaken in my impression. I believed that you had been sent here for another purpose altogether.' He was silent for another moment, then shook his head, smiling broadly again. 'It was my error then. No matter. You shall be provided with whatever you require, and I shall personally inform you as to the most efficacious route into the forest.'

One of the rishis made as if to speak but was silenced by a look from the sage.

'Maha-dev, do tell us what you were speaking of a moment ago. What is this evil menace you mentioned? Is it some wild predator that troubles your ashramites?'

Sage Agastya sighed. 'It is no matter. You are honoured guests. I must not burden you with our petty troubles. Please, eat some more. We do not boast of a fine table as you princes and you, my lady, must be accustomed to. But the fruits of this region are renowned for their sweetness, and the melons are particularly good this time of year. They will nourish you and prepare you for the rest of your arduous journey.'

Faced with the maharishi's insistence, Rama was unable to press the matter further. Controlling his curiosity, he ate some of the proffered melon – it was every bit as sweet as promised. Sita ate as well, pointing to the bowl of grapes to let him know discreetly that they were good too. He took some. They were sweet, and the large seeds were easy to remove. He would have wished for some jamuns, rasbhurries or ber, but none had been served and he didn't want to ask for them. Well, they were going into the deep forest; surely they would find any number of berry and other fruits growing wild everywhere. Food for exiles.

They spoke of minor matters for a while, mostly relating to Rama's and Lakshman's visits to Ananga-ashrama and Siddashrama, and Guru Vashishta and Brahmarishi Vishwamitra. Sage Agastya was very eager to know about various rituals and practices and how they were followed in Ayodhya. He also had questions about Mithila, especially about Sita's father Maharaja Janak and his renowned patronage of brahmanical studies.

They had finished the meal and the bowls had been cleared away. Several of the senior rishis of the ashram were seated to one side of the hut by this time, listening unobtrusively to their conversation. Agastya urged Sita to speak more about her father, and several of the other rishis added their voices to his.

To please them, Sita narrated an anecdote depicting her father's dedication to the search for spiritual wisdom. 'He had performed a lavish sacrifice once and distributed many gifts. Wise men from Kuru and Panchala attended the ceremony and my father wished to learn who among them all was the wisest. So he ordered his men to fasten ten gold coins between the horns of each of a thousand cows and had the cows driven into a pen. Then he told the venerable brahmins that the one among them who could prove he was the wisest of all could drive home all the cows.'

As Rama watched Sita tell her tale, he felt eyes watching him intently. He glanced over at the part of the room where the other rishis were seated. All of them were listening intently to Sita, some of the older ones nodding their heads happily. Clearly they relished having visitors and hearing of such things.

Except for one of the rishis, a relatively younger man, with only a little grey peppering his mostly black hair, and a face marred by an odd discoloration, like white-skin fungus, except that his skin had turned more pale green than white. The rishi was staring at Rama, and when Rama's eyes found his, he blinked rapidly and lowered his gaze in deference to the honourable visitor. Yet, Rama observed, he did not look at Sita or pay much attention to her story. Rama continued to watch the rishi with the discoloured face without making his observation evident; after a while, the brahmin's eyes crept inevitably back to Rama. Rama felt a sense of disappointment issuing from the man. He had been one of those who had started to speak when Maharishi Agastya had turned the topic away from the initial mention of the evil menace. Something was definitely troubling him.

Sita had reached the end of her story. 'As Maharishi Yajnavalkya's pupil, who was but a novice yet, began to lead away the cows, an outraged brahmin shouted, "How presumptuous!" And yet another cried out, "Yajnavalkya, do you truly believe you are the wisest here?" Janak restored quiet and allowed Yajnavalkya to explain his pupil's presumptiveness . . . The guru faced the hostile gathering calmly and said,' and here Sita looked around with a coy smile. '"I salute the wisest. But I want those cows."'

The rishis roared with laughter. Several slapped their thighs. One elderly rishi – Rama thought he was the same one who had been keeping the foragers away from the vegetable patch, and not doing a very good job of it – laughed so much he choked, and had to be given water to drink by his fellow rishis. 'More, more,' said the doe-challenged rishi when he had recovered his power of speech. Sita beamed. She would have obliged happily, Rama, knew, but the maharishi intervened.

'Rishiyon, we must not detain our guests further. You heard them say they wish to proceed towards Dandaka-van at the earliest. Let us now wish them a good voyage and see them off at the gates.'

Rama glanced at the rishis. The one with the discoloured face showed his disappointment clearly, looking down at the floor. Others seemed unhappy as well, yet unwilling to speak contrary to their guru.

Agastya stood with a little difficulty, favouring his right hip. He sighed with the unmistakable weariness of age, and took hold of a staff laid against the wall of the hut. Rama glanced idly at the staff, and saw something unusual.

At once he found his opening.

Speaking with apparent nonchalance, he said, 'Maha-dev, we city-dwellers have long heard tales of the dreaded Dandaka-van. Since our childhood we have been told hair-raising stories of demons and supernatural beings prowling the woods.'

Lakshman understood what Rama was up to and added his own voice: 'Indeed, maha-dev, we were told that the forest is infested with wild predators as well as Asuras.'

Sita added: 'Since we are proceeding there to reside, we would appreciate anything you could tell us in this regard, maha-dev.'

Sage Agastya stroked his beard thoughtfully, his forehead

wrinkled with concentration. He could hardly ignore their queries, Rama knew, and waited patiently for his answer.

Instead, it was another voice that spoke first. The rishi with the discoloured face stepped forward. 'Maha-dev, if I may speak . . . ?'

Agastya looked troubled. He turned his wise, tired eyes to the rishi.

Finally he nodded. 'Speak, Somashrava.'

The rishi's face was pinched with intensity, the discolorations on his forehead and cheek seeming to change colour as he grew more agitated. 'The stories you heard are true. Demons abound within the deep woods. After leaving our ashram, you will find only one more brahmin on your route. That is the venerable sage Atri and his legendary wife Anusuya. But beyond their domicile you will find no more brahmin inhabitants. After you cross the confluence of the rivers, travel over Chitrakut hill and Panchvati grove, then cross the Godavari, you will see only wilderness. A desolate spiritual wasteland, beautiful and alluring in its physical temptations, like a honey trap laid out to entice and imprison mortals with fleshly desires. No mortal who enters those woods ever returns . . . at least, they do not return as mortals.'

Somashrava fell silent after this astonishing speech, after a look from his guru, even though it was evident that he had much more to say. The rishi's emotions had changed visibly while narrating these few details; his discolorations had turned from their green tinge into an almost reddish hue.

Rama asked, 'Do you fear attacks by these Asuras?'

Rishi Somashrava looked at his guru. Sage Agastya remained silent, his long face and high cheekbones still with disapproval.

Lakshman spoke. 'Why else would you have walled in

your ashram, maha-dev, if not to keep out something that threatens you?'

Somashrava began to speak again, in a headlong rush. 'All the other sages have fled this region. Once there were many ashrams here—'

'Enough,' Agastya said quietly. 'Rajkumars, rajkumari . . . you need not trouble yourself with these matters. We will deal with these inconveniences as they arise. It is an inevitable part of our penance and a small price to pay for eventual spiritual enlightenment.'

Somashrava looked as if he would cry out. The discolorations on his face were turning blackish now. Rama wondered if the colour changes reflected the rishi's emotional state or were caused by some unrelated factor.

Rama suggested politely, 'It would be helpful if we heard the whole matter, guru-dev. After all, we are now residents of these parts too, virtually neighbours. And as neighbours, we must share our troubles.'

Agastya sighed, laying a wrinkled white-haired arm on Rama's shoulder. 'My son – for you are as a son to me – we are far more fortunate than some of us realise. These environs, where our ashram is situated, are relatively peaceful and tranquil yet. Compared to the Dandaka-van into which your brave trio ventures, we are almost safe and sound here. You, on the other hand, will have far more contentious matters to contend with within those formidable woods. What Somashrava has told you is all true. Be on your guard night and day inside that terrible place. There are perils that would infatuate any mortal and sway him from the path of common reason. If you were not pupils of Guru Vashishta and the great Vishwamitra, achievers of such notable feats of kshatriya bravery, I would have entreated you not to go any further, for it would mean certain destruction. As it is, I give you all my blessings for a safe exile and shall offer special prayers to the Lord Brahma daily until your fourteen years are over and you pass this way once more.'

'Why will you not tell them?'

Somashrava's voice quivered with frustration and anger. 'Why will you not tell them about the gandharva? That murderer of my brother and father and of so many other innocents among our brahmacharyas? These men are champions, heroes of the Bhayanak-van, cleansers of the cursed Southwoods, slayers of Tataka and her demon hordes, challengers of Ravana, and of Parsurama. Already, their deeds are the stuff of history. Then why will you not tell them about our bane? They can help us. They can slay the creature and avenge our lost friends . . . and my blood-relatives.'

Agastya didn't react angrily at Somashrava's unexpected and unorthodox outburst, as Rama expected. Instead, the sage looked sad. 'Because it is not their karma, Somashrava. They are merely passing through our habitat on their way to their own destination. We cannot divert them from their intended goal and ask them to solve our problems.'

'Why not?' Somashrava demanded, his voice and tone still respectful and controlled, but trembling with urgent desperation. Rama could see tears bunching in the corners of the rishi's eyes. The tears were yellowish black in colour. 'They are kshatriyas, we are brahmins at a holy outpost, expanding the realm of brahman. The code of the kshatriyas says that we may call upon any of them to protect us and defend us from aggressors, be they human or inhuman. It is their dharma to fight for our survival.'

'True,' Agastya said. 'But the code of the kshatriyas does not apply to exiles. Being banished, they are now bound only by the terms of their banishment. Rama, Sita and Lakshman need only stay in the Dandaka-van and survive the fourteen years. Nothing else is required of them. As exiles, they exist outside the Laws of Manu.'

Outside the law. *Outlaws*. It was hard hearing oneself described with that word, even though it was spoken by a wise and sympathetic tongue, and was undeniably accurate. The truth was not easy for Rama to accept. *An outlaw in my own kingdom, that is what I am now become.*

Somashrava was silenced momentarily by his guru's argument. Still, the rishi was searching for some counter-argument, unwilling to concede the point that easily. His father and brother, he had said. And many other brahmacharyas as well? No wonder the poor brahmin was beside himself with grief. Rama looked around and saw, as he had sensed, the door of the hut crowded with the faces of acolytes. The entire population of the ashram had gathered outside the hut, listening eagerly to the debate. The silent pleading in the eyes of the little brahmacharyas told its own story. Rama noticed now for the first time that one of them had an arm missing, another an eye, a third a leg, a fourth had an ugly scar on his bald head and neck . . . He guessed that these crippled ones had been inside one of the huts when the visitors had entered the ashram, not among the more active acolytes. No doubt Rishi Somashrava's own facial discoloration had been caused by some similar encounter with the berserker in question.

He turned to Sage Agastya without hesitation. 'Mahadev, permit me to speak my mind. All that you have said is undeniably true. Your knowledge of dharma and the laws of my ancestor Manu are unquestionable. Yet even though the code no longer applies to us exiles, outlaws as we are for these fourteen years, yet we still carry our weapons for our own protection. We intend to use them freely to defend ourselves and our loved ones against any aggressors. And what else art thou and thy ashramites if not beloved to us, who love all things that serve brahman? So, I ask you humbly and in all deference to your greater years and wisdom, allow us this opportunity to serve you. Not to avenge those who have been struck down, but because we wish it. We would not choose to turn our backs on such a menace, for who is to say that he might not follow us and attack us while we sleep? One Asura downed is one Asura fewer for us to fear in Dandaka-van. Let us face and destroy this evil that plagues you, and gain spiritual satisfaction for ourselves as well. Show us this gandharva and we will kill him.'

'Here.'

Rishi Somashrava crouched down by the peepal tree and pointed to a spot on the ground, near the trunk. A large stain discoloured the leaf-strewn earth, spreading outwards in smaller splotches, the way blood might splash out of a human body if it was slashed open. As the rishi glanced up over his shoulder to see his reaction, Rama was struck by the peculiar similarity between the stain on the ground and the tree trunk, and the discoloration on Somashrava's face.

Lakshman moved past Rama and crouched beside the rishi. 'This is where the last attack happened?'

'Yes, rajkumar. The rakshasa snatched the young boy as he was collecting water at the stream nearby.' Somashrava pointed back the way they had come, in the direction of the brook they had passed a few dozen yards back, within sight of the ashram walls. Neither the brook nor the wall was visible from here, though. 'His screams caught my attention. I came running and tried to grab hold of the boy's legs as he was being dragged away. But the demon was too strong. The boy screamed in agony, and his limbs would have been ripped apart had I held on. So I was forced to let go, and I attempted to strike the demon with my lathi.' The rishi pointed at some fragments of wood lying nearby. They looked like splinters left over from wood-chopping. 'As you can see, the creature simply caught the lathi in its teeth and shattered it to bits. Then it roared at me, as if it was taunting me to do anything further, swung around,' Somashrava turned quickly, reliving the incident; Lakshman and Rama moved back to give him space, 'and its tail rose up into the air and struck me a blow across my face. It knocked me all the way to . . .' he ran to a sapling over twenty yards away, 'this place. I fell unconscious. When I awoke, I found only these bloodstains spattered here by this peepal, and no sign of the monster or even a trail.'

Sita asked, 'And that caused your skin to . . . change colour?'

Somashrava touched his discoloured face, now an angry reddish-brown. 'Yes. Nothing will remove it, neither ayurvedic herbs or remedies, nor invocations and penance.'

And perhaps you are secretly proud of that. For the rishi clearly wore the mark like a warrior's wound now, an exterior symbol that revealed the inner rage that burned within him. Rage like that often didn't end with revenge, Rama knew; it ate away at the person until he became a facsimile of the very thing he hated. But he kept his thoughts to himself. Somashrava had enough on his mind without needing unsolicited advice.

'Very well, Somashrava,' Rama said. 'We will deal with this matter now. You may return to the ashram. Thank you for showing us the place where the demon was last seen.'

Somashrava hesitated. 'I wish to stay with you here tonight. To help . . . hunt the beast.'

Rama saw Lakshman glance at him over the rishi's shoulder. Lakshman shook his head once, meaningfully.

'Rishi Somashrava,' Rama said, 'perhaps it is best if

you leave this part to us. This will undoubtedly be a night fraught with great peril. My brother and I, as also my wife, are trained at the art of the hunt—'

'So was I,' Somashrava said quickly. 'I was born in the kshatriya varna, raised and trained in the calling of a Kashi spearman. But my father had sworn an oath to surrender his eldest son to the pursuit of brahman. When my brother was killed in these woods by the same rakshasa, my father then sent me in his place, to fulfil the promise. He was visiting me once when he decided to try and hunt the rakshasa himself. He was killed as well.'

Rama raised his eyebrows. 'The spearmen of Kashi are renowned across the Arya nations.'

Somashrava nodded proudly. 'And I was a front-runner. I am in my fortieth year now. I trained until I was a score and five years. I was told I would be taken as an Indradhanush-man in another two years.'

Lakshman nodded slowly, impressed. The Indradhanush unit of Kashi was similar to the Vajra of Kosala, an elite fighting squad which hand-picked only the best of the best warriors. Rama re-assessed the brahmin. This explained the man's emotional demeanour, and the greater leeway Sage Agastya had allowed him.

Somashrava added quietly, 'I heard my father's screams after he was taken by the beast. They continued almost all of that night. The next day, I found parts of his body scattered across several miles.'

His tone was the opposite of anger. Now that action was finally being taken, he seemed calmer, more able to deal with the past. Rama saw Lakshman shrugging, deferring to him, and came to a decision.

'In that case, you may stay, Somashrava,' he said. 'Another pair of eyes and hands is always welcome.'

*   *   *

Sita knew that smell. It was the fragrance of temple flowers. She had placed a garland like that around the deity of Sri, the Mother-Creator, every morning since she could recall. The smell of those saffron hued blossoms was imprinted indelibly on her sense-memory. She sat up straighter. She was on a plain wooden platform on the peepal tree, one of two such that Lakshman and Rama and the rishi had rigged. Lakshman and Somashrava were on the other platform, while Rama and she sat on this one. Rama was behind her, facing the other way. They sat back to back, to cover every direction. She turned her head slightly, lowering her sword. She could feel the warmth of Rama's breath on her cheek as he turned his head, sensing her movement. She knew better than to turn around or speak loudly, despite her certainty that the creature they were hunting was nearby.

'Temple flowers,' she whispered.

There was no response at first. Then Rama said softly, sounding perplexed, 'Where? I don't see them.' He added, 'Or smell them.'

She turned around fully then. It was so remarkable that Rama couldn't smell the flowers, she couldn't believe it. Was he teasing her? No. He wouldn't do that. Rama took combat very seriously, she knew that already. Lakshman had sauntered and joked and chatted with Somashrava before nightfall, but Rama had grown deathly still and sober as the hours passed, almost as if he was preparing himself for the act of taking life yet again. *Because he doesn't like killing. Even when it's righteous.*

'It's so strong. How can you not smell it?' she said, keeping her voice just low enough for him to hear her. She glanced around cautiously. 'It smells as if it's right below this very—'

She looked up, realising suddenly, too late, that the

smell wasn't coming from below as she had foolishly assumed. This wasn't some temple maiden walking home after her visit to the nearest mandir for darshan. It was an Asura, a rakshasa no less, and they could as easily attack—

'*From above, Rama!*' she cried as the dark, grotesque shape fell on her like a jungle cat from the high branches. She tried to get the sword up in time as the apparition enveloped her like a flying bat out of hell. It was swatted aside by a powerful clawed forelimb and vanished over the edge of the platform. Then the beast had her by the throat, choking her so she couldn't speak or breathe, and by the waist, and by the thighs as well, clenching her in an enormously powerful grip with sharp-clawed limbs that dug into her flesh like pincers, drawing blood, and she was lifted as easily as a rag doll, horizontally at first, then up and away. She felt a moment of shocking weight-lessness and felt wind billow at her face, the tips of branches raking her arms and ankles, and she knew that the beast had leapt to another tree. *That's how it hunts without ever being seen. It uses the trees to move around!* No wonder the rishis had said it always appeared from nowhere and disappeared with its victims. It took them up into the trees. The tigers of the mangroves in southern Banglar hunted this way. Fishermen who trawled the creeks of the mangrove forest in that region were used to tigers leaping from trees, snatching away a grown man from the boat in which he was seated, and disappearing into the trees before his companions had time to even emit a cry. The beast that carried her felt more powerful even than a Banglar tiger.

She heard Rama's voice, shouting commands to Lakshman and Somashrava. She heard the zip-zip sound of two arrows being loosed in quick succession, and knew that Lakshman had fired. Immediately she heard Rama's voice admonishing his brother: 'It has Sita!' The creature carrying her swerved to avoid the arrows, in mid-air literally, and twisted its body around, slamming sideways into a thick trunk. It clung on tenaciously for a moment, growling, then was away again, leaping through the air, travelling from tree to tree far faster than even a very swift runner could cover by sprinting across the same distance. *They'll never be able to catch us if it moves this fast*, she thought, then something hit her temple with a sound like a stick snapping, and she lost consciousness.

She woke to the sight of temple flowers. They were littered around her, on the clean-brushed platform on which she lay, fresh and fragrant. She waited for the throbbing in her head to slow. Trying not to give her wakeful state away before she had to, she pressed her hands to her body, trying to feel her condition. Her limbs felt intact, and there were no wounds on her midriff as might have been expected. If the creature fed on its victims, as most rakshasas did, then this one hadn't taken a bite of her yet. Or not that she could make out. She became aware of a peculiar yet intensely familiar sound from above her. Slowly, cautiously, she opened her left eye very slightly, for she was lying on her right side, curled up, and through the slitted eye she glimpsed the source of the sound. It was so surprising she almost sat up at once.

They were temple bells, swaying softly in the wind, tinkling together. She was lying on a temple altar, before the deity. From the damp, closed feel of the place, and the cold rock slab beneath her body, she felt certain it was some kind of cave.

She took three shallow breaths and released them very slowly, careful not to let her chest heave, or blow away any dust on the floor beside her. Though there wasn't much of that to speak of. The ground had been cleaned so painstakingly, it would have passed muster in her father's palace. She opened her right eye this time, just a fraction, and saw the familiar black stone effigy with its top flattened on four sides, representing the four faces of the Creator. Brahma. She was in a temple devoted to Lord Brahma.

'I know you are awake, stree.'

The voice was a cultured one, delicately nuanced with a classical accent, the kind of Sanskrit Sita had heard the older sages speak in her father's religious councils. *It's maya*, she warned herself. Asura illusions.

But she turned to look at the speaker anyway, unable to resist.

It was her abductor. As she had suspected during the flight through the trees, the Asura was no simple rakshasa. Its head and limbs – all six of them – were closer to a feline predator, while its torso, the back of its head, spine and tapering tail resembled a large lizard. She estimated its length to be perhaps twelve feet from head to tail-tip. Its overall colouring was a dusty rust-black mottled with greenish patches, an effective camouflaging in the trees. It sat in the centre of the cave, the roof curved above it like a roughly shaped upturned bowl. Behind it was a low-ceilinged, narrow passageway that she guessed led outside. The sound of water dripping steadily came from somewhere behind her – beyond the shrine, which meant that the cave probably went further inside. For a moment, just a fraction of an instant, she thought she heard voices as well: a faint distant whispering. Then there was only the touch of the wind on her right cheek and the fragrance of temple flowers, beneath which she smelt her own hair, in which leaves and bark had entangled in her abduction through the treetops.

She raised herself, not speaking, just examining the Asura with watchful eyes.

It showed its large fangs in a leering expression. 'Do not fear, stree. He will come for you soon. Already I sense him approaching the other side of the mound in which this cave is set. I made sure to leave a trail even a blind kshatriya would be able to follow, snapping branches and stalks off all the way home. And he is as excellent a hunter as I expected.'

Keep it talking. Until you think of some way to escape, keep it engaged in conversation. 'What manner of being are you?'

It made that leering face again. Slobber dripped from its jaws. 'I thought that was obvious, woman. An Asura! Just don't ask what species or race or varna. The ones who cursed me into this condition weren't very particular about my fitting into the social order!'

She found its impeccable language and manner more disturbing than if it had simply behaved the brutish way most rakshasas were expected to behave.

'What is this place? Some ancient Brahma shrine you chose to desecrate?'

It issued a coughing sound that was probably laughter. 'Desecrate? Look again. I built this shrine myself. I alone maintain it. I am the pujari of this temple.'

She was taken aback. 'Pujari? If by pujari you mean the temple attendant, then tell me, what kind of pujari slaughters brahmins and brahmacharyas and abducts women?'

It nodded its lizard-lion head. 'An excellent question. But now your consort approaches the cave entrance. The time for dialogue is past.'

Sita's heart skipped a beat. Could it be telling the truth? So then it was using her to lure Rama into its lair. That was why she remained alive and unharmed yet. Over her head, the temple bells tinkled again softly, and she felt a gentle breeze touch her right cheek. It was blowing in from the cave entrance. Then it was not far to the opening. If Rama was really approaching, he would be within hearing distance . . .

'*Rama, beware!*' she cried, throwing herself off the stone slab and on to the rough cave floor. She rolled behind the deity, seeking the passageway she was certain lay there. Her shouted words echoed in the narrow confines of the cave, ringing back and forth, mingling with the tinkling of the temple bells, and a moment later the coughing laughter of the beast. She rose to a half-crouch, and ran forward – stopped dead in her tracks by an unbroken rock wall which tapered up so sharply, she almost struck her head on the curved overhang. She looked around in desperation, but there was no escape this way. She had been wrong. The sound of water was still faintly audible, dripping in some other subterranean chamber, but there was a wall of rock between this cave and that one. Her plan had failed.

Again the faint whispering sound came to her, louder now than before. She turned a full circle, searching for an aperture, a hole, anything. But only the blank wall of the rockface rose above her, sloping to meet her head.

She turned back the way she had come, certain she would now face her death. But the space between the rear of the deity and the sharply curving cave wall was empty. The creature had remained where it sat, certain in its knowledge that she would find no escape route that way. She could still hear it, coughing out its odd laugh. The sound of her echoes had almost died away.

Suddenly the cave exploded with resounding noise, running feet, the metallic sounds of a spearhead glancing off the cave wall, and voices . . . There would be hardly any point in remaining silent in a cave, after all.

Sita came out from behind the stone effigy of Brahma just as Rama, Lakshman and Somashrava emerged into the cave. The lizard Asura was between her and them, and as he stopped directly before it, Rama's sightline met hers. She saw the flash of relief in his eyes when he took in her uninjured condition.

Then he charged at the Asura.

Rama's sword flashed in the flickering light of the cave as he struck the Asura. Following a beat behind him, Lakshman leapt too, wielding his sword. Both brothers circled the beast, their swords moving as though wielded by the same person. The flashing blades of Kosala steel bit hard into the lizard-beast's uppermost limbs, slicing easily through their meaty thickness. It roared with agony as both upper limbs were hewed from its body. Reddish-black ichor spurted from the gaping wounds. The severed arms fell writhing to the cave floor, oozing fluids.

The brothers were followed by Somashrava, his spear raised. The kshatriya-turned-brahmin ran the spear into the belly of the beast, piercing it with a sound that made Sita flinch despite her years of training as a warrior princess. So ferocious was the brahmin's assault, the spear passed through the Asura's body and burst out from the creature's back, glistening in the light of the temple diyas. Ichor dripped in a steady stream, pooling on the cave floor. The brahmin roared with fury and tried valiantly to remove the spear, but his effort only resulted in it breaking off at the handle with a resounding crack.

By this time, Rama and Lakshman had spun around and taken up defensive stances, ready for the creature's expected retaliation. The look on Lakshman's face was more a grimace than a grin. He exhaled in perfect unison with Rama, and in that instant Sita envied the brothers their closeness. How many times had she attempted to interest her sister and cousins in the arts of combat, without success? Had they been as inclined as she to be as well-prepared as any male kshatriya, she would have moved with them at a moment like this one, like four devis at work.

Both brothers paused, still waiting for the beast to make its next move. Rama's face was impassive, his eyes glinting darkly, his stance impeccable. Even Nakhudi would have been proud to fight beside him, Sita thought. And felt the twinge of pain that was her heart calling out for her companion. *This is your only family now*, she told herself sternly, focusing on the crisis at hand. *Rama and Lakshman. Be grateful that they are here to defend and fight for you – just as you would fight for them had you but a sword right now.*

After a long moment of inaction, Rama and Lakshman exchanged a surprised glance. Their defensive stances faltered ever so slightly; they had expected instant retaliation after such a brutal assault. So had Sita.

Yet the creature did nothing. It simply sat there and waited. Its wounds gushed ichor-blood, its jaws yawned open, releasing involuntary moans of pain that reverberated through the cave, vibrating in Sita's very bones. But it made not a single move to fight back or even defend itself.

Lakshman and Rama looked more uncertain. The creature was wounded sorely, but it was still formidable enough to be dangerous. One swipe of its leathery tail could sweep them off their feet. Its remaining limbs were still tipped with razor-sharp claws, its gaping maw was lined with teeth a tiger would have envied. Why then was it not attacking?

Somashrava turned to Rama. 'Kill it!' he shouted over and over in a frenzy akin to madness. 'Kill the demon of Chitrakut!'

The creature made no move, even though Somashrava, carried away by his desire for long-awaited vengeance, had stepped close enough for it to bite off his head if it pleased. Rama and Lakshman saw this and moved forward, raising their swords again.

Sita took a step forward too, loath to enter the circle of violence unarmed. 'Rama, Lakshman! Wait.'

Both paused, glancing at her by flicking their eyes yet keeping their heads towards the creature, ready for any demonaic surprises.

'This is no ordinary Asura,' she said. 'It is a devotee of Brahma. Look at this shrine beside me. The creature claims to be the pujari of this temple. It speaks the old tongue, like the ancient seers. It spoke kindly to me and did not touch me once.'

'It abducted you,' Lakshman said. 'It is a slayer of innocent children and brahmins. What devotee of Brahma slays his own fellow brahmins?'

'Kill it then. But first ask it who it really is, why it does what it does. There must be some reason why it does these things. I wish to know it if possible,' she pleaded.

The beast coughed, spraying ichor-blood with each effusion. Somashrava ignored the spray that discoloured his ang-vastra and dhoti. Rama and Lakshman turned their full attention back to it, expecting something to happen. Only Sita knew that the creature was laughing. Laughing, at a time like this! Its voice was hoarse with pain yet its immaculate accent was still in place. 'The girl is foolishly deluded. This is no time for talk. Kill me, kshatriya. Plunge your sword into my heart, lop off my head, and avenge the brahmins I slew.'

Rama and Lakshman stared at the creature. Even Somashrava was taken aback for a moment. Then the brahmin recovered his wits, yelling, 'It seeks to deceive us, rajkumars! Do not be fooled by its silken tongue. Slay the beast! Slay the beast!'

Somashrava searched around frantically for a weapon to replace his spear. He cried out in triumph, picking up a rusted mace lying half concealed by dried leaves near the entrance of the cave; no doubt it had belonged to some long-dead warrior who had sought to battle the creature within its lair. Hefting the mace, he swung it as hard as he could, pounding it against the creature's chest, once, twice, and yet again. Each time the beast emitted a cry of pain, issuing spouts of its vital fluid. The third blow, swung with all of Somashrava's strength, struck it with such impact that it was violently turned around perforce. It now faced Sita – and the shrine of Brahma. She saw the sunken pits in its chest where the mace had crushed its bones and ribcage. It slumped forward, bleeding from its multiple wounds. The brahmin stepped back, exhausted by his effort.

'Good, good,' it coughed softly. 'Pain is good, it is what I deserve for all my crimes. But even infinite blows will not kill me, brave brahmin. Only my saviour can free my soul from this cursed body-cage. You, who art the consort of the woman I abducted, I beg of you . . . slay me now. It is what I desire devoutly.'

Rama stepped forward, his face a cross between puzzlement and distrust. 'Why do you not fight? You abducted my beloved, left a trail for us to follow, led us here into your lair, yet you do not defend yourself or your home. Fight us and I will give you an honourable death.'

'Honourable?' The beast emitted a choking noise that might have been its version of a chuckle. Life-fluids oozed from its mouth. 'I do not deserve any honour. Just a swift, brutally effective end will suffice. Kill me now!'

'I will kill you, monster!' Somashrava had turned the mace around, and now plunged its end into the creature's side, below its second limb, into the soft meat of its underarm. The rusted weapon penetrated several inches, and stuck. The creature wailed in pain. Sita resisted the urge to cover her ears. This was not the way Asuras were supposed to die, speaking immaculate Sanskrit and begging to be slain, not lifting a claw to defend themselves. Rama was right. The creature should fight back at least.

'Foolish one!' it cried out. 'I tell you, none of you will kill me though you may pound and hack at me for all eternity. I am destined to die at the hands of only one mortal. And he is here before me. I knew him by his scent the moment he stepped into the bounds of Chitrakut vale.' It pointed a claw at Rama. 'You alone are the saviour that was promised me, my last enemy.'

'Then why did you not attack me in the tree?' Rama shouted, torn between confusion and caution. 'Why did you abduct my wife?'

The creature paused to cough out some part of its innards, spitting the offal out on to the cave floor at Somashrava's feet. He did not move an inch, the mace retrieved and held again at the ready as he listened suspiciously. 'Because I wished to die here. Before the shrine of my lord,' it said, its voice weakening.

Sita came up beside Rama. 'Rama, I don't understand this. What does this mean? Why won't the creature fight?'

'I don't understand it either,' Rama said grimly. 'But I cannot slay a creature that does not fight me. It would be murder. Even its abducting you does not justify my committing such an act.'

'We know its past crimes,' Lakshman said. 'You would be doing the just thing if you executed it for those atrocities.'

'Your brother speaks truly, rajkumar,' Somashrava said. He still held the mace menacingly, ready to strike at the beast again. 'This creature deserves to die a thousand deaths for all the lives it took.' He raised the mace and swung it down like a mallet. Sita could hear the unmistakable sound of bones crunching beneath the weight of the weapon's head. The creature roared with fresh pain as its right rear foot lay shattered. Somashrava shouted above the roars: 'Kill it, Rama, and avenge my father's and brother's deaths! Or I will inflict such violence upon it that even death would be a blessed relief in comparison.'

'Yes!' the beast roared in fresh agony. 'Punish me, Rama! Kill me now! Rajkumar Rama? That is how your companions address you, is it not? Whoever you may be, I beg of you, free my soul from this cursed body, release me from the cycle of pain inflicted and pain suffered. Give me my moksh, I beg of you!'

Sita called out: 'First answer these questions. Who are you? Do you have a name? What is this curse you speak of? Why is only Rama able to kill you?'

The creature moaned and rolled its eyes, finding Sita. 'If I tell you what you wish to know, will you prevail upon your husband to release me?'

Sita shook her head. 'He follows his dharma and will do as he must. Even a mountain cannot move him once his mind is made up. But answer my questions and perhaps you may say something that changes his mind.'

The creature's eyes released two fat yellow tears. They rolled down its muzzle and hung at the rim of its jawline, catching the light of the diyas.

'Very well then. I will answer your questions. You wish to know my name? I am Viradha. A gandharva in the court of Lord Indra.'

'Indra? The king of the city of the devas? How could a demon such as yourself be a servant in the court of heaven? Do not lie, monster, or I will shatter your other limb as well with this mace.' Somashrava moved to allow himself access to the limb in question.

The creature groaned. One teardrop shook, then broke free and splattered on the ground. It was lost in the pool of vital fluids that had seeped out of its wounds. 'I know it is difficult to believe, yet why would I lie when it can only prolong my pain? Listen to me. I was once a gandharva in Lord Indra's court, but I fell from favour.'

'How did you become what you are now?' Sita asked. 'What are you anyway?'

'I was overcome by a lust for acquiring wealth beyond my means. This led me to commit many sins which plunged me further into acts of wrongdoing. Over time I became a devotee of Lord Kubera, the treasurer of the devas. I sought to absolve all my wrongdoings by committing my crimes in the name of Kubera. Kubera learned of my misuse of his name and cursed me. He turned me into this thing you see before you, a creature that can never walk on two legs but must crawl and slide across the dirt of the ground.'

Somashrava lowered the mace. It was heavy, and the brahmin blinked as he considered the Asura's words.

Lakshman asked, 'And why do you call my brother your saviour? Why is he alone destined to kill you?'

The creature that was once Viradha groaned. The other teardrop shivered at the rim of its jaw, but remained fixed. 'After I was cursed by Kubera and thrown down to the mortal plane in this place, the vale of Chitrakut, I regretted my past sins and began to repent. In my desperation I turned towards Lord Brahma, because those who worship Brahma-dev must eschew all wealth and worldly possessions. I built this shrine so I could worship in secret and prayed night and day to the Creator. Finally, Lord Brahma appeared before me. When he asked me what I wished in return for my long penance, I said I desired to be a brahmin.'

'A brahmin?' Somashrava put the mace down, gaping in surprise. 'You? A brahmin? Impossible!' Yet he asked, with evident curiosity, 'What was Brahma-dev's response?'

'He said my wish would be granted, but only after I was released from this body. And that would only happen when a certain kshatriya came to Chitrakut and felled me. Until then, I had to live in this vale and prey on any who dared to inhabit it.'

'But you attacked brahmins! Children! You killed my father and brother!' Somashrava shouted.

'I did the task that Brahma-dev had appointed me to do. I do not say I liked what I did. Yet it made a certain kind of sense. Only brahmins and brahmacharyas came to these desolate woods. If I continued attacking them, sooner or later a kshatriya would come to find me and put an end to the demon of Chitrakut.' The beast sighed wearily. 'Many did come over the years, but none was the one destined to slay me. Until today.'

They were all silent, considering the import of the creature's words. Sita shook her head, amazed. It was almost too fantastic to believe, yet why would the creature lie? Especially when all it sought was its own demise.

She touched Rama's shoulder. He looked at her. 'I believe it. I feel it speaks the truth.'

Lakshman shrugged. 'In any case, it wants what we want: to be dead. Kill it, Rama. Free it for another life, or end the menace. Either way you will perform a great service to the brahmins of Chitrakut as well as to this tortured soul.'

Even Somashrava agreed, his face still red with anger. 'Yes. Kill it anyway, Rajkumar Rama. One way or other, its life must end today.'

Rama was silent. Sita waited for him to make his decision, knowing that to try to sway him was useless, yet hoping with all her heart that he would do as they all wished. She could not bear to see the poor beast suffer any more. Killing Asuras in self-defence was one thing. This was needless suffering.

Before anyone knew what was happening, the creature moved. It swung around with frightening speed, surprising them all with the suddenness of its reaction. Before Sita could blink, it had grasped her by the waist with its still functional middle limbs. It swung her up into the air, toward its jaws. 'Slay me now or I will tear out your wife's throat and drink her pulsing blood! One more life means nothing to me in the service of Brahma!' The words were a cry rather than a threat, yet its jagged teeth were poised above Sita's slender throat.

Rama's reaction was even swifter than the creature's action. Before Sita knew what had happened, she found herself falling to the cave floor. She landed hard on her shoulder, wrenching it slightly, but managing belatedly to roll with the fall. Something landed beside her, spattering wetly on the rock floor. The creature's middle limb, the one which had caught and held her up to its maw. She turned in time to see Rama straddling the creature's nether body, his sword swinging in a fatal arc. As the sword bit into the creature's neck, she saw the beast open its mouth one last time in that same leering grin. Then the sword cut through and through, decapitating it.

A moment later, the beast's head landed with a thud on the far side of the cave, rolling twice before coming to a halt. Sita could see the lizard eyes, still living. The mouth emitted a sigh that might only have been the last breath escaping, but she knew better. Then the creature's eyes shut and it was at peace. She looked back over her shoulder, confirming a doubt: the beast's eyes had looked at the stone effigy of Brahma as it died, asking the Creator's blessings one final time.

They left Sage Agastya's ashram the morning after slaying the beast Viradha. Every single brahmin came out to bid them farewell, even the crippled and maimed ones who normally worked indoors. Sita's heart went out to one little brahmacharya held up by two of his older brethren; one arm was severed at the elbow and both his legs were missing below the mid-thighs. He could not have been more than ten years of age. With some difficulty, he raised his sole hand to wave at her bravely. She waved back.

'If only killing the demon had undone all the evil it did here as well,' she said, 'then perhaps I could live with the knowledge that it was Lord Brahma himself who sent it here. Though I still wouldn't be able to understand *why* the Creator would send such a creature to torment the innocent people of Chitrakut.'

Rama finished adjusting Lakshman's rig. 'If we could understand the ways of the devas, we would be devas.'

Lakshman peered over his shoulder, checking the repaired rig, which had broken in the furious pursuit through the woods the night before. 'Rama's right, Sita-bhabhi. Everything fits a larger purpose. Brahma-dev must have some great plan, or he would not have sent the demon to this place. Besides, each one of us has his own karma. The brahmins who died or were injured, they must be paying the karmic cost of some past misdeed too.'

Sita knew Lakshman and Rama were both right but was still reluctant to concede the point. 'Even so. It just seems to be so cruel.'

Rama turned to her. 'Nature seems cruel too, Sita. So many innocents die or are maimed in natural disasters every year. Nature doesn't do these things deliberately. It's only seeking to maintain its own balance, and if in doing so it inadvertently causes suffering to a few, well, then it also ensures the survival of many. Think of the demon Viradha as a force of nature, no different from any typhoon, flood or earthquake.' To underline his point, he gestured at the ashram gates crowded by happy brahmacharyas, waving and chanting benevolent slokas at them.

She would have said something in response to that, but just then Lakshman announced he was finally ready. They turned back together and waved at the brahmins of Chitrakut ashram. They had already said their farewells and shown their respects to Sage Agastya earlier that morning; after washing themselves clean in the river, they had even found time for darshan at the various shrines. The temple of Brahma in the cave of the demon Viradha would be cleaned and maintained by the ashramites; it would henceforth stand as a memorial to those who had been taken by the creature.

They set out at a brisk pace. The success of the night before had energised them, given both Rama and Lakshman a vigour that had been less evident before they arrived at Chitrakut. Only Sita felt less than vigorous, and vaguely dissatisfied with the detour to Agastya's ashram. Instead of receiving the ashirwaad of the maharishi and spending a few peaceful hours in the last human company they would find for a long while, the visit had turned into the very apotheosis of her expectation. She still cringed inwardly at the memory of the brutal violence in the cave.

She glanced at Rama as they walked through a dense grove of manai, the slender creepers hanging down like the tresses of celestial apsaras. Rama was intent on ducking his head to avoid it striking the fibrous ends of the manai. He didn't seem troubled by the events of the previous night. But then, that was Rama. He might have misgivings about taking a life and engaging in violence, but once engaged, he put all his energies into completing the task, no matter how brutal the slaughter. She had witnessed him in action on at least four separate occasions now – at their first meeting in the encounter with the bear-slayers, at the Pit of Vasuki, in the duel with Parsurama, and last night. In fact, ever since meeting Rama, her life seemed to have been one violent encounter after another. It was true that she had been raised a warrior princess, but she had never desired war or combat. She had desired only to be able to defend herself and her loved ones against any aggressive assault. She guessed that Rama felt similarly, in that all the fights he'd been involved in had been for the purpose of helping thwart some aggressor's attack. But he was also more eager than the average kshatriya to engage in such encounters, volunteering his services where they were required. It was different before, she admitted to herself reluctantly, *but we are married now*. Surely that counted for something.

She tried to convince herself that her shocking abduction by Viradha was not the cause of her concern over Rama's repeated engagements with violence, but it was difficult. After all, despite Rama being right beside her, skin to skin, the demon had been able to pluck her up and away. If it had truly intended harm, she would have been dead before she reached the cave, or worse, eaten alive within that rocky grotto long before Rama and the others even reached there. It was a sobering thought, and the more distance she put between herself and the place where it had happened, the more relieved she felt to be away. What if she, or even Rama or Lakshman for that matter, had been maimed, losing a limb or an eye in that fight? Would life truly be no different than it was before? It wasn't that she feared being maimed itself. She was willing to take whatever challenges life brought her, and face them head-on. But to choose to participate in violence, as they had done the night before, was to choose to accept such maimings and loss of life as inevitable. For sooner or later, as all kshatriyas knew, violence took its toll. The memory of those crippled brahmacharya acolytes, their little bodies misshapen by their losses, tugged at her heart. Was it not enough that she and her husband were in exile? That they would be removed from human civilisation and companionship for fourteen long years? Forced to live deep within a hostile jungle where they would face any number of natural wild animals and predators, and even the occasional Asura? Was it not enough that violence would find them and they would be forced to defend themselves against it, remaining vigilant night and day? Did they have to add to that heavy burden and risk by additionally going out in search of more violence? Seeking to invoke aggression upon dangerous beasts like Viradha?

As the morning wore down into noonday and grew into afternoon, Sita's mind churned with the same line of thought. At one point, she felt almost grateful that they were far from civilisation. Had they remained in

Ayodhya, who knew how many people in distress might have come to Rama's doorstep, begging his intercession in some case or other. That, after all, was the inevitable responsibility of any prince or king, to protect his people. The Arya nations did not believe in sending out champions to fight their fights. She did not know how she would have dealt with the constant stress of Rama venturing out to subdue this riot or settle that dispute, or hunt down that Asura. She would never be able to be that Sita now. That choice had been denied her the instant her husband had been exiled – and had accepted the exile unquestioningly. Now, all she had was Rama – and Lakshman, of course, wonderful jovial Lakshman. And virtually nothing else. And if she was to pass fourteen years in this hostile wilderness, surely the least she should have was Rama's presence beside her, not his absence on account of him running off to champion some desperate cause or other.

On the other hand, she mused, as they passed through a surprising though brief patch of pilai – a sandy stretch with shells which crunched underfoot, indicating that a river had flown through here at some point, or perhaps even an ancient ocean in aeons past – at least in the Dandaka-van there would be no more people who would continually seek out Rama to champion their causes. He might be kept busy wielding his sword or firing his bow daily to ensure their survival in hostile environs, but that would be in their own defence. He would stay close by her at all times, not venture forth to slay some berserk rakshasa or perform some miraculous feat of valour for any brahmarishi who invoked his services under the brahmin-kshatriya code. And that, she concluded, was probably the only assurance she had. There were no more lost causes to champion in here, except their own.

They had crossed the pilai land and climbed up into a hilly region, winding up and down repeatedly. Ahead of them, Lakshman slowed and called a halt.

'I sense plentiful game here,' he said. 'I'll hunt us down some food and we can take a brief respite before continuing. According to Somashrava's directions, this hilly territory we're walking through means that we're a few hours' march from Chitrakut hill. After we take some nourishment, we can press on and be there before nightfall. We will camp there as the sage suggested when we were parting. It is the most appropriate site in this region.'

He had removed his bow and began to string it deftly as he spoke. Rama nodded. 'I will stay with Sita. You catch us some light game. Nothing large. Perhaps just a small beast. We do not wish to eat too heartily when we have hours yet to march. I will build a fire while you hunt.'

Sita's mind pictured a rabbit or a brace of squirrels skinned and skewered on a stick over a fire. Her stomach churned. 'Rama,' she said, catching hold of his shoulder, 'I will find and pluck us some herbs. We can wash them and eat them raw. They will be nourishing enough for our needs.'

Lakshman frowned. 'Herbs? To season the meat, you mean? There's no need for that. Roasted meat has its own fine taste.' He patted his flat stomach. 'It's been two days since we ate meat, with Guha that was.'

'No!' she said, louder than she'd intended. Both brothers looked at her, surprised. 'No,' she repeated, softer. 'I meant there's no need to hunt.' She gestured at the sky, visible in glimpses through the trees. 'It will take up precious time. I would rather reach our destination earlier. We can always sup there more heartily, to celebrate our new homecoming.'

'That's a fine idea,' Lakshman said. 'But we should eat something now. I haven't eaten a morsel since yesterday and the good brahmins only fed us fruits!'

'I will pluck herbs,' she insisted. 'They will be nourishing enough. As Rama said, we ought to eat lightly, to travel the quicker. That way, we will waste no time hunting or building a fire.'

Lakshman's face changed and he seemed about to argue the point, but Rama nodded approvingly. 'Sita speaks wisely. Let us take a quick respite and lunch on herbs and roots. We can always hunt at Chitrakut hill, after we pick out the spot for our domicile.'

He smiled as he slapped Lakshman on the back. 'We are in forest exile after all, my brother. Herbs and roots, remember? Herbs and roots!'

Lakshman muttered something about herbs and roots marrying one another and keeping out of everyone else's way, but acquisced without further debate. He left his bow strung and ready but put it aside reluctantly as Sita went about the task of ferreting out something edible. The pickings were slim, for the region was too wild and hilly for the most nourishing herbs or shrubs to flourish. After several moments of searching, she finally found some bitter-root and some sister-of-spinach leaf. She washed them in a little spring nearby, Rama watching over her alertly, and offered them to her husband and brother-in-law. The root and leaf looked very meagre in Lakshman's broad hands, but he took them uncomplainingly, munching noisily. His face altered visibly when he chewed into the bitter-root, but he managed to keep chewing and swallowing without uttering a word of complaint. That made her feel guilty. Would it have been so bad if she had allowed him to hunt down some small creature? Yes! If she could have her way, she would not want either brother firing a single arrow or unsheathing their swords again unless it was a matter of their own survival. And, merciful Sri knew, there would be instances enough for such defensive actions in the fourteen years to come. If she could do anything to reduce the violence they inflicted, it would go a long way to alleviating the heartsickness she felt.

Lakshman looked up suddenly, stopping in mid-chew. When he spoke, he revealed a mouthful of half-eaten leaves and root. 'Did you hear that?' He stood, taking up his bow and notching an arrow to the cord.

Rama slid his sword out slowly.

Sita put down the banana leaf on which she was holding her food.

They waited.

Someone, or something, for this was Chitrakut, was coming through the brush. Two bushes grew together, their leaves forming a light barrier. Sita watched as the stalks of the bushes were bent back slowly, to allow a body to pass through. She held her breath as the leaves parted to reveal the face of the approaching visitor.

Her first impression, completely absurd of course, was that it was Nakhudi. She had harboured fantasies of the rani-rakshak tracking her all this while, determined to follow her mistress to the ends of the earth to fulfil her oath of lifelong fealty. Almost immediately, she knew that the head emerging through the parted leaves was too low-set to belong to the statuesque Jat. Her second, equally absurd thought was that it was her mother. Which was even more uncanny, for she had never seen her mother, ever.

She blinked and wiped her mind free of these delusions.

And saw the woman who stood in the clearing, staring dully at the raised sword and drawn bow of Rama and Lakshman, both pointed at her.

12

The woman gasped with astonishment and lowered her head at once.

'My lords?' she said in a quavering voice. 'I am no threat to thee.'

Lakshman took a step forward, keeping his arrow trained on the stranger. 'Show your face.'

Reluctantly, her head jerking as she drew nervous, gasping breaths, the woman raised her head. She was an elderly woman, Sita saw, her face wreathed with wrinkles, her nose large and hooked, her jaw large but weak. She wore garments in the tribal style, brightly coloured reds and yellows, but they had faded and worn away with overuse and were little more than too-often-patched swatches of cloth stitched together. She was about Sita's height, perhaps slightly taller, though it was hard to tell with her bent the way she was, and her entire aspect – the stringy, dirty white hair, the thin, grimy, wrinkled neck, jutting shoulder-points, bony frame, tattered garments, the unravelling jute sack that she carried, clutched in one withered fist – bespoke extreme poverty. Her fair skin and pale, almost colourless – but very faintly greenish – eyes told a story of a life spent foraging and sifting for scant nourishment. She walked with the weary tread of one who had been beaten down often by life and kept her back bent in expectation of further beatings. She gazed dully from one armed man to the other, as if knowing that she might be struck down by them for no good reason, and prepared to accept that as easily as any fate.

Rama lowered and sheathed his sword. Lakshman lowered his arrow a notch, but kept it strung.

'She could be an Asura in human guise,' Lakshman said.

Rama hesitated, his hand still on his sword-grip.

Sita moved forward. 'No.'

She went to the woman and touched her face, then her shoulder. The woman did not so much as flinch or blink, taking the examination with the same choiceless lack of response with which she'd viewed her possible death. Sita felt nothing but bone and skin beneath the weathered cloth.

'She is no Asura,' she said. 'Only an old tribal woman.'

Lakshman made a disgusted noise. 'That's obvious. Had she been an Asura, she would have torn you to bits by now, my good sister-in-law!'

Sita ignored him. 'Namaskar,' she said to the woman. 'I am Sita Janaki, travelling to Chitrakut hill with my husband and my brother-in-law. We apologise for greeting you with such aggression. We were informed to beware of demons in these woods.'

The woman said meekly, 'Aye, my lady. Demons there are plentiful in Chitrakut. And even more in the forests beyond the hill, in Panchvati groves. But I am only Shabbri, a poor forager. I cause nobody no harm.'

Sita turned and looked pointedly at Lakshman. He rolled his eyes but said no more. Rama came over to the woman.

'Namaskar. I am Rama of Ayodhya, husband of Sita Janaki.'

The woman's eyes remained downcast, unwilling to meet Rama's. 'I am Shabbri, a poor forager,' she repeated dully. 'Master,' she added.

'Where do you hail from, Shabbri-devi? Where is your family? Your clan?'

The woman started. 'Oh no, sire. Do not address me so. I am no devi. Merely a lowly outcast. Solitary and homeless, I wander these woods of Chitrakut and live off the land. I cause nobody no harm, nohow.'

'Alone? Here? How do you survive? Do you not fear the wild beasts and the demons?'

'What have I to fear? I who have nothing and no one? The demons do not desire such as me. For they are mostly rakshasas, descended of the line of their lord, Ravana of Lanka, and, being so, are therefore descendants of the line of Pulastya and all of higher caste than myself. They will not touch me or allow my shadow to fall upon them for fear they will be polluted.'

Sita raised her eyebrows, glancing at Rama to see his reaction. She had never heard of flesh-eating demons who avoided low-castes for fear of polluting their souls, but obviously the old woman believed in them. She thought it more likely that the woman had fortuitously escaped harm until now, or was not fleshy and appetising enough for the rakshasas to trouble themselves over. Rama shrugged too, as if to say, *Well, what's the point in arguing?* Sita agreed silently.

She touched the old woman's hand. 'Come, Shabbri. Sit with us and share our meal. We have not much but you are welcome to eat a bite with us.'

Shabbri drew back fearfully from Sita's touch. 'You must not touch me, my lady. I am of the lowest gotra. You will be polluted by me.' Her eyes flickered to one side then the other. 'I should make my way from here.

You are clearly of high birth and varna, from your speech and manner and weaponry. It is not right that I should tarry here in your presence.'

Rama took a step forward, as if to stop the woman. 'Wait. I wish to speak with you a little. We are new to these woods and would welcome any help.'

Shabbri glanced up fearfully, not at Rama's eyes, but off to one side. 'What help can one such as I offer thou, sire? Allow me to leave before I commit the sin of caste-offence and earn the wrath of my superiors.'

Sita felt sorry for the old woman. She had obviously been treated badly in her time. She reached out and took the woman's hand, intending to clasp it and show the frightened forager that she did not care about such things as caste-offences and varna demarcations. Instead, she startled the old woman, who jerked her hand back. It happened to be the hand clutching the jute sack, and Sita caught the mouth of the sack instead of Shabbri's hand. The woman lost her grip on it, and the sack fell on to the ground between them, spilling its contents.

Rama exclaimed aloud as he saw the small rounded objects that emerged from the jute bag.

He bent down, picking up one of the fallen objects and bringing it to his face. He sniffed it curiously. A look of wonderment came over him. The change transformed his face completely. He looked like the boy Sita recalled faintly from her childhood memories. Not Rama the rakshasa-slayer, champion of Bhayanak-van, and performer of other great feats of valour. Simply Rama the boy.

'Ber,' he said reverentially. 'Ripe ber.'

The old woman had fallen in her haste to retreat from the outstretched hand. Sita bent down and offered her hand again. 'Please,' she said. 'I do not care for caste-laws. Take my hand and rise.'

The old woman's eyes were big and wide. Still she struggled to rise on her own, but found no purchase on the leafy shrubs. Finally she accepted Sita's offer and allowed herself to be helped up. But she balked and whimpered when Sita's hand accidentally touched her feet.

'No, mistress, it is not right, not right. Shabbri is an outcast, most wretched of all varnas.'

Sita looked at her firmly. 'My father says that there are no castes in the eyes of the devas, only good people and bad. Tell me, do you consider yourself a good person or a bad one?'

Shabbri looked uncertain, her eyes darting away. 'Shabbri has done no one no harm.'

Sita nodded. 'You are clearly a good person. You have nothing to fear. When your soul is finally freed from the cycle of rebirth and attains moksh, you will ascend to Swarga-lok the same as any brahmin or brahmacharya. My father knows this implicitly, and he has spent his entire life studying theology.'

Shabbri stared nervously at Sita, who smiled reassuringly. After a moment, Shabbri smiled back shakily.

Then she looked past Sita and cried out.

Rama was picking up the fallen wildberries and popping them into the sack. Shabbri took a step towards him, then stopped, still subservient to a lifetime of self-training. She shook her head, speaking with her head lowered.

'No, master. You must not touch those. They are Shabbri's food for today.' She added hesitantly, 'Perhaps for the next several days.'

Rama finished gathering up the berries and came over, holding out the sack. 'I was collecting them for you. Our apologies for startling you, maa. We will not steal your meal, you need have no fear on that account. I was hoping you could show us where you found these ber, that we might pluck our own.'

Shabbri kept her head lowered, but her hand crept out and took the sack. Still, Sita noted, she was careful not to let her hand touch Rama's.

'It would be my great honour, master. I found these in a patch some four or five yojanas west of here.'

'West,' Rama repeated, his mouth closing tightly. He glanced in that direction. It was quite contrary to the way they were travelling, which was south-east. He looked at Lakshman, who was seated on the same fallen tree they had been sitting on when Shabbri had appeared. Lakshman raised his eyebrows but made no comment. Rama sighed. 'That would delay us. I suppose plucking ber will have to wait.'

'Like eating rabbit meat,' Lakshman said drily. His fallen herbs and roots lay underfoot, ignored. He rubbed his bare belly pointedly. Sita rolled her eyes at him. He grinned wryly, to show that he was only jesting . . . well, half jesting. Even Sita's stomach felt ill nourished.

Shabbri hesitated, having caught some if not all the import of this last exchange. Her eyes darted to Sita. She seemed to have gained a smidgen of confidence, Sita was pleased to note. 'Yes?' Sita asked, encouraging.

'My lady,' Shabbri said haltingly, 'I would like nothing better than to offer your lord my entire lot of ber. I can always find more before sundown, and Shabbri does not require much herself.'

'That is very generous of you, maa. My husband is inordinately fond of ber. The only thing he likes as much is kairee. Perhaps we could offer you a trade. We are travelling to Chitrakut hill, to take up residence there. Once we arrive at that location, my husband and brother-in-law will hunt us a good meal. If you come with us, we will gladly provide you with as much food as you like from our own cookfire. It would be only fair, if we are to sample your ber.'

'Indeed,' Rama said. 'If you can bring us ber from time to time, you may eat as often as you like with us.' He smiled. 'Your ber smell very fresh and ripe. I daresay they are quite juicy and sweet too.'

Shabbri's eyes opened wide again as Sita spoke, growing large and round with each sentence. When Rama spoke, though, she exclaimed and shook her head rapidly. 'Nay, master. Nay. I am honoured beyond words by your generosity. Never has any high-caste treated Shabbri with such kindness before. I will gladly fetch you all the ber you desire. But you must not eat of those I have collected in this sack.'

She clutched the mouth of the sack tighter, holding it with both hands.

Lakshman rose from his seat, frowning. 'What's so special about these ber? Are they intended for someone? Or as an offering?' Foods offered to deities could not be eaten, although a portion, called prasadam, could be taken by the worshippers after being sanctified by a brahmin priest. Some tribes offered sacrificial offerings of fruit and vegetables in place of the traditional animal balidaans.

Shabbri shook her head. 'Nay, my lord, it is not for that reason.' She continued shaking her head wordlessly.

Sita put a hand on the old woman's shoulder. 'What is it, then, maa? Do not fear to speak openly. We will not forcibly take your ber from you, nor will we coerce you if you do not wish to share it. You may speak your mind.'

Tears welled up in the old lady's eyes. 'You have addressed me as maa, milady. No one has called Shabbri mother since . . . since . . . a long time. I will tell you why I cannot offer you my ber, much as I would wish to, but . . . I will whisper it.'

She leaned her head closer, speaking just loud enough for Sita to hear, though not the men.

Sita smiled, nodding in understanding. So, it was that simple.

She turned to Rama. 'She has a habit of checking each ber as she plucks it. To see if it's sweet enough. She likes them very sweet. The ones that are over-ripe or raw she leaves for the bears, she says, who like them that way. She only keeps the sweetest ones in her sack.'

Rama smiled. 'Is that all?'

'That's it. If anything, she would be honoured if she could offer you nourishment. Among her people, to feed a higher caste, especially a lord of some note, as she believes you are, is a great punya.'

Rama nodded. Punya, or a redeeming act, was the opposite of paap, or sin. 'That is well and good, but the caste rules do not interest me as much as those very attractive fruit. Shabbri-maa, I would be honoured if you would allow me to eat a few of your ber.'

'Parantu . . . jhoota!' Shabbri gasped, unable to comprehend how a person like Rama would deign to eat a low-caste's once-bitten food.

Rama smiled. 'You are like a mother in age to me. I will imagine that my own mother nibbled at them to choose the sweetest ones for my pleasure. May I, maa?'

He reached out his hand. Shabbri stared at the outstretched hand in a daze. Then, as with a great effort, she raised the sack and handed it to Rama. Rama took it, smiling his thanks, and dug inside. He pulled out a ber. Sita could see the tiny bite-mark on one side where Shabbri had tasted it. Rama put the ber to his mouth and took a bite of it. Juice spilt down his chin. He chewed, closing his eyes.

'Swarga,' he said. *Heavenly.*

Suddenly, Shabbri laughed. And like wax before a flame, her features melted and transformed.

13

Sita lurched back in amazement. Lakshman exclaimed and strung his bow, shouting to Rama to step aside.

The old woman's face and body rippled like a reflection in a pond over which a wind was blowing. It shimmered in the hazy light of high afternoon, and sparkled briefly, before stabilising into a shimmering white corona.

Rama stood transfixed, the half-eaten ber in his hand, staring at the apparition that had replaced the old tribal woman. He knew he ought to be drawing his sword and paying heed to Lakshman's shouts, but he felt no fear or alarm at the supernatural transformation of the outcast. Instead, he felt a great sense of calm and contentment, the kind of feeling he associated as a young boy with lying with his head in his mother's lap and falling asleep listening to her sing his favourite lullabies. A sense of being protected and safe. It was a feeling he hadn't experienced in the past several days; quite the opposite, in fact. And because of this, it suffused his body with a great lethargy.

The being that stood in the place of the one called Shabbri was also an old woman. Her features were as lined and weathered as Shabbri's had been, but they were subtly different. This woman seemed nobler somehow, more majestic; though if pressed to describe how, Rama would not have been able to explain it. It would take a kavya to do justice to the fine nuances. But the overall effect was one of great wisdom and power. She was clad all in white, an ascetic's ang-vastra that wound about her slender frame from shoulder to ankle. Her deeply scored and lined face, white hair, light, almost grey eyes, and parched withered skin all spoke of great austerities endured, sacrifices made, penance paid.

'Namaskar, Rama Chandra,' she said in a voice that was so light he hardly felt she was speaking – she might have been whispering into his mind itself. 'Welcome to Dandaka-van.'

Lakshman moved beside Rama, his bow still held at the ready, the arrow aimed directly at the old woman's breast. Lakshman's arm was trembling with anger, or perhaps it was simply fear made rage; for once Rama could not tell. 'Who are you? Show your true form! Are you a rakshasi? A yaksi? Show your real form, demon!'

The old woman smiled. 'I am no rakshasi. I am Anasuya, restorer of the Ganga. You may know me as the wife of Sage Atri, whose hermitage is west of Sage Agastya's ashram, near the domiciles of the sages Sarabhanga and Sutiksna.'

Sage Agastya had mentioned to them that Atri and Anasuya and the other sages dwelled nearby, but the way to their ashrams had been some way off their path and they had resolved to visit the sages later.

That is why I chose to come to you, Rama Chandra. My business with you could not wait.

Rama spoke quietly to Lakshman. 'Brother, lower your bow.'

Lakshman glanced at him sharply, a retort on his tongue, but he saw Rama's face and held back his words. He lowered the bow slowly. Rama didn't know if he was relieved that the woman was not an Asura, or disappointed. The latter seemed more likely.

Your brother's heart is brimming with anger like a cup filled to overflowing. You must guide him in channelling this anger into more productive forms of energy.

'Yes,' Rama said, then stopped. He looked around, realising that nobody else had spoken aloud. Yet he had heard Anasuya's voice.

I speak to your mind directly, for you have opened yourself to receive me so graciously. I may speak thus when something is needed to be said that is not for the ears of others. But now I revert to audible speech.

'I apologise for startling you, Rajkumar Lakshman,' she said. 'But when I first sensed your presence in this part of the forest, I could not resist testing the already legendary qualities of yourself, your sister-in-law Sita, and your brother Rama.'

'Testing?' Sita said dubiously. 'So that was why you disguised yourself as the low-caste tribal woman?'

Anasuya smiled. Her smile was like a white sun dawning over dark mountain ridges, bearing gifts of warmth and light and inner illumination. Rama felt the very synapses of his brain speed up and flow more smoothly, as if he might be able to solve the mysteries of the universe as long as he was bathed in the light of that glorious smile. It was akin to the feeling of being taken over by the shakti of the maha-mantras Bala and Atibala, but without the more aggressive, warrior-like qualities of that state.

Lakshman still looked suspicious. 'Why an outcast? Why that whole charade about not wanting to offend us, and not sharing your ber? What kind of test was that?'

'A necessary test, and one that you all passed with flying colours.' Anasuya seemed undaunted by Lakshman's barely concealed hostility. She turned the warmth of her gaze back to Rama, who felt his very toes tingle with energy. 'Especially you, Rama Chandra. You would eat the half-bitten wildberries of a tribal outcast. Amazing.'

Rama basked in the glow of her approbation, but felt compelled to speak his mind honestly. 'Maha-rati,' he said, addressing her by the title of Great Light, which seemed appropriate. 'You praise me overmuch. The varnas, castes and gotras were designed to aid people to work together more productively, especially in the larger cities. To divide up the occupations and enable speciali-sation and better craftsmanship. Not to divide and distin-guish negatively, or to prejudice our perception and treatment of some groups because of their occupations. A given task may be unclean, such as sweeping wetrooms or collecting nightsoil, but that does not make the person himself or herself unclean.'

Anasuya sighed. A soft wind swept through the bower, rustling fallen leaves around their feet. Lakshman's eyes flicked this way and that, alert to any deception or subterfuge. 'A mature and enlightened view, more so for one of your tender age. Sadly, there are many less know-ledgeable souls who choose to embrace such biased views. Their numbers increase with each passing decade, I note sadly, suggesting a disturbing trend. And as you know, even one prejudiced mind is one too many. It takes only one rotten berry to spoil the whole sack. Which is why I say your act was not just symbolic, but a great event. You did not simply pass my test today, you passed the test of time itself.'

She swept on without giving him a chance to protest mildly against this unbridled praise. 'Not only did you ignore any kind of caste prejudice in your treatment of Shabbri, you also swept aside all class protocol. You are a prince after all, a king in exile. Yet you behaved with that grime-streaked forest forager as if she were a noble person in your father's court. Truly, you have deserved your growing reputation. And I say this as one who does not offer praise lightly. But let me not embarrass you any further. You have a journey to complete, a house to raise, and a new life to settle down to; I will not cause you to tarry much longer.'

She reached behind her and drew out a bow and a quiver. At the sight of the weapon, Rama saw Lakshman tense instantly, his hand flying to the arrow he still held loosely on the cord. Rama's hand touched his brother's shoulder, and Lakshman relaxed again, reluctantly.

Anasuya held out the bow. 'Take this, Rama. As you can see, it is decorated with gold and jewels and constructed unlike any ordinary bow. It belonged to Vishnu, and was made for him by Vishwakarma, builder, smith and forger of the devas. It is my husband Atri's wish that I give it to you.'

Rama joined his hands. 'Maha-rati, Anasuya, I cannot accept such a divine gift. This bow is beyond value. I have not done anything to deserve its ownership.'

She shook her head. 'Still you deny your achievements? You are much too humble for your own good, Rama. Be honest, if not vain! You have already been given one bow of Vishnu, by the brahmin Parsurama, which you neglected to carry with you into exile, choosing only ordinary weapons that would befit any kshatriya in your father's army.'

'The terms of my exile were clear, maha-rati. I was to take no personal possessions. These weapons are indeed the regular issue from the palace armoury. Under kshatriya law it is permissible for me to bear them as an essential means of self-defence.'

She chuckled softly. 'Even now you explain law to me?

Do not feel it necessary to justify your every act, Rama. You are already the epitome of dharma. The Bow of Vishnu you were given vanished from the palace the instant you exited Ayodhya, for it was meant only for your use. This bow I now hand to you is the very same one, for such celestial weapons exist outside of time and space as mortals understand these concepts. Take it this time, for it is given to you after you have entered exile, and there is no law against that.'

Still Rama hesitated, not reaching out for the jewelled bow.

She sighed. 'You still believe in your heart that you have not earned the right to bear this bow, am I right? Then know this, Rama. You will earn the right very shortly. Do not think I give the bow to you out of the goodness of my heart alone! It will serve you well in the dark days that lie ahead. For you have a mission to fulfil and you require this bow in order to fulfil that mission.'

'Mission?' Sita stepped forward, her hands joined respectfully but her face troubled. 'What mission do you speak of, maa?'

Anasuya smiled at Sita. 'The fulfilment of his dharma.'

Sita's face cleared at once. 'Maa,' she said simply, bowing her head. That effulgent smile had worked its magic on her as well. Yet even beneath the beatific expression that wreathed Sita's face as Anasuya turned her smile upon her, Rama saw the anxiety writhing.

She is gravely troubled, Rama. There has been too much violence done in too short a time. She fears that you will meet the inevitable consequence of all those who live by violence. You know what it is I speak of.

Yes, I do. Rama found himself answering as simply as thinking the words. *I do not know how to appease her fears.*

Then do not appease them.

Rama was surprised.

You do not engage in violence for its own sake, or to meet your own ends. You do so to serve dharma. Either she understands and accepts that, or she does not. That is her choice to make, her briar crown to wear. Not yours. Do you follow my meaning?

Rama nodded. 'For dharma then,' he said, reaching out.

Anasuya handed him the bow. It felt unbearably heavy at first, as if it would drag him to the ground and lie there immovably, like an elephant's anchor-weight. But the instant he held it in both hands, it felt just like any ordinary bow. A little lighter, if anything. Not very different from the bow he already wore on his back, except that the angle of the curve was different, and the wood was an unfamiliar grain, one that he had never seen before.

Indeed, for the tree is not of this plane. That is why it will not bear any ordinary arrow to touch it.

'But then . . .'

Anasuya held out an arrow. He did not know where she had got it from, but when he looked up after examining the bow it was in her hand, offered to him. He took it without argument. It gleamed like gold, and felt as heavy as if it were made of the metal. Then, like the bow, it seemed to change its quality and felt almost like any ordinary arrow. Almost, but not quite.

'This arrow belonged to Lord Brahma. It is not a magical arrow in the usual sense of the word. But it possesses abilities.'

'Abilities,' Rama repeated. The arrow was of a different woodgrain from the bow. It felt too thick to be fast enough or effective across long distances.

'Do not be deceived by its appearance. It has the ability to be whatever you wish it to be. You have but to will it. It takes its power from two things: the mind of its wielder and that of its target. An evil man cannot use it against a good man. Nor can a good man use it in a wrong cause. But to a good man who uses it in a just cause, Rama, it will do whatever you will it to do.'

'Whatever I will it?' Rama looked uncertainly at the arrow. It did not seem all that special, now that he had held it for a few moments. But when he had first touched it, while still in Anasuya's hands . . .

'Just so. If you will it to be a dozen arrows flying simultaneously to a dozen different targets, it will do exactly that. Or to fly across a great distance to strike a single minute target – so long as you can spy that target with your naked eye. After it has accomplished its task, it will disappear from the target and reappear within your quiver. You need only wait as long as it takes to reach one target before firing it again at another, and you shall never want for more arrows.'

Lakshman looked at the arrow with great interest. Anasuya's gifts had dispelled his last doubts and he was listening and watching the proceedings keenly. Rama hoped that she would have a gift for Lakshman as well. He doubted whether this bow and arrow was usable by anyone beside himself.

Not for him. For he must learn the lesson of self-control first. He is too eager to embrace violence, to take lives. Your example will keep him from straying off the path of dharma, Rama. But I do have gifts for your wife.

Anasuya handed Sita a shimmering garment woven from fine shining filament, a necklace, bangles, earrings, and other feminine ornaments, all cast in white gold as pristine as Anasuya herself. Sita accepted the gifts with a beatific expression on her face. Rama sensed the unspoken communication that passed between the two.

Then Anasuya returned her attention to Rama. *She is blessed to have you for a husband, Rama.*

And I am blessed to have her for my wife. Aloud he said, 'Blessed are we to receive such great gifts, my lady. Yet tell us if you will, what is this mission you wish us to undertake?'

'Not I. I would wish you only a decade and four years of peaceful exile and blissful harmony. It is not my mission, and I only come here to give you these gifts and a warning.'

'A warning?' Lakshman asked, frowning.

'Yes. You are on your way to Chitrakut, are you not?'

'Yes,' Sita said, clutching her gifts to her chest. Her voice sounded less anxious than before, but Rama caught the stress that she was trying hard not to reveal. 'That is a good place to build our home, is it not? The sage Agastya—'

'Advised you wisely. Chitrakut is a peaceful hill, and you will find much happiness there. But the place to the south of the hill, the plainsland that the ancients named Panchvati . . .'

'Yes?'

'You would do well not to venture there. Whatever the temptation.'

'Why not?' Lakshman's tone was more curious than concerned. He was challenged by the warning. 'Are there demons there? We can fight demons, can we not, Rama? We do not fear them.'

Anasuya's corona of white light shimmered reddish for a moment. Then she continued in a quiet tone: 'There are worse things than demons in this world, young Lakshman. You would do well to remember that not all battles can be fought with the skill of arms.'

'But the Bow of Vishnu, the Arrow of Brahma-dev?'

Lakshman asked, his eyes bright, his chin raised defiantly. 'Why would you give us these if not for a battle?'

Rama was about to admonish his brother, when Anasuya responded: 'The weapons are for your defence. They are not meant to be used to start violence, only to defend yourself against any violence that may be directed at you.'

Lakshman shook his head, irritated. 'What is the difference? Sometimes one has to strike first in order to defend oneself against a stronger, stealthier foe. Asuras do not ask politely before starting a fight!'

Anasuya's eyes narrowed. *Watch him closely, Rama. Your brother has much to learn about Asuras, warfare, and himself. It is his self-righteous outrage at the injustice of your exile that fuels his anger. He must understand that he cannot set one wrong right by committing further wrongs. Not by slaughtering a thousand Asuras can he achieve the justice he seeks.*

Aloud she said, 'When the time comes, my friends, you will fight for your lives, and so be it. I pray that the things I have given you will be of some use at that unfortunate time. But I believe that this violence, like all violence, can be prevented.'

'How?' Rama's question was genuine. 'Tell us and we will do as you ask. We do not wish any further bloodshed.'

'In that case, Rama, do not shed any blood.'

Lakshman cocked his head. 'But what if—'

'There are no what-ifs, rajkumar,' she said sharply. 'Simply a choice between himsa and ahimsa.' Violence and non-violence. 'Lay down your arms as long as you dwell in Chitrakut, draw no blood, and you may see your fourteen years pass without incident.'

'Lay down our arms?' Lakshman shook his head sceptically. 'We are kshatriyas. It is our dharma to fight the fights that need fighting.'

'And to know when not to fight.' Anasuya drew a deep breath, then resumed in a less harsh tone. 'All I ask is that you do not draw first blood, or be the one to initiate the violence. This is the missive I came to give you: go to Chitrakut and live there in peace and harmony, all the years of your exile if you can. But if you are lured away by temptation, and tricked into committing an act of violent aggression against another being, be it mortal, animal or Asura, then the devas alone protect you. With those words I leave you now. Go in peace, Rajkumar Rama, Rajkumar Lakshman, Rajkumari Sita.'

Her extremities shimmered and blurred briefly, and then she was gone, leaving them alone once more in the forest. Rama looked down and saw that the sack of ber was still lying at his feet where he had dropped it. He bent and picked it up.

14

They built their hut on the top of Chitrakut hill. To the north and east the hill sheered away in a steep cliffside, falling a hundred and fifty feet to the river Godavari. Running downhill to the west was a long unbroken line of mahua trees, bursting with new life in the height of spring. Behind their hut was a grove of banyan, some almost as large and as ancient as the Nyagrodha of the Nisadas. Beyond that, further to the south, was an unlikely assortment of peepal, fir, elm and even a few walnuts. And farther that way the hill sloped gently into the region known as Panchvati, a vast, thickly forested plain that seemed to stretch as far as the eye could discern – all the way to the western ocean, Lakshman insisted.

Even if it did not reach the ocean, it was still a formidable wilderness, and one they knew now that they must not venture into. That left a great area for them to inhabit, and they hardly needed any of it. Even Lakshman did not question Anasuya's warning not to venture in that direction; Rama realised that the new, angrier Lakshman resented being given such a restrictive prohibition, but he also knew better than to disobey it and endanger them all. And so, as that spring wore on to give way to an idyllic summer, they found at Chitrakut a brief respite. A season of rest.

They built their hut facing north-east. Not only because it let the sun shine in directly each morning, but because it faced both their homes – Kosala was north, and Videha east. *We are still looking back then*, Rama told himself, working on the thatched roof of the hut beside his brother, as Sita used the traditional mixture of dung and mud and straw to lay the floor of their domicile.

By day, the Dandaka-van hardly lived up to its ominous reputation. The picturesque view from the hill, especially from the short promontory overlooking the confluence, was idyllic enough to attract them every morning during their brief respites from house-building. After the hut was fully constructed and they began work on the fore-garden and rear vegetable patch, they began going farther south, down the Panchvati side of the hill, as it came to be called among them, but never across the river that marked their self-affixed boundary. The view on the Panchvati side was picturesque enough to inspire royal artists – and exiled lovers. Rama and Sita loved to sit here and watch the sun go down until it was time for their sandhyavandana. Rama could imagine seers falling into transcendental trances in such scenic surroundings, lost in their tapasya for years on end. The sense of communion with nature was palpable; he could feel the forest growing around him, living, breathing, speaking its verdant dialect.

By night, it became clear why Panchvati was so notorious. After dusk, the benign artistic vista gave way to a darker side. The howls, roars and grunts of predators carried clearly through the thin mud-and-straw walls of their little house atop the hill. Often by day, when one of them went out foraging for firewood or fruit, they would spy bear tracks, panther or leopard paw-prints, wild boar droppings, wolf markings, and signs of a variety of other denizens of the wild. For unlike Asuras, who were notoriously disdainful of crossing water, even a relatively less sanctified river such as the Godavari, the beasts of the wilderness roved where they pleased. It was not the fact that predators prowled around them all night that was alarming, it was the sheer number that was overwhelming. Everywhere they looked, there was evidence of some species or other having marked the area, sharpened its claws on a tree, killed and eaten, leaving gnawed carcasses; constant reminders that this was their territory, not the true home of these three hairless visitors who walked on two legs.

They had several encounters with these predators. Some inadvertent, as when Lakshman returned once with his face and chest blood-spattered, claiming to have been set upon by a leopard lurking in the trees above. Or when Rama and Sita were collecting flowers for their prayers, heard a grunting sound, and looked up to see a bear twice as tall as Rama. He had reached slowly, cautiously for his bow, the jewelled one that Anasuya had given him and which he had never let out of his sight since, but Sita had thrown him an imploring look that tore at his soul, and he had given the bear the benefit of the doubt. After several moments of raising itself upon hind legs, sniffing the air and chuffing loudly, the bear finally dropped back on all fours and trundled away westwards, dismissing them completely.

Other encounters he did not always tell Sita about. These were the more frequent, less pleasant run-ins, with boars or wolves or even wildcat, that did not allow any room for pacifism or error. He had to simply draw and shoot, or be mauled, raked, gutted or otherwise fall casualty to the inevitable cycle of violence that was simply nature's way of going about its daily business. He did not consider these almost daily encounters to be violence per se; they were simply a way of life in the deep forest, an unavoidable part of survival.

Lakshman was less amenable to Sita's new insistence on pacifism. He returned the very first night with two antelopes, a doe, a small hog, and a brace of rabbits. It took him three trips to fetch the carcasses, and when they were all finally piled up outside the hut, Sita blanched and gave him a dressing-down such as he had probably never received from Guru Vashishta back in gurukul. Lakshman took the admonishments with equanimity. When Sita was done, he thanked her politely and without any trace of sarcasm for trying to help him curb his violent ways, then calmly discussed how plentiful the game was on the southern hillside, and how he was thinking of sacrificing an antelope every evening in the ancient style. It was as if both were equally natural to Lakshman: hunting and killing for their needs, and Sita's desire for pacifism. And in a sense they were, Rama found himself agreeing silently: both violence and the desire for peace co-existed naturally in nature, constantly seeking a balance. Neither could rule exclusively, for then life itself would cease: some species would proliferate while others would die out, or be outnumbered. And human society, in its youthful remove from savagery – it was after all only ten thousand years or so since humankind had gained the first glimmers of social understanding – was still largely a reflection of its natural progenesis. Perhaps some day, if there were more humans upon the face of Prithvi than animals, violence truly could end; but what of human violence against other humans? Might not that increase to compensate for the lack of the older varieties of violence? This was the kind of contemplation that occupied Rama's mind.

They found a pond in a depression in the hill, lush

with lotus flowers. By day the large floating flowers opened to show their pink-petalled blossoms to the sun; by night they closed up like an acolyte joining palms in a namaskar to bid Surya-deva goodnight. When they discovered this place, Rama and Sita began spending more time here than anywhere else. They even neglected their unfinished hut, Lakshman all but pushing them out after the morning meal, saying, 'Go, let me do my dharma.' He was quite serious about it. He took his chores in exile literally to be his dharma. And so they were according to scripture, for the Vedic rotes praised those who served others, reserving for them the special blessings of the devas. Lakshman worked by day, and hunted every night after dusk, growing visibly leaner. One morning when Rama went out of the hut to greet the rising sun, he stood at the edge of the cliff near their hut and looked down at the river rushing by below. He saw a figure down by the riverbank, walking lithely to the water with a freshly plucked lotus in hand. It took him a moment to recognize the figure as Lakshman, so much had his brother changed in these few months.

Rama changed too. But not in the same way as Lakshman. If anything, he grew towards the opposite direction. After his first doubtful resistance, he began to yield to Sita's new embrace of ahimsa the Vedic creed of non-violent co-existence. He began to look back upon his adventures in the Bhayanak-van and afterwards as necessary evils, acts of dharma that he committed out of painful necessity. Thinking about his past actions itself brought about a change. He let these churning thoughts and half-percolated insights simmer within, preferring silent contemplation to discourse and debate. That had always been his way. Even as a young shishya at Guru Vashishta's gurukul he had always been more silent than his fellow pupils. Yet when the guru called upon him to answer a question, he always seemed to have the answer. It was as if he observed all, assimilated everything, processed it in his system, and achieved a level of understanding that was deeper than any amount of intellectual debate could produce. That was one reason why his gurus had always been pleased by him. The Arya way of learning laid special emphasis on silent contemplation. *Each shishya is a school unto himself*, the gurus always said. *And the student must become the teacher in order to understand the lesson.*

Rama couldn't claim to have become a guru. But he did feel closer to understanding the essential elusive mysteries of life than he had been before leaving Ayodhya. Life there had been so . . . busy. Always the press of people, opinions, comments, rumours, news, decisions, sabhas. There was little time to simply be oneself. To expand and build. The emphasis was always on imbibing and absorbing, to becoming a receptacle for other people's opinions, wants, dislikes, desires. Not on finding out what one thought, wanted, liked, sought. In the hustle and bustle of even the most learned gatherings it was difficult to hear oneself speak at times, let alone think. Surely such volatile discussion did lead to some greater understanding over time; but it was equally as certain that the individual could find the same understanding by another path, the lonely but far truer path of self-contemplation. Combined with the physical exercise of the body to ensure proper breathing, channelling of energies and healthier functionality, this Arya art, named yoga, was unfortunately losing its pride of place as a necessity for all, and being relegated to the practice of only forest hermits, seers and sadhus. Rama and Sita, and Lakshman too when he was free of his endless chores, performed their yogic exercises every day, as much as their daily religious oblations and rituals. And over time, Rama felt, they grew more comfortable with themselves, with each other, and most of all with their circumstances.

And in this gentle manner, exile grew slowly into a way of life. Neither undesirable nor desirable; simply a fact of life, like being born male or female, tall or short, dark or fair, western or eastern.

Sita was weeding in the vegetable garden behind the hut, and thinking idle afternoon thoughts when she heard the curious sound of a woman singing a Sanskrit ballad.

It was mid-afternoon on a Shanivar in the fourth month of their exile. The summer had turned hot and humid, and both Rama and she had taken to retreating into the cool shade of their hut to escape the heat of the day, snatching an hour or two of rest. It was searing hot beneath the high-angled sun, the very birds falling silent or staying put in the shade of leafy branches until the sun angled westward and the shadows lengthened. There was less to do as well. Lakshman had toiled the hardest, working like a demon possessed through the spring, turning from the finished hut to the garden, even trimming the nearby hedges, cutting away the wild unruly grass surrounding their compound to root out the snakes that frequented the patch, and was currently engaged on a project to mark out a pathway all the way down to the riverside. He was away right now, somewhere on the eastern side of the hill, or perhaps by the river, where he loved to swim.

Rama was inside the hut, napping in that easy way he had of slipping into deep, restful sleep anywhere, any time. Sita had been lying on her pallet in the hut beside him just moments ago, but she had grown restless in the still, breezeless confines and had finally risen, seeking out something to occupy herself that would pass the time until Rama awoke or Lakshman returned. She had settled on weeding only because it would keep her in the shade of the hut – at least until the sun traversed to this side – and was something she had been putting off for the past week.

She was on her hands and knees, carefully pulling unwanted stalks from the tomato patch, and thinking about whether it would be all right for them to build a raft and travel downriver a little way. It would be something to do, and as long as they only set foot on the northern bank, that should satisfy the terms of Anasuya's warning. She thought she would speak to Rama about it when he woke, and that was when she heard the singing.

It was a familiar aria, one that had been around since much before her time. A romantic lyric from a famous Sanskrit rendition of the Sakuntala legend. In the play the song was sung by Raja Dushyanta to Sakuntala at their first encounter. The raja had lost his way in the forest while hunting, and came across a beautiful maiden bathing and frolicking in a lotus pond. The song was his way of expressing how he felt upon witnessing this vision of female perfection. It sounded more than a little strange coming from a woman, but oddly appropriate. After all, the details of the song were concerned more with aesthetic generalities rather than specific references to the female anatomy, in sharp departure from most Sanskrit songs. It was one of the reasons Sita had always loved the song, not just for its heart-breaking melody, almost underlining the essential sadness of the play's storyline itself, but because it stayed far away from the typical clichéd descriptions of bosoms and more intimate details of womanly physique. Instead, Dushyanta's song spoke of the glow on Sakuntala's face, the light in her eyes, the rapturous look when she spied a golden fish in the pond and tried to clasp it.

Sita stood up, brushing her hair out of her face with the back of her muddy hands. That smeared mud on her forehead and temple but she was unaware of it. She peered over the low bamboo fence that Lakshman had constructed to keep foraging animals out of their garden – and out of the hut too, for the animals of Chitrakut were unused to humans and unusually bold. All she could see was the line of mahua trees, still and dry in the rasping summer heat. The sun was already riding westward, throwing the shadow of the trees of the southern thicket a yard or more on the grassy field. She raised her hand, trying to see more clearly into the shade of the thicket, but the glare was directly in her eyes and the shadows between the close-growing trees were too dense. The singing continued from that direction. She waited, expecting the singer to emerge at any moment; it still sounded as if she was approaching.

But after a moment the singing grew softer and more distant, as if the singer were moving farther away. Sita bit her lip in impatience. She glanced back at the hut. Rama hadn't emerged, so he was probably still sleeping. If she ran inside to wake him up, they would waste precious time debating what to do, and the stranger in the woods might disappear. But her bow and arrow were right beside the entrance to the hut, where she had left it when she came out to do her weeding. She might not eat flesh any more, but she never went anywhere without a weapon close at hand. Not since Viradha had she been unarmed.

She ran back to the wall, picked up the bow and arrow, and, slinging it easily across her shoulder, slipped through the bamboo gate and went sprinting into the woods in search of the singing stranger.

15

The singing continued as Sita made her way cautiously through the woods. She kept looking back at first, stealing glances at the hut. When she saw that she would lose sight of it, only a few dozen yards into the thicket, she hesitated, but the song drew her. She couldn't believe that any Asura would be wandering across Chitrakut hill, singing songs from Sanskrit dramas. And what Asura would pick this particular song, a song that captured the essence of love and longing so effectively that it was rumoured to be sung by kings to queens on their wedding nights? She smiled. Not just a rumour; Rama had sung it to her on their wedding night. It was one of the cherished happy memories she had of that fateful night, before things began to go completely wrong. She had to see this woman, speak with her. Surely she was some sadhuni from an ashram, collecting fruit or flowers, who had wandered too far by mistake? Or perhaps even a messenger sent by either Atri and Anasuya or Agastya who had failed to see the hut, nestled as it was on the northern ridge of the hill? Sita was certain it was one of these explanations, and that drove her on boldly. Besides, she was armed and still within earshot of the hut. Sound travelled a long way in Chitrakut.

The singing stopped. She paused, trying to see through

the trees, but she still couldn't catch any sight of the woman. When the silence lengthened, she started forward at a faster pace, breaking into a run. She already had a fair idea where the singer had been heading and she slowed down as she reached the familiar clearing. Yes. It was the lotus pond where Rama and she loved to sit in the evenings.

Beside the lotus pond, bending down to reach for one of the beautiful pink blossoms, was a girl clad in a white ang-vastra draped in the ascetic style, tightly around the waist and hips and loosely around one shoulder, diagonally. A small woven cane basket sat on the bank of the pond beside her; there were flowers in it. Her hair was matted in the traditional hermit style, confirming her sadhuni status. She was slender and well shaped, and the first glimpse Sita had of her outstretched arm, the curve of her neck, and her left profile all suggested that she was pretty in a rustic, naïve way. She was speaking softly to the nearest lotus flower, her voice melodious and low.

'Come to me, my pretty lotus blossom. I will place you gently in my basket and take you to my guru. She will be pleased to offer you at our evening darshan. What finer destiny can you have than to pass through the hands of the venerated Sage Anasuya, offered to the devas?'

The girl reached further, her fingers brushing the surface of the water lightly. The effect was enough to make the lotus drift away from her. Sita watched silently, stepping closer, completely unnoticed by the sadhuni.

'How silly of me! Do not go away. I meant to bring you closer, not push you farther away. Come now, my pretty kamal. Come to . . .'

The girl stretched out, reaching her hand in one final effort to touch the edge of the lotus and pull it closer. This time she leaned too far, losing her balance. She gasped and began to windmill her arms, trying to keep from toppling into the water.

'Devi!' she cried, starting to fall.

Sita sprinted forward, shooting out her hand and grabbing hold of the girl. She had to drop the bow and arrow to do so, and grasped the sadhuni around her slender waist as best as she could manage. Inevitably she pulled too hard, and both she and the girl fell back on the sloping bank of the lotus pond. The girl's feet kicked the edge of the water, splashing both of them.

'Devi protect me!' the girl exclaimed, twisting out of Sita's grasp. She lurched to her feet unsteadily, turning to look at her rescuer, not with gratitude, but with terror. She stood, shaking, staring wide-eyed at Sita.

'Demon!' she said. 'You are one of the legendary demons of Panchvati my guru warned me about!'

Sita smiled, amused that *she* should be mistaken for a demon. 'But we are in Chitrakut. Panchvati is across the river.' She gestured to her left, southwards.

The girl took several steps backward. Her eyes were set wide apart, large and almond-shaped. *Like a doe.* Even her behaviour was doe-like, nervous, quick-moving, shivering. 'Don't be scared,' Sita said. 'I heard your song and followed. When I saw you were about to fall into the pond . . .'

The girl remained silent, staring. She had turned her head to one side, away from Sita, as if she might bolt at any second. *Like a doe, frozen in a tiger's sights, wanting to bolt yet too terrified to break the impasse.* And to think that only only moments earlier Sita had thought that she might be an Asura!

Sita spread her hands, showing they were empty. 'I mean you no harm. I am Sita of Mithila. My husband, his brother-in-law and I live here in Chitrakut. Our hut is only a hundred yards or so up the hill. I can show you if you like.'

The girl shuddered violently then glanced behind her, as if fearing some new deception.

'Wait,' Sita said. 'I heard you say your guru is Anasuya. Is that so?'

At the mention of Anasuya, the girl nodded reluctantly. Sita indicated the robe she had on. 'This robe was given to me by Anasuya herself.'

The girl stared at the robe, then back at Sita's face. 'How do I know you are telling the truth? That you are not a demoness seeking to carry me across the river as a prize for your demon brothers? I know how you demonesses come out to seek wives for your brother demons!'

Sita was losing patience. This was absurd. 'All right,' she said at last. 'If you do not believe me, so be it. But it was your singing that drew me here. That song . . . it means something special to me. A happier time, before I came here. Not that I am not happy here, but . . . You sang it so soulfully, I simply had to see who you were.'

And then, on an impulse, she sang a snatch of verse from the song herself:

'Light, precious light, how you draw me like a moth to a flame . . .'

The girl stopped shivering and staring. Slowly, she smiled. She stepped forward hesitantly.

'You can sing,' she said. 'My guru says that no Asura could sing a love song, not the way a human can . . .'

She came forward. She smiled at Sita. 'Forgive me, my sister. I have heard such stories . . . And I had already wandered too far from my ashram, seeking out the very best flowers I could find. For today is my first day serving the sages Anasuya and Atri. I wished to please them.'

'There's no need to apologise,' Sita said, relieved. 'I

feared the exact same thing at first. That is why . . .' she turned to point behind her, 'I brought my bow and quiver with me, for protection.'

The girl turned her large doe eyes to look at the fallen bow and quiver, arrows spilled out from it and splayed like the spokes of a hand-fan. She came forward.

'Well met, sister Sita,' she said, embracing her in the warm style of rural Aryas.

'Well met, sister . . . ?'

'Supanakha,' the girl said, her breath redolent of an aroma Sita found hauntingly familiar but couldn't quite place. 'Your sister, Supanakha.'

And then she embraced Sita again, in a grip so powerful Sita felt her very ribcage would shatter and pierce her heart. She had no breath left to even scream. Something was forced into her mouth, something tasting foul and ripe and liquorish, then a cloudbank descended and engulfed her in its wet, dark maw.

Rama woke from strange, unsettling dreams. He didn't recall exactly what he had done in those dreams, but it was something grossly immoral. And in return for his immoral transgression, Sita and Lakshman were condemned to a terrible fate. This was all he remembered, but as hard as he tried, he could recall no details. It wasn't difficult to understand the sub-context of that dream; he had been wrestling with the consequences of the choices he had made for the past several weeks. What if, he had asked himself once, he had left Sita behind, just as Lakshman had left Urmila behind, and what if he had left Lakshman behind as well, and had come into exile alone? Would that have been so terrible? So much worse than this?

The answer was yes. It would have been unbearable. For with Sita and Lakshman with him, he felt as content as he would have done back in Ayodhya. Not as comfortable, certainly; not as indolent and able to wallow in luxury, of course. But every bit as content, surely. The truth was, he was happy. And he was happy because he had brought his wife and brother into exile with him. It was a selfish happiness, for all happiness was selfish. And inevitably, as the season had given way to summer, and a sense of tranquillity and harmony had fallen upon their simple rustic life here at Chitrakut, that very happiness had roused its twin emotion, guilt.

He sighed and rose from the disarrayed pallet, strewn across the floor by his tossing and turning. His body was wreathed with sweat, his ang-vastra soaked through and through. He took it off and wound it around his arm as he went out of the hut. He was in the habit of washing his own clothes after sandhyavandana. If he could stop Lakshman from doing it; Lakshman seemed to do everything so quickly and efficiently, Rama had to make an effort to ensure he did his own chores first, or they would be done by Lakshman in no time. He smiled. No wonder he was having guilty dreams. He was still living like a king here, in this rustic kingdom of Chitrakut. Lakshman made sure of that.

The late-afternoon sunshine was bright and piercing after the relative dimness of the hut. It took him a moment to accept that the sun was angled much lower than he had expected. When he realised how low it had travelled, he shook his head in disbelief. He had slept away the whole afternoon! It was the mangoes he had eaten before noon. Three of them, large and golden and bursting with ecstasy, their flesh dripping sweet sticky juice with every bite. He rubbed his belly, sighing. At this rate he would grow as fat as his father.

'Sita?'

He walked around the hut, expecting her to be in the garden, planting some new herb or vegetable. The garden was her pet project these days. It was coming along quite nicely, he was pleased to say. One good monsoon and they would be able to harvest their own food right here in their own back yard, instead of having to walk all the way upriver to that patch half a yojana away. And then he would probably grow even fatter without that exercise! He would have to start waking Lakshman at dawn and go running through the woods every morning, if only to keep his body fit. Not that he was really in any danger of fattening up – his stomach was still as firm as a drum – but it would give him something to do. It felt strange, not having done anything for so many months. Rest was good. But so was work. He craved something to do. Even hunting. At least it kept one's senses sharpened. Perhaps he could coax Sita into going on a hunt. There were far too many wild boar in the hills to the north. It wouldn't hurt to bring down a few, aid the natural cycle and balance the population.

He stopped short.

He had completed a full circuit of their property. Sita was nowhere in sight.

'Sita?' he called out.

After a moment, the answer came from behind him, on the wind. 'Here, my love.'

He turned to see her walking towards him, coming from the direction of the woods. She looked radiant and alive, her cheeks flushed, her face lit up with a vitality he hadn't seen for days . . . or months, actually. She looked as she had the day of the swayamvara in Mithila. Like a woman in search of her own destiny, and if she didn't like the first choice she saw, she would garland the next one, or the one after . . .

'Rama,' she said breathlessly. She had been running.

She caught his hand and swung him around, laughing. He swung around with her, smiling too. The wheeling made them dizzy and they fell to the ground, rolling on the soft kusa grass of their front yard. She pulled up a handful and sprinkled it over his head. Grass clung to his sweat-sticky neck and upper arms, prickling his skin. Her hair had come unravelled, and strands of it lay across her face and shoulders. She looked enormously attractive to him just then, and as her eyes watched him, he saw his own desire reflected in her face as well.

He laughed. 'So what makes my beloved wife so childishly playful this summer afternoon?'

She grinned. 'Something wonderful happened.'

'What?'

'I'm married to you!'

He raised himself on his elbow, looking down at her. 'You have been married to me for months now! What makes you act as giddy as a new bride of a sudden?'

She put her head down abruptly, her hair falling across her face, concealing her eyes. 'Yes, but I just remembered how wonderful it is.'

'What is?'

She raised her face to him. Hair lay across her face in wild, unruly strands. A faint twinge of doubt tweaked his mind. What had got into her? He had never seen Sita like this before. Not even when—

'That I'm married to you! It's wonderful! A miracle! We should celebrate it!'

She reached up and caught hold of his hand, pulling him down towards her. 'We should celebrate it!'

He smiled at her excitement. 'And we shall. But first we have to go to the river.'

She sat up and clapped her hands together. 'That's good too. Let's go and bathe in the river!'

He laughed. 'That we shall. But not in the way you mean. I speak of our sandhyavandana. Have you collected the flowers yet?'

She peered up at him, shading her eyes from the sun, which was low in the western sky now. 'Flowers?'

'For the evening ritual, Sita.'

She shrugged, looking down at the ground, and began plucking up handfuls of grass. 'I'm tired of rituals and ceremonies. We are in exile, are we not? Everything else deprived us, our homes, our kingdoms, all wealth and comfort. At least we still have each other. Can we not enjoy that much at least as we please?'

He was puzzled now. She sound strange, almost resentful. It was an abrupt change of mood, totally unlike Sita. 'Yes, of course. And we do share one another's companionship; it is what makes our exile so bearable, even wonderful at times. Only this afternoon I was thinking of how I would have passed fourteen years without you or Lakshman, and I realised—'

'Lakshman.'

'What?'

She looked up abruptly. 'Where is he? Your brother?'

This was very peculiar. 'I don't know. I slept the afternoon away.' He grinned sheepishly. 'Lazy buffalo that I am. He must be down by the river, working on that pathway.'

She was silent for a moment. Then suddenly, in another unexpected change of mood, she smiled seductively up at him. 'Let's go into the hut.'

He frowned.

'We will. But first we have to gather flowers for the evening ritual—'

'To hell with the evening ritual,' she said sharply. Then, reverting to the same silky, seductive tone: 'Rama, I am unhappy. Being in exile is not easy. Comfort me. Give me the warmth of your companionship.'

He stared at her.

He felt as if a large insect were trailing its feelers across his back. He resisted the urge to turn around. 'I thought I heard singing as I slept. Earlier in the afternoon. Was that you?'

She smiled. 'You remember that song?'

'Which one?'

'You know. The one we sang together the night of our wedding.'

'The song from the play of Dushyanta and Sakuntala?'

'Yes.' She seemed pleased. 'That's the one.'

He chose his words very carefully. 'You mean the song from the play *Sakuntala*, don't you?'

'Yes, yes. From *Sakuntala and Dushyanta*. The same. The lovers' song.'

'Remember the last time we sang that song?' He spoke with deliberate casualness.

'Just the other night, was it not, my love?' She smiled up at him coyly. 'But lovers ought to do more than sing love songs.'

He felt his spine grow cold. Ice ran into his veins. 'Stand up.'

She held her arms up to him, beckoning him alluringly. 'Come, lie with me.'

'I said, stand up.' His voice was curt now, with no tenderness or hint of pretence.

She looked up at him, a puzzled expression in her brown eyes. 'What is it? Did I say something wrong, my love?'

'Many things. But I would have guessed even had you not spoken a word. Did you truly think you could deceive me so easily?'

She pouted. 'Why are you speaking so harshly to me, my lord? It is I, Sita. Your wife.'

He laughed. 'No. You are not Sita. You are not my wife.'

16

Lakshman paused to examine his handiwork. The line of thick, bushy darbha grass was trimmed as close as he could manage with just a sword. He leaned forward, running the palm of his hand across the top of the neatly trimmed grass. It felt like fur, a bearcoat perhaps, or shaggy sheep's wool.

He stood up, satisfied. Sweat dripped down his back and shoulders. He stretched, easing the tension from his body. Slowly he grew aware of the sun on his shoulders, and on the ground. The afternoon had crept into evening without him knowing. He had been absorbed in his work. Cutting grass away to clear a path didn't need that much concentration; keeping a wary eye out for the proliferation of snakes did.

He looked uphill, at the winding pathway of neatly cut grass, just about a yard in width. Every few yards or so a dark tangle lay off to one side or the other, some easily visible, others hidden by the grass. Those tangles, looking like so many lengths of coloured twine, some black, some green, some speckled, dotted, matted . . . those were all snakes that he had had to kill to clear the pathway. Three nests had lain directly on the pathway – the route he had marked as the most accessible from hut to river. It had taken almost a week of patient, risky work, clearing away the snakes, emptying out the nests and filling in the holes to prevent them from coming back – leaving a partial snake eggshell or two in the filled-in hole was a good deterrent – and then undertaking the arduous task of mowing the grass, with only his sword for the task. His back ached pleasantly from the task, his shoulders and neck were sore, but it was done at last. Now, when he or Sita or Rama went down to the river carrying a mud pot for water, they wouldn't have to constantly look out for snakes underfoot. Or avoid the snake nests and climb through thorn bushes or down crumbling rocky slopes. They could walk along the path as comfortably as Ayodhyans along Suryavansha Avenue.

He smiled at his own simile. Suryavansha Avenue. That was funny. Then again, perhaps he should name his newly made path. Who knew? Some day people might come to look at the spot where they had lived in exile, and stare and point at these things. There, they would say, looking at this pathway down the hillside, that was cut by Lakshman to ease his brother's and bhabhi's thrice-daily trips to the river. Hmm. If this little path was going to become such a legend, it ought to have a name. What should he call it? Definitely not Suryavansha Avenue! He grinned at his own wit.

He glanced up, remembering how the path seemed to wind around the hill like a necklace if seen from the river, and instantly the word rekha came to mind. Rekha, meaning line or border. Yes, that was good, for after Anasuya's warning, the river had become their border. But rekha alone was too general, too vague. How could he make it more specific? Hmm. How had their ancestors named roads and places in Ayodhya? After themselves of course. Raghuvamsha Avenue, Manu Sabagraha, Aja Marg . . . So why not Lakshman Rekha? It had a ring to it.

Did it sound vain? Not really. After all, he'd made the pathway, hadn't he? So it was his right to name it. Lakshman Rekha, then. It had a nice ring to it, Lakshman's Borderline.

He stood, grinning to himself, feeling absurd. Now all he needed was a few dozen PFs to patrol the path, and then it would truly be a border. Until then—

The scream rang out through the heavy afternoon silence, piercing and shrill. As suddenly as it had begun, it broke off, as if someone had covered the woman's mouth in mid-scream.

He froze momentarily, just long enough to try to make out the direction and distance of the scream's origin.

Then he broke into a sprint, running straight uphill, up the path he had just finished clearing. The wind hissed in his ears as he ran, like the ghosts of the snakes he had slaughtered.

Rama backed away from the woman lying on the grass. She had released the maya-jal, the Asura spell that had transformed her body and features to make her appear to be Sita. The changes themselves were mainly physical, he saw, as she struggled and writhed with the morphing that was enlarging bones, growing fur, and otherwise altering the very structure of her body into something wholly inhuman. She was some kind of Asura. A yaksi, he guessed, for they possessed the power to morph. But there was rakshasa blood in her as well. He could see the unmistakable demoniac signs that were so typical of the rakshasa species – the nubs of horns on the crown of her skull, the sharp ridges of bone along her upper spine, the shaggy-haired ears . . . A crossbreed then, a yaksi-rakshasi. And she had used a spell in addition to her natural morphing abilities, for while morphing enabled her to take human form convincingly, it took sorcery to make her look and sound like a specific human; in this case, Sita.

And where was Sita then? What had this she-demon done with her? His anger threatened to rise. He fought it down with an effort, determined to see this through calmly, no matter what. *No matter what*.

The morph completed, she threw back her head and issued a brief shrill scream that she herself choked off midway. She stood before him on all fours now, a creature covered with fur like a golden leopard, but with the wide-set eyes and snubby nose of a deer. A scar on her left flank caught his eye, sparking some memory, but he couldn't follow the thought through to its end. It was not relevant. Nothing else was relevant except learning where Sita was and getting her back safe and sound. And to do that, he must play cat-and-mouse with this demoness.

She growled softly at him, sleek and beautiful in her own primal way. He had a feeling she would not want for mates among her own species – or among any Asura species, for that matter. Her allure was evident, alien and animalistic though it was.

'I thought that form pleased you,' she said, her natural voice throaty, husky. 'I know how much value you mortals lay on outward appearances. Why then did you spurn me? Where you not convinced by my bhes-bhav?'

He cleared his throat. 'Your bhes-bhav was perfect. It was not your guise that gave you away.'

'What was it then?' She sniffed at herself. 'I even assumed her fetid mortal odour to please you.'

'There is more to being a mortal than mere physicality. The last time my wife and I sang that song was on our wedding night, months ago,' he added. 'It was also the first night of our exile and not one we are likely to forget.' He did not add that that night seemed another age now.'

She cocked her head, staring at him. Her feral green eyes bored into him with a frank lustfulness. It was interesting that he could tell that she was aroused despite the gulf of difference between their species. He noted the fact in a lesser part of his mind for future reference.

'Tell me then,' she purred. 'Tell me what pleases you, and I will do it. Whatever you desire, I can become that. I have talents no mortal woman can dream of. Ways to pleasure you that you never thought possible. We will fill the forest with our cries of pleasure and be the envy of every mating couple in this wilderness. We will be lovers of legend and lore, like your Sakuntala and Dushyanta, or Nala and Damyanti . . .'

Taking him by surprise, she sang a line from the song of Sakuntala. 'Light, precious light, how you draw me like a moth to a flame . . .'

'Stop.' He was shocked to find his hands trembling. Control. *Remember Sita. First find Sita. Then deal with this . . . creature.*

She took a step closer, then another, her body moving with feline grace. Her lithely muscled body rippled beneath the sleek, lustrous fur. Her lambent eyes glowed with longing, phosphorescent in the shade of the thatched overhang before the hut. 'Rama, my Rama . . . my beloved. I only wish to love you.'

'Stop it.' His voice was firmer now, decisive.

She came another two steps closer, then three. Now he could smell her odour. Distinctive and overwhelming. Unlike any creature he had smelled before. A combination of wildcat and Asura and, yes, mortal too. For the scent she had stolen from Sita still remained in the mix, and it was that which he found unsettling in the extreme.

'I will give you Lanka,' she said.

He was startled by the sudden change of topic.

'My cousin Ravana, your arch-enemy, was felled by the Brahm-astra you wielded at Mithila. He lies in a coma now, beyond recovery it seems. His wife and brother pray night and day, keeping a round-the-clock vigil at the shrine of Shiva on the mound Nikumbhila. But there has been no change in his condition for months. He is beyond salvaging, a mere husk from which the aatma has long fled.'

'Why are you telling me this?'

She licked her chops, her tongue a deep fleshy scarlet. 'Lanka has no lord now. It is yours for the taking.'

'Mine?' His voice sounded unnaturally loud. He forced himself to modulate it. 'Why would I want anything to do with a place like Lanka?'

She shrugged her catlike shoulders, looking away coyly for a moment. 'You are a king without a kingdom, Lanka is a kingdom without a king.'

'An Asura kingdom.'

'Ah.' She spoke as if he had said something she had never considered before. 'Yes. I see. Well, Lanka was not always a kingdom of Asuras. Ravana made it so when he wrested it from his half-brother Kubera. He used his sorcery to open the gateways to Narak and fetch up his Asura hordes. He turned it into the hell it was until recently.'

'Was?'

'Riots. Civil war. The Asuras have nigh decimated one another. The few survivors that remain limp through the ruins, licking their wounds, unable to even rebuild their homes without authoritative leadership. You could marshal them, bring order to chaos. Bring shiploads of mortals if you please. Turn it into an island-paradise! You could be lord of Lanka and do with it as you will. You could even make it a kingdom of . . . what is that word you mortals bandy about?'

'Dharma,' he said without hesitation.

She sniffed. 'You could make it a kingdom of dharma. Lanka lies supine, yours for the taking. Embrace it. Seed it with your own seed. With your dharma.'

'And where do you fit into all this?'

She sidled past him, around him. He felt something sleek and furry trail across the backs of his thighs, caress his lower back. Her tail. She craned her head, looking up with those sultry, mesmerising eyes. 'I will be your queen. Your paramour. Your wife.'

'I already have a wife.'

She smiled slowly, a smile that took for ever. 'Do you?'

His hand shot out, snatched up the sword leaning against the wall of the hut. He had been edging towards it these past several moments, distracting her with conversation. He brought it round and put the point to her neck in one lightning-swift motion. He pressed it in, drawing a bead of blood, enough to let her know he meant business.

'I do. And now you must take me to her.' He added with the same immaculately polite tone: 'If you please.'

Lakshman held his breath as Rama's hand shot out, grasped the sword and brought it to bear neatly on the Asura's throat. The creature froze, outmanoeuvred. *Well done, bhai,* he applauded silently. Another moment or two and Lakshman would have made his move. The only reason he had held back until now was because the creature was dangerously close to Rama, and because he believed implicitly that Rama would regain control of the situation. He always did.

Now he watched as Rama had more words with the strange creature. Then, with a contemptuous flick of its tail, the beast turned and began walking on all fours towards the southern woods. Rama walked beside it, keeping his sword within slashing range.

Lakshman waited until they had passed over the grassy ridge, out of sight, then sprinted forward. He paused at the hut, peering inside. 'Bhabhi?' he called. 'Sita?'

He hadn't expected a response, but his heart still sank when none was received. That meant that he had read the situation correctly. The creature he had just seen with Rama had somehow lured Sita away from the hut, probably while Rama napped in the afternoon, and now Rama was forcing it to lead him to the place where it had left Sita . . . Bound? Unconscious? Or . . .

He pushed the thought away, and loped up the ridge, reaching the top in time to see Rama and the Asura disappear into the shadows of the thicket. He sprinted after them, staying low and moving as silently as a hunter tracking deadly prey.

17

She lay by the lotus pond, curled up on the bank. At first sight he experienced one terrible heart-stopping moment when he was certain she was dead. Then he felt her pulse, and it was beating, albeit faintly. Her face was slick with sweat, her mouth slack, her breathing shallow.

He turned to the demoness. She was seated on her haunches on the sloping bank, watching him with stark envy.

'I fed her black lotus. She is under its influence. She will sleep long and deep. Her dreams will be fantastic and intense. When she awakens she will be well. You need not fear for her.'

Rama felt rage well up within him, as thick as the dark that fell upon this very wood on a moonless night. Three lightning-swift steps and he was within striking distance of the creature again, his blade to her throat. It took a great effort of will not to cut her to bloody ribbons. If this beast . . . this shape-shifter . . . this demoness had harmed Sita, how could he spare its life? He could not. This did not fall within the purview of Anasuya's warning, did it? How could he let an Asura who had hurt Sita – or worse – simply walk away untouched? Yet he maintained control of his emotions, banking his anger. Of all the difficult things he had been called upon to do in the past few months, this was the hardest.

Not killing was harder by far than killing.

She watched him. And waited.

He turned and struck the sword into the nearest tree trunk. It was a neem. Bark split with a crackling sound, sap splattered. He had to pull hard to retrieve the imbedded blade.

He heard her make a sound and turned quickly. He was alert to the point where he could hear a grasshopper cricking to his right, and if he wished, he could have swept his sword and sliced the insect in half without even seeing it with his eyes. He breathed, seeking calm and balance.

She sat exactly as she had before, unmoving. Her eyes glistened darkly in the shadowy dimness of the thicket. She was crying, if it could be called crying.

He tried to calm himself. 'I can make you happy,' she said. 'Bear you children. Bring you—'

'I do not wish to speak with you,' he said, cutting her off. 'Nor hear any other words you have to say.'

She stared up at him silently, eyes glistening. Something changed in her face, and he could not read her expression any more. She was too alien. How could she ever think that she could be . . . what had she said? . . . his queen, his paramour, his *wife*? Disgust swelled up, filling the space that rage had only partially vacated.

'I only wish to love you,' she said. 'Can you not understand that?'

He breathed before replying. 'Understand it, yes. Accept it, no. You are Asura, of a demon race. I am mortal, a being of dharma. What you desire can never be. Not if you offer me all the kingdoms in all the planes of existence to rule over. All that I desire, I already have. And that does not include you.'

She was so silent, he thought she would explode with rage. Instead, she only shook her head from side to side, like a cat shaking off water.

'Rama, I love you, I wish to give you everything, wealth, power, glory . . . I will give you Lanka! Even the inert body of Ravana the ten-headed to do with as you please.'

He was silent, but she could read the anger in his bunched shoulder muscles as plainly as the expression on his wine-dark face.

'If you wish,' she swallowed, feeling her pride stick in her gullet but forcing it down, 'if you wish, I will accept the position of second wife. You may still keep that hairless mortal wench. But do not spurn me thus. I have followed you and watched you since before you left Ayodhya. My love for you has grown too strong to be dismissed out of hand.' She lowered her head, tasting her own shame. 'If I must beg, then beg I shall. But I will be your wife, and you my husband. I have willed it so.'

He turned to her. His voice was deathly quiet. 'Then will it otherwise. For you will never have me. Now, heed me well. I am setting you free. Go back to your lair in Lanka, to your Asura brethren. I spare you this time because I have taken a vow.' He pointed at Sita's prone form. 'A vow for her sake. I will spill no more blood. Go now. And never return. For the next time you show yourself, I may not be as loath to spill your blood as I am today.'

He turned his back upon her, directing his attention to Sita once more. 'Go now,' he said. 'Go!'

He bent over Sita, clearing the hair from her face, rubbing her cheeks. 'Sita? Sita' His voice was as gentle now as it had been harsh a moment ago. 'My love, it is I, Rama.'

After a moment, he rose and went down to the edge of

the pond. Dipping the end of his ang-vastra into the water, he returned to Sita and began wiping her face with the wet cloth. He let a few drops fall on to her brow, gently.

Supanakha watched him silently. Her anger rose within her uncontrollably. So this was her fate then? This was her reward for all these months of patience and faith. This was how the dark Asura gods rewarded her for her offerings and her prayers. With harsh words, the tip of a sword at her throat, and an admonition to leave and never return. A threat to spill her blood should she ever come back again. And for what? For this hollow-boned mortal female who could not stomach a wedge of black lotus. That flat-bellied furless black-eyed weakling.

She snarled silently, her jaws opening and snapping shut in rage.

Rama rose again and went down to the pond for more water. He used his sword to reach out and draw a lotus towards the bank. He put the sword down, and bent over to pick up the lotus, raising it up like a bowl filled with water, intending to carry it back to Sita.

Supanakha chose that instant to act. Bunching her powerful hind muscles, she leapt across the yards that separated her from the humans. She landed with a roar, straddling Sita's unconscious body. In an instant, she had the mortal woman in her grasp, her bared claws at Sita's face and belly.

Rama cried out, spinning around and flinging the lotus at her, even as he lunged for his sword. Supanakha ducked her head instinctively, and the lotus, filled with pond water, splashed on Sita's face. Supanakha saw Rama roll over in a somersault, rising with his sword in his hand.

He crouched before her. 'Release her! She has no part in this. It is me you seek, is it not? Then fight me! Leave her out of this.'

Supanakha snarled. 'She is the only reason you spurn me. By killing her, I remove the obstacle in my path. You must accept me as your wife then.'

Rama's eyes were like daggers of fire. 'Foolish she-devil. Nothing you do can make me marry you. Do you not understand that yet? I was ready to let you leave unharmed, because I had some sympathy for your emotions, and because of my desire to abjure violence. But if you harm a hair on Sita's head, I will visit such violence upon you as you never dreamed possible.'

'You lie!' she screamed. 'You love me! It is only this mortal wench that keeps you from admitting it. Let me kill her and we will be man and wife. Please, Rama. It is the only way!'

Before Rama could respond or act, a figure leapt into the clearing, directly behind Supanakha. Lakshman, brandishing his sword, struck her with his fist in the back of her neck, at the tender spot just beneath her skull. Startled, the she-demon released her grip on Sita, and spun around with the ferocity of a predator to face her new assailant.

Rama leaped forward, catching Sita with his left arm before she fell. She lurched in his grasp, coughing and choking. He moved her to one side, out of harm's way, lowering her to the ground, setting her head back against the trunk of a peepal. She coughed violently, spitting up fragments of bluish-black stuff. It was the black lotus weed that the demoness had fed her – she must have not swallowed it all. She spat it up, retching drily. Her eyes were red and struggling to focus, but she was awake and aware, he saw. He thanked the devas silently.

'Wait here, my love,' he said, then kissed her quickly and turned back to the fray.

Lakshman had the creature backed up against the

trunk of a mahua. Supanakha snarled, baring her fangs and claws, but Lakshman's sword moved in a blur, hissing through the air to her left and right, fencing her in.

'What do you think, she-demon?' he said. 'Would I make you a good husband? Will you marry me now that my brother has spurned you?'

Supanakha roared with anger and pain.

'Lakshman,' Rama said quietly. 'Do not taunt and play with her.'

'What else would you have me do, bhai? Turn my back on her as you did? Have her leap upon Sita once more, this time to end her life?'

Rama was astonished. 'Lakshman, what are you—'

'I saw you spare this creature's life, Rama. And I saw how she repaid your trust and mercy. Have you not learned from all our encounters with Asuras that they are never to be trusted or spared? We must treat them the way they treat us, with no mercy or quarter.'

'Then they will continue to treat us the same,' Rama said. 'And the circle of violence will spin round and round, unbreakable as the serpent Vasuki, swallowing its own tail for all infinity. No, Lakshman, I understand your anger. It is directed at the demoness for daring to enter our peaceful lives and wreak havoc. But heed my words now. The only way to end this violence is by ending violence itself! Do you hear me? End it, Lakshman. Put aside your sword and let her leave peacefully.'

Lakshman did not turn to look at Rama, for that would have meant taking his eyes off Supanakha. But his astonishment was obvious from the way he replied. 'Let her leave? Put aside my sword? Rama, are you in your right mind? She will tear me apart! She will kill us all if we let our guard down. You saw how she acted when you turned your back on her and put down your sword.'

'Supanakha,' Rama said. 'I give you one more chance. If your purpose truly is to gain my love, then heed me well.'

To Lakshman's surprise, the demoness stopped snarling and listened silently to Rama's words, her head cocked to one side. But her eyes remained fixed on Lakshman, boring into him like twin arrows.

'Harming Sita or my brother will not win you my love. It will only earn you my hatred. As of this moment, I feel sympathy for you. If you attack any of us again, that sympathy will turn to distrust. I will make my brother put down his sword in a moment. I give you leave to walk away unharmed. Do you agree to end this feud here and now and leave peacefully?'

Supanakha's eyes remained on Lakshman even as she replied. 'I do not like it, but I will do it, because you have willed it so. And because I still have faith that some day you will learn to love me, Rama. For that reason alone I shall go from here. But one day we will be united. That much I believe.'

Rama sighed. 'Go quickly and in peace. Lakshman, put down your sword and step aside. Give her room to leave.'

Lakshman stared at the Asura, and she stared back. 'Rama, you cannot believe anything this beast says. She will promise anything to break free. Even if she walks away now, outnumbered and outmatched as she is, she will not let the matter end here. She will return. You heard what she said. She still believes you will marry her some day. She will return when you and I are not close by, and assassinate Sita, as she sought to do today. Let us kill her right now, and end this menace once and for all.'

'No!' Rama strode forward. 'Lakshman, do as I say!

Release her at once. As your brother, I command you.'

Lakshman's body was stiff with anger. But he backed away slowly, lowering his sword. 'As you say, Rama.'

Supanakha, pressed back against the tree and forced to stand on her hind legs until now, dropped to all fours again. She licked her chops roughly, twitching her tail as she turned away, her muscles tensing as she prepared to run. She turned her head to look at Rama one last time.

'I will return,' she purred softly. 'And you will be mine, Rama. Even if I have to bring fourteen thousand of my rakshasa brothers to make you agree, you will be my husband. I swear it by the name of Shiva.'

Lakshman's head snapped up. 'You see? I told you, Rama! Treacherous demon!'

His sword flicked out, moving in a blur. It slashed once, then twisted and slashed a second time, then a third. With each slash it sliced off a part of Supanakha's flesh. The first cut took her nose, leaving a spurting, gaping hole in the centre of her face. The second sliced off her left ear, the third took her right ear. She howled in pain and humiliation, leaping back. Lakshman's fourth slash sliced the empty air where she had stood a moment ago. She screamed once, then leapt backwards, upending herself head over heels. A flash of her pale-furred belly, and then she had vanished into the shadows of the woods.

'Lakshman!' Rama shouted, running forward. He caught his brother's arm and turned it, taking hold of his sword. 'I told you, no violence!'

'That's why I did not kill her, bhai,' Lakshman said calmly.

Rama stared in the direction that Supanakha had disappeared. Moments later, the sound of another anguished wail rose from ahead. It was at least a hundred yards away, and receding. He shook his head in frustration.

'You should not have done that, Lakshman,' he said sadly. 'You should not have.'

Then he turned and walked away from his brother, dropping his sword by his feet as he went.

Lakshman stood alone, staring into the woods, listening to the echoes of Supanakha's howls until they grew too faint to hear. After he could hear no more, he bent to retrieve his sword, and turned to follow his brother and sister-in-law back home.

18

Jatayu peered through the early-morning mists over Panchvati, seeking out its destination. Time was when it could have spotted the hill of Chitrakut beside the Godavari river from a mile high. Now, even flying a mere four or five hundred yards above the ground, it was struggling to make out the terrain below. It dropped lower, searching grimly. If it had read the signs correctly, there was not much time left. It must find its destination swiftly or its mission would be pointless. It peered blurrily through the morning haze, flying lower and lower. Caution, it warned itself, any lower and it might lose these high currents. It was a chore getting airborne these days, and flying too low could mean a forced landing in low terrain. There were rksas in these parts, and the bear races and Jatayu had never been very good friends. There was a time when Jatayu had hunted bears, relishing them the way a mortal might relish sweet savouries. Bears had a way of remembering such things. It had a feeling that if it were to come down in bear territory in its present bedraggled state, it would soon become a savoury itself. Even as withered and haggard as it was, it would still provide nourishment enough for a dozen bears for a few nights.

It scanned the rolling terrain with increasing frustration,

cursing the circumstances that had left it so crippled and infirm. Its vision, like its strength, had never been the same since those last days in Lanka. When the island-kingdom had burned in a series of shocking explosions, Jatayu had been caught wholly unawares, singed and burned badly. It had lost much of its feathers, and a fair bit of flesh as well. It would never soar the high skies as it once had, looking down on even the highest condors and eagles with a proud, disdainful eye. But most of all, it had lost its greatest talent: sight. Where once it could spy a pregnant female cobra curled around her nest from two miles high, it was now having difficulty finding a hill and a river from five hundred yards! It was almost wholly blind in one eye, and the other was only slightly less damaged. It was lucky if it could find itself a calf or a lamb or two these days.

The curve of the rising sun crested the distant mountains, sending rays of light sweeping across the hazy forest-carpeted land. Jatayu looked up involuntarily, and a glittering refraction caught its one good eye. Water. A lake perhaps. No, a river.

A river! It changed course slowly, painfully. The muscles that worked its finer wing movements were injured too, scorched in the explosions. It flew eastwards, squinting against the effulgence of the rising sun. It struggled to rise a little higher, just enough to put it out of the direct rays of the sun. It took a great deal more work than it once had. To think that just six months earlier it could fly from Lanka to Ayodhya and back in mere days. Ah, to be that Jatayu once more.

A hundred yards higher, then another fifty, then fifty more . . . Yes! Now it could see the hill beside the river. That must be it. No wonder it had not found it sooner. It had been scouring much too far to the south-west.

Foolish Jatayu. Foolish, withered, blind Jatayu. To think that you were once the king of vultures. Second only to the great Garuda, lord of all birdkind. And Ravana promised you not long ago that if you did as he bade you, helped his invasion of the mortal realm succeed, then you would be lord. Above even mighty Garuda. And now look at you, your flocks lost, your master reduced to a mindless palsy, your aerie atop the black fortress burned in the destruction of Lanka, yourself only a hollow shade of your former self. Alas, poor Jatayu. What is left that you can do? What great victories can you achieve now?

Perhaps none. But it could still do something of note. However small or minor that act might be, it could still attempt at least to redeem itself. To pay the penance for its past mistakes. Earn a small copper coin to place on the empty side of the scales of karma, to balance against the formidable tonne-weight of its past sins and crimes.

It set its man-like jaw and changed course grimly, heading for the hill named Chitrakut, and the hut atop that hill.

Sita had not spoken a word since the day of Supanakha's attack. Rama did not press her. He had been largely silent as well, speaking neither to her nor to Lakshman. He was no longer angry with Lakshman. He knew that his brother had done what he thought was right at the time; the devas knew that Rama himself had desired nothing more than to raise his sword and cut that she-devil down where she stood. But regardless of how they felt, the fact remained: they had transgressed. Sage Anasuya's warning had been crystal clear – do not draw first blood. They had done so. And now they could only wait silently to see what the consequences might be. He did not think they would be benign, but he still prayed daily.

They were returning from their morning rituals, by the path that Lakshman had made. He had finished it the day of the attack, Rama recalled. Since then, Lakshman had undertaken no new hobby or chore. They had all gone about their daily business, doing what must be done but not much more. There had been no laughter, no easy chatter. It was as if a cloud had come to rest over Chitrakut hill, a dark, brooding cloud that muffled all old emotions and stifled all new ones. Their half-hearted attempts at conversation were still-born, their faces sombre. Even the deer and rabbits that Sita had taken to feeding daily in the field behind their hut seemed to sense the change, staring fitfully at them, perhaps surprised by their silence, perhaps reading their hearts.

The rising sun was just starting to peek over the horizon as they reached the top of the hill. Another few yards and the hut was in view. It was a beautiful morning, with nary a cloud yet in sight. Any day now, the rains must come; it was past their time already. But not today. Surely not today. The sky was the blue of a northman's eyes, clear and speckless. The wind was still cool, if humid, a blessed relief from the steaming heat of the summer afternoons. The newly cut grass underfoot was soft and pleasantly prickly, like a thick pelt rug.

A shadow fell across them.

Rama ignored it at first, continuing to walk towards the hut. Then he remembered: no clouds.

And even if there was one overhead, the shadow moved too swiftly to be a cloud in this gentle breeze.

He stopped and looked up.

'Lakshman,' he snapped.

'I see it, bhai.' Lakshman's voice was subdued but alert.

It was a jatayu. The largest Rama had ever seen. No. He had seen one this large before . . . at Mithila. When he and Lakshman had stood at the top of the Sage's Brow, reciting the mantras that unleashed the Brahm-astra. The sky had been full of such flying Asuras. And the one at the fore, leading that winged regiment, had been a man-vulture like this one.

The creature issued a scree as it saw them looking up. It flew past them, beyond the hill and a hundred yards farther east, then began a slow turn, curving back.

'It seeks us,' Lakshman said quietly. He did not add what he normally would have said, that perhaps they ought to prepare to defend themselves.

Rama indicated a spot a few yards further. A kind of promontory jutting out over the river vale. He stopped there, Sita and Lakshman close behind. He glanced at Sita. She met his look with an expression that contained no discernible emotion at first. Then she reached out and squeezed his arm. He nodded, thanking her for the reassurance. He removed his bow from his shoulder and set it by his side, casually held. Lakshman followed his example.

The jatayu approached the hill again, the rising sun backlighting it. Rama could see the sun shining through gaps in its feathers. That could mean only one thing. The creature was injured, its plumage severely damaged. As it came closer, slowing in preparation to land, he saw that its underbelly and wings had been singed badly, burnt black in patches. From the awkward way it moved, he sensed it was still hurting from those wounds.

With a final scree, the bird-beast landed on the promontory. It flapped its wings several times, its enormous claws scratching yard-long rents in the grassy surface as it struggled to get a firm grip. The wind from that flapping was enough to flatten Rama's river-dampened garments against his body. A powerful stench of charred flesh came to him.

Finally, the jatayu settled down. Its hooked beak turned this way, then that, several times. Rama saw that it had lost most of the vision in its left eye; that was why it was turning its head, to look at each of them in turn with its remaining good eye.

'Jatayu,' Rama said. 'That is your name, is it not?'

'Aye,' the bird-creature said in a high-pitched tone, then made a noise in its throat as if trying to re-accustom itself to human speech. 'Jatayu,' it continued in a lower tone. 'The first of its name.'

The legendary Jatayu itself. Rama was impressed and saddened both at once. As a young boy, hearing the tales of such creatures of myth and legend, he had dreamed some day of coming face to face with them. Never in those dreams had he imagined the circumstances to be as they were now. 'How come you to this sorry state, my winged friend?'

Jatayu bowed its bald head briefly, as if unable to meet Rama's eyes. It spoke in a broken patois that betrayed how long it had been since it had spoken anything other than Asura dialects. 'Once was Jatayu friend and ally of mortals. Your own ancestors called it friend, as you did just now. But many things changed over time. For too long now, it has been in the service of Ravana, lord of Asuras.'

'Yes,' Rama said slowly. 'I thought it was you I saw in the skies above Mithila, leading your flocks in battle against us.'

'Jatayu admits it. It was at that very battle for Mithila that Jatayu lost its flocks.'

'And suffered these grievous injuries as well?'

'Nay. These were the result of Lanka's burning. When the island-kingdom was torn apart by civil war these months past, following its master's descent into mindless coma.'

'I see.' Then the demoness had spoken truly. Lanka was a spent force, Ravana no longer a power to reckon with. 'And what business brings Jatayu here to Chitrakut hill this summer morning?'

Jatayu hesitated, scratching its claws restlessly. They were still strong and sharp enough to gouge out foot-deep depressions in the ground. 'It wishes to make amends. Jatayu has done much for which it is ashamed. It knows it has not long to live now, with such grievous wounds and its powers enfeebled. In its infirmity and old age, it would like to try and balance its karma.'

'A noble intention, nobly stated,' Rama said. A spark of hope sprang up in his breast. He had feared at first sight that the giant flying creature had been yet another demon sent to plague them in their exile. But now he thought it might be a gift from the other side, from the side that so often stood by and watched without offering a helping hand. A rare gift from the forces of brahman, like the jewelled bow and golden arrow given by Anasuya. 'How may I help Jatayu achieve this noble goal? Tell me, old friend of my forefathers.'

Jatayu's half-blinded eyes betrayed its surprise. 'Rama is kind. Jatayu has done nothing but spy on his people, attack and murder them, and even attempt to attack Rama himself. Yet Rama speaks to Jatayu with respect and love.'

Rama went closer to the bird-beast, ignoring the awful stench of burned and rotting flesh, mingled with the natural unwashed odour of bird. He placed a hand on the edge of the creature's wing, feeling the powerful but damaged muscle beneath the leathery hide. 'Because I feel the same way as you do, old one. Jatayu seeks to atone for its past sins. So does Rama.'

'Rama?' Jatayu cocked its head. 'What sins does Rama

have to atone for? You are a soldier of dharma. Even Ravana feared you for your adherence to dharma. The force of brahman has ever been strong with you, Rama. You are gifted with great prowess because of your adherence to dharma and the path of brahman.'

'Yet Rama has misused that very prowess. I have taken too many lives, my friend. It must stop. I must make amends for the blood I have spilled. That is why I seek only ahimsa now. The code of non-violence.'

Jatayu's pupils flared. Each of those enormous grey-green orbs was as large as Rama's head. They stared at him, and he could see his own image reflected in them. 'That will not be possible, Rama. You cannot embrace ahimsa. Not today. Perhaps some other day, in the distant future. But not today. Nay.'

'What does Jatayu mean? Why do you say these words?'

Jatayu wheezed, releasing a foul breath that told Rama more eloquently than the external wounds how badly the giant vulture-beast was really injured. 'Because Jatayu comes here today to warn Rama and his companions. A terrible storm approaches Chitrakut. Rama and his companions must leave, must return to Ayodhya and seek aid. He must do so at once, for time is scarce. Even as we speak, the storm grows every closer to this peaceful hill. Before nightfall on this very day it will break here like a cloudburst. And if Rama remains here, he will be washed away.'

Rama shook his head. 'I don't understand. What is this storm you speak of? What comes?'

'Supanakha,' Jatayu said. 'The demoness. She has sought the aid of her brothers Khara and Dushana. They are the last survivors of Lanka's army, lost at sea and separated from the rest of the invading armada, and somehow spared by the Brahm-astra. They have inhabited the seaward plains south of Chitrakut, and even now they make their way northwards, seeking you out. Seeking to avenge their sister's humilation and mutilation at your hands. I saw them start out two days past, and it is no more than three days' march from thence to hence. They will arrive here sometime today.' It hung its head briefly. 'Jatayu would have come sooner, but it is ashamed to admit that it took two full days to make up its mind. Only this day, in the still, silent hours before dawn, was Jatayu so assailed by its conscience that it rose out of the tree it slept in and flew north to Chitrakut, seeking to redress its past sins, seeking to warn you, Rama.'

Rama patted the bird's underside reassuringly. 'You did well, old one. You have indeed paid a measure towards the balancing of your karma today. Thank you for your warning.'

Both Sita and Lakshman had come forward on hearing Jatayu's revelations. Lakshman said thoughtfully, 'Two rakshasas, and Supanakha herself. That is all you saw, old one? Just these three?'

Jatayu squawked. 'Would that it were so, Lakshman. If it were merely three rakshasas, Jatayu would not trouble you with warnings. You would dispatch them in mere moments. Nay, it is Jatayu's sorrow to inform you that Khara and Dushana's army of demons is great in number. Not as great as the army you felled at Mithila, surely, but for three kshatriyas alone in this wilderness, they are still too many. You must retreat at once to your city, someplace where you can find your own army to defend yourselves against these rakshasas.'

Rama smiled sadly. 'That is not possible, Jatayu. Rama is in exile. I can go no more to my city or my people to ask their help. Whatever befalls me now, I must face it

alone. Tell me, how great was the number of rakshasas
you saw? How are they armed? What war machines do
they possess?'

'They are armed heavily, and armoured as well. Their
siege machines were lost at sea with their sunken ship.
They do not deem it necessary to build more to confront
three mortal kshatriyas in a thatched hut. But I cannot
describe their numbers in the mortal way. I can only tell
you how great a distance they covered as they marched.
It was—'

'Fourteen thousand rakshasas,' Rama said.

All three of them looked at him. He nodded. 'That is
the number Supanakha named. Do you recall it,
Lakshman?'

'Yes,' Lakshman said slowly. '"Fourteen thousand of
my rakshasa brothers" she called them. Then she was
speaking the truth.'

'About that, as about all else, it would seem,' Rama
said. 'So now we know their numbers. An army of fourteen thousand rakshasas marches to do war with us.'

'What will we do, Rama?' Lakshman asked. 'Shall I
go to Guha and ask him for help? Or—'

'No, Lakshman,' Rama said. 'We shall not ask anyone
for help. Nor shall we go anywhere. This is our home
now, and we shall stay here. If we must go anywhere then
it can only be southwards, further into exile. We can never
turn our faces back towards Ayodhya again, not until our
fourteen years are past. You know these things as well as
I do.'

'Yes, but Rama, the rakshasa army . . . how will we
defend ourselves?'

'We will not. We shall await them and attempt to
parley. Perhaps we can make them see the futility of
violence, as we have learned to see it.'

Lakshman shook his head impatiently. 'And if we cannot convince them? Then what?'

'Then we die.'

19

Supanakha's anger had begun to ebb. The pain in her severed nose and ears had faded somewhat over the past several days. Her brothers had refused to treat the wounds with herbs, as it was against rakshasa custom. A wounded rakshasa must heal its wounds naturally or die. It was the rakshasa way of culling out the sick and old and infirm – and if it meant the loss of the young and wounded as well, so be it. Despite their strenuous objections, she had found some of the herbs she had learned of during her observations of mortals and applied them herself. The exposed flesh still gaped rawly, but the pain had subsided and so had the bleeding. At least she could think for the first time since the shameful encounter.

They were marching through dense forest, the only sound their boots tramping the leafy undergrowth. It was a considerable noise, multiplied fourteen thousand times. The trees they passed beneath had no birds, the woods no animals; all had fled at the sound of their approach, clearing their way from the south-western coast to these Panchvati plains. She marched at the head of the force, alongside her brothers. They were both armoured, as she was, Khara bearing his favourite killing device, an over-sized axe-like weapon with a blade as large as a bull's haunch, and Dushana his legendary mace, as long as a full-grown mortal, and as thick and heavy, with ugly spikes set into its business end. All three of them wore helmets with the shape and insignia of the boar tribe, for that was their clan. Strictly speaking, Supanakha was tiger, but then again, she was also part-yaksi, part-mortal, and the devas knew what else. It was enough that she was their sister, and so she wore the boar clan helmet, though the real reason she had put it on was to conceal her gaping facial wounds. She was sick of everyone staring at them while talking to her or passing by. She had already struck down a half-dozen rakshasas who had been too slow to look away, or had committed the fatal error of making a comment or sniggering when she passed them by.

They were approaching the river, she knew. She could smell it ahead, perhaps two miles, no more. Soon they would be crossing the Godavari and marching up Chitrakut hill. And at Rama's doorstep. She should be glad. She should be feeling exultant right now. Soon they would be ripping apart that flimsy hut and doing much the same to its inhabitants. She would have her vengeance. Both Khara and Dushana had special plans in store for Sita, and after they were done with her she would look a great deal worse than Supanakha. And then it would be Lakshman's turn, for he must pay the price for humiliating her.

Among rakshasas, killing was considered lawful combat, no matter what the circumstances. But mutilation was deemed an insult. The logic was that if you truly had a grouse, you would simply kill the subject of your hatred and be done with it. But to deliberately mutilate or maim someone left the subject less complete, and therefore inferior to his or her fellow rakshasas. There were no crippled rakshasa children, not even those born that way; they were suffocated, drowned or even eaten by their own parents before they could be seen by the rest of the clan. A rakshasa born deformed was considered to have been mutilated by the devas. What had been done to Supanakha was deemed far, far worse than if she had been killed and left as food for vultures. It was this humiliation that had convinced Khara and Dushana to assemble their legions so swiftly for this campaign. Not that they needed much persuading; since their fortuitous survival at sea and their miraculous escape from the Brahm-astra, they were desperate for some opportunity to prove their valour in combat. They could not return to Lanka, or what was left of it, unless they had faced enemies and won a battle at the very least.

This was the first real opportunity, apart from a few minor skirmishes with bandit gangs, and the bear and ape clans that inhabited the southern plains. And what greater glory than to face and defeat the very mortal who had decimated the rest of the Asura armies, and reduced the great Ravana to a slobbering, mindless whelp? The roar that their soldiers had raised when they heard the news was ear-shattering. A chance to kill Rama? Every rakshasa in existence would sign on without hesitation. By rakshasa law, the one who actually killed him would be eligible to claim lordship of all the rakshasa clans. For Rama had defeated their lord, and by doing so was himself eligible to take Ravana's place. So by killing Rama now, any rakshasa would be able to crown himself lord of rakshasas. Every one of these fourteen thousand bloodthirsty brutes to her rear had visions of lordship filling their minuscule brains at this instant. It was a powerful motivator, more effective than the whips of kumbha-rakshasas or the commands of their leaders. Once the fray began, it would be hard to keep any of these rakshasas from rushing at Rama to stake his claim.

Which was why Supanakha had kept her own misgivings to herself. Now, as they approached the river and Dushana sent an order rippling down the line to halt, she felt even more uneasy. She was beginning to wish that she had done as she had first been inclined; had she retreated into the forest for a while to heal from her wounds and heal her wounded heart as well, she would have arrived at a different solution. Instead, she had rushed straight to Khara's lair and spilled out the whole sordid tale, weeping like any spurned mortal woman. She regretted that now. It had been one more humiliation to add to the list.

But the time for second thoughts was long past. They were at the Godavari now. She caught her breath as they emerged from the canopy of trees on to the open bank of the river. It was mid-afternoon, almost the same hour as the one in which she had tricked Sita into following her into the woods. Dushana strode away, shouting orders to line up alongside the riverbank. Rakshasas did not march in particularly neat formations – neatness of any kind was antithetical to their nature – but they could stand in reasonable order on a riverbank, or against a stone wall.

They swarmed out of the trees in their thousands, filling the Godavari's southern bank all the way to the treeline. Their armour caught the afternoon sunlight and gleamed, sending dazzling reflections that criss-crossed the far side of the river like beams of light penetrating the shadows of the thicket.

Supanakha stood on a high rock with Khara as Dushana gave the order to fell tree trunks. The plan was to build a pontoon bridge across the river. The Godavari was not very wide, barely twenty yards across at this point, and while it flowed fairly rapidly, it was not the roaring deluge of spring or the swollen overflow of the monsoons. There were any number of oaks and walnuts in the south woods that would span that length. Khara estimated aloud, for Supanakha's benefit, that it would take no more than an hour or two to fell and trim the trunks and hoist them across the river. A couple of hours and a couple of dozen casualties. For rakshasas, while not terrified of the Godavari, still bore a deep-rooted aversion to all fresh flowing water. Once in that river, every one of these hulking killing machines was about as powerful as a flailing kitten.

She raised her eyes, tilting her helmet just so to avoid getting sunlight in her eyes. It wasn't hard. Already the sun was falling behind them. It was at most two hours to sundown, maybe less. She sniffed and scanned the north slope. It was too thickly wooded, but she found the promontory ridge protruding out from the top of the hill. She had watched Rama come there often, and just as often she had clung to trees and shadows on that side of the river, watching as he had performed his riverside rituals. She sighed involuntarily, remembering how hopeful she had felt then, how full of dreams and ambitions – and lust.

Khara snarled, attracting her attention. She came out of her reverie and looked at him, scowling. 'What?'

He snorted. 'I am finding no sport in this fight. This Rama of yours. How can he possibly face a force of this size?' He spat into the river. 'It will be like slaughtering babes in their beds.'

'Are you having second thoughts, brother?'

He laughed, grunting noisily. On the bank below, Khara paused and glanced up suspiciously before continuing to yell orders at the nearest men. 'What do you take me for, sister?'

'A murderer of children and an eater of their innards, usually while they're still alive. Or is that only your hobby?' she purred at him.

He shrugged off her attempt at provocation. 'Shut up, Supanakha. I am trying to think of a way to make this honourable.'

'Honourable? Why does it have to be honourable?' But she listened curiously.

'What achievement will I boast of afterwards? Slaying three mortals? There's almost not a rakshasa there,' he swept his hand across the riverbank, 'who won't claim to have done as much.'

'They may have killed brahmins and sadhus. Tapasvis intent on praying to their devas in their ashrams, brahmacharyas barely old enough to tie their own pig-tails. These are kshatriyas, brother. Not just any kshatriyas. The champions of Bhayanak-van. Slayers of Tataka and her demon hordes.'

'Invokers of the Brahm-astra. Challengers of Parsurama. Yes, yes, I know, I know.' He held up a hand. 'But that was all before, when they still possessed the shakti of the maha-mantras given by the brahmarishi-who-was-once-a-warrior. Now they are ordinary mortals again, denuded of all power, abilities, even their own mortal armies and their walled fortress-city.' He snorted, spewing fluids. 'Ayodhya the Unconquerable. Undefeated. Unbesieged. Uninvaded.' He gestured at the wild overgrown hillside across the river. 'Where is their Ayodhya now? Where are their akshohini? Their war elephants? Or even their maha-shakti? They have nothing. They are just mortals with steel in their fists. And never mind fourteen thousand; fourteen of my men are too many to bring down three mortal kshatriyas, no matter who they are or what they may have done before.'

Supanakha smiled sweetly. She had glimpsed a way to appease her own flickering conscience as well as satisfy Khara's tumescent rakshasa ego. 'Would you care to wager on that?'

He turned to her, his burnished helmet flashing dazzling light into her eyes. 'What?'

She purred softly, enticing and taunting at the same time. 'A wager. I say that fourteen of your rakshasas, your finest champions even, cannot stalk and kill Rama. What say you?'

'I say you must be madder than I thought, sister, or richer than I knew! What do you offer in wager?'

She leaned over and whispered into his ear. The light in his eyes almost matched the gleam of his helmet. 'Sister Supanakha,' he said, grinning wide enough to reveal even his rearmost bone-breaker teeth, 'you have yourself a wager.'

He turned and shouted to Dushana to pick out fourteen of the best assassins in their ranks.

Supanakha raised her eyes to the hilltop once more. *Now, my proud beloved, we will see if you are as good a warrior as you are a husband and a brother.*

Lakshman came sprinting from the promontory. Rama and Sita were sitting in the grassy field, feeding a doe and two infant deer leaves out of their palms. The deer looked up nonchalantly as Lakshman ran up.

'They are at the river, Rama. From the way they are felling trees, it's clear they mean to breach it. I think they will be across before sundown.'

Rama nodded. 'Good.' He continued feeding the deer. The infants stumbled over each other's feet in their eagerness to get at the leaves, which crunched in their jaws briefly before disappearing.

Lakshman stared at him. 'Good? Is that all you have to say? It's an army, Rama. A very well-trained one. Supanakha was there at the fore with her brothers; they wear the boar clan sigil. If you listen you can just hear the roaring of their hordes.'

Sita raised her head curiously. The sound of distant roaring was audible, like a far-off waterfall.

'Rama, what would you have me do? Shall I choose a vantage spot in the trees across the river and start picking them off?'

'How many would you kill, Lakshman? Ten? Twenty? A hundred? Even two hundred? It would hardly make a difference, my brother.'

'Then what is your plan? Will you take your jewelled bow and golden arrow? The gifts Anasuya gave you? If you use them, you can slay them from right up here, from the top of the hill.' He pointed back at the promontory. 'She said the arrow could kill any number of targets at any distance. All you have to do is will it, and the entire force will be destroyed. It will be like unleashing the Brahm-astra at Mithila.'

Rama shook his head. 'Lakshman, I will not use the bow and arrow that Anasuya gave me.' One of the little deer also shook his head, as if in imitation.

'But she said you were to use them to defend yourself in such an eventuality. That is why she gave them to you.'

'Possibly. But she also gave us all express instructions not to invoke any violence. Not to draw first blood. Do you remember that as well?' Rama glanced up at Lakshman as he asked the question.

Lakshman sighed, sinking to his knees in the grass. 'Yes, of course I remember. But I did not simply attack someone unprovoked. That she-devil meant to destroy us all. To kill Sita. To seduce you. I said she would come back if we spared her, and I was right. She has come back. With an army to destroy us!'

Rama shook his head. 'The army would not have come if we hadn't hurt her. We took a vow of non-violence. You broke it. That is what led to this pass.'

Lakshman held his head in his hands. 'All right. If you wish to blame me, then blame me. I did it. Instead of releasing the demoness unharmed, I cut her nose and ears off. But it was *I* that did that, Rama. Not you, nor Sita. You are still free to do your dharma. Protect yourself, protect your wife, our home. If need be, I will defend my own self.'

Rama's hands were empty of leaves. He showed his palms to the deer, who licked both eagerly. He turned to Lakshman. 'If need be, I will defend us all, Lakshman. It's quite likely I will have to do just that before this day is over. If so, then so be it. I am not pleased to have to take up arms again, but I cannot simply let us be slaughtered by rakshasas either.'

Lakshman smiled in relief, his teeth flashing white in his dark, sunburned face. 'Then you will use the Bow of Vishnu and the Arrow of Brahma!'

'No.'

Lakshman's smile faded. 'But you just said you will fight.'

'With my usual weapons, yes. With all the skills at my command. Using all the knowledge and talent and strength I possess, of course. But no more celestial weapons. No more extermination from afar. That is too potent a shakti. It breeds a lust for power that is more dangerous than violence itself. No, I will fight with my own bare hands if I have to, but I will fight as a mortal man. As a kshatriya.'

'Against fourteen thousand rakshasas? Rama, it is impossible.'

Rama nodded. 'Possibly. If that is my karma, then I will see it through to the end.'

'And Sita? Will you let her die too? Or be taken as a rakshasa slave? You know how they treat mortal women who are taken as spoils of war. And Supanakha must have a special hell in store for her. As also for me. Will you let me die too, bhai?'

Rama stood up. Lakshman stood too, facing Rama head on.

'No, Lakshman. I do not believe that any of us will die. I cannot swear to it, for which man knows what his future truly holds, but I will only say this: that is not the future I have planned for us.'

Lakshman stared uncertainly. 'Then what is it you have planned? What do you intend to do?'

'Survive,' Rama said.

He walked away from Lakshman, in the direction of the hut.

20

The sun was at the western horizon when they breached the river. Khara had seethed with impatience all the while. He had asked repeatedly if there were any who could swim across the river. After the fourth or fifth time, Dushana had suggested softly that if he kept repeating that question, the men would grow insolent and ask their general whether *he* could swim. That shut Khara up. He had waited while the whole operation dragged on. Supanakha enjoyed his irritation. She knew that his impatience was to win the wager. He wanted the prize she had offered him. And he believed it was his for the taking. All he had to do was send his assassins across and they would do the job, click-click-snap, as easy as a pisaca clacking its mandibles.

As the last log was put into place, a fresh roar went up from the assembled rakshasas. They had been quiet the past hour, waiting with as much impatience as their general. Everyone had been told by now about the special mission on which the hand-picked assassins were being sent. They were disgruntled about it. Many felt it was unfairly depriving the rest of them the opportunity to be the first to sup on the legendary Rama's innards. But discipline and a lust for battle kept them in check. Now that the bridge was made, they were excited again, eager to have their share of the blood-letting. *Not much blood to let, though,* Supanakha thought. *And if my suspicions are right, then no mortal blood at all.*

Khara gave the order for the assassins to cross. They sprinted across the bridge, the logs shifting and rolling beneath their weight but holding quite well. It had taken about a dozen rakshasa lives to get the logs that secure. The first team had failed to tie their vines tightly enough and had had their throats torn out and been pushed backwards into the river. After that, the bridge-building had gone much better.

The fourteen rakshasas reached the far bank and disappeared into the shadows of the woods. Supanakha glimpsed a reflection or two off their armour as they made their way up the slope, each taking a different route, all vying for the honour of reaching their intended target first.

Beside her, Khara smiled and snorted noisily, spewing phlegm. 'Ready to lose your wager, sister dear?'

She smiled her best catty smile at him. 'Ready to lose fourteen rakshasas?'

He laughed at her wit, continuing to spew noisily.

She turned away, wrinkling her face in disgust. She almost wished that Rama would kill all his assassins. Almost. But not quite. Now that the time had come, she found she wanted vengeance after all.

Vengeance and Sita. She had plans for that woman who had blocked her dreams. Very painful, long-drawn-out plans.

Rama spied the first assassin when he was still a hundred yards from the hut.

He stood up and stepped out of the shade of their thatched forecourt. He was unarmed.

'There is no point hiding,' he called out. 'I see you. Come forward and you will not be harmed. I only wish to speak with you.'

There was no response.

Rama took another few steps towards the field. He knew the rakshasa was hiding just behind a small rise in the grass. 'I have a message for you to take to your leader.'

The rakshasa remained where he was.

Rama walked out to him, stopping when he was a dozen yards away. 'Go back to your commander. Tell him that Rama does not wish to fight him or his army. Tell him to take his forces and go and I will not pursue him or take offence at his coming here. Carry this message, and you can prevent this war.'

In response, the rakshasa rose from his hiding place and sprang at Rama, a spear raised. He had taken perhaps three steps, the spear about to launch, when an arrow struck him in the throat, halting him dead in his tracks. He spun around, blood gurgling from his throat, and fell face down in the grass. His spear pitched forward and stuck, quivering, a yard from Rama.

Rama glanced back. He could see Lakshman and Sita by the wall of the hut, their bows redrawn and ready to fire again. He sighed and nodded.

This was going to be hard.

He glanced in the direction of the woods. He could sense the other assassins watching him, weighing how best to cover that sizeable expanse of open field without being cut down. He decided to make it easier for them.

He began walking towards the treeline. Behind him, he heard Lakshman call out. He ignored the shout and walked on. He knew what Lakshman was trying to say. He was worried that Rama would walk out of arrow range.

Rama stopped fifty yards short of the treeline.

'I do not wish you harm,' he said. 'You can see I am unarmed. If you will speak with me, I will have words with you. Come out and show yourselves.'

A muffled grunt was the only answer. Two javelins and one deftly aimed arrow flew towards him. The javelins fell an inch short and two inches long, but the arrow flew straight towards his heart. He spun around, moving into its line of flight. When he had completed a full circle, the arrow was clutched in his fist. He held it up for them to see, then opened his hand and dropped it on the grass.

'Take this message to your commander. Rama refuses to fight. Go home in peace and you will not be harmed.'

And he turned his back on the woods and began walking towards the hut again. He prayed silently as he took one step, then two, then three, hoping beyond hope . . .

But the attack came as swiftly as the javelins and the arrow. Nine of them, all sprinting across the field like Ayodhyan Vajra kshatriyas in a short-race, all eager to reach him first and have pride of kill, all with blades drawn ready to take him at close quarters.

He turned and ran towards them.

Three of them grunted with surprise, and slowed. The rest continued regardless. He leapt as two of them failed to resist the temptation and threw their blades. The sharpened steel flew past him, glinting coldly in the evening sunlight, slicing the air where he had stood a moment ago. He landed on the chest of one rakshasa, crushing his windpipe, used him as a launching pad, somersaulted in mid-air, knocked another's face crooked, breaking his neck, struck a third on the septum with his heel, knocking him unconscious, and landed with both feet on a fourth one, smashing his knife into his own chest. Then he rolled across the grass, snatched up a sword in passing, cut another rakshasa's legs from under him, and locked swords with a sixth for two, three slashes before swiping the blade across the demon's face, drawing a howl of outrage.

When he turned to face the last three, they were already fallen, arrows in their throats. More arrows came swishing around him, dropping the others who were able, or foolish enough, to attempt to rise again.

Ten down. Four to go.

He turned and saw Lakshman and Sita walking out of the shadow of the hut, heading towards him. He was already at the limit of their arrow range.

Behind them, he saw the shapes rise from over the lip of the promontory, sprinting towards Sita and Lakshman.

'Lakshman!' he cried, snatching up a javelin and running forward with it. He stopped abruptly, using the balls of his feet to halt, as if on the tip of a precipice, and released the missile. The javelin flew true to its target, striking an assassin who was about to loose an arrow at Sita. She had turned and dropped to her knee by then, firing off two quick bolts. Lakshman took the last rakshasa.

They met in the centre of the field. Sita seemed a little wan and shaken, but otherwise all right.

'Well,' Lakshman said impassively. 'So much for your parley.'

Rama shook his head. 'This wasn't the parley. I was just trying to avoid taking their lives. Now we must go to the river and address their general. That's our last hope.'

Lakshman's eyes flashed but his voice was measured. 'And if he also replies the way his assassins did?'

Rama sighed. 'Then we defend ourselves as best we can.'

Lakshman hesitated as Rama began to turn away. 'Rama . . .'

'Yes?'

'At least carry Anasuya's weapons. Show them to Khara and Dushana and Supanakha. They know the power of celestial weaponry. Maybe showing them will convince them that they cannot win against you.'

'I can't do that unless I'm really prepared to use the weapons, Lakshman. You know that. No, we'll either win this fight with what we have, or . . .' He shrugged. 'Or we'll try to stop it.'

Lakshman sighed and followed him.

Khara peered across the river curiously. 'Ah, I think one returns now.'

His soldiers had seen the shadow moving among the trees as well. They sent up a rousing cheer, calling out lewd comments in the rakshasa dialect. The cheer died out abruptly as they saw the figure emerging from the trees on the far bank.

Supanakha started, her heart pounding within her ribcage as she recognised Rama's dark, almost bluish skin and aquiline features even across the breadth of the river. Beside her, Khara swore a curse on his mother's corpse, and spat. 'What is he doing there, still alive? How did he get past my assassins?'

'He killed them, brother. That's how.'

Khara snorted. 'Impossible! Those were the best of my best. If I sent them into Lanka to assassinate Ravana, they would not fail. How could a puny mortal best them?'

Supanakha replied quietly: 'Listen and learn, brother. He speaks now.'

Khara made another gruntlike sound but stayed silent. So did the army. Supanakha guessed they were too shocked at the sight of the very man they had come to kill standing calmly across the river, facing all fourteen thousand of them as if he were simply come to deliver a speech to an assembly. *And in a sense, he has*, she thought with an excitement bordering on glee.

Rama called out above the sound of the river. 'Generals Khara and Dushana, I am Rama Chandra of Ayodhya. My brother and my wife and I are here in exile, living in Chitrakut. We live here in peace, causing no harm to anyone. What happened with your sister was a mistake. She attempted to kill my wife, and my brother . . . he could not stay his hand. But we do not wish to kill. That is why he mutilated her but spared her life. She did what she did because she wishes to be my wife. That is not possible. I am already happily wed. I gently ask Supanakha to forgo this matter and end this feud here and now. I forgive her for trying to harm my wife, and I ask her forgiveness for the hurt my brother caused her as well. I request you all, in all humility, go back to where you came from. Leave us in peace.'

In the silence that followed, Supanakha heard only two sounds: Khara gnashing his teeth and the pounding of her own heart. She felt it would burst at any instant at the rate it was pumping blood.

Khara snarled loudly enough to be heard across the river – and by all his soldiers. 'Where are my rakshasas?' he shouted hoarsely. 'I sent fourteen across to you. Where are they now?'

Rama bent his head regretfully. 'I asked them to leave in peace as I am asking you now. They would not listen. I hope you will be wise enough to do so.'

Khara snorted, his effluents spraying the soldiers below

the rock on which he stood. He leapt down from the rock, landing on the riverbank. His arms struck several of his own soldiers, knocking them to the ground. He lunged at the nearest tree, a sala. Grasping it around the trunk, he exerted his powerful arms and back. Groaning, it began to break free of the loose alluvial soil. Khara roared as it tore free, mud-sodden roots hanging from the bottom. He ran to the edge of the river, tree in his arms, and flung it with a great effort. It flew across the river in a sharp arc and landed on the far side. Rama leapt aside when he saw it coming, but it struck his foot as he moved and knocked him down.

Slowly a great blood-chilling cry rose from the throats of the assembled rakshasas.

As Rama rose to his feet unsteadily on the north bank, Khara roared out like an enraged lion, 'When we wear our armour and pick up our blades, mortal, we do not return home without having conquered. Pick up your sword and fight like a kshatriya now. Or die like a brahmin. But the only peace you will have from us is the peace of death when we send you to the netherworld, where even Yama-dev will not be able to tell from your fragments whether you were once mortal, Asura or something in between!'

And he ran forward, leaping on to the log-bridge, and cried out to the assembled rakshasas: 'To me! To me! To war!'

'To war!' they replied, and rushed for the bridge, following their commander.

21

Sita watched the rakshasas swarming the bridge. Their exultant charge was soon cut short. The bridge was only wide enough for them to cross one at a time, and since they were clumsy and large-bodied, the going was not as steady as on flat land. Khara made it across easily enough, stumbling only once, but his legions struggled and fell, too eager, too clumsy, too quick. Several were washed away downriver, screaming before they sank like stones and were rolled away. Those behind them proceeded with more caution but were pushed by the ones waiting their turn. Dushana saw the chaos and ran about shouting orders. He succeeded in restoring some discipline to the crossing and it proceeded more regularly. Yet even with these obstacles, several dozen rakshasas were already across, and all would cross in another hour or two.

She heard arrows singing through the air above her as Lakshman fired nonstop. His aim was lethal. On the river-bank Rama stood and fought off those that made it through the onslaught of Lakshman's arrows. Already five rakshasas lay dead around him, and seven or eight more had been killed by Lakshman. But as Rama said earlier, how many could they kill, just the two of them? A hundred? Two hundred? Five hundred? Even at Bhayanak-van, she knew, there had been no more than that number, give or take a hundred. And they had been strengthened by the maha-mantras then, as well as accompanied by Brahmarishi Vishwamitra's invocations. Here they had only their wits and their weapons, and Sita feared . . . no, she *knew* . . . it would not be enough.

A decision reached, she turned and sprinted up the hill, climbing as fast as her legs would take her. It was good she did not wait a moment longer, because then she would have seen Rama receive his first wound, a slashing cut across the left bicep.

Lakshman fired arrows faster than he had ever fired before, but still he knew it was not fast enough. Already he had seen Rama cut four times . . . no, five now . . . and yet there were hardly a few dozen rakshasa corpses on the north bank. The narrow crossing-bridge was an unexpected ally, slowing down the progress of the rest of the army. But already those following had learned from watching their earlier comrades, and none were falling into the river any more. He watched as the line of crossing rakshasas was given a barked command by Dushana and they began sprinting across the log-bridge. Lakshman speeded up his shooting, trying to keep up with the increase in pace of those crossing, but it cost him his aim. He saw two of his arrows inflict mere flesh wounds, the rakshasas roaring with pain but stumbling on towards Rama. Also, his supply of arrows, while yet plentiful, was not inexhaustible, unlike the magically refilled quiver in the Bhayanak-van battle. In a little while he would have to drop the bow and arrow, grab his sword, and leap down from this tree, joining Rama on the bank below. Then they would be reduced to fighting back to back. And how long could that go on? *How many rakshasas are our lives worth?* It sounded like a bad joke.

He forced back the tears that threatened to obscure his vision and put every ounce of skill and talent he had into his shooting. His hands blurred as the cord took, tautened and released arrow after arrow, dropping rakshasas on the bank below until those behind had to clamber over the corpses to get to Rama.

And yet they kept on coming, like an ocean. Wave after wave of inhuman hatred and rage.

Rama did not feel the wounds on his body, but he knew he was being cut too often. He did not fear injury or pain. He only dreaded being hamstrung too badly to continue fighting. The pile of rakshasas around him was three deep, forming a natural defensive circle. But the ones clambering over those bodies had the advantage of extra height, in addition to their natural tallness, and their heavily downslashing weapons were growing too difficult for him to hold back. He would have to fall back in a moment, to the edge of the trees, and then make his way uphill slowly, fighting every step of the way. He had expected that. Had been prepared to fight them all the way until his back was to the wall of his hut. If that was what lay in store for him, he would accept it.

Even through the haze of combat, he sensed the sky darken. The snouts of rakshasas pressing him in were shadowed suddenly, their feral eyes gleaming in the dimness. He could not chance a sideways look, but he could tell that the sun was low in the sky, almost at the horizon. But not yet set. Then he remembered that morning, when a similar shadow had fallen upon him, and a surge of hope sprang to his heart.

A scree came from above, piercing through the roar of battle and the shouts of rakshasas clamouring for their chance to fight Rama.

A howl of outrage rose from the collective throats of the rakshasas on the far bank and on the bridge. Those on the north bank made the fatal mistake of looking back to see what ailed their comrades, and it was the last sight they saw. Lakshman's arrows and Rama's flashing sword cut down the dozen or so rakshasas before they had a chance to raise their weapons.

Only then did Rama get an opportunity to raise his head and look up, as all the rakshasas were doing.

When he did, a smile came to his face. He wiped at his eyes, smearing more blood and rakshasa offal across his forehead. 'Jatayu,' he said softly. 'Welcome back, old one.'

Jatayu cried out again, wheeling over the Godavari, trying to make sure it timed its descent exactly. It was important it made no errors. It had taken a long time finding a suitable boulder, and twice as long getting airborne with the damn thing clutched in its claws. Every flap of its wings had felt as if it would be the last. When the Godavari came into view, it felt so relieved, it could have fallen into the river itself, going down with the boulder. Ah, that would be bliss. To die doing such a good deed. But alas, it had much more to do to redress its past wrongs. Much more karma to balance.

It settled for swooping as low as it could above the narrow log-bridge. From this height, the bridge looked like a stick of straw placed over a little stream.

Jatayu released the boulder, feeling one of its claws snap off with a wrenching pain as it caught on a sharp edge. It was jerked sideways, losing its balance, and began to wheel around in a spiral. It took it several heart-stopping seconds to regain control of its flight and catch a current sufficiently strong to lift it high, high above the arrows that the rakshasas on the south bank were sending towards it. They fell too low to hurt Jatayu.

Then again, Jatayu didn't need to be struck by any arrows to die. It knew it was dying anyway.

Supanakha saw the boulder fall from the clutches of the man-vulture and leapt backwards to safety. She had only just reached the branch of the nearest tree, clinging to it with all four claws, when the enormous rock struck the bridge. The double row of logs lashed together were hit squarely in the middle, at their weakest point. The rock ploughed through them, snapping them like twigs. It crushed several rakshasas who were directly beneath it as well, the impact throwing those who were also on the bridge into the flowing river. The bridge sank into the water, the wood snapping and cracking as it broke free, and then there was just so much flotsam and shards floating downriver, along with about a hundred of Supanakha's brethren.

She watched the mayhem from her vantage point, her eyes dancing with glee. Khara was beside himself with rage, yelling curses at the flying beast above, now rising well out of range of the puny arrows that Dushana and his soldiers were firing up at it. Ah, what a stroke of genius. It would take the rakshasas another two hours to rebuild the bridge, and she would wager everything she had that if and when they did, the jatayu would be back, carrying another boulder.

She wished Khara had had the guts to cross the bridge himself, as he had started to do. But the oversized fool had egged his soldiers on, while falling back himself, moving aside to let the rank and file cross. Now he was still on this side of the river, yelling himself blue in the face without any effect.

She looked across the river and her heart sank. Rama! He was so covered in blood, he looked red. She hoped it wasn't all his blood, but knew better. She had watched the way he had stood his ground, giving no quarter and taking none. He must have a dozen wounds, some deeper than others. She watched him ignore the hail of arrows that Dushana was ordering his soldiers to fire, the piled corpses of the rakshasas he had slain giving him suffi-cient cover to stand and recover his strength. He swiped at his face, smearing more blood across his brow instead of clearing it.

She licked her chops. Suddenly she wanted Rama more than she had ever wanted him before.

Rama and Lakshman sat beneath the banyan tree in which Lakshman had been ensconced. They were both exhausted. Lakshman had taken an arrow to the thigh too, a lucky shot or perhaps a very good one. They sat with their backs to the trunk, lines of sweat running down Lakshman's body, lines of sweat and blood down Rama's.

'They will find a way across eventually,' Lakshman said finally. 'They can build three bridges at once instead of one. Or five. Or ten. They have enough numbers to do it. Jatayu will not be able to stop them all at once. One way or another, they will get across.'

'Yes,' Rama said.

'And once they have crossed in large enough numbers, they need not come at us in ones and twos as they are forced to do now because of the bridge. They will regroup on this bank, then launch an assault on a wider front, surrounding us completely. We cannot fight on all sides at once, even if we stand back to back.'

'Yes,' Rama said.

'And once they have us surrounded, it is only a matter

of time. How many wounds can we sustain and still fight on? How many slashes can we deflect? How many corpses . . .' Lakshman trailed off, as if he had lost the thread of his argument.

'Yes,' Rama said again, wearily.

Lakshman rose to his feet. 'Rama.'

'Yes,' Rama said. He did not look up.

Lakshman reached down and shook Rama's shoulder. 'Bhai.'

Rama looked up. He saw only Lakshman's arm and his face. Lakshman was looking uphill.

Rama heard a sound and was on his feet in an instant, sword in hand. He gazed up the path, peering through the lengthening shadows. The sun was at the horizon, the air suffused with the golden glow that presaged the purple glamour of dusk in Chitrakut.

He saw figures moving through the trees, coming down the pathway. He gestured to Lakshman, who was already setting an arrow to his bow in readiness.

Rama looked around for Sita, remembered that Lakshman had told him she had left soon after the crossing began, running uphill, and bit back an exclamation. He prayed that these rakshasas, however they had managed to get across the river, had not stopped to check the hut.

The first of the figures stepped into view. This time Rama spoke the exclamation that had leapt to his tongue just a moment ago. Lakshman lowered his bow.

Somashrava strode forward, his white dhoti tied at mid-thigh in the wrestler's fashion. He carried a bow and a quiver. Following on his heels came a line of men and women, all armed with bows and quivers, several carrying swords and other weapons. None of them was young, and they were a motley bunch. Their clothes were as ragged and worn as their faces, their weapons cracked and rusted, and their bearing unlike any kshatriyas either Rama or Lakshman had seen before. But their faces were well fed, if lean from exertion and activity, and their eyes were sharp and alert.

Somashrava embraced Rama warmly, uncaring of his blood-smeared body. 'Rama,' he said. 'It is good to see you again. And you, Lakshman,' he said, embracing Lakshman too.

'And you as well, Somashrava,' Rama replied. 'But what does this mean?'

Somashrava gestured upwards. 'Our mutual friend from the skies came this morning. It spoke to Sage Agastya and told him of your plight. I entreated the sage to let me come to your aid. We marched all day without rest, and I feared we would be too late. But we saw the jatayu drop the rock on the bridge as we reached the crest of Chitrakut hill, and we saw how bravely you two fought. Truly, Rama, all that they say about you is too little praise. You fight like all the great heroes of legend combined into one man.'

Rama shrugged off the compliments. 'Who are your companions, Somashrava? They do not look like brahmacharyas.'

Somashrava gestured to the others to come forward. They came slowly, reluctantly, as if shy of making Rama's acquaintance. He noticed the way none of them would meet his gaze. Strange. And one or two of them even looked vaguely familiar. If he did not know them personally, he was sure he knew their type. Yes. As the last one stepped into view, Rama knew beyond doubt who these people were.

'These are friends of my late father and my late brother. All good men and women. All of them have suffered losses to the demons of this region. All share one common goal. To see every last Asura in this part of the world exterminated or driven away for good. It is no mere coincidence that they were passing by the ashram at almost the same time that Jatayu brought its message. For all things serve Brahma's purpose.'

'Yes,' said the last man, sauntering forward with a sardonic smile on his face. Rama heard Lakshman's sharp intake of breath as he recognised the man as well. 'Even such things as this, a partnership of princess and poachers. Strange, is it not, Rajkumar Rama?'

And the man that Rama knew as Bearface bowed with a flourish, his mutilated face split in a wide grin.

22

Before either Rama or Lakshman could say a word, the sound of another pair of feet came to them. Sita burst into sight, her hair wild and windblown, her manner agitated.

She blinked in surprise at the gathering but ran straight to Rama. She clutched his hand. 'Rama, they are gone.'

He frowned. 'Sita. What—'

'The Bow of Vishnu, the Arrow of Brahma. They are not in the place where they were kept. They have vanished.'

'Why were you seeking them?'

She hesitated. 'Watching you fight . . . I could not bear it. If we are to die defending ourselves against the rakshasas of Chitrakut, surely we can use the bow and the arrow as well, can we not? I was going to fetch them and urge you to use them. I was the one who held you to Anasuya's warning the strictest, so it's only right that I should be the one to release you of that hold. But I could not find them, Rama. They're gone!'

Rama shook his head. 'Yes, I know. Anasuya told me they would. She spoke to me in my mind besides the words she spoke to us aloud. She told me that the celestial weapons were not meant to be used just for our personal defence but to uphold dharma in a righteous fight. They will return to me when that time comes. I did not wish to tell you or Lakshman earlier because I knew you both believed that we could not fight the rakshasas without those weapons. They were your last hope. I could not bear to take that from you.'

She stared at him in the fading daylight. 'But then, how will we—' She stopped and looked around, remembering the crowd surrounding them. 'Who are these people? Somashrava? You, here?'

'Yes, my lady,' he said gravely. Briefly he explained for her benefit how he had come to be here. 'There are more of us gathering. We have sent word for all to assemble on this north bank of the Godavari. We will make our stand here with Rama and Lakshman and yourself, rajkumari.'

Sita turned to Rama. He nodded. 'You see now? We thought it was hopeless. But it isn't. Where there was one, there were three. And where there are three, now there are many. And more will come. We will stand together and fight, my love. We will fight them with all our wit and skill and strength. And in the end, we will triumph.'

Bearface stepped forward. 'Moving words, my lady. And sound ones. I can't say as your husband and I have met on friendly terms before. But this here fight is our fight as well. We have long waged war against the demons of this region; even before Ravana's troops came, there were always demons here. Viradha, whom I am told you killed, was one of them. But never have we dared to risk open war with them.' He gestured at the river. 'What we saw while coming downhill earlier, that kind of fighting, alone against that multitude . . .' He shook his head. 'Never have I seen the likes of it. We are not all Ayodhyans. Not even fit to call ourselves Aryas, most of us. Back in the civilised world we would be considered brigands, outlaws, poachers, thieves, vagrants. But here we are all human. Like yourselves. And this has now become a war between mortals and demons. Because as you saw, they will not rest until they have wiped us out. And so we cannot rest until they are all wiped out. If you will have us, my lord Rama, I will be proud to fight beside you. I do not speak for these other men, for we consider ourselves free men and servants of nobody, not even princes of Ayodhya, begging your pardon. But I think they too will be inclined to help balance the odds in this battle.'

He held out his hand in a kshatriya's greeting. Rama looked at it, then at Sita and Lakshman. Somashrava watched anxiously. Rama took the hand, clasping it close to his chest and clapping his other hand over the other man's fist. Bearface did the same. A ragged cheer rose from the rest of the group. One by one they came forward to greet Rama and introduce themselves. Another small group of four arrived in the interim and were brought up to speed.

A scree from overhead interrupted them all.

Rama went out to the riverbank and looked up. A few arrows began flying at once, but they were half-heartedly aimed. The destruction of the bridge had shocked and disheartened the rakshasas. He saw Jatayu flying overhead. The man-vulture pointed upriver with its winged arm, then turned slowly, and pointed downriver as well. Rama understood.

He turned back to the ragged gathering of allies. 'The enemy has split into groups. Upriver as well as down. They will be building more bridges and attempting to cross again.' He explained to them what Lakshman had been arguing earlier. 'If we stay here, sooner or later we will be overwhelmed.' He paused, looking at Bearface. 'Unless you think your numbers will match theirs?'

Bearface snorted. 'Nowhere near, friend. At most we

can expect two or three hundred. And that includes women and children. Although you can count almost everyone old enough to walk as a fighter.'

Rama nodded. He wasn't surprised. 'Then we have only one chance of winning this war.'

'What's that?' Bearface asked with interest.

Rama looked around at the expectant faces of the outlaws, at the shining face of Somashrava, so eager to do right, at Sita and at Lakshman. 'You understand that this war may not be ended in a day, or a week, or even a year? I cannot promise you how long it will take. All I can promise is that it will end some day, and we will win it in the end. If you can stand strong for that long, then we have a chance. If you expect to win every skirmish, every battle, then you may as well leave now.'

Bearface hawked and spat to one side. A rakshasa body happened to come in the way of his oral missile. 'Friend Rama, we have been fighting all our lives. For some of us, who are older, the Last Asura War never truly ended; it is still going on. That is why we have no truck with your cities and your civilised rules. We know that those are only temporary. This enmity between mortals and Asuras? This is for ever! We have fought all our lives; why should we be afraid of a few years more? Right, folks?'

'Aye,' they said in unison.

Rama nodded, pleased. 'Good. Then listen to me carefully. If we are to thwart the enemy's attempts today, we must do the opposite of what he expects.'

'Which is?' Lakshman asked eagerly.

Rama glanced back over his shoulder at the river, lit by the last rays of the setting sun. 'He is trying to cross to this side, to attack us. We must go across the river, outflank him and attack from behind.'

Utter silence met his announcement. He cleared his

throat and went on, 'We will not break his back, of course. But if we strike hard and then melt away into the darkness, then strike again at another place and disappear again . . . we will draw the rakshasas back the way they came. When they think we are on that side, we—'

'Circle round and attack them on this side, and keep outflanking them until they don't know where we are and where we'll strike next. That's classic Vajra strategy.' The voice that spoke these words came from the back of the group, where the shadows were too heavy now for even Rama to see clearly.

'That they are,' Rama admitted. 'Do you have a problem with that?'

The speaker shook his head. 'Nay,' he said. 'I was once a Vajra kshatriya. It is a good plan.'

A sound attracted their attention. A man came crashing through the undergrowth. He stopped short at the sight of Bearface, addressing his words alternately to the outlaw leader and to Rama, at whom he glanced with fearful admiration. 'Their second bridge is ready,' he said breathlessly. 'They are about to cross soon. What are our plans? Stand and fight? Or flee?'

Bearface looked at Rama, then at the rest of the group that surrounded them, waiting anxiously.

'We do as Rama orders,' Bearface said at last. 'We cross the river and strike them from behind.'

The man's face fell. 'Cross . . . the river?'

Bearface waved to one of his associates. 'Dharu, explain the plan to him. Get the word out. We have to move quickly, or they'll all be on this bank before we're on that one.'

'How do we cross?' Lakshman asked Rama quietly as the others began shooting last-minute instructions and orders, preparing themselves for the crossing.

'We swim. The Godavari isn't very deep. The others already know that, as they must swim to and fro fairly often.'

He nodded. 'I doubt the rakshasas are taking much comfort in that right now.'

Somashrava came up. 'We're all ready when you are, Rama. You propose to move right away, don't you?'

'We must. For this to work.'

'Good,' he said. 'Ratnakar knows a good spot a few hundred yards upstream from here. We can cross over in minutes, without the rakshasas seeing us.'

Rama nodded. 'We'll cross there then.' He caught Somashrava's shoulder. 'You trust him, this Ratnakar?'

'Who, Bearface? Of course, my prince. I trust him with my life.'

'Then I will too. Lead on.'

Rama looked around one last time at the band of supporters gathered in the fading light. It was no army. Not even a company of PFs. But it was all he had. Lakshman and Sita looked at him expectantly, their faces more hopeful now that the odds were improved. After months of isolation it did feel good to be with others, to have the reassurance that you weren't fighting alone, that the fight was for more than just one's own self-defence.

He raised his sword and led them through the fading twilight, across the river, into battle.

GLOSSARY

This 21st-century retelling of The Ramayana freely uses words and phrases from Sanskrit as well as other ethnic Indian languages. Many of these have widely varying meanings depending on the context in which they're used – and even depending on whether they were used in times ancient, medieval or present-day. This glossary explains their meanings according to their contextual usage in this book rather than their strict dictionary definitions. AKB.

aagya: permission.

aangan: entrance; courtyard.

aaram: rest.

aarti: prayer ceremony.

aatma: spirit; soul.

aatma-hatya: suicide.

acamana: ritual offering of water to Surya the sun-god at sunrise and sunset.

agar: black gummy stuff of which joss sticks are made.

agarbatti: incense prayer sticks made of agar; joss sticks.

agni: fire; fire-god.

agnihotra: fire-sacrifice; offering to the fire-god agni. Originally, in Vedic times, this meant an animal-sacrifice. Later, as the Vedic faith evolved into vegetarian-favouring Hinduism, it became any ritual fire-offering. The origin of the current-day Hindu practice of anointing a fire with ghee (clarified butter) and other ritual offerings.

Aja-putra: literally, son of Aja, in which Aja was the previous Suryavansha king of Ayodhya; it was common to refer to Aryas as 'son of (father's name)'; e.g. Rama would be addressed as 'Dasaratha-putra'.

akasa-chamber: from the word 'akasa' meaning sky. A room with the ceiling open to the sky, used for relaxation.

akhada: wrestling square.

akshohini: a division of the army

with representation from the four main forces – battle elephants, chariots with archers, armoured cavalry, and infantry.

amrit: nectar of the devas; the elixir of eternal life, one of many divine wonders produced by the churning of the oceans in ancient pre-Vedic times. The central cause of the original hostility between the devas and the Asuras, in which the Asuras sought the amrit in order to gain immortality like the devas but the devas refused them the amrit.

an-anga: bodiless.

anarth ashram: orphanage.

anashya: indestructible.

an-atmaa: soulless.

angoor: grape.

ang-vastra: length of cloth covering upper body – similar to the upper folds of a Roman toga; any bodily garment.

anjan: kohl; kajal.

apsara: any of countless beautiful danseuses in the celestial court of lord Indra, king of the devas.

arghya: the traditional washing of the feet, used to ceremonially welcome a visitor, literally by washing the dust of the road off his feet.

artha: meaning, purpose, motive. Taken together, artha, karma and dharma form the trifold foundation of Vedic philosophy.

Arya: literally, noble or pure. Commonly mispelled and mispronounced as 'Aryan'. A group of ancient Indian warrior tribes believed to have flourished for several millennia in the period before Christ. Controversially thought by some historians to have been descended from Teutonics who migrated to the Indian sub-continent and later returned – although current Indian historical scholars reject this view and maintain that the Aryas were completely indigenous to the region. Recent archaeological evidence seems to confirm that the Aryas migrated *from* India to Europe, rather than the other way around. Both views have their staunch supporters.

asana: a yogic posture, or series of postures similar to the kathas of martial arts – which are historically believed to have originated from South-Central India and have the same progenesis as yoga.

ashirwaad: blessings.

Ashok: a boy's given name.

ashubh: inauspicious.

ashwamedha: the horse ceremony. A declaration of supremacy issued by a king, tantamount to challenging one's neighbouring kingdoms to submit to one's superior strength.

astra: weapon.

Asura: anti-god: literally, a-Sura or anti-Sura, where Sura meant the clan of the gods and anyone who stood against them was referred to as an a-Sura. Loosely used to describe any demonic creature or evil being.

atee-sundar: very beautiful. Well done or well said.

atma-brahman: soul force; one's given or acquired spiritual energy.

atman: soul; spirit.

Awadhi: Ayodhyan commonspeak;

the local language, a dialect of Hindi.

awamas: the moon's least visible phase.

awamas ki raat: moonless night.

Ayodhya: the capital city of Kosala.

Ayodhya-naresh: master of Ayodhya. King.

ayushmaanbhav: long life; generally used as a greeting from an elder to a younger, as in 'live long'.

baalu: bear (see also rksa).

badmash: rascal, scoundrel, mischievous one.

bagh: big cat, interchangeably used for lion, tiger and most other related species of large, predatory cat.

bagheera: panther or leopard.

baithak-sthan: rest-area; lounge.

balak: boy.

balidaan: sacrifice.

bandara: monkey; any simian species.

barkha: rainstorm.

ber: a variety of wild Indian berry, yellowish-reddish outside, white inside, very juicy and sweetish.

bete: child.

bhaang: an intoxicating concoction made by mixing the leaf of the poppy plant with hand-churned buttermilk. Typically consumed at Holi celebrations by adult Hindus. Also smoked in hookahs or traditional bongs as pot.

bhaangra: robust and vigorous north Indian (punjabi) folk dance.

bhade bhaiya: older brother.

bhagyavan: blessed one; fortunate woman.

bhai: brother.

bhajan: a devotional chant.

bhakti: devotion.

bharat-varsha: the original name for India; literally, *land of bharata* after the ancient Arya king Bharata.

bhashan: lecture.

bhayanak: frightening, terrifying.

bhes-bhav: physical appearance.

bhindi: ladyfinger, okra.

bhojanshalya: dining hall.

bhor: extreme; as in *bhor suvah*: extreme (early) morning.

bhung: useless; negated.

bindi: a blood-red circular dot worn by Hindu women on their foreheads to indicate their married status. Now worn in a variety of colours and shapes as a fashion accessory.

brahmachari: see brahmacharya.

brahmacharya: a boy or man who devotes the first 25 years of his life to prayer, celibacy, and the study of the Vedic sciences under the tutelage of a brahmin guru.

brahman: the substance of which all matter is created. Literally, the stuff of existence.

brahmarishi: an enlightened holy man who has attained the highest level of grace; literally, a rishi or holy man, whom Brahma, creator of all things, has blessed.

brahmin: the priestly caste. Highest in order.

buddhi: intellect; mind; intelligence.

chacha: uncle; father's younger brother.

chaddar: sheet.

Chaitra: the month of spring; roughly corresponds to the latter half of March and first half of April.

charas: opium.

chaturta: cleverness.

chaukat: a square. Most Indian houses were designed as a square, with an entrance on one wall and the house occupying the other three walls. In the centre was an open chaukat where visitors (or intruders) could be seen from any room in the house.

chaupat: an ancient Indian war strategy dice game, universally acknowledged to be the original inspiration for chess, played on a flat piece of cloth or board by rolling bone-dice to decide moves, involving pieces representing the four akshohini of the Arya army – elephants, chariot, foot-soldiers, knights.

chillum: toke; a smoking-pipe used to inhale charas (opium).

chini kulang: a variety of bird.

choli: breast-cloth; a garment used to cover a woman's upper body.

chotti: pig-tail.

chowkidari: the act of guarding a person or place like a sentry or chowkidar.

chudail: banshee; female ghost; witch.

chunna: lime-powder or a mixture of lime-powder and water; used to whitewash outer or inner walls; also eaten in edible form in paan or mixed directly with tobacco.

chunnri: a strip of cloth used by a woman to cover her breasts and cleavage, also used to cover the head before elders or during prayer.

chupp-a-chuppi: hide and seek.

crore: one hundred hundred thousand; one hundred lakhs; ten million.

daiimaa: brood-mother, clan-mother, wet nurse, governess. A woman serving first as midwife to the expecting mother, then later as wet-nurse, governess and au pair.

dakshina/guru-dakshina: ritual payment by a kshatriya to a brahmin on demand.

daku: dacoit; highway bandit; jungle thief.

danav: a species of Asura.

darbha: a variety of thick grass.

darshan: the Hindu act of gazing reverentially upon the face of a divine idol, an essential part of worship; literally, *viewing*.

dasya: slave; servant.

Deepavali: the predominant Indian Hindu festival, the festival of lights. Also known as Diwali.

desh: land; country; nation.

deva: god. Several Indian devas have their equivalents in Greek and Norse mythology.

dev-astra: weapon of the devas; divine weapon.

dev-daasi/devdasi: prostitute.

devi: goddess.

dhanush-baan: bow and arrows.

dharma: sacred duty. A morally binding code of behaviour. The cornerstone of the Vedic faith.

dharam-patni: wife; literally, 'partner in dharma'.

dharamshala: a traditional rest-house on Indian roads in times past, where travellers could partake of free shelter and simple nourishment. Literally, 'shelter of dharma'.

dhobi: washerman (of clothes).

dhol: drum.

dollee: palanquin; travelling chair.

dosa: a flat crisp rice-pancake, a staple of South Indian cuisine.

dhoti: a white cotton lower garment, worn usually by Indian men.

diya: clay oil lamp.

drishti: vision; view; sight.

dumroo: a small x-shaped drum with sounding tassels. Dumroo-wallah, or He who Plays The Dumroo, refers to Lord Shiva the Destroyer, who plays the dumroo to make all of us monkeys (mortals) dance to his rhythm.

gaddha: donkey.

gaddhi: seat; literally, a cushion.

gaja-gamini: elephant-footed.

gandharva: forest nymph; when malevolent, also a species of Asura.

ganga-jal: sacred Ganges water.

ganja: charas; opium.

garuda: eagle, after the mythic giant magical eagle Garuda, the first-of-his-name, a major demi-god believed to be the creator and patron deity of all birdkind.

gauthan: village; any rural settlement.

gayaka: singer.

Gayatri: a woman's given name; also the most potent mantra of Hindus, recited before beginning any venture, or even at the start of one's day to ensure strength and success.

gharial: a sub-species of reptilian predator unique to the Indian sub-continent, similar to crocodiles and alligators in body but with a sword-shaped mouth.

ghat: literally, low-lying hill. Burning ghat usually refers to the places in which Hindu bodies are traditionally cremated.

gobi: common term for cauliflower as well as cabbage.

gotra: sub-caste.

govinda: goatherd.

gulmohur: a species of Asian tree that produces beautiful red flowers in winter.

guru/guruji: a teacher, generally associated with a sage. The 'ji' is a sign of respect; it literally means 'sir', and can be added after any male name or title: eg, Ramaji.

guru-dakshina: see dakshina.

guru-dev: guru who is as a god, or deva; divine teacher.

gurukul: a guru's hermitage for scholars; a forest ashram school where students resided, maintaining the ashram and its grounds while being taught through lectures in the open air.

gurung: a variety of bird.

hai: ave; hail; woe. An exclamation.

halwai: maker of sweets.

hatya: murder.

havan: sacrificial offering.

hawaldar: constable.

himsa: violence, bodily harm.

Holi: a major Indian festival and feast day, celebrated to mark the end of winter and the first day of spring, the last rest day before the start of the harvest season; celebrated with the throwing of coloured powders and coloured waters symbolising the colours of spring, and the eating of sweetmeats (mithai) and the drinking of bhaang.

Ikshwaku: the original kshatriya ancestral clan from which the Suryavansha line sprang. After the founder, Ikshwaaku.

imli ka butta: tamarind.

Indra: god of thunder and war. Equivalent to the Norse god Thor or the Greek god Ares.

indra-dhanush: literally, Indra's bow; a rainbow.

ishta: religious offering.

jadugar: magician.

jagganath: relentless and unstoppable Hindu god of war; another name for Ganesha; juggernaut.

Jai: boy's given name; hail.

Jai Mata Ki: Praise be to the Mother-Goddess.

Jai Shree: Praise be to Sri (or Shree), Divine Creator.

jaise aagya: as you wish; your wish is my command.

jal murghi: a variety of Indian bird; literally, water-fowl.

jal-bartan: vessel for drinking water.

jaldi: quickly; in haste.

jalebi: Indian sweet, made by pouring dough into a tureen of boiling oil in spiralling shapes, removed, then drenched in sugar-syrup.

jamun: a common variety of Indian berry-like fruit, purplish-black, deliciously sour.

janayu: ceremony marking the coming of age, usually of a brahmin male. Also known as thread ceremony.

Jat: a proud, violently inclined, North Indian clan.

jatayu: vulture, after Jatayu, the first-of-its-name, the giant hybrid man-vulture, second only to Garuda in its leadership of bird-kind.

jhadi-buti: literally, herbs and roots; herbal medicines.

jhadoo: Indian broom.

jhilli: a variety of Indian bird.

ji: yes (respectfully).

johar ka roti: a flat roasted pancake made from barley-flour.

johari: jeweller.

kaand: a section of a story; literally, a natural joint on a long stick of sugarcane or bamboo, used to mark off a count.

kabbadi: a game played by children and adults alike. India's official national sport.

kachua: tortoise.

kaho: speak.

kai-kai: harsh cawing sound.

kairee: a raw green mango, used to make pickle.

kajal: kohl.

kala: black.

kala jaadu: black magic.

kala kendra: art council.

kalakaar: artist.

kalarappa: ancient South Indian art of man-to-man combat, universally acknowledged to be the progenitor of Far Eastern martial arts – learned by visiting Chinese delegates and later adapted and evolved into the modern martial arts.

kalash: a brass or golden pot of a specific design, filled with rice and anointed ritually, tipped over by a new bride to bring prosperity into the house during her home-coming ceremony. A symbol of the good fortune brought by a new wife to her husband's home.

Kali: the goddess of vengeance. An avatar of the universal devi.

Kali-Yuga: the Age of Kali, prophesied to be the last and worst age of human civilisation.

Kama: god of love. The equivalent of the Greek Eros or sometimes Cupid.

kamasutra: the science of love.

karmic: pertaining to one's karma.

karya: deeds.

kasturi: deer-musk.

katha: story.

kathputhli: puppet.

kavee: poet.

kavya: poem.

kesar: saffron, extremely valuable then and now as an essential spice used in Indian cooking; traditionally given as a gift by kings to one another; worth several times more than its weight in gold.

khaas: special; unique.

khatiya: cot; bed.

khazana: treasure-trove; treasury.

khottey-sikkey: counterfeit coin/s.

khukhri: a kind of North Indian machete, favoured by the hilly gurkha tribes.

kintu: but; however.

kiran: ray (usually of light); a girl or boy's given name.

koel/koyal: Indian song-bird.

Kosala: a North-Central Indian kingdom believed to have flourished for several millennia before the start of the Christian era.

koyal: Indian song-bird.

krodh: wrath.

kshatriya: warrior caste. The highest of four castes in ancient India, the armed defenders of the tribe, skilled in martial combat and governance. Kings were always chosen from this caste. Later, with the Hindu shift towards pacifism and non-violence, the brahmin or priestly caste became predominant, with kshatriyas shifting into the second-highest position in contemporary India.

kumbha-rakshasa: dominant species of demons, lording over their fellow rakshasas as well as other Asura species because of their considerable size and strength; named after Kumbhakarna, the mammoth giant brother of Ravana, who grew to mountainous proportions owing to an ancient curse that condemned him to absorb the physical mass of any living thing he killed or ate. Unlike Kumbhakarna, the kumbhas (for short), do not grow larger with each kill or meal.

kumkum: red powder.

kundalee: horoscope.

kurta: an upper garment with a round neck, full sleeves. Like a shirt but slipped over the head like a tee shirt.

kusa or kusalavya: a lush variety of grass found in Northern and North-Central India, long-bladed and thick.

lakh: a hundred thousand.

langot: loin-cloth.

lingam: a simple unadorned representation of Lord Shiva, usually made of roughly carved black stone, shaped like an upward moulded pillar of stone with a blunt head that is traditionally anointed. Typically regarded by some Western scholars as a phallic object; a controversial view which has been repeatedly disproven by Indian scholars and study of ancient Vedic texts.

lohit: iron.

lota: a small metal pot with a handle, used to carry water.

lungi: a common lower-body garment; a sheet of cloth wrapped around the waist once or more times and tucked in or knotted, extending to the ankles; unisexual but more often worn by men.

maa: mother.

maang: the centre point of the hairline on a person's forehead.

magarmach: Indian river crocodile.

maha: great. As in maha-mantra, maha-raja, maha-bharata, maha-guru, maha-dev, etc.

mahadev: great one.

mahal: palace; mansion; manse.

maharuk: a variety of Indian tree.

maha-mantra: supreme mantra or verse, such as the maha-mantra Gayatri. A potent catechism to ward off evil and ensure the success of one's efforts.

mahout: elephant-handler.

mahseer: a variety of Indian fish.

mahua: a variety of Indian tree.

manai: a variety of Indian tree with heavy creepers.

manch: literally, platform or dais; also, a gathering of elders or leaders of a community.

mandala: a purified proscribed circle.

mandap: a ceremonial dais on which prayer rituals and other ceremonies are conducted.

mandir: temple.

mangalsutra: a black thread necklace worn by a married woman as proof of her marital status.

mann: mind.

mantra: an invocation to the devas

mantri: minister.

marg: road.

marg-darshak: guide, mentor, guru.

marg-saathi: fellow-traveller; companion on the road.

martya: human; all things pertaining to humankind.

mashaal: torch.

masthi: mischief.

matka: earthen pot.

maya: illusion.

mayini: witch, demoness.

melas: country fairs, carnivals.

mithai: traditional Indian sweetmeats.

mithaigalli: sweetmeat lane; a part of the market where the halwais (mithai-makers) line up their stalls.

mithun: Indian bison; a species of local buffalo.

mochee: cobbler.

mogra: a strongly scented white flower that blooms very briefly; worn by Indian women in their hair.

moksh: salvation.

mudra: gesture, especially during a dance performance; a symbolic action.

muhurat: an auspicious date to initiate an important undertaking. Even today in India, all important activities – marriages, coronations, the start of a a new venture – are always scheduled on a day and time found suitable according to the panchang (Hindu almanac) or muhurat calendar.

mujra: a sensual dance.

naachwaali: dancing-girl or courtesan.

naashta: breakfast; also, an early evening refreshment (equivalent of the British 'tea').

naga: any species of snake; a species of Asura.

nagin: female cobra.

namak: salt.

namaskar/namaskaram: greetings. Usually said while joining one's palms together and bowing the head forward slightly. A mark of respect.

namaskara: see namaskar.

nanga: naked.

Narak: Hell.

naresh: lord, master. A royal title used to address a maharaja, the equivalent of 'your highness'.

natya: dance.

nautanki: song-and-dance melo-drama, a cheap street play.

navami: an infant's naming day.

neem: an Indian tree whose leaves and bark are noted for their proven, highly efficacious medic-inal properties.

nidra: an exalted, transcendental meditative state, a kind of yogic sleep.

odhini: woman's garment used specifically to cover the head, similar to pallo.

Om Hari Swaha: Praise be to the Creator, Amen.

Om Namay: Praise be the Name of . . .

paan: the leaf of the betelnut plant, in which could be wrapped a variety of edible savouries, espe-cially pieces of supari and chewing tobacco.

pahadi: a hill dweller or mountain man. Often used colloquially to connote a rude, ill-educated and ill-mannered person.

paisa: in the singular, a penny, the smallest individual unit of coinage, then and now. In the generic, money.

palai: sandy ground. Also pilai, or pillai.

palas: a variety of Indian flowering tree.

pallo: the top fold of a woman's

sari, used to conceal the breasts and cleavage of the wearer.

panchayat: a village committee usually of five (panch) persons.

parantu: but; however.

pari: angel; fairy.

parikrama: a ritual demonstrating one's devotion to a given deity, often consisting of walking several (hundred) times around a temple as well as the performance of related rituals and prayers.

patal: the lowermost level of narak, the lowest plane attain-able in existence.

patang: kite.

payal: a delicately carved chain of tiny bells, usually of silver, worn as an anklet by women.

peda: a common, highly popular Indian sweet made of milk and sugar.

peepal: a species of tree with hanging roots and vines.

phanas: jackfruit.

phera: ritual circling of a sacred fire.

phool mala: flower-garland.

pisaca; a species of Asura.

pitashree: revered father.

pitchkarees: water-spouts; portable hand-pumps used by children in play.

pooja: prayer.

pradhan-mantri: prime minister.

Prajapati: Creator; The One Who Made All Living Things; also used as a term for butterflies, which are believed to represent the spirit of the Creator.

pranaam: a high form of namaste or greeting.

pranayam: a yogic method of breathing that enables biofeed-back and control of the senses.

prarthana: intense, devout prayer.

prasadam: food blessed by the devas in the course of prayer; a sacramental offering.

prashna-uttar: question-answer.

pravachan: monologue or lecture, usually by a guru or mentor; to be imbibed in rapt silence.

Prithvi: Earth.

pundit: priest; master of religious ceremonies.

purnima: full moon; full moon night.

purohit: see pundit.

pushpak: a flying vehicle described in ancient Indian texts, anti-gravitational devices whose technological basis was said to be once known but is now forgotten; also 'chariots of the gods'.

putra: son.

raag: a scale in Indian classical music, consisting of a certain blend of notes in a related confluence, designed to produce a specific effect on the environment. E.g. Raag Bhairav was said to be capable of inducing rain, Raag Deepak to cause oil lamps to light.

raat ki rani: colloquial name for a common Indian flower that blooms only at night; literally, 'queen of the night'.

rabadi: a popular Indian dessert of thickened sweetened milk, over-boiled until the water drains and only thick layers of cream remain.

raja: king; liege; clan-chieftain.

raje: a more affectionate form of 'raja'. The 'e' suffix to a name ending in a vowel indicates intimacy and warmth.

raj-gaddhi: throne; seat of the king.

rajkumar: prince.

rajkumari: princess.

raj-marg: king's way; royally protected highway or road.

rajya sabha: king's council of ministers, a meeting of the same.

rakshak: protector.

rakshasas: a variety of Asura; roughly equivalent to the Western devil or demon. Singular/male: rakshas or rakshasas. Singular/feminine: rakshasi. Plural /both: rakshasas.

rang: colour; usually, coloured powder.

rang-birangi: colourful.

rangoli: the traditional Indian art of creating elaborate patterns on floors, usually at the entrances of domiciles, by carefully sprinkling coloured powder.

ras: juice.

rasbhurries: a very sweet, sticky and juicy wild berry; literally, 'juice-filled'.

rath/s: chariot/s.

rawa: a type of flour.

rishi: sadhu.

rksa: black mountain bear.

rudraksh: red beads, considered sacred by Hindus.

rupaiya: rupee. The main unit of currency in India even today.

rudraksh maala: a Hindu rosary or prayer-bead necklace strung with rudraksh beads.

sabha: committee; parliament.

sadhu: literally, 'most holy' or 'most auspicious'; also used to denote a penitent hermit; holy man.

sadhuni: a female sadhu or woman whose life is dedicated to prayer and worship.

saivite: worshipper of Lord Shiva.

sakshi: a woman's close female friend.

sala: a variety of Indian tree.

samabhavimudra: celestial meditative stance.

samadhi: memorial.

samasya: problem, situation.

samay chakra: the chariot wheel of Time, turning relentlessly as god rides across the universe. A cornerstone of Hindu belief.

samjhe: 'understood?'

sammelan: a friendly gathering; a meeting.

sandesh: message.

sandhyavandana: evening oblation; ritual offering of water and prayer to the sun at sunset; see also acamana.

Sanskriti: Arya culture and tradition.

sanyas: renunciation from the world; the process by which one gives up all one's worldly possessions, attachments and relationships, taking sanyas, and becoming a 'sanyasi'.

saprem: supreme.

Satya-Yuga: Age of Truth.

sautan: husband's second wife; one's rival for a husband's affections.

savdhaan: caution.

seema: borderline; boundary.

senapati: commander of armed forces, a general.

sesa: rabbit.

shaasan: a type of low-lying couch with a backrest or armrest.

shagun: a variety of Indian tree; an auspicious event or occurrence.

shakti: strength, power, force. Used to describe divine power of a god, as in Kali-shakti or Goddess Kali's power.

shama: forgiveness. Colloquially, 'excuse me'.

Shani: god of weapons and destruction. Equivalent to the Greek god Saturn.

Shanivar: Day of Shani; now marked as Saturday because Shani is believed to correspond to Saturn; but probably a quite different day in the ancient Vedic calendar.

shantam: quiet, calm, serene; literally, 'be at peace'.

shanti: colloquialisation of shantam.

shastra: a science; an area of study.

shatru: enemy.

shikhaar: the hunt.

shikhsa: education; learning.

shishya/s: student/s of a guru.

shraap: curse; terrible invocation.

Shravan: a month in the Hindu calendar; usually the month of the rains; also, a boy's given name.

siddh: successful; blessed.

silbutta: grinding stone and board; pestle and mortar.

sindhoor: a blood-red powder used in marital rituals. Traditionally applied by a husband on his wife's hairline (maang) to indicate her status as a married woman. Hence, unmarried women and widows are not permitted to wear sindhoor. Although a bindi (dot) is now used as a modern equivalent and worn universally as a fashion accessory.

siphai: soldier; guard.

sitaphal: a variety of Indian fruit with sweet milky pods.

sloka: sacred verse.

smriti: hidden; secret.

soma: wine made from the soma plant; a popular wine in ancient India.

sona: gold.

spasa: spy, informant.

stree-hatya: murder of a woman.

sudra: the lowest caste, usually relegated to cleaning, hunting, tanning and other undesirable activities. The lowest in order.

suhaag raat: wedding night.

supari: betelnut.

Suryavansha: the Solar Dynasty, a line of kings that ruled over Kosala; literally, the clan of the sun-god, Surya.

su-swagatam: welcome; the traditional ritual greeting offered to a visitor.

sutaar: carpenter.

swaha: a term used to denote the auspicious and successful completion of a sloka or recitation; corresponds to the Latin 'Amen'.

swami: master; lord; naresh.

Swarga-lok/a: Heaven.

swayamvara: a ceremonial rite during which a woman of marriagable age was permitted to select a suitable husband. Eligible men wishing to apply would line up to be inspected by the bride-to-be. On finding a suitable mate, she would indicate her choice by placing the garland around his neck.

taal: rhythm; beat.

tabla: an Indian percussion instrument, a kind of drum sounded by striking the heel of the palm and the tips of the fingers.

tamasha: a show; performance; common street play.

tandav: the frenzied sexually charged celestial dance of Shiva the Destroyer by which he generates enough shakti to destroy the entire universe that Brahma the Creator may recreate it once again.

tanpura: an Indian stringed musical instrument.

tandoor: an Indian barbecue.

tann: body.

tantrik: a worshipper of physical energy and sensual arts.

tapasvi: one who endures penance, usually with an aim to acquiring spiritual prowess.

tapasya: penance.

teko: prostrate one's head, touching the forehead to the ground as a demonstration of devotion and obeisance.

thakur: lord; landowner.

thali: a round metal platter used for eating meals or for storing prayer items. The Indian equivalent of the Western 'dinner plate'.

thrashbroom: a broom with harsh bristles, used for beating rugs and mattresses.

three worlds: Swarga-lok, Prithvi, Narak. Literally, Heaven, Earth, Hell.

tilak: ash or colour anointment on one's forehead, indicating that one has performed one's ritual prayers and sacrifices and is blessed with divine grace to perform one's duties.

tirth yatra: pilgrimage.

Treta-Yuga: Age of Reason.

trimurti: the holy Hindu trinity of Brahma, Vishnu and Shiva, respectively the Creator, Preserver and Destroyer.

trishul: trident.

tulsi: a variety of Indian plant known for its efficacious medicinal properties and regarded as a symbol of a happy and secure household; always grown in the courtyard of a house and prayed to daily by the woman of the house; also, a woman's given name.

upanisad: an ancient sacred Indian text.

uraga: a species of Asura.

vaid: physician trained in the art of Ayur-vaidya, the ancient Indian study of herbal medicine and healing.

vaisya: the trading or commercial caste. Third in order.

vajra: lightning bolt.

van: forest, jungle. Pronounced to rhyme with 'one'.

vanar: bandara; simian; any monkey species, but most commonly used to denote apes, especially the intelligent anthropomorphic talking apes of this saga, forthcoming in Armies of Hanuman; Book Four of The Ramayana.

vanash: a variety of Indian tree.

varna: caste; literally, occupational level or group.

varsha: rain; a woman's given name.

Veda: the sacred writings of the ancient Arya sages, comprising meditations, prayers, observations and scientific treatises on every conceivable human area of interest; the basis of Indian culture.

vetaal: a species of Asura; somewhat similar to the Western concept of 'vampire' but not usually synonymous.

vidya: knowledge.

vinaashe: destruction; death.

yagna: religious fire-ritual.

yaksi: a female yaksa; a species of Asura capable of shape-shifting; closely corresponding to (but not identical to) the Western concept of Elves.

Yama: Yama-raj, lord of death and king of the underworld; literally Death personified as a large powerfully built dark-skinned man with woolly hair, who rides a black buffalo and carries a bag of souls.

yash: fame; adoration; admiration.

yoganidra: the supreme state of transcendence while meditating, usually indicated by the eyes being partly open yet seeing only the apparent nothingness of brahman; a divine near-sleep-like state.

yojana: a measurement of distance in ancient India, believed to have been equivalent to around nine miles.

yoni: female sexual organ; the 'yang' of 'yin and yang'.

yuga: age; historical period.